W9-BLH-292

WITHDRAWN FROM
COLLECTION

THE GRAVEYARD BOOK

THE GRAVEYARD BOOK

Based on the novel by: NEIL GAIMAN

Adapted by: P. CRAIG RUSSELL

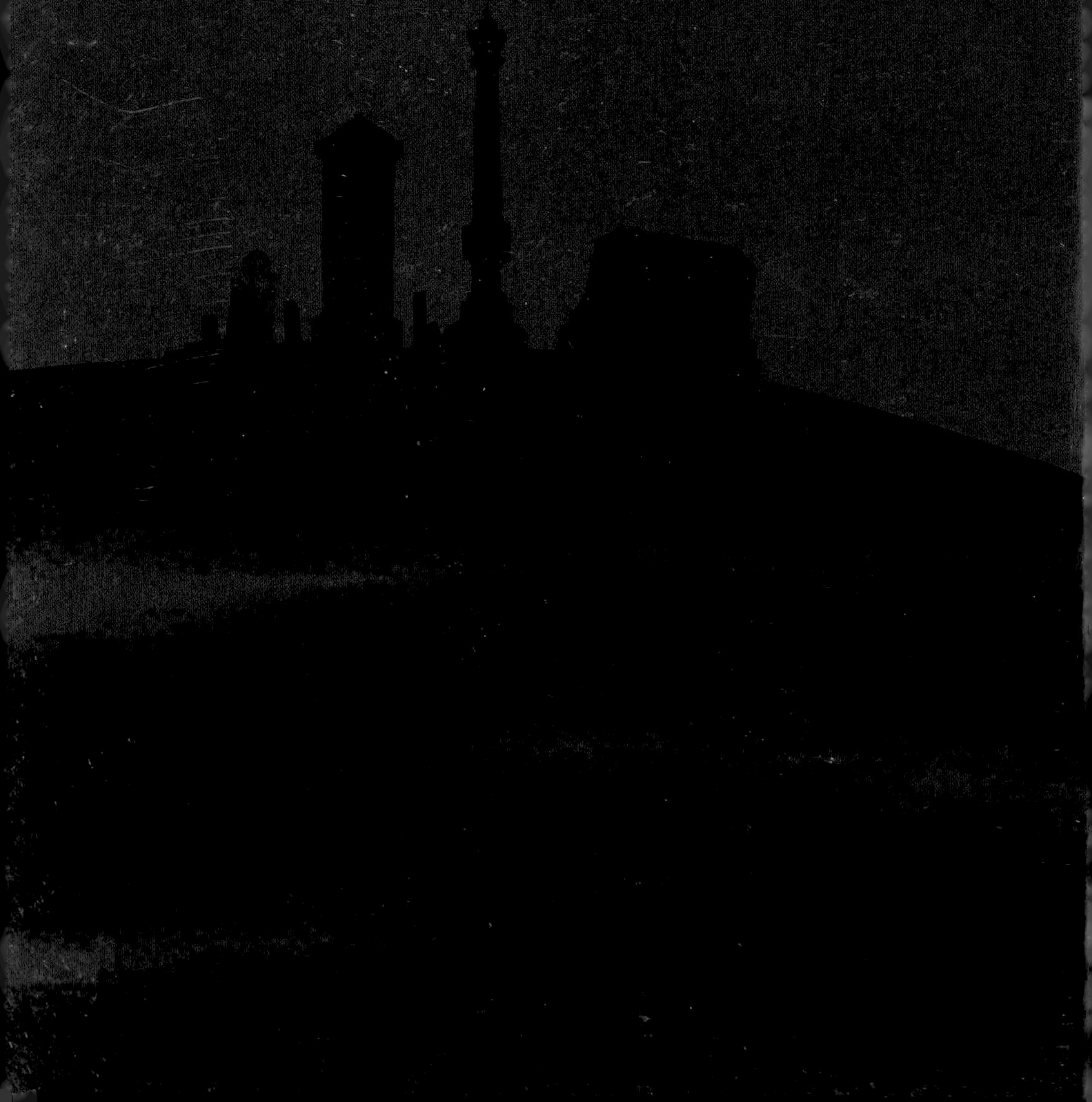

Illustrated by:
P. CRAIG RUSSELL
STEPHEN B. SCOTT
KEVIN NOWLAN
GALEN SHOWMAN
TONY HARRIS
JILL THOMPSON
DAVID LAFUENTE
SCOTT HAMPTON

Colorist: LOVERN KINDZIERSKI

Letterer: RICK PARKER

HARPER

An Imprint of HarperCollins*Publishers*

The Graveyard Book Graphic Novel

Text copyright © 2008 by Neil Gaiman

Illustrations copyright © 2014 by P. Craig Russell

All rights reserved. Manufactured in China.

No part of this book may be used or reproduced in any manner

whatsoever without written permission except in the case of brief

quotations embodied in critical articles and reviews. For information

address HarperCollins Children's Books, a division of HarperCollins

Publishers, 195 Broadway, New York, NY 10007.

www.harpercollinschildrens.com

Library of Congress catalog card number: 2013953799

ISBN 978-0-06-242188-3

Lettering by Rick Parker

Typography by Brian Durniak

16 17 18 19 20 SCP 10 9 8 7 6 5 4 3 2 1

First Edition

To Brooke and Andrew, Jadon and Josiah, and Naomi and Emmeline
(and special thanks to Galen Showman
and Scott Hampton for service above and beyond)
—P.C.R.

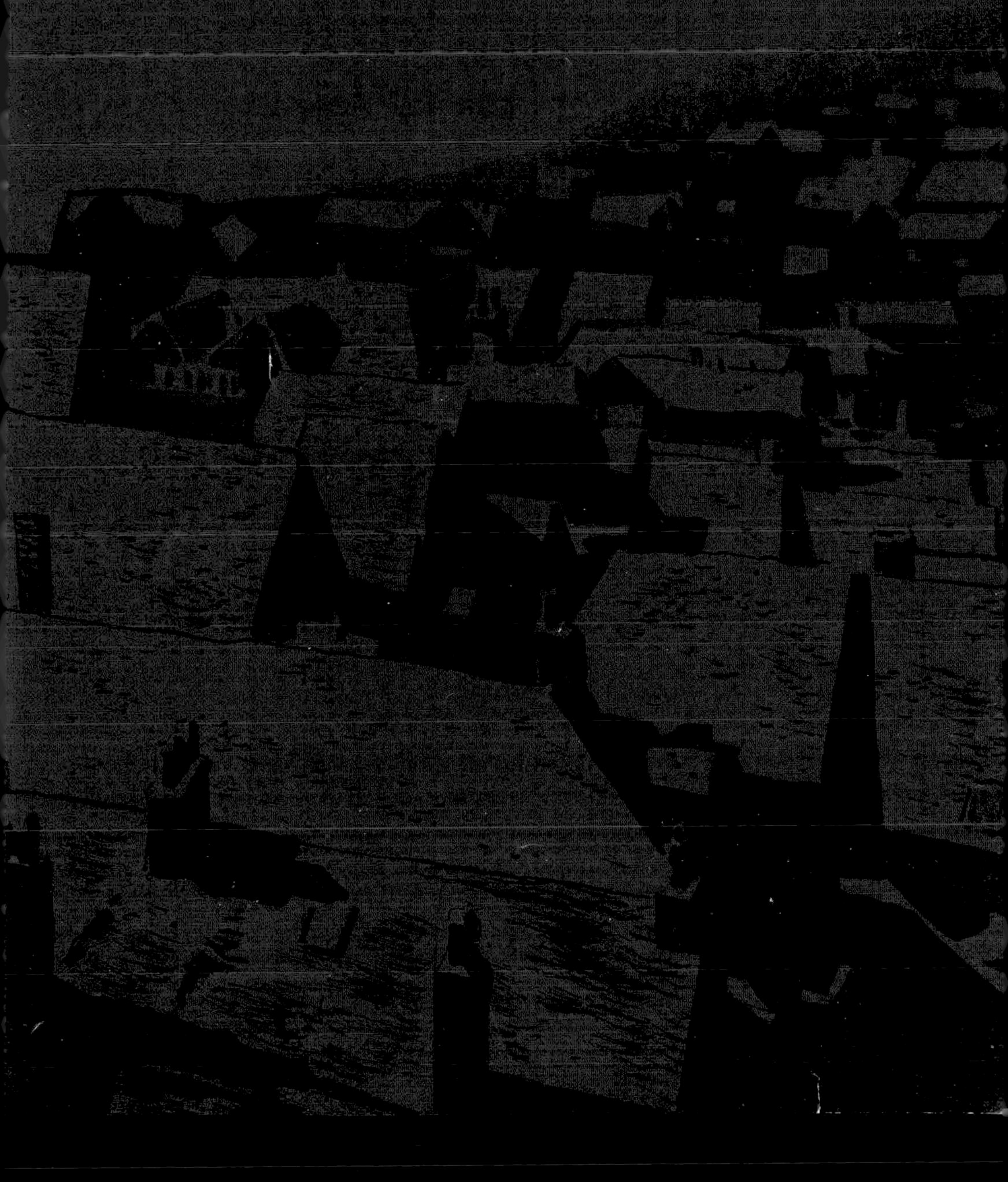

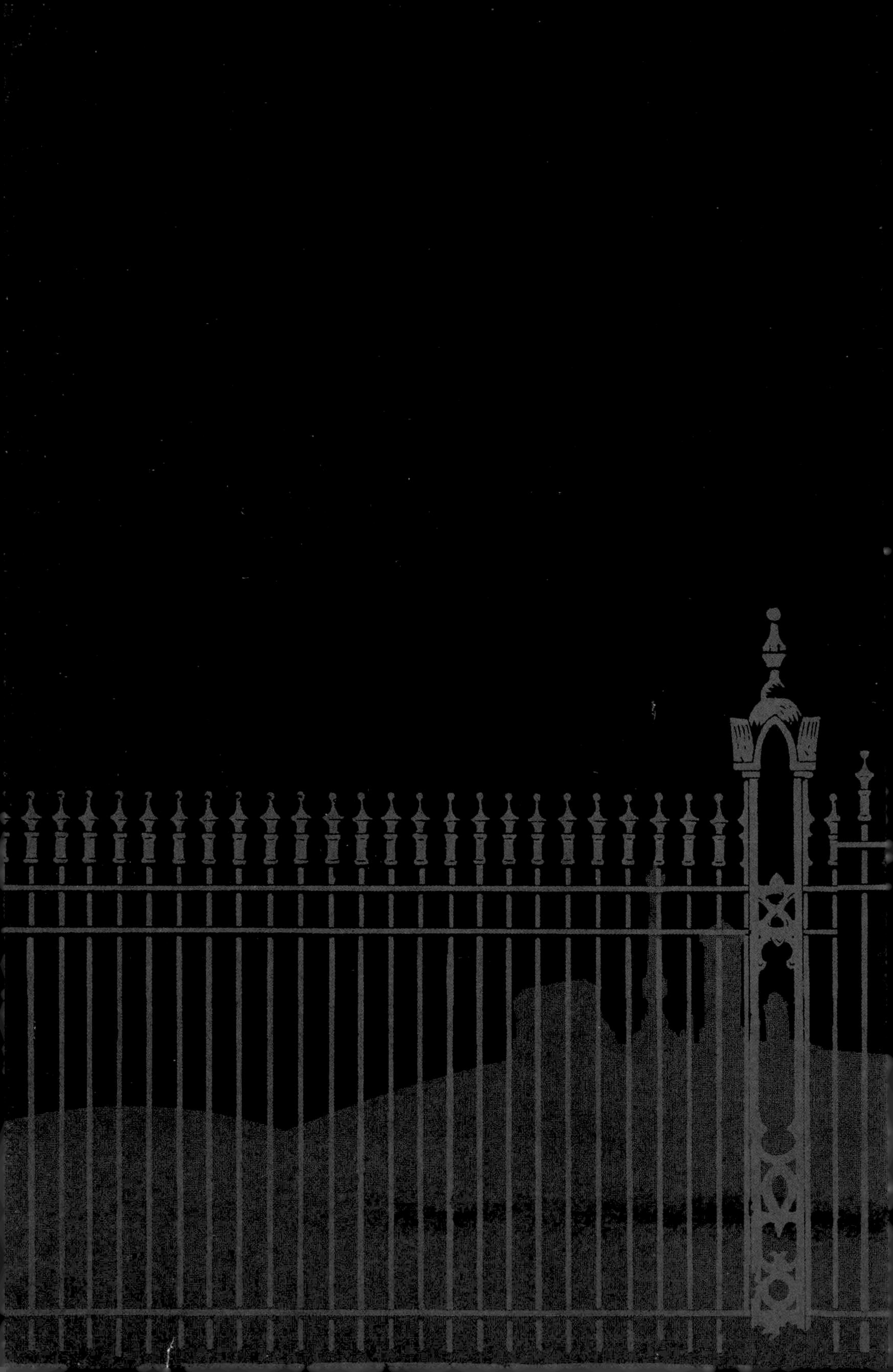

THE GRAVEYARD BOOK

VOLUME 1

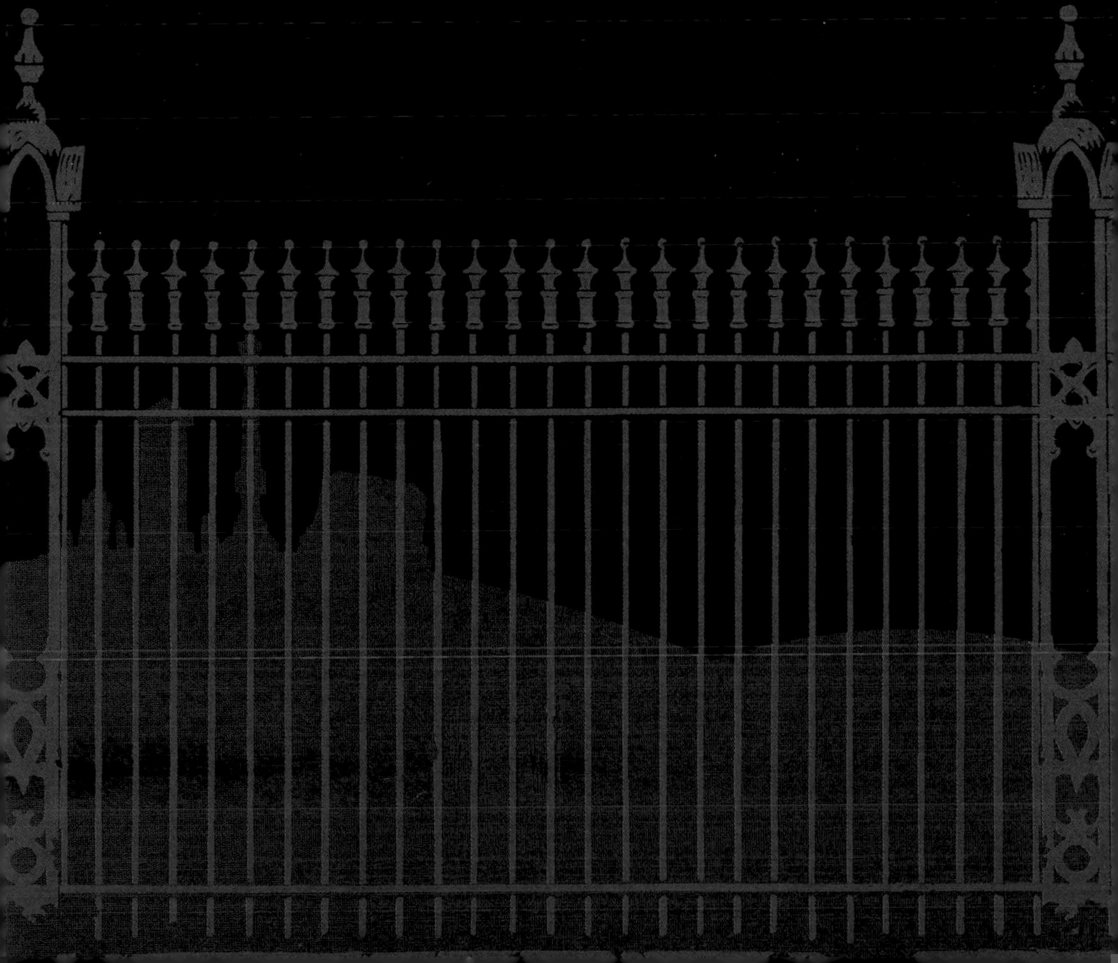

1
How Nobody Came to the Graveyard

Illustrated by Kevin Nowlan

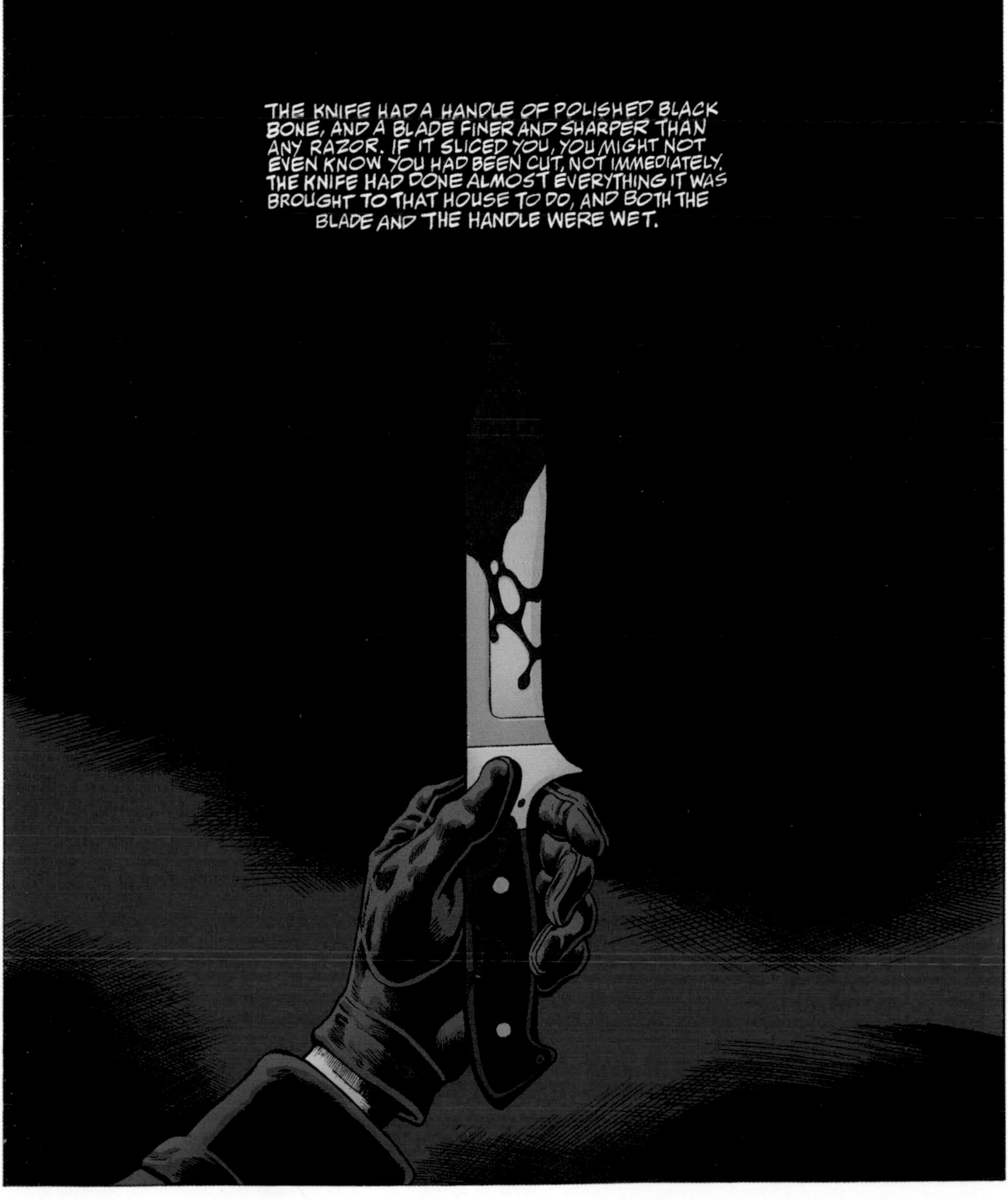
THE KNIFE HAD A HANDLE OF POLISHED BLACK BONE, AND A BLADE FINER AND SHARPER THAN ANY RAZOR. IF IT SLICED YOU, YOU MIGHT NOT EVEN KNOW YOU HAD BEEN CUT, NOT IMMEDIATELY. THE KNIFE HAD DONE ALMOST EVERYTHING IT WAS BROUGHT TO THAT HOUSE TO DO, AND BOTH THE BLADE AND THE HANDLE WERE WET.

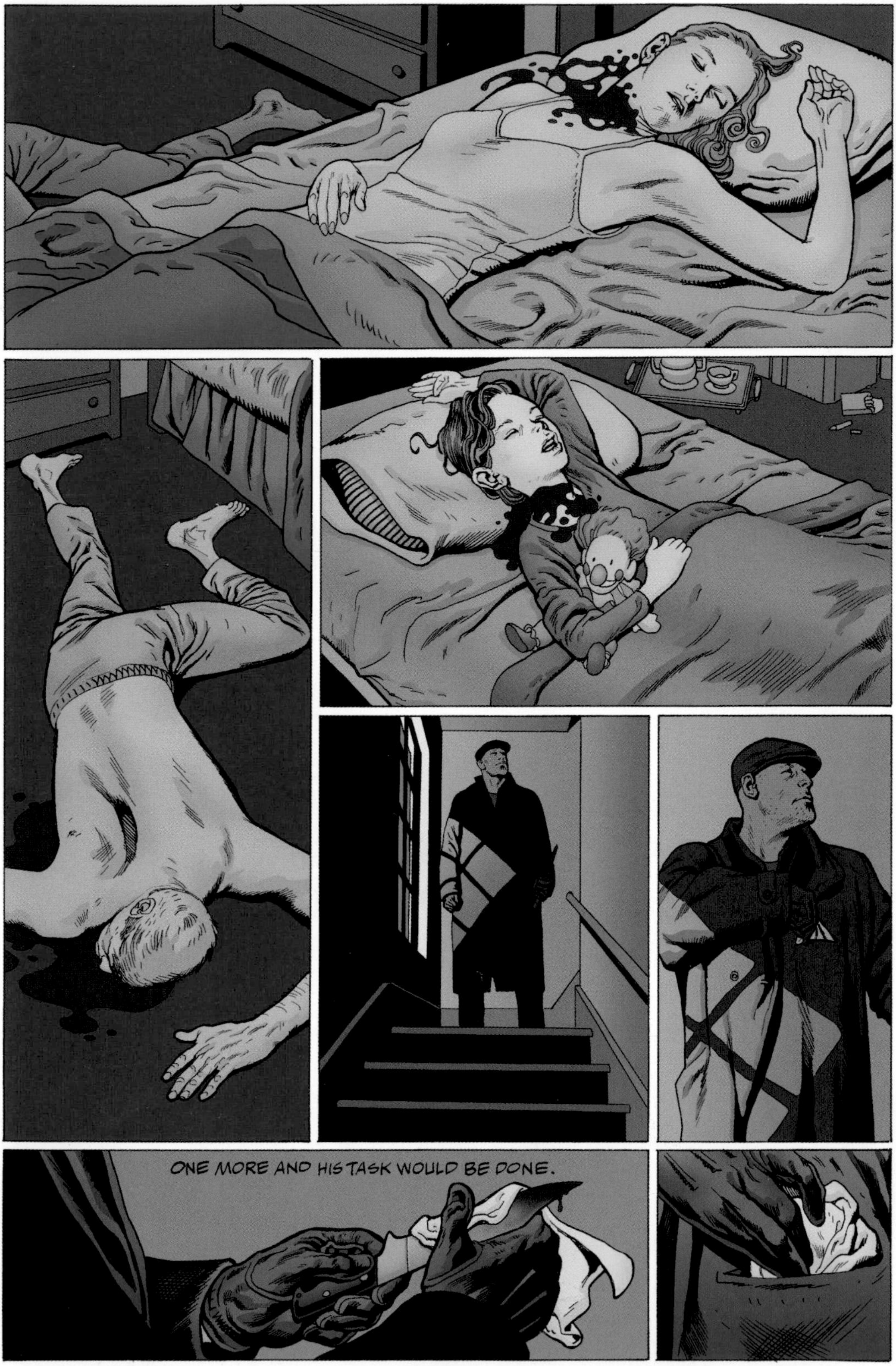
ONE MORE AND HIS TASK WOULD BE DONE.

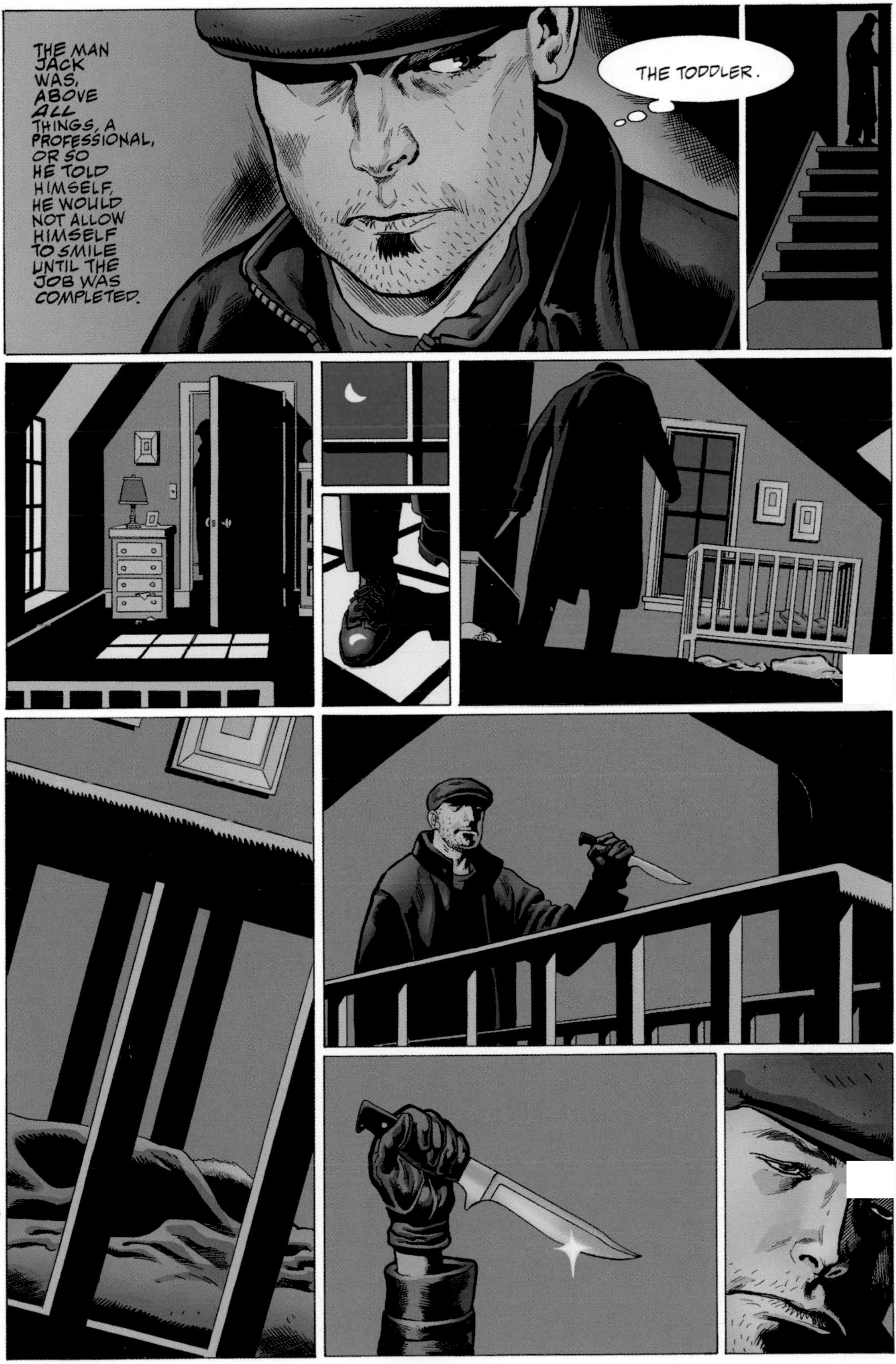
THE MAN JACK WAS, ABOVE ALL THINGS, A PROFESSIONAL, OR SO HE TOLD HIMSELF. HE WOULD NOT ALLOW HIMSELF TO SMILE UNTIL THE JOB WAS COMPLETED.
THE TODDLER.

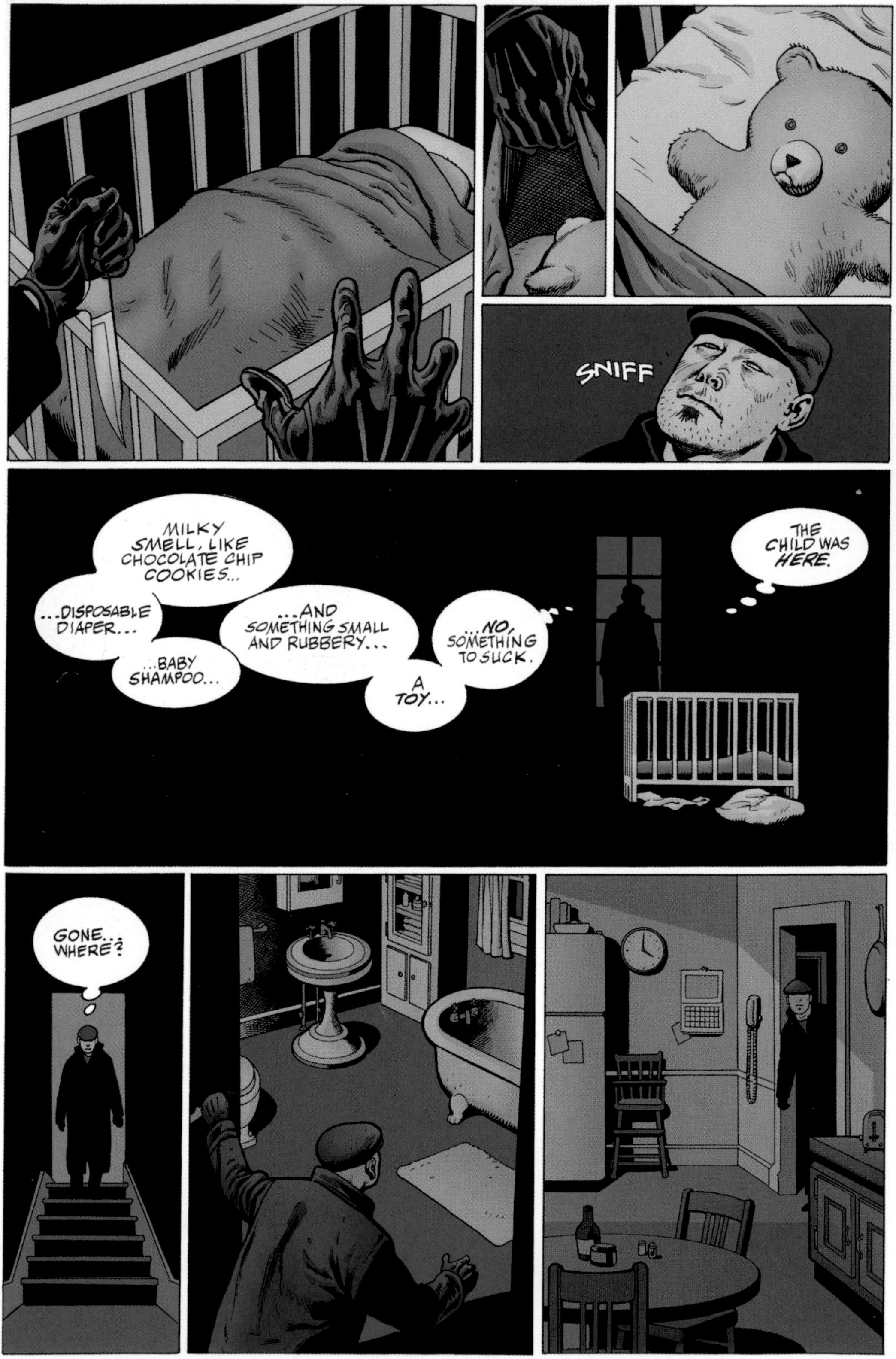
SNIFF
MILKY SMELL, LIKE CHOCOLATE CHIP COOKIES...
...DISPOSABLE DIAPER...
...BABY SHAMPOO...
...AND SOMETHING SMALL AND RUBBERY...
A TOY...
...NO, SOMETHING TO SUCK.
THE CHILD WAS HERE.
GONE... WHERE?

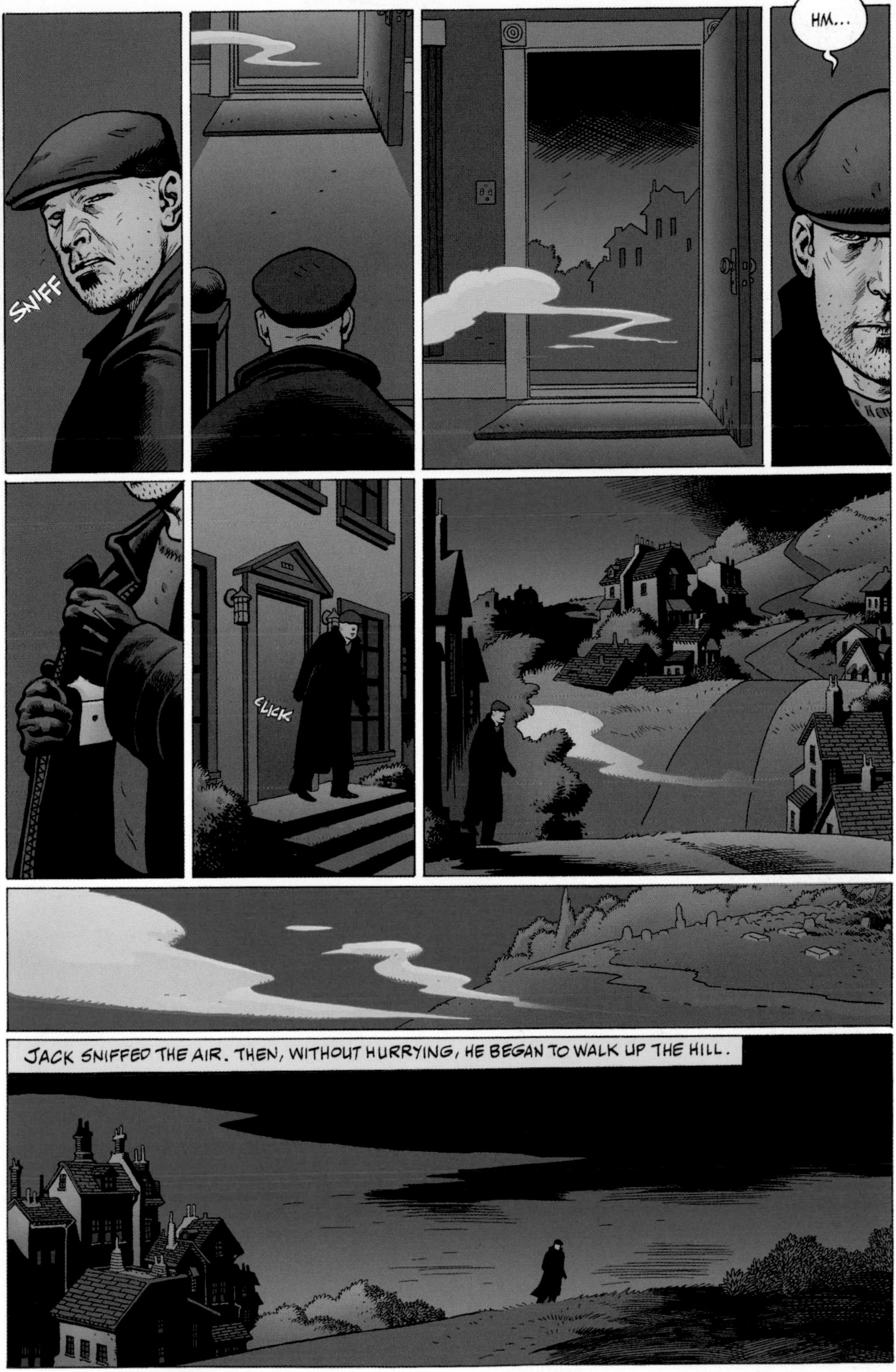
SNIFF
HM...
CLICK
JACK SNIFFED THE AIR. THEN, WITHOUT HURRYING, HE BEGAN TO WALK UP THE HILL.

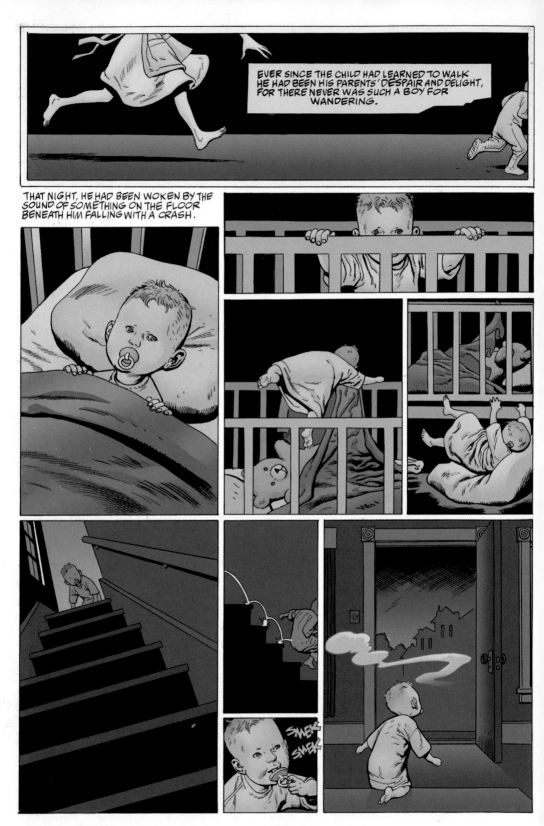

EVER SINCE THE CHILD HAD LEARNED TO WALK HE HAD BEEN HIS PARENTS' DESPAIR AND DELIGHT, FOR THERE NEVER WAS SUCH A BOY FOR WANDERING.

THAT NIGHT, HE HAD BEEN WOKEN BY THE SOUND OF SOMETHING ON THE FLOOR BENEATH HIM FALLING WITH A CRASH.

SMEK
SMEK

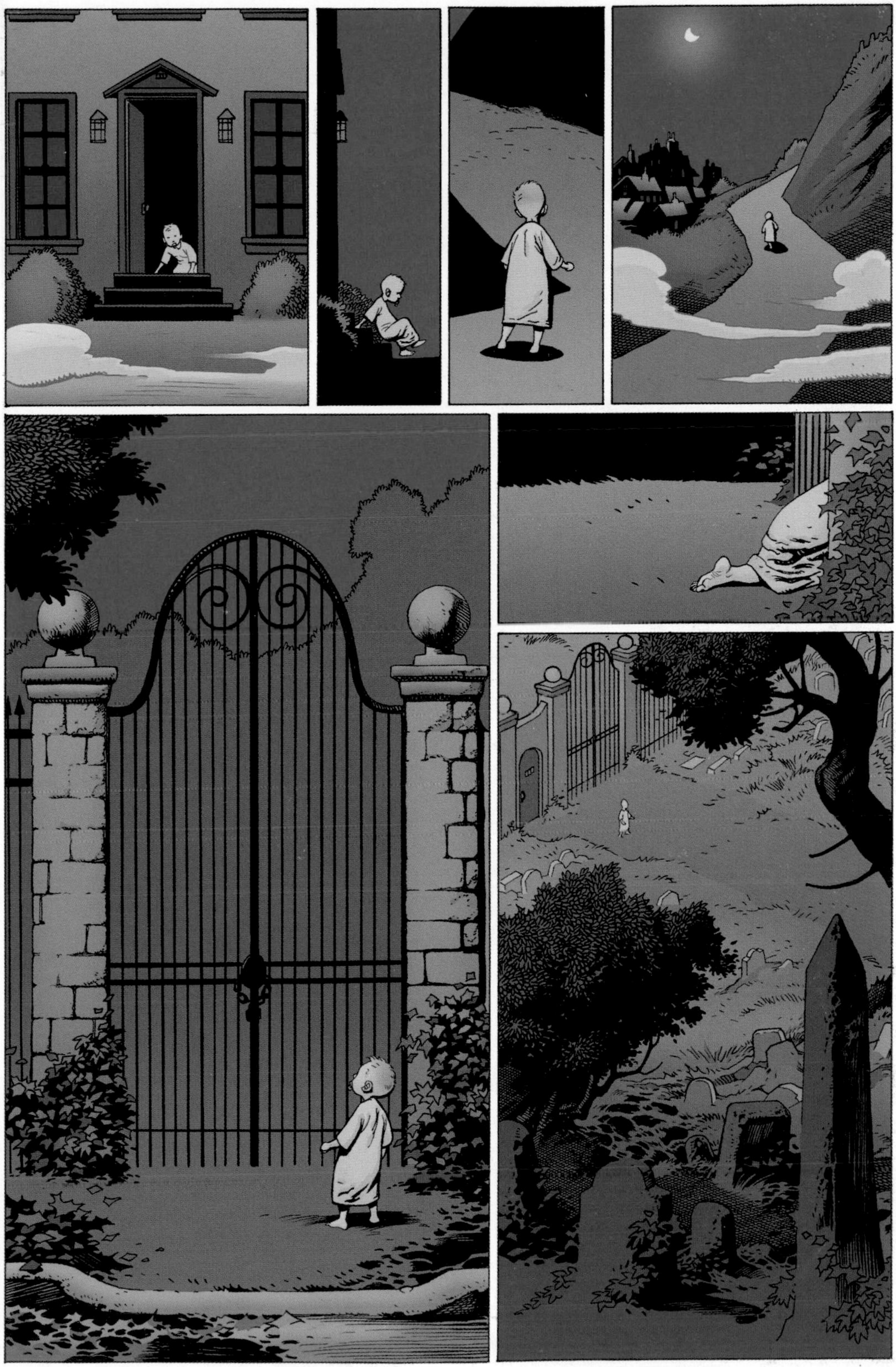

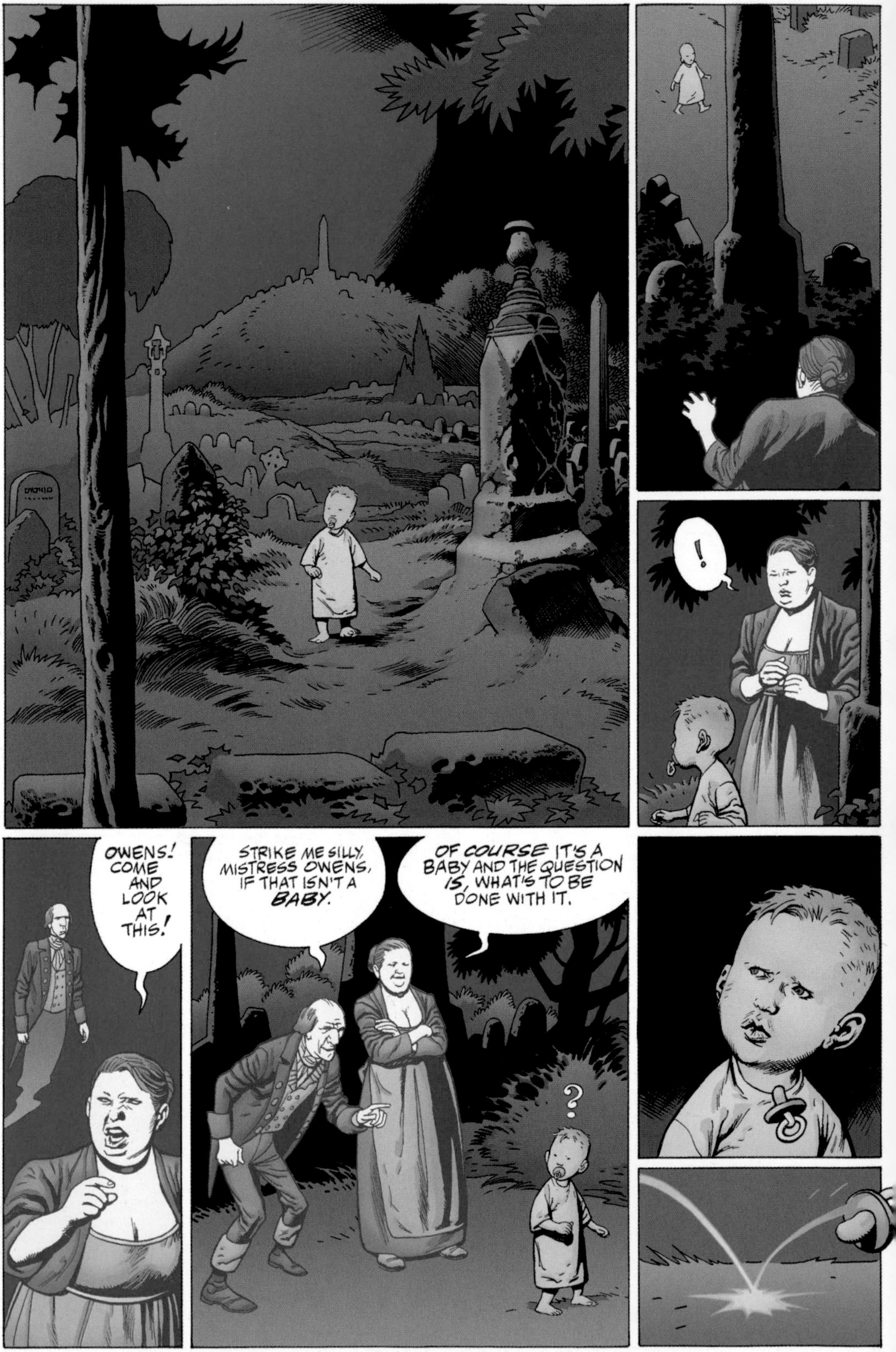
!
OWENS! COME AND LOOK AT THIS!
STRIKE ME SILLY, MISTRESS OWENS, IF THAT ISN'T A BABY.
OF COURSE IT'S A BABY AND THE QUESTION IS, WHAT'S TO BE DONE WITH IT.
?

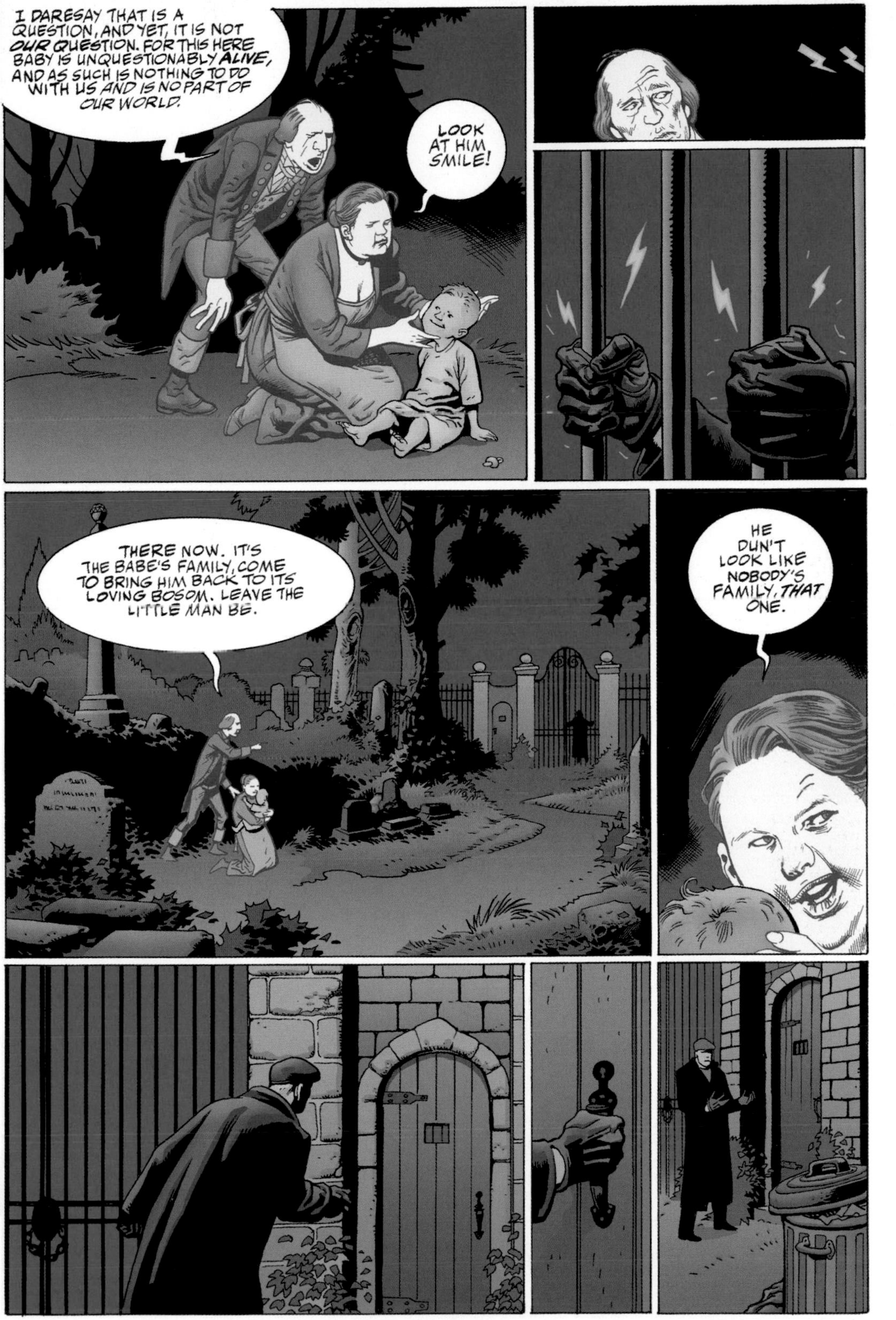
I DARESAY THAT IS A QUESTION, AND YET, IT IS NOT OUR QUESTION. FOR THIS HERE BABY IS UNQUESTIONABLY ALIVE, AND AS SUCH IS NOTHING TO DO WITH US AND IS NO PART OF OUR WORLD.
LOOK AT HIM SMILE!
THERE NOW. IT'S THE BABE'S FAMILY, COME TO BRING HIM BACK TO ITS LOVING BOSOM. LEAVE THE LITTLE MAN BE.
HE DUN'T LOOK LIKE NOBODY'S FAMILY, THAT ONE.

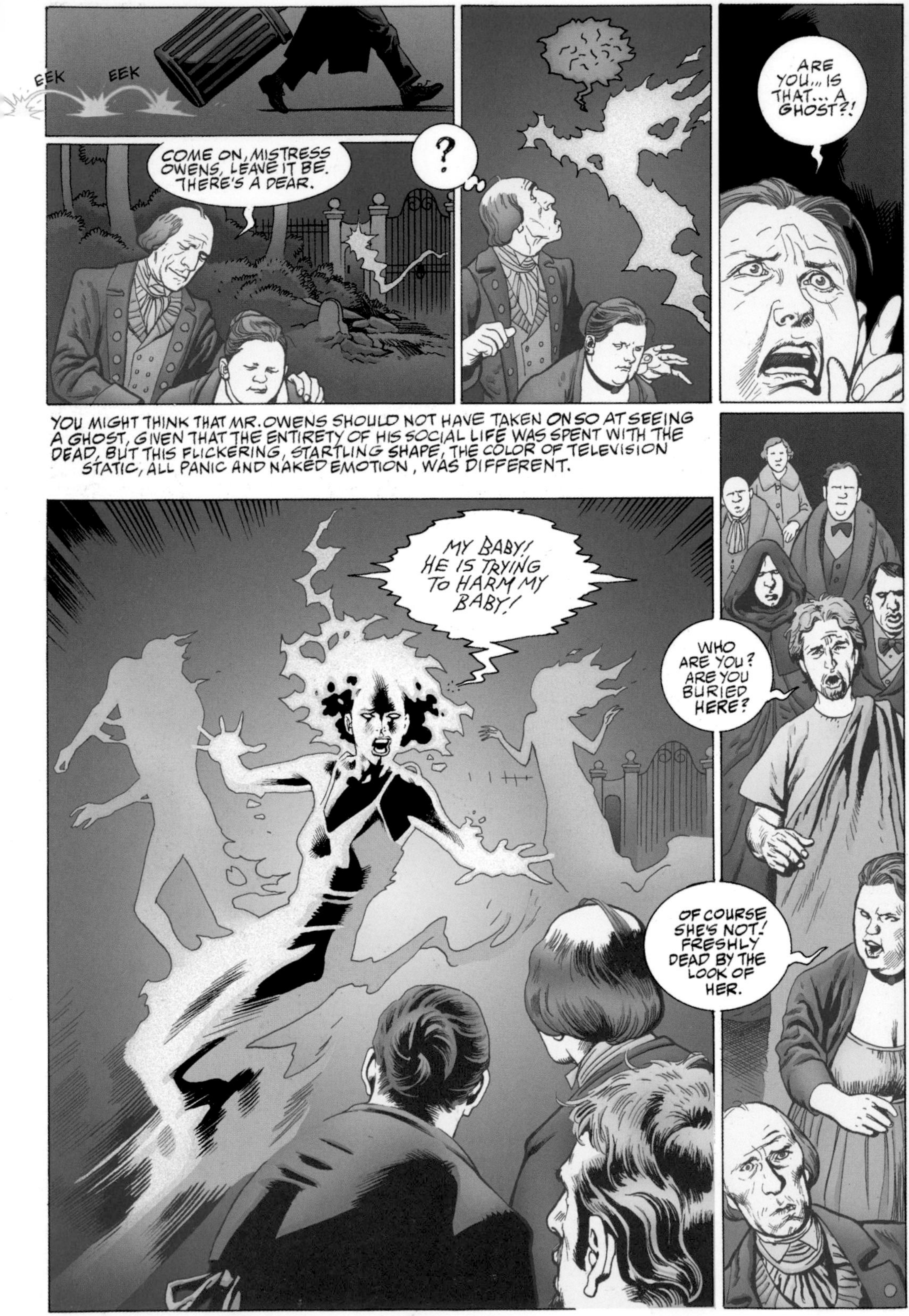
EEK
EEK
COME ON, MISTRESS OWENS, LEAVE IT BE. THERE'S A DEAR.
?
ARE YOU... IS THAT... A GHOST?!
YOU MIGHT THINK THAT MR. OWENS SHOULD NOT HAVE TAKEN ON SO AT SEEING A GHOST, GIVEN THAT THE ENTIRETY OF HIS SOCIAL LIFE WAS SPENT WITH THE DEAD, BUT THIS FLICKERING, STARTLING SHAPE, THE COLOR OF TELEVISION STATIC, ALL PANIC AND NAKED EMOTION, WAS DIFFERENT.
MY BABY! HE IS TRYING TO HARM MY BABY!
WHO ARE YOU? ARE YOU BURIED HERE?
OF COURSE SHE'S NOT! FRESHLY DEAD BY THE LOOK OF HER.

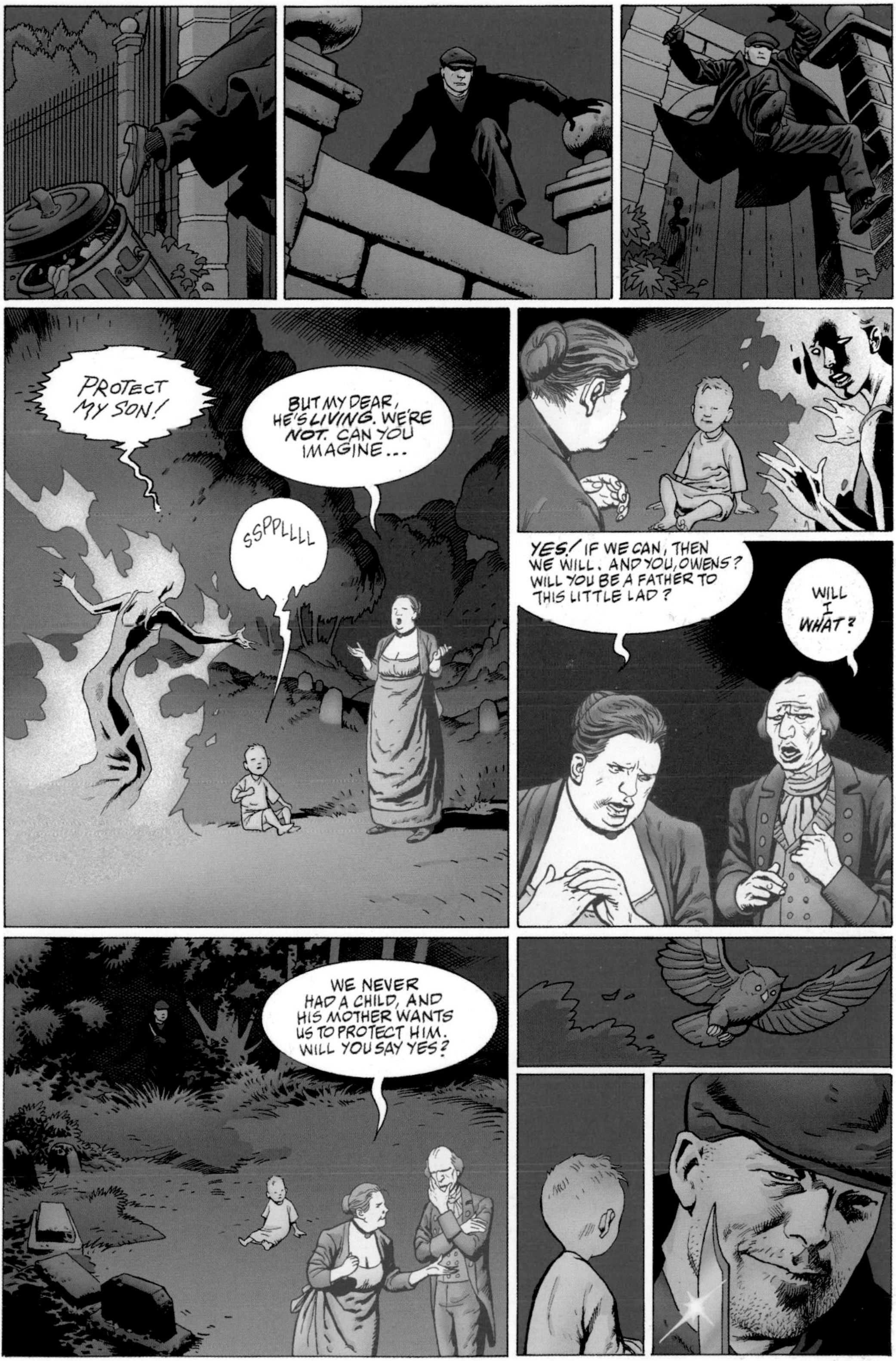
PROTECT MY SON!
BUT MY DEAR, HE'S LIVING. WE'RE NOT. CAN YOU IMAGINE...
SSPPLLLL
YES! IF WE CAN, THEN WE WILL. AND YOU, OWENS? WILL YOU BE A FATHER TO THIS LITTLE LAD?
WILL I WHAT?
WE NEVER HAD A CHILD, AND HIS MOTHER WANTS US TO PROTECT HIM. WILL YOU SAY YES?

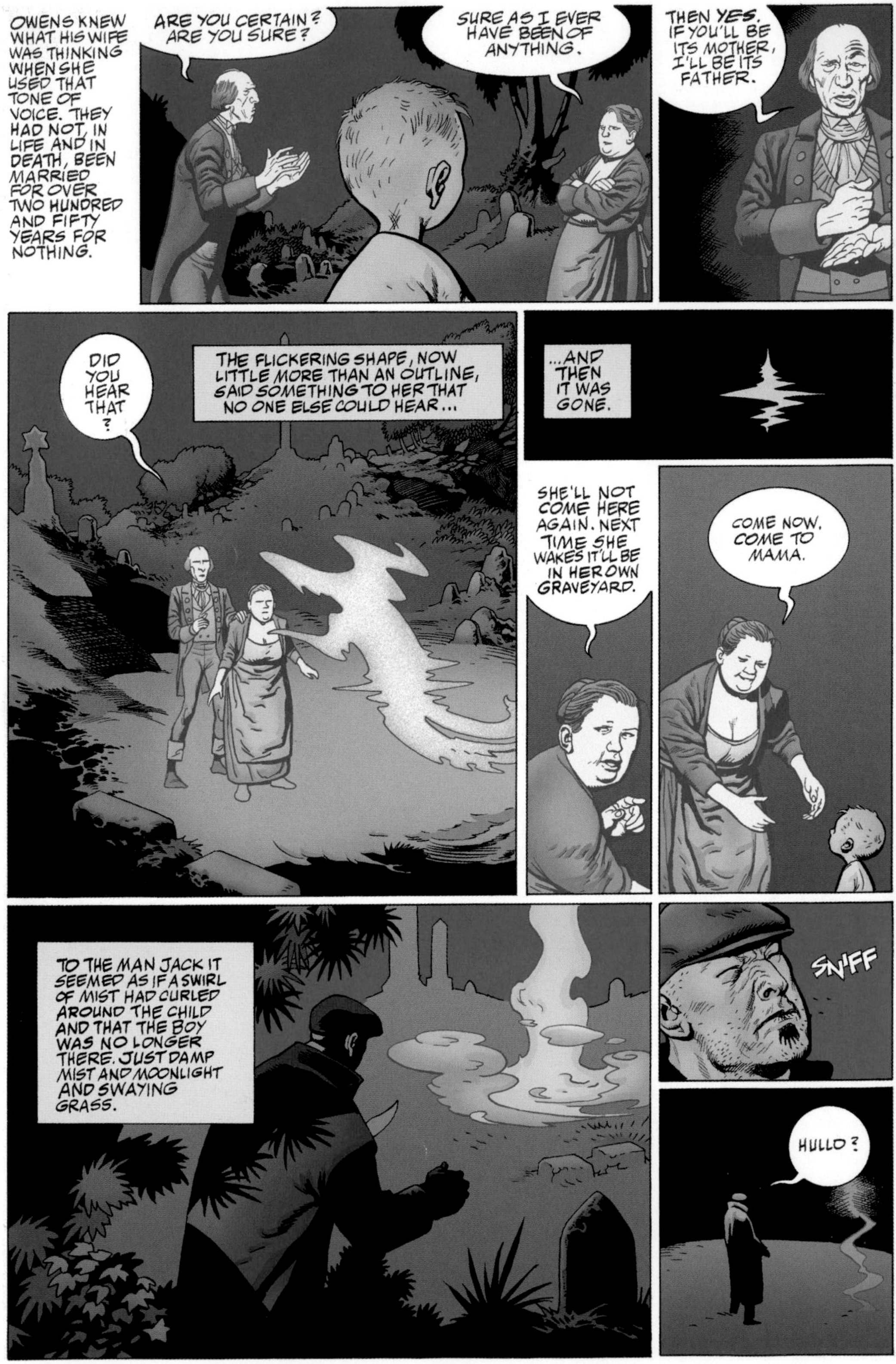
OWENS KNEW WHAT HIS WIFE WAS THINKING WHEN SHE USED THAT TONE OF VOICE. THEY HAD NOT, IN LIFE AND IN DEATH, BEEN MARRIED FOR OVER TWO HUNDRED AND FIFTY YEARS FOR NOTHING.
ARE YOU CERTAIN? ARE YOU SURE?
SURE AS I EVER HAVE BEEN OF ANYTHING.
THEN YES. IF YOU'LL BE ITS MOTHER, I'LL BE ITS FATHER.
DID YOU HEAR THAT?
THE FLICKERING SHAPE, NOW LITTLE MORE THAN AN OUTLINE, SAID SOMETHING TO HER THAT NO ONE ELSE COULD HEAR...
...AND THEN IT WAS GONE.
SHE'LL NOT COME HERE AGAIN. NEXT TIME SHE WAKES IT'LL BE IN HER OWN GRAVEYARD.
COME NOW. COME TO MAMA.
TO THE MAN JACK IT SEEMED AS IF A SWIRL OF MIST HAD CURLED AROUND THE CHILD AND THAT THE BOY WAS NO LONGER THERE. JUST DAMP MIST AND MOONLIGHT AND SWAYING GRASS.
SNIFF
HULLO?

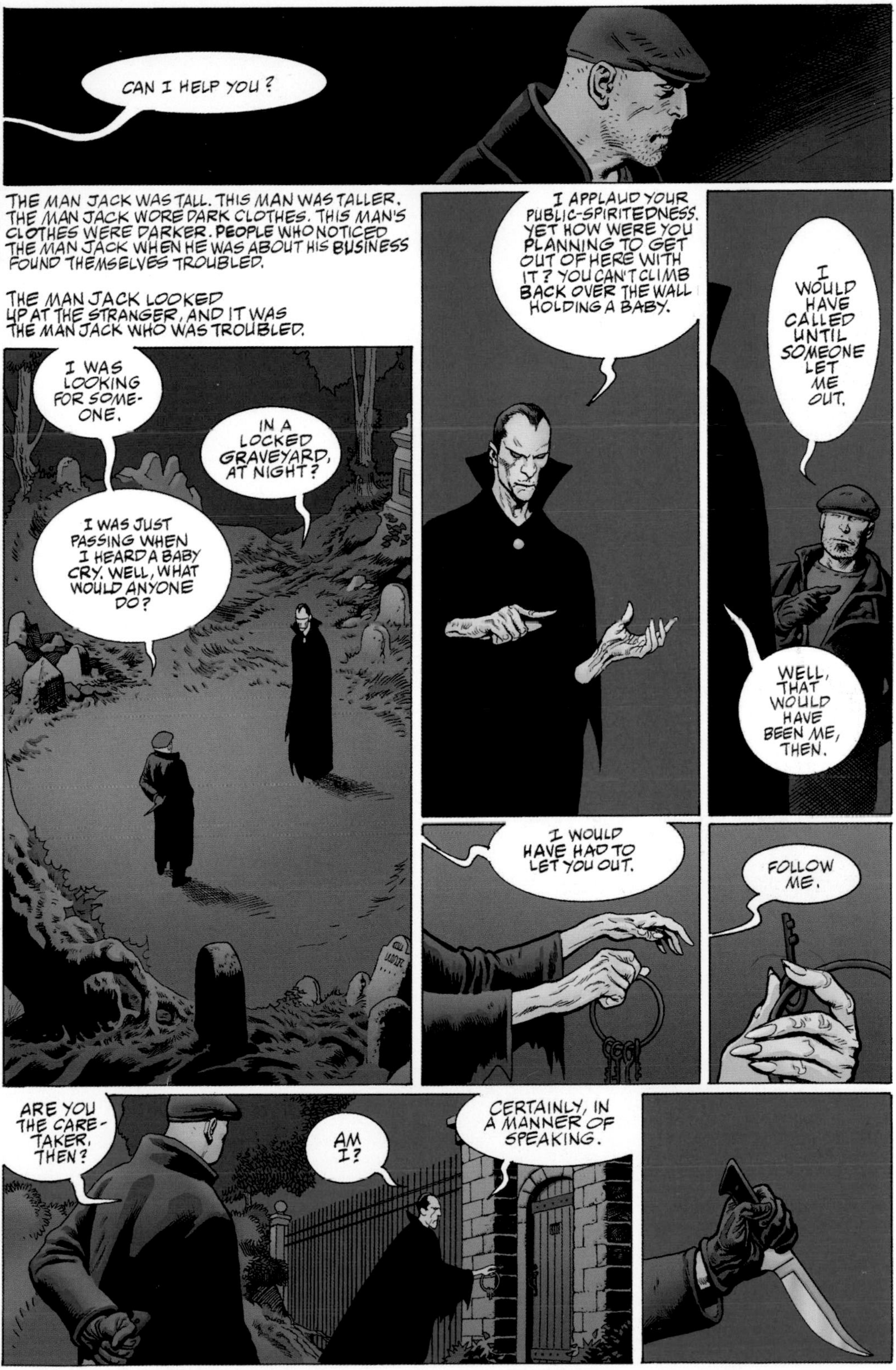
CAN I HELP YOU?
THE MAN JACK WAS TALL. THIS MAN WAS TALLER. THE MAN JACK WORE DARK CLOTHES. THIS MAN'S CLOTHES WERE DARKER. PEOPLE WHO NOTICED THE MAN JACK WHEN HE WAS ABOUT HIS BUSINESS FOUND THEMSELVES TROUBLED.
THE MAN JACK LOOKED UP AT THE STRANGER, AND IT WAS THE MAN JACK WHO WAS TROUBLED.
I WAS LOOKING FOR SOME-ONE.
IN A LOCKED GRAVEYARD, AT NIGHT?
I WAS JUST PASSING WHEN I HEARD A BABY CRY. WELL, WHAT WOULD ANYONE DO?
I APPLAUD YOUR PUBLIC-SPIRITEDNESS. YET HOW WERE YOU PLANNING TO GET OUT OF HERE WITH IT? YOU CAN'T CLIMB BACK OVER THE WALL HOLDING A BABY.
I WOULD HAVE CALLED UNTIL SOMEONE LET ME OUT.
WELL, THAT WOULD HAVE BEEN ME, THEN.
I WOULD HAVE HAD TO LET YOU OUT.
FOLLOW ME.
ARE YOU THE CARE-TAKER, THEN?
AM I?
CERTAINLY, IN A MANNER OF SPEAKING.

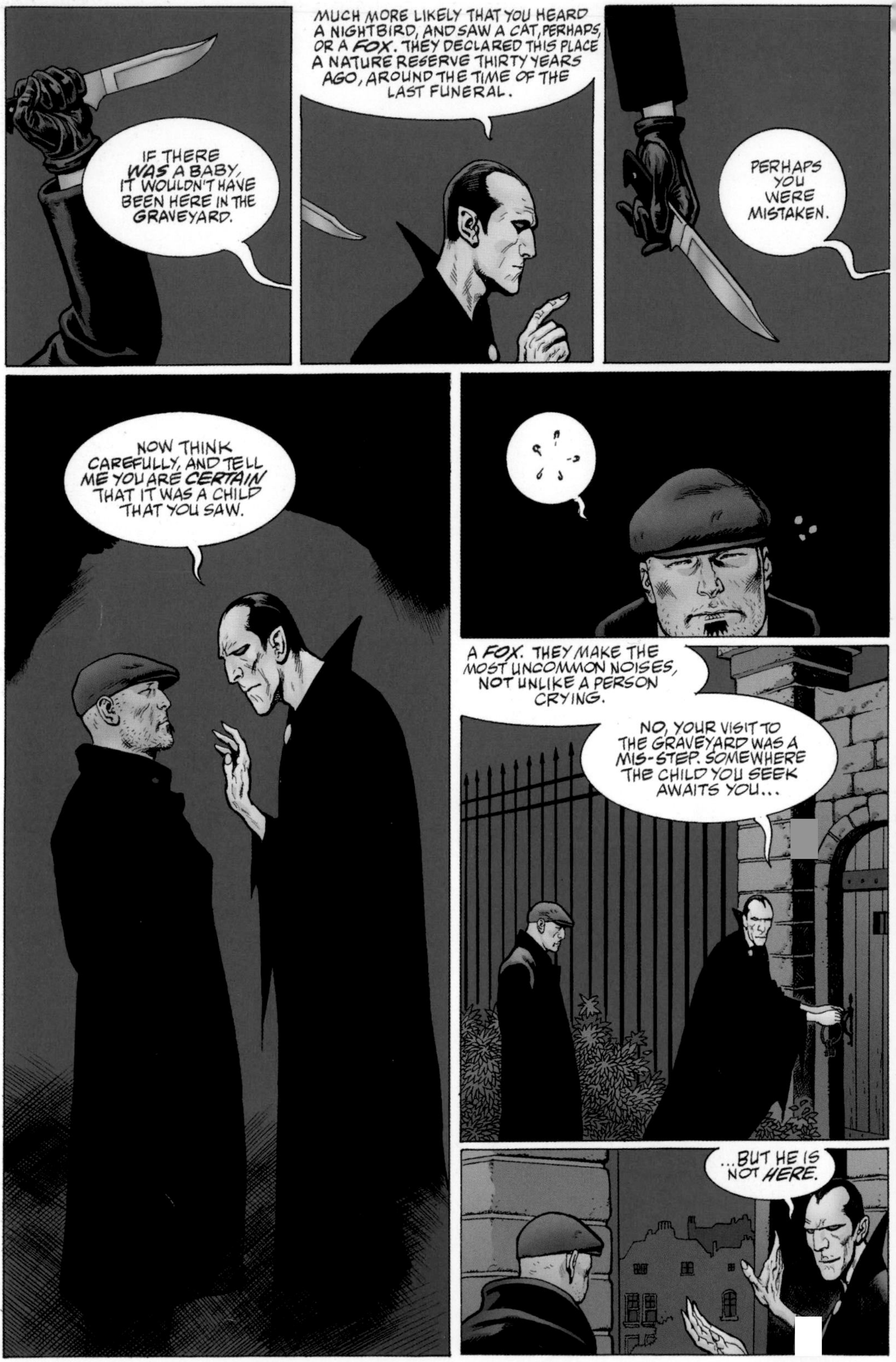
IF THERE WAS A BABY, IT WOULDN'T HAVE BEEN HERE IN THE GRAVEYARD.
MUCH MORE LIKELY THAT YOU HEARD A NIGHTBIRD, AND SAW A CAT, PERHAPS, OR A FOX. THEY DECLARED THIS PLACE A NATURE RESERVE THIRTY YEARS AGO, AROUND THE TIME OF THE LAST FUNERAL.
PERHAPS YOU WERE MISTAKEN.
NOW THINK CAREFULLY, AND TELL ME YOU ARE CERTAIN THAT IT WAS A CHILD THAT YOU SAW.
A FOX. THEY MAKE THE MOST UNCOMMON NOISES, NOT UNLIKE A PERSON CRYING.
NO, YOUR VISIT TO THE GRAVEYARD WAS A MIS-STEP. SOMEWHERE THE CHILD YOU SEEK AWAITS YOU...
...BUT HE IS NOT HERE.

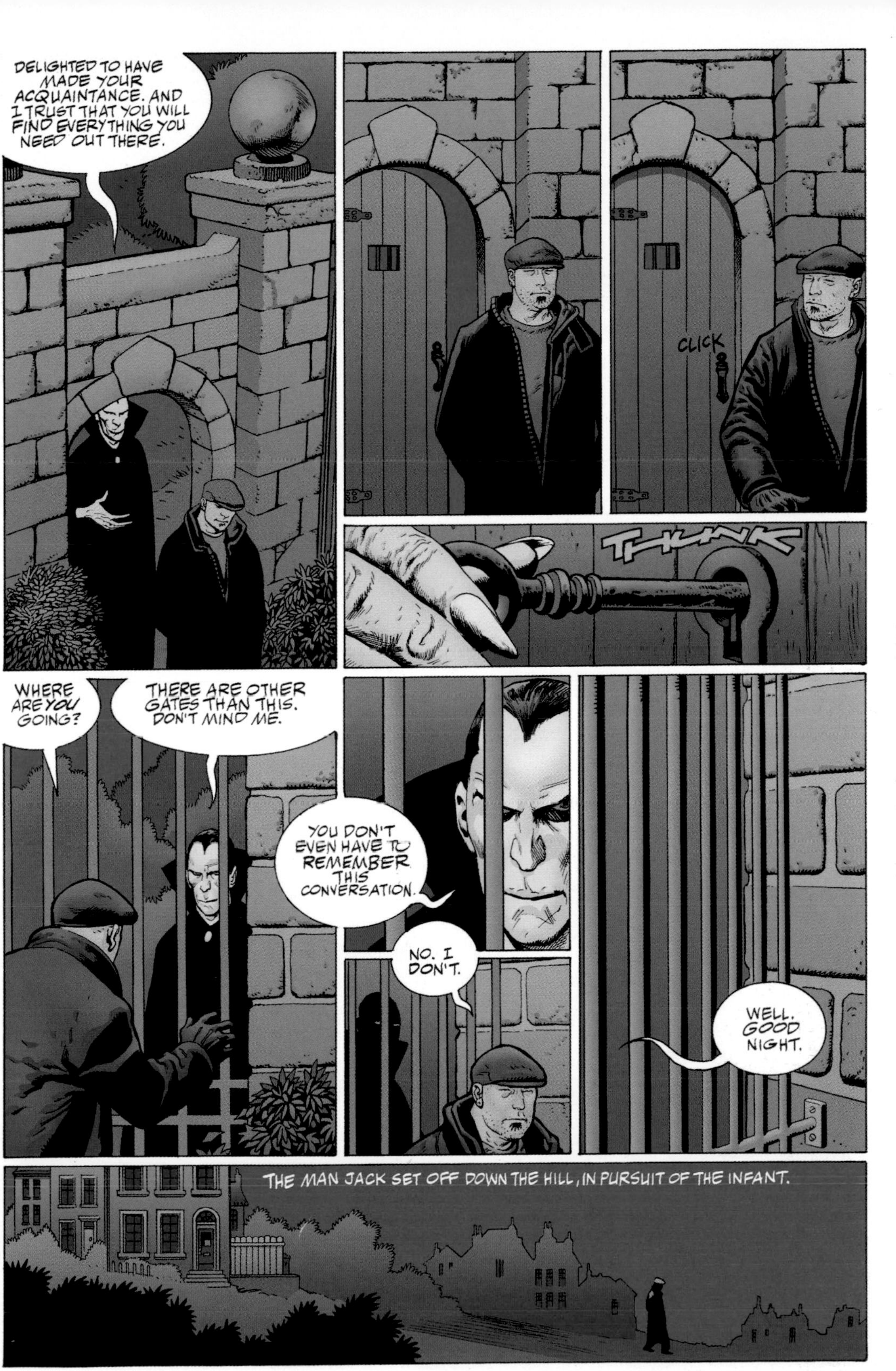
DELIGHTED TO HAVE MADE YOUR ACQUAINTANCE. AND I TRUST THAT YOU WILL FIND EVERYTHING YOU NEED OUT THERE.
CLICK
THUNK
WHERE ARE YOU GOING?
THERE ARE OTHER GATES THAN THIS. DON'T MIND ME.
YOU DON'T EVEN HAVE TO REMEMBER THIS CONVERSATION.
NO. I DON'T.
WELL. GOOD NIGHT.
THE MAN JACK SET OFF DOWN THE HILL, IN PURSUIT OF THE INFANT.

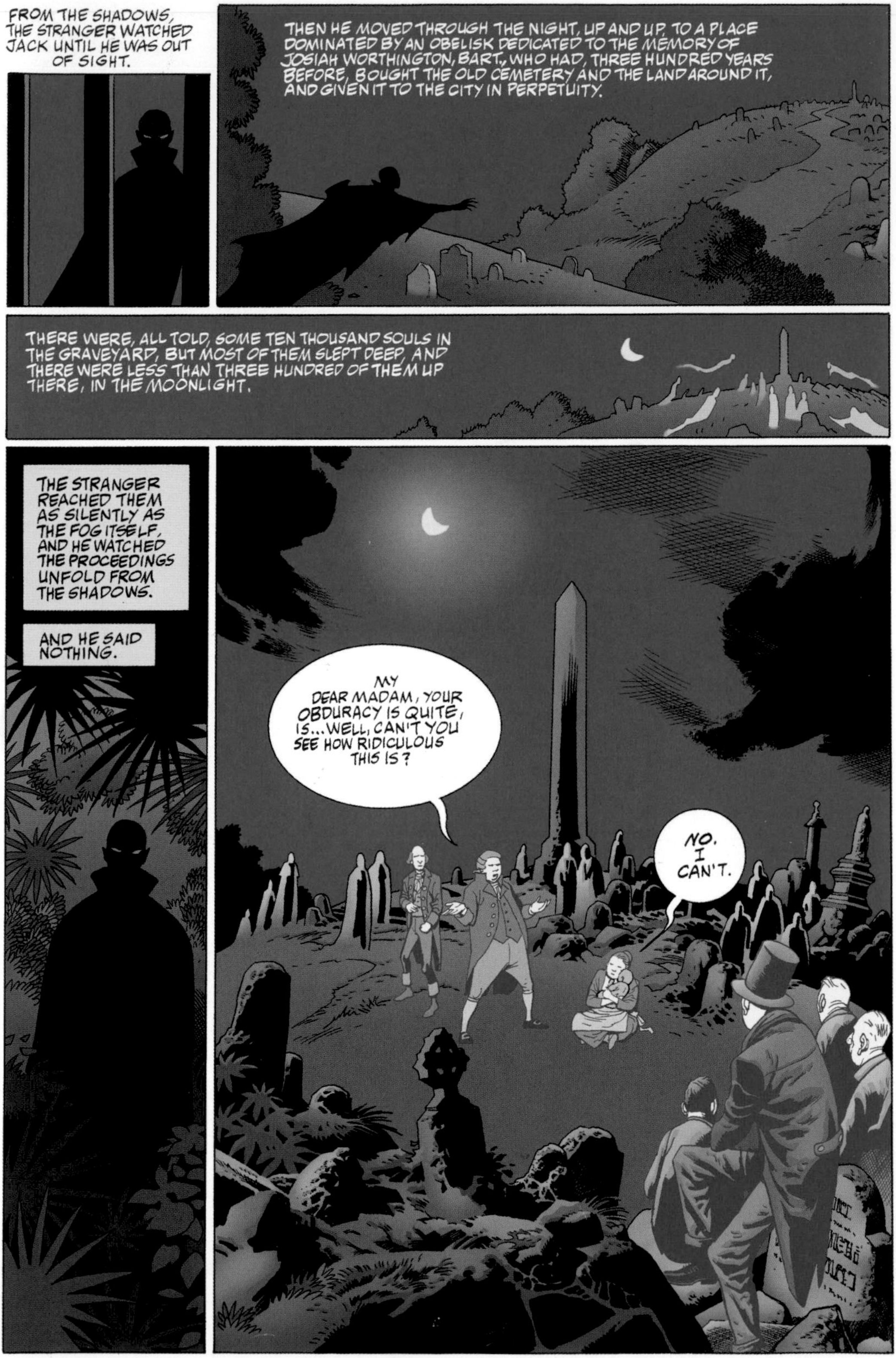
FROM THE SHADOWS, THE STRANGER WATCHED JACK UNTIL HE WAS OUT OF SIGHT.
THEN HE MOVED THROUGH THE NIGHT, UP AND UP, TO A PLACE DOMINATED BY AN OBELISK DEDICATED TO THE MEMORY OF JOSIAH WORTHINGTON, BART., WHO HAD, THREE HUNDRED YEARS BEFORE, BOUGHT THE OLD CEMETERY AND THE LAND AROUND IT, AND GIVEN IT TO THE CITY IN PERPETUITY.
THERE WERE, ALL TOLD, SOME TEN THOUSAND SOULS IN THE GRAVEYARD, BUT MOST OF THEM SLEPT DEEP, AND THERE WERE LESS THAN THREE HUNDRED OF THEM UP THERE, IN THE MOONLIGHT.
THE STRANGER REACHED THEM AS SILENTLY AS THE FOG ITSELF, AND HE WATCHED THE PROCEEDINGS UNFOLD FROM THE SHADOWS.
AND HE SAID NOTHING.
MY DEAR MADAM, YOUR OBDURACY IS QUITE, IS...WELL, CAN'T YOU SEE HOW RIDICULOUS THIS IS?
NO. I CAN'T.

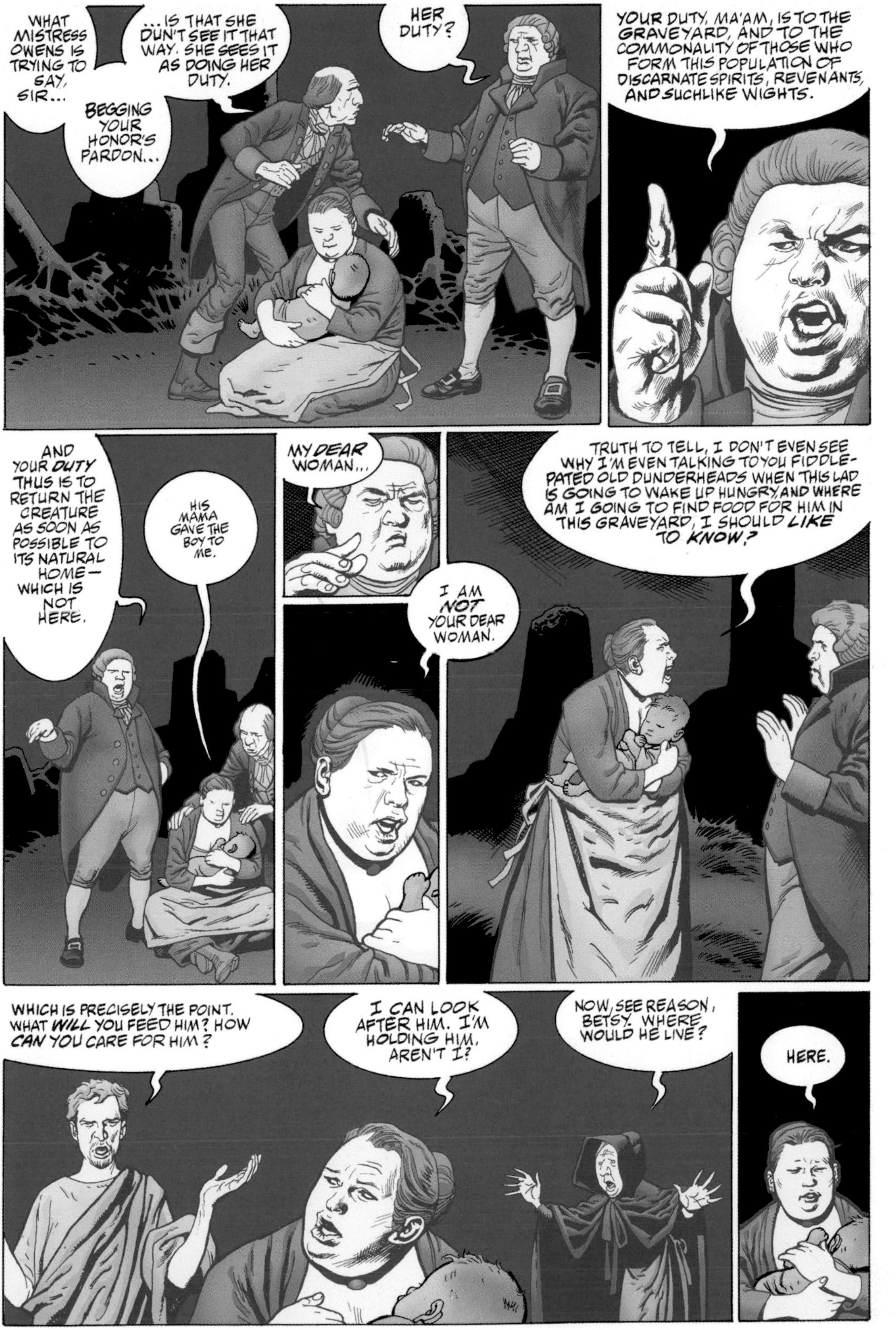
WHAT MISTRESS OWENS IS TRYING TO SAY, SIR...
...IS THAT SHE DON'T SEE IT THAT WAY. SHE SEES IT AS DOING HER DUTY.
BEGGING YOUR HONOR'S PARDON...
HER DUTY?
YOUR DUTY, MA'AM, IS TO THE GRAVEYARD, AND TO THE COMMONALITY OF THOSE WHO FORM THIS POPULATION OF DISCARNATE SPIRITS, REVENANTS, AND SUCHLIKE WIGHTS.
AND YOUR DUTY THUS IS TO RETURN THE CREATURE AS SOON AS POSSIBLE TO ITS NATURAL HOME— WHICH IS NOT HERE.
HIS MAMA GAVE THE BOY TO ME.
MY DEAR WOMAN...
I AM NOT YOUR DEAR WOMAN.
TRUTH TO TELL, I DON'T EVEN SEE WHY I'M EVEN TALKING TO YOU FIDDLE-PATED OLD DUNDERHEADS WHEN THIS LAD IS GOING TO WAKE UP HUNGRY, AND WHERE AM I GOING TO FIND FOOD FOR HIM IN THIS GRAVEYARD, I SHOULD LIKE TO KNOW?
WHICH IS PRECISELY THE POINT. WHAT WILL YOU FEED HIM? HOW CAN YOU CARE FOR HIM?
I CAN LOOK AFTER HIM. I'M HOLDING HIM, AREN'T I?
NOW, SEE REASON, BETSY. WHERE WOULD HE LIVE?
HERE.

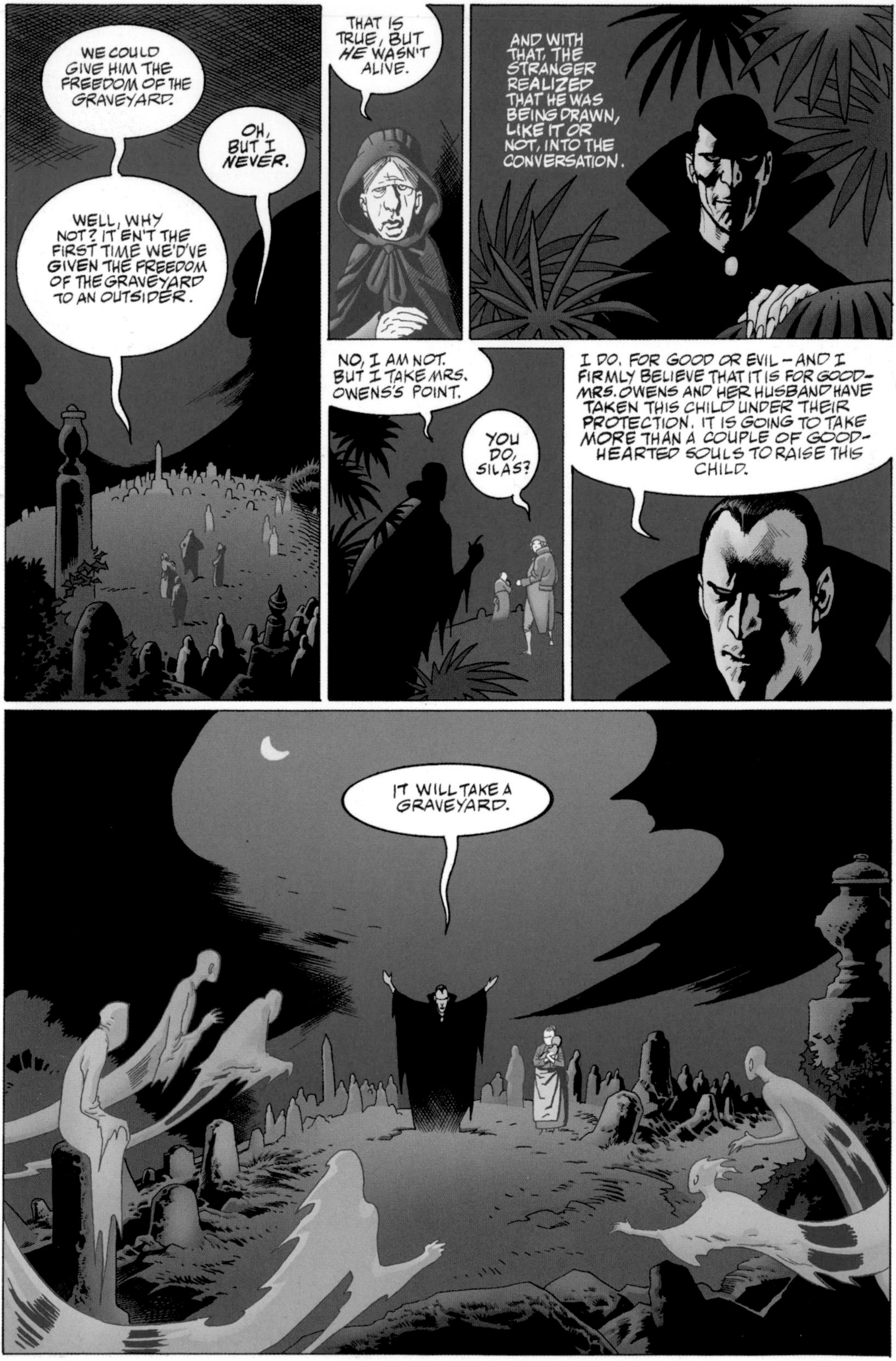
WE COULD GIVE HIM THE FREEDOM OF THE GRAVEYARD.
OH, BUT I NEVER.
WELL, WHY NOT? IT EN'T THE FIRST TIME WE'D'VE GIVEN THE FREEDOM OF THE GRAVEYARD TO AN OUTSIDER.
THAT IS TRUE, BUT HE WASN'T ALIVE.
AND WITH THAT, THE STRANGER REALIZED THAT HE WAS BEING DRAWN, LIKE IT OR NOT, INTO THE CONVERSATION.
NO, I AM NOT. BUT I TAKE MRS. OWENS'S POINT.
YOU DO, SILAS?
I DO. FOR GOOD OR EVIL – AND I FIRMLY BELIEVE THAT IT IS FOR GOOD – MRS. OWENS AND HER HUSBAND HAVE TAKEN THIS CHILD UNDER THEIR PROTECTION. IT IS GOING TO TAKE MORE THAN A COUPLE OF GOOD-HEARTED SOULS TO RAISE THIS CHILD.
IT WILL TAKE A GRAVEYARD.

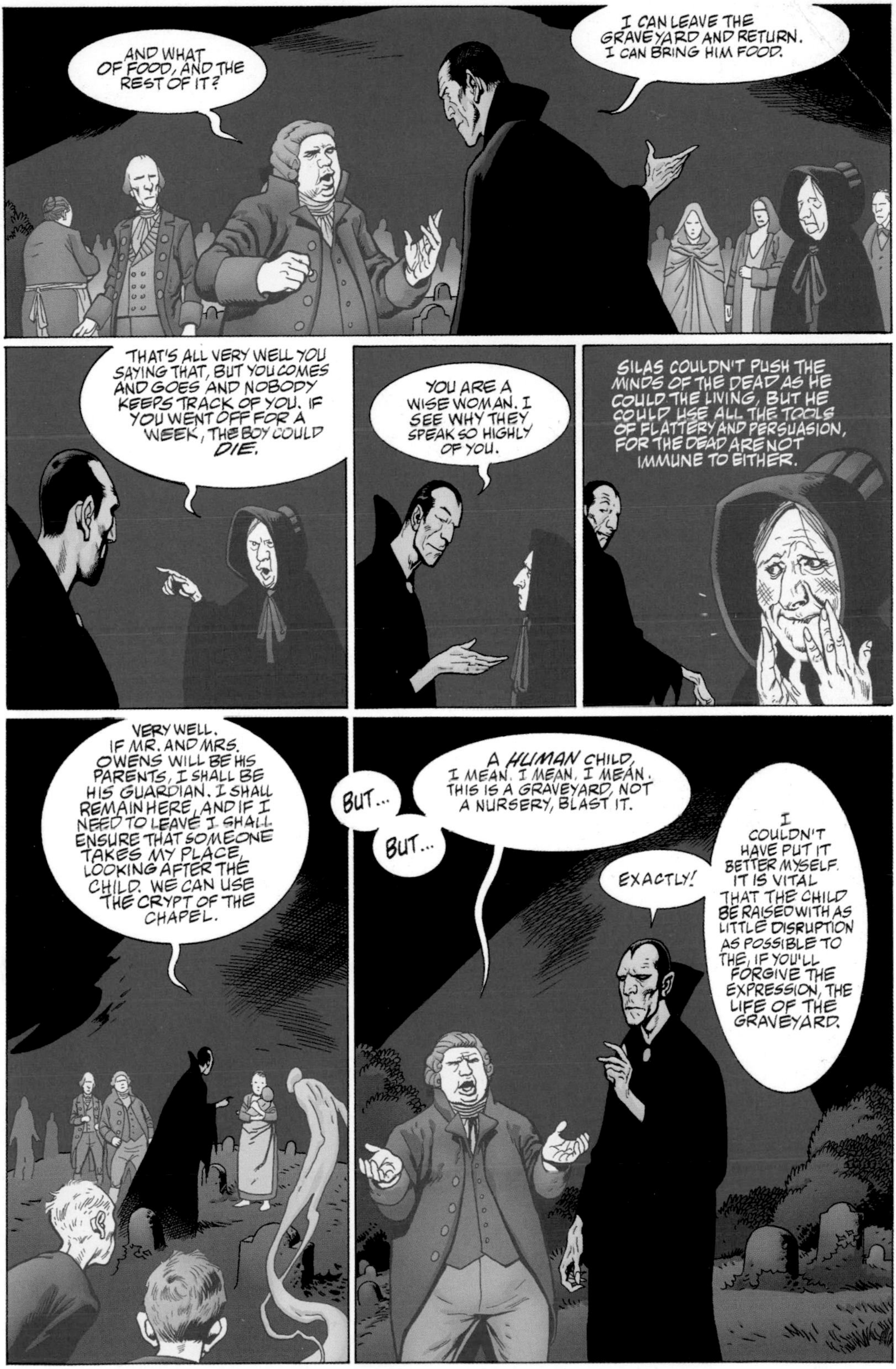
AND WHAT OF FOOD, AND THE REST OF IT?
I CAN LEAVE THE GRAVEYARD AND RETURN. I CAN BRING HIM FOOD.
THAT'S ALL VERY WELL YOU SAYING THAT, BUT YOU COMES AND GOES AND NOBODY KEEPS TRACK OF YOU. IF YOU WENT OFF FOR A WEEK, THE BOY COULD DIE.
YOU ARE A WISE WOMAN. I SEE WHY THEY SPEAK SO HIGHLY OF YOU.
SILAS COULDN'T PUSH THE MINDS OF THE DEAD AS HE COULD THE LIVING, BUT HE COULD USE ALL THE TOOLS OF FLATTERY AND PERSUASION, FOR THE DEAD ARE NOT IMMUNE TO EITHER.
VERY WELL. IF MR. AND MRS. OWENS WILL BE HIS PARENTS, I SHALL BE HIS GUARDIAN. I SHALL REMAIN HERE, AND IF I NEED TO LEAVE I SHALL ENSURE THAT SOMEONE TAKES MY PLACE, LOOKING AFTER THE CHILD. WE CAN USE THE CRYPT OF THE CHAPEL.
BUT...
BUT...
A HUMAN CHILD, I MEAN. I MEAN. I MEAN. THIS IS A GRAVEYARD, NOT A NURSERY, BLAST IT.
EXACTLY!
I COULDN'T HAVE PUT IT BETTER MYSELF. IT IS VITAL THAT THE CHILD BE RAISED WITH AS LITTLE DISRUPTION AS POSSIBLE TO THE, IF YOU'LL FORGIVE THE EXPRESSION, THE LIFE OF THE GRAVEYARD.

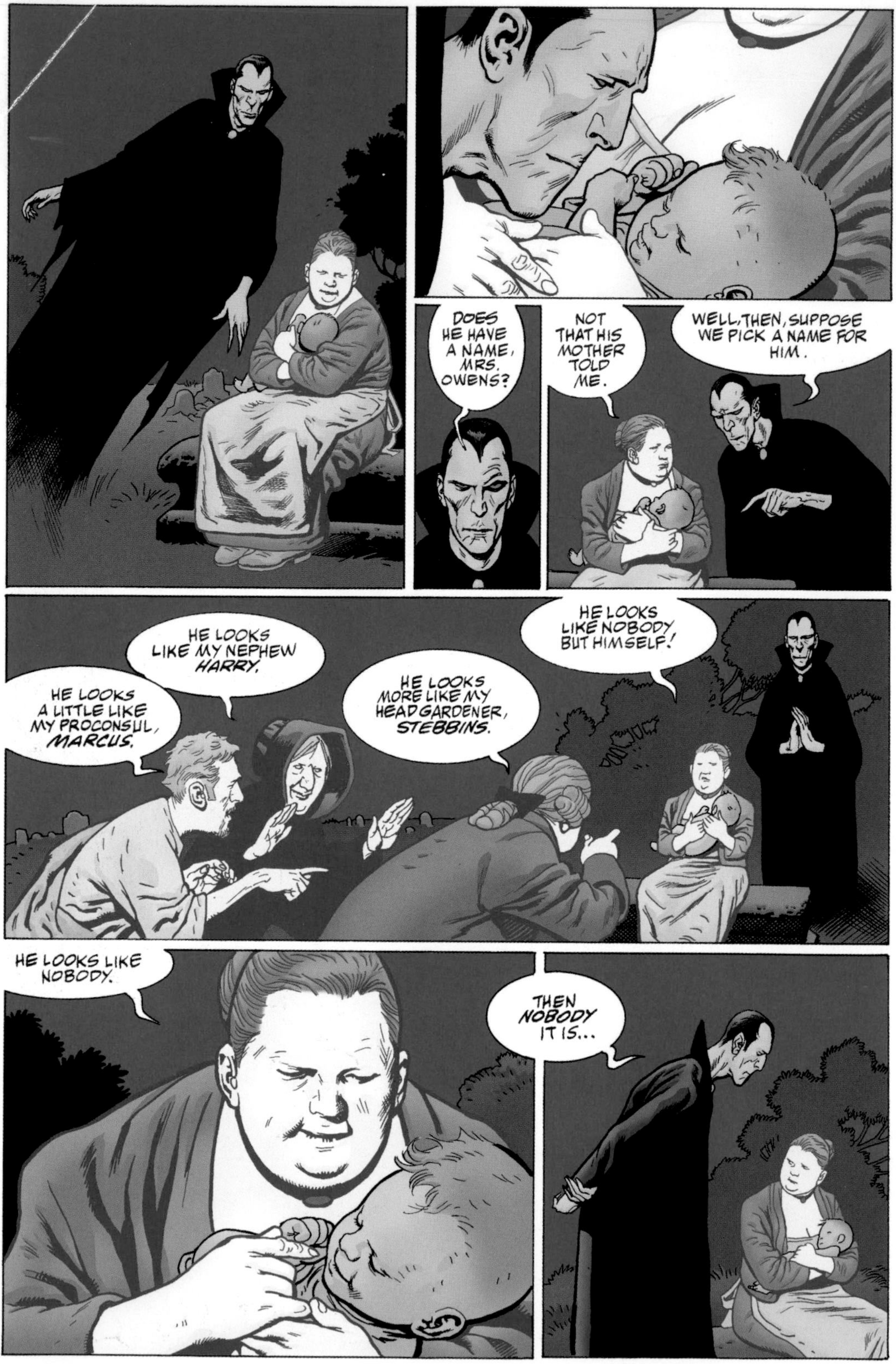
DOES HE HAVE A NAME, MRS. OWENS?
NOT THAT HIS MOTHER TOLD ME.
WELL, THEN, SUPPOSE WE PICK A NAME FOR HIM.
HE LOOKS A LITTLE LIKE MY PROCONSUL, MARCUS.
HE LOOKS LIKE MY NEPHEW HARRY.
HE LOOKS MORE LIKE MY HEAD GARDENER, STEBBINS.
HE LOOKS LIKE NOBODY BUT HIMSELF!
HE LOOKS LIKE NOBODY.
THEN NOBODY IT IS...

...NOBODY OWENS.

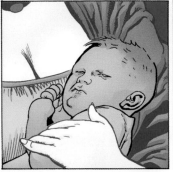

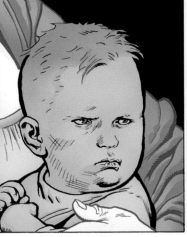

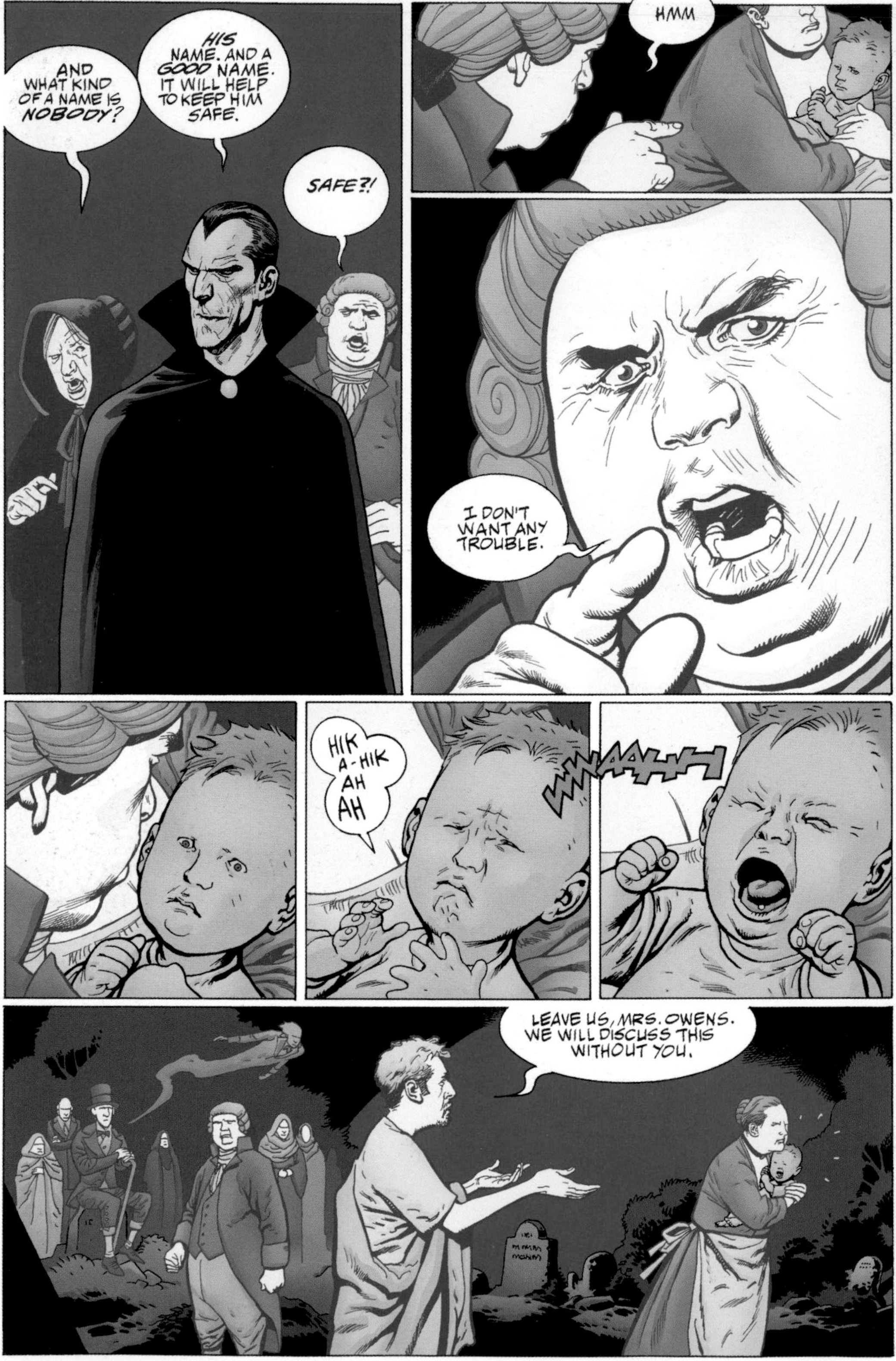
AND WHAT KIND OF A NAME IS NOBODY?
HIS NAME. AND A GOOD NAME. IT WILL HELP TO KEEP HIM SAFE.
SAFE?!
HMM
I DON'T WANT ANY TROUBLE.
HIK A-HIK AH AH
WAAHH
LEAVE US, MRS. OWENS. WE WILL DISCUSS THIS WITHOUT YOU.

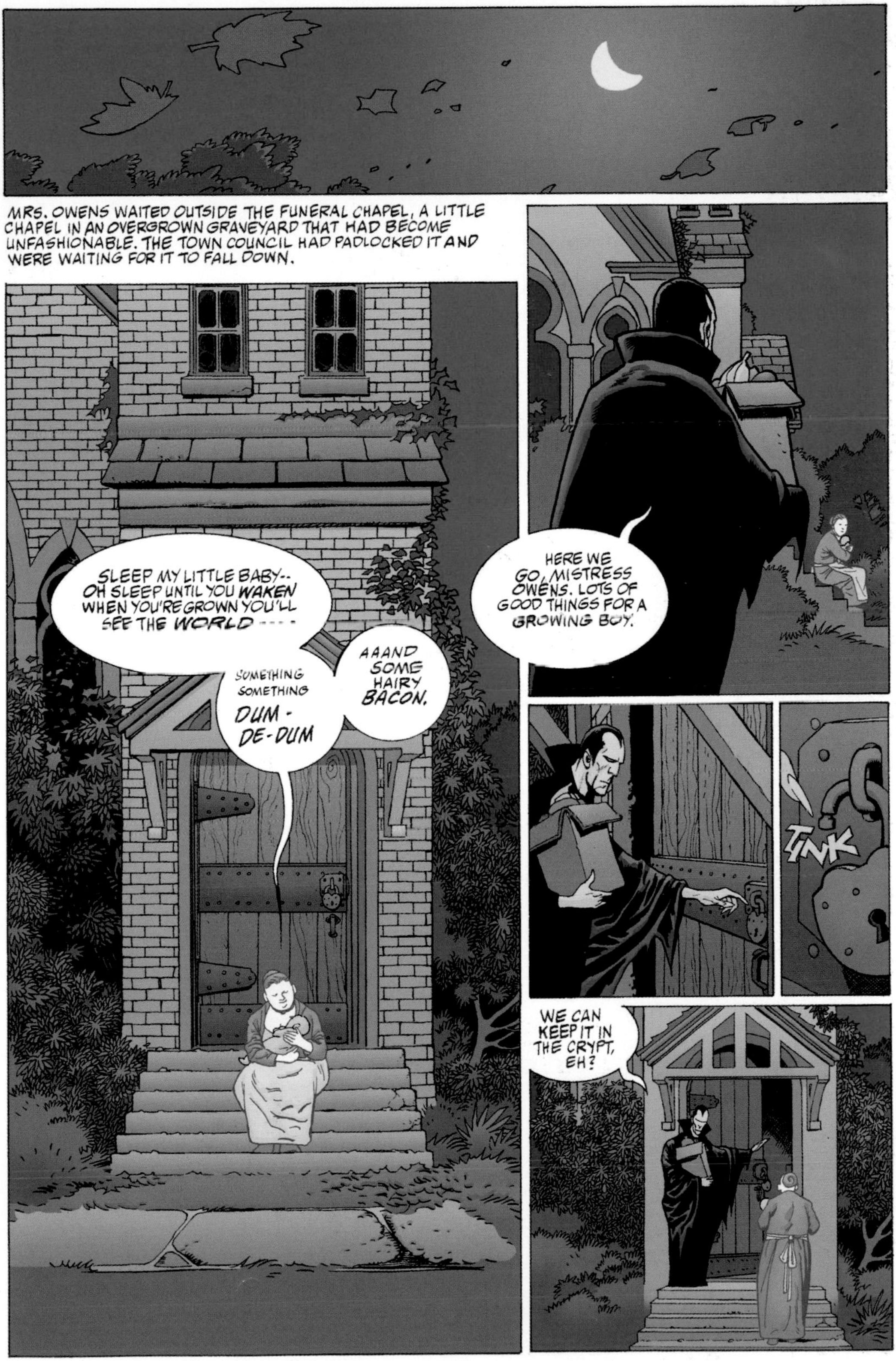
MRS. OWENS WAITED OUTSIDE THE FUNERAL CHAPEL, A LITTLE CHAPEL IN AN OVERGROWN GRAVEYARD THAT HAD BECOME UNFASHIONABLE. THE TOWN COUNCIL HAD PADLOCKED IT AND WERE WAITING FOR IT TO FALL DOWN.
SLEEP MY LITTLE BABY-- OH SLEEP UNTIL YOU WAKEN WHEN YOU'RE GROWN YOU'LL SEE THE WORLD----
SOMETHING SOMETHING DUM-DE-DUM
AAAND SOME HAIRY BACON.
HERE WE GO, MISTRESS OWENS. LOTS OF GOOD THINGS FOR A GROWING BOY.
TINK
WE CAN KEEP IT IN THE CRYPT, EH?

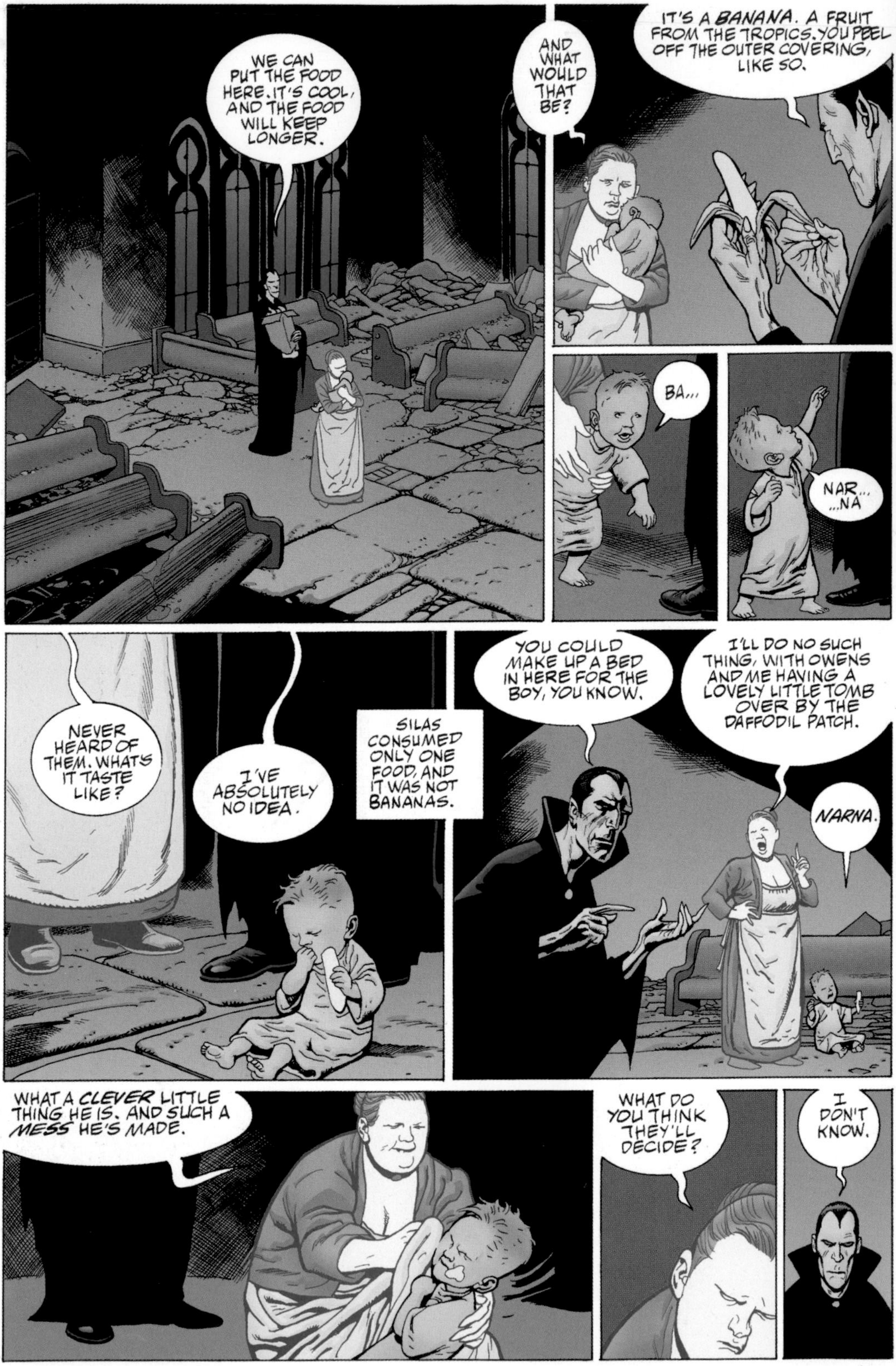
WE CAN PUT THE FOOD HERE. IT'S COOL, AND THE FOOD WILL KEEP LONGER.
AND WHAT WOULD THAT BE?
IT'S A BANANA. A FRUIT FROM THE TROPICS. YOU PEEL OFF THE OUTER COVERING, LIKE SO.
BA...
NAR... ...NA
NEVER HEARD OF THEM. WHAT'S IT TASTE LIKE?
I'VE ABSOLUTELY NO IDEA.
SILAS CONSUMED ONLY ONE FOOD, AND IT WAS NOT BANANAS.
YOU COULD MAKE UP A BED IN HERE FOR THE BOY, YOU KNOW.
I'LL DO NO SUCH THING, WITH OWENS AND ME HAVING A LOVELY LITTLE TOMB OVER BY THE DAFFODIL PATCH.
NARNA.
WHAT A CLEVER LITTLE THING HE IS. AND SUCH A MESS HE'S MADE.
WHAT DO YOU THINK THEY'LL DECIDE?
I DON'T KNOW.

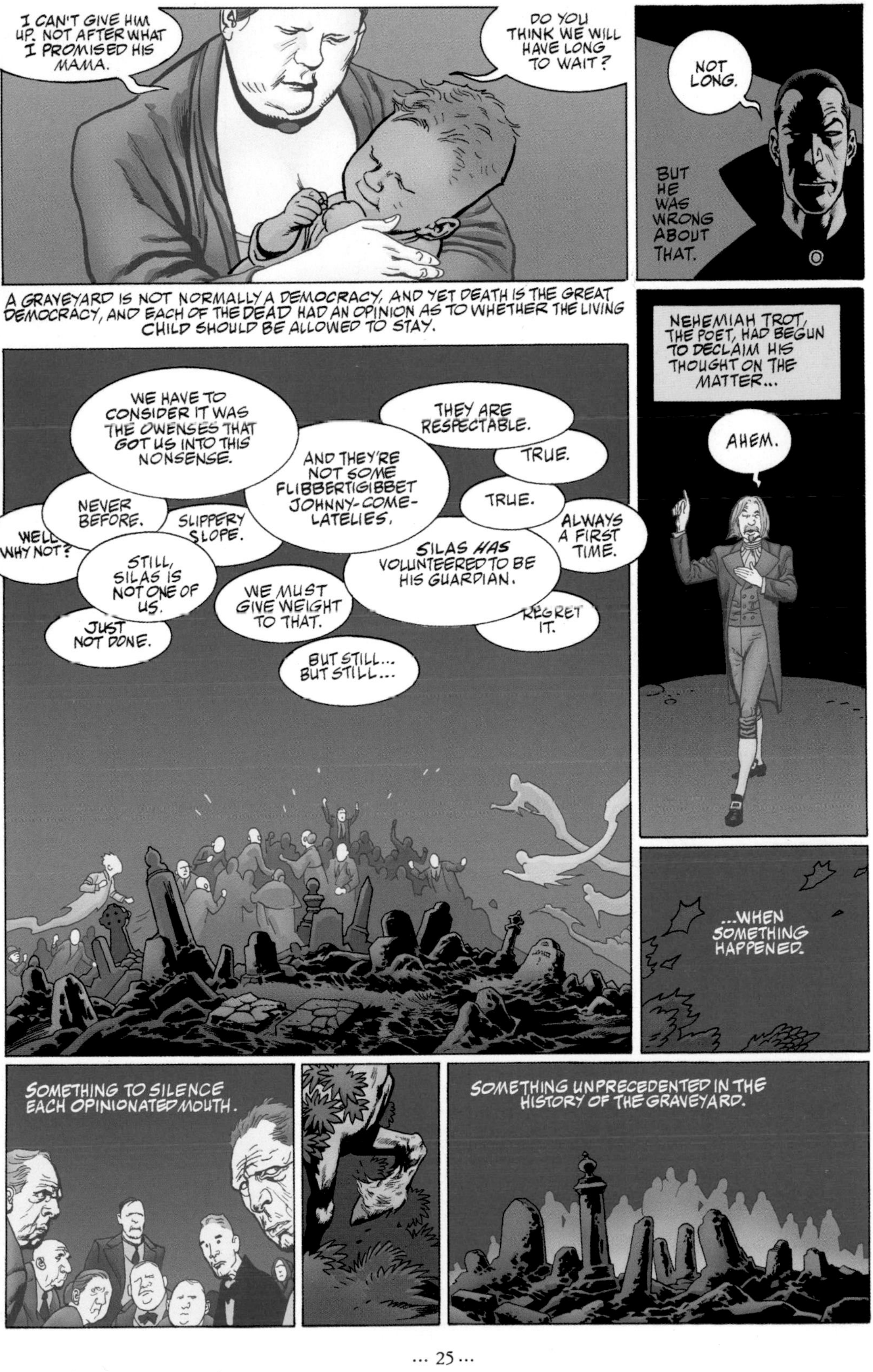
I CAN'T GIVE HIM UP. NOT AFTER WHAT I PROMISED HIS MAMA.
DO YOU THINK WE WILL HAVE LONG TO WAIT?
NOT LONG.
BUT HE WAS WRONG ABOUT THAT.
A GRAVEYARD IS NOT NORMALLY A DEMOCRACY, AND YET DEATH IS THE GREAT DEMOCRACY, AND EACH OF THE DEAD HAD AN OPINION AS TO WHETHER THE LIVING CHILD SHOULD BE ALLOWED TO STAY.
WE HAVE TO CONSIDER IT WAS THE OWENSES THAT GOT US INTO THIS NONSENSE.
THEY ARE RESPECTABLE.
TRUE.
AND THEY'RE NOT SOME FLIBBERTIGIBBET JOHNNY-COME-LATELIES.
TRUE.
NEVER BEFORE.
SLIPPERY SLOPE.
WELL, WHY NOT?
ALWAYS A FIRST TIME.
STILL, SILAS IS NOT ONE OF US.
SILAS *HAS* VOLUNTEERED TO BE HIS GUARDIAN.
WE MUST GIVE WEIGHT TO THAT.
REGRET IT.
JUST NOT DONE.
BUT STILL... BUT STILL...
NEHEMIAH TROT, THE POET, HAD BEGUN TO DECLAIM HIS THOUGHT ON THE MATTER...
AHEM.
...WHEN SOMETHING HAPPENED.
SOMETHING TO SILENCE EACH OPINIONATED MOUTH.
SOMETHING UNPRECEDENTED IN THE HISTORY OF THE GRAVEYARD.

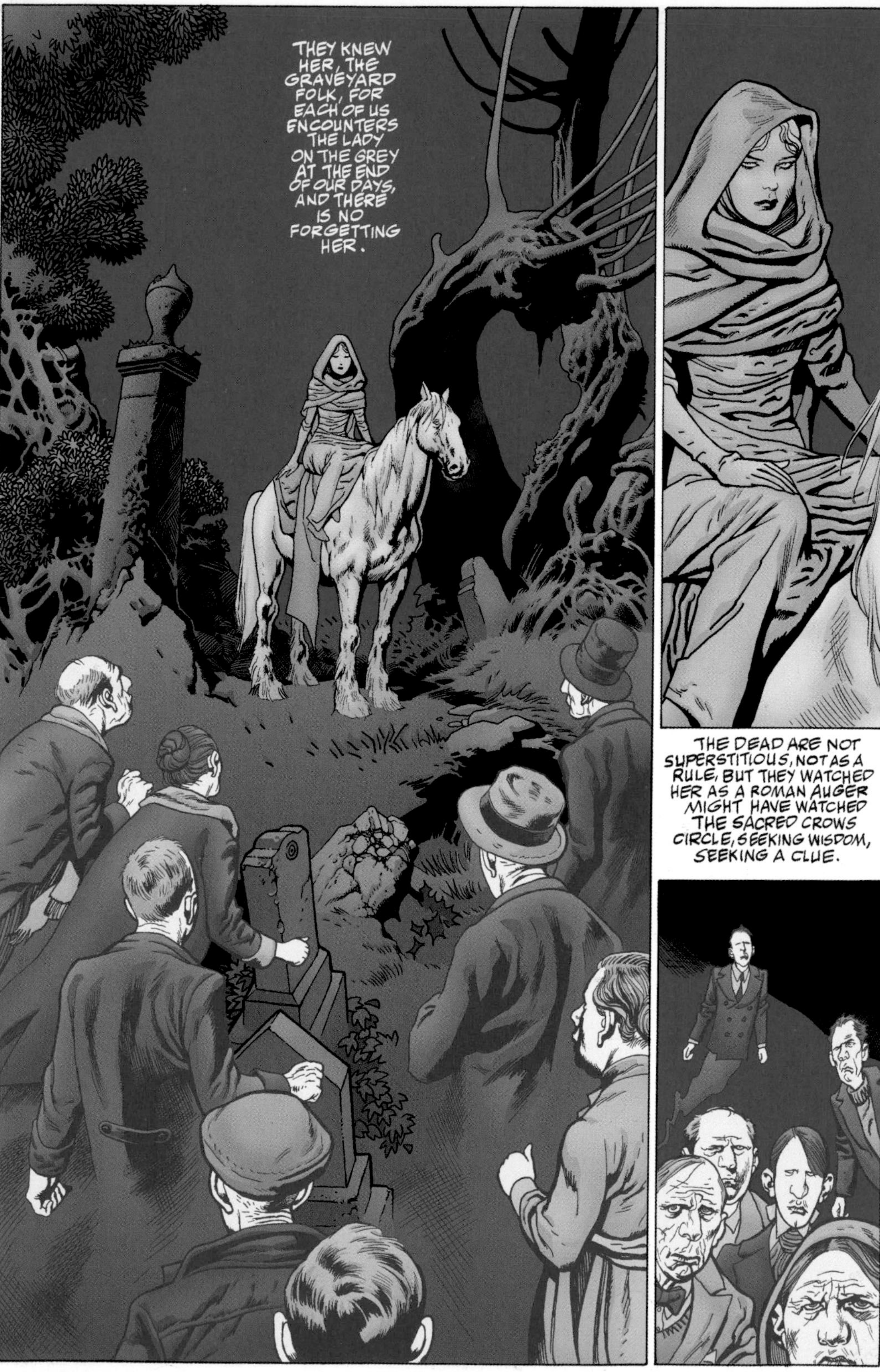
THEY KNEW HER, THE GRAVEYARD FOLK, FOR EACH OF US ENCOUNTERS THE LADY ON THE GREY AT THE END OF OUR DAYS, AND THERE IS NO FORGETTING HER.
THE DEAD ARE NOT SUPERSTITIOUS, NOT AS A RULE, BUT THEY WATCHED HER AS A ROMAN AUGER MIGHT HAVE WATCHED THE SACRED CROWS CIRCLE, SEEKING WISDOM, SEEKING A CLUE.

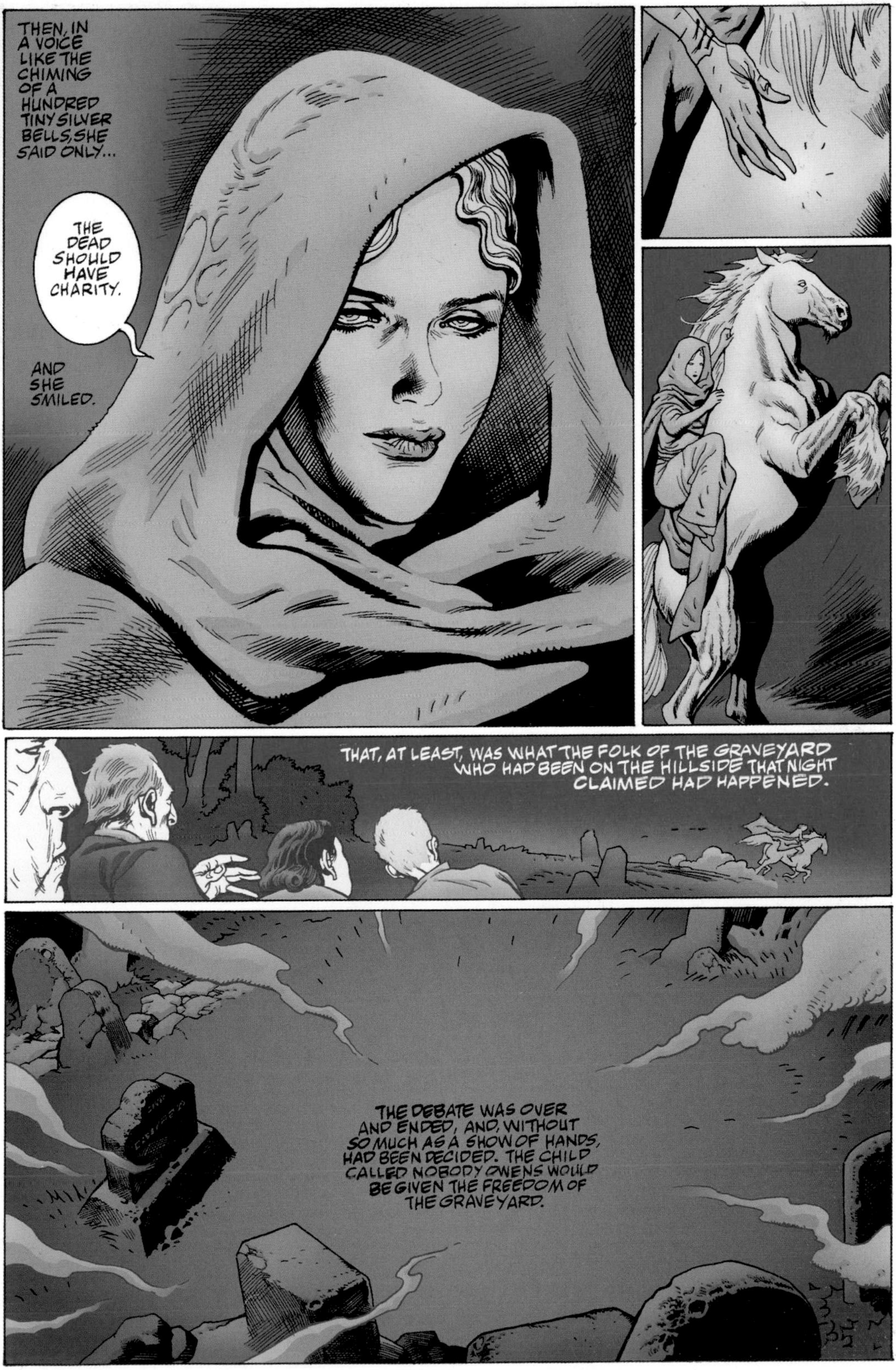
THEN, IN A VOICE LIKE THE CHIMING OF A HUNDRED TINY SILVER BELLS, SHE SAID ONLY...
THE DEAD SHOULD HAVE CHARITY.
AND SHE SMILED.
THAT, AT LEAST, WAS WHAT THE FOLK OF THE GRAVEYARD WHO HAD BEEN ON THE HILLSIDE THAT NIGHT CLAIMED HAD HAPPENED.
THE DEBATE WAS OVER AND ENDED, AND, WITHOUT SO MUCH AS A SHOW OF HANDS, HAD BEEN DECIDED. THE CHILD CALLED NOBODY OWENS WOULD BE GIVEN THE FREEDOM OF THE GRAVEYARD.

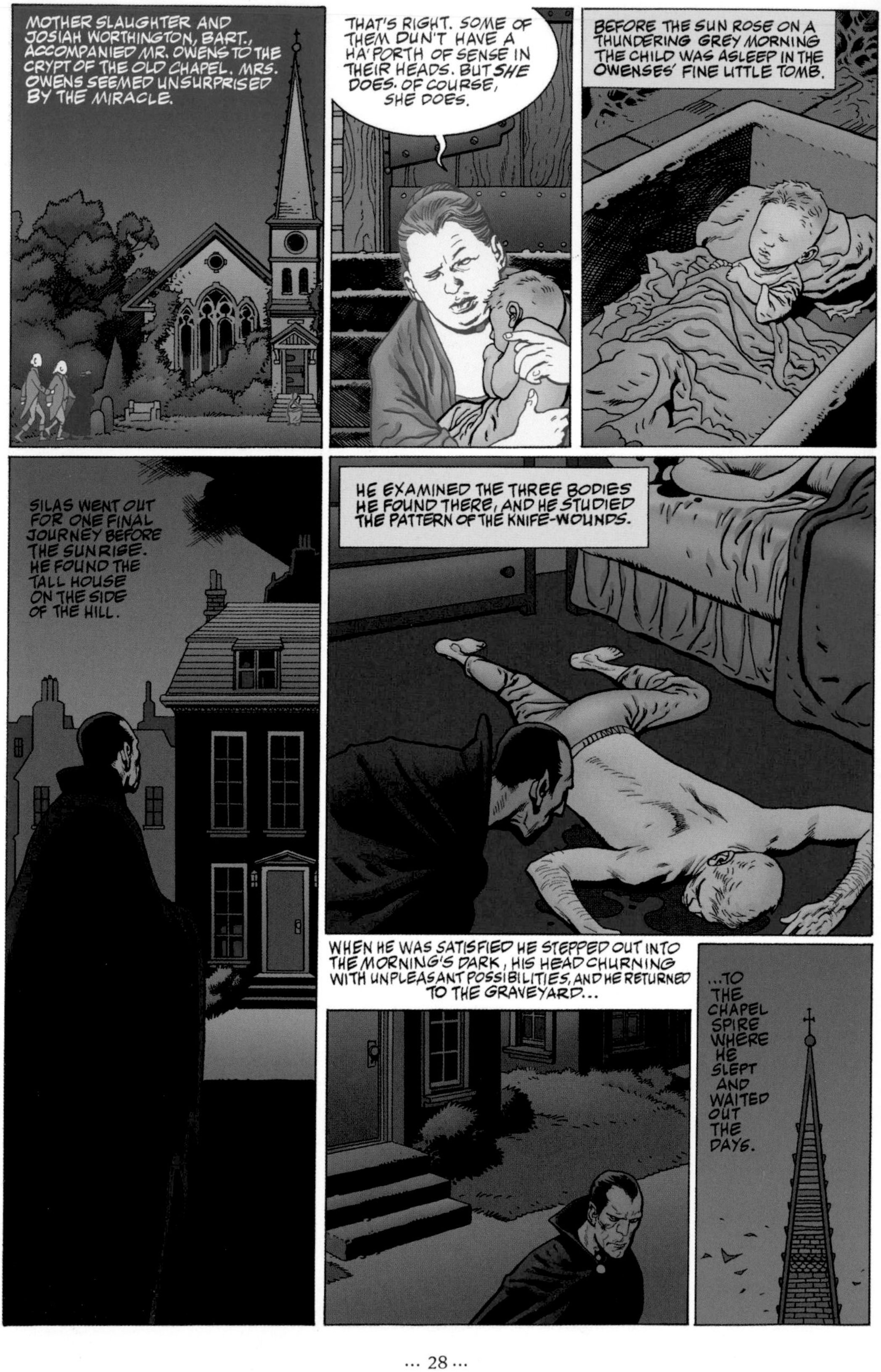
MOTHER SLAUGHTER AND JOSIAH WORTHINGTON, BART., ACCOMPANIED MR. OWENS TO THE CRYPT OF THE OLD CHAPEL. MRS. OWENS SEEMED UNSURPRISED BY THE MIRACLE.
THAT'S RIGHT. SOME OF THEM DUN'T HAVE A HA'PORTH OF SENSE IN THEIR HEADS. BUT SHE DOES. OF COURSE, SHE DOES.
BEFORE THE SUN ROSE ON A THUNDERING GREY MORNING THE CHILD WAS ASLEEP IN THE OWENSES' FINE LITTLE TOMB.
SILAS WENT OUT FOR ONE FINAL JOURNEY BEFORE THE SUNRISE. HE FOUND THE TALL HOUSE ON THE SIDE OF THE HILL.
HE EXAMINED THE THREE BODIES HE FOUND THERE, AND HE STUDIED THE PATTERN OF THE KNIFE-WOUNDS.
WHEN HE WAS SATISFIED HE STEPPED OUT INTO THE MORNING'S DARK, HIS HEAD CHURNING WITH UNPLEASANT POSSIBILITIES, AND HE RETURNED TO THE GRAVEYARD...
...TO THE CHAPEL SPIRE WHERE HE SLEPT AND WAITED OUT THE DAYS.

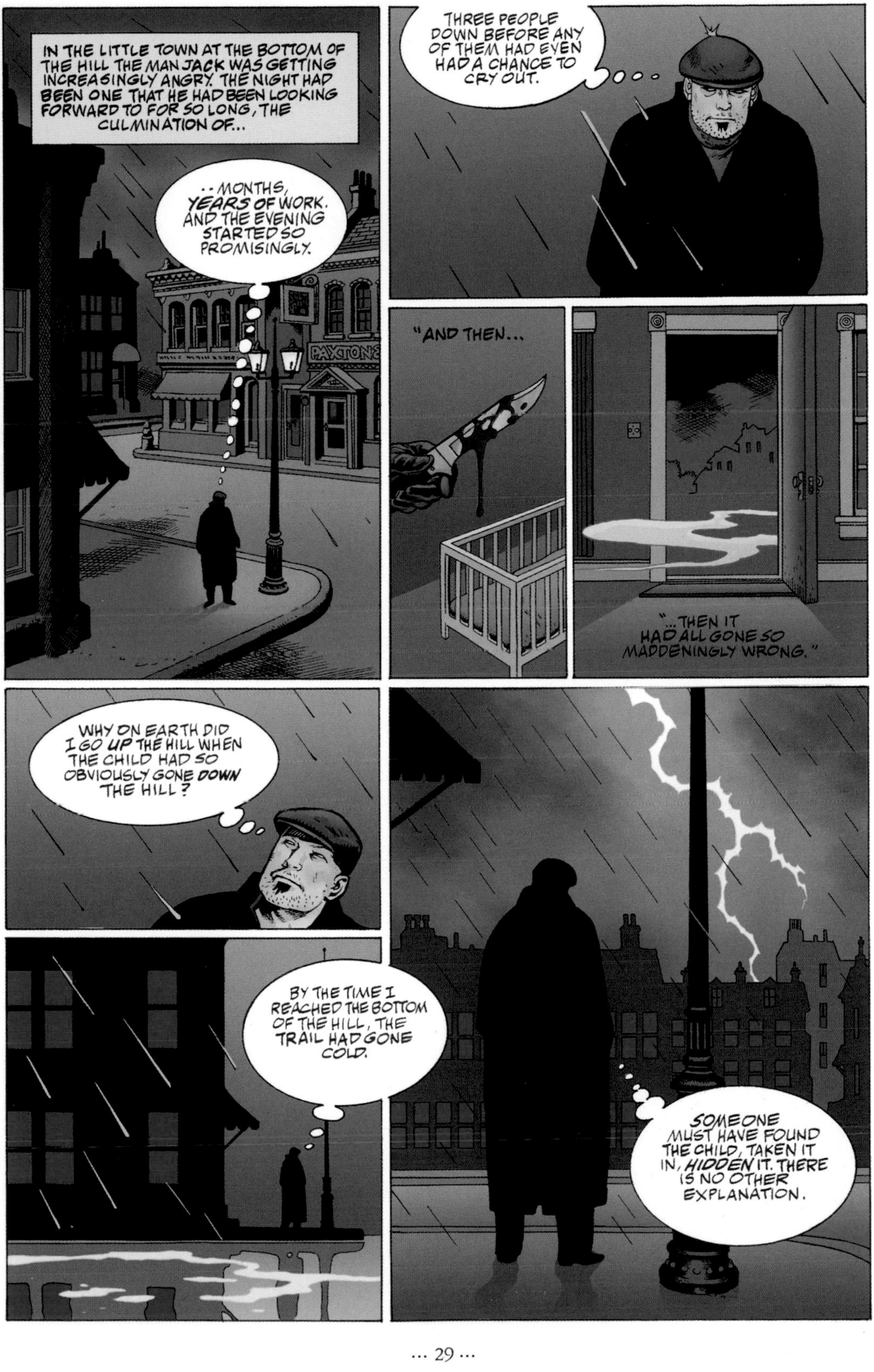
IN THE LITTLE TOWN AT THE BOTTOM OF THE HILL THE MAN JACK WAS GETTING INCREASINGLY ANGRY. THE NIGHT HAD BEEN ONE THAT HE HAD BEEN LOOKING FORWARD TO FOR SO LONG, THE CULMINATION OF...
..MONTHS, YEARS OF WORK. AND THE EVENING STARTED SO PROMISINGLY.
PAXTONS
THREE PEOPLE DOWN BEFORE ANY OF THEM HAD EVEN HAD A CHANCE TO CRY OUT.
"AND THEN...
"...THEN IT HAD ALL GONE SO MADDENINGLY WRONG."
WHY ON EARTH DID I GO UP THE HILL WHEN THE CHILD HAD SO OBVIOUSLY GONE DOWN THE HILL?
BY THE TIME I REACHED THE BOTTOM OF THE HILL, THE TRAIL HAD GONE COLD.
SOMEONE MUST HAVE FOUND THE CHILD, TAKEN IT IN, HIDDEN IT. THERE IS NO OTHER EXPLANATION.

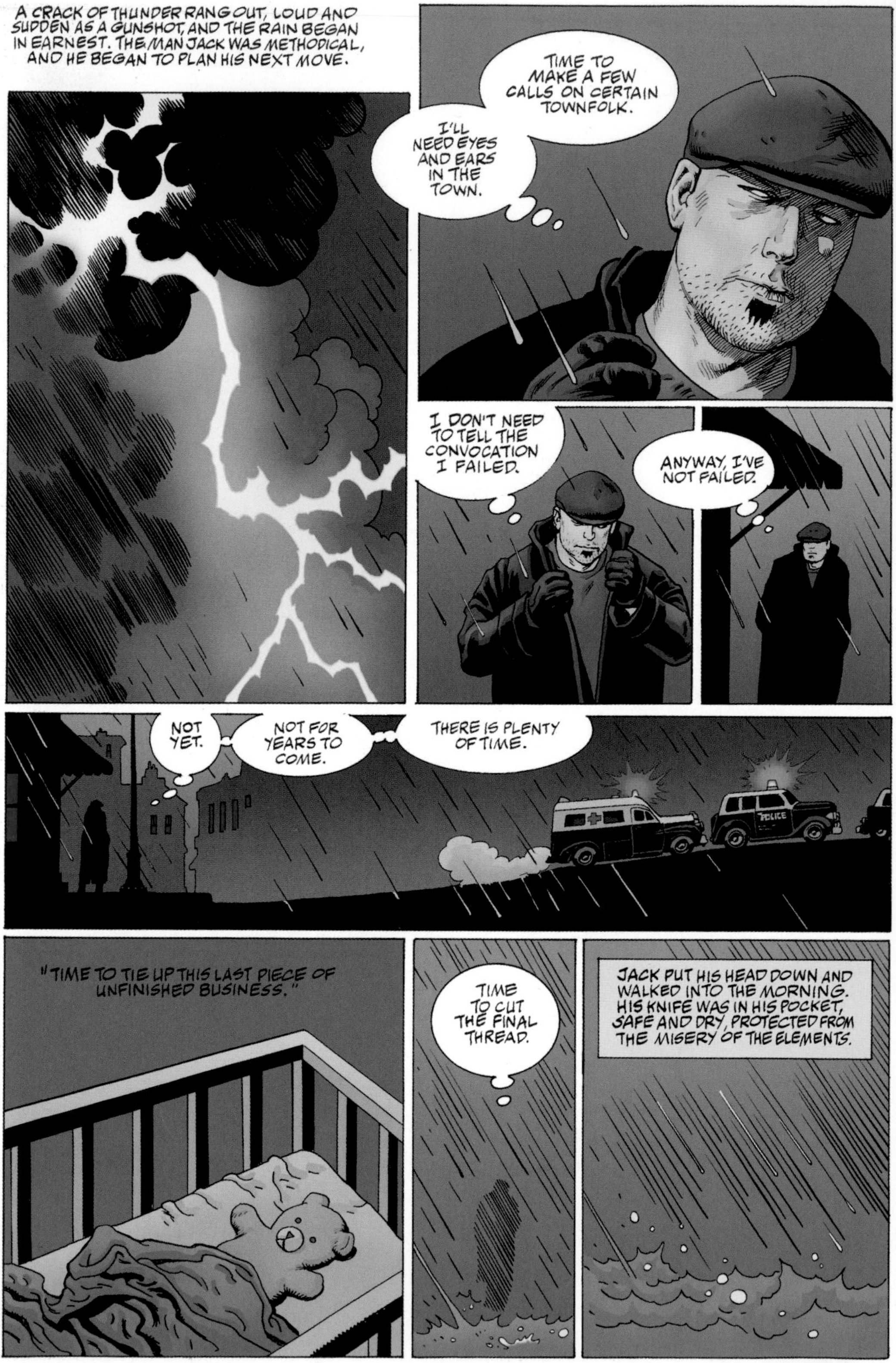
A CRACK OF THUNDER RANG OUT, LOUD AND SUDDEN AS A GUNSHOT, AND THE RAIN BEGAN IN EARNEST. THE MAN JACK WAS METHODICAL, AND HE BEGAN TO PLAN HIS NEXT MOVE.
TIME TO MAKE A FEW CALLS ON CERTAIN TOWNFOLK.
I'LL NEED EYES AND EARS IN THE TOWN.
I DON'T NEED TO TELL THE CONVOCATION I FAILED.
ANYWAY, I'VE NOT FAILED.
NOT YET.
NOT FOR YEARS TO COME.
THERE IS PLENTY OF TIME.
POLICE
"TIME TO TIE UP THIS LAST PIECE OF UNFINISHED BUSINESS."
TIME TO CUT THE FINAL THREAD.
JACK PUT HIS HEAD DOWN AND WALKED INTO THE MORNING. HIS KNIFE WAS IN HIS POCKET, SAFE AND DRY, PROTECTED FROM THE MISERY OF THE ELEMENTS.

2
The New Friend

Illustrated by P. Craig Russell

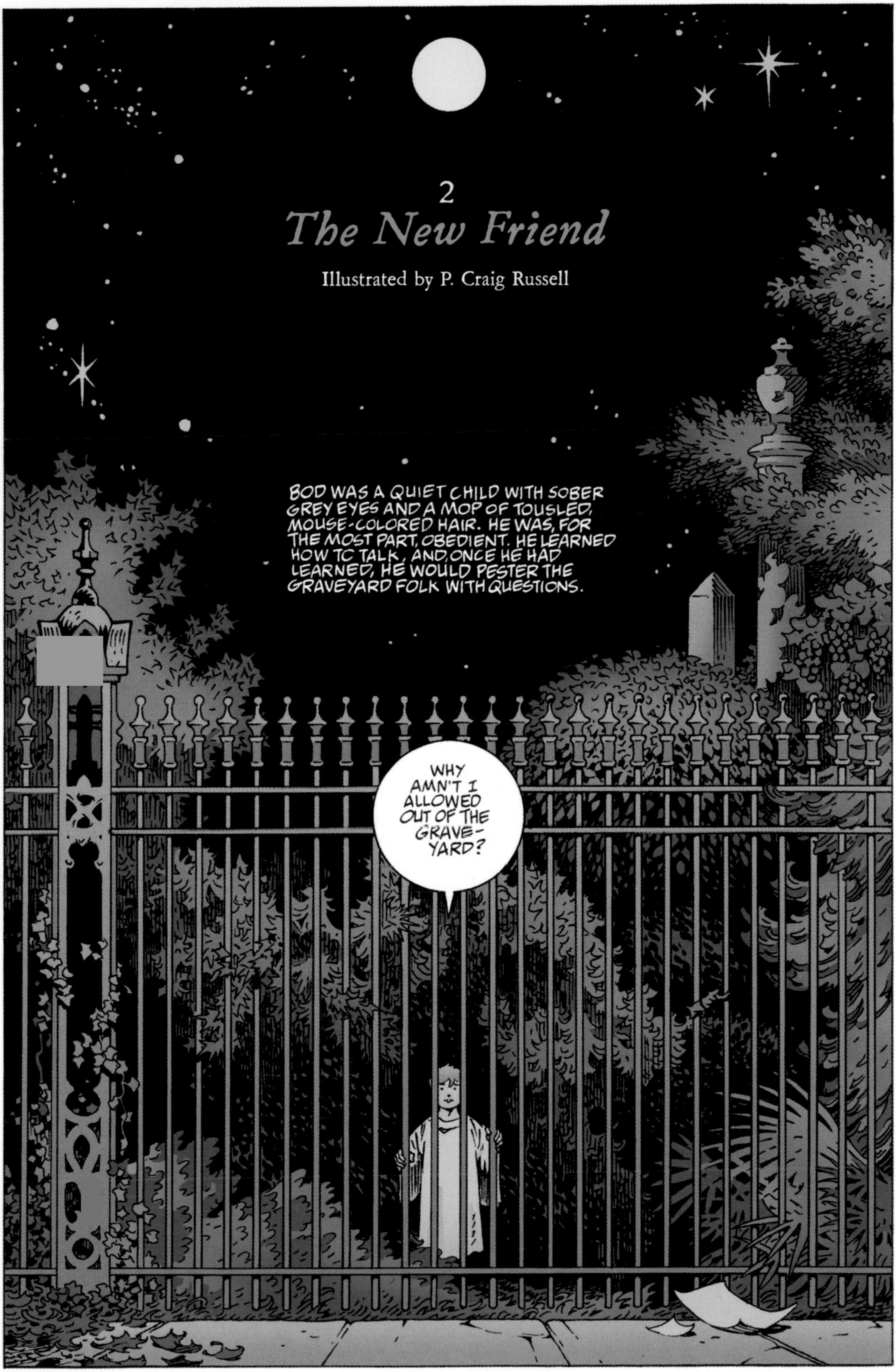
BOD WAS A QUIET CHILD WITH SOBER GREY EYES AND A MOP OF TOUSLED, MOUSE-COLORED HAIR. HE WAS, FOR THE MOST PART, OBEDIENT. HE LEARNED HOW TO TALK, AND, ONCE HE HAD LEARNED, HE WOULD PESTER THE GRAVEYARD FOLK WITH QUESTIONS.
WHY AMN'T I ALLOWED OUT OF THE GRAVE-YARD?

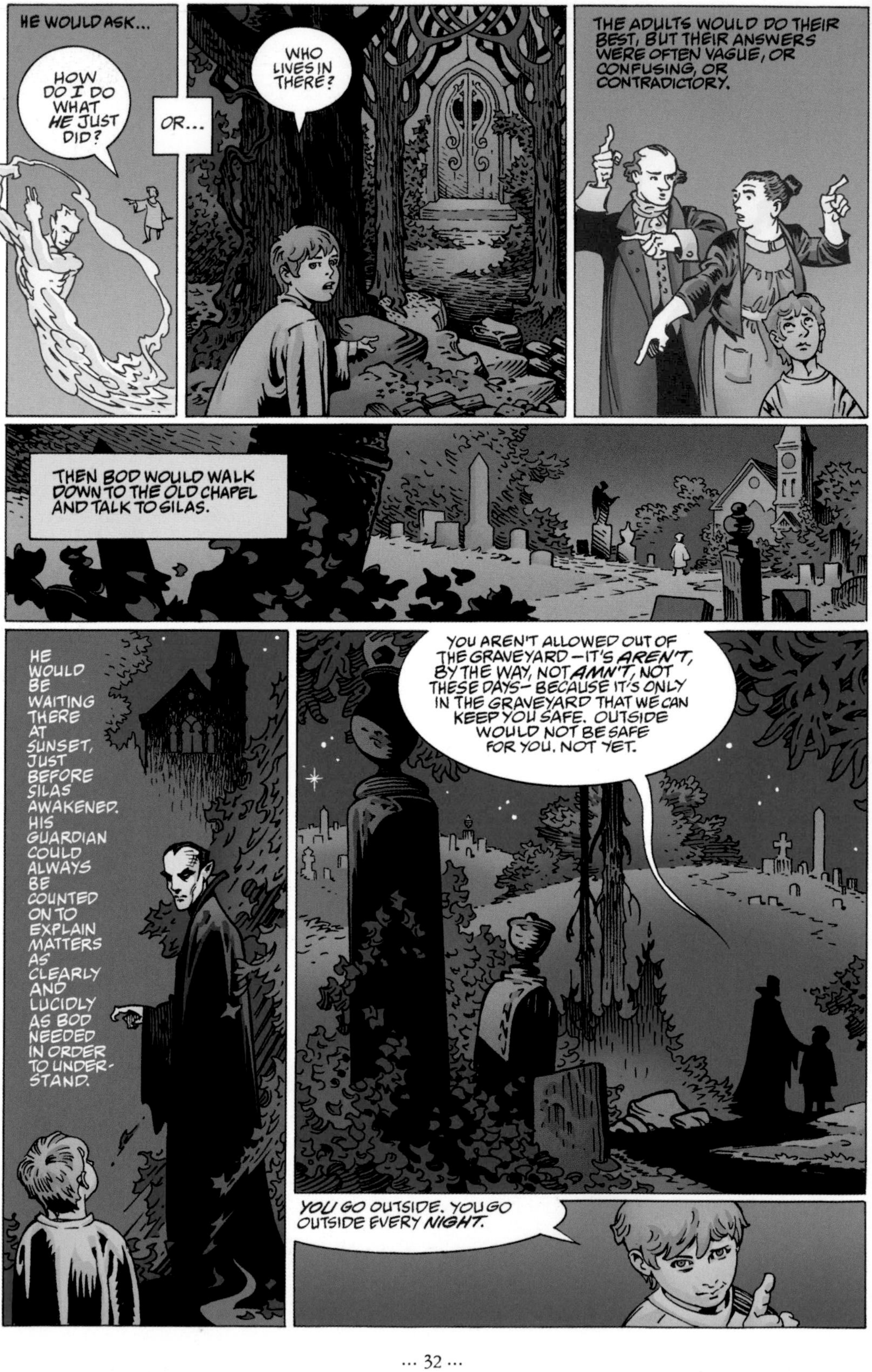

HE WOULD ASK...
HOW DO I DO WHAT HE JUST DID?
OR...
WHO LIVES IN THERE?
THE ADULTS WOULD DO THEIR BEST, BUT THEIR ANSWERS WERE OFTEN VAGUE, OR CONFUSING, OR CONTRADICTORY.
THEN BOD WOULD WALK DOWN TO THE OLD CHAPEL AND TALK TO SILAS.
HE WOULD BE WAITING THERE AT SUNSET, JUST BEFORE SILAS AWAKENED. HIS GUARDIAN COULD ALWAYS BE COUNTED ON TO EXPLAIN MATTERS AS CLEARLY AND LUCIDLY AS BOD NEEDED IN ORDER TO UNDER-STAND.
YOU AREN'T ALLOWED OUT OF THE GRAVEYARD—IT'S AREN'T, BY THE WAY, NOT AMN'T, NOT THESE DAYS—BECAUSE IT'S ONLY IN THE GRAVEYARD THAT WE CAN KEEP YOU SAFE. OUTSIDE WOULD NOT BE SAFE FOR YOU. NOT YET.
YOU GO OUTSIDE. YOU GO OUTSIDE EVERY NIGHT.

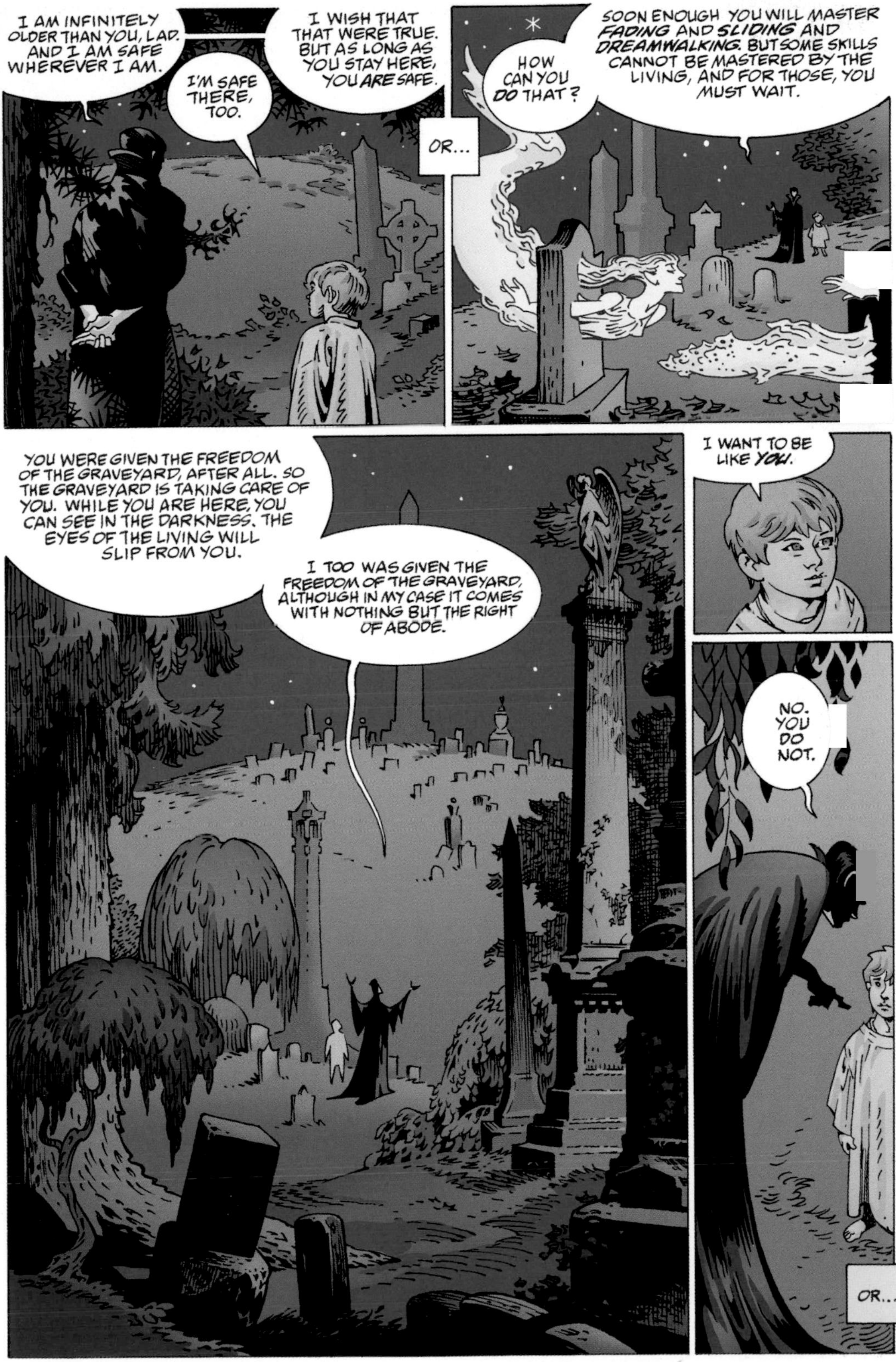

I AM INFINITELY OLDER THAN YOU, LAD. AND I AM SAFE WHEREVER I AM.
I'M SAFE THERE, TOO.
I WISH THAT THAT WERE TRUE. BUT AS LONG AS YOU STAY HERE, YOU ARE SAFE.
OR...
HOW CAN YOU DO THAT?
SOON ENOUGH YOU WILL MASTER FADING AND SLIDING AND DREAMWALKING. BUT SOME SKILLS CANNOT BE MASTERED BY THE LIVING, AND FOR THOSE, YOU MUST WAIT.
YOU WERE GIVEN THE FREEDOM OF THE GRAVEYARD, AFTER ALL. SO THE GRAVEYARD IS TAKING CARE OF YOU. WHILE YOU ARE HERE, YOU CAN SEE IN THE DARKNESS. THE EYES OF THE LIVING WILL SLIP FROM YOU.
I TOO WAS GIVEN THE FREEDOM OF THE GRAVEYARD, ALTHOUGH IN MY CASE IT COMES WITH NOTHING BUT THE RIGHT OF ABODE.
I WANT TO BE LIKE YOU.
NO. YOU DO NOT.
OR...

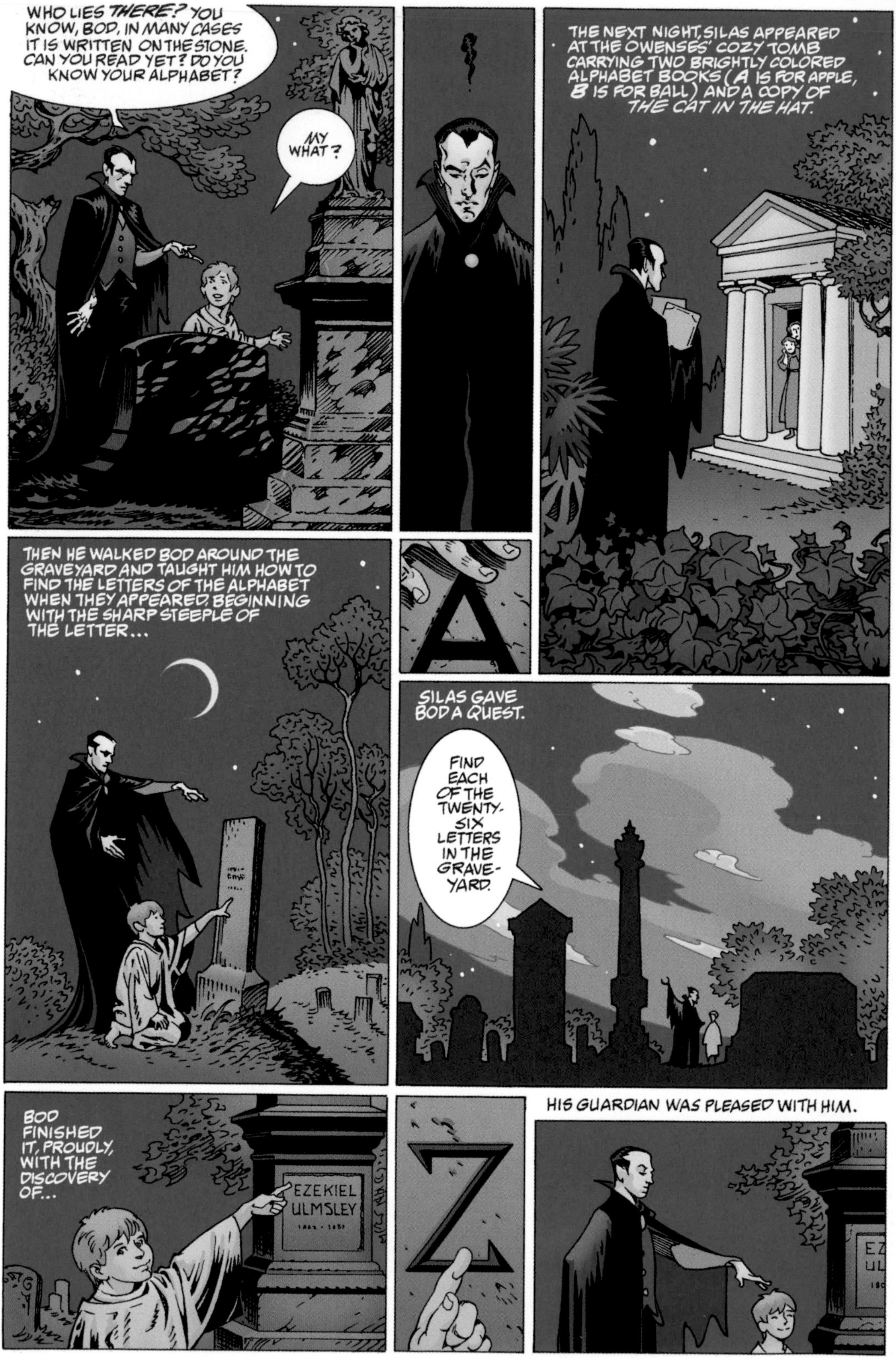
WHO LIES THERE? YOU KNOW, BOD, IN MANY CASES IT IS WRITTEN ON THE STONE. CAN YOU READ YET? DO YOU KNOW YOUR ALPHABET?
MY WHAT?
!
THE NEXT NIGHT, SILAS APPEARED AT THE OWENSES' COZY TOMB CARRYING TWO BRIGHTLY COLORED ALPHABET BOOKS (A IS FOR APPLE, B IS FOR BALL) AND A COPY OF THE CAT IN THE HAT.
THEN HE WALKED BOD AROUND THE GRAVEYARD AND TAUGHT HIM HOW TO FIND THE LETTERS OF THE ALPHABET WHEN THEY APPEARED, BEGINNING WITH THE SHARP STEEPLE OF THE LETTER...
A
SILAS GAVE BOD A QUEST.
FIND EACH OF THE TWENTY-SIX LETTERS IN THE GRAVEYARD.
BOD FINISHED IT, PROUDLY, WITH THE DISCOVERY OF...
EZEKIEL ULMSLEY
Z
HIS GUARDIAN WAS PLEASED WITH HIM.

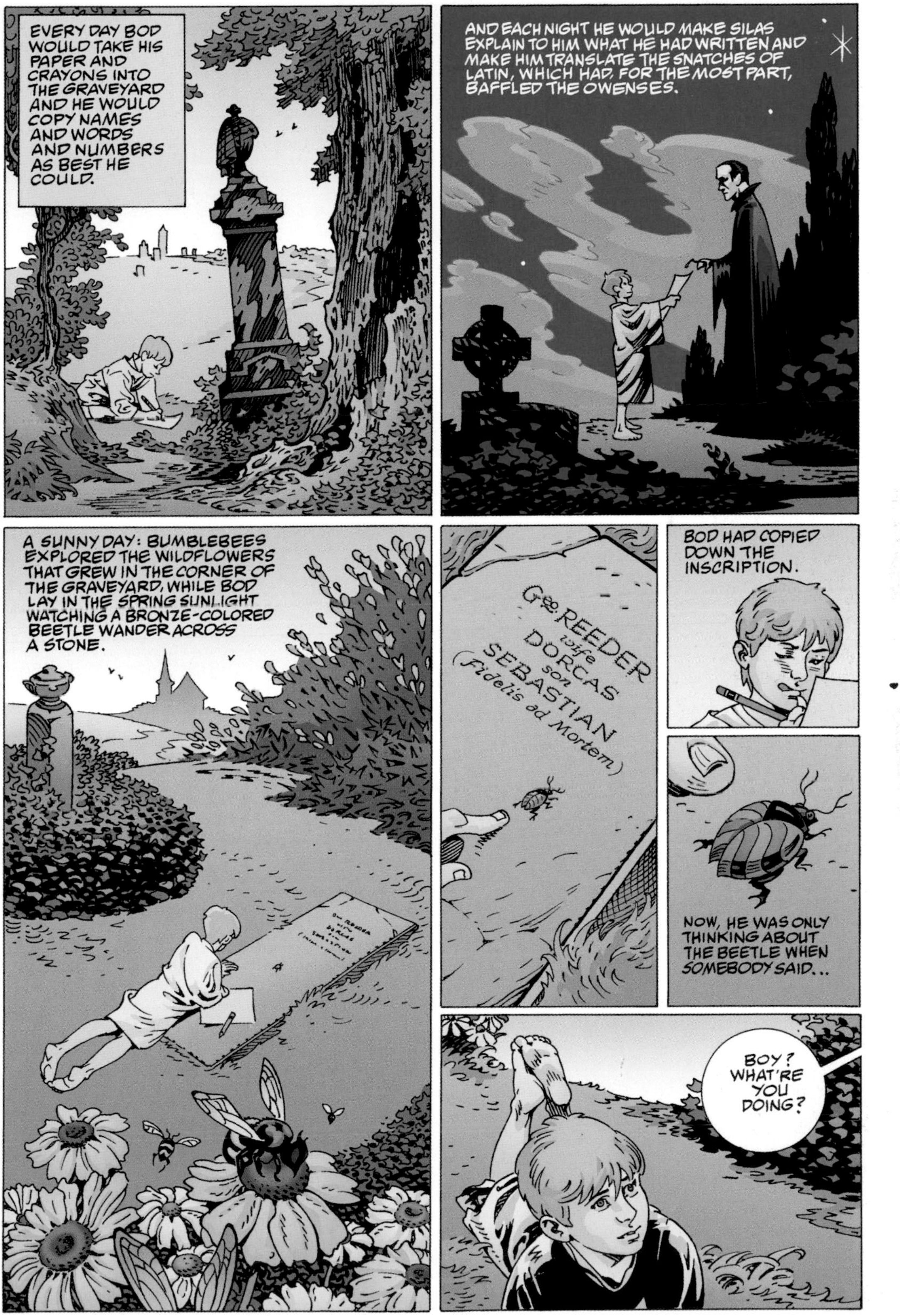
EVERY DAY BOD WOULD TAKE HIS PAPER AND CRAYONS INTO THE GRAVEYARD AND HE WOULD COPY NAMES AND WORDS AND NUMBERS AS BEST HE COULD.
AND EACH NIGHT HE WOULD MAKE SILAS EXPLAIN TO HIM WHAT HE HAD WRITTEN AND MAKE HIM TRANSLATE THE SNATCHES OF LATIN, WHICH HAD, FOR THE MOST PART, BAFFLED THE OWENSES.
A SUNNY DAY: BUMBLEBEES EXPLORED THE WILDFLOWERS THAT GREW IN THE CORNER OF THE GRAVEYARD, WHILE BOD LAY IN THE SPRING SUNLIGHT WATCHING A BRONZE-COLORED BEETLE WANDER ACROSS A STONE.
Geo. REEDER
wife
DORCAS
son
SEBASTIAN
(Fidelis ad Mortem)
BOD HAD COPIED DOWN THE INSCRIPTION.
NOW, HE WAS ONLY THINKING ABOUT THE BEETLE WHEN SOMEBODY SAID...
BOY? WHAT'RE YOU DOING?

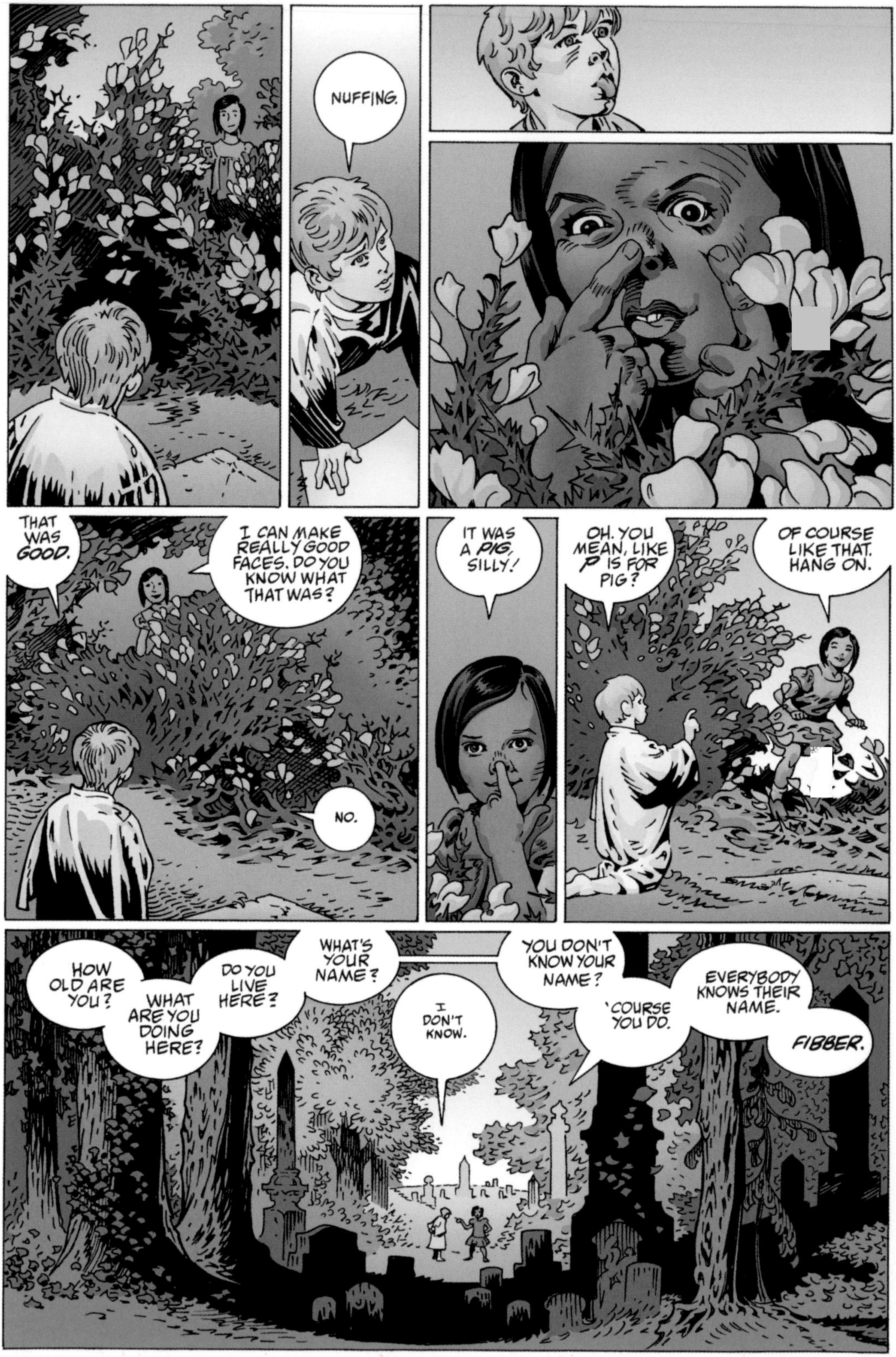
NUFFING.
THAT WAS GOOD.
I CAN MAKE REALLY GOOD FACES. DO YOU KNOW WHAT THAT WAS?
NO.
IT WAS A PIG, SILLY!
OH. YOU MEAN, LIKE P IS FOR PIG?
OF COURSE LIKE THAT. HANG ON.
HOW OLD ARE YOU?
WHAT ARE YOU DOING HERE?
DO YOU LIVE HERE?
WHAT'S YOUR NAME?
I DON'T KNOW.
YOU DON'T KNOW YOUR NAME?
'COURSE YOU DO.
EVERYBODY KNOWS THEIR NAME.
FIBBER.

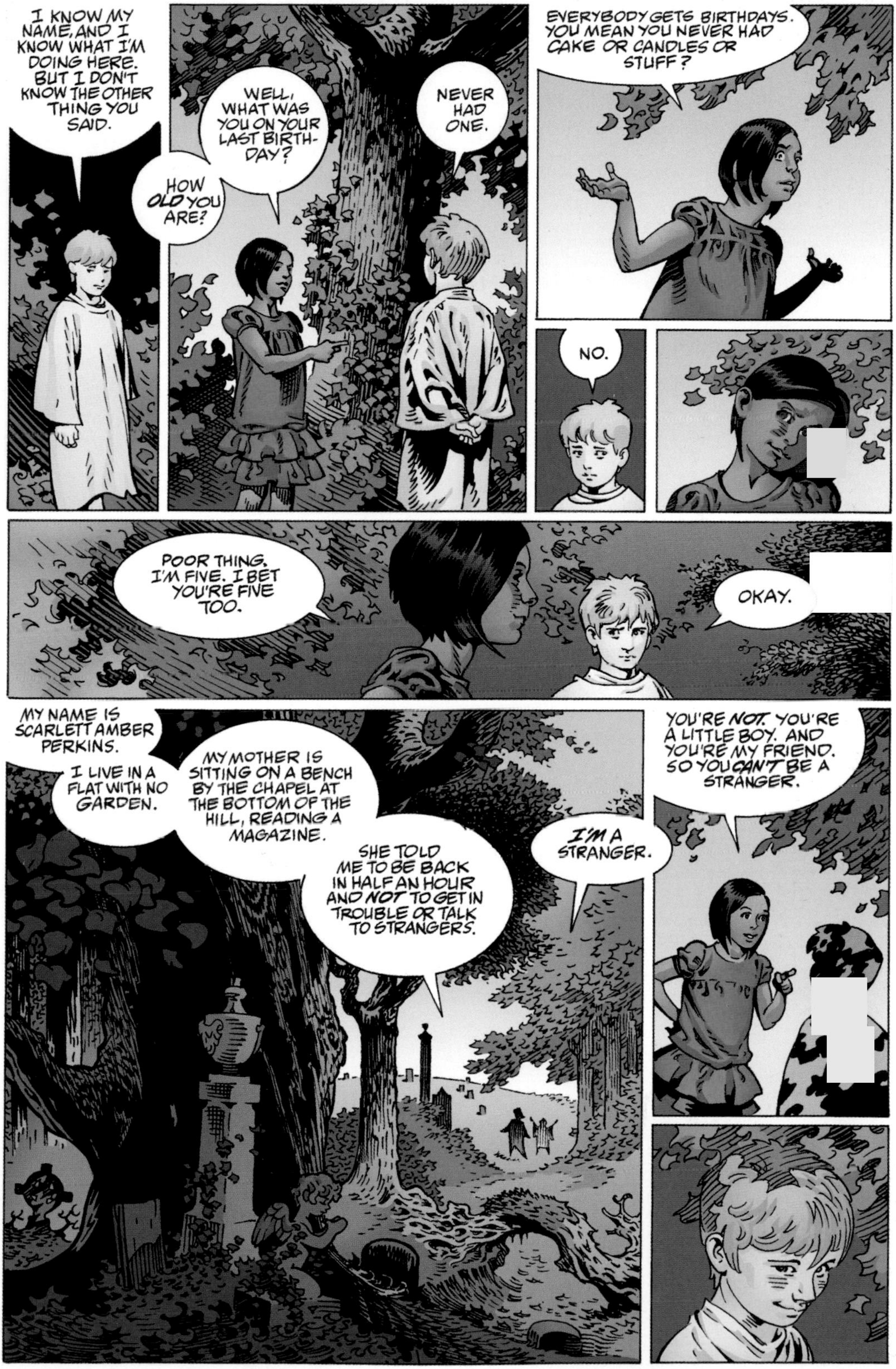
I KNOW MY NAME, AND I KNOW WHAT I'M DOING HERE. BUT I DON'T KNOW THE OTHER THING YOU SAID.
HOW OLD YOU ARE?
WELL, WHAT WAS YOU ON YOUR LAST BIRTHDAY?
NEVER HAD ONE.
EVERYBODY GETS BIRTHDAYS. YOU MEAN YOU NEVER HAD CAKE OR CANDLES OR STUFF?
NO.
POOR THING. I'M FIVE. I BET YOU'RE FIVE TOO.
OKAY.
MY NAME IS SCARLETT AMBER PERKINS.
I LIVE IN A FLAT WITH NO GARDEN.
MY MOTHER IS SITTING ON A BENCH BY THE CHAPEL AT THE BOTTOM OF THE HILL, READING A MAGAZINE.
SHE TOLD ME TO BE BACK IN HALF AN HOUR AND NOT TO GET IN TROUBLE OR TALK TO STRANGERS.
I'M A STRANGER.
YOU'RE NOT. YOU'RE A LITTLE BOY. AND YOU'RE MY FRIEND. SO YOU CAN'T BE A STRANGER.

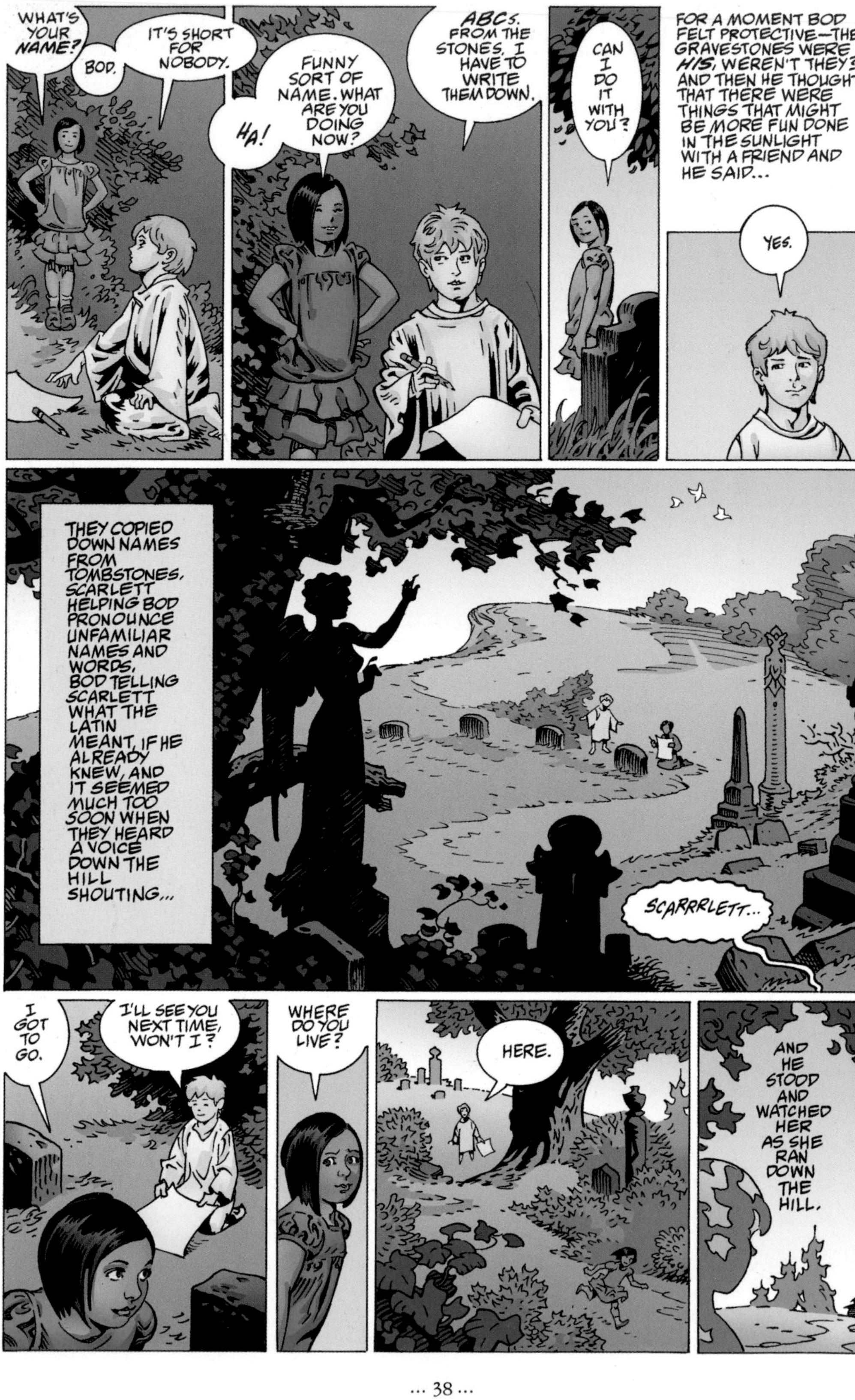
WHAT'S YOUR NAME?
BOD.
IT'S SHORT FOR NOBODY.
HA!
FUNNY SORT OF NAME. WHAT ARE YOU DOING NOW?
ABCs. FROM THE STONES. I HAVE TO WRITE THEM DOWN.
CAN I DO IT WITH YOU?
FOR A MOMENT BOD FELT PROTECTIVE—THE GRAVESTONES WERE HIS, WEREN'T THEY?—AND THEN HE THOUGHT THAT THERE WERE THINGS THAT MIGHT BE MORE FUN DONE IN THE SUNLIGHT WITH A FRIEND AND HE SAID...
YES.
THEY COPIED DOWN NAMES FROM TOMBSTONES, SCARLETT HELPING BOD PRONOUNCE UNFAMILIAR NAMES AND WORDS, BOD TELLING SCARLETT WHAT THE LATIN MEANT, IF HE ALREADY KNEW, AND IT SEEMED MUCH TOO SOON WHEN THEY HEARD A VOICE DOWN THE HILL SHOUTING...
SCARRRLETT...
I GOT TO GO.
I'LL SEE YOU NEXT TIME, WON'T I?
WHERE DO YOU LIVE?
HERE.
AND HE STOOD AND WATCHED HER AS SHE RAN DOWN THE HILL.

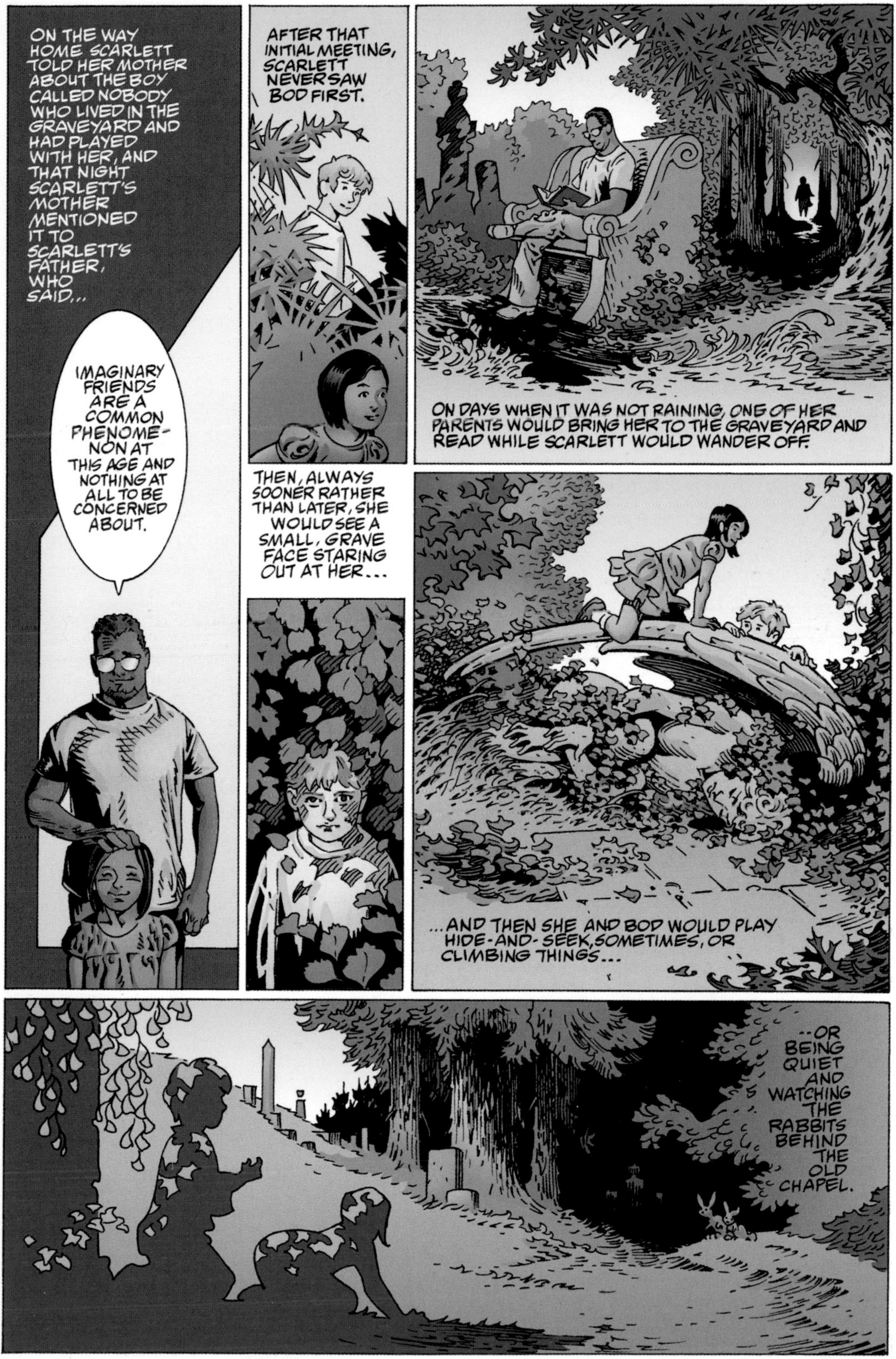

ON THE WAY HOME SCARLETT TOLD HER MOTHER ABOUT THE BOY CALLED NOBODY WHO LIVED IN THE GRAVEYARD AND HAD PLAYED WITH HER, AND THAT NIGHT SCARLETT'S MOTHER MENTIONED IT TO SCARLETT'S FATHER, WHO SAID,...
IMAGINARY FRIENDS ARE A COMMON PHENOMENON AT THIS AGE AND NOTHING AT ALL TO BE CONCERNED ABOUT.
AFTER THAT INITIAL MEETING, SCARLETT NEVER SAW BOD FIRST.
ON DAYS WHEN IT WAS NOT RAINING, ONE OF HER PARENTS WOULD BRING HER TO THE GRAVEYARD AND READ WHILE SCARLETT WOULD WANDER OFF.
THEN, ALWAYS SOONER RATHER THAN LATER, SHE WOULD SEE A SMALL, GRAVE FACE STARING OUT AT HER...
...AND THEN SHE AND BOD WOULD PLAY HIDE-AND-SEEK, SOMETIMES, OR CLIMBING THINGS...
...OR BEING QUIET AND WATCHING THE RABBITS BEHIND THE OLD CHAPEL.

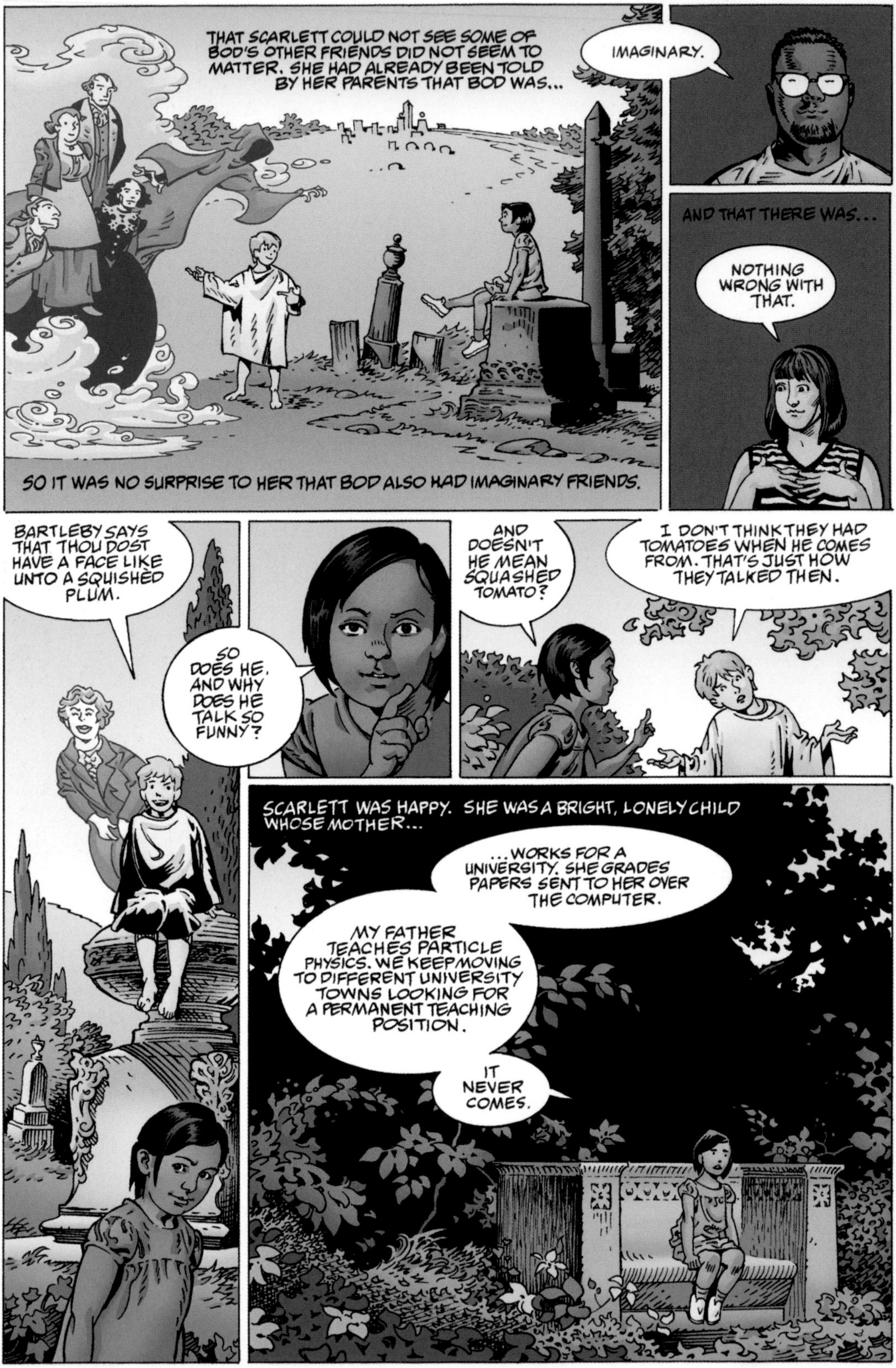

THAT SCARLETT COULD NOT SEE SOME OF BOD'S OTHER FRIENDS DID NOT SEEM TO MATTER. SHE HAD ALREADY BEEN TOLD BY HER PARENTS THAT BOD WAS...
IMAGINARY.
AND THAT THERE WAS...
NOTHING WRONG WITH THAT.
SO IT WAS NO SURPRISE TO HER THAT BOD ALSO HAD IMAGINARY FRIENDS.
BARTLEBY SAYS THAT THOU DOST HAVE A FACE LIKE UNTO A SQUISHED PLUM.
SO DOES HE. AND WHY DOES HE TALK SO FUNNY?
AND DOESN'T HE MEAN SQUASHED TOMATO?
I DON'T THINK THEY HAD TOMATOES WHEN HE COMES FROM. THAT'S JUST HOW THEY TALKED THEN.
SCARLETT WAS HAPPY. SHE WAS A BRIGHT, LONELY CHILD WHOSE MOTHER...
...WORKS FOR A UNIVERSITY. SHE GRADES PAPERS SENT TO HER OVER THE COMPUTER.
MY FATHER TEACHES PARTICLE PHYSICS. WE KEEP MOVING TO DIFFERENT UNIVERSITY TOWNS LOOKING FOR A PERMANENT TEACHING POSITION.
IT NEVER COMES.

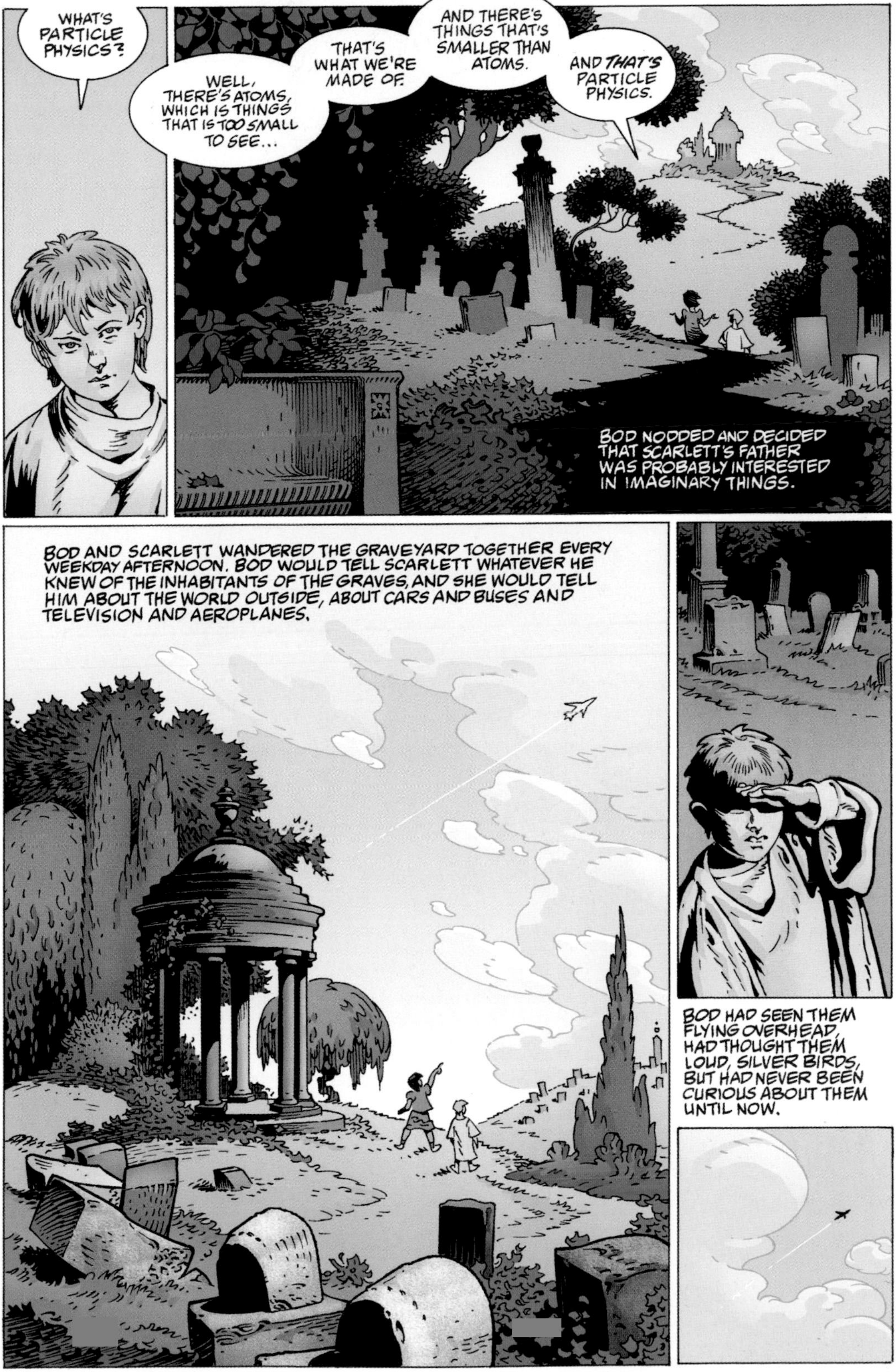
WHAT'S PARTICLE PHYSICS?
WELL, THERE'S ATOMS, WHICH IS THINGS THAT IS TOO SMALL TO SEE...
THAT'S WHAT WE'RE MADE OF.
AND THERE'S THINGS THAT'S SMALLER THAN ATOMS.
AND THAT'S PARTICLE PHYSICS.
BOD NODDED AND DECIDED THAT SCARLETT'S FATHER WAS PROBABLY INTERESTED IN IMAGINARY THINGS.
BOD AND SCARLETT WANDERED THE GRAVEYARD TOGETHER EVERY WEEKDAY AFTERNOON. BOD WOULD TELL SCARLETT WHATEVER HE KNEW OF THE INHABITANTS OF THE GRAVES, AND SHE WOULD TELL HIM ABOUT THE WORLD OUTSIDE, ABOUT CARS AND BUSES AND TELEVISION AND AEROPLANES.
BOD HAD SEEN THEM FLYING OVERHEAD, HAD THOUGHT THEM LOUD, SILVER BIRDS, BUT HAD NEVER BEEN CURIOUS ABOUT THEM UNTIL NOW.

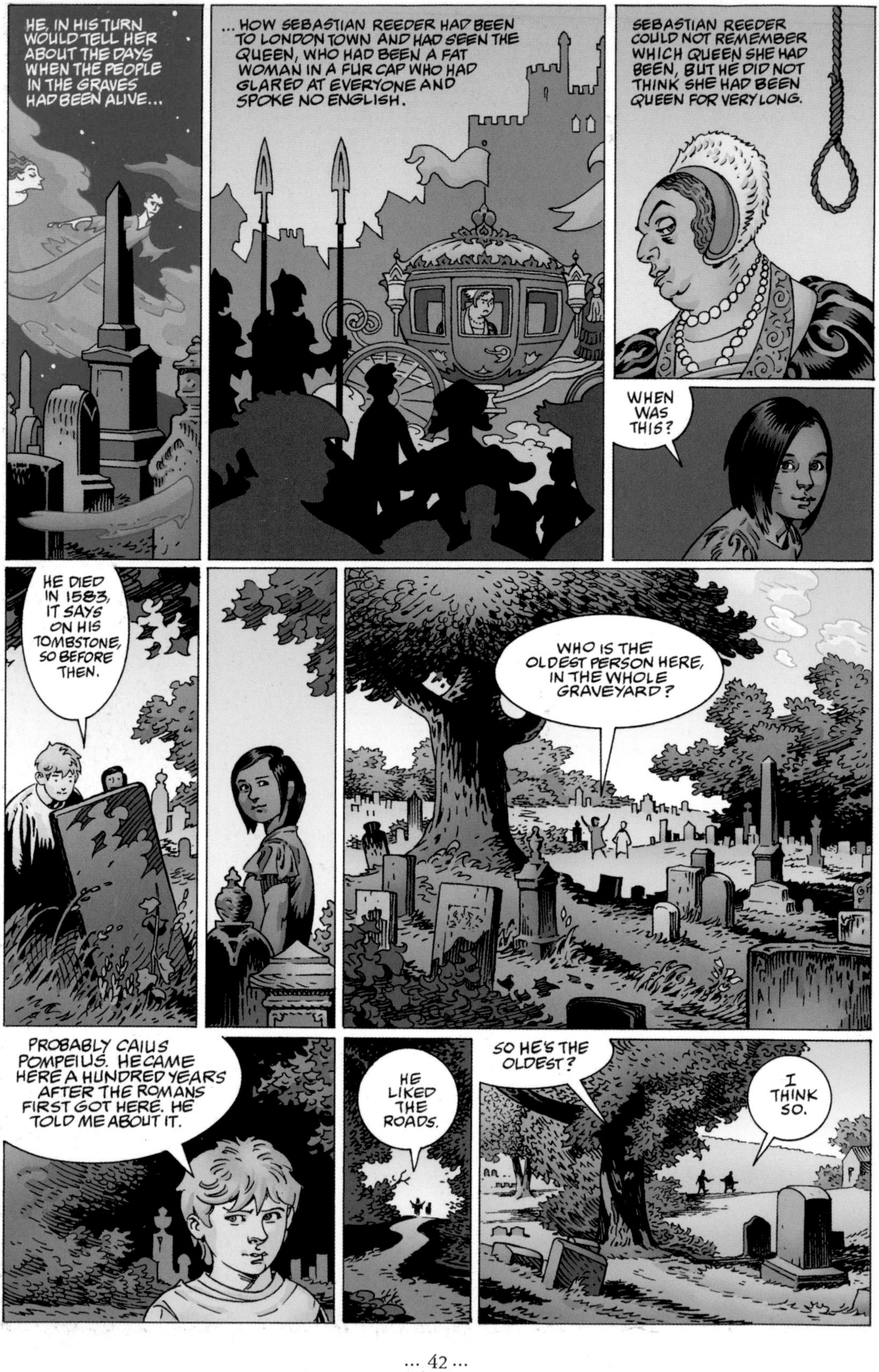
HE, IN HIS TURN WOULD TELL HER ABOUT THE DAYS WHEN THE PEOPLE IN THE GRAVES HAD BEEN ALIVE...
...HOW SEBASTIAN REEDER HAD BEEN TO LONDON TOWN AND HAD SEEN THE QUEEN, WHO HAD BEEN A FAT WOMAN IN A FUR CAP WHO HAD GLARED AT EVERYONE AND SPOKE NO ENGLISH.
SEBASTIAN REEDER COULD NOT REMEMBER WHICH QUEEN SHE HAD BEEN, BUT HE DID NOT THINK SHE HAD BEEN QUEEN FOR VERY LONG.
WHEN WAS THIS?
HE DIED IN 1583, IT SAYS ON HIS TOMBSTONE, SO BEFORE THEN.
WHO IS THE OLDEST PERSON HERE, IN THE WHOLE GRAVEYARD?
PROBABLY CAIUS POMPEIUS. HE CAME HERE A HUNDRED YEARS AFTER THE ROMANS FIRST GOT HERE. HE TOLD ME ABOUT IT.
HE LIKED THE ROADS.
SO HE'S THE OLDEST?
I THINK SO.

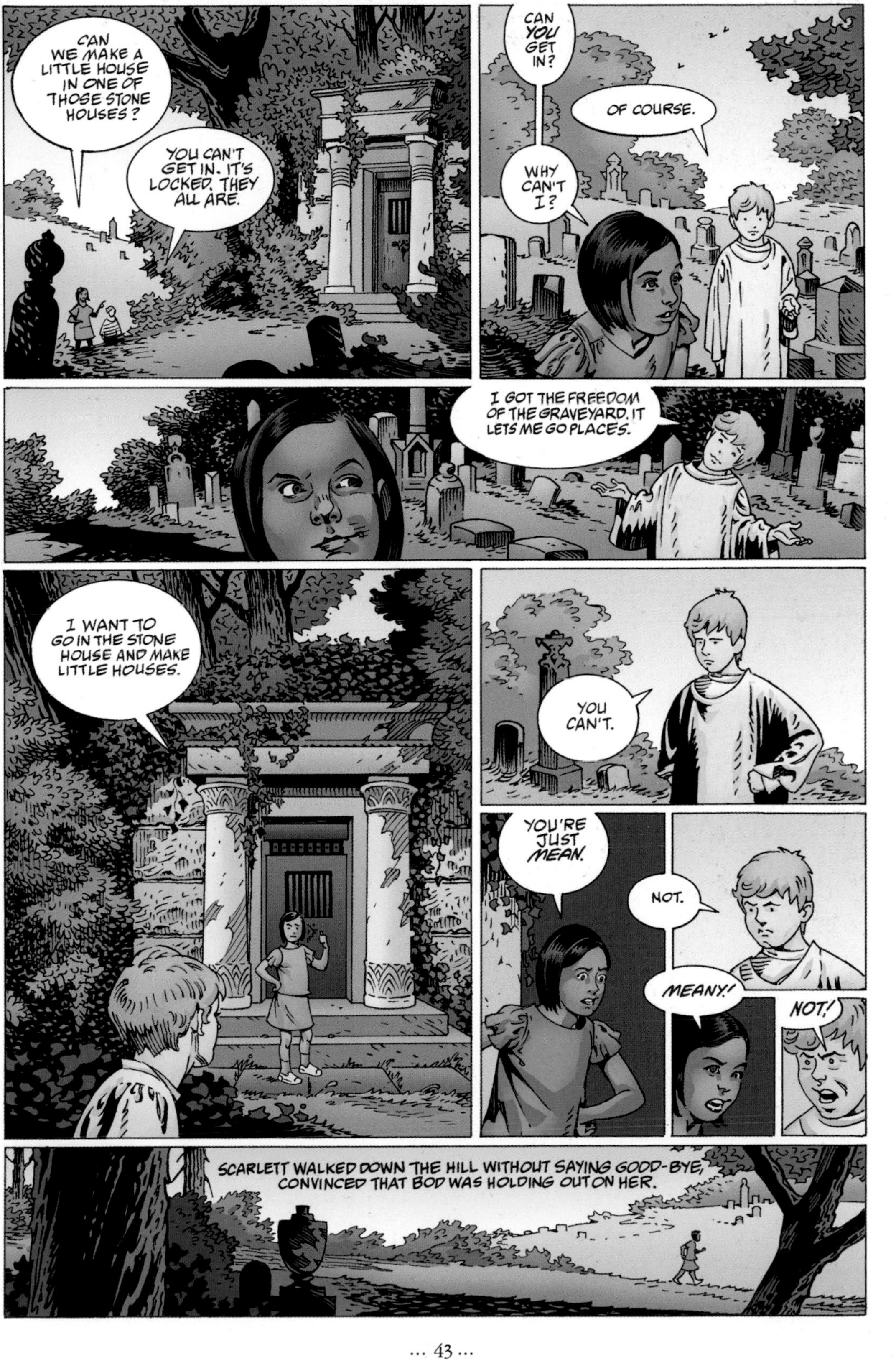
CAN WE MAKE A LITTLE HOUSE IN ONE OF THOSE STONE HOUSES?
YOU CAN'T GET IN. IT'S LOCKED. THEY ALL ARE.
CAN YOU GET IN?
OF COURSE.
WHY CAN'T I?
I GOT THE FREEDOM OF THE GRAVEYARD. IT LETS ME GO PLACES.
I WANT TO GO IN THE STONE HOUSE AND MAKE LITTLE HOUSES.
YOU CAN'T.
YOU'RE JUST MEAN.
NOT.
MEANY!
NOT!
SCARLETT WALKED DOWN THE HILL WITHOUT SAYING GOOD-BYE, CONVINCED THAT BOD WAS HOLDING OUT ON HER.

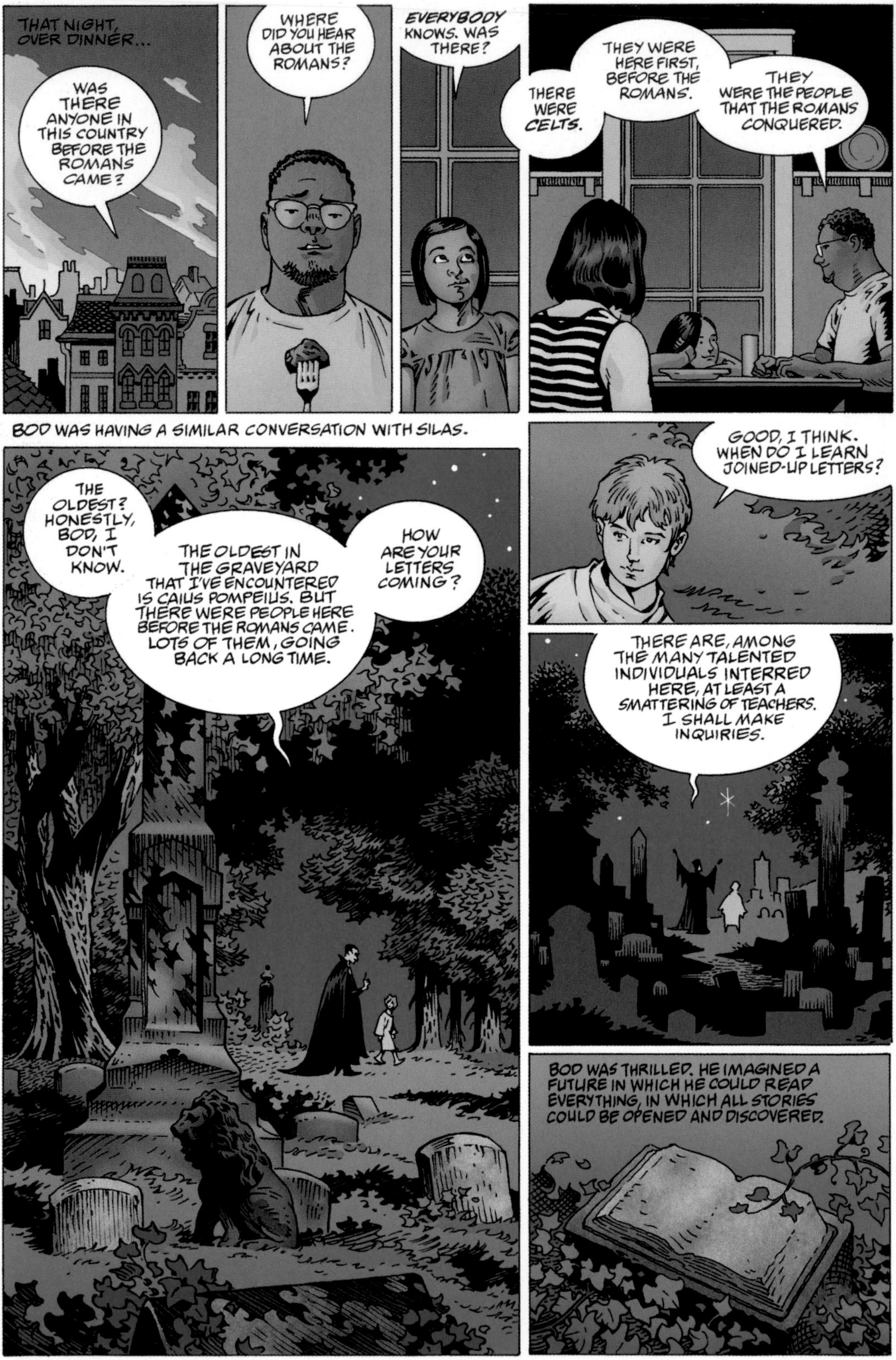
THAT NIGHT, OVER DINNER...
WAS THERE ANYONE IN THIS COUNTRY BEFORE THE ROMANS CAME?
WHERE DID YOU HEAR ABOUT THE ROMANS?
EVERYBODY KNOWS. WAS THERE?
THERE WERE CELTS.
THEY WERE HERE FIRST, BEFORE THE ROMANS.
THEY WERE THE PEOPLE THAT THE ROMANS CONQUERED.
BOD WAS HAVING A SIMILAR CONVERSATION WITH SILAS.
THE OLDEST? HONESTLY, BOD, I DON'T KNOW.
THE OLDEST IN THE GRAVEYARD THAT I'VE ENCOUNTERED IS CAIUS POMPEIUS. BUT THERE WERE PEOPLE HERE BEFORE THE ROMANS CAME. LOTS OF THEM, GOING BACK A LONG TIME.
HOW ARE YOUR LETTERS COMING?
GOOD, I THINK. WHEN DO I LEARN JOINED-UP LETTERS?
THERE ARE, AMONG THE MANY TALENTED INDIVIDUALS INTERRED HERE, AT LEAST A SMATTERING OF TEACHERS. I SHALL MAKE INQUIRIES.
BOD WAS THRILLED. HE IMAGINED A FUTURE IN WHICH HE COULD READ EVERYTHING, IN WHICH ALL STORIES COULD BE OPENED AND DISCOVERED.

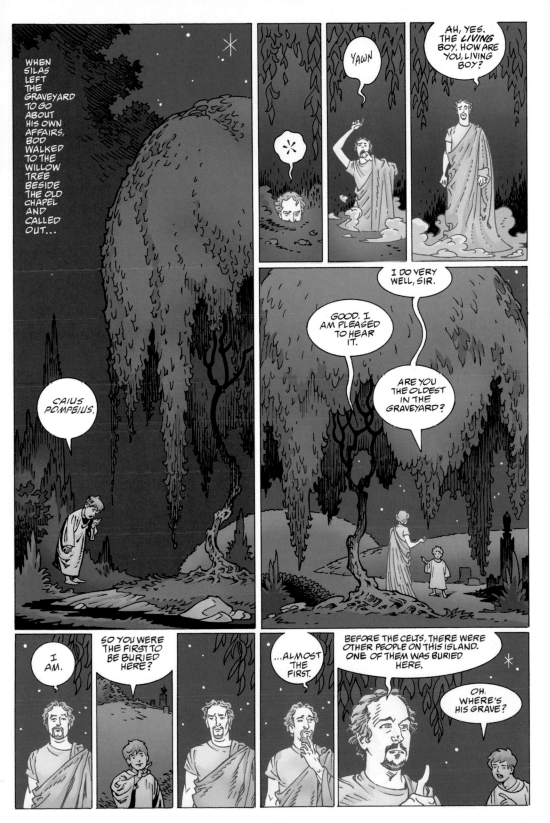

WHEN SILAS LEFT THE GRAVEYARD TO GO ABOUT HIS OWN AFFAIRS, BOD WALKED TO THE WILLOW TREE BESIDE THE OLD CHAPEL AND CALLED OUT...

YAWN

AH, YES. THE *LIVING* BOY. HOW ARE YOU, LIVING BOY?

CAIUS POMPEIUS.

I DO VERY WELL, SIR.

GOOD. I AM PLEASED TO HEAR IT.

ARE YOU THE OLDEST IN THE GRAVEYARD?

I AM.

SO YOU WERE THE FIRST TO BE BURIED HERE?

...ALMOST THE FIRST.

BEFORE THE CELTS, THERE WERE OTHER PEOPLE ON THIS ISLAND. ONE OF THEM WAS BURIED HERE.

OH. WHERE'S HIS GRAVE?

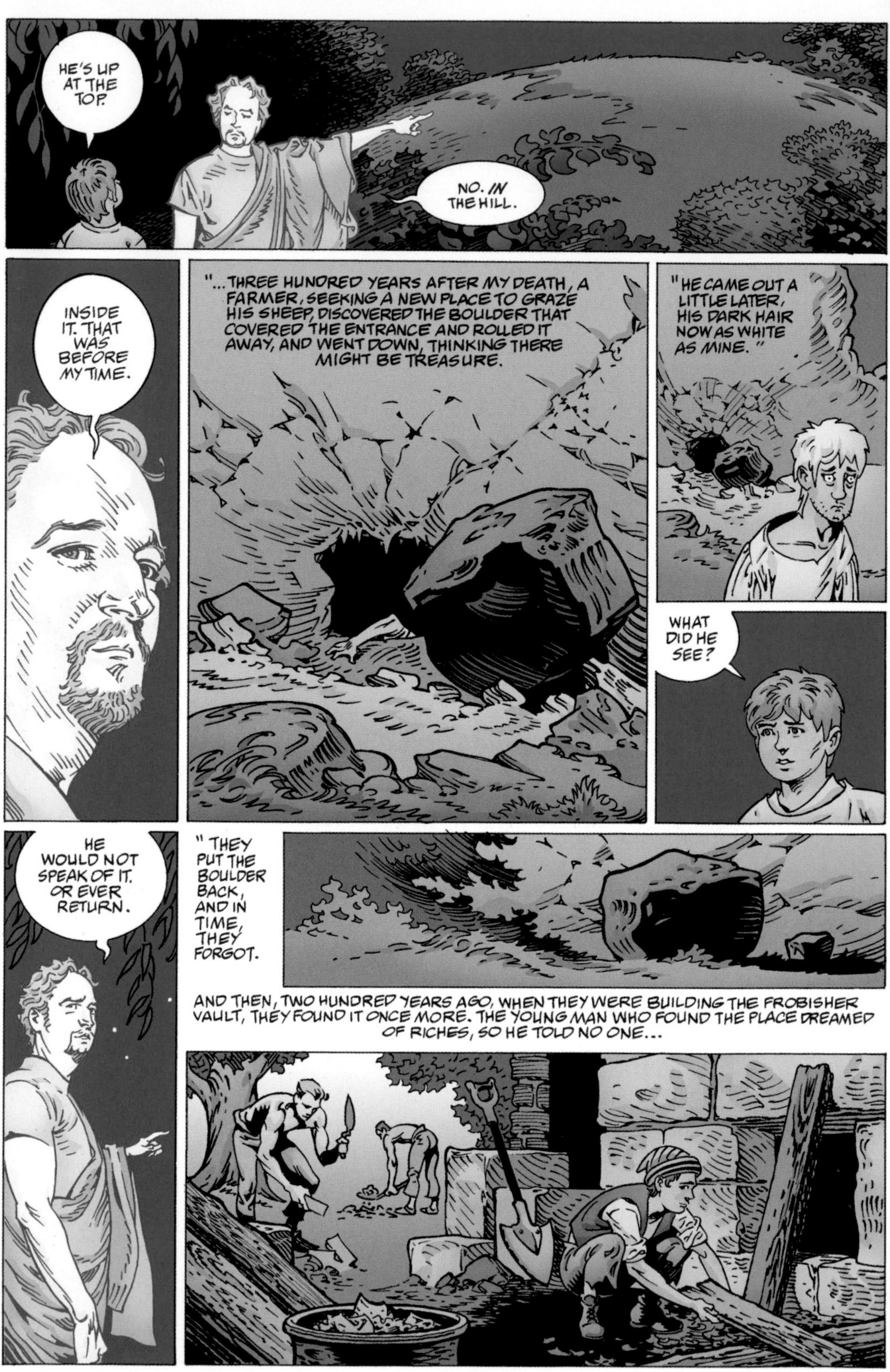

HE'S UP AT THE TOP?
NO. IN THE HILL.
INSIDE IT. THAT WAS BEFORE MY TIME.
"...THREE HUNDRED YEARS AFTER MY DEATH, A FARMER, SEEKING A NEW PLACE TO GRAZE HIS SHEEP, DISCOVERED THE BOULDER THAT COVERED THE ENTRANCE AND ROLLED IT AWAY, AND WENT DOWN, THINKING THERE MIGHT BE TREASURE.
"HE CAME OUT A LITTLE LATER, HIS DARK HAIR NOW AS WHITE AS MINE."
WHAT DID HE SEE?
HE WOULD NOT SPEAK OF IT, OR EVER RETURN.
"THEY PUT THE BOULDER BACK, AND IN TIME, THEY FORGOT.
AND THEN, TWO HUNDRED YEARS AGO, WHEN THEY WERE BUILDING THE FROBISHER VAULT, THEY FOUND IT ONCE MORE. THE YOUNG MAN WHO FOUND THE PLACE DREAMED OF RICHES, SO HE TOLD NO ONE...

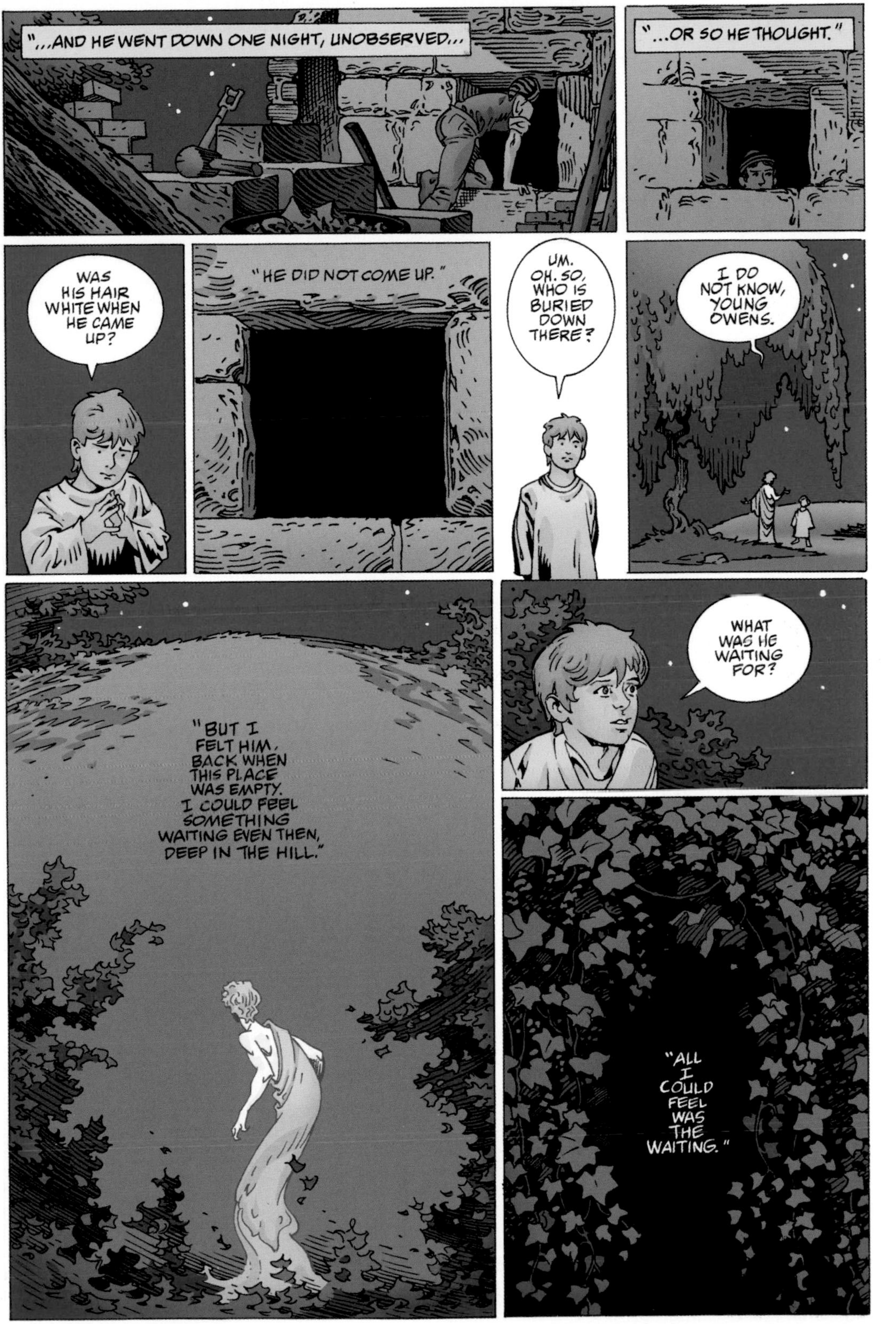
"...AND HE WENT DOWN ONE NIGHT, UNOBSERVED...
"...OR SO HE THOUGHT."
WAS HIS HAIR WHITE WHEN HE CAME UP?
"HE DID NOT COME UP."
UM. OH. SO, WHO IS BURIED DOWN THERE?
I DO NOT KNOW, YOUNG OWENS.
"BUT I FELT HIM, BACK WHEN THIS PLACE WAS EMPTY. I COULD FEEL SOMETHING WAITING EVEN THEN, DEEP IN THE HILL."
WHAT WAS HE WAITING FOR?
"ALL I COULD FEEL WAS THE WAITING."

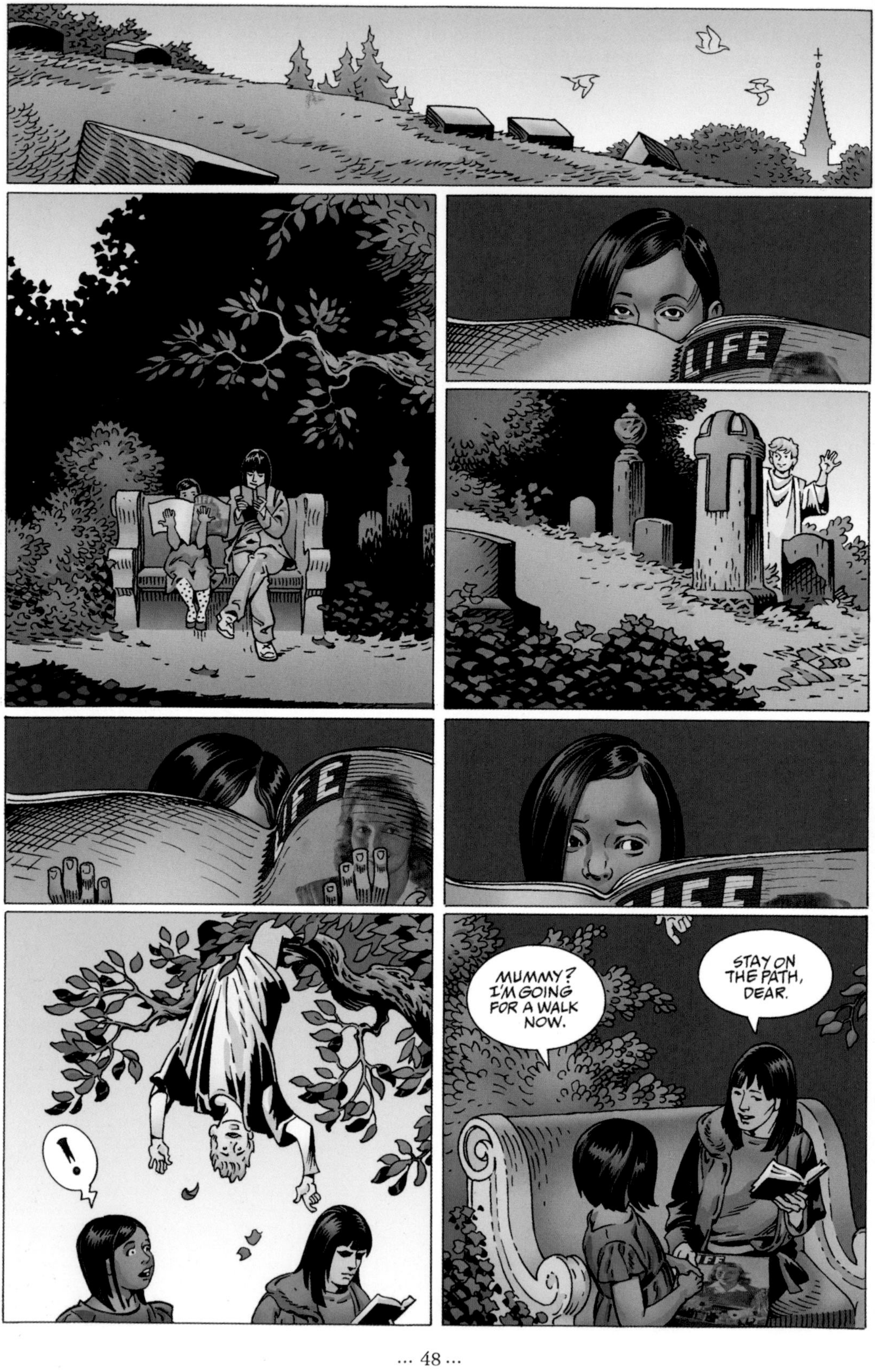
!
MUMMY? I'M GOING FOR A WALK NOW.
STAY ON THE PATH, DEAR.

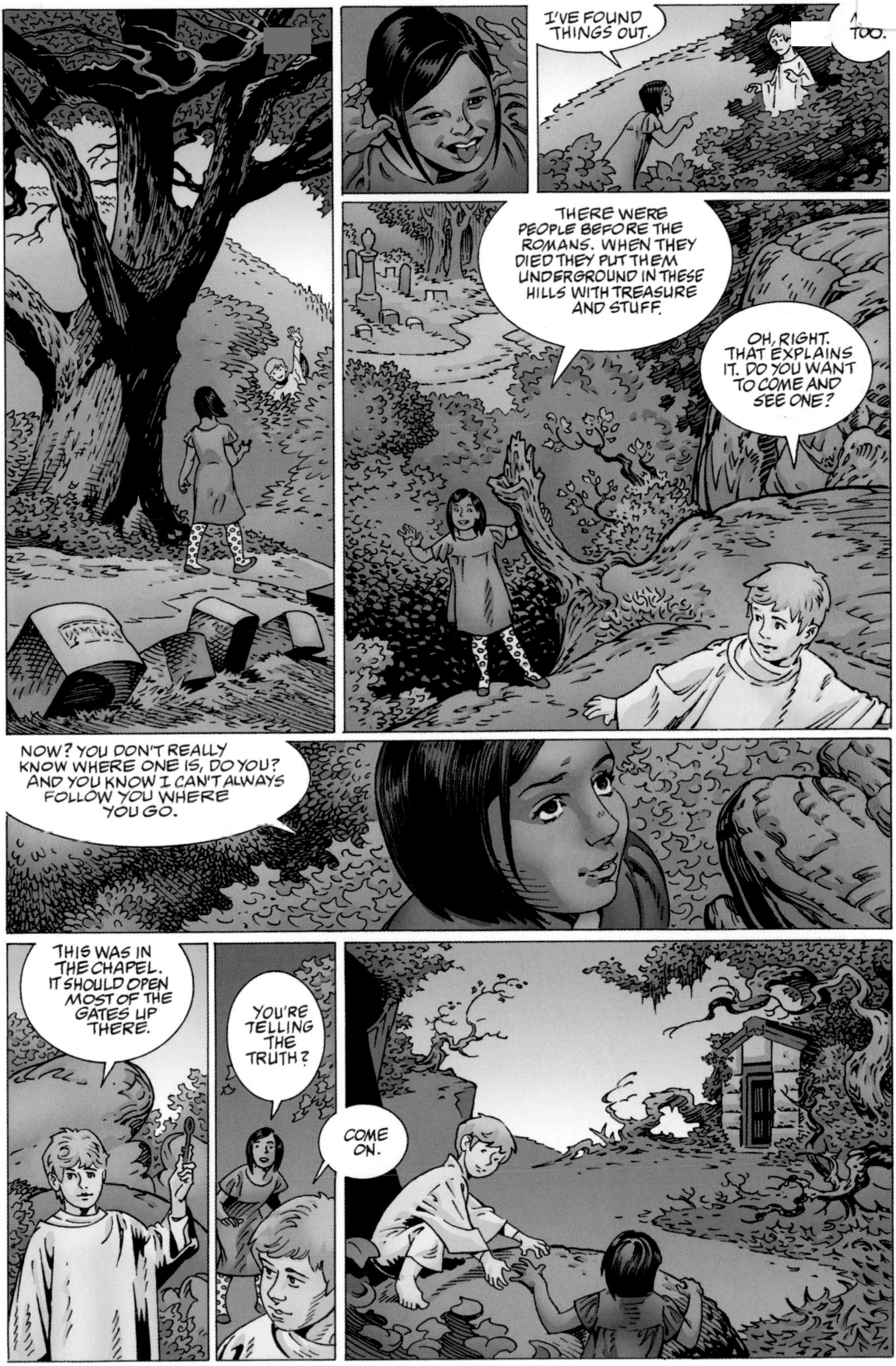
I'VE FOUND THINGS OUT.
TOO.
THERE WERE PEOPLE BEFORE THE ROMANS. WHEN THEY DIED THEY PUT THEM UNDERGROUND IN THESE HILLS WITH TREASURE AND STUFF.
OH, RIGHT. THAT EXPLAINS IT. DO YOU WANT TO COME AND SEE ONE?
NOW? YOU DON'T REALLY KNOW WHERE ONE IS, DO YOU? AND YOU KNOW I CAN'T ALWAYS FOLLOW YOU WHERE YOU GO.
THIS WAS IN THE CHAPEL. IT SHOULD OPEN MOST OF THE GATES UP THERE.
YOU'RE TELLING THE TRUTH?
COME ON.

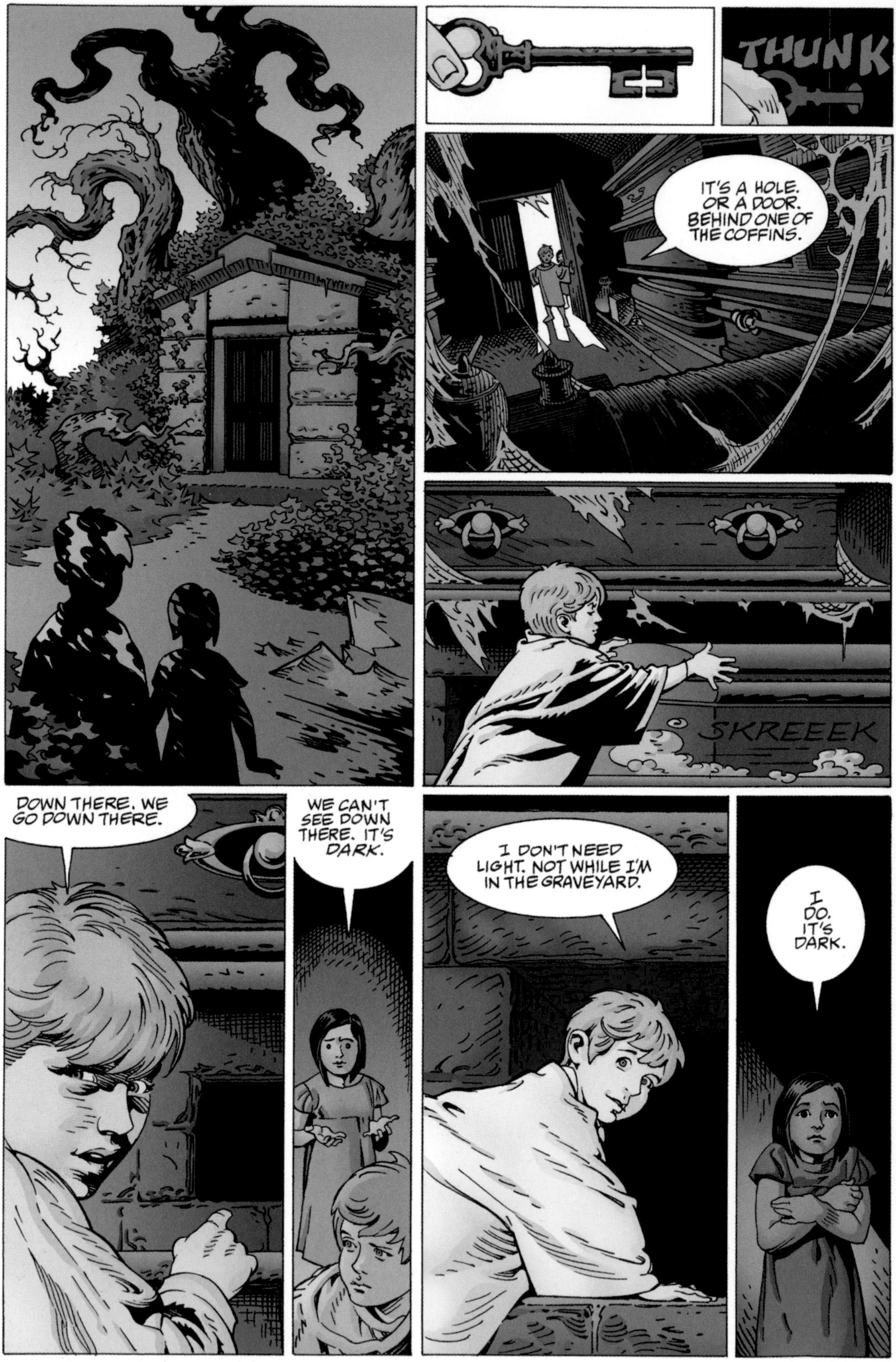
THUNK
IT'S A HOLE. OR A DOOR. BEHIND ONE OF THE COFFINS.
SKREEEK
DOWN THERE. WE GO DOWN THERE.
WE CAN'T SEE DOWN THERE. IT'S DARK.
I DON'T NEED LIGHT. NOT WHILE I'M IN THE GRAVEYARD.
I DO. IT'S DARK.

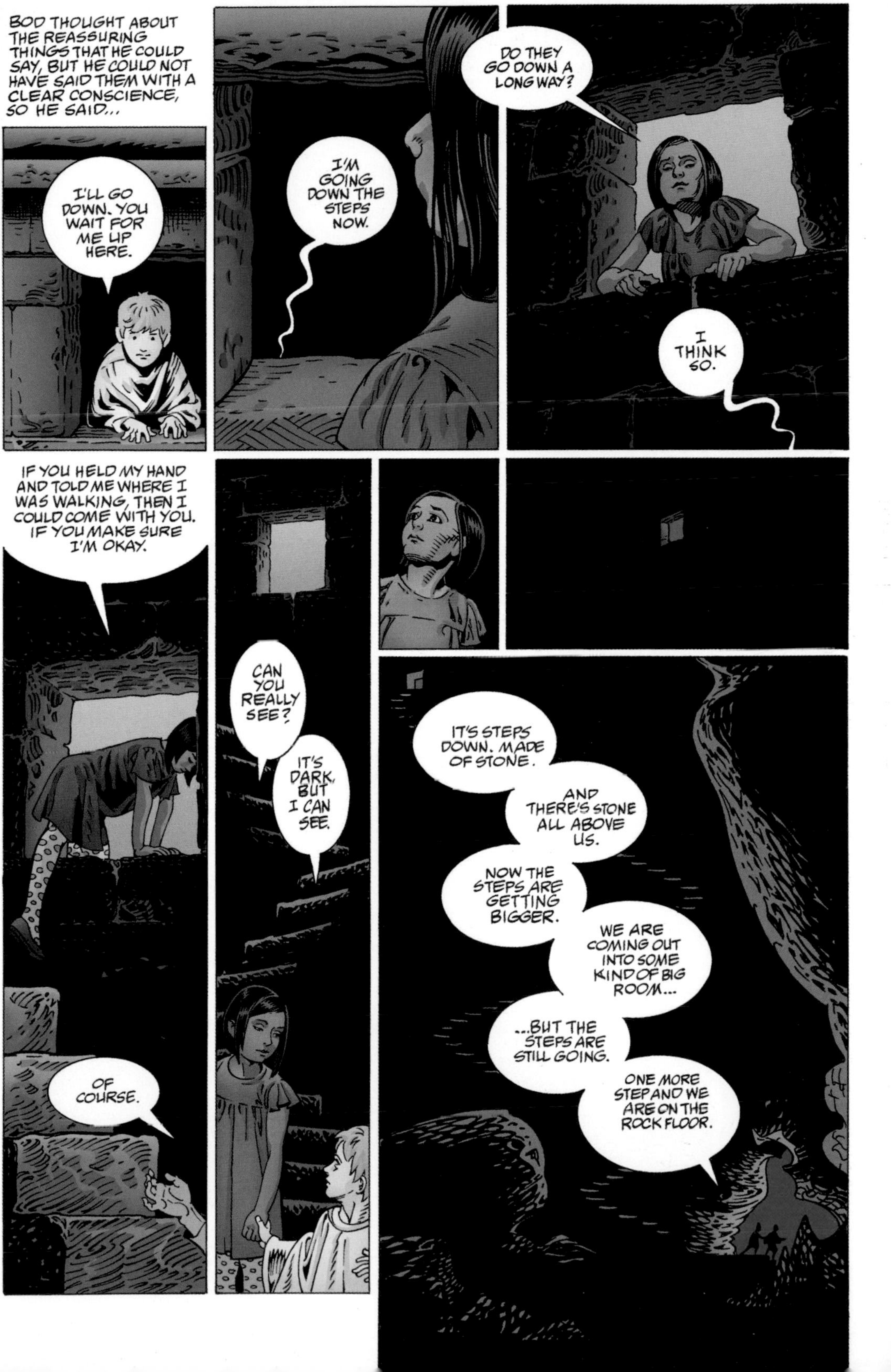
BOD THOUGHT ABOUT THE REASSURING THINGS THAT HE COULD SAY, BUT HE COULD NOT HAVE SAID THEM WITH A CLEAR CONSCIENCE, SO HE SAID...
I'LL GO DOWN. YOU WAIT FOR ME UP HERE.
I'M GOING DOWN THE STEPS NOW.
DO THEY GO DOWN A LONG WAY?
I THINK SO.
IF YOU HELD MY HAND AND TOLD ME WHERE I WAS WALKING, THEN I COULD COME WITH YOU. IF YOU MAKE SURE I'M OKAY.
OF COURSE.
CAN YOU REALLY SEE?
IT'S DARK, BUT I CAN SEE.
IT'S STEPS DOWN. MADE OF STONE.
AND THERE'S STONE ALL ABOVE US.
NOW THE STEPS ARE GETTING BIGGER.
WE ARE COMING OUT INTO SOME KIND OF BIG ROOM...
...BUT THE STEPS ARE STILL GOING.
ONE MORE STEP AND WE ARE ON THE ROCK FLOOR.

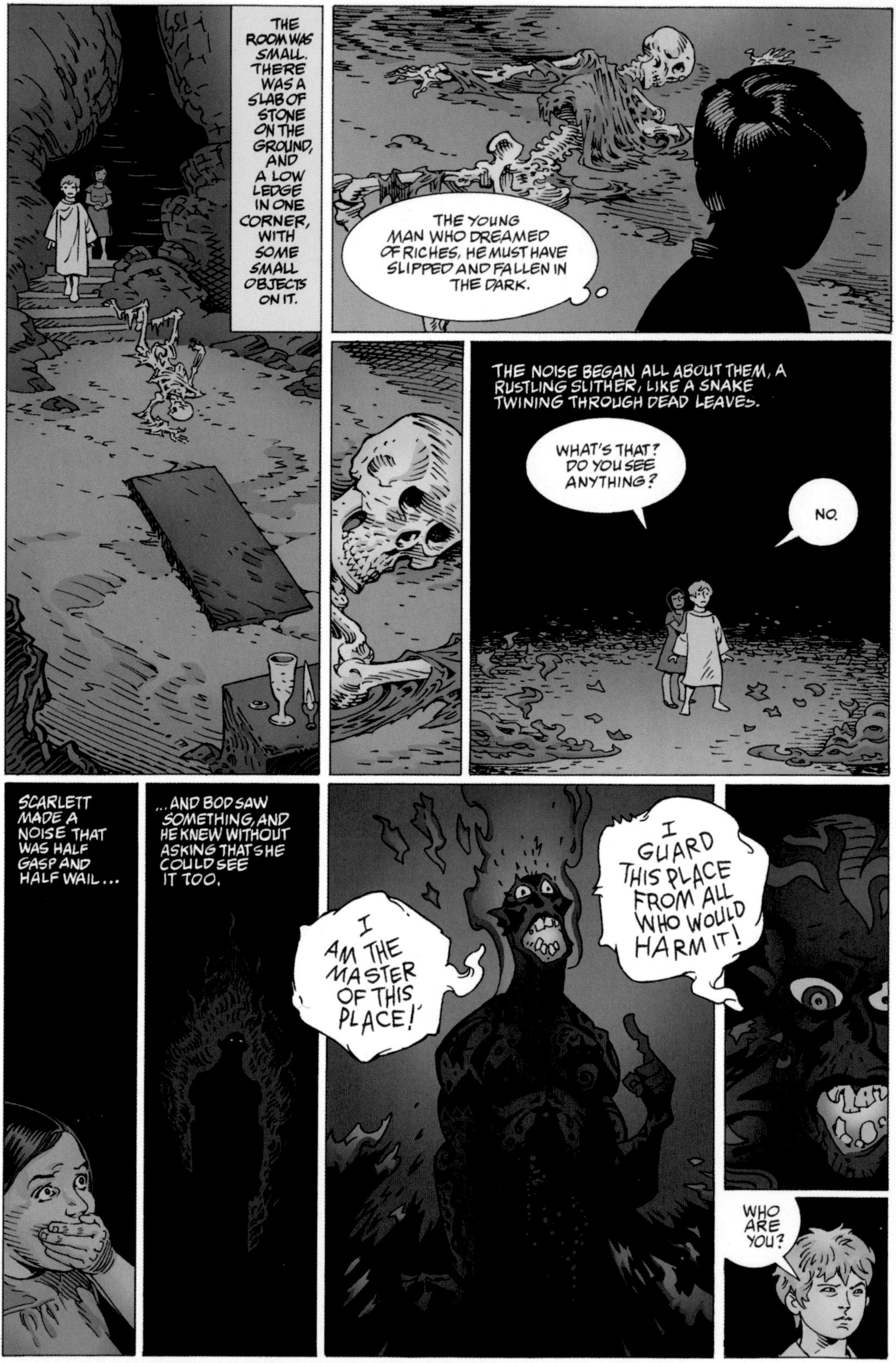
THE ROOM WAS SMALL. THERE WAS A SLAB OF STONE ON THE GROUND, AND A LOW LEDGE IN ONE CORNER, WITH SOME SMALL OBJECTS ON IT.
THE YOUNG MAN WHO DREAMED OF RICHES, HE MUST HAVE SLIPPED AND FALLEN IN THE DARK.
THE NOISE BEGAN ALL ABOUT THEM, A RUSTLING SLITHER, LIKE A SNAKE TWINING THROUGH DEAD LEAVES.
WHAT'S THAT? DO YOU SEE ANYTHING?
NO.
SCARLETT MADE A NOISE THAT WAS HALF GASP AND HALF WAIL...
...AND BOD SAW SOMETHING, AND HE KNEW WITHOUT ASKING THAT SHE COULD SEE IT TOO.
I AM THE MASTER OF THIS PLACE!
I GUARD THIS PLACE FROM ALL WHO WOULD HARM IT!
WHO ARE YOU?

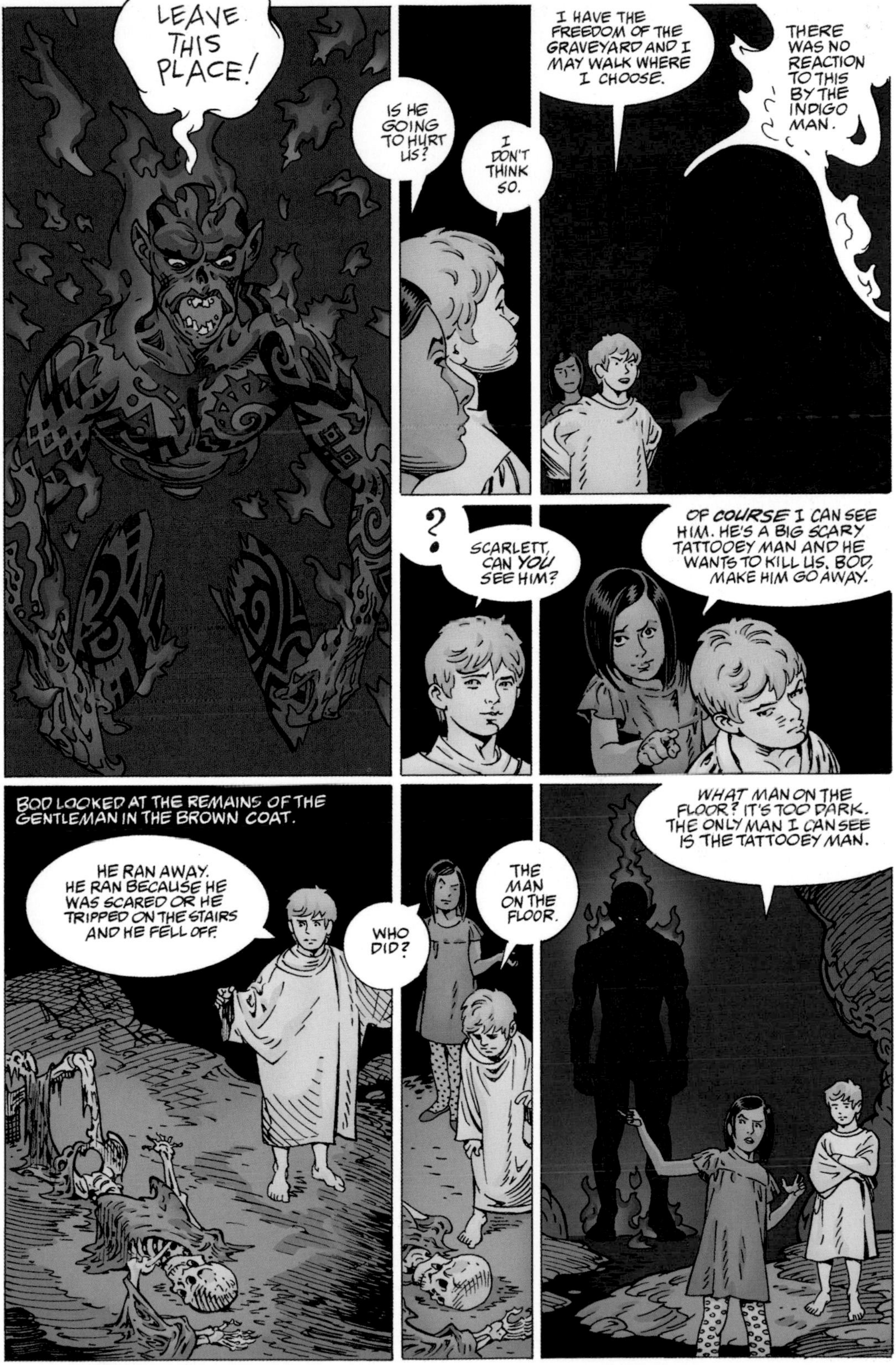
LEAVE THIS PLACE!
IS HE GOING TO HURT US?
I DON'T THINK SO.
I HAVE THE FREEDOM OF THE GRAVEYARD AND I MAY WALK WHERE I CHOOSE.
THERE WAS NO REACTION TO THIS BY THE INDIGO MAN.
?
SCARLETT, CAN YOU SEE HIM?
OF COURSE I CAN SEE HIM. HE'S A BIG SCARY TATTOOEY MAN AND HE WANTS TO KILL US. BOD, MAKE HIM GO AWAY.
BOD LOOKED AT THE REMAINS OF THE GENTLEMAN IN THE BROWN COAT.
HE RAN AWAY. HE RAN BECAUSE HE WAS SCARED OR HE TRIPPED ON THE STAIRS AND HE FELL OFF.
WHO DID?
THE MAN ON THE FLOOR.
WHAT MAN ON THE FLOOR? IT'S TOO DARK. THE ONLY MAN I CAN SEE IS THE TATTOOEY MAN.

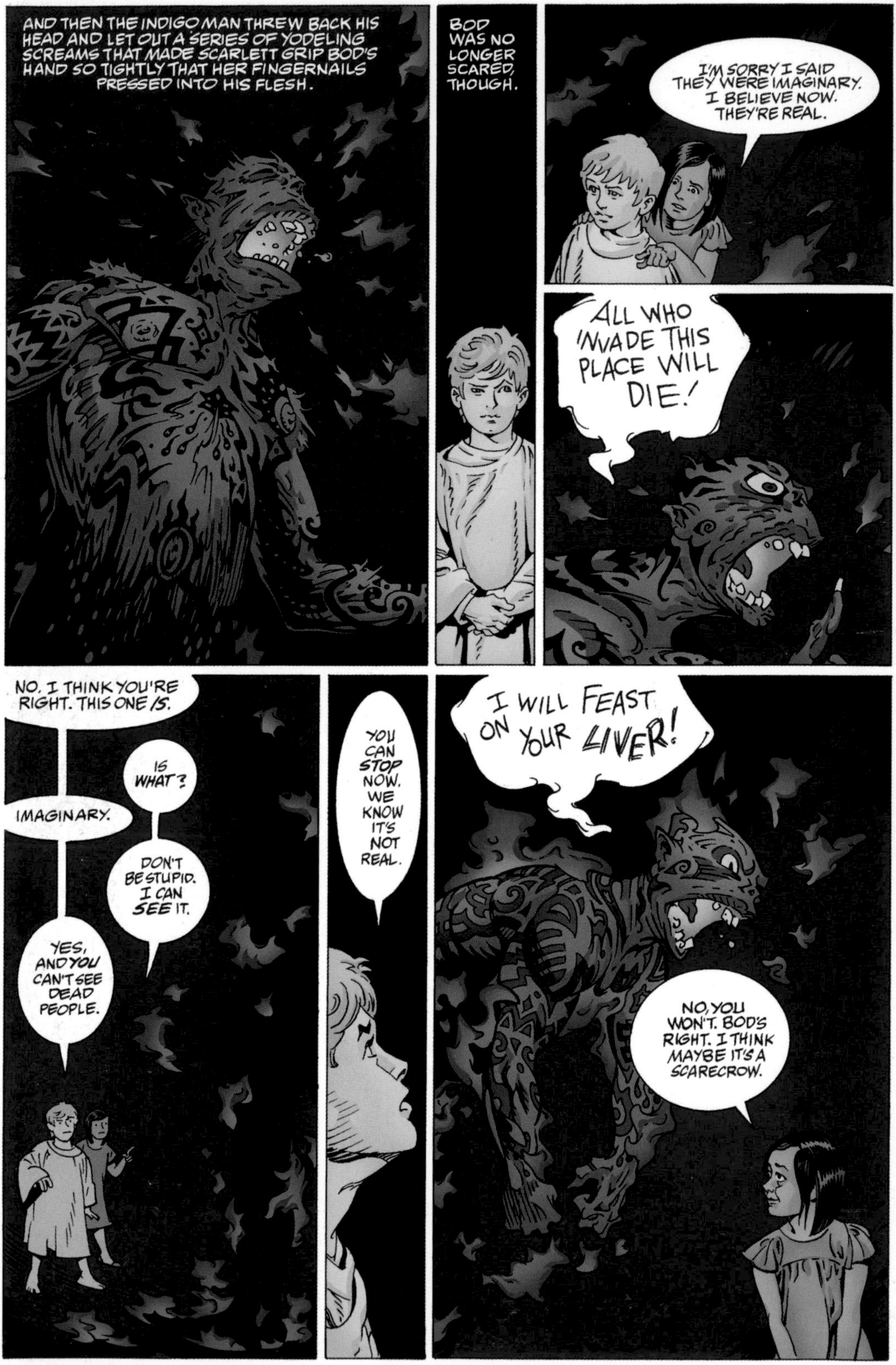
AND THEN THE INDIGO MAN THREW BACK HIS HEAD AND LET OUT A SERIES OF YODELING SCREAMS THAT MADE SCARLETT GRIP BOD'S HAND SO TIGHTLY THAT HER FINGERNAILS PRESSED INTO HIS FLESH.
BOD WAS NO LONGER SCARED, THOUGH.
I'M SORRY I SAID THEY WERE IMAGINARY. I BELIEVE NOW. THEY'RE REAL.
ALL WHO INVADE THIS PLACE WILL DIE!
NO. I THINK YOU'RE RIGHT. THIS ONE IS.
IS WHAT?
IMAGINARY.
DON'T BE STUPID. I CAN SEE IT.
YES, AND YOU CAN'T SEE DEAD PEOPLE.
YOU CAN STOP NOW. WE KNOW IT'S NOT REAL.
I WILL FEAST ON YOUR LIVER!
NO, YOU WON'T. BOD'S RIGHT. I THINK MAYBE IT'S A SCARECROW.

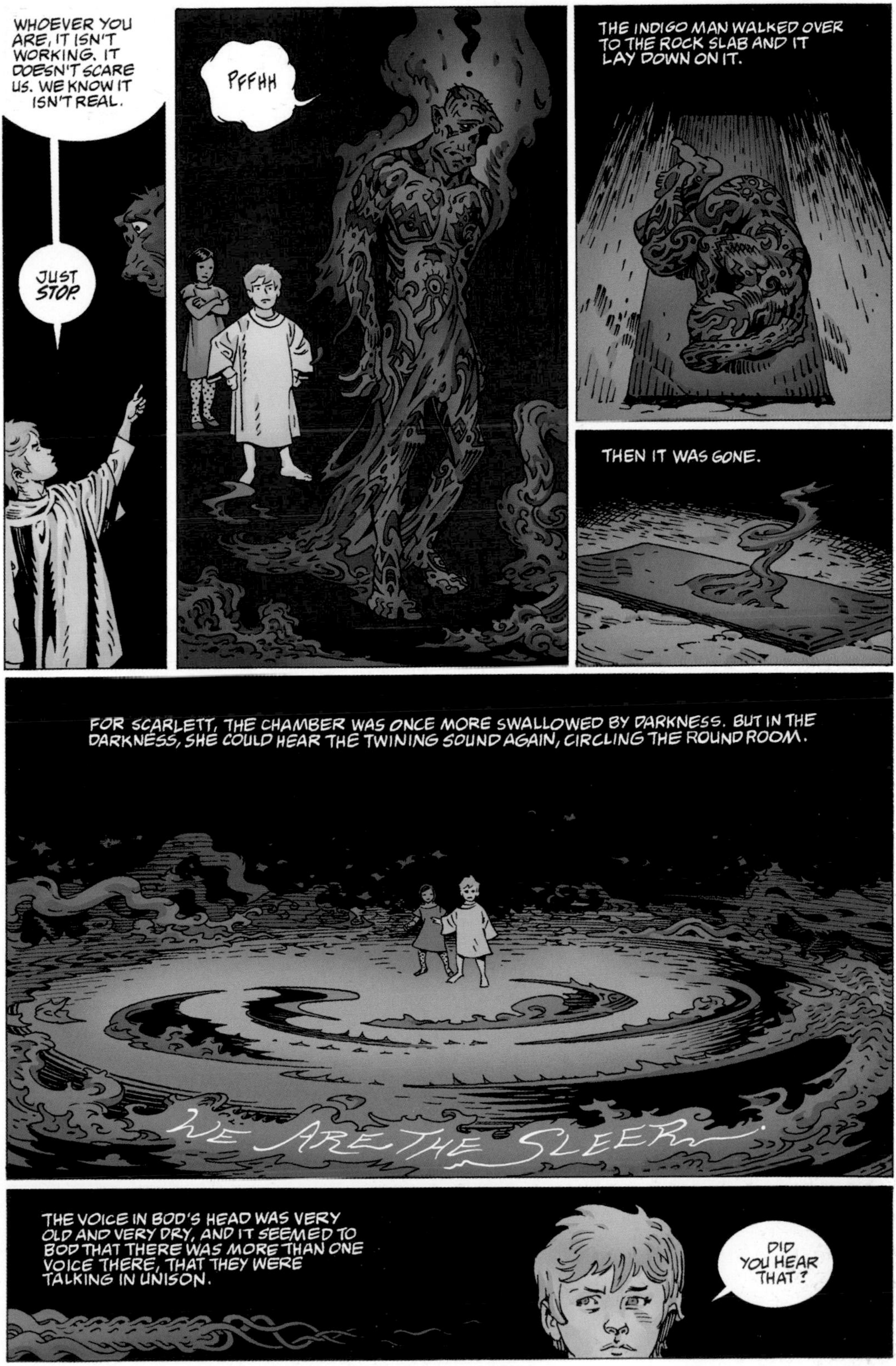

WHOEVER YOU ARE, IT ISN'T WORKING. IT DOESN'T SCARE US. WE KNOW IT ISN'T REAL.
JUST STOP.
PFFHH
THE INDIGO MAN WALKED OVER TO THE ROCK SLAB AND IT LAY DOWN ON IT.
THEN IT WAS GONE.
FOR SCARLETT, THE CHAMBER WAS ONCE MORE SWALLOWED BY DARKNESS. BUT IN THE DARKNESS, SHE COULD HEAR THE TWINING SOUND AGAIN, CIRCLING THE ROUND ROOM.
WE ARE THE SLEER.
THE VOICE IN BOD'S HEAD WAS VERY OLD AND VERY DRY, AND IT SEEMED TO BOD THAT THERE WAS MORE THAN ONE VOICE THERE, THAT THEY WERE TALKING IN UNISON.
DID YOU HEAR THAT?

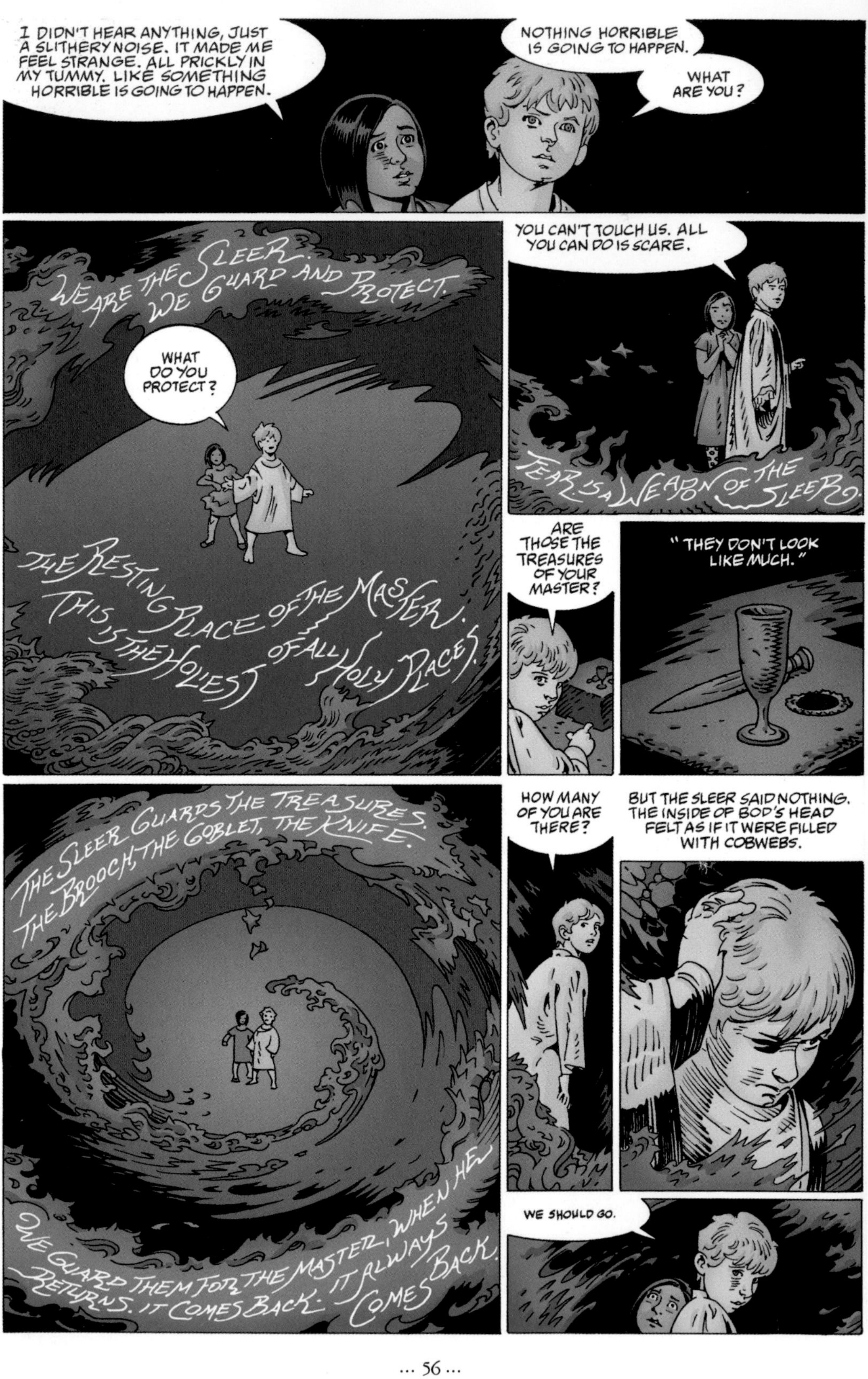

I DIDN'T HEAR ANYTHING, JUST A SLITHERY NOISE. IT MADE ME FEEL STRANGE. ALL PRICKLY IN MY TUMMY. LIKE SOMETHING HORRIBLE IS GOING TO HAPPEN.
NOTHING HORRIBLE IS GOING TO HAPPEN.
WHAT ARE YOU?
WE ARE THE SLEER. WE GUARD AND PROTECT.
WHAT DO YOU PROTECT?
THE RESTING PLACE OF THE MASTER. THIS IS THE HOLIEST OF ALL HOLY PLACES.
YOU CAN'T TOUCH US. ALL YOU CAN DO IS SCARE.
FEAR IS A WEAPON OF THE SLEER.
ARE THOSE THE TREASURES OF YOUR MASTER?
"THEY DON'T LOOK LIKE MUCH."
THE SLEER GUARDS THE TREASURES. THE BROOCH, THE GOBLET, THE KNIFE.
WE GUARD THEM FOR THE MASTER, WHEN HE RETURNS. IT COMES BACK. IT ALWAYS COMES BACK.
HOW MANY OF YOU ARE THERE?
BUT THE SLEER SAID NOTHING. THE INSIDE OF BOD'S HEAD FELT AS IF IT WERE FILLED WITH COBWEBS.
WE SHOULD GO.

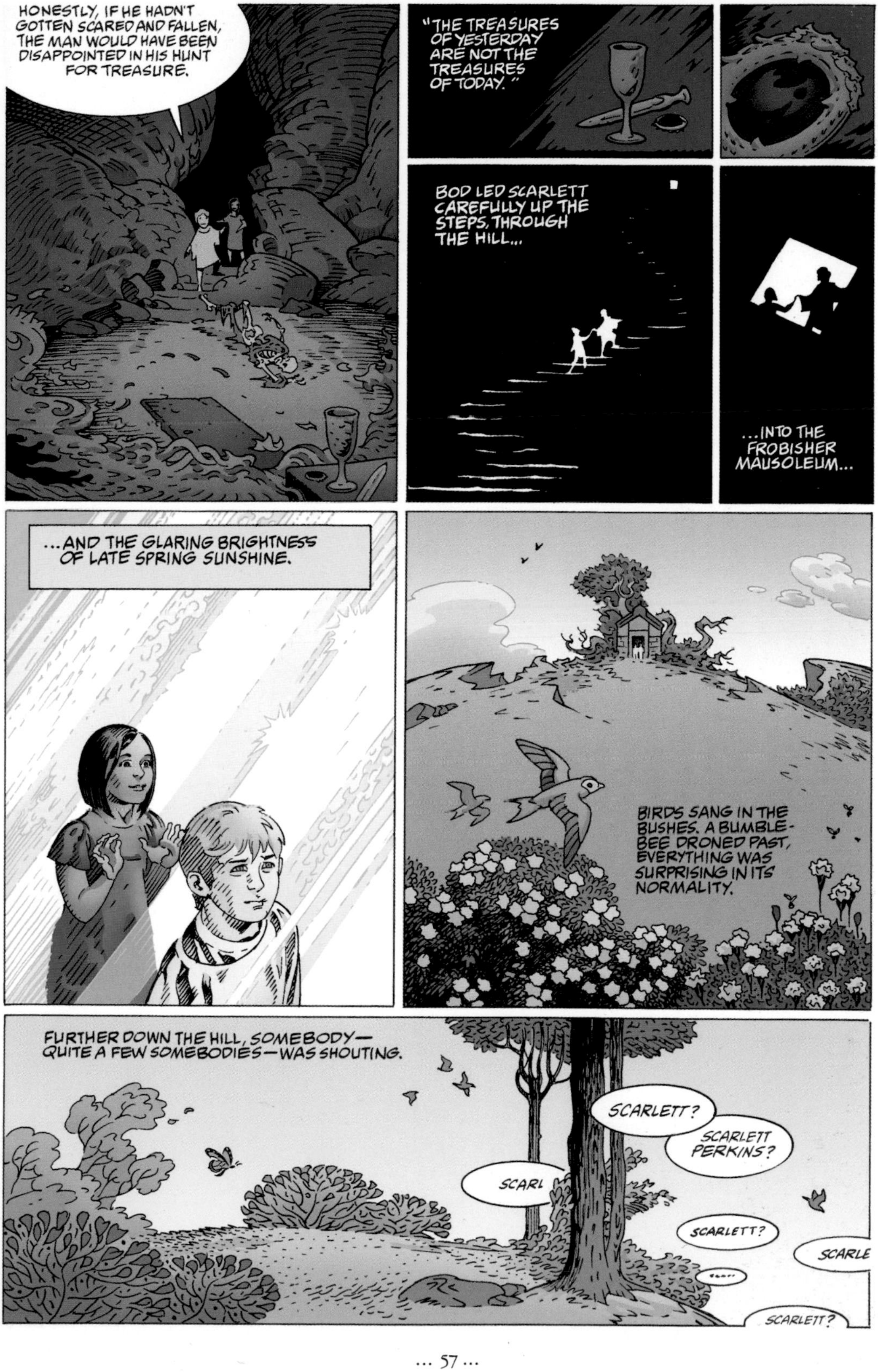
HONESTLY, IF HE HADN'T GOTTEN SCARED AND FALLEN, THE MAN WOULD HAVE BEEN DISAPPOINTED IN HIS HUNT FOR TREASURE.
"THE TREASURES OF YESTERDAY ARE NOT THE TREASURES OF TODAY."
BOD LED SCARLETT CAREFULLY UP THE STEPS, THROUGH THE HILL...
...INTO THE FROBISHER MAUSOLEUM...
...AND THE GLARING BRIGHTNESS OF LATE SPRING SUNSHINE.
BIRDS SANG IN THE BUSHES. A BUMBLE-BEE DRONED PAST, EVERYTHING WAS SURPRISING IN ITS NORMALITY.
FURTHER DOWN THE HILL, SOMEBODY— QUITE A FEW SOMEBODIES—WAS SHOUTING.
SCARLETT?
SCARLETT PERKINS?
SCARL
SCARLETT?
SCARLE
SCARLETT?

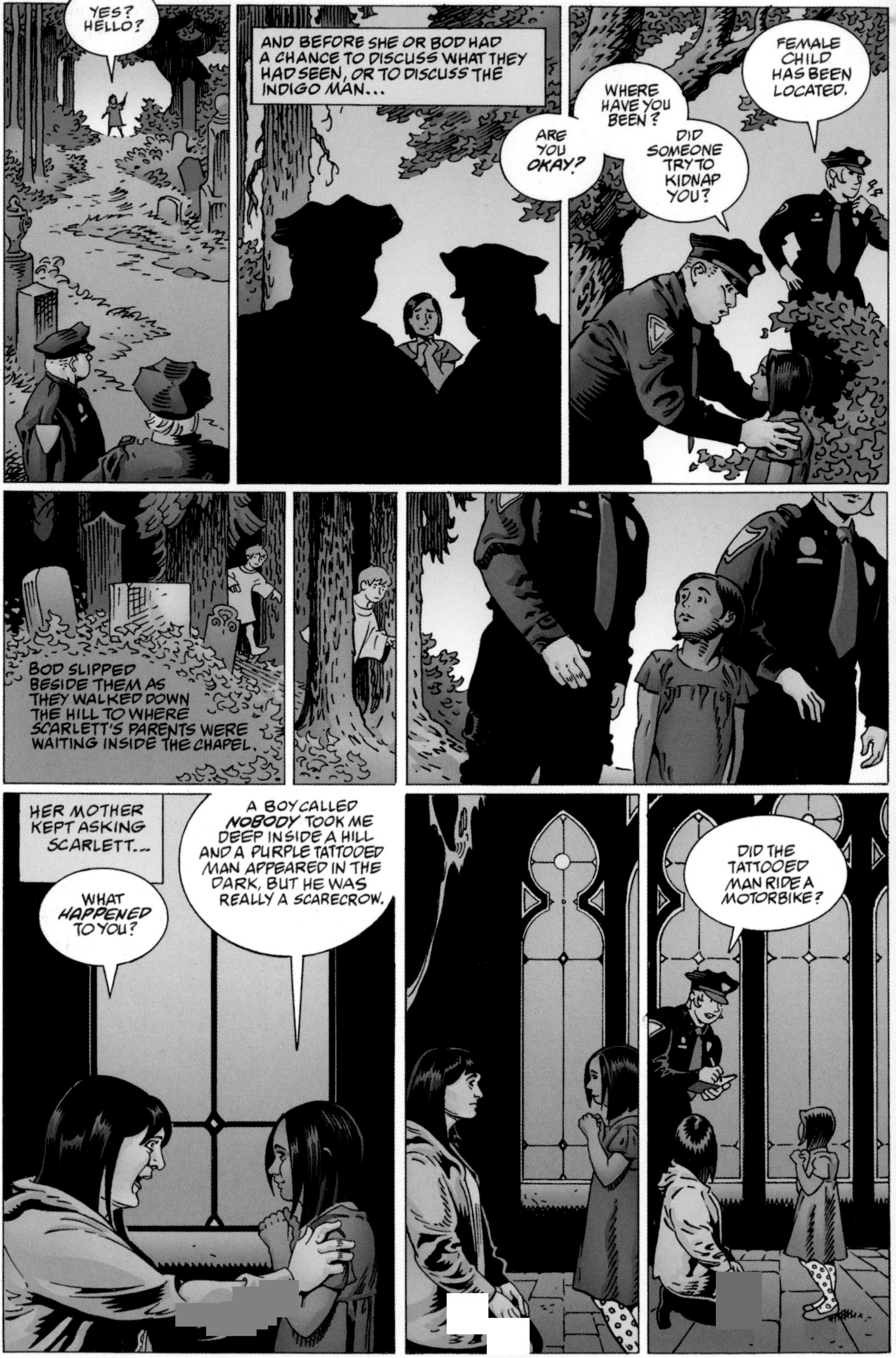
YES? HELLO?
AND BEFORE SHE OR BOD HAD A CHANCE TO DISCUSS WHAT THEY HAD SEEN, OR TO DISCUSS THE INDIGO MAN...
ARE YOU OKAY?
WHERE HAVE YOU BEEN?
DID SOMEONE TRY TO KIDNAP YOU?
FEMALE CHILD HAS BEEN LOCATED.
BOD SLIPPED BESIDE THEM AS THEY WALKED DOWN THE HILL TO WHERE SCARLETT'S PARENTS WERE WAITING INSIDE THE CHAPEL.
HER MOTHER KEPT ASKING SCARLETT...
WHAT HAPPENED TO YOU?
A BOY CALLED NOBODY TOOK ME DEEP INSIDE A HILL AND A PURPLE TATTOOED MAN APPEARED IN THE DARK, BUT HE WAS REALLY A SCARECROW.
DID THE TATTOOED MAN RIDE A MOTORBIKE?

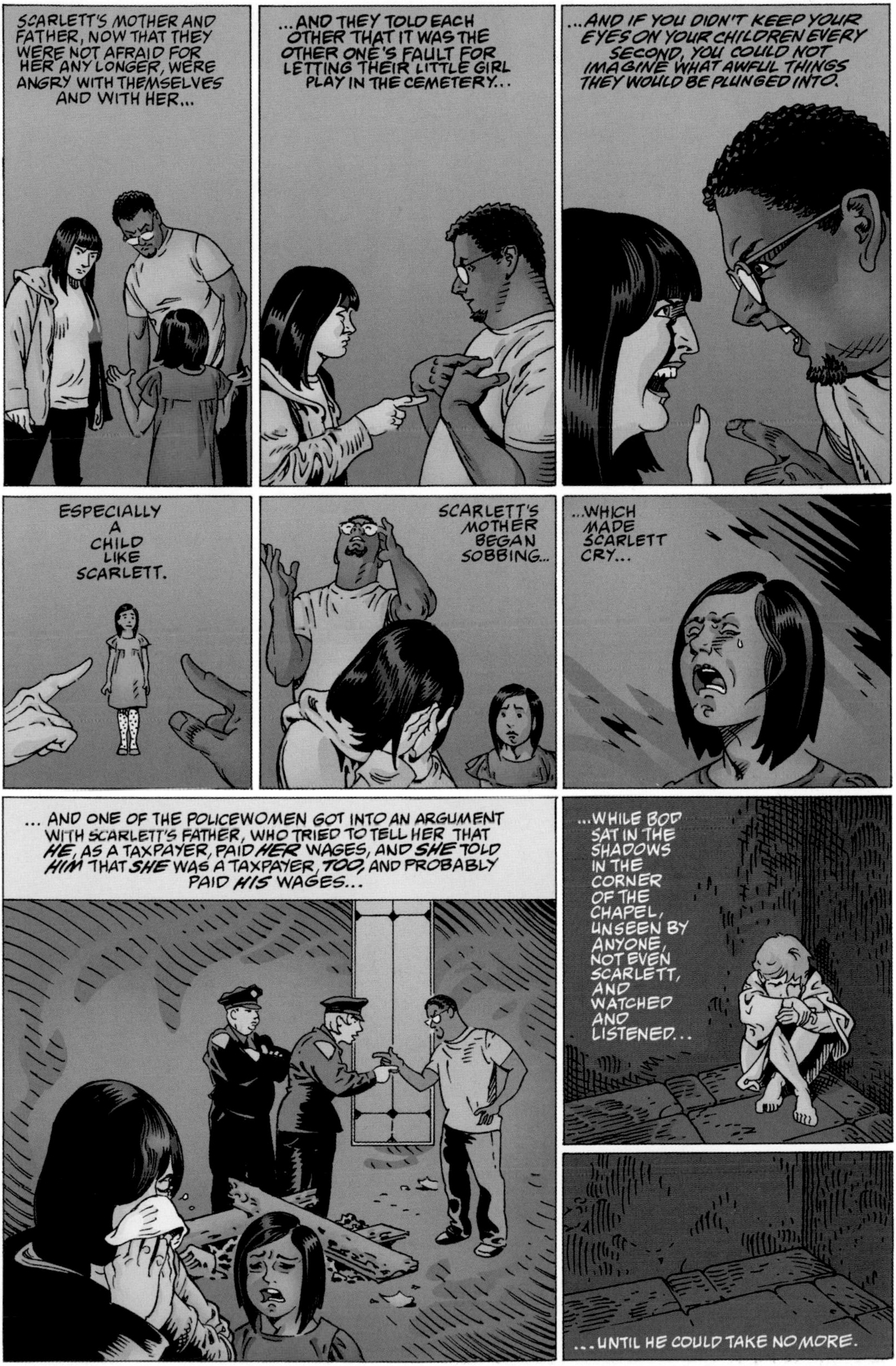
SCARLETT'S MOTHER AND FATHER, NOW THAT THEY WERE NOT AFRAID FOR HER ANY LONGER, WERE ANGRY WITH THEMSELVES AND WITH HER...
...AND THEY TOLD EACH OTHER THAT IT WAS THE OTHER ONE'S FAULT FOR LETTING THEIR LITTLE GIRL PLAY IN THE CEMETERY...
...AND IF YOU DIDN'T KEEP YOUR EYES ON YOUR CHILDREN EVERY SECOND, YOU COULD NOT IMAGINE WHAT AWFUL THINGS THEY WOULD BE PLUNGED INTO.
ESPECIALLY A CHILD LIKE SCARLETT.
SCARLETT'S MOTHER BEGAN SOBBING...
...WHICH MADE SCARLETT CRY...
... AND ONE OF THE POLICEWOMEN GOT INTO AN ARGUMENT WITH SCARLETT'S FATHER, WHO TRIED TO TELL HER THAT HE, AS A TAXPAYER, PAID HER WAGES, AND SHE TOLD HIM THAT SHE WAS A TAXPAYER, TOO, AND PROBABLY PAID HIS WAGES...
...WHILE BOD SAT IN THE SHADOWS IN THE CORNER OF THE CHAPEL, UNSEEN BY ANYONE, NOT EVEN SCARLETT, AND WATCHED AND LISTENED...
...UNTIL HE COULD TAKE NO MORE.

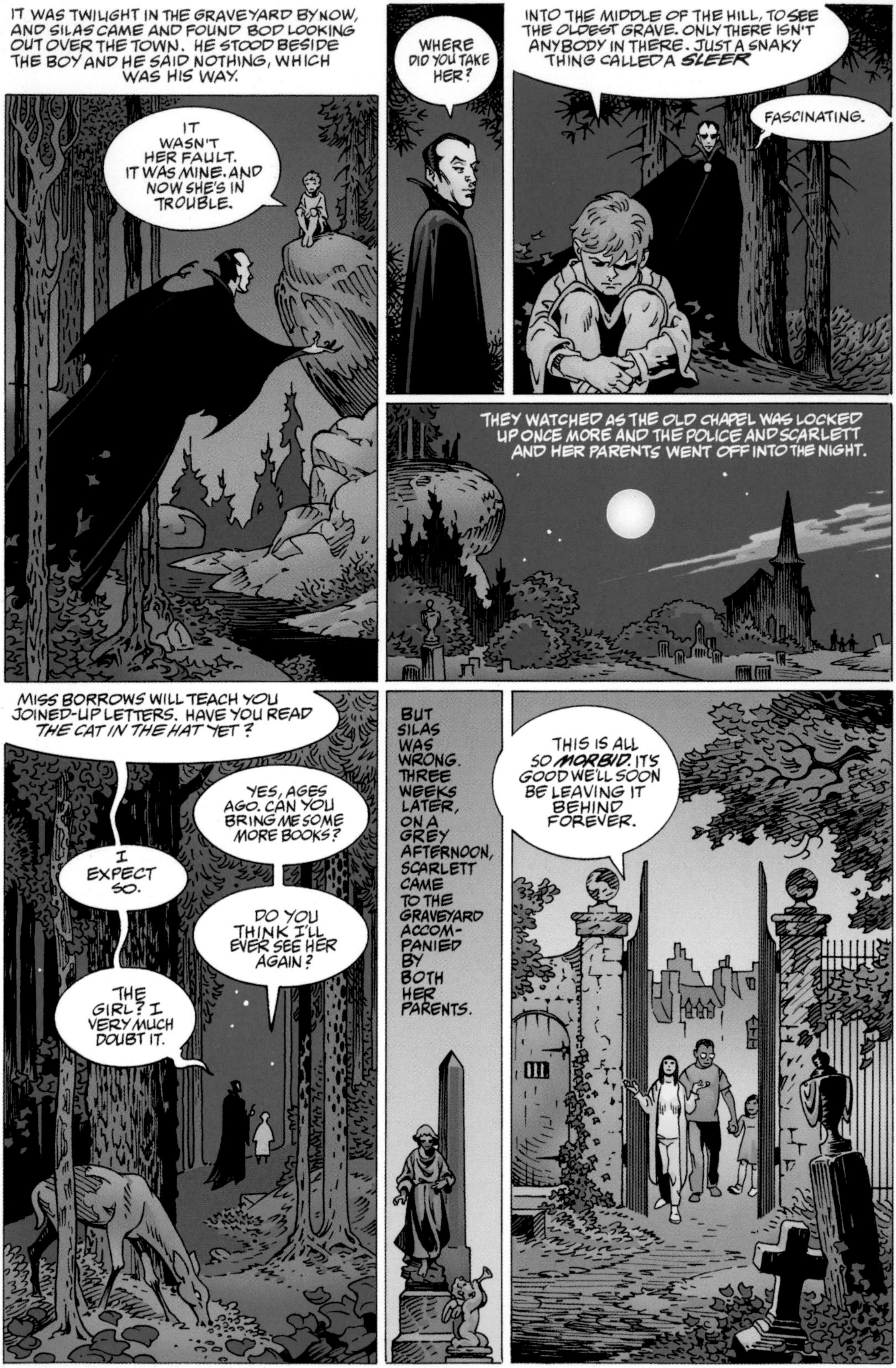
IT WAS TWILIGHT IN THE GRAVEYARD BY NOW, AND SILAS CAME AND FOUND BOD LOOKING OUT OVER THE TOWN. HE STOOD BESIDE THE BOY AND HE SAID NOTHING, WHICH WAS HIS WAY.
IT WASN'T HER FAULT. IT WAS MINE. AND NOW SHE'S IN TROUBLE.
WHERE DID YOU TAKE HER?
INTO THE MIDDLE OF THE HILL, TO SEE THE OLDEST GRAVE. ONLY THERE ISN'T ANYBODY IN THERE. JUST A SNAKY THING CALLED A SLEER
FASCINATING.
THEY WATCHED AS THE OLD CHAPEL WAS LOCKED UP ONCE MORE AND THE POLICE AND SCARLETT AND HER PARENTS WENT OFF INTO THE NIGHT.
MISS BORROWS WILL TEACH YOU JOINED-UP LETTERS. HAVE YOU READ THE CAT IN THE HAT YET?
YES, AGES AGO. CAN YOU BRING ME SOME MORE BOOKS?
I EXPECT SO.
DO YOU THINK I'LL EVER SEE HER AGAIN?
THE GIRL? I VERY MUCH DOUBT IT.
BUT SILAS WAS WRONG. THREE WEEKS LATER, ON A GREY AFTERNOON, SCARLETT CAME TO THE GRAVEYARD ACCOMPANIED BY BOTH HER PARENTS.
THIS IS ALL SO MORBID. IT'S GOOD WE'LL SOON BE LEAVING IT BEHIND FOREVER.

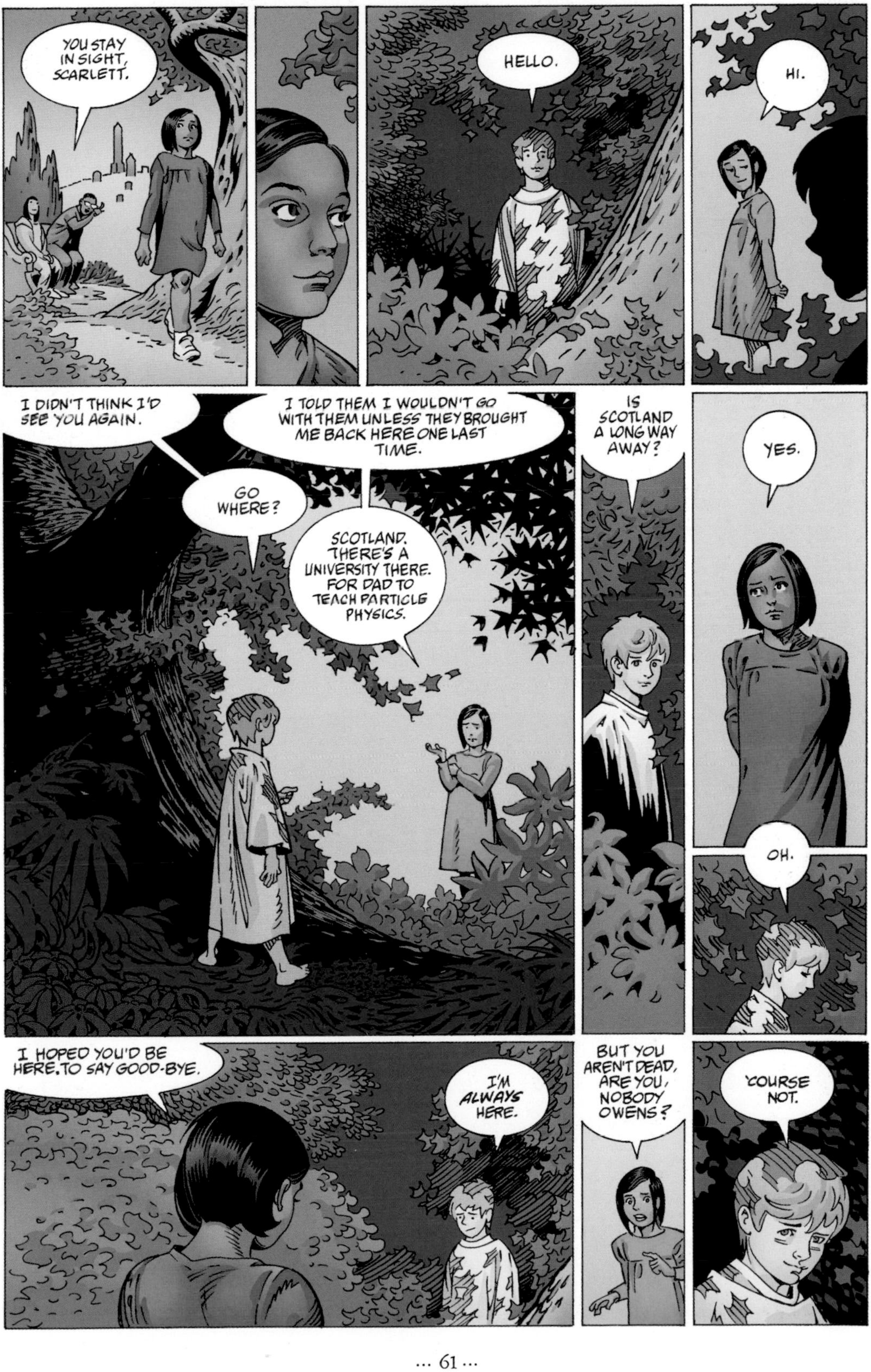

YOU STAY IN SIGHT, SCARLETT.
HELLO.
HI.
I DIDN'T THINK I'D SEE YOU AGAIN.
I TOLD THEM I WOULDN'T GO WITH THEM UNLESS THEY BROUGHT ME BACK HERE ONE LAST TIME.
GO WHERE?
SCOTLAND. THERE'S A UNIVERSITY THERE. FOR DAD TO TEACH PARTICLE PHYSICS.
IS SCOTLAND A LONG WAY AWAY?
YES.
OH.
I HOPED YOU'D BE HERE. TO SAY GOOD-BYE.
I'M ALWAYS HERE.
BUT YOU AREN'T DEAD, ARE YOU, NOBODY OWENS?
'COURSE NOT.

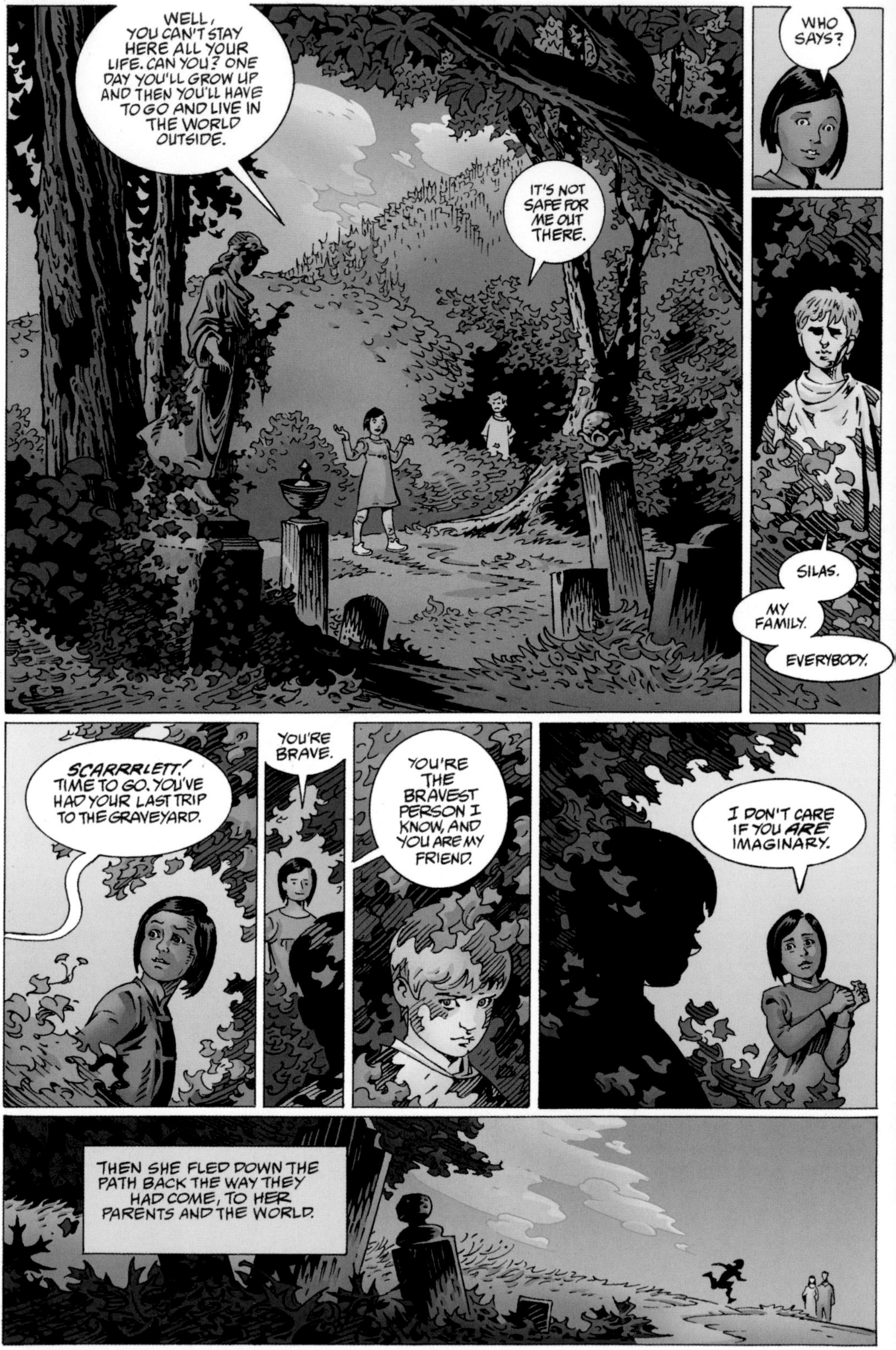
WELL, YOU CAN'T STAY HERE ALL YOUR LIFE. CAN YOU? ONE DAY YOU'LL GROW UP AND THEN YOU'LL HAVE TO GO AND LIVE IN THE WORLD OUTSIDE.
IT'S NOT SAFE FOR ME OUT THERE.
WHO SAYS?
SILAS.
MY FAMILY.
EVERYBODY.
SCARRRLETT! TIME TO GO. YOU'VE HAD YOUR LAST TRIP TO THE GRAVEYARD.
YOU'RE BRAVE.
YOU'RE THE BRAVEST PERSON I KNOW, AND YOU ARE MY FRIEND.
I DON'T CARE IF YOU *ARE* IMAGINARY.
THEN SHE FLED DOWN THE PATH BACK THE WAY THEY HAD COME, TO HER PARENTS AND THE WORLD.

3
The Hounds of God

Illustrated by Tony Harris and Scott Hampton

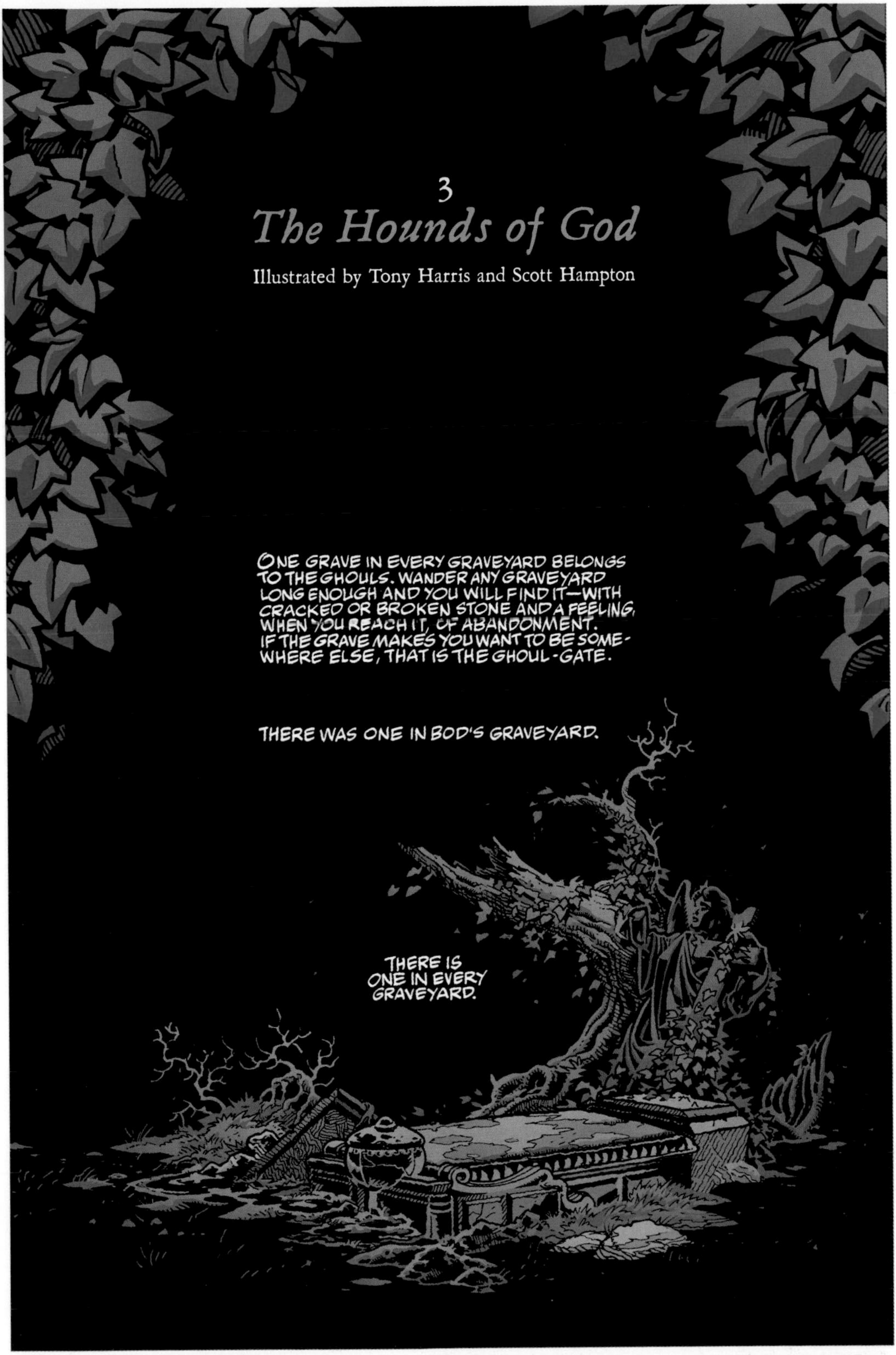
ONE GRAVE IN EVERY GRAVEYARD BELONGS TO THE GHOULS. WANDER ANY GRAVEYARD LONG ENOUGH AND YOU WILL FIND IT—WITH CRACKED OR BROKEN STONE AND A FEELING, WHEN YOU REACH IT, OF ABANDONMENT. IF THE GRAVE MAKES YOU WANT TO BE SOMEWHERE ELSE, THAT IS THE GHOUL-GATE.
THERE WAS ONE IN BOD'S GRAVEYARD.
THERE IS ONE IN EVERY GRAVEYARD.

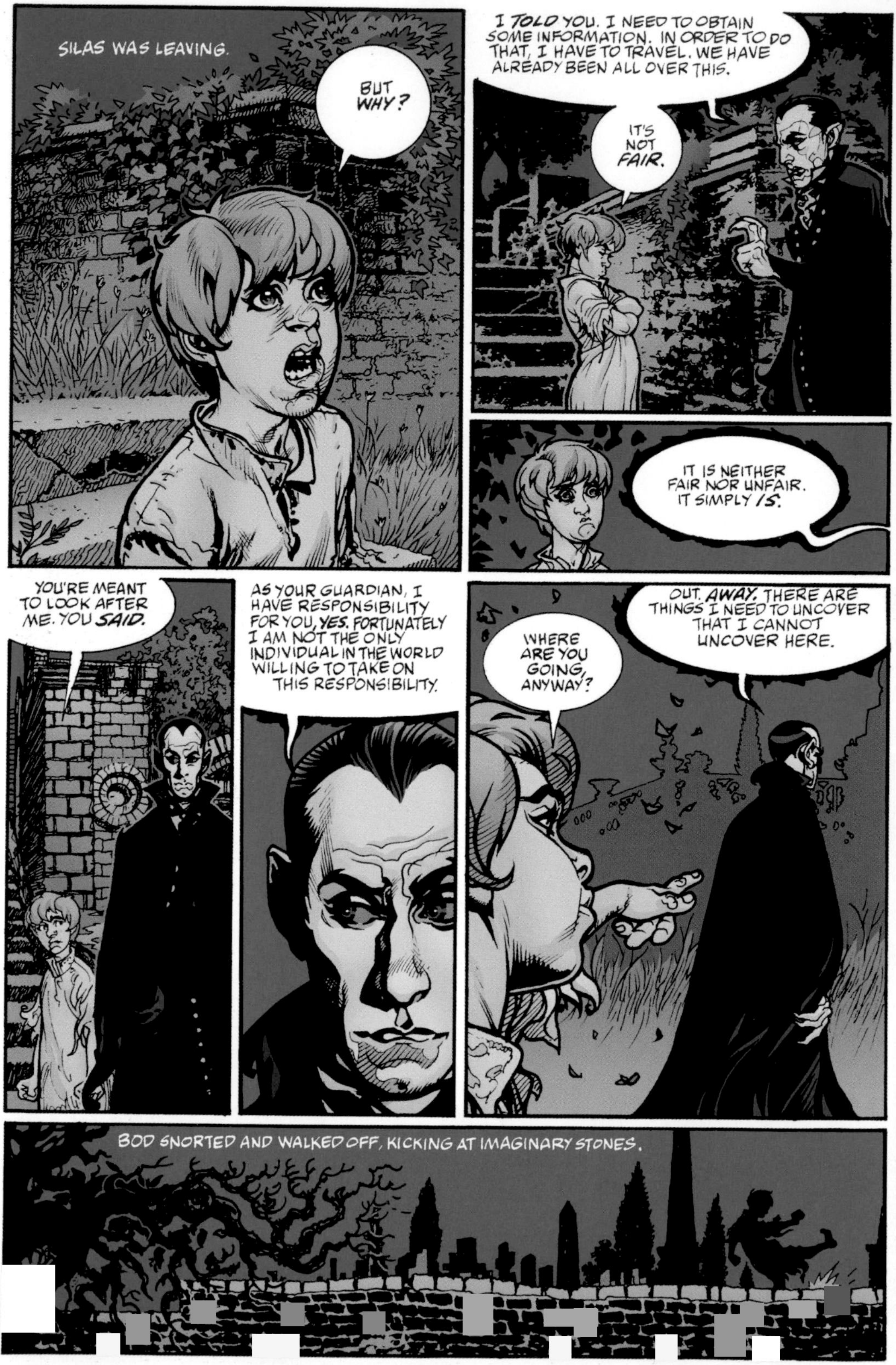
SILAS WAS LEAVING.
BUT WHY?
I TOLD YOU. I NEED TO OBTAIN SOME INFORMATION. IN ORDER TO DO THAT, I HAVE TO TRAVEL. WE HAVE ALREADY BEEN ALL OVER THIS.
IT'S NOT FAIR.
IT IS NEITHER FAIR NOR UNFAIR. IT SIMPLY IS.
YOU'RE MEANT TO LOOK AFTER ME. YOU SAID.
AS YOUR GUARDIAN, I HAVE RESPONSIBILITY FOR YOU, YES. FORTUNATELY I AM NOT THE ONLY INDIVIDUAL IN THE WORLD WILLING TO TAKE ON THIS RESPONSIBILITY.
WHERE ARE YOU GOING, ANYWAY?
OUT. AWAY. THERE ARE THINGS I NEED TO UNCOVER THAT I CANNOT UNCOVER HERE.
BOD SNORTED AND WALKED OFF, KICKING AT IMAGINARY STONES.

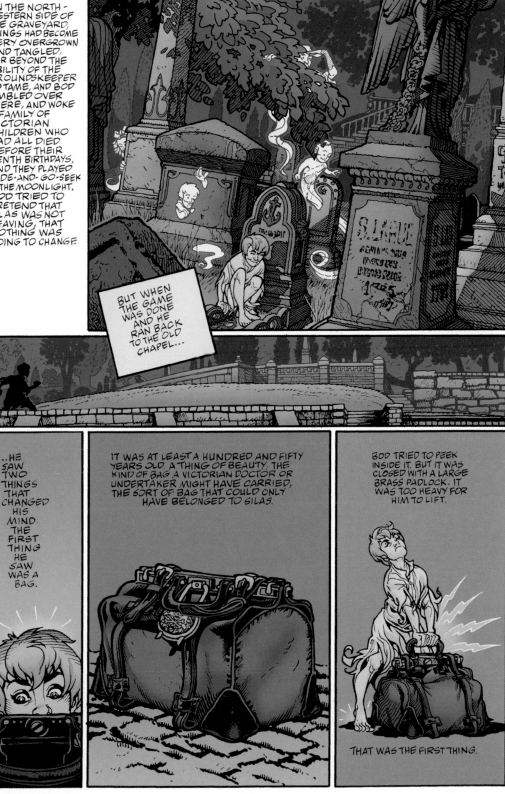

ON THE NORTH-WESTERN SIDE OF THE GRAVEYARD, THINGS HAD BECOME VERY OVERGROWN AND TANGLED, FAR BEYOND THE ABILITY OF THE GROUNDSKEEPER TO TAME, AND BOD AMBLED OVER THERE, AND WOKE A FAMILY OF VICTORIAN CHILDREN WHO HAD ALL DIED BEFORE THEIR TENTH BIRTHDAYS, AND THEY PLAYED HIDE-AND-GO-SEEK IN THE MOONLIGHT. BOD TRIED TO PRETEND THAT SILAS WAS NOT LEAVING, THAT NOTHING WAS GOING TO CHANGE.

BUT WHEN THE GAME WAS DONE AND HE RAN BACK TO THE OLD CHAPEL...

...HE SAW TWO THINGS THAT CHANGED HIS MIND. THE FIRST THING HE SAW WAS A BAG.

IT WAS AT LEAST A HUNDRED AND FIFTY YEARS OLD, A THING OF BEAUTY, THE KIND OF BAG A VICTORIAN DOCTOR OR UNDERTAKER MIGHT HAVE CARRIED, THE SORT OF BAG THAT COULD ONLY HAVE BELONGED TO SILAS.

BOD TRIED TO PEEK INSIDE IT. BUT IT WAS CLOSED WITH A LARGE BRASS PADLOCK. IT WAS TOO HEAVY FOR HIM TO LIFT.

THAT WAS THE FIRST THING.

... 65 ...

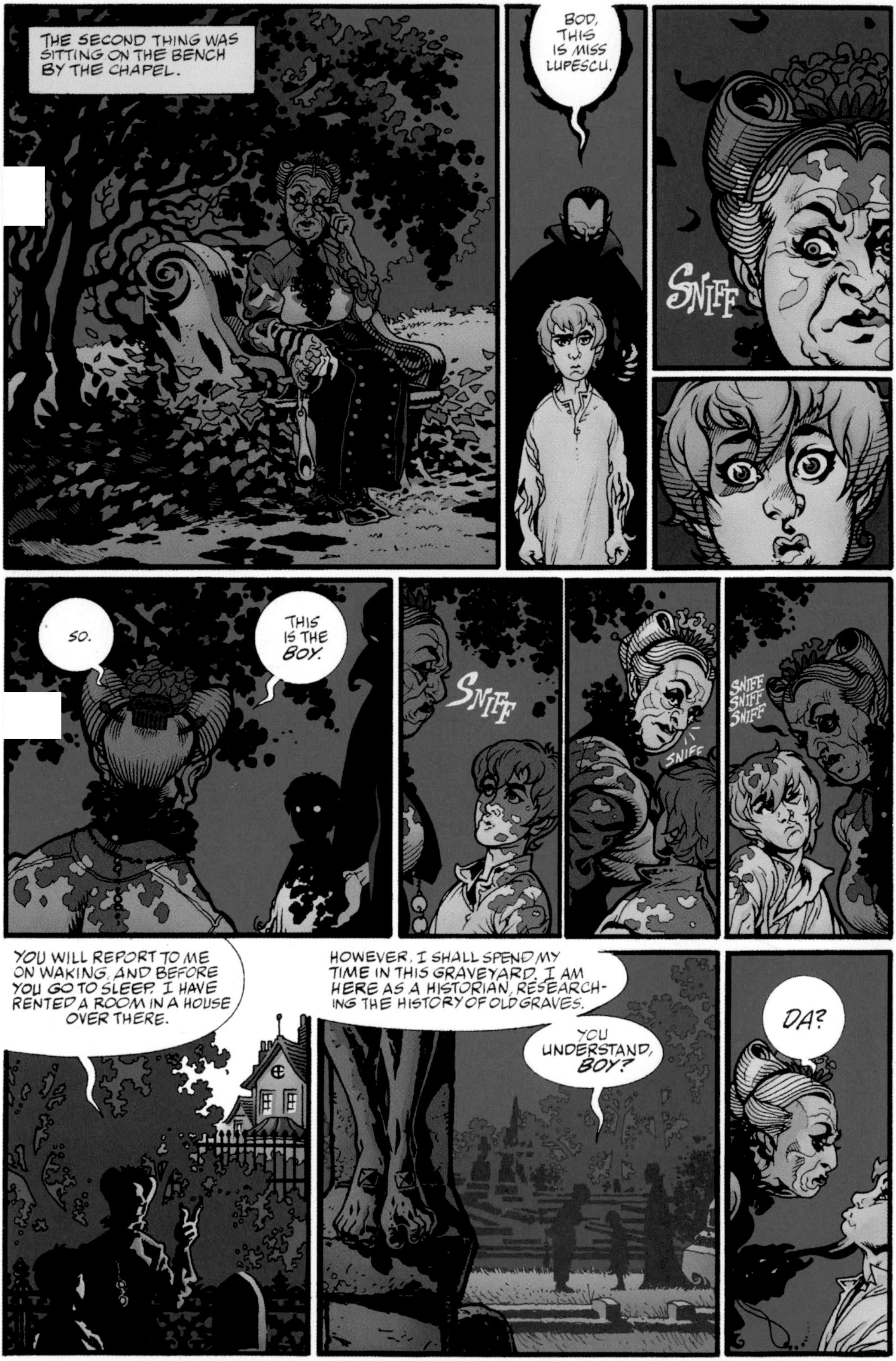
THE SECOND THING WAS SITTING ON THE BENCH BY THE CHAPEL.
BOD, THIS IS MISS LUPESCU.
SNIFF
SO.
THIS IS THE BOY.
SNIFF
SNIFF
SNIFF SNIFF SNIFF
YOU WILL REPORT TO ME ON WAKING, AND BEFORE YOU GO TO SLEEP. I HAVE RENTED A ROOM IN A HOUSE OVER THERE.
HOWEVER, I SHALL SPEND MY TIME IN THIS GRAVEYARD. I AM HERE AS A HISTORIAN, RESEARCHING THE HISTORY OF OLD GRAVES.
YOU UNDERSTAND, BOY?
DA?

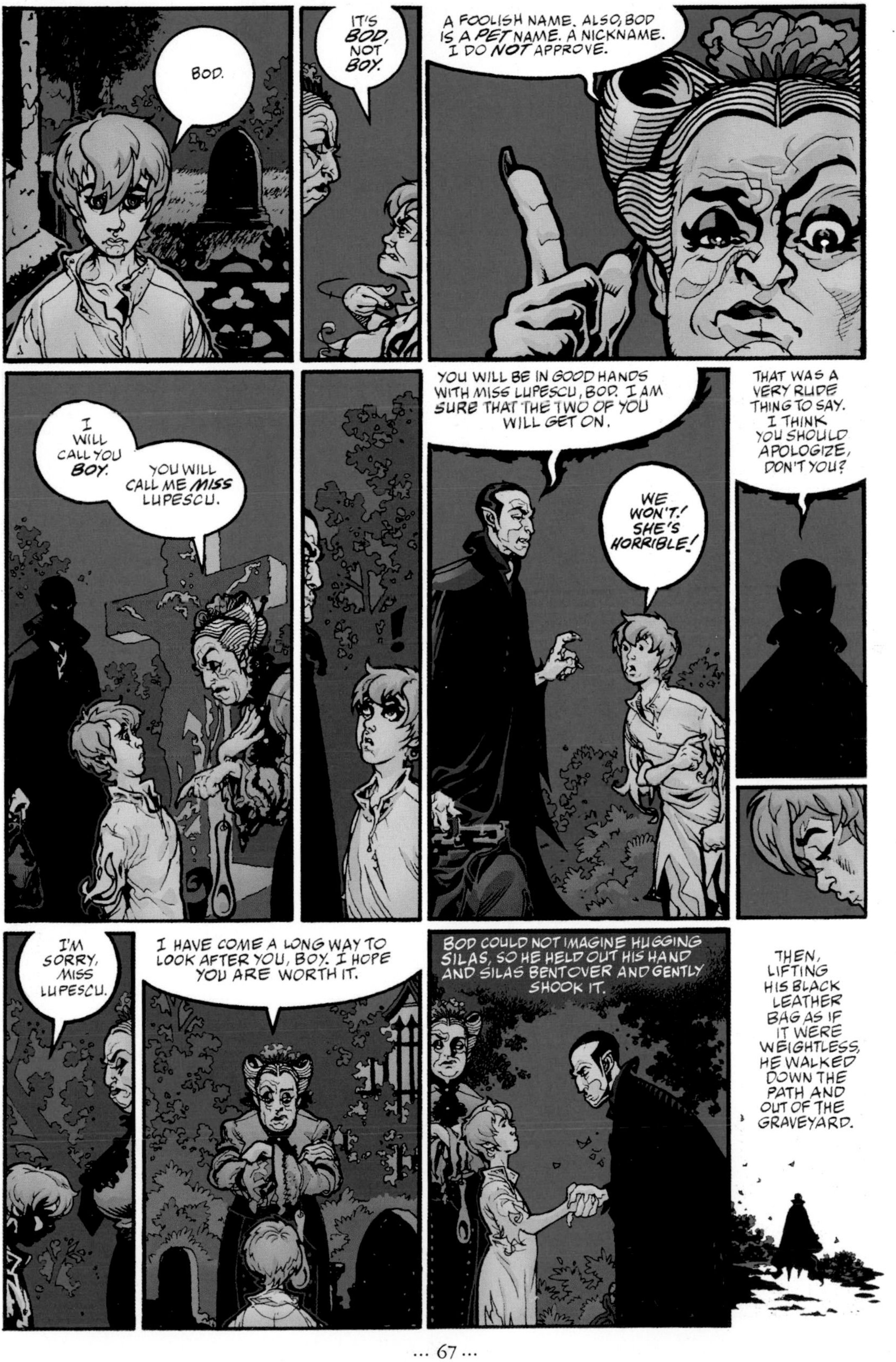
BOD.
IT'S BOD, NOT BOY.
A FOOLISH NAME. ALSO, BOD IS A PET NAME. A NICKNAME. I DO NOT APPROVE.
I WILL CALL YOU BOY.
YOU WILL CALL ME MISS LUPESCU.
!
YOU WILL BE IN GOOD HANDS WITH MISS LUPESCU, BOD. I AM SURE THAT THE TWO OF YOU WILL GET ON.
WE WON'T! SHE'S HORRIBLE!
THAT WAS A VERY RUDE THING TO SAY. I THINK YOU SHOULD APOLOGIZE, DON'T YOU?
I'M SORRY, MISS LUPESCU.
I HAVE COME A LONG WAY TO LOOK AFTER YOU, BOY. I HOPE YOU ARE WORTH IT.
BOD COULD NOT IMAGINE HUGGING SILAS, SO HE HELD OUT HIS HAND AND SILAS BENT OVER AND GENTLY SHOOK IT.
THEN, LIFTING HIS BLACK LEATHER BAG AS IF IT WERE WEIGHTLESS, HE WALKED DOWN THE PATH AND OUT OF THE GRAVEYARD.

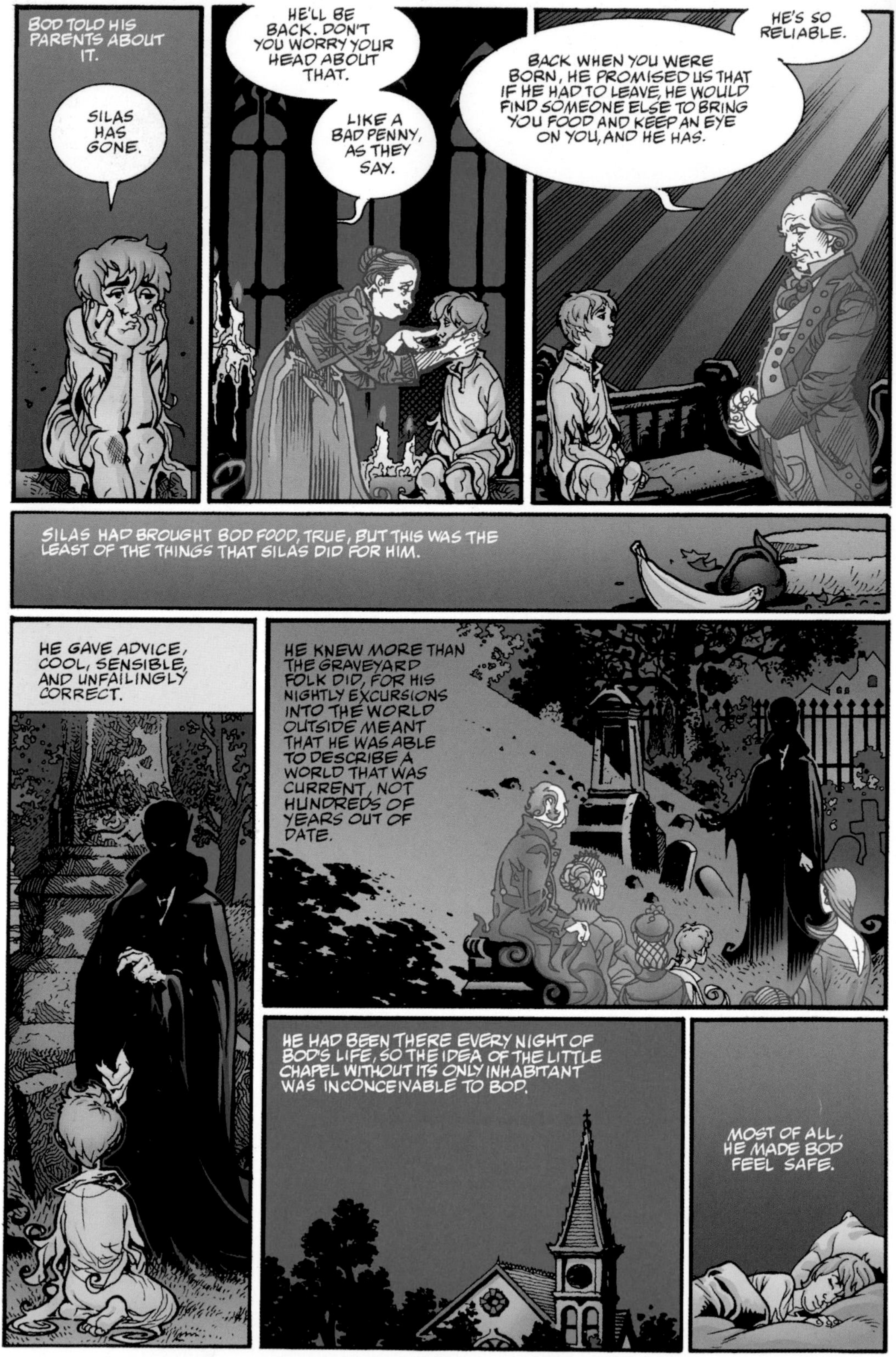
BOD TOLD HIS PARENTS ABOUT IT.
SILAS HAS GONE.
HE'LL BE BACK. DON'T YOU WORRY YOUR HEAD ABOUT THAT.
LIKE A BAD PENNY, AS THEY SAY.
BACK WHEN YOU WERE BORN, HE PROMISED US THAT IF HE HAD TO LEAVE, HE WOULD FIND SOMEONE ELSE TO BRING YOU FOOD AND KEEP AN EYE ON YOU, AND HE HAS.
HE'S SO RELIABLE.
SILAS HAD BROUGHT BOD FOOD, TRUE, BUT THIS WAS THE LEAST OF THE THINGS THAT SILAS DID FOR HIM.
HE GAVE ADVICE, COOL, SENSIBLE, AND UNFAILINGLY CORRECT.
HE KNEW MORE THAN THE GRAVEYARD FOLK DID, FOR HIS NIGHTLY EXCURSIONS INTO THE WORLD OUTSIDE MEANT THAT HE WAS ABLE TO DESCRIBE A WORLD THAT WAS CURRENT, NOT HUNDREDS OF YEARS OUT OF DATE.
HE HAD BEEN THERE EVERY NIGHT OF BOD'S LIFE, SO THE IDEA OF THE LITTLE CHAPEL WITHOUT ITS ONLY INHABITANT WAS INCONCEIVABLE TO BOD.
MOST OF ALL, HE MADE BOD FEEL SAFE.

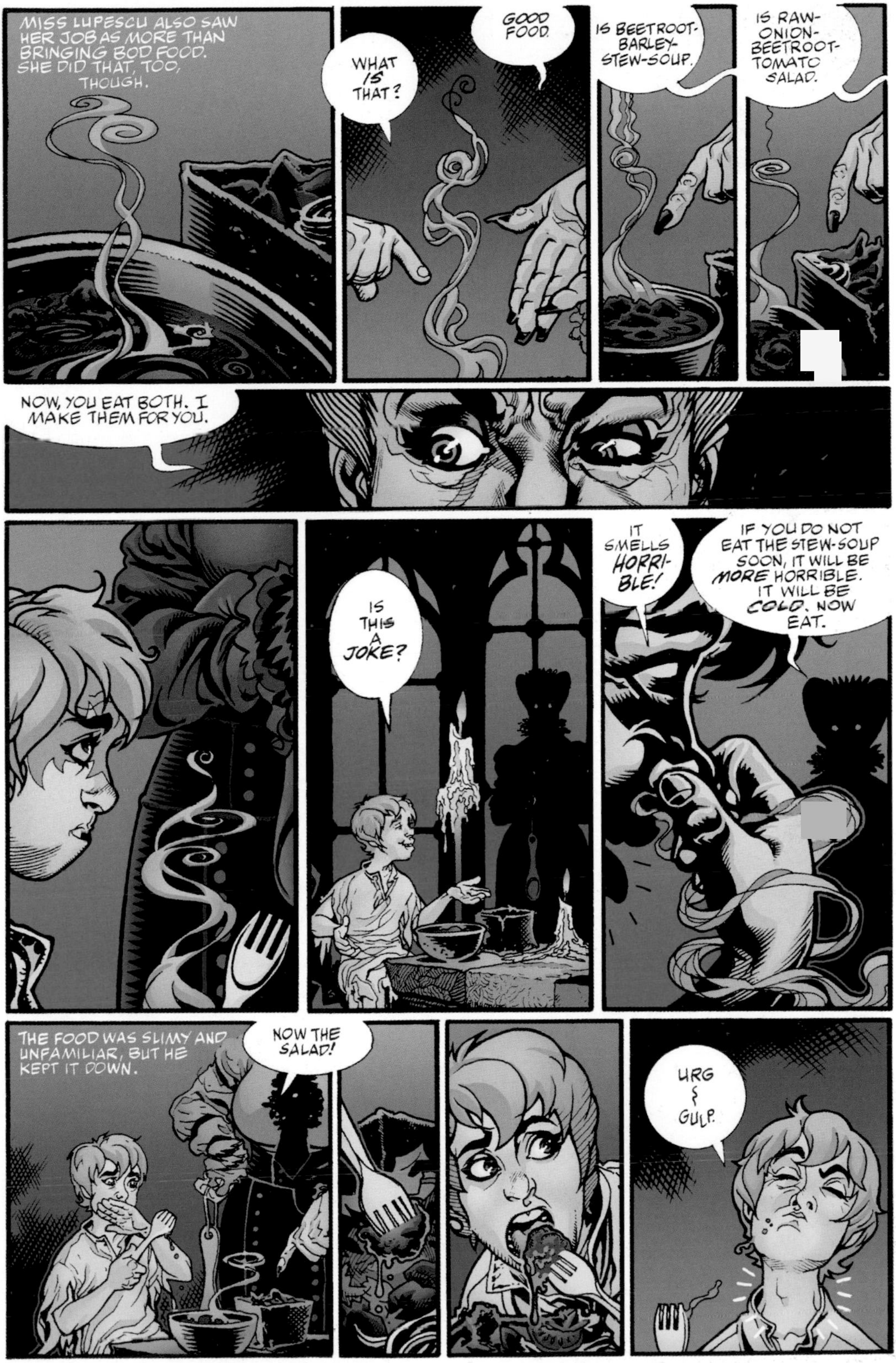

MISS LUPESCU ALSO SAW HER JOB AS MORE THAN BRINGING BOD FOOD. SHE DID THAT, TOO, THOUGH.
WHAT IS THAT?
GOOD FOOD.
IS BEETROOT-BARLEY-STEW-SOUP.
IS RAW-ONION-BEETROOT-TOMATO SALAD.
NOW, YOU EAT BOTH. I MAKE THEM FOR YOU.
IS THIS A JOKE?
IT SMELLS HORRIBLE!
IF YOU DO NOT EAT THE STEW-SOUP SOON, IT WILL BE MORE HORRIBLE. IT WILL BE COLD. NOW EAT.
THE FOOD WAS SLIMY AND UNFAMILIAR, BUT HE KEPT IT DOWN.
NOW THE SALAD!
URG & GULP.

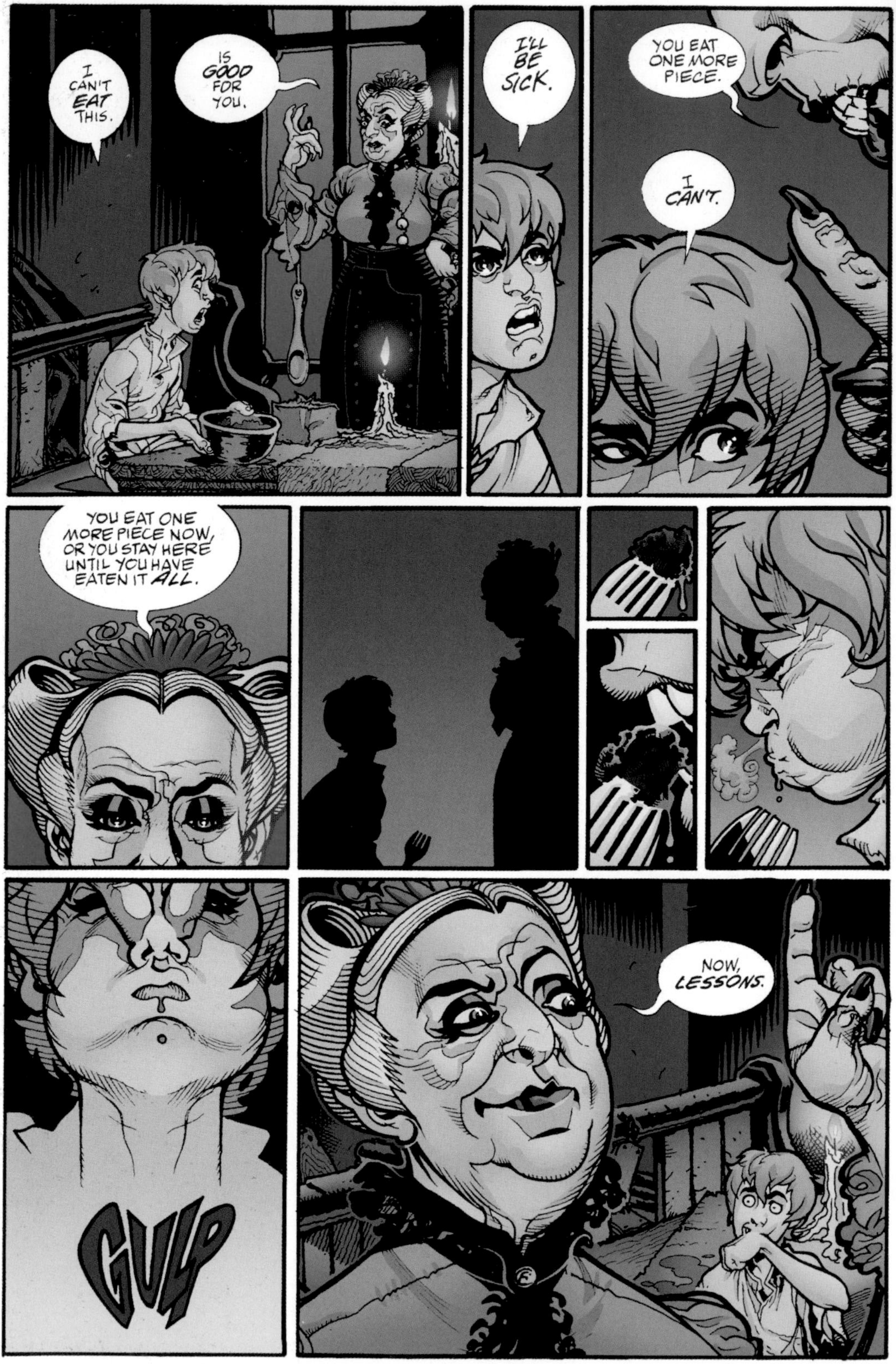
I CAN'T EAT THIS.
IS GOOD FOR YOU.
I'LL BE SICK.
YOU EAT ONE MORE PIECE.
I CAN'T.
YOU EAT ONE MORE PIECE NOW, OR YOU STAY HERE UNTIL YOU HAVE EATEN IT ALL.
GULP
NOW, LESSONS.

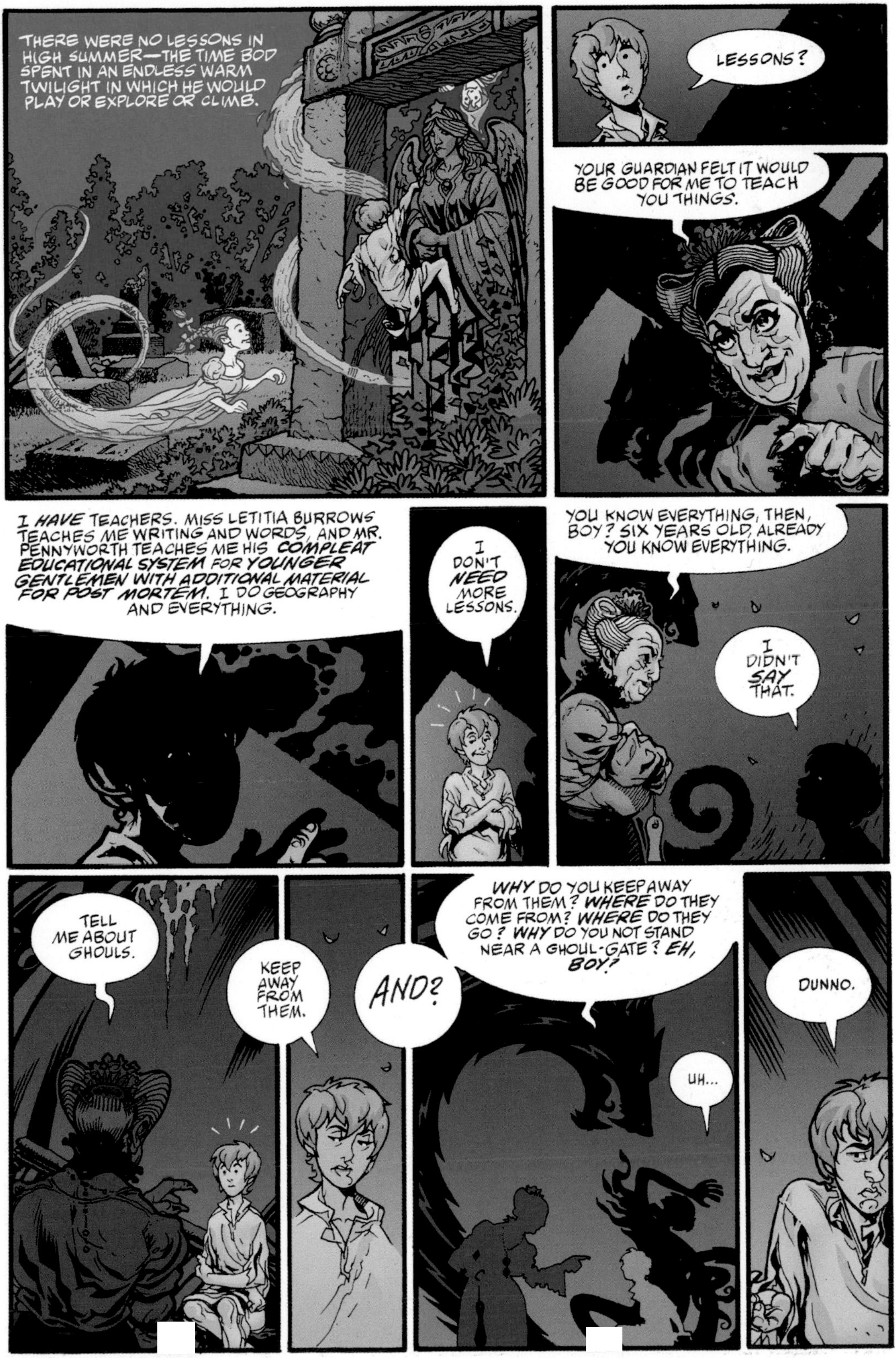
THERE WERE NO LESSONS IN HIGH SUMMER—THE TIME BOD SPENT IN AN ENDLESS WARM TWILIGHT IN WHICH HE WOULD PLAY OR EXPLORE OR CLIMB.
LESSONS?
YOUR GUARDIAN FELT IT WOULD BE GOOD FOR ME TO TEACH YOU THINGS.
I HAVE TEACHERS. MISS LETITIA BURROWS TEACHES ME WRITING AND WORDS, AND MR. PENNYWORTH TEACHES ME HIS COMPLEAT EDUCATIONAL SYSTEM FOR YOUNGER GENTLEMEN WITH ADDITIONAL MATERIAL FOR POST MORTEM. I DO GEOGRAPHY AND EVERYTHING.
I DON'T NEED MORE LESSONS.
YOU KNOW EVERYTHING, THEN, BOY? SIX YEARS OLD, ALREADY YOU KNOW EVERYTHING.
I DIDN'T SAY THAT.
TELL ME ABOUT GHOULS.
KEEP AWAY FROM THEM.
AND?
WHY DO YOU KEEP AWAY FROM THEM? WHERE DO THEY COME FROM? WHERE DO THEY GO? WHY DO YOU NOT STAND NEAR A GHOUL-GATE? EH, BOY?
UH...
DUNNO.

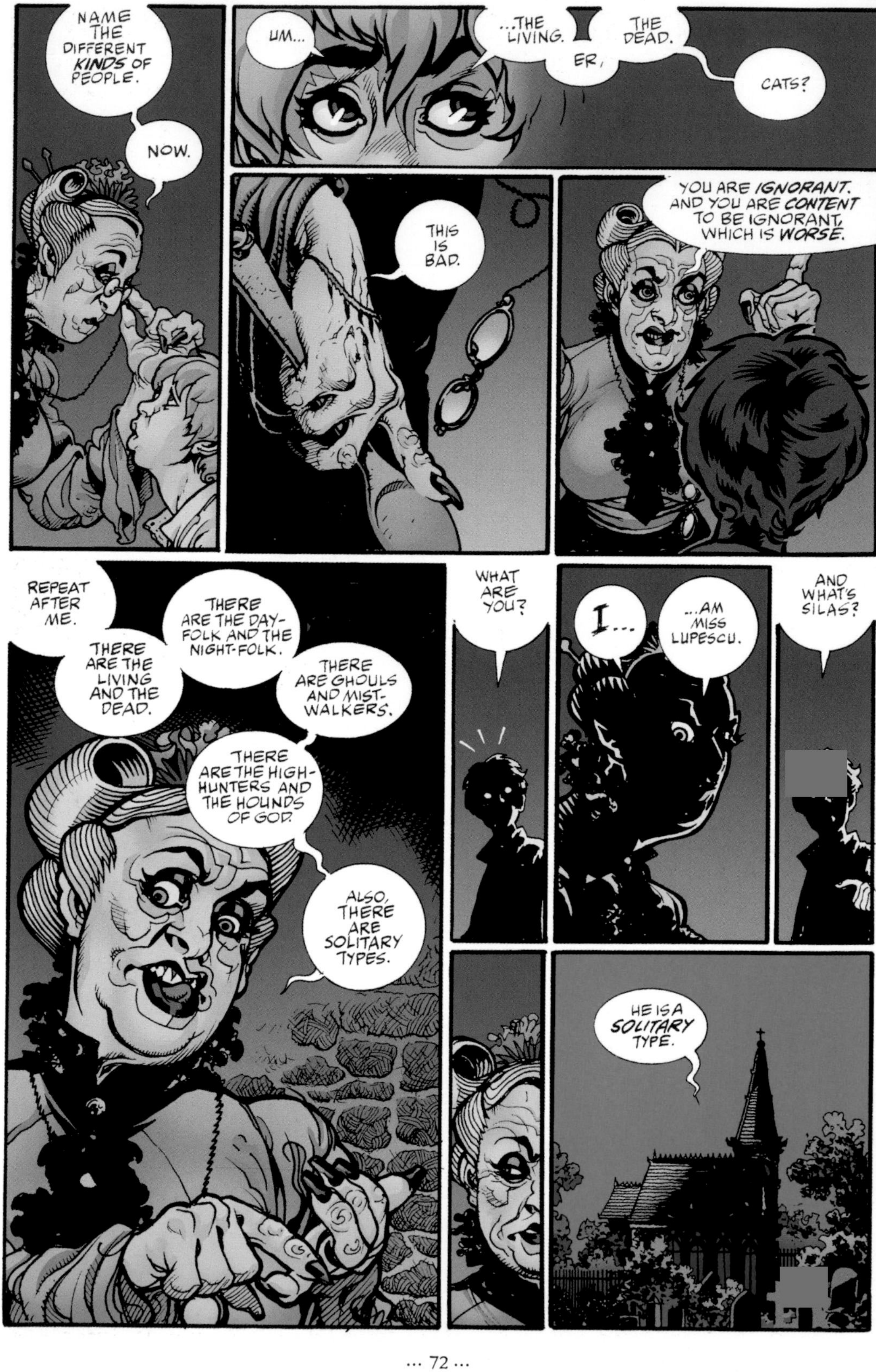
NAME THE DIFFERENT KINDS OF PEOPLE.
NOW.
UM...
...THE LIVING.
ER,
THE DEAD.
CATS?
THIS IS BAD.
YOU ARE IGNORANT. AND YOU ARE CONTENT TO BE IGNORANT, WHICH IS WORSE.
REPEAT AFTER ME.
THERE ARE THE LIVING AND THE DEAD.
THERE ARE THE DAY-FOLK AND THE NIGHT-FOLK.
THERE ARE GHOULS AND MIST-WALKERS.
THERE ARE THE HIGH-HUNTERS AND THE HOUNDS OF GOD.
ALSO, THERE ARE SOLITARY TYPES.
WHAT ARE YOU?
I...
...AM MISS LUPESCU.
AND WHAT'S SILAS?
HE IS A SOLITARY TYPE.

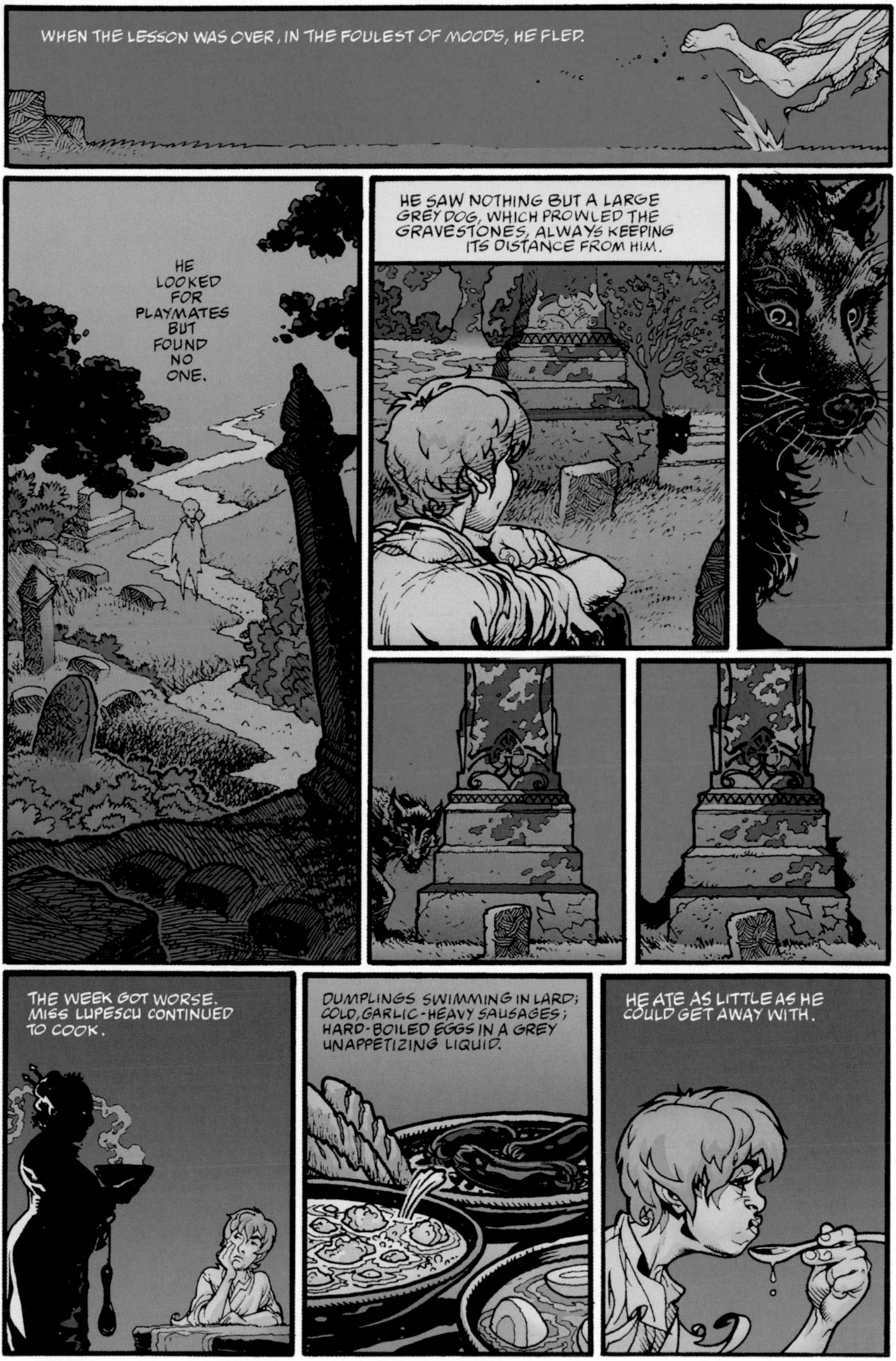
WHEN THE LESSON WAS OVER, IN THE FOULEST OF MOODS, HE FLED.
HE LOOKED FOR PLAYMATES BUT FOUND NO ONE.
HE SAW NOTHING BUT A LARGE GREY DOG, WHICH PROWLED THE GRAVESTONES, ALWAYS KEEPING ITS DISTANCE FROM HIM.
THE WEEK GOT WORSE. MISS LUPESCU CONTINUED TO COOK.
DUMPLINGS SWIMMING IN LARD; COLD, GARLIC-HEAVY SAUSAGES; HARD-BOILED EGGS IN A GREY UNAPPETIZING LIQUID.
HE ATE AS LITTLE AS HE COULD GET AWAY WITH.

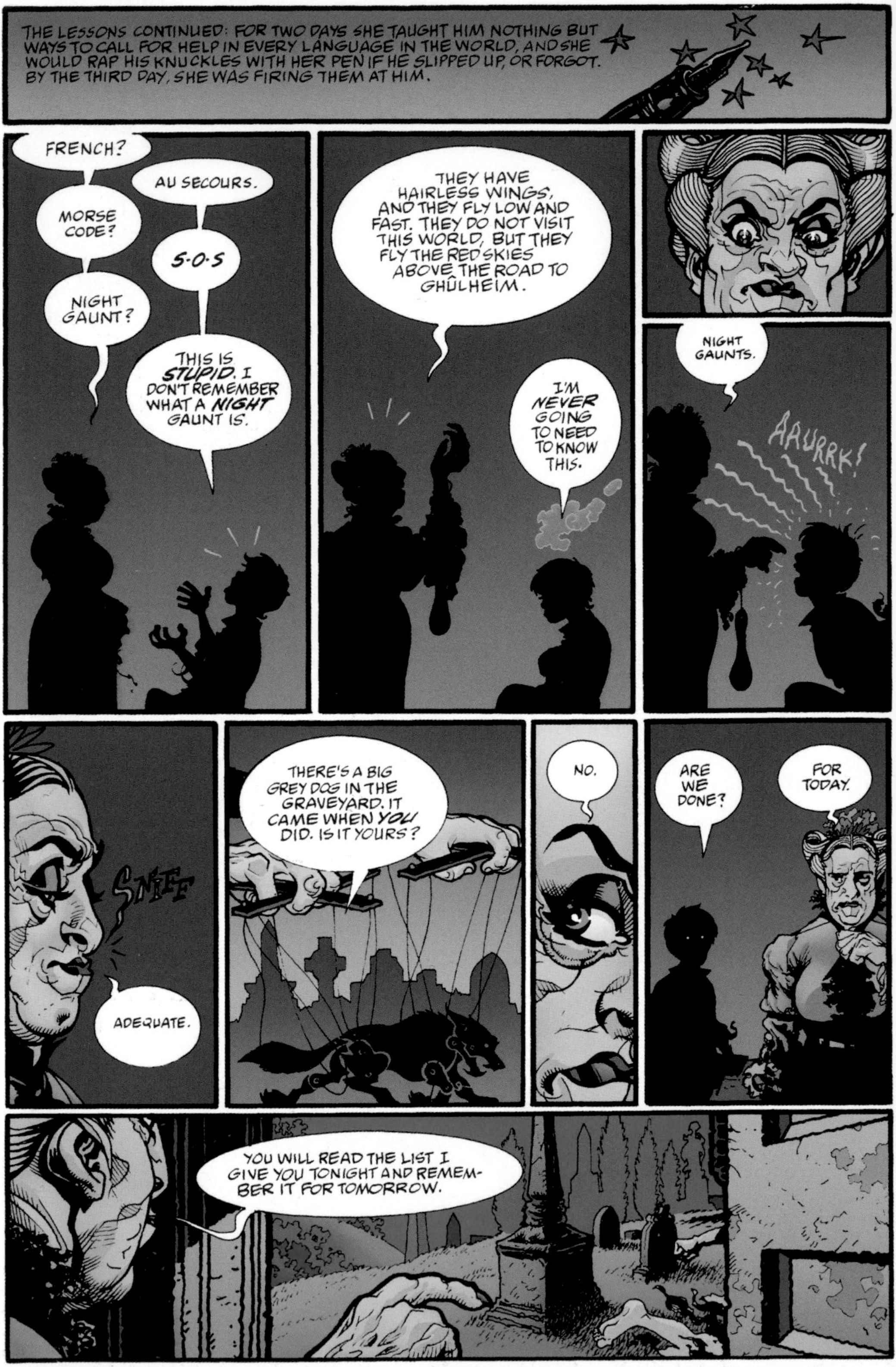
THE LESSONS CONTINUED: FOR TWO DAYS SHE TAUGHT HIM NOTHING BUT WAYS TO CALL FOR HELP IN EVERY LANGUAGE IN THE WORLD, AND SHE WOULD RAP HIS KNUCKLES WITH HER PEN IF HE SLIPPED UP, OR FORGOT. BY THE THIRD DAY, SHE WAS FIRING THEM AT HIM.
FRENCH?
AU SECOURS.
MORSE CODE?
S-O-S
NIGHT GAUNT?
THIS IS STUPID. I DON'T REMEMBER WHAT A NIGHT GAUNT IS.
THEY HAVE HAIRLESS WINGS, AND THEY FLY LOW AND FAST. THEY DO NOT VISIT THIS WORLD, BUT THEY FLY THE RED SKIES ABOVE THE ROAD TO GHÛLHEIM.
I'M NEVER GOING TO NEED TO KNOW THIS.
NIGHT GAUNTS.
AAURRK!
SNIFF
ADEQUATE.
THERE'S A BIG GREY DOG IN THE GRAVEYARD. IT CAME WHEN YOU DID. IS IT YOURS?
NO.
ARE WE DONE?
FOR TODAY.
YOU WILL READ THE LIST I GIVE YOU TONIGHT AND REMEMBER IT FOR TOMORROW.

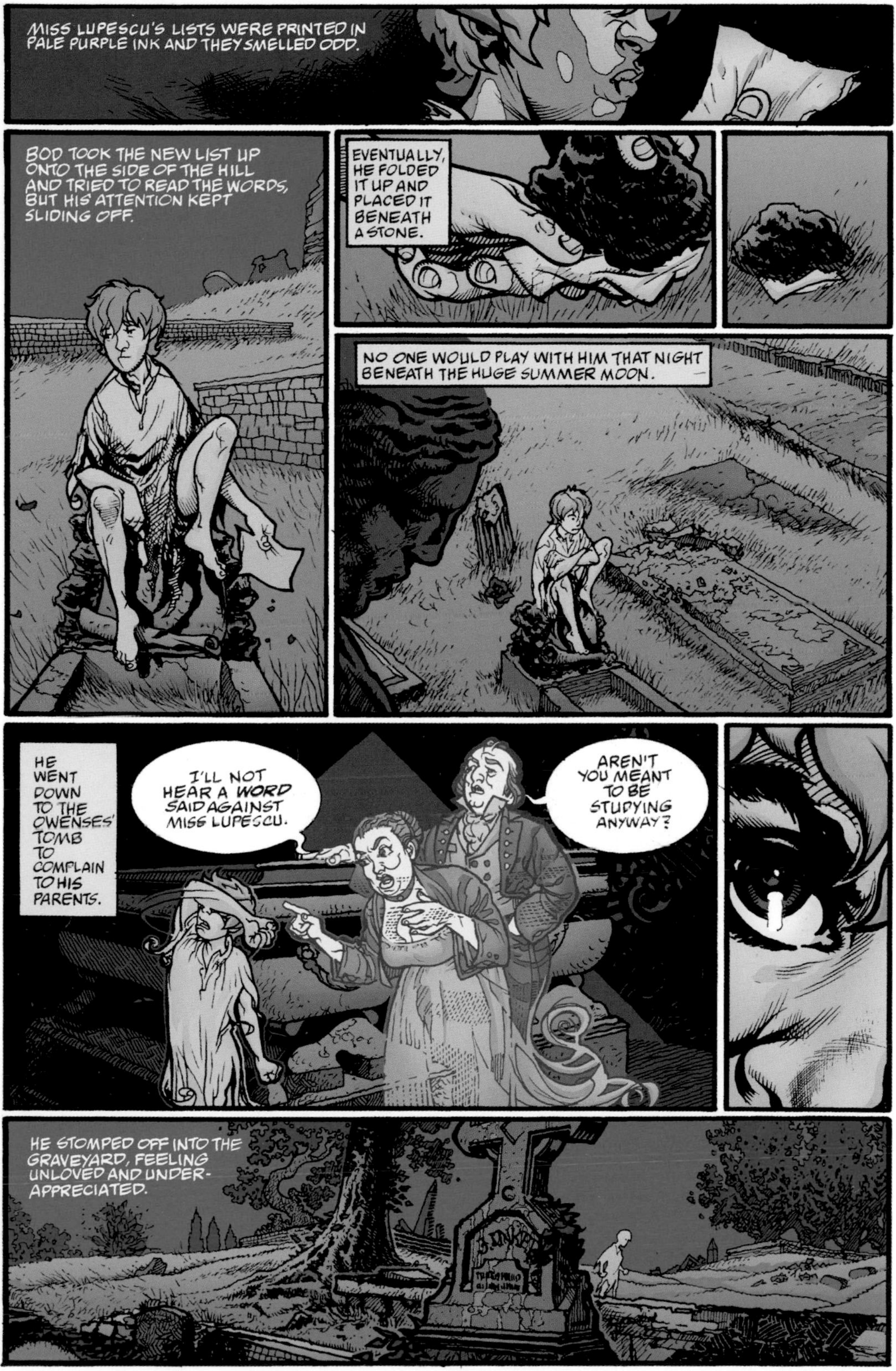
MISS LUPESCU'S LISTS WERE PRINTED IN PALE PURPLE INK AND THEY SMELLED ODD.
BOD TOOK THE NEW LIST UP ONTO THE SIDE OF THE HILL AND TRIED TO READ THE WORDS, BUT HIS ATTENTION KEPT SLIDING OFF.
EVENTUALLY, HE FOLDED IT UP AND PLACED IT BENEATH A STONE.
NO ONE WOULD PLAY WITH HIM THAT NIGHT BENEATH THE HUGE SUMMER MOON.
HE WENT DOWN TO THE OWENSES' TOMB TO COMPLAIN TO HIS PARENTS.
I'LL NOT HEAR A WORD SAID AGAINST MISS LUPESCU.
AREN'T YOU MEANT TO BE STUDYING ANYWAY?
HE STOMPED OFF INTO THE GRAVEYARD, FEELING UNLOVED AND UNDER-APPRECIATED.

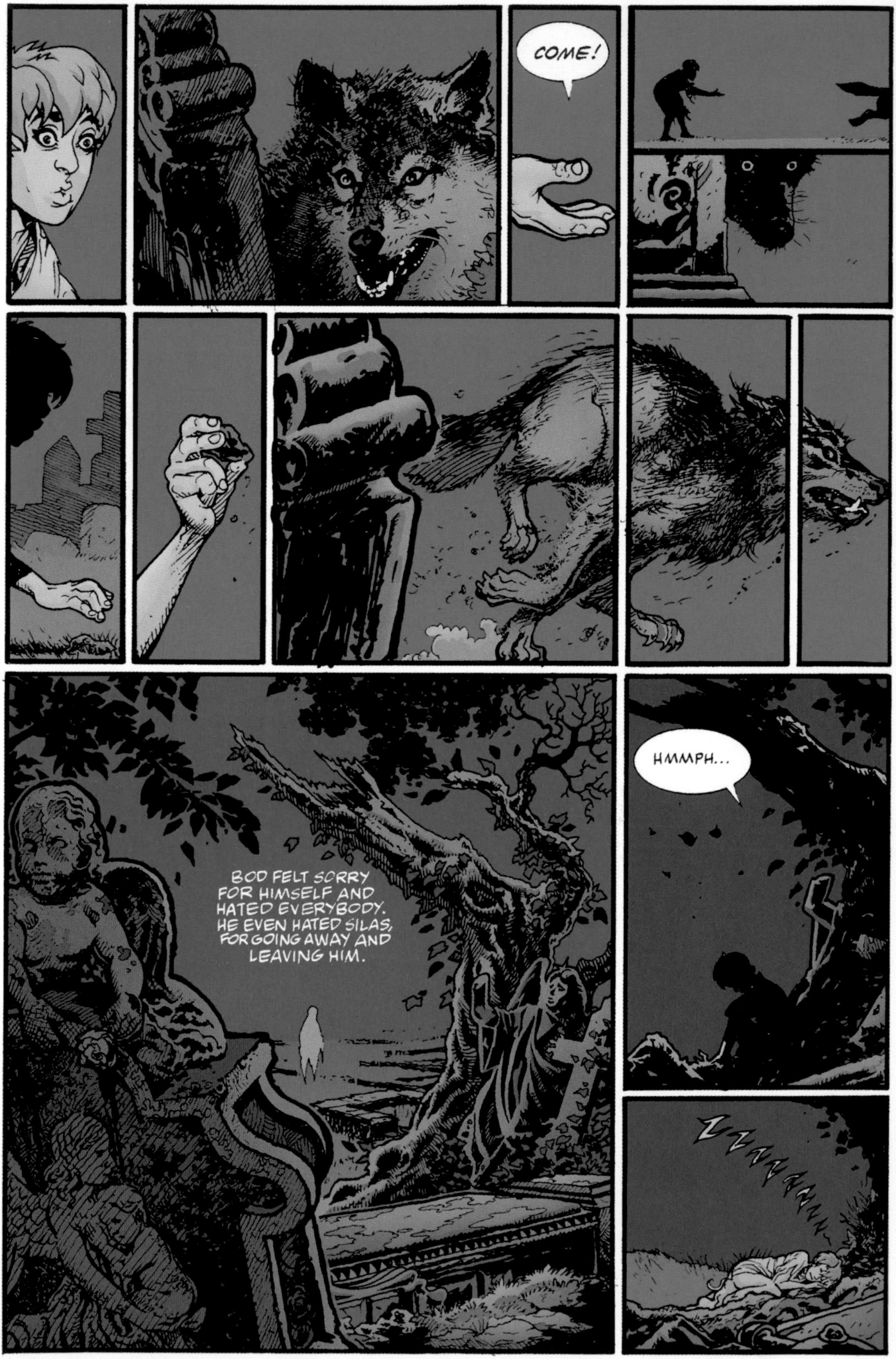
COME!
BOD FELT SORRY FOR HIMSELF AND HATED EVERYBODY. HE EVEN HATED SILAS, FOR GOING AWAY AND LEAVING HIM.
HMMPH...
ZZZZZZZ

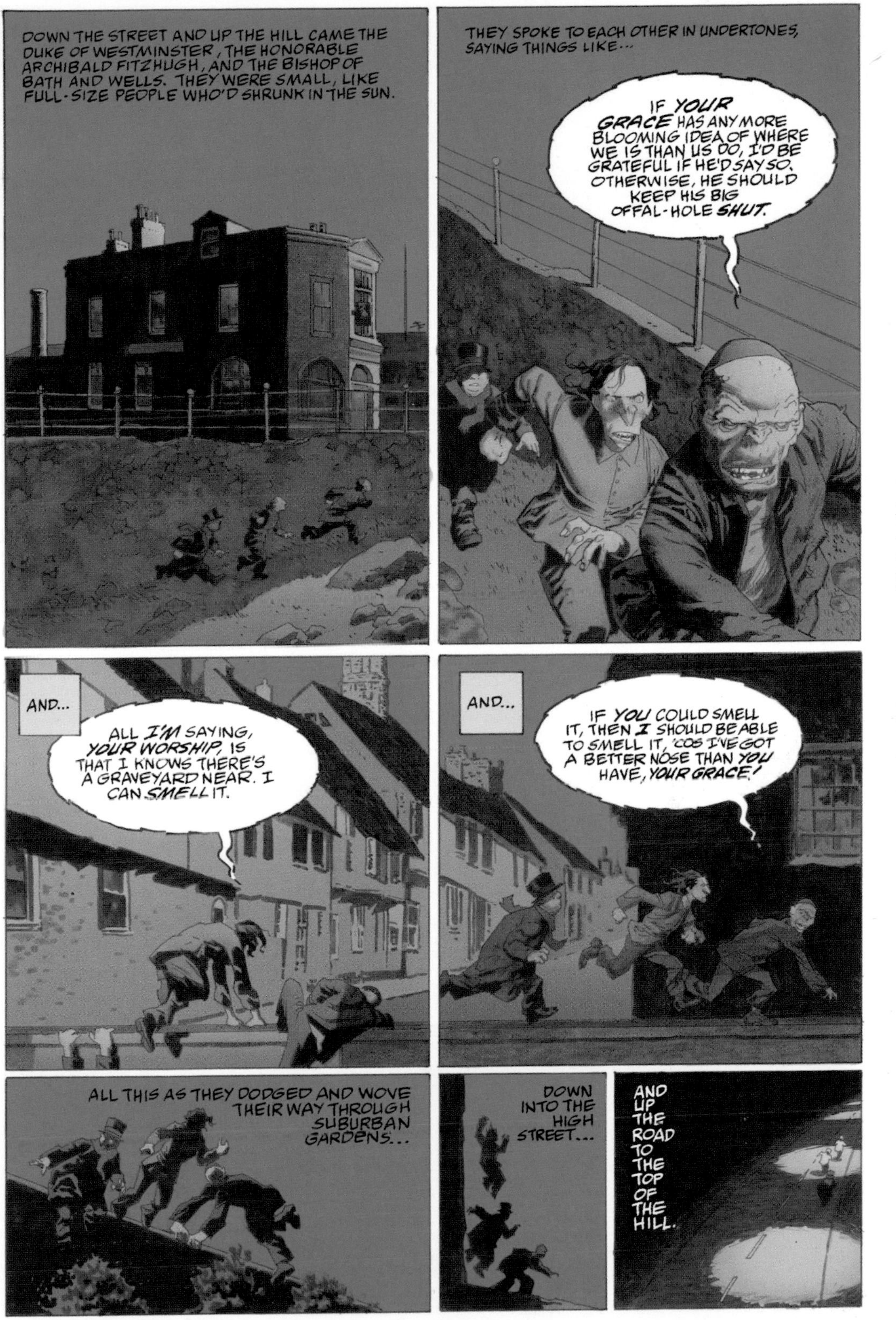
DOWN THE STREET AND UP THE HILL CAME THE DUKE OF WESTMINSTER, THE HONORABLE ARCHIBALD FITZHUGH, AND THE BISHOP OF BATH AND WELLS. THEY WERE SMALL, LIKE FULL-SIZE PEOPLE WHO'D SHRUNK IN THE SUN.
THEY SPOKE TO EACH OTHER IN UNDERTONES, SAYING THINGS LIKE...
IF YOUR GRACE HAS ANY MORE BLOOMING IDEA OF WHERE WE IS THAN US DO, I'D BE GRATEFUL IF HE'D SAY SO. OTHERWISE, HE SHOULD KEEP HIS BIG OFFAL-HOLE SHUT.
AND...
ALL I'M SAYING, YOUR WORSHIP, IS THAT I KNOWS THERE'S A GRAVEYARD NEAR. I CAN SMELL IT.
AND...
IF YOU COULD SMELL IT, THEN I SHOULD BE ABLE TO SMELL IT, 'COS I'VE GOT A BETTER NOSE THAN YOU HAVE, YOUR GRACE!
ALL THIS AS THEY DODGED AND WOVE THEIR WAY THROUGH SUBURBAN GARDENS...
DOWN INTO THE HIGH STREET...
AND UP THE ROAD TO THE TOP OF THE HILL.

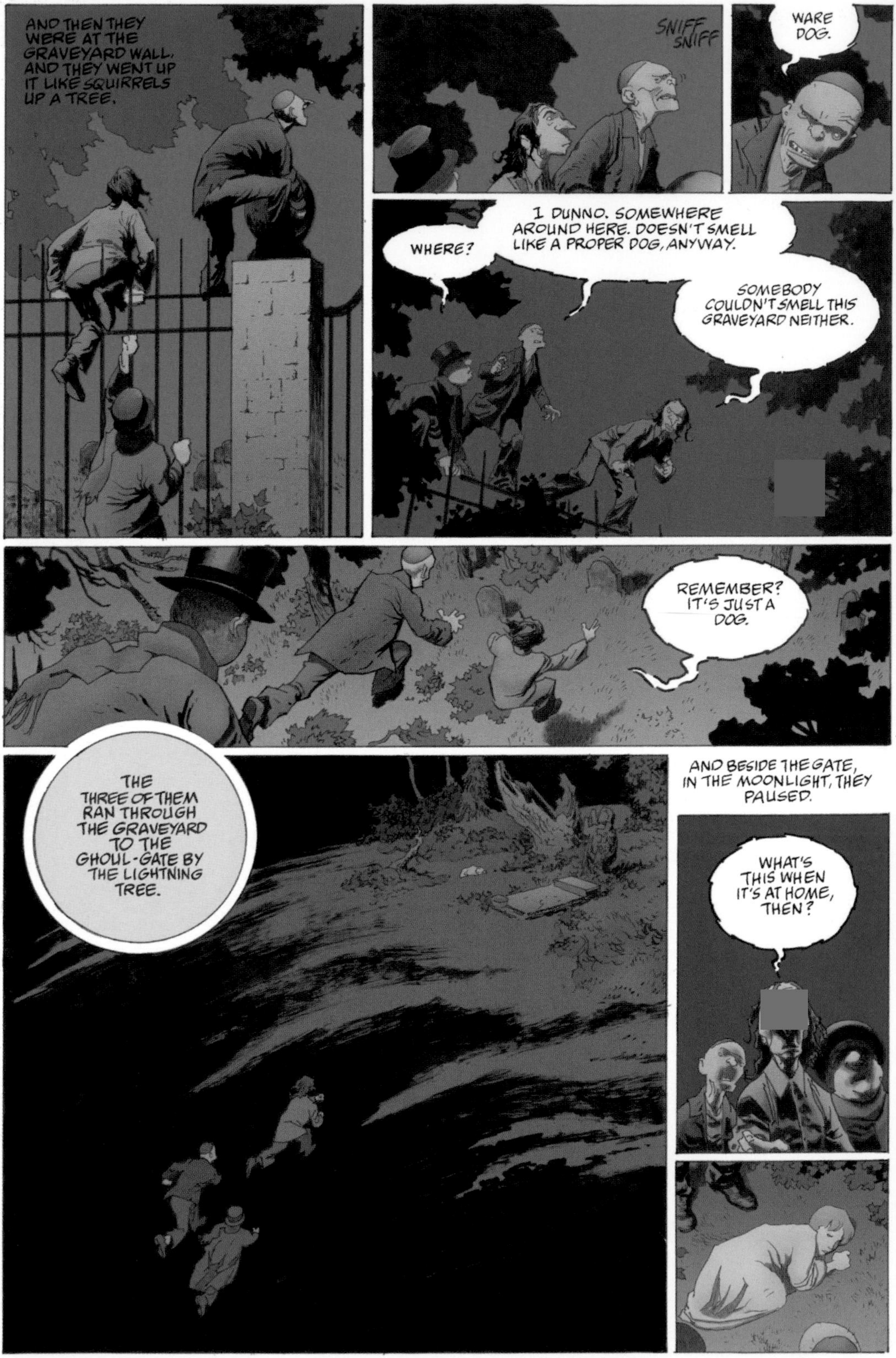
AND THEN THEY WERE AT THE GRAVEYARD WALL, AND THEY WENT UP IT LIKE SQUIRRELS UP A TREE.
SNIFF SNIFF
WARE DOG.
WHERE?
I DUNNO. SOMEWHERE AROUND HERE. DOESN'T SMELL LIKE A PROPER DOG, ANYWAY.
SOMEBODY COULDN'T SMELL THIS GRAVEYARD NEITHER.
REMEMBER? IT'S JUST A DOG.
THE THREE OF THEM RAN THROUGH THE GRAVEYARD TO THE GHOUL-GATE BY THE LIGHTNING TREE.
AND BESIDE THE GATE, IN THE MOONLIGHT, THEY PAUSED.
WHAT'S THIS WHEN IT'S AT HOME, THEN?

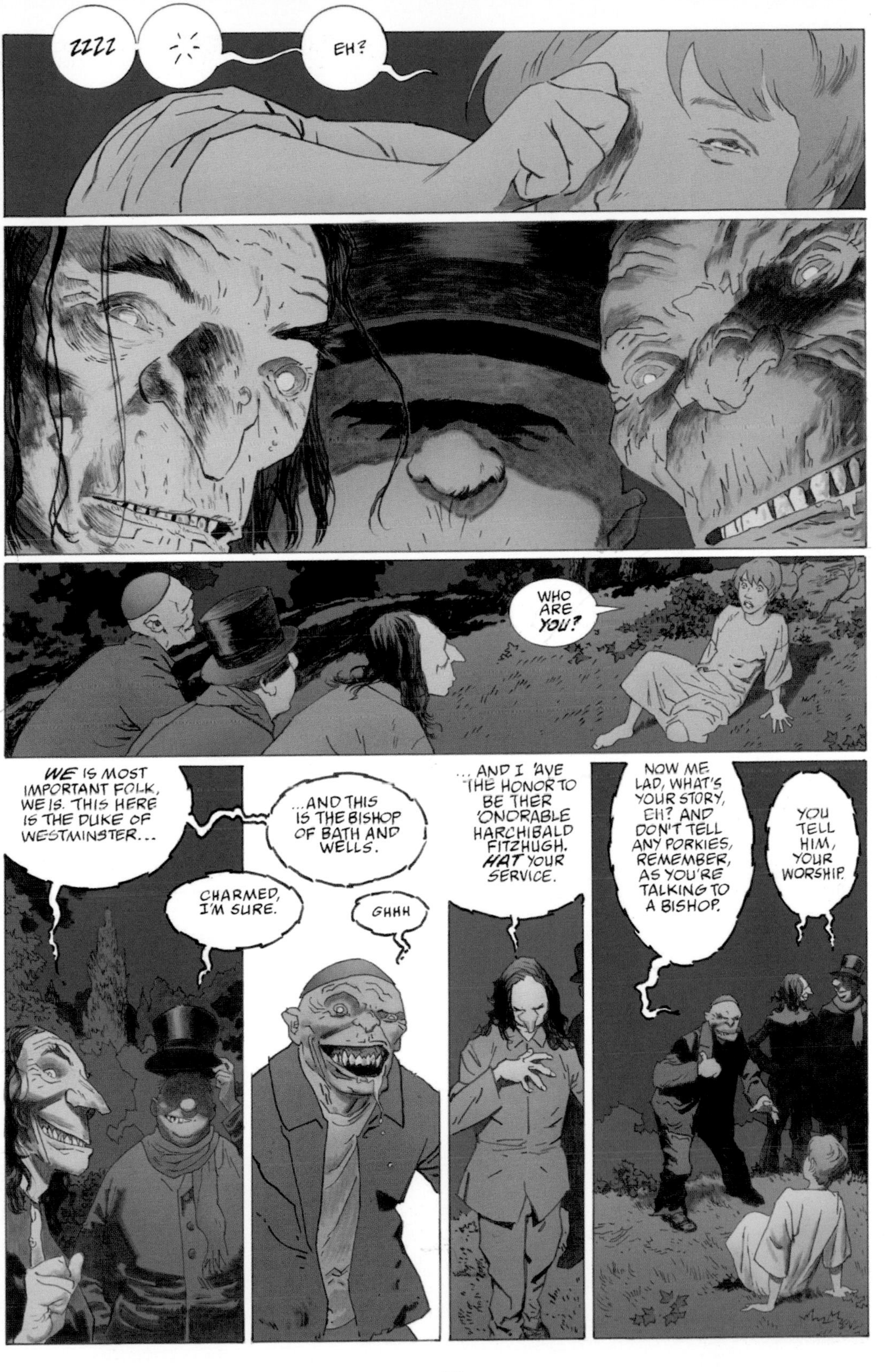
ZZZZ
EH?
WHO ARE YOU?
WE IS MOST IMPORTANT FOLK, WE IS. THIS HERE IS THE DUKE OF WESTMINSTER...
CHARMED, I'M SURE.
...AND THIS IS THE BISHOP OF BATH AND WELLS.
GHHH
...AND I 'AVE THE HONOR TO BE THER 'ONORABLE HARCHIBALD FITZHUGH. HAT YOUR SERVICE.
NOW ME LAD, WHAT'S YOUR STORY, EH? AND DON'T TELL ANY PORKIES, REMEMBER, AS YOU'RE TALKING TO A BISHOP.
YOU TELL HIM, YOUR WORSHIP.

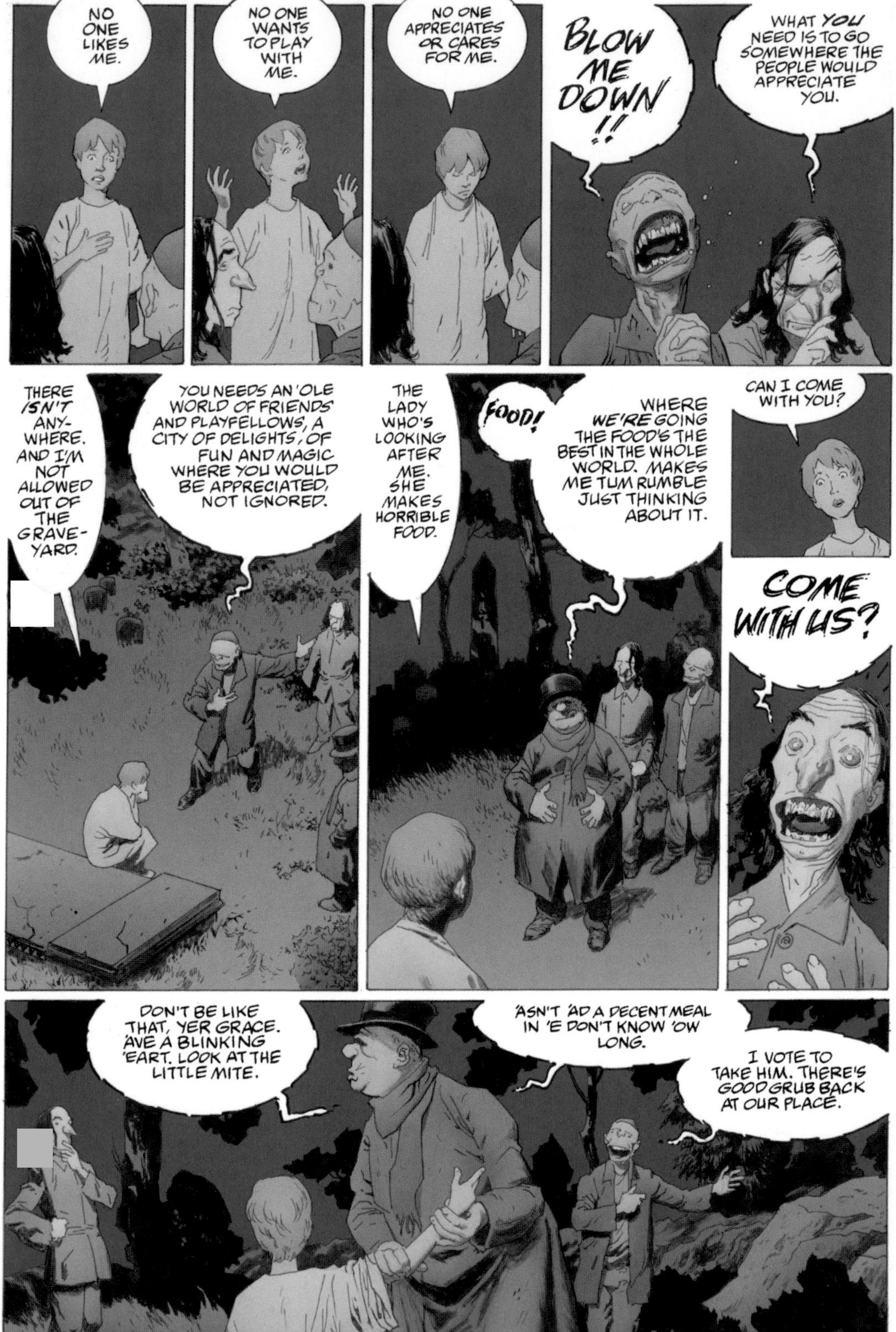
NO ONE LIKES ME.
NO ONE WANTS TO PLAY WITH ME.
NO ONE APPRECIATES OR CARES FOR ME.
BLOW ME DOWN!!
WHAT YOU NEED IS TO GO SOMEWHERE THE PEOPLE WOULD APPRECIATE YOU.
THERE ISN'T ANYWHERE. AND I'M NOT ALLOWED OUT OF THE GRAVEYARD.
YOU NEEDS AN 'OLE WORLD OF FRIENDS AND PLAYFELLOWS, A CITY OF DELIGHTS, OF FUN AND MAGIC WHERE YOU WOULD BE APPRECIATED, NOT IGNORED.
THE LADY WHO'S LOOKING AFTER ME. SHE MAKES HORRIBLE FOOD.
FOOD!
WHERE WE'RE GOING THE FOOD'S THE BEST IN THE WHOLE WORLD. MAKES ME TUM RUMBLE JUST THINKING ABOUT IT.
CAN I COME WITH YOU?
COME WITH US?
DON'T BE LIKE THAT, YER GRACE. 'AVE A BLINKING 'EART. LOOK AT THE LITTLE MITE.
'ASN'T 'AD A DECENT MEAL IN 'E DON'T KNOW 'OW LONG.
I VOTE TO TAKE HIM. THERE'S GOOD GRUB BACK AT OUR PLACE.

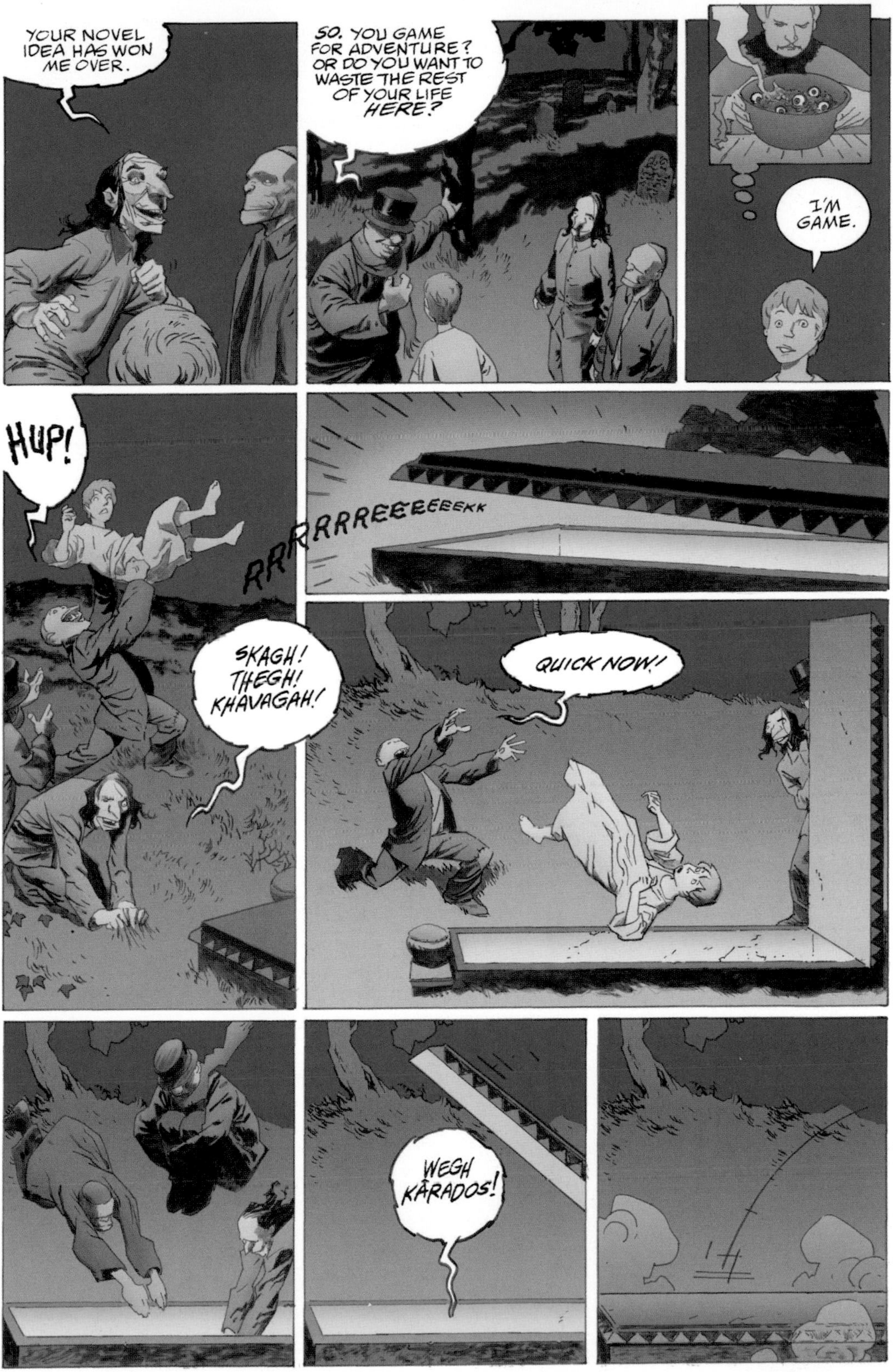
YOUR NOVEL IDEA HAS WON ME OVER.
SO. YOU GAME FOR ADVENTURE? OR DO YOU WANT TO WASTE THE REST OF YOUR LIFE HERE?
I'M GAME.
HUP!
RRRRRREEEEEEEKK
SKAGH! THEGH! KHAVAGAH!
QUICK NOW!
WEGH KĀRADOS!

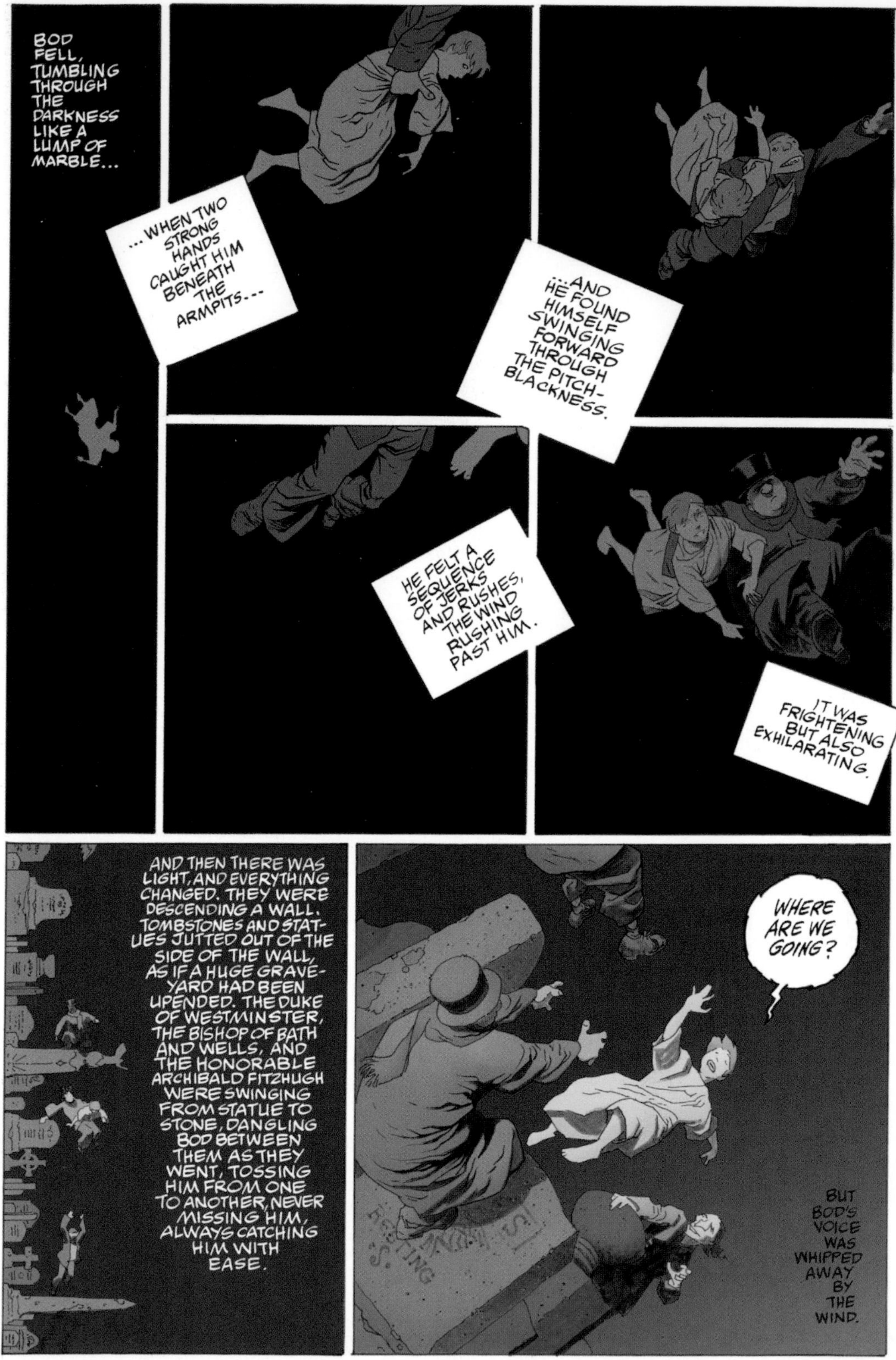
BOD FELL, TUMBLING THROUGH THE DARKNESS LIKE A LUMP OF MARBLE...
...WHEN TWO STRONG HANDS CAUGHT HIM BENEATH THE ARMPITS...
...AND HE FOUND HIMSELF SWINGING FORWARD THROUGH THE PITCH-BLACKNESS.
HE FELT A SEQUENCE OF JERKS AND RUSHES, THE WIND RUSHING PAST HIM.
IT WAS FRIGHTENING BUT ALSO EXHILARATING.
AND THEN THERE WAS LIGHT, AND EVERYTHING CHANGED. THEY WERE DESCENDING A WALL. TOMBSTONES AND STATUES JUTTED OUT OF THE SIDE OF THE WALL, AS IF A HUGE GRAVEYARD HAD BEEN UPENDED. THE DUKE OF WESTMINSTER, THE BISHOP OF BATH AND WELLS, AND THE HONORABLE ARCHIBALD FITZHUGH WERE SWINGING FROM STATUE TO STONE, DANGLING BOD BETWEEN THEM AS THEY WENT, TOSSING HIM FROM ONE TO ANOTHER, NEVER MISSING HIM, ALWAYS CATCHING HIM WITH EASE.
WHERE ARE WE GOING?
BUT BOD'S VOICE WAS WHIPPED AWAY BY THE WIND.

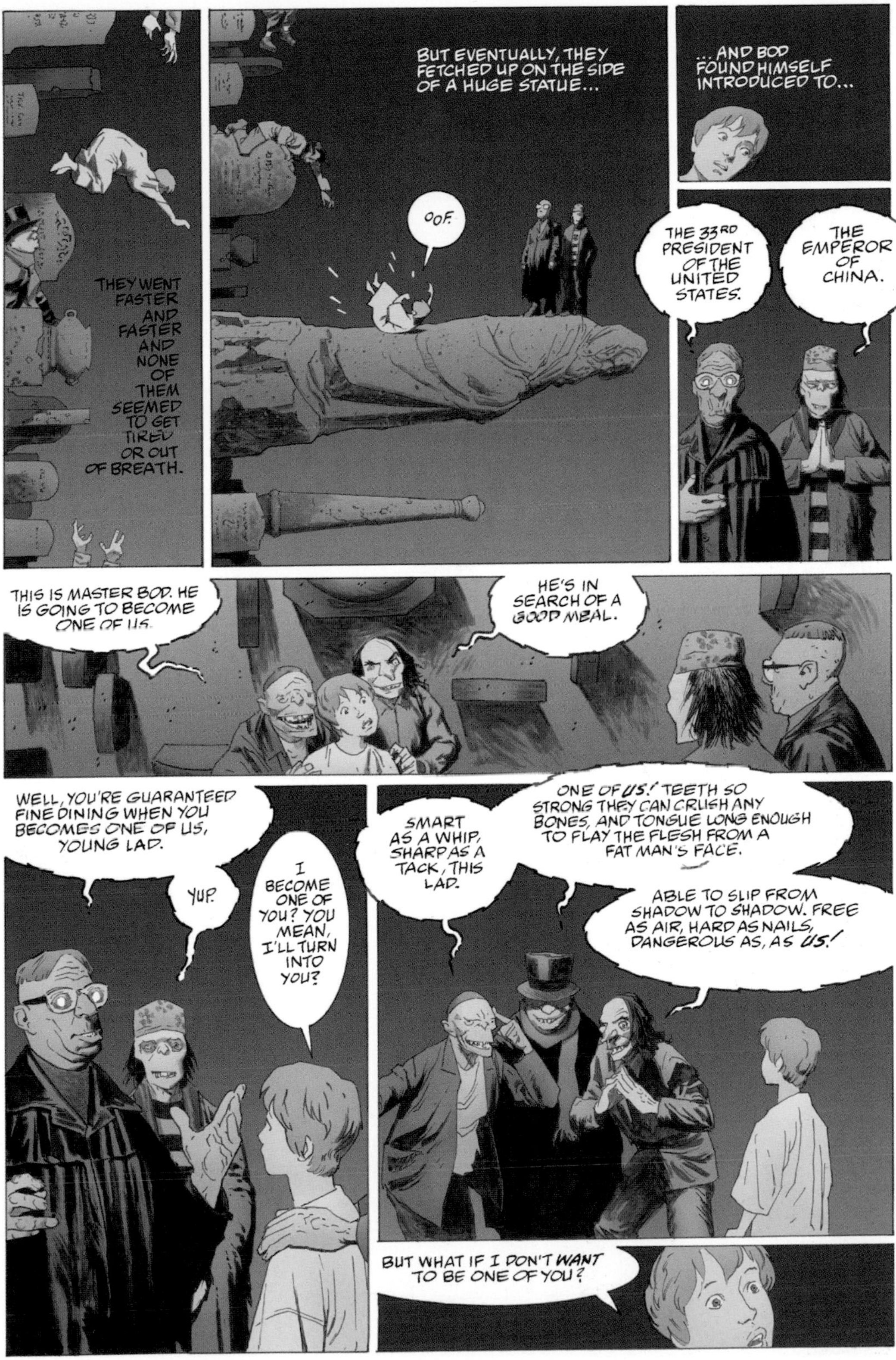

THEY WENT FASTER AND FASTER AND NONE OF THEM SEEMED TO GET TIRED OR OUT OF BREATH.
BUT EVENTUALLY, THEY FETCHED UP ON THE SIDE OF A HUGE STATUE...
OOF.
...AND BOD FOUND HIMSELF INTRODUCED TO...
THE 33RD PRESIDENT OF THE UNITED STATES.
THE EMPEROR OF CHINA.
THIS IS MASTER BOD. HE IS GOING TO BECOME ONE OF US.
HE'S IN SEARCH OF A GOOD MEAL.
WELL, YOU'RE GUARANTEED FINE DINING WHEN YOU BECOMES ONE OF US, YOUNG LAD.
YUP.
I BECOME ONE OF YOU? YOU MEAN, I'LL TURN INTO YOU?
SMART AS A WHIP, SHARP AS A TACK, THIS LAD.
ONE OF US! TEETH SO STRONG THEY CAN CRUSH ANY BONES, AND TONGUE LONG ENOUGH TO FLAY THE FLESH FROM A FAT MAN'S FACE.
ABLE TO SLIP FROM SHADOW TO SHADOW. FREE AS AIR, HARD AS NAILS, DANGEROUS AS, AS US!
BUT WHAT IF I DON'T WANT TO BE ONE OF YOU?

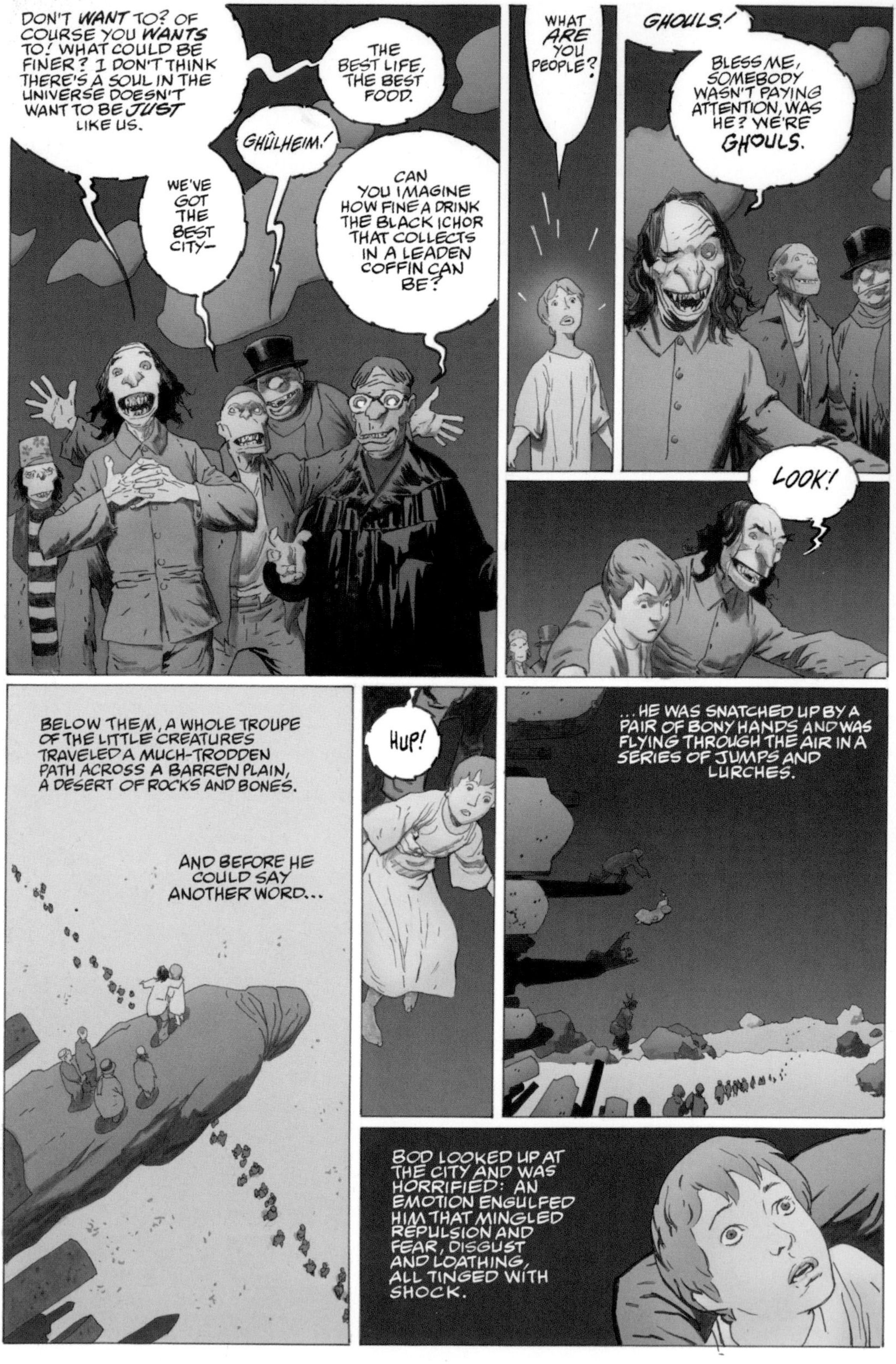
DON'T WANT TO? OF COURSE YOU WANTS TO! WHAT COULD BE FINER? I DON'T THINK THERE'S A SOUL IN THE UNIVERSE DOESN'T WANT TO BE JUST LIKE US.
THE BEST LIFE, THE BEST FOOD.
WE'VE GOT THE BEST CITY—
GHÛLHEIM!
CAN YOU IMAGINE HOW FINE A DRINK THE BLACK ICHOR THAT COLLECTS IN A LEADEN COFFIN CAN BE?
WHAT ARE YOU PEOPLE?
GHOULS!
BLESS ME, SOMEBODY WASN'T PAYING ATTENTION, WAS HE? WE'RE GHOULS.
LOOK!
BELOW THEM, A WHOLE TROUPE OF THE LITTLE CREATURES TRAVELED A MUCH-TRODDEN PATH ACROSS A BARREN PLAIN, A DESERT OF ROCKS AND BONES.
AND BEFORE HE COULD SAY ANOTHER WORD...
HUP!
...HE WAS SNATCHED UP BY A PAIR OF BONY HANDS AND WAS FLYING THROUGH THE AIR IN A SERIES OF JUMPS AND LURCHES.
BOD LOOKED UP AT THE CITY AND WAS HORRIFIED: AN EMOTION ENGULFED HIM THAT MINGLED REPULSION AND FEAR, DISGUST AND LOATHING, ALL TINGED WITH SHOCK.

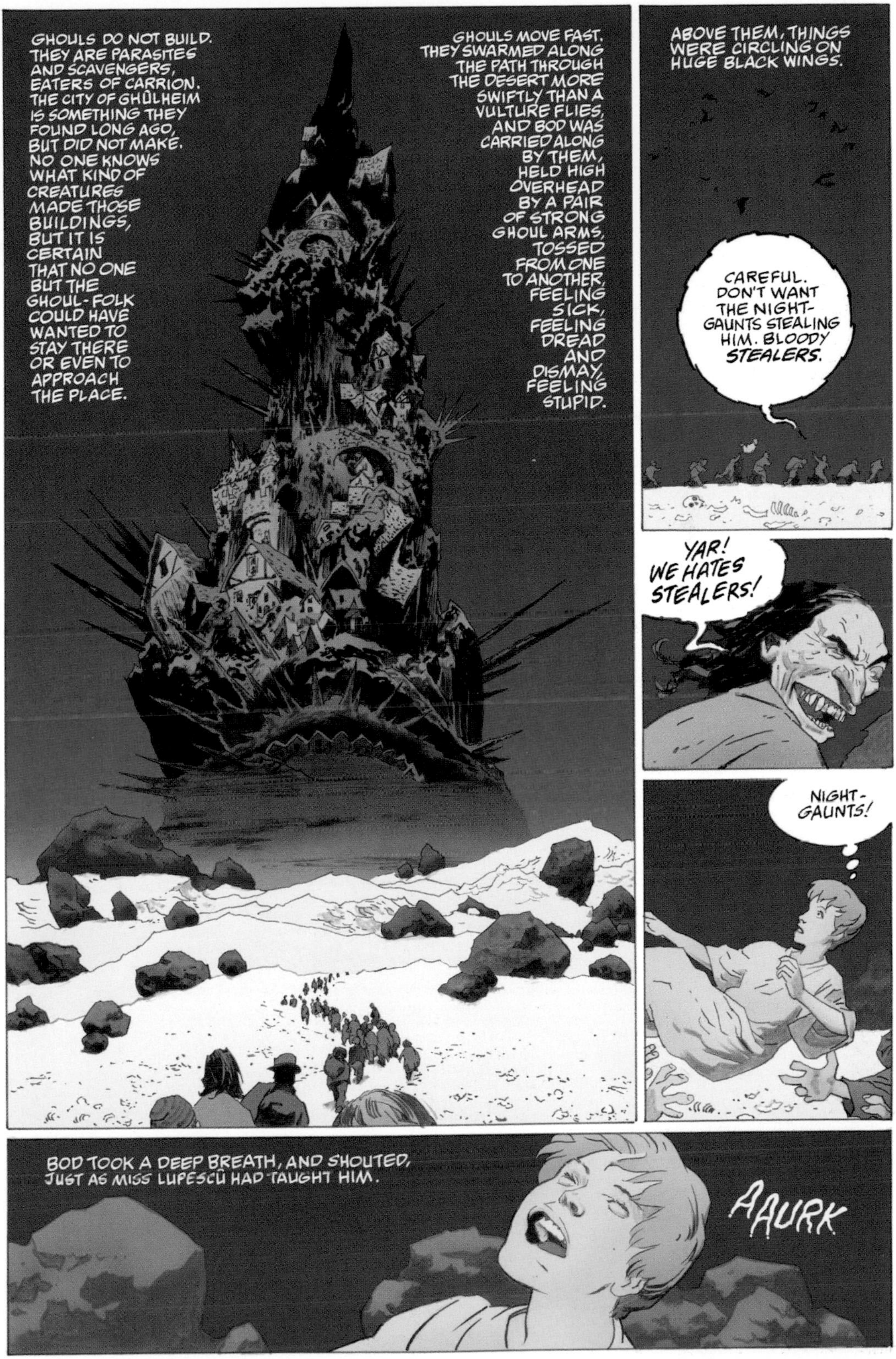
GHOULS DO NOT BUILD. THEY ARE PARASITES AND SCAVENGERS, EATERS OF CARRION. THE CITY OF GHÛLHEIM IS SOMETHING THEY FOUND LONG AGO, BUT DID NOT MAKE. NO ONE KNOWS WHAT KIND OF CREATURES MADE THOSE BUILDINGS, BUT IT IS CERTAIN THAT NO ONE BUT THE GHOUL-FOLK COULD HAVE WANTED TO STAY THERE OR EVEN TO APPROACH THE PLACE.
GHOULS MOVE FAST. THEY SWARMED ALONG THE PATH THROUGH THE DESERT MORE SWIFTLY THAN A VULTURE FLIES, AND BOD WAS CARRIED ALONG BY THEM, HELD HIGH OVERHEAD BY A PAIR OF STRONG GHOUL ARMS, TOSSED FROM ONE TO ANOTHER, FEELING SICK, FEELING DREAD AND DISMAY, FEELING STUPID.
ABOVE THEM, THINGS WERE CIRCLING ON HUGE BLACK WINGS.
CAREFUL. DON'T WANT THE NIGHT-GAUNTS STEALING HIM. BLOODY STEALERS.
YAR! WE HATES STEALERS!
NIGHT-GAUNTS!
BOD TOOK A DEEP BREATH, AND SHOUTED, JUST AS MISS LUPESCU HAD TAUGHT HIM.
AAURK

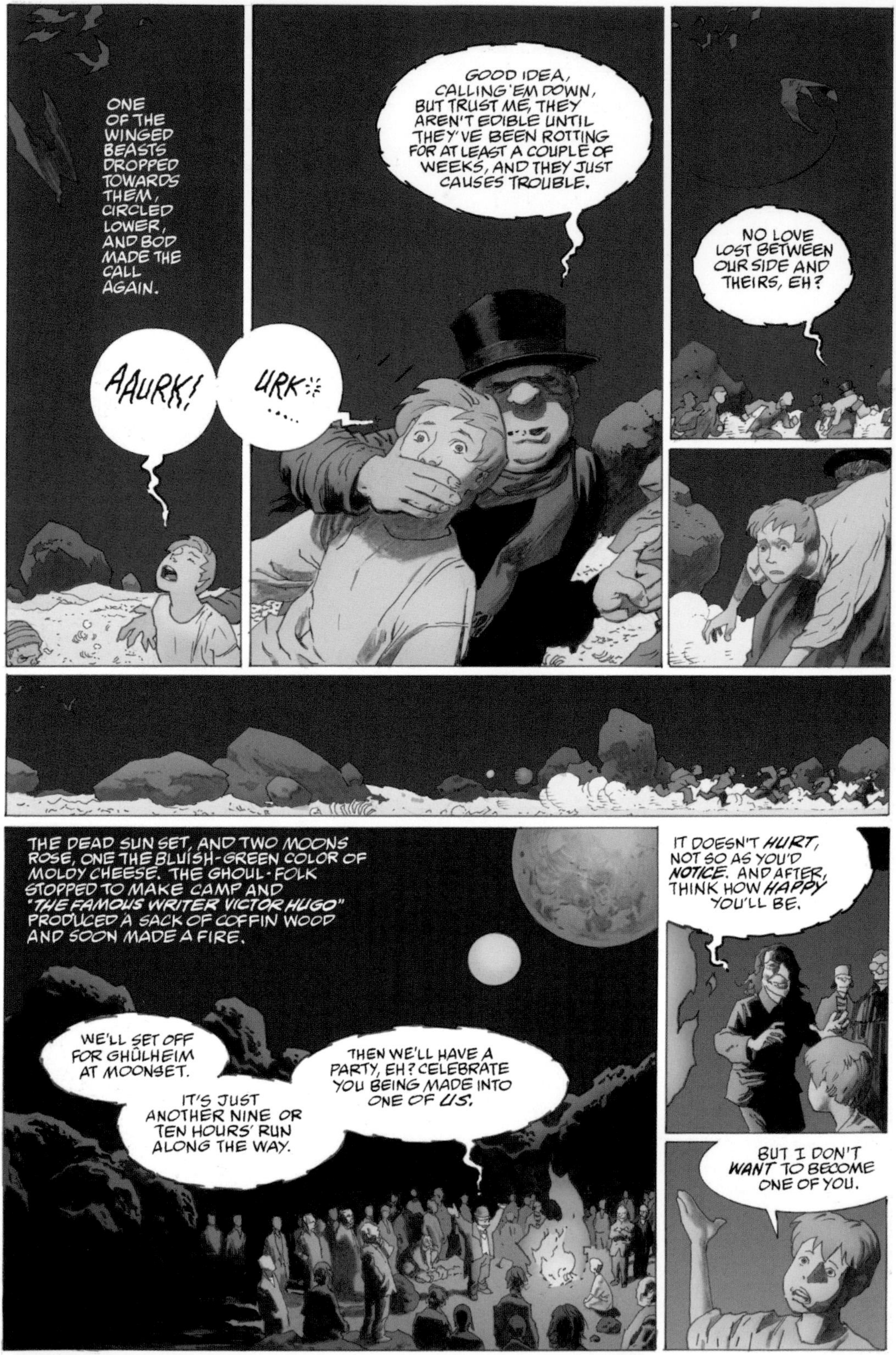
ONE OF THE WINGED BEASTS DROPPED TOWARDS THEM, CIRCLED LOWER, AND BOD MADE THE CALL AGAIN.
AAURK!
URK.....
GOOD IDEA, CALLING 'EM DOWN, BUT TRUST ME, THEY AREN'T EDIBLE UNTIL THEY'VE BEEN ROTTING FOR AT LEAST A COUPLE OF WEEKS, AND THEY JUST CAUSES TROUBLE.
NO LOVE LOST BETWEEN OUR SIDE AND THEIRS, EH?
THE DEAD SUN SET, AND TWO MOONS ROSE, ONE THE BLUISH-GREEN COLOR OF MOLDY CHEESE. THE GHOUL-FOLK STOPPED TO MAKE CAMP AND "THE FAMOUS WRITER VICTOR HUGO" PRODUCED A SACK OF COFFIN WOOD AND SOON MADE A FIRE.
WE'LL SET OFF FOR GHÛLHEIM AT MOONSET.
IT'S JUST ANOTHER NINE OR TEN HOURS' RUN ALONG THE WAY.
THEN WE'LL HAVE A PARTY, EH? CELEBRATE YOU BEING MADE INTO ONE OF US.
IT DOESN'T HURT, NOT SO AS YOU'D NOTICE. AND AFTER, THINK HOW HAPPY YOU'LL BE.
BUT I DON'T WANT TO BECOME ONE OF YOU.

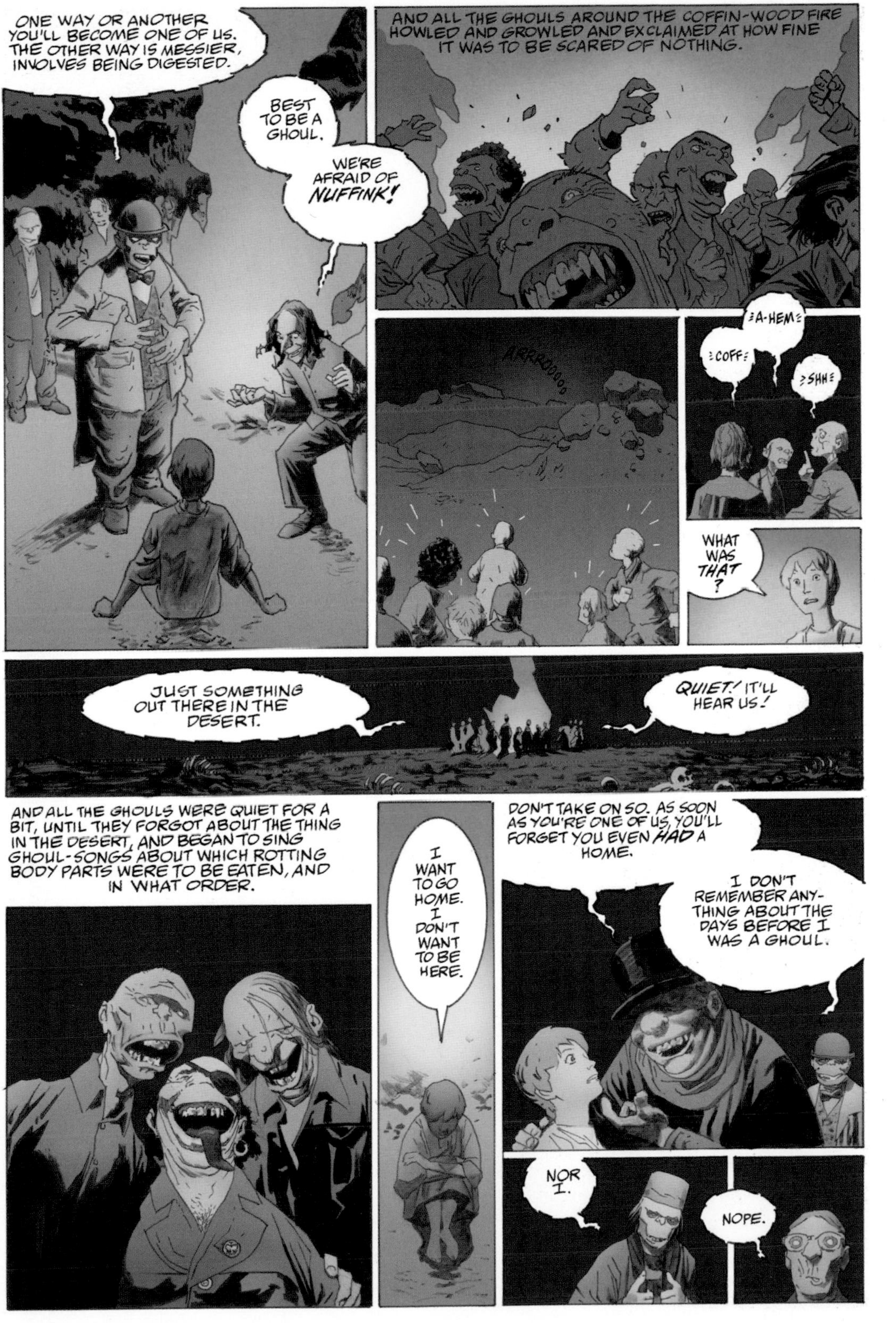
ONE WAY OR ANOTHER YOU'LL BECOME ONE OF US. THE OTHER WAY IS MESSIER, INVOLVES BEING DIGESTED.
BEST TO BE A GHOUL.
WE'RE AFRAID OF NUFFINK!
AND ALL THE GHOULS AROUND THE COFFIN-WOOD FIRE HOWLED AND GROWLED AND EXCLAIMED AT HOW FINE IT WAS TO BE SCARED OF NOTHING.
ARRROOOOO
A-HEM
COFF
SHH
WHAT WAS THAT?
JUST SOMETHING OUT THERE IN THE DESERT.
QUIET! IT'LL HEAR US!
AND ALL THE GHOULS WERE QUIET FOR A BIT, UNTIL THEY FORGOT ABOUT THE THING IN THE DESERT, AND BEGAN TO SING GHOUL-SONGS ABOUT WHICH ROTTING BODY PARTS WERE TO BE EATEN, AND IN WHAT ORDER.
I WANT TO GO HOME. I DON'T WANT TO BE HERE.
DON'T TAKE ON SO. AS SOON AS YOU'RE ONE OF US, YOU'LL FORGET YOU EVEN HAD A HOME.
I DON'T REMEMBER ANYTHING ABOUT THE DAYS BEFORE I WAS A GHOUL.
NOR I.
NOPE.

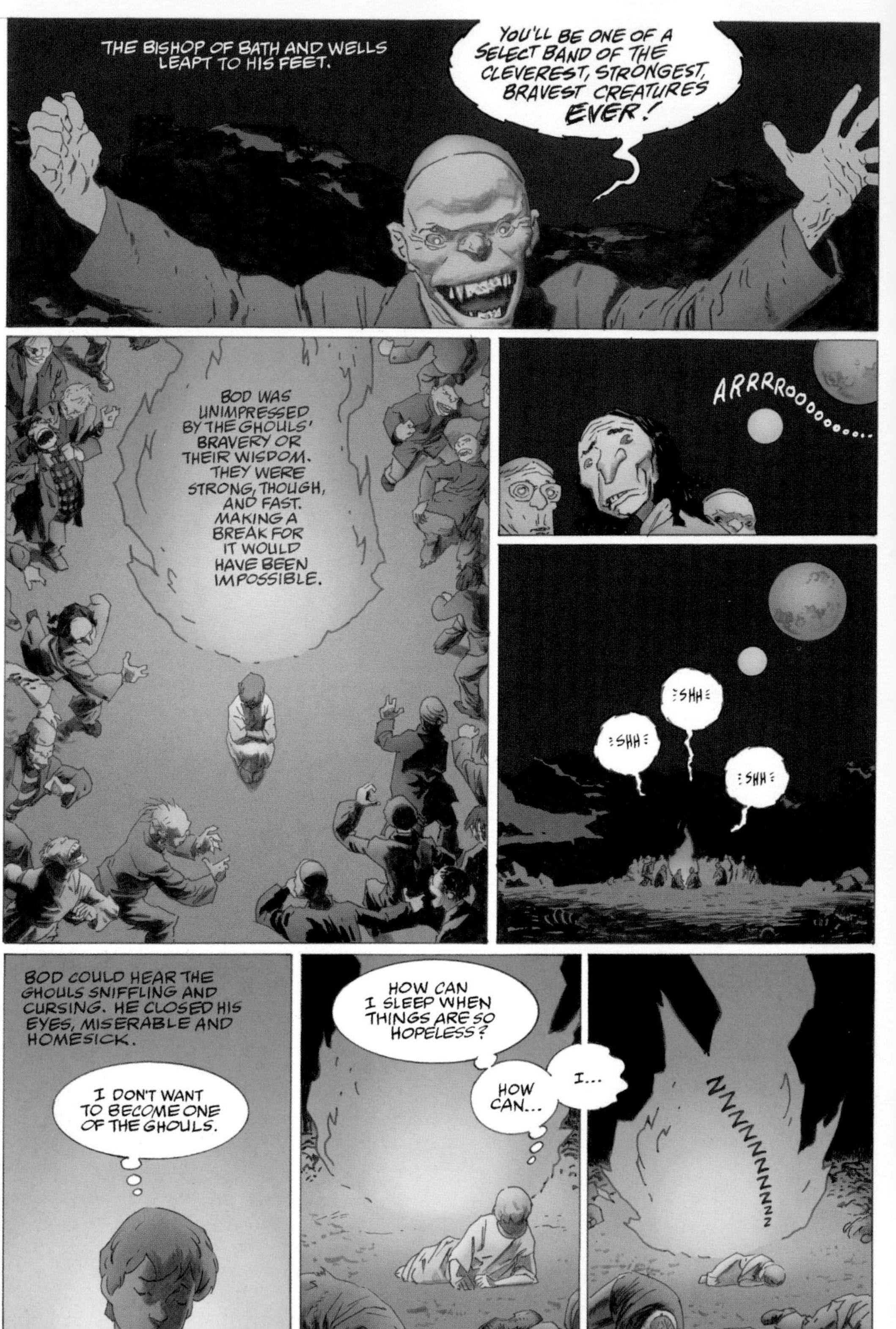
THE BISHOP OF BATH AND WELLS LEAPT TO HIS FEET.
YOU'LL BE ONE OF A SELECT BAND OF THE CLEVEREST, STRONGEST, BRAVEST CREATURES EVER!
BOD WAS UNIMPRESSED BY THE GHOULS' BRAVERY OR THEIR WISDOM. THEY WERE STRONG, THOUGH, AND FAST. MAKING A BREAK FOR IT WOULD HAVE BEEN IMPOSSIBLE.
ARRRROOOOOOO.....
SHH
SHH
SHH
BOD COULD HEAR THE GHOULS SNIFFLING AND CURSING. HE CLOSED HIS EYES, MISERABLE AND HOMESICK.
I DON'T WANT TO BECOME ONE OF THE GHOULS.
HOW CAN I SLEEP WHEN THINGS ARE SO HOPELESS?
HOW CAN...
I...
ZZZZZZZZZZZ

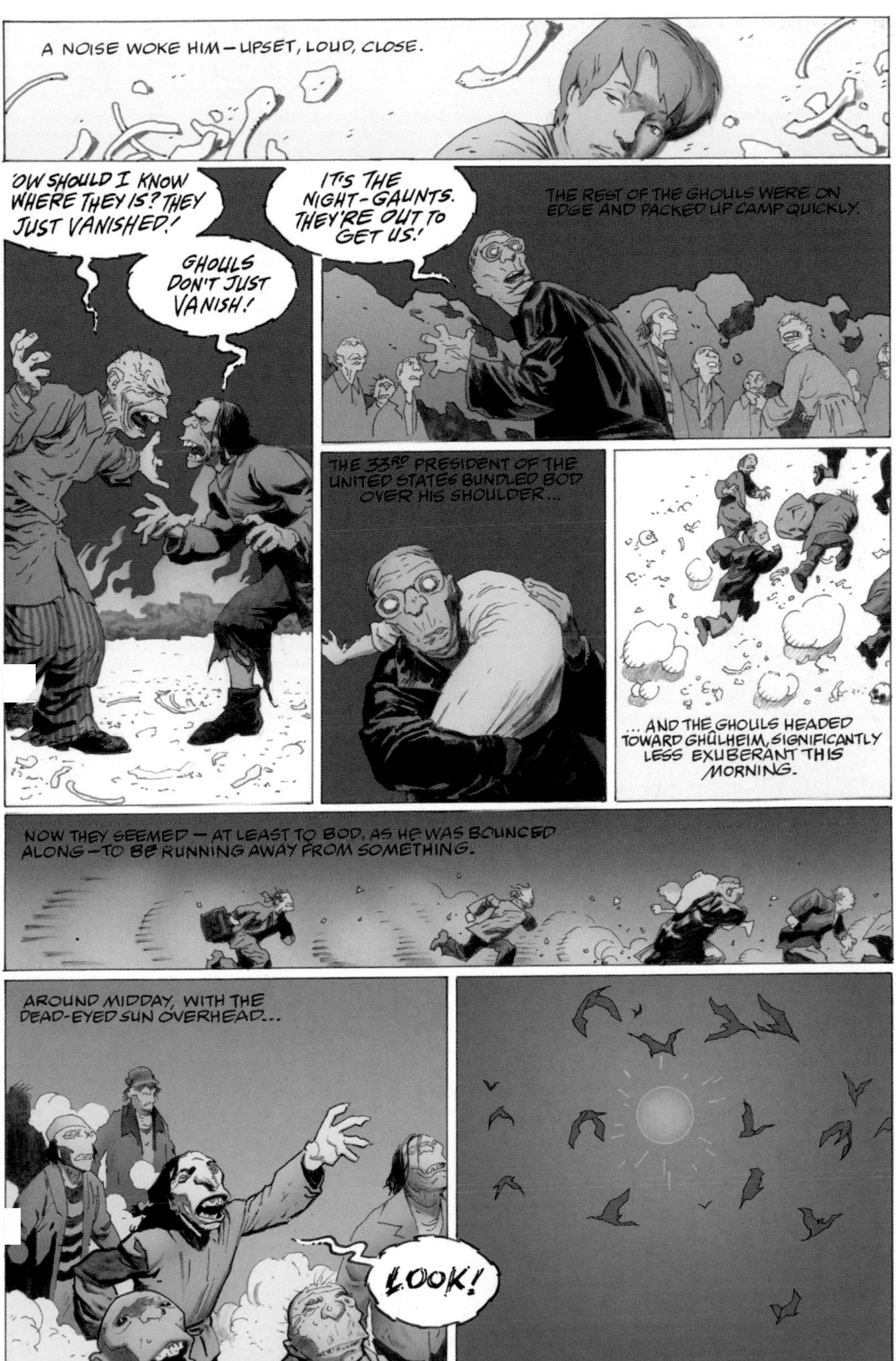
A NOISE WOKE HIM—UPSET, LOUD, CLOSE.
'OW SHOULD I KNOW WHERE THEY IS? THEY JUST VANISHED!
GHOULS DON'T JUST VANISH!
IT'S THE NIGHT-GAUNTS. THEY'RE OUT TO GET US!
THE REST OF THE GHOULS WERE ON EDGE AND PACKED UP CAMP QUICKLY.
THE 33RD PRESIDENT OF THE UNITED STATES BUNDLED BOD OVER HIS SHOULDER...
...AND THE GHOULS HEADED TOWARD GHÛLHEIM, SIGNIFICANTLY LESS EXUBERANT THIS MORNING.
NOW THEY SEEMED—AT LEAST TO BOD, AS HE WAS BOUNCED ALONG—TO BE RUNNING AWAY FROM SOMETHING.
AROUND MIDDAY, WITH THE DEAD-EYED SUN OVERHEAD...
LOOK!

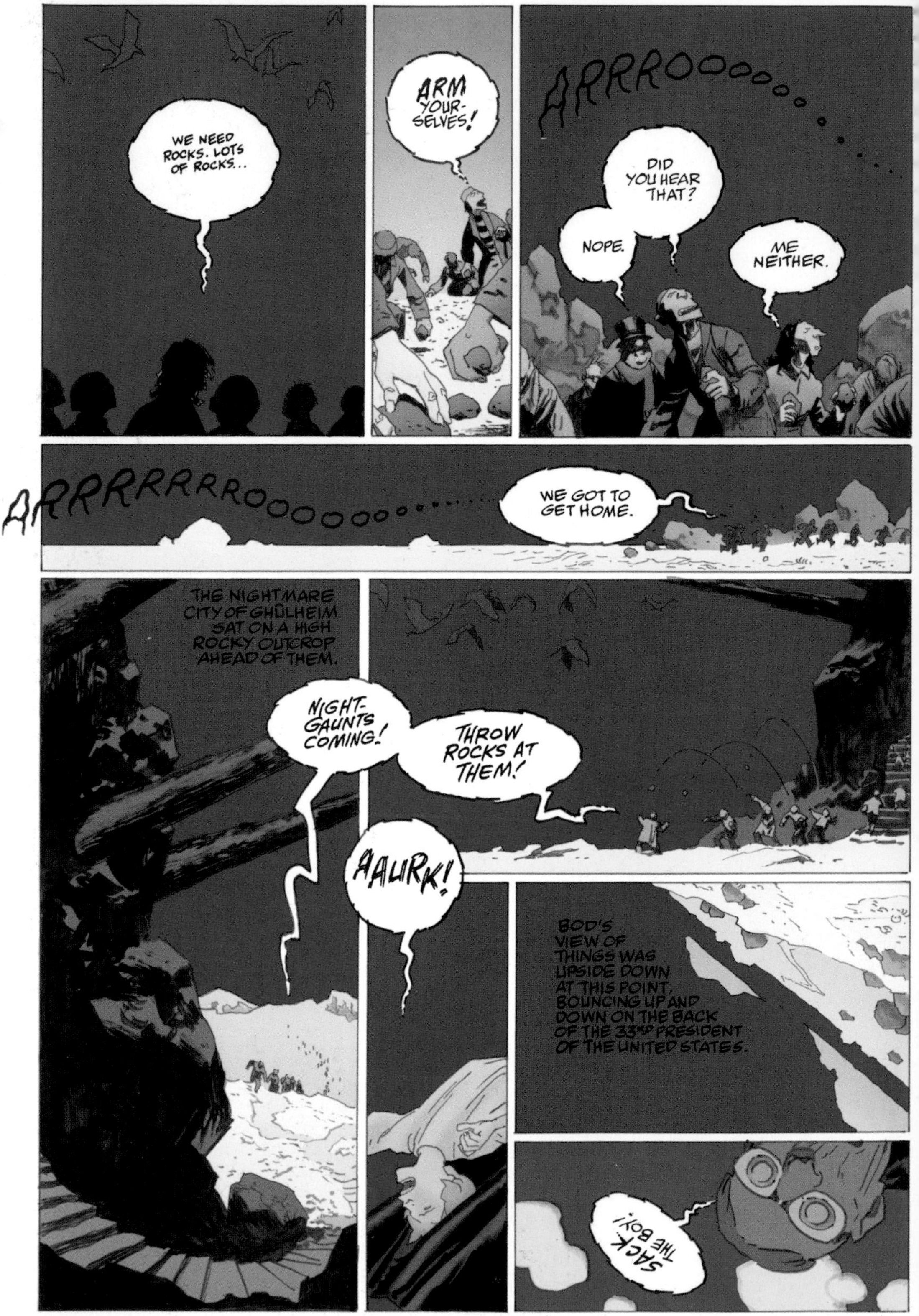
WE NEED ROCKS. LOTS OF ROCKS...
ARM YOUR-SELVES!
ARRROOOOOOOOO.......
DID YOU HEAR THAT?
NOPE.
ME NEITHER.
ARRRRRRRROOOOOOOOO.......
WE GOT TO GET HOME.
THE NIGHTMARE CITY OF GHÛLHEIM SAT ON A HIGH ROCKY OUTCROP AHEAD OF THEM.
NIGHT-GAUNTS COMING!
THROW ROCKS AT THEM!
AAURK!
BOD'S VIEW OF THINGS WAS UPSIDE DOWN AT THIS POINT, BOUNCING UP AND DOWN ON THE BACK OF THE 33RD PRESIDENT OF THE UNITED STATES.
SACK. THE BOY!

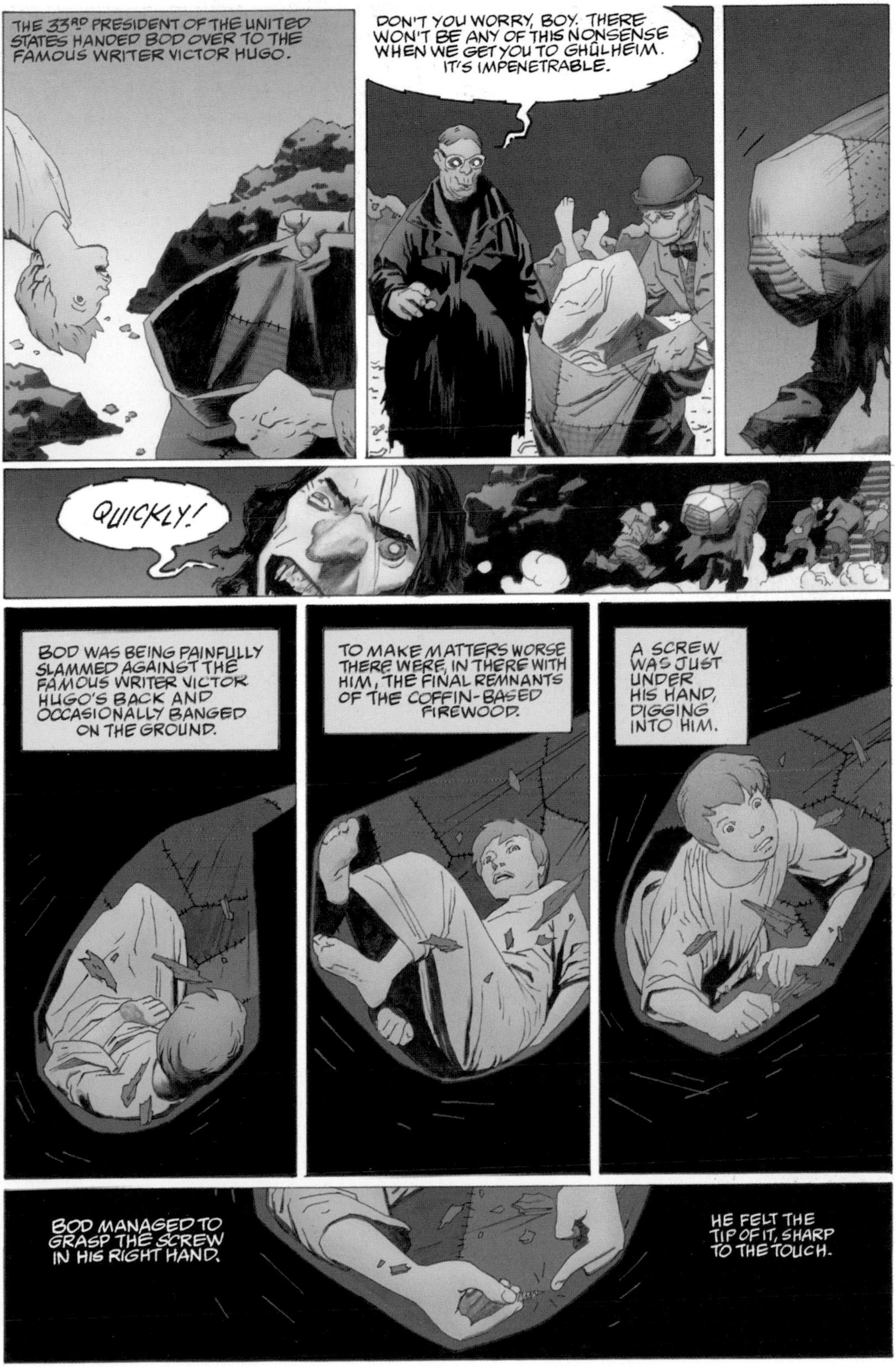
THE 33RD PRESIDENT OF THE UNITED STATES HANDED BOD OVER TO THE FAMOUS WRITER VICTOR HUGO.
DON'T YOU WORRY, BOY. THERE WON'T BE ANY OF THIS NONSENSE WHEN WE GET YOU TO GHÛLHEIM. IT'S IMPENETRABLE.
QUICKLY!
BOD WAS BEING PAINFULLY SLAMMED AGAINST THE FAMOUS WRITER VICTOR HUGO'S BACK AND OCCASIONALLY BANGED ON THE GROUND.
TO MAKE MATTERS WORSE THERE WERE, IN THERE WITH HIM, THE FINAL REMNANTS OF THE COFFIN-BASED FIREWOOD.
A SCREW WAS JUST UNDER HIS HAND, DIGGING INTO HIM.
BOD MANAGED TO GRASP THE SCREW IN HIS RIGHT HAND.
HE FELT THE TIP OF IT, SHARP TO THE TOUCH.

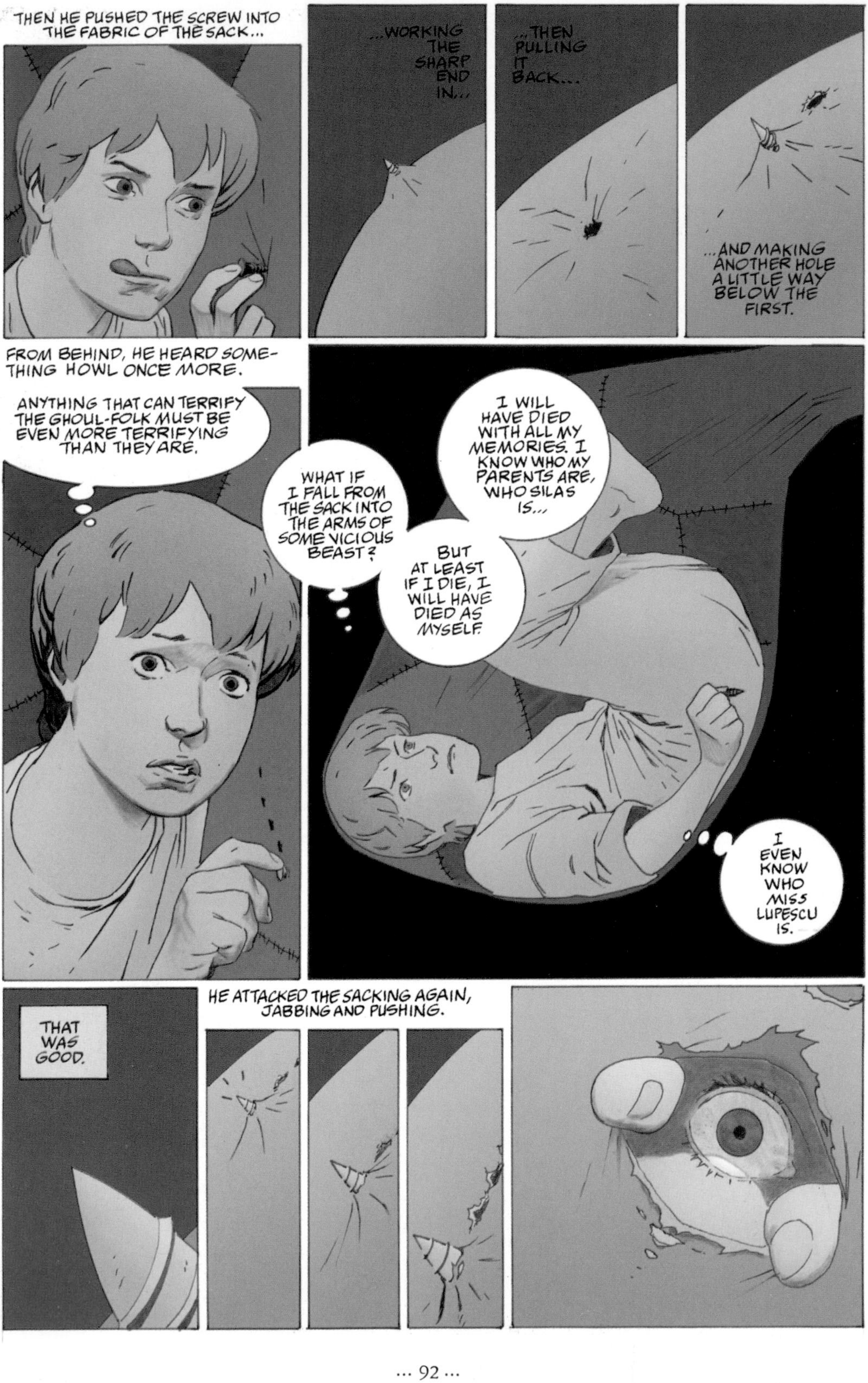
THEN HE PUSHED THE SCREW INTO THE FABRIC OF THE SACK...
...WORKING THE SHARP END IN...
...THEN PULLING IT BACK...
...AND MAKING ANOTHER HOLE A LITTLE WAY BELOW THE FIRST.
FROM BEHIND, HE HEARD SOMETHING HOWL ONCE MORE.
ANYTHING THAT CAN TERRIFY THE GHOUL-FOLK MUST BE EVEN MORE TERRIFYING THAN THEY ARE.
WHAT IF I FALL FROM THE SACK INTO THE ARMS OF SOME VICIOUS BEAST?
I WILL HAVE DIED WITH ALL MY MEMORIES. I KNOW WHO MY PARENTS ARE, WHO SILAS IS...
BUT AT LEAST IF I DIE, I WILL HAVE DIED AS MYSELF.
I EVEN KNOW WHO MISS LUPESCU IS.
THAT WAS GOOD.
HE ATTACKED THE SACKING AGAIN, JABBING AND PUSHING.

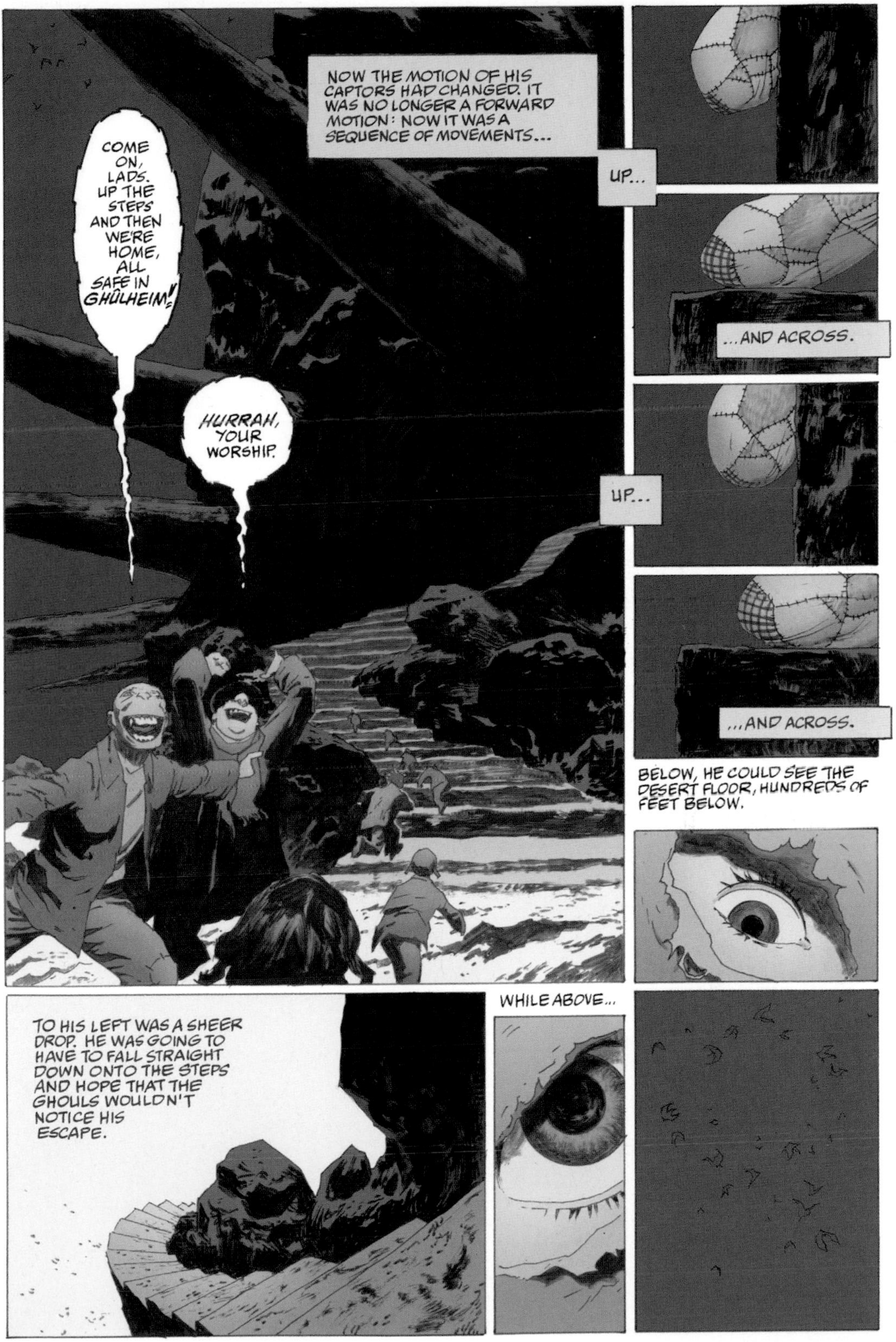
NOW THE MOTION OF HIS CAPTORS HAD CHANGED. IT WAS NO LONGER A FORWARD MOTION: NOW IT WAS A SEQUENCE OF MOVEMENTS...
COME ON, LADS. UP THE STEPS AND THEN WE'RE HOME, ALL SAFE IN GHÛLHEIM!
HURRAH, YOUR WORSHIP.
UP...
...AND ACROSS.
UP...
...AND ACROSS.
BELOW, HE COULD SEE THE DESERT FLOOR, HUNDREDS OF FEET BELOW.
TO HIS LEFT WAS A SHEER DROP. HE WAS GOING TO HAVE TO FALL STRAIGHT DOWN ONTO THE STEPS AND HOPE THAT THE GHOULS WOULDN'T NOTICE HIS ESCAPE.
WHILE ABOVE...

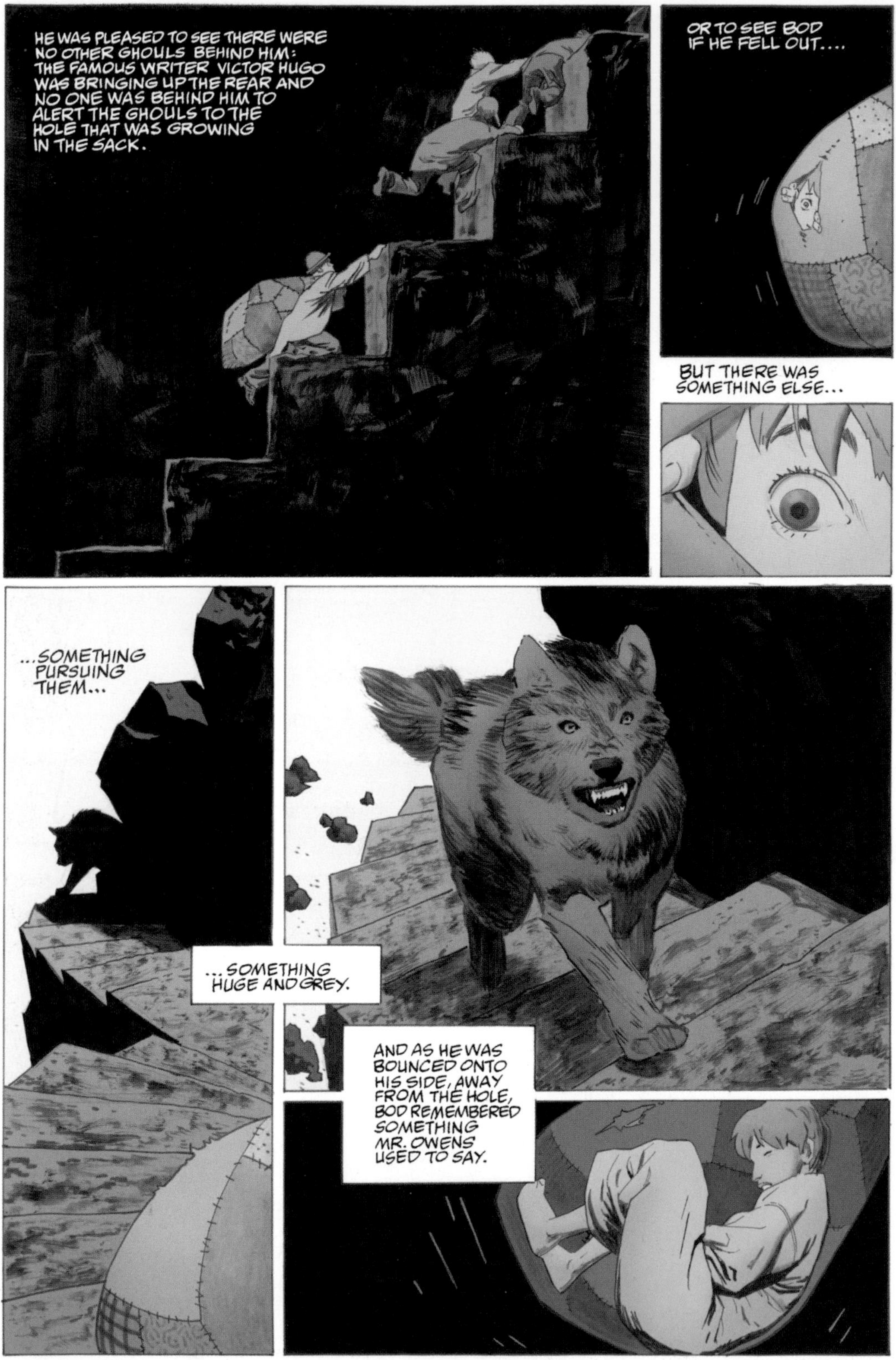
HE WAS PLEASED TO SEE THERE WERE NO OTHER GHOULS BEHIND HIM: THE FAMOUS WRITER VICTOR HUGO WAS BRINGING UP THE REAR AND NO ONE WAS BEHIND HIM TO ALERT THE GHOULS TO THE HOLE THAT WAS GROWING IN THE SACK.
OR TO SEE BOD IF HE FELL OUT....
BUT THERE WAS SOMETHING ELSE...
...SOMETHING PURSUING THEM...
...SOMETHING HUGE AND GREY.
AND AS HE WAS BOUNCED ONTO HIS SIDE, AWAY FROM THE HOLE, BOD REMEMBERED SOMETHING MR. OWENS USED TO SAY.

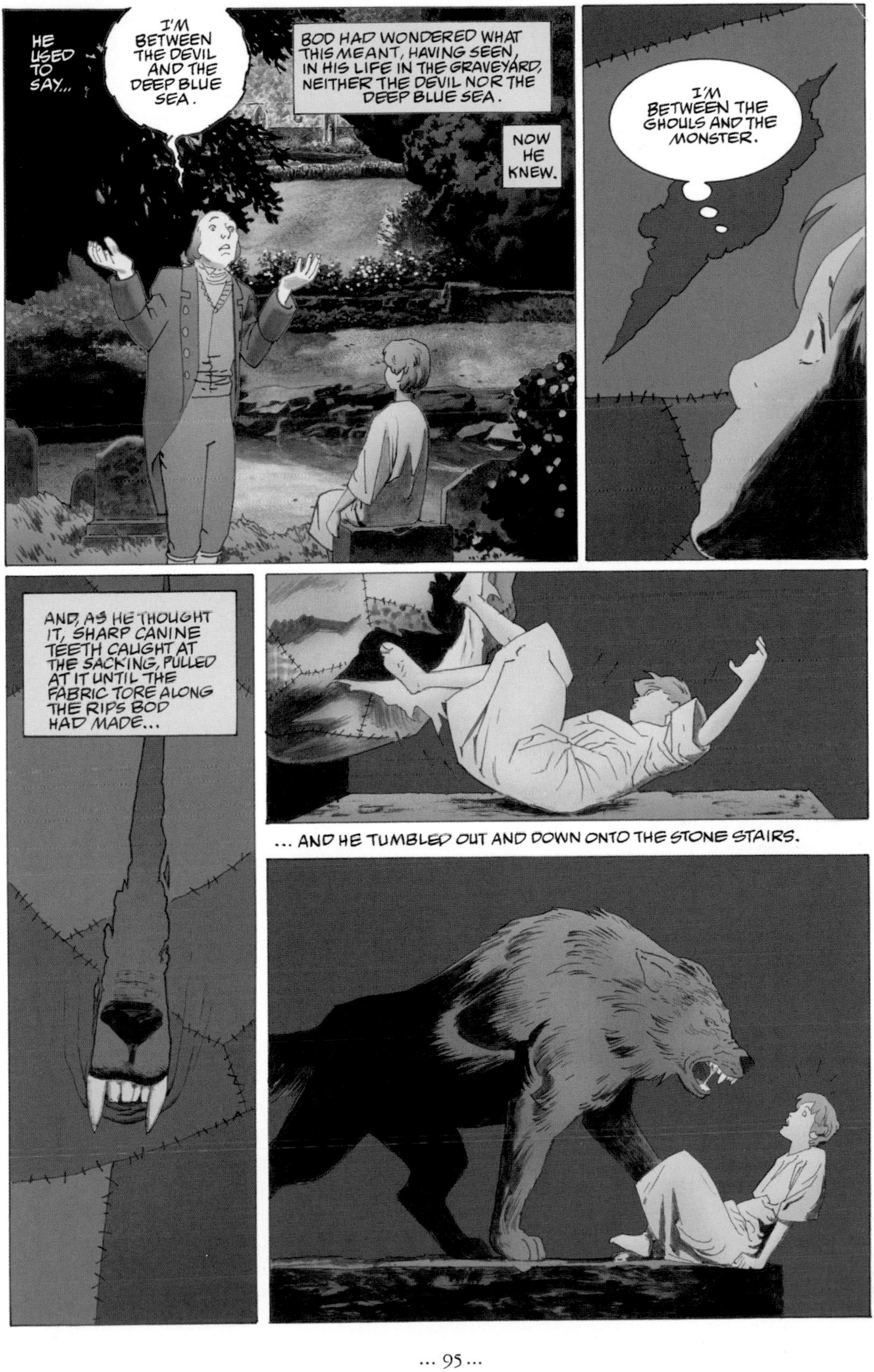
HE USED TO SAY...
I'M BETWEEN THE DEVIL AND THE DEEP BLUE SEA.
BOD HAD WONDERED WHAT THIS MEANT, HAVING SEEN, IN HIS LIFE IN THE GRAVEYARD, NEITHER THE DEVIL NOR THE DEEP BLUE SEA.
NOW HE KNEW.
I'M BETWEEN THE GHOULS AND THE MONSTER.
AND, AS HE THOUGHT IT, SHARP CANINE TEETH CAUGHT AT THE SACKING, PULLED AT IT UNTIL THE FABRIC TORE ALONG THE RIPS BOD HAD MADE...
... AND HE TUMBLED OUT AND DOWN ONTO THE STONE STAIRS.

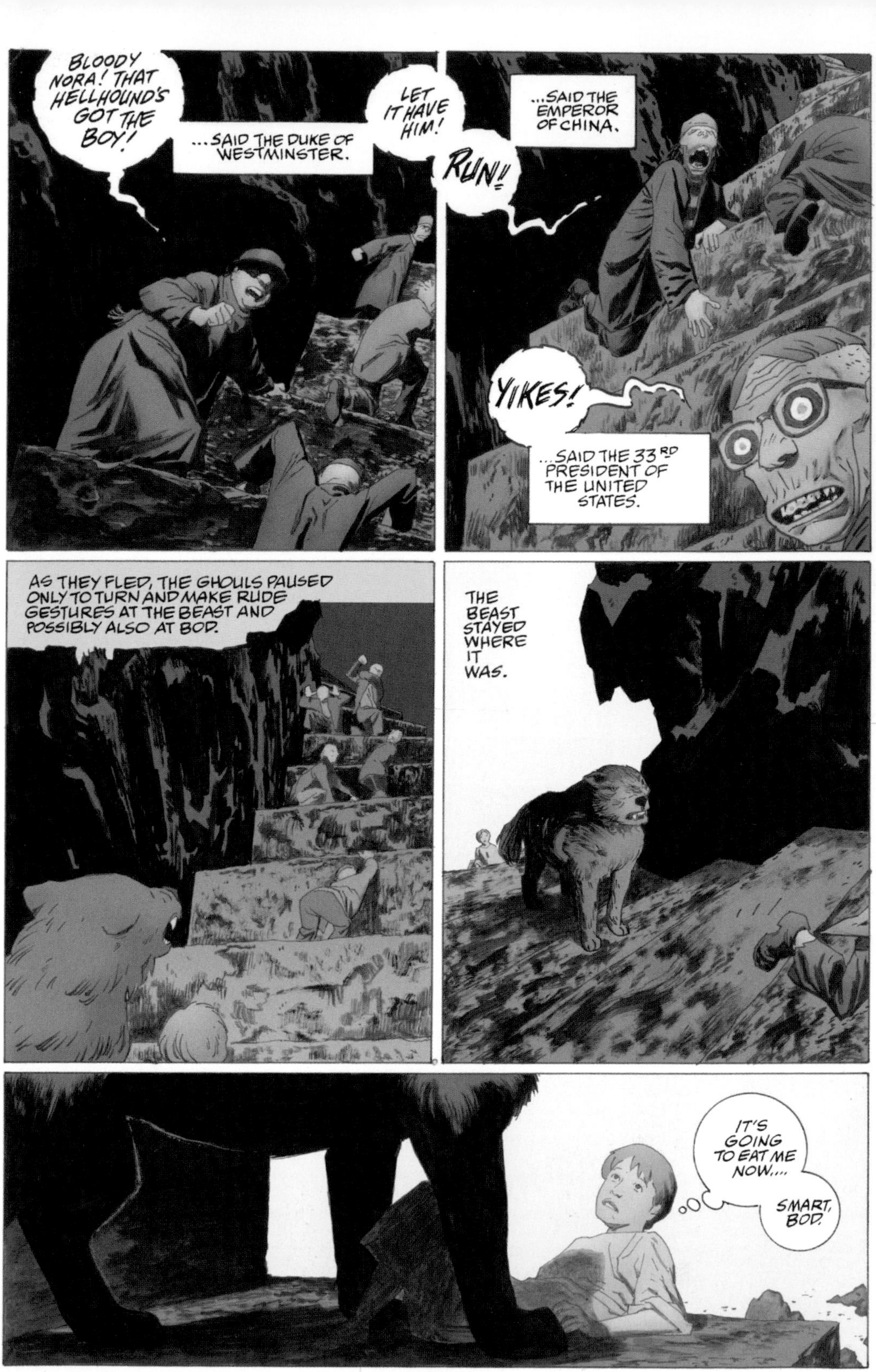

BLOODY NORA! THAT HELLHOUND'S GOT THE BOY!
...SAID THE DUKE OF WESTMINSTER.
LET IT HAVE HIM!
RUN!!
...SAID THE EMPEROR OF CHINA.
YIKES!
...SAID THE 33RD PRESIDENT OF THE UNITED STATES.
AS THEY FLED, THE GHOULS PAUSED ONLY TO TURN AND MAKE RUDE GESTURES AT THE BEAST AND POSSIBLY ALSO AT BOD.
THE BEAST STAYED WHERE IT WAS.
IT'S GOING TO EAT ME NOW....
SMART, BOD.

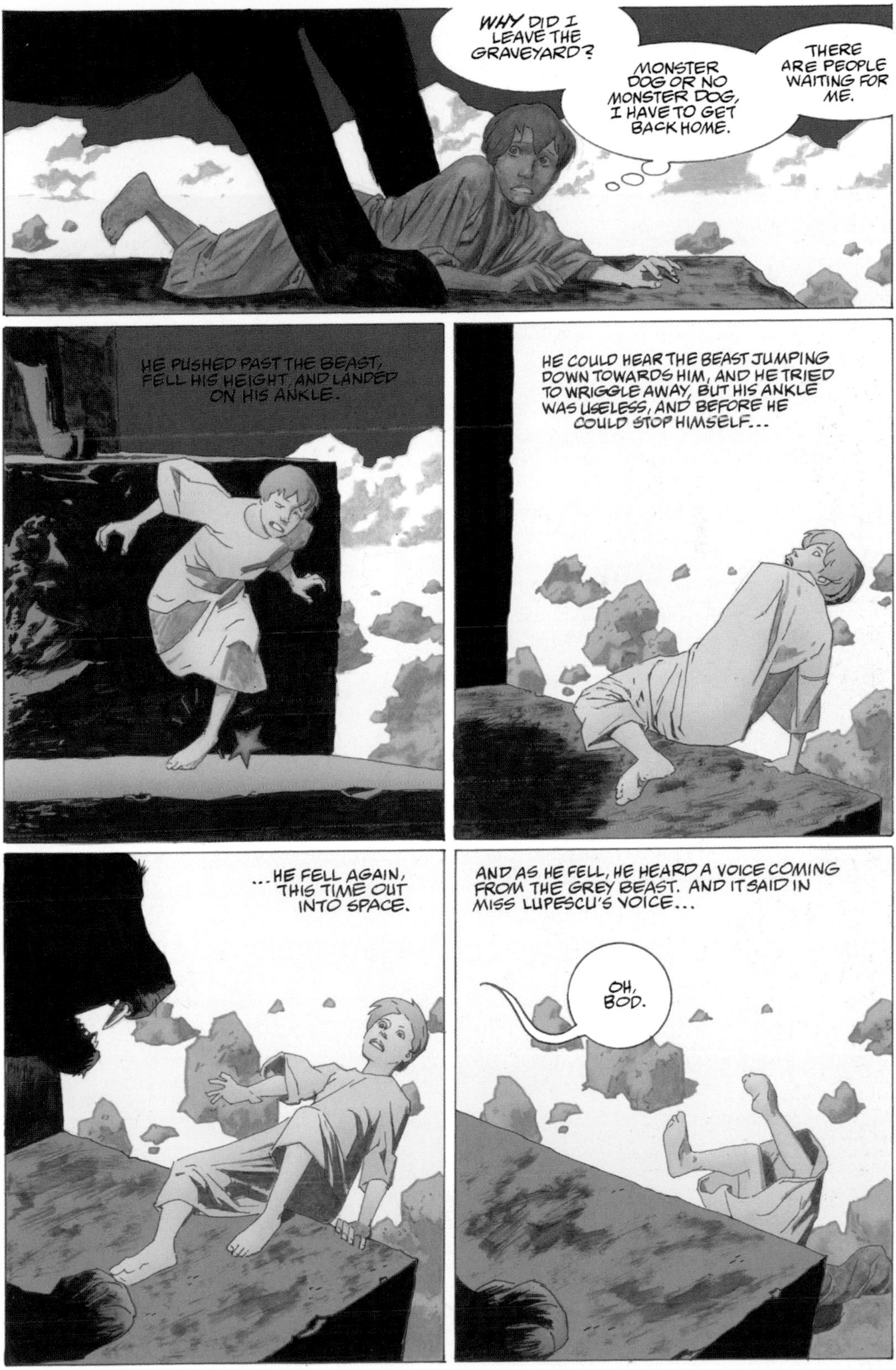
WHY DID I LEAVE THE GRAVEYARD?
MONSTER DOG OR NO MONSTER DOG, I HAVE TO GET BACK HOME.
THERE ARE PEOPLE WAITING FOR ME.
HE PUSHED PAST THE BEAST, FELL HIS HEIGHT, AND LANDED ON HIS ANKLE.
HE COULD HEAR THE BEAST JUMPING DOWN TOWARDS HIM, AND HE TRIED TO WRIGGLE AWAY, BUT HIS ANKLE WAS USELESS, AND BEFORE HE COULD STOP HIMSELF...
...HE FELL AGAIN, THIS TIME OUT INTO SPACE.
AND AS HE FELL, HE HEARD A VOICE COMING FROM THE GREY BEAST. AND IT SAID IN MISS LUPESCU'S VOICE...
OH, BOD.

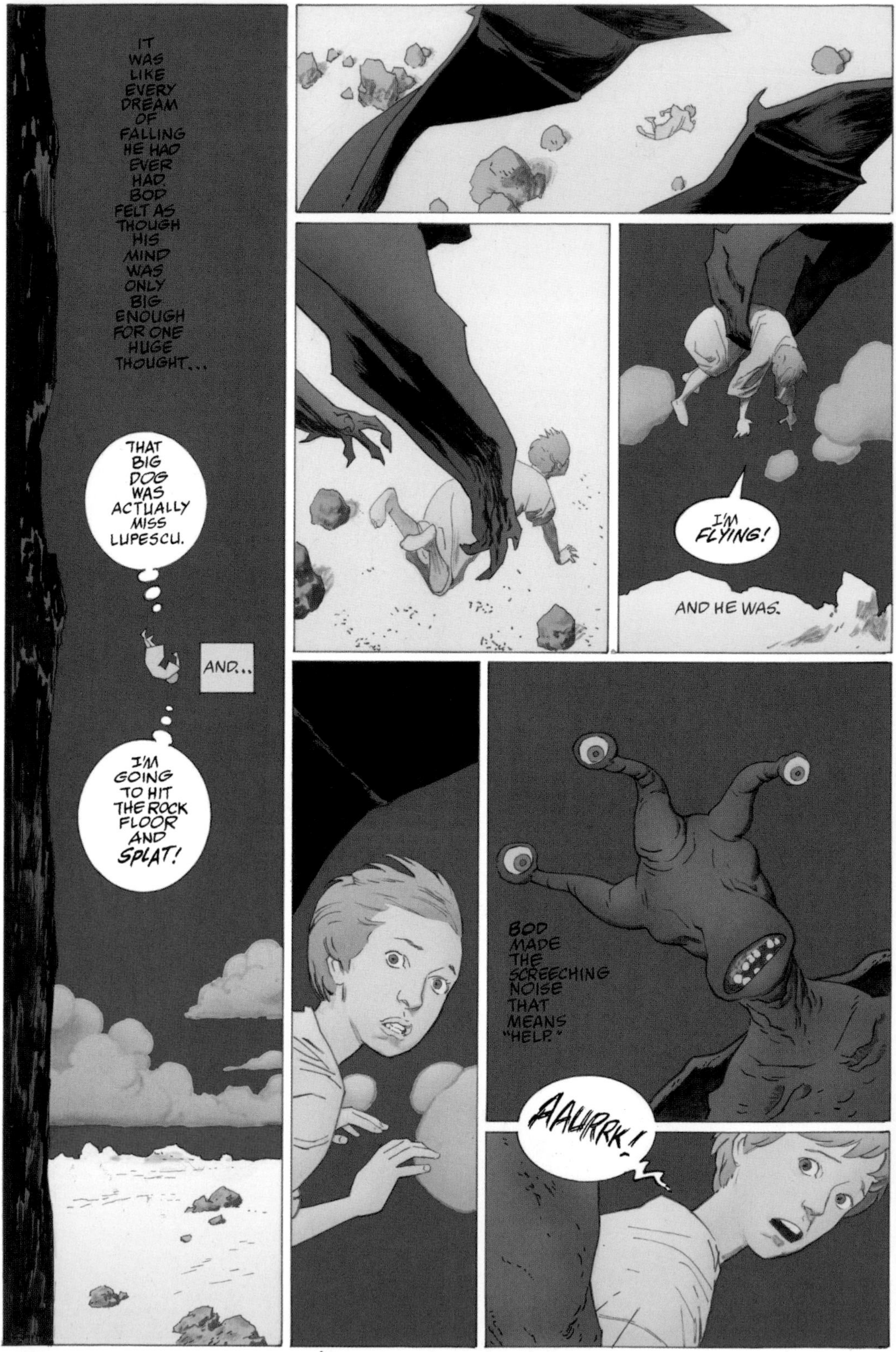

IT WAS LIKE EVERY DREAM OF FALLING HE HAD EVER HAD. BOD FELT AS THOUGH HIS MIND WAS ONLY BIG ENOUGH FOR ONE HUGE THOUGHT...
THAT BIG DOG WAS ACTUALLY MISS LUPESCU.
AND...
I'M GOING TO HIT THE ROCK FLOOR AND SPLAT!
I'M FLYING!
AND HE WAS.
BOD MADE THE SCREECHING NOISE THAT MEANS "HELP."
AAURRK!

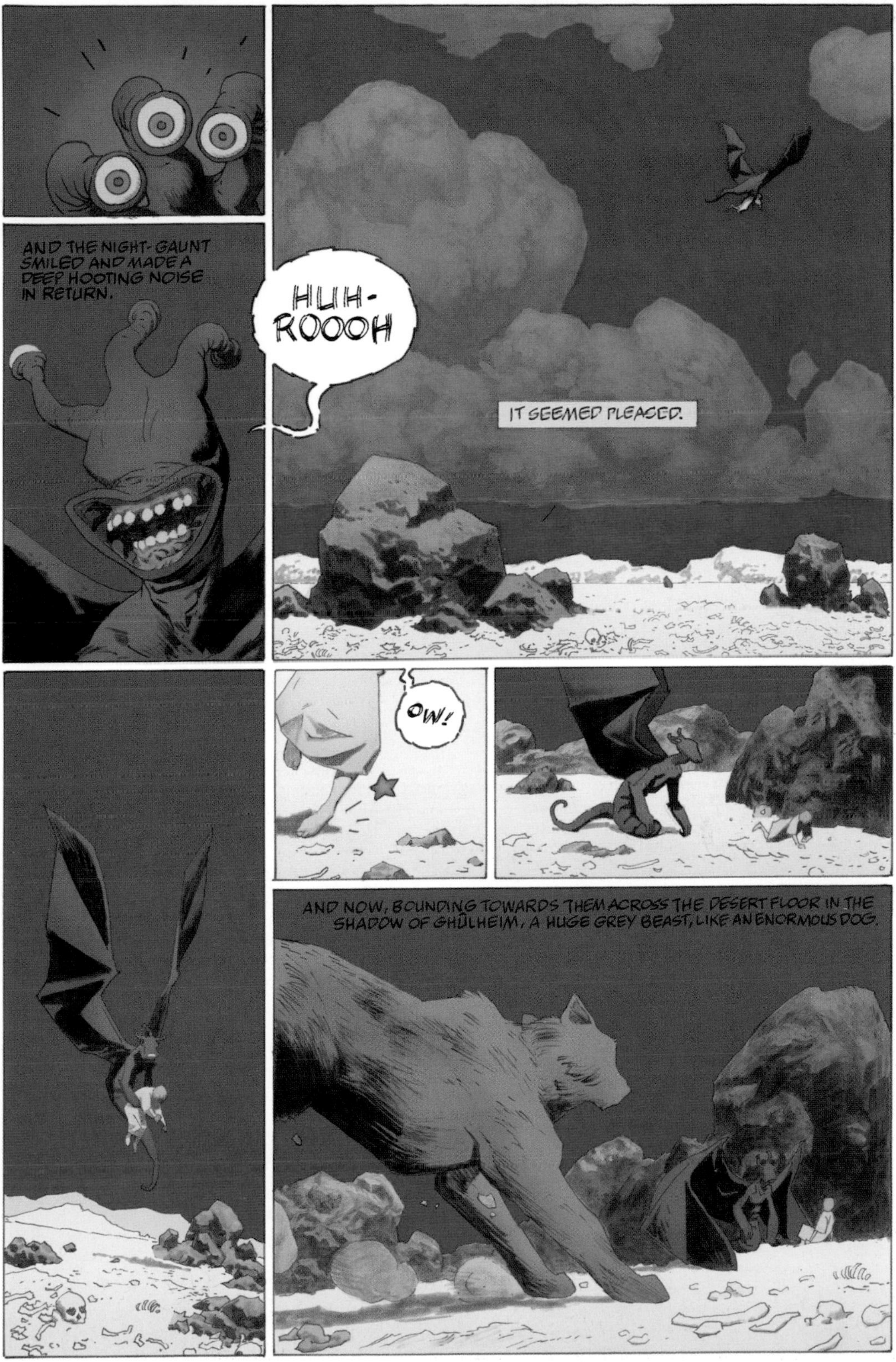
AND THE NIGHT-GAUNT SMILED AND MADE A DEEP HOOTING NOISE IN RETURN.
HUH-ROOOH
IT SEEMED PLEASED.
OW!
AND NOW, BOUNDING TOWARDS THEM ACROSS THE DESERT FLOOR IN THE SHADOW OF GHÛLHEIM, A HUGE GREY BEAST, LIKE AN ENORMOUS DOG.

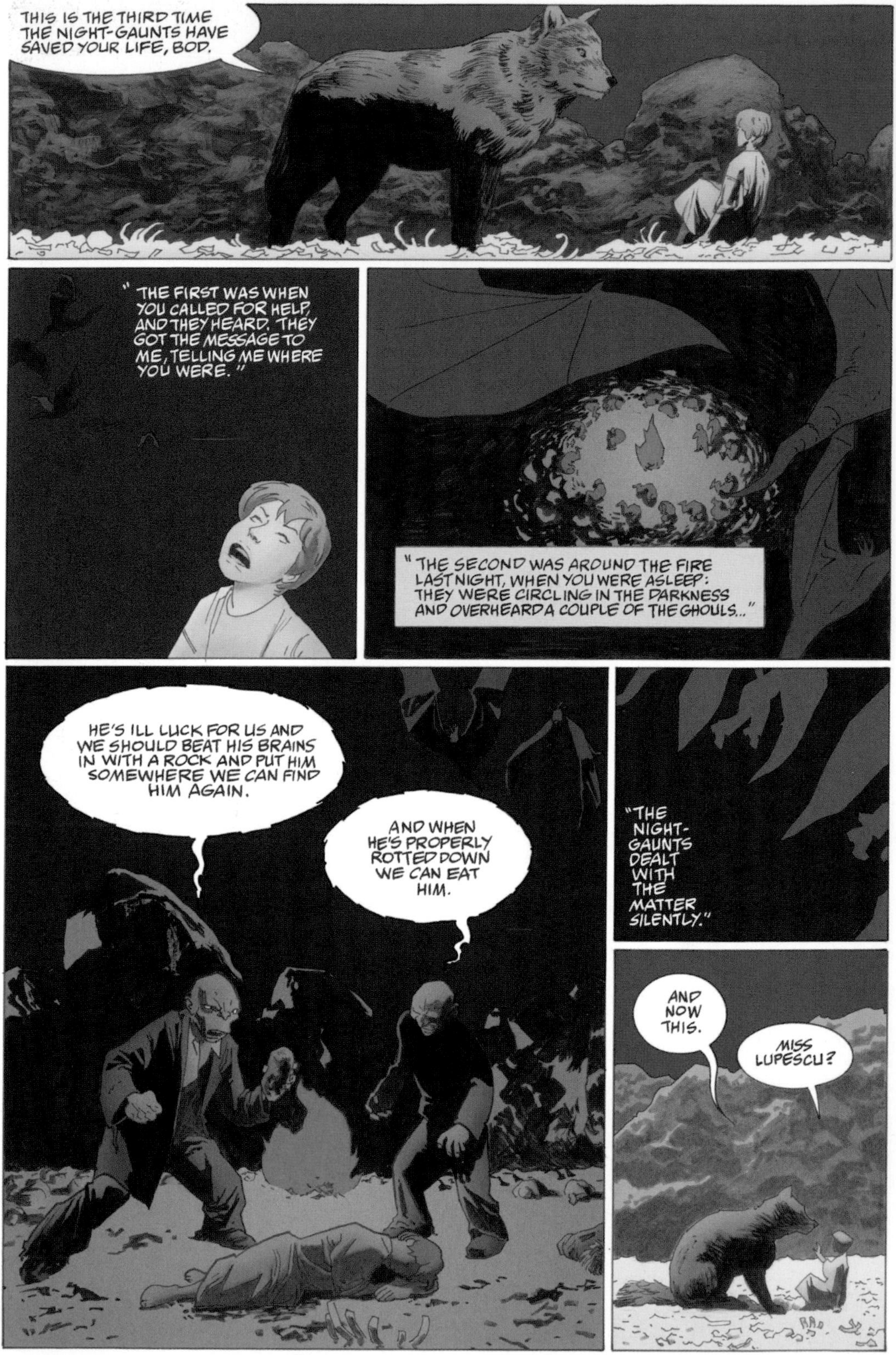
THIS IS THE THIRD TIME THE NIGHT-GAUNTS HAVE SAVED YOUR LIFE, BOD.
"THE FIRST WAS WHEN YOU CALLED FOR HELP, AND THEY HEARD. THEY GOT THE MESSAGE TO ME, TELLING ME WHERE YOU WERE."
"THE SECOND WAS AROUND THE FIRE LAST NIGHT, WHEN YOU WERE ASLEEP: THEY WERE CIRCLING IN THE DARKNESS AND OVERHEARD A COUPLE OF THE GHOULS..."
HE'S ILL LUCK FOR US AND WE SHOULD BEAT HIS BRAINS IN WITH A ROCK AND PUT HIM SOMEWHERE WE CAN FIND HIM AGAIN.
AND WHEN HE'S PROPERLY ROTTED DOWN WE CAN EAT HIM.
"THE NIGHT-GAUNTS DEALT WITH THE MATTER SILENTLY."
AND NOW THIS.
MISS LUPESCU?

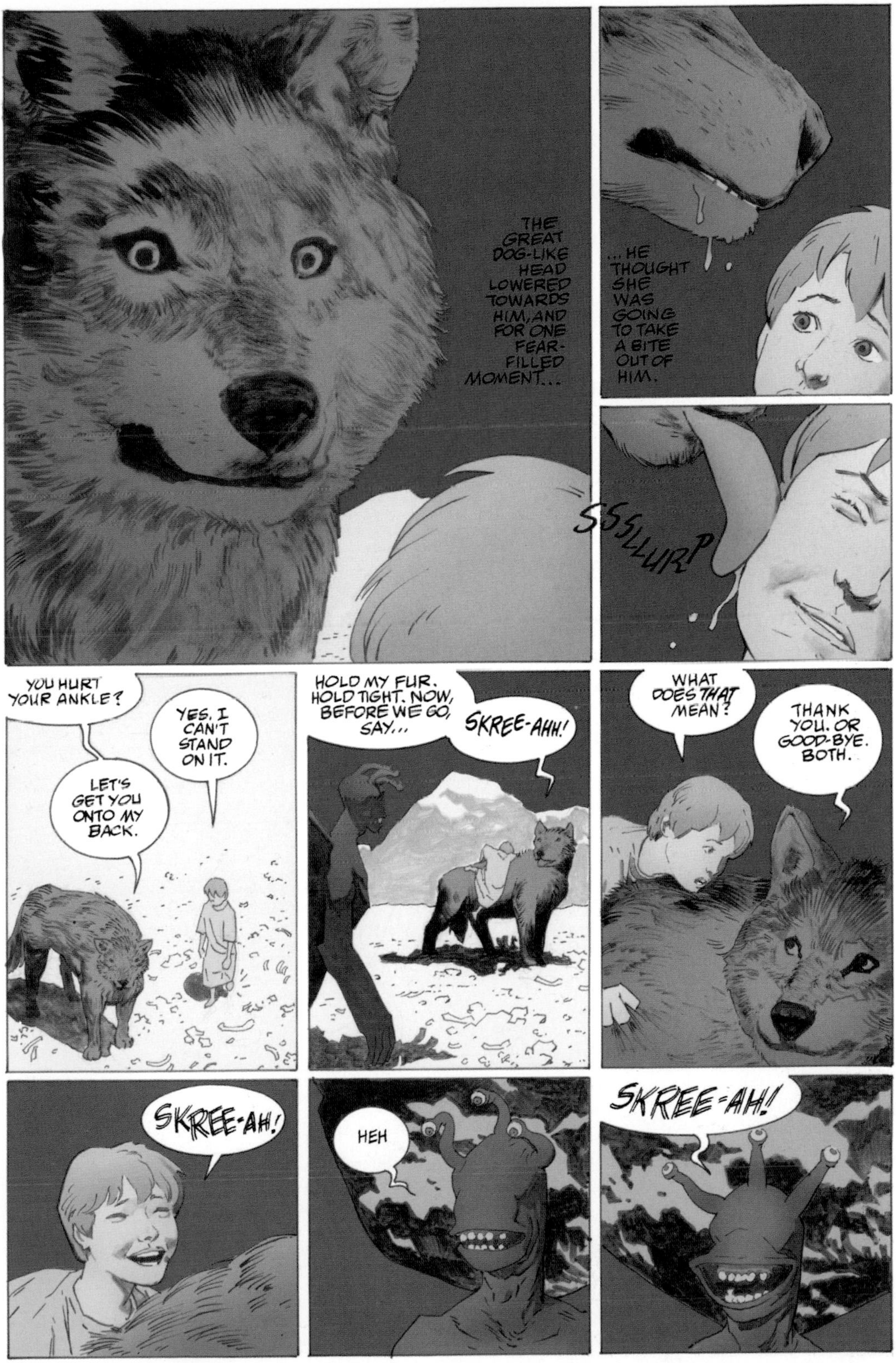
THE GREAT DOG-LIKE HEAD LOWERED TOWARDS HIM, AND FOR ONE FEAR-FILLED MOMENT...
...HE THOUGHT SHE WAS GOING TO TAKE A BITE OUT OF HIM.
SSSLLURP
YOU HURT YOUR ANKLE?
YES. I CAN'T STAND ON IT.
LET'S GET YOU ONTO MY BACK.
HOLD MY FUR. HOLD TIGHT. NOW, BEFORE WE GO, SAY...
SKREE-AHH!
WHAT DOES THAT MEAN?
THANK YOU. OR GOOD-BYE. BOTH.
SKREE-AH!
HEH
SKREE-AH!

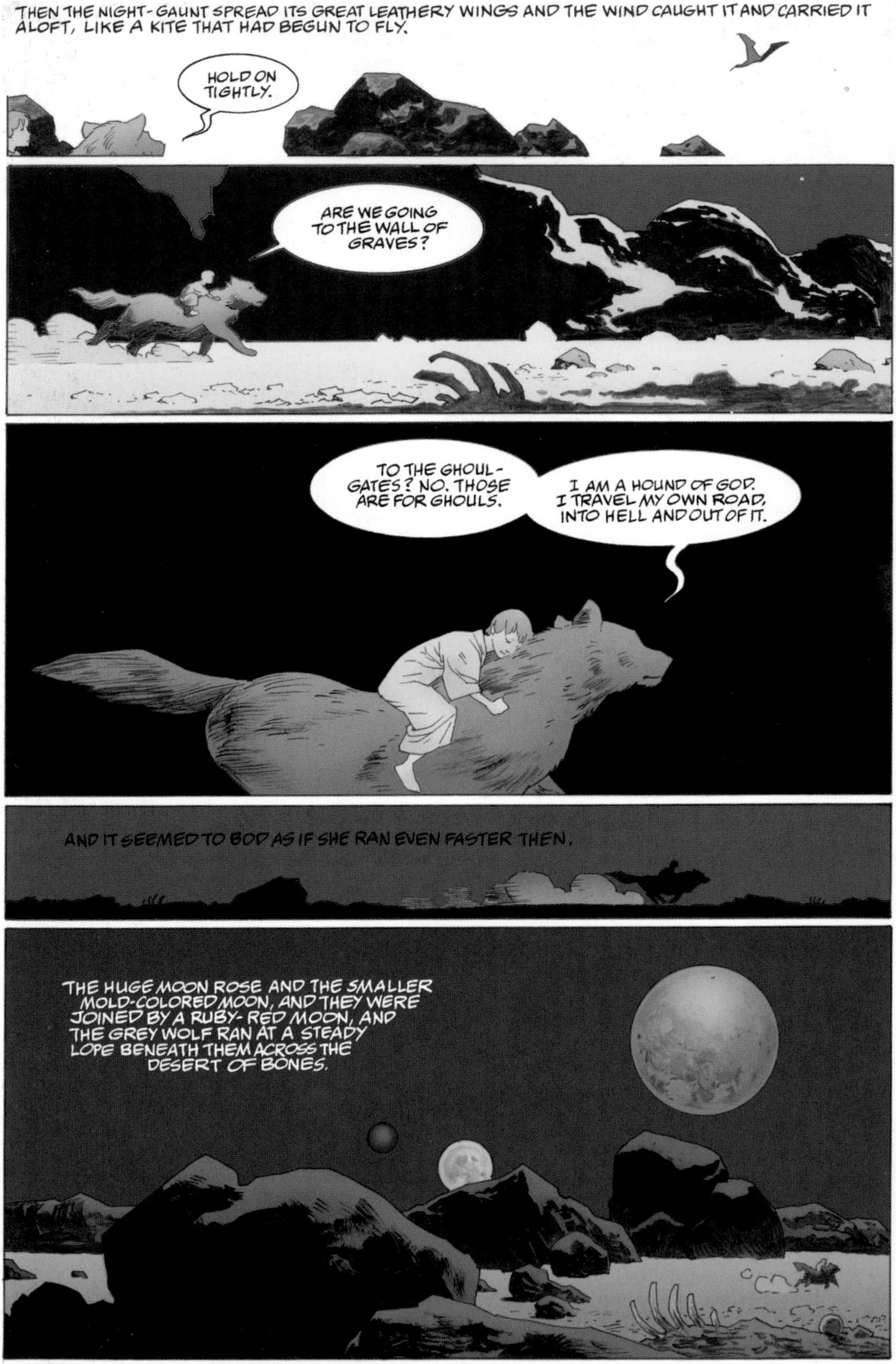
THEN THE NIGHT-GAUNT SPREAD ITS GREAT LEATHERY WINGS AND THE WIND CAUGHT IT AND CARRIED IT ALOFT, LIKE A KITE THAT HAD BEGUN TO FLY.
HOLD ON TIGHTLY.
ARE WE GOING TO THE WALL OF GRAVES?
TO THE GHOUL-GATES? NO. THOSE ARE FOR GHOULS.
I AM A HOUND OF GOD. I TRAVEL MY OWN ROAD, INTO HELL AND OUT OF IT.
AND IT SEEMED TO BOD AS IF SHE RAN EVEN FASTER THEN.
THE HUGE MOON ROSE AND THE SMALLER MOLD-COLORED MOON, AND THEY WERE JOINED BY A RUBY-RED MOON, AND THE GREY WOLF RAN AT A STEADY LOPE BENEATH THEM ACROSS THE DESERT OF BONES.

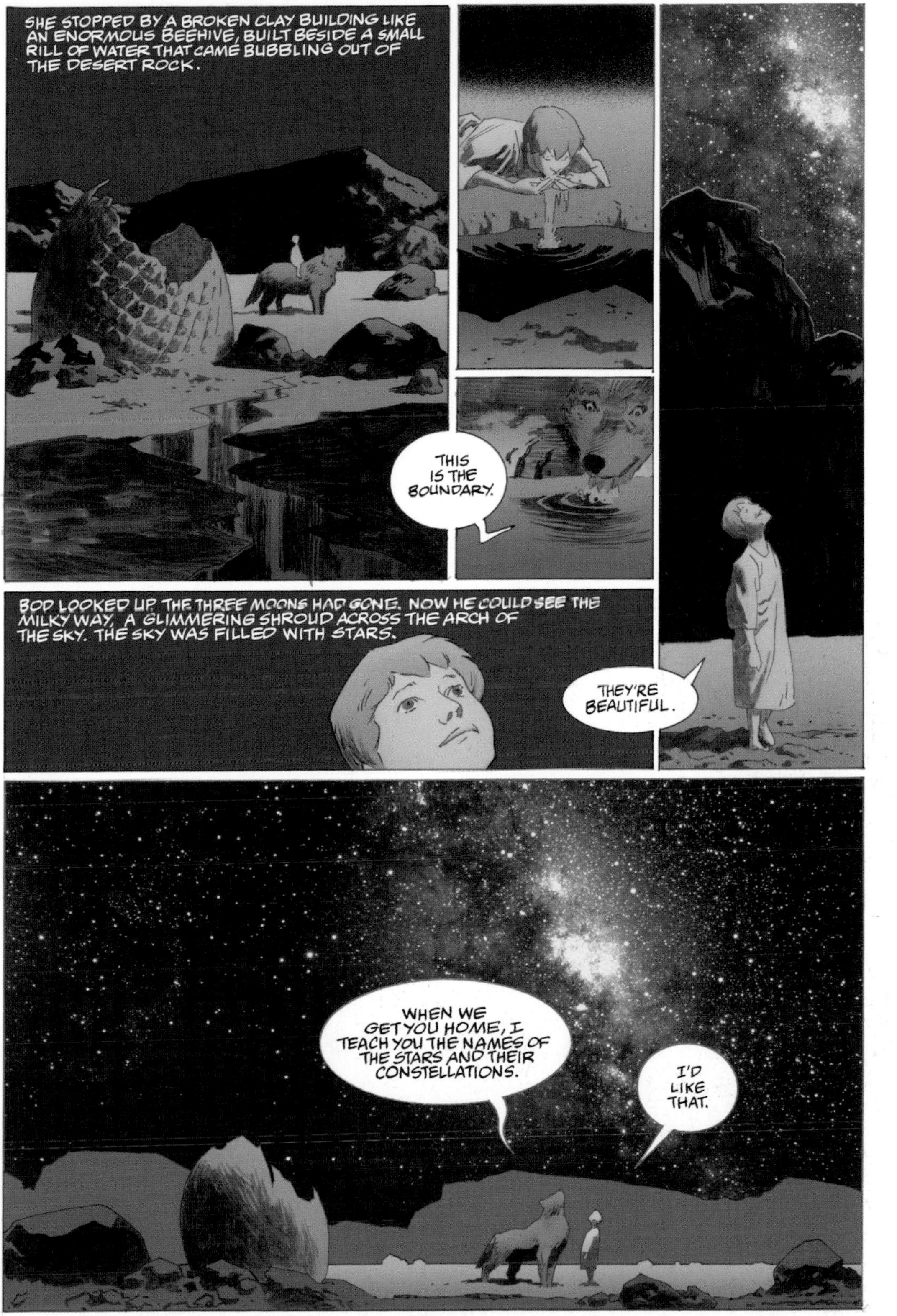
SHE STOPPED BY A BROKEN CLAY BUILDING LIKE AN ENORMOUS BEEHIVE, BUILT BESIDE A SMALL RILL OF WATER THAT CAME BUBBLING OUT OF THE DESERT ROCK.
THIS IS THE BOUNDARY.
BOD LOOKED UP. THE THREE MOONS HAD GONE. NOW HE COULD SEE THE MILKY WAY, A GLIMMERING SHROUD ACROSS THE ARCH OF THE SKY. THE SKY WAS FILLED WITH STARS.
THEY'RE BEAUTIFUL.
WHEN WE GET YOU HOME, I TEACH YOU THE NAMES OF THE STARS AND THEIR CONSTELLATIONS.
I'D LIKE THAT.

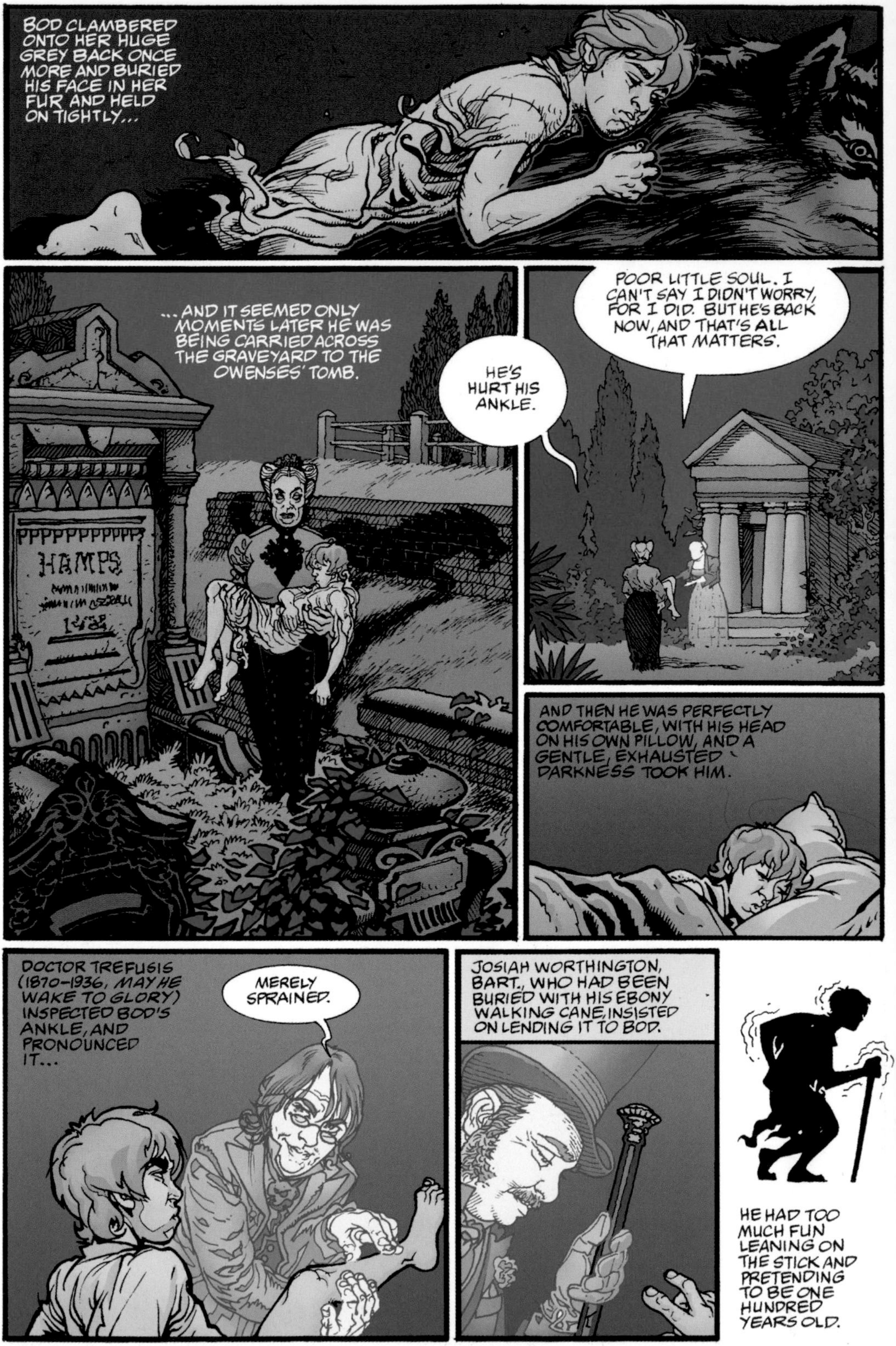

BOD CLAMBERED ONTO HER HUGE GREY BACK ONCE MORE AND BURIED HIS FACE IN HER FUR AND HELD ON TIGHTLY...
...AND IT SEEMED ONLY MOMENTS LATER HE WAS BEING CARRIED ACROSS THE GRAVEYARD TO THE OWENSES' TOMB.
HAMPS
HE'S HURT HIS ANKLE.
POOR LITTLE SOUL. I CAN'T SAY I DIDN'T WORRY, FOR I DID. BUT HE'S BACK NOW, AND THAT'S ALL THAT MATTERS.
AND THEN HE WAS PERFECTLY COMFORTABLE, WITH HIS HEAD ON HIS OWN PILLOW, AND A GENTLE, EXHAUSTED DARKNESS TOOK HIM.
DOCTOR TREFUSIS (1870–1936, MAY HE WAKE TO GLORY) INSPECTED BOD'S ANKLE, AND PRONOUNCED IT...
MERELY SPRAINED.
JOSIAH WORTHINGTON, BART., WHO HAD BEEN BURIED WITH HIS EBONY WALKING CANE, INSISTED ON LENDING IT TO BOD.
HE HAD TOO MUCH FUN LEANING ON THE STICK AND PRETENDING TO BE ONE HUNDRED YEARS OLD.

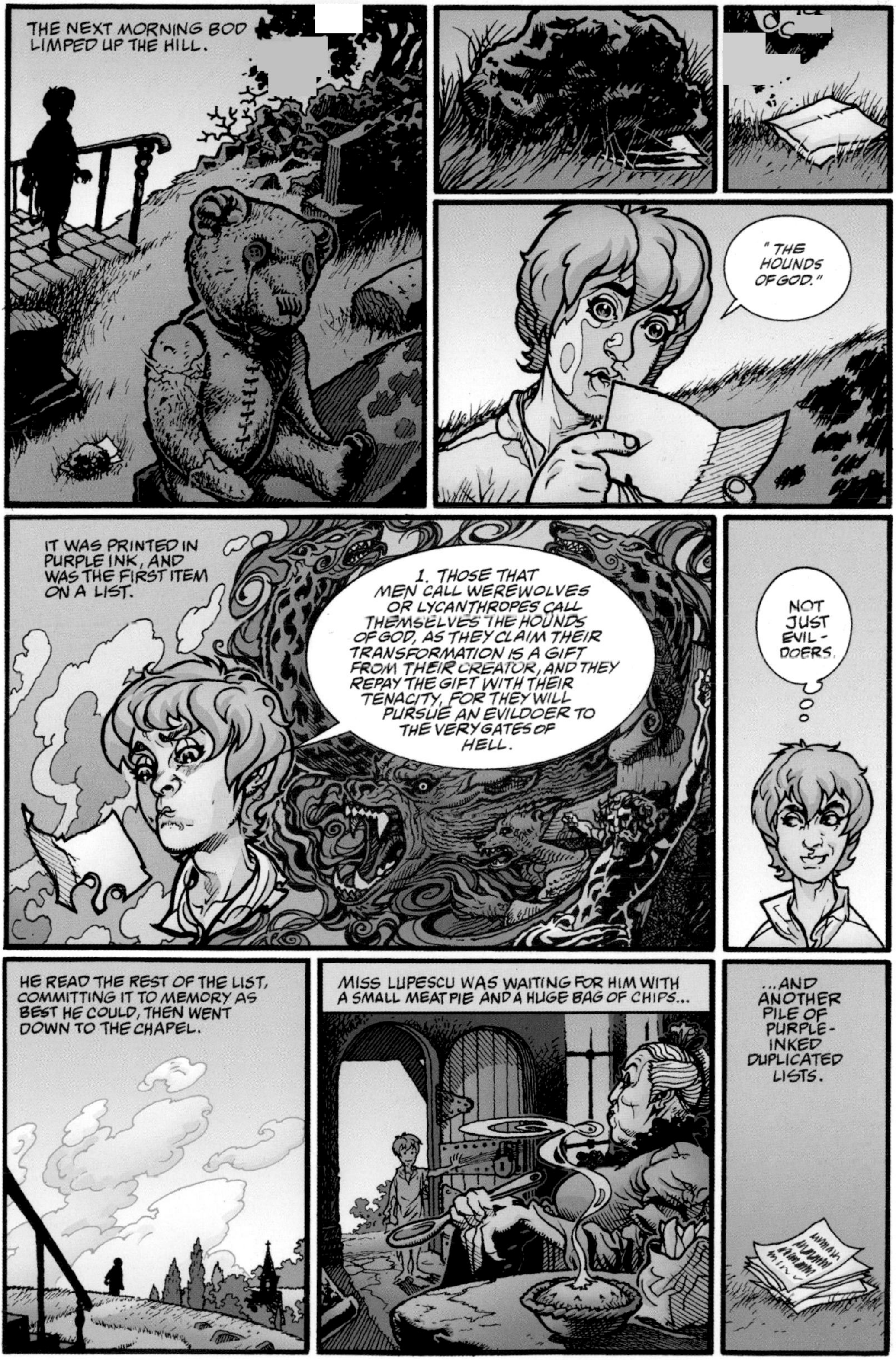

THE NEXT MORNING BOD LIMPED UP THE HILL.
"THE HOUNDS OF GOD."
IT WAS PRINTED IN PURPLE INK, AND WAS THE FIRST ITEM ON A LIST.
1. THOSE THAT MEN CALL WEREWOLVES OR LYCANTHROPES CALL THEMSELVES THE HOUNDS OF GOD, AS THEY CLAIM THEIR TRANSFORMATION IS A GIFT FROM THEIR CREATOR, AND THEY REPAY THE GIFT WITH THEIR TENACITY, FOR THEY WILL PURSUE AN EVILDOER TO THE VERY GATES OF HELL.
NOT JUST EVIL-DOERS.
HE READ THE REST OF THE LIST, COMMITTING IT TO MEMORY AS BEST HE COULD, THEN WENT DOWN TO THE CHAPEL.
MISS LUPESCU WAS WAITING FOR HIM WITH A SMALL MEAT PIE AND A HUGE BAG OF CHIPS...
...AND ANOTHER PILE OF PURPLE-INKED DUPLICATED LISTS.

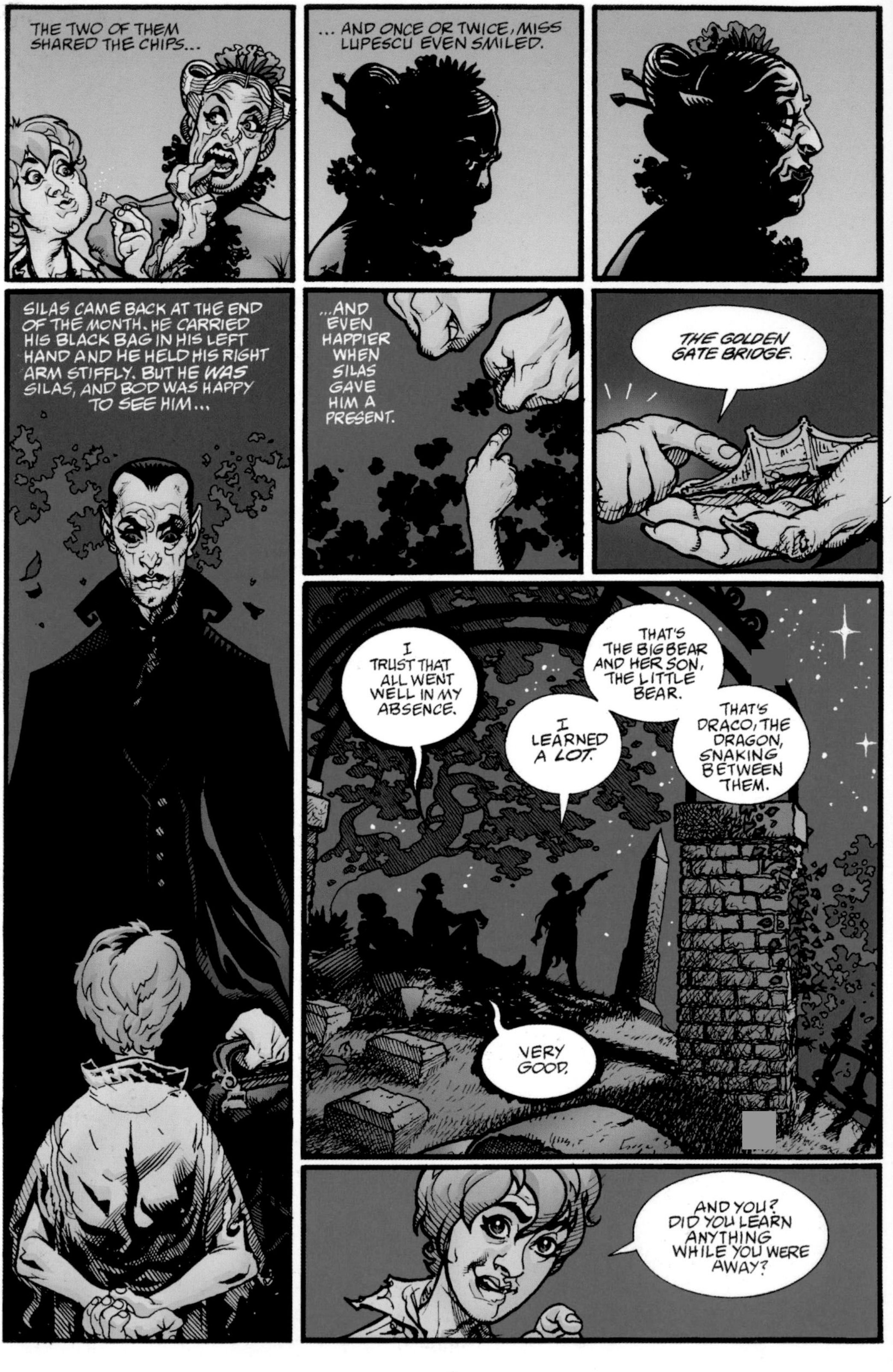
THE TWO OF THEM SHARED THE CHIPS...
... AND ONCE OR TWICE, MISS LUPESCU EVEN SMILED.
SILAS CAME BACK AT THE END OF THE MONTH. HE CARRIED HIS BLACK BAG IN HIS LEFT HAND AND HE HELD HIS RIGHT ARM STIFFLY. BUT HE WAS SILAS, AND BOD WAS HAPPY TO SEE HIM...
...AND EVEN HAPPIER WHEN SILAS GAVE HIM A PRESENT.
THE GOLDEN GATE BRIDGE.
I TRUST THAT ALL WENT WELL IN MY ABSENCE.
I LEARNED A LOT.
THAT'S THE BIG BEAR AND HER SON, THE LITTLE BEAR.
THAT'S DRACO, THE DRAGON, SNAKING BETWEEN THEM.
VERY GOOD.
AND YOU? DID YOU LEARN ANYTHING WHILE YOU WERE AWAY?

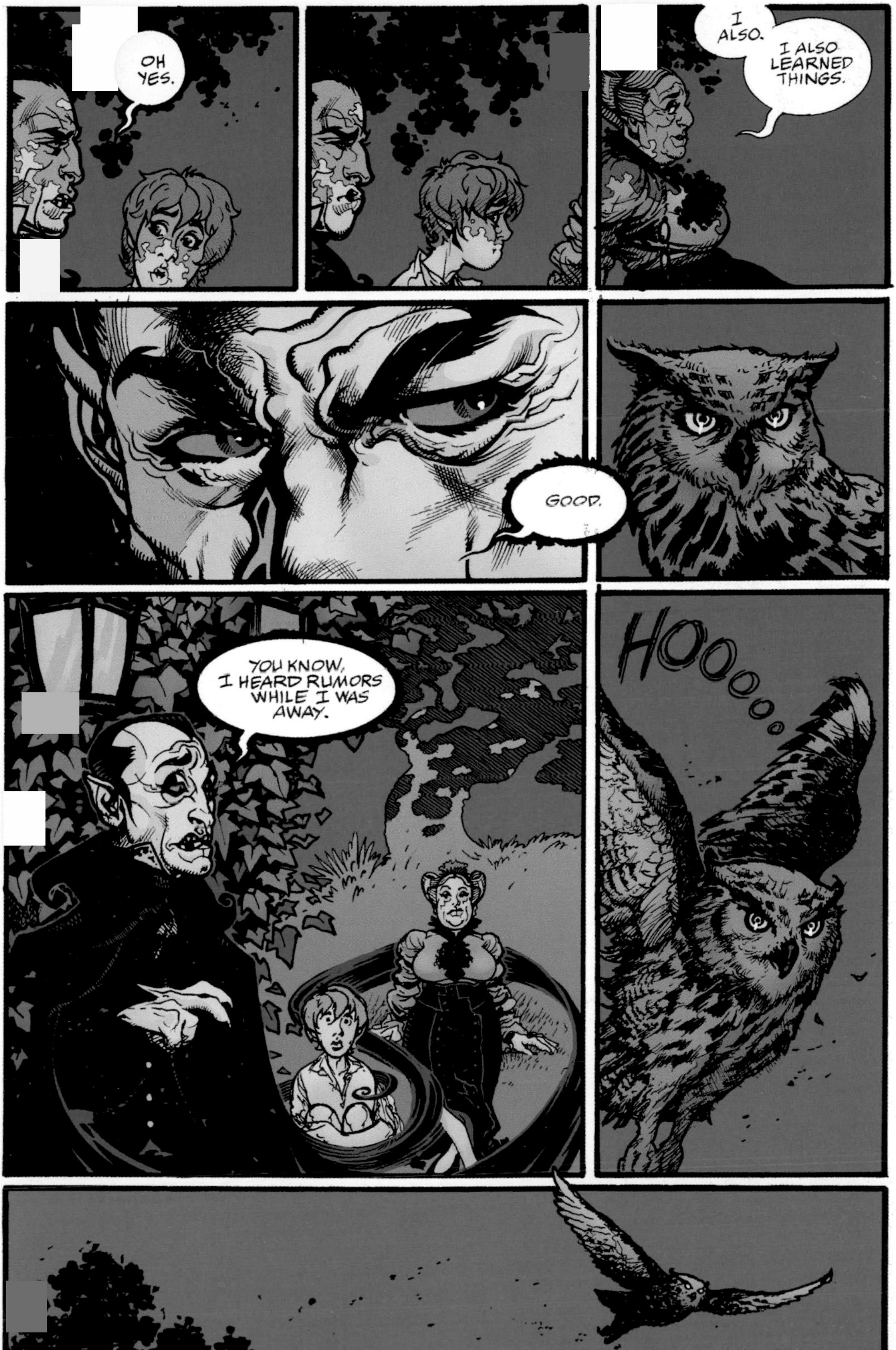
OH YES.
I ALSO.
I ALSO LEARNED THINGS.
GOOD.
YOU KNOW, I HEARD RUMORS WHILE I WAS AWAY.
HOOoooo

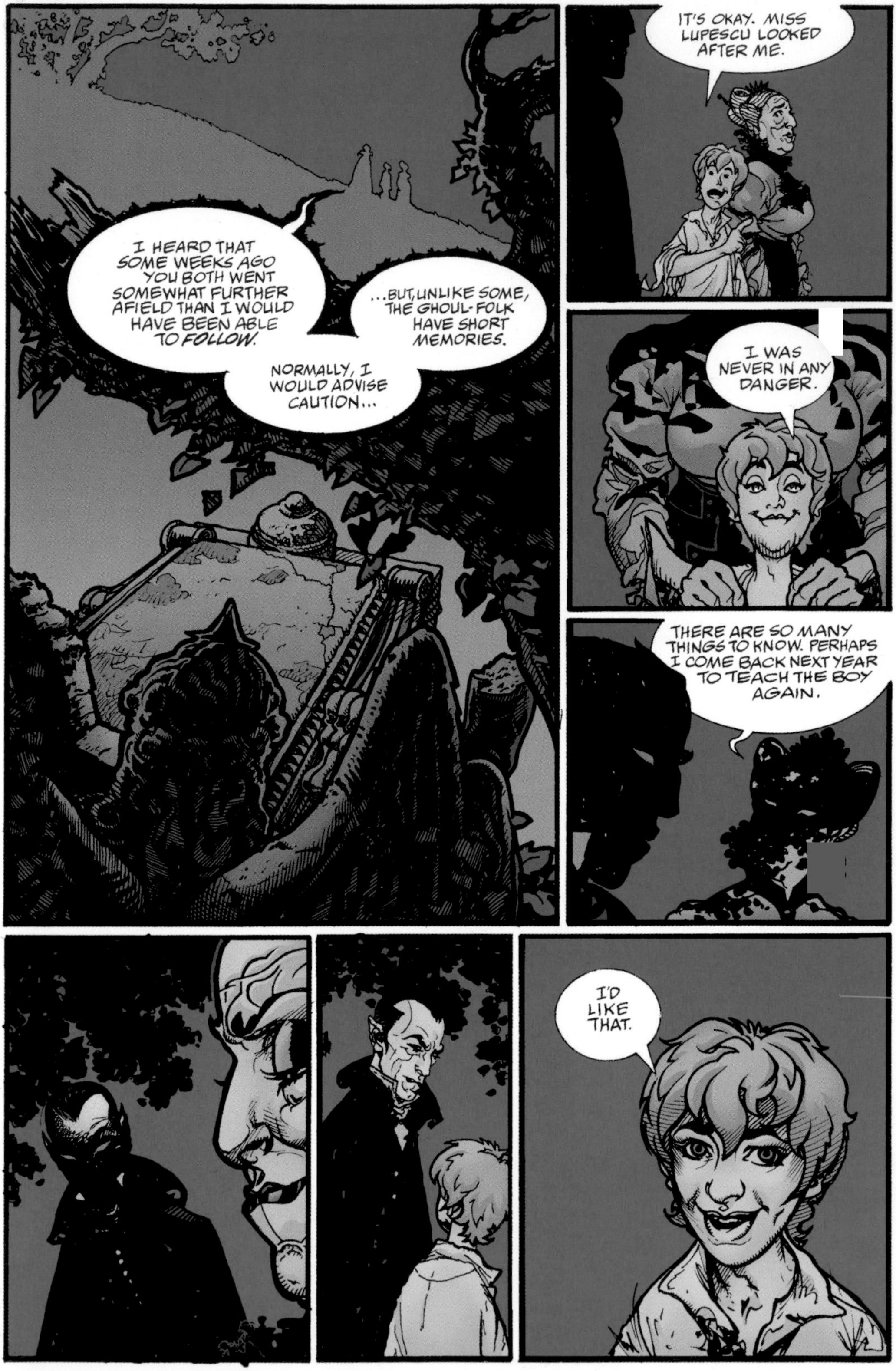
I HEARD THAT SOME WEEKS AGO YOU BOTH WENT SOMEWHAT FURTHER AFIELD THAN I WOULD HAVE BEEN ABLE TO FOLLOW.
NORMALLY, I WOULD ADVISE CAUTION...
...BUT, UNLIKE SOME, THE GHOUL-FOLK HAVE SHORT MEMORIES.
IT'S OKAY. MISS LUPESCU LOOKED AFTER ME.
I WAS NEVER IN ANY DANGER.
THERE ARE SO MANY THINGS TO KNOW. PERHAPS I COME BACK NEXT YEAR TO TEACH THE BOY AGAIN.
I'D LIKE THAT.

4
The Witch's Headstone

Illustrated by Galen Showman

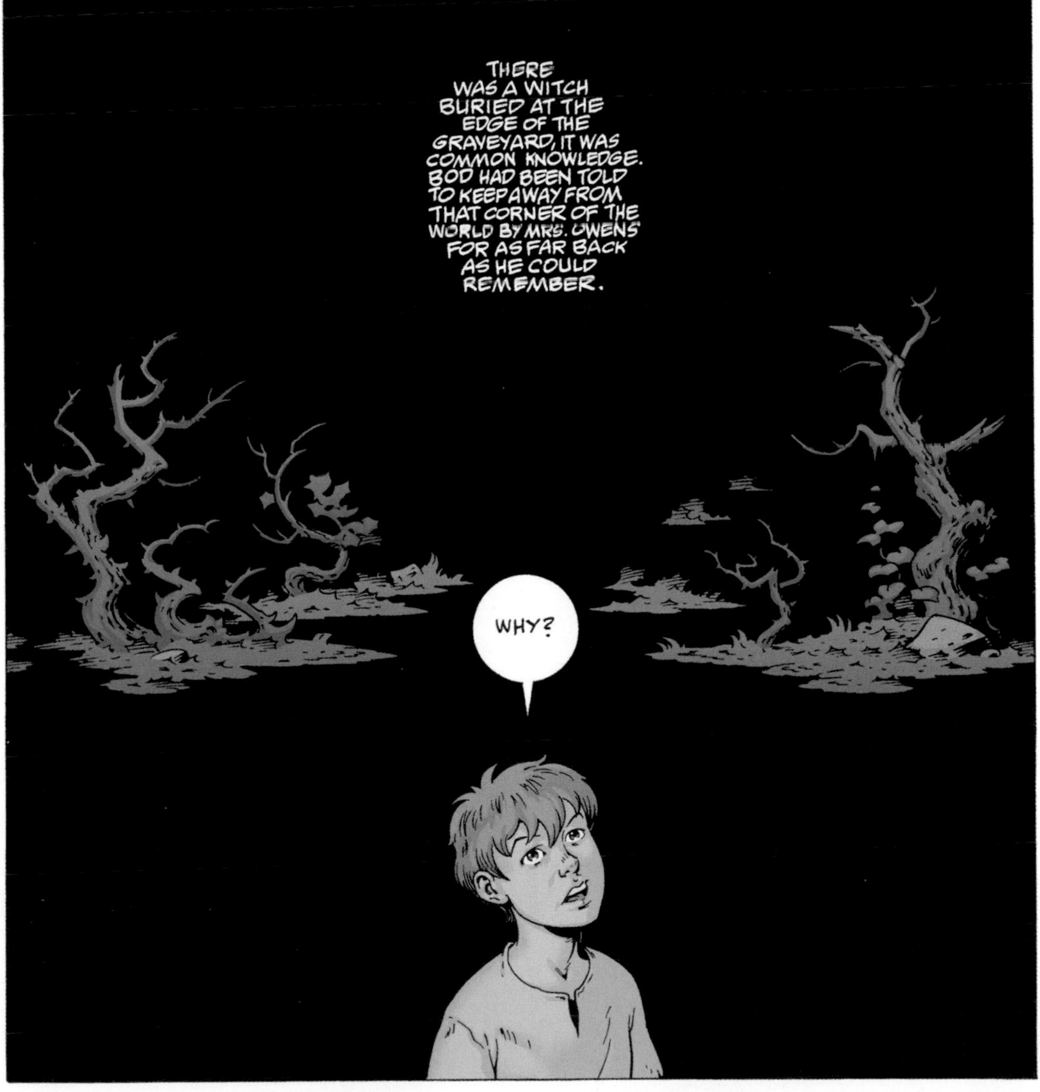
THERE WAS A WITCH BURIED AT THE EDGE OF THE GRAVEYARD, IT WAS COMMON KNOWLEDGE. BOD HAD BEEN TOLD TO KEEP AWAY FROM THAT CORNER OF THE WORLD BY MRS. OWENS FOR AS FAR BACK AS HE COULD REMEMBER.
WHY?

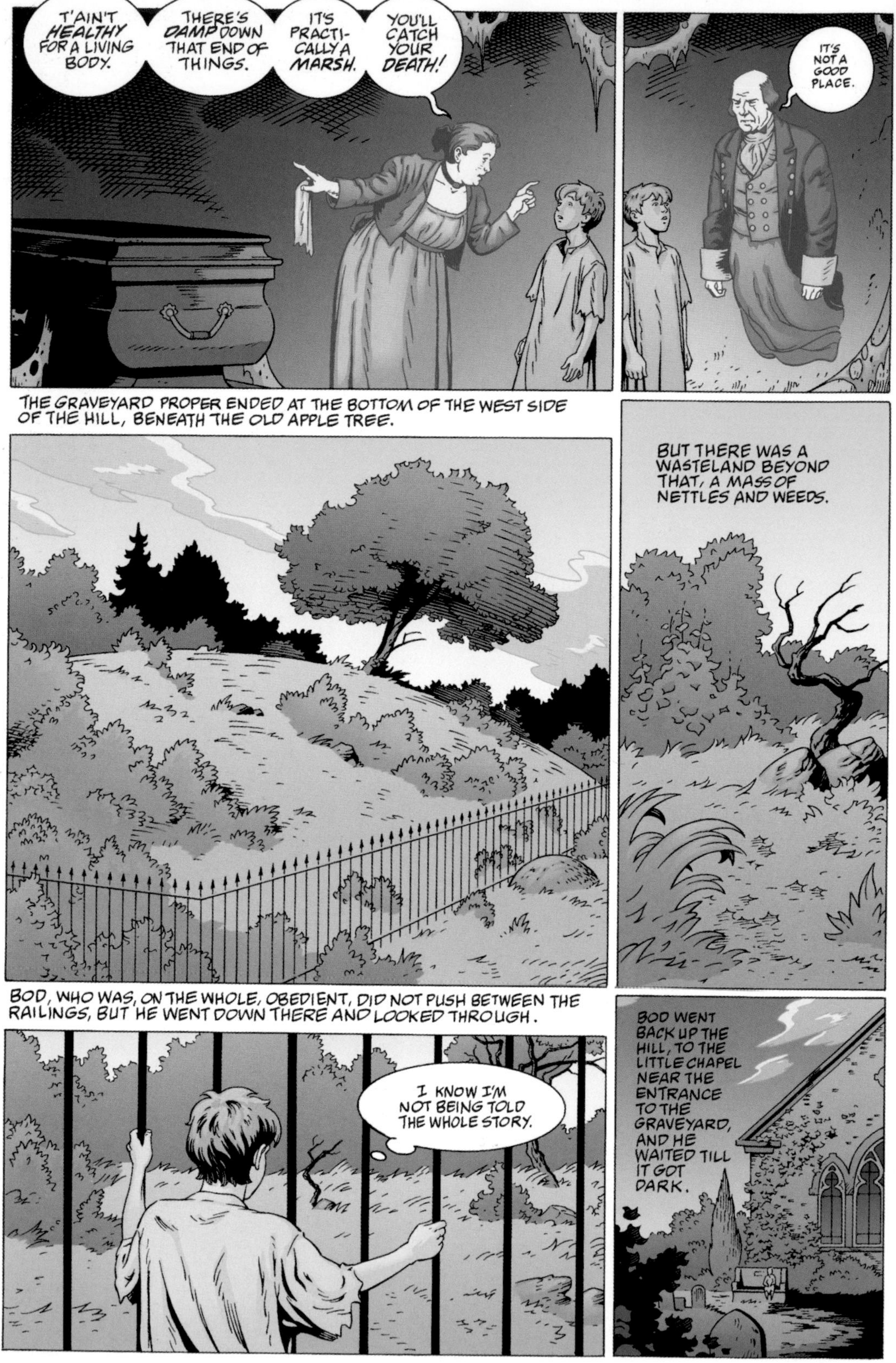
T'AIN'T HEALTHY FOR A LIVING BODY.
THERE'S DAMP DOWN THAT END OF THINGS.
IT'S PRACTI-CALLY A MARSH.
YOU'LL CATCH YOUR DEATH!
IT'S NOT A GOOD PLACE.
THE GRAVEYARD PROPER ENDED AT THE BOTTOM OF THE WEST SIDE OF THE HILL, BENEATH THE OLD APPLE TREE.
BUT THERE WAS A WASTELAND BEYOND THAT, A MASS OF NETTLES AND WEEDS.
BOD, WHO WAS, ON THE WHOLE, OBEDIENT, DID NOT PUSH BETWEEN THE RAILINGS, BUT HE WENT DOWN THERE AND LOOKED THROUGH.
I KNOW I'M NOT BEING TOLD THE WHOLE STORY.
BOD WENT BACK UP THE HILL, TO THE LITTLE CHAPEL NEAR THE ENTRANCE TO THE GRAVEYARD, AND HE WAITED TILL IT GOT DARK.

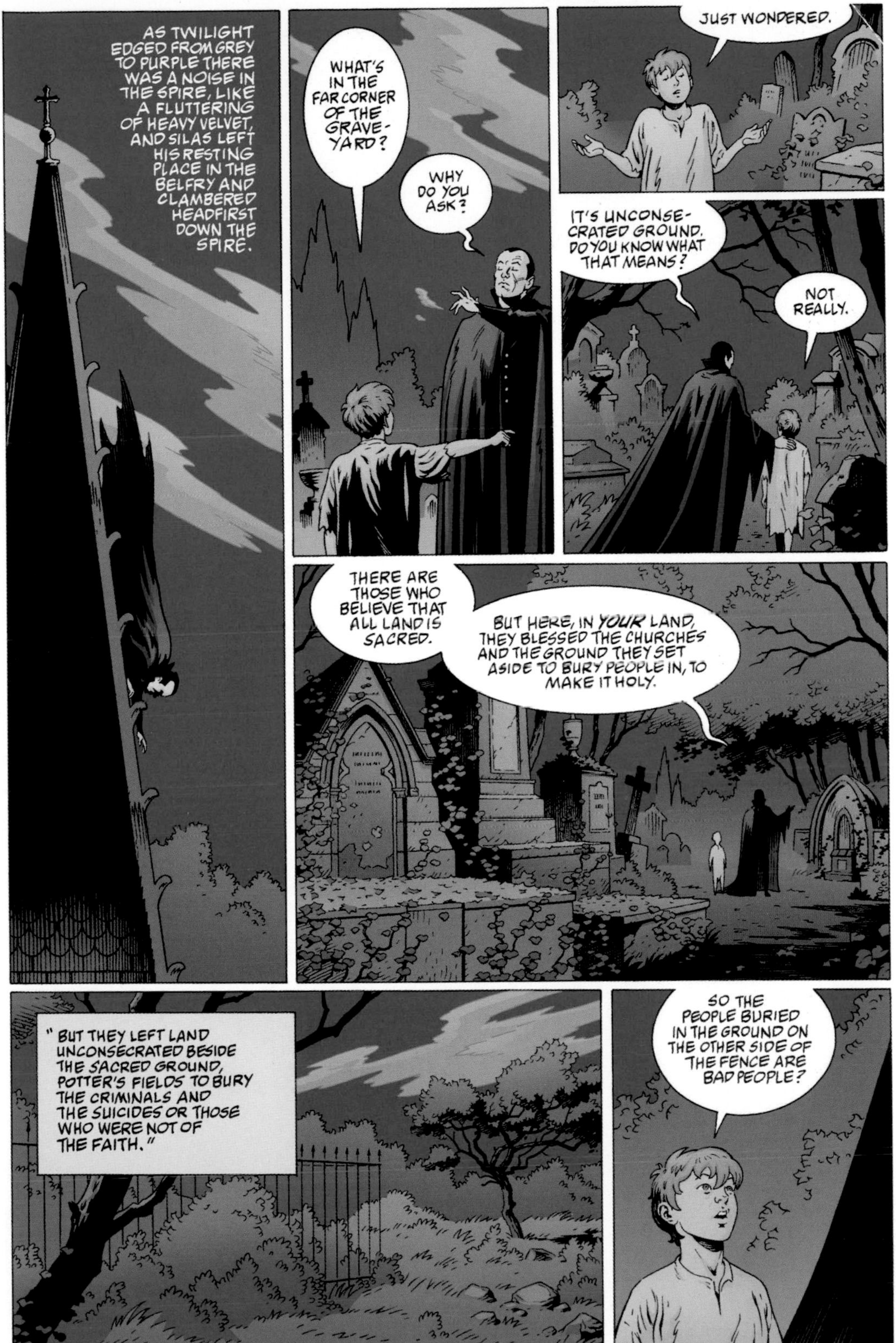
AS TWILIGHT EDGED FROM GREY TO PURPLE THERE WAS A NOISE IN THE SPIRE, LIKE A FLUTTERING OF HEAVY VELVET, AND SILAS LEFT HIS RESTING PLACE IN THE BELFRY AND CLAMBERED HEADFIRST DOWN THE SPIRE.
WHAT'S IN THE FAR CORNER OF THE GRAVE-YARD?
WHY DO YOU ASK?
JUST WONDERED.
IT'S UNCONSE-CRATED GROUND. DO YOU KNOW WHAT THAT MEANS?
NOT REALLY.
THERE ARE THOSE WHO BELIEVE THAT ALL LAND IS SACRED.
BUT HERE, IN YOUR LAND, THEY BLESSED THE CHURCHES AND THE GROUND THEY SET ASIDE TO BURY PEOPLE IN, TO MAKE IT HOLY.
"BUT THEY LEFT LAND UNCONSECRATED BESIDE THE SACRED GROUND, POTTER'S FIELDS TO BURY THE CRIMINALS AND THE SUICIDES OR THOSE WHO WERE NOT OF THE FAITH."
SO THE PEOPLE BURIED IN THE GROUND ON THE OTHER SIDE OF THE FENCE ARE BAD PEOPLE?

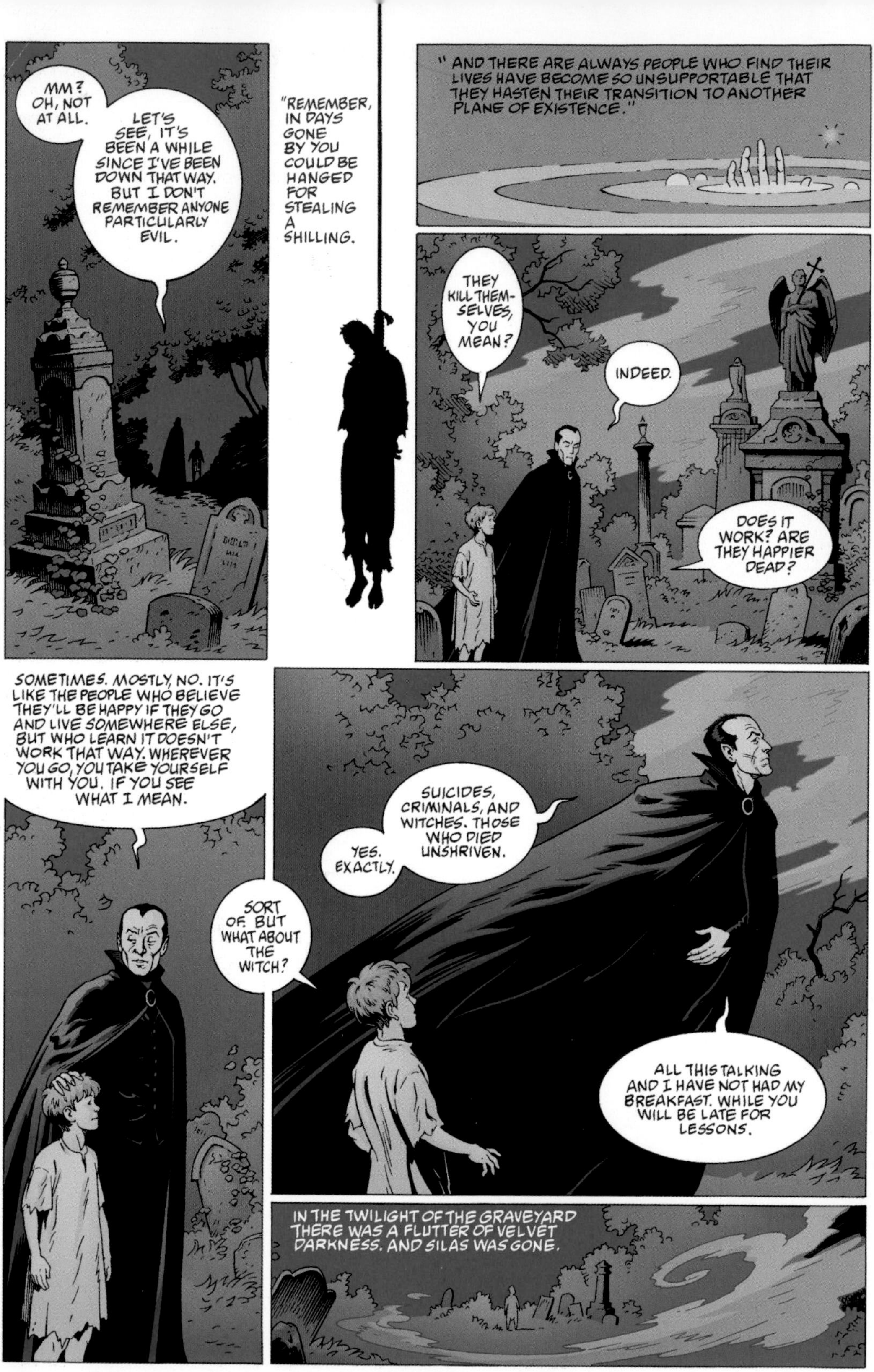
MM? OH, NOT AT ALL.
LET'S SEE, IT'S BEEN A WHILE SINCE I'VE BEEN DOWN THAT WAY. BUT I DON'T REMEMBER ANYONE PARTICULARLY EVIL.
"REMEMBER, IN DAYS GONE BY YOU COULD BE HANGED FOR STEALING A SHILLING.
"AND THERE ARE ALWAYS PEOPLE WHO FIND THEIR LIVES HAVE BECOME SO UNSUPPORTABLE THAT THEY HASTEN THEIR TRANSITION TO ANOTHER PLANE OF EXISTENCE."
THEY KILL THEMSELVES, YOU MEAN?
INDEED.
DOES IT WORK? ARE THEY HAPPIER DEAD?
SOMETIMES. MOSTLY, NO. IT'S LIKE THE PEOPLE WHO BELIEVE THEY'LL BE HAPPY IF THEY GO AND LIVE SOMEWHERE ELSE, BUT WHO LEARN IT DOESN'T WORK THAT WAY. WHEREVER YOU GO, YOU TAKE YOURSELF WITH YOU. IF YOU SEE WHAT I MEAN.
SORT OF. BUT WHAT ABOUT THE WITCH?
SUICIDES, CRIMINALS, AND WITCHES. THOSE WHO DIED UNSHRIVEN.
YES. EXACTLY.
ALL THIS TALKING AND I HAVE NOT HAD MY BREAKFAST. WHILE YOU WILL BE LATE FOR LESSONS.
IN THE TWILIGHT OF THE GRAVEYARD THERE WAS A FLUTTER OF VELVET DARKNESS. AND SILAS WAS GONE.

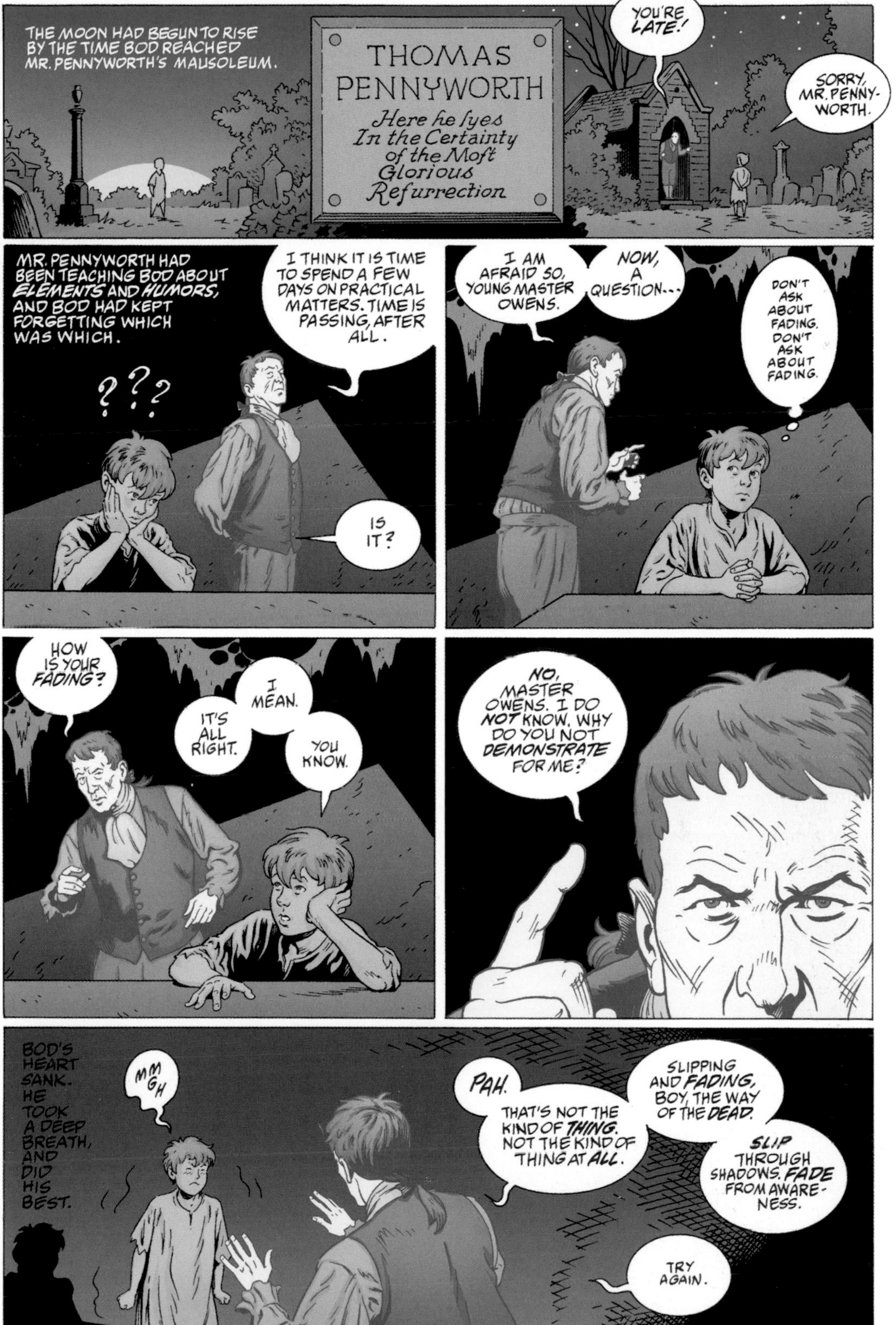
THE MOON HAD BEGUN TO RISE BY THE TIME BOD REACHED MR. PENNYWORTH'S MAUSOLEUM.
THOMAS PENNYWORTH
Here he lyes In the Certainty of the Moft Glorious Refurrection
YOU'RE LATE!
SORRY, MR. PENNY-WORTH.
MR. PENNYWORTH HAD BEEN TEACHING BOD ABOUT ELEMENTS AND HUMORS, AND BOD HAD KEPT FORGETTING WHICH WAS WHICH.
I THINK IT IS TIME TO SPEND A FEW DAYS ON PRACTICAL MATTERS. TIME IS PASSING, AFTER ALL.
???
IS IT?
I AM AFRAID SO, YOUNG MASTER OWENS.
NOW, A QUESTION...
DON'T ASK ABOUT FADING. DON'T ASK ABOUT FADING.
HOW IS YOUR FADING?
IT'S ALL RIGHT.
I MEAN.
YOU KNOW.
NO, MASTER OWENS. I DO NOT KNOW. WHY DO YOU NOT DEMONSTRATE FOR ME?
BOD'S HEART SANK. HE TOOK A DEEP BREATH, AND DID HIS BEST.
MMGH
PAH.
THAT'S NOT THE KIND OF THING. NOT THE KIND OF THING AT ALL.
SLIPPING AND FADING, BOY, THE WAY OF THE DEAD.
SLIP THROUGH SHADOWS. FADE FROM AWARE-NESS.
TRY AGAIN.

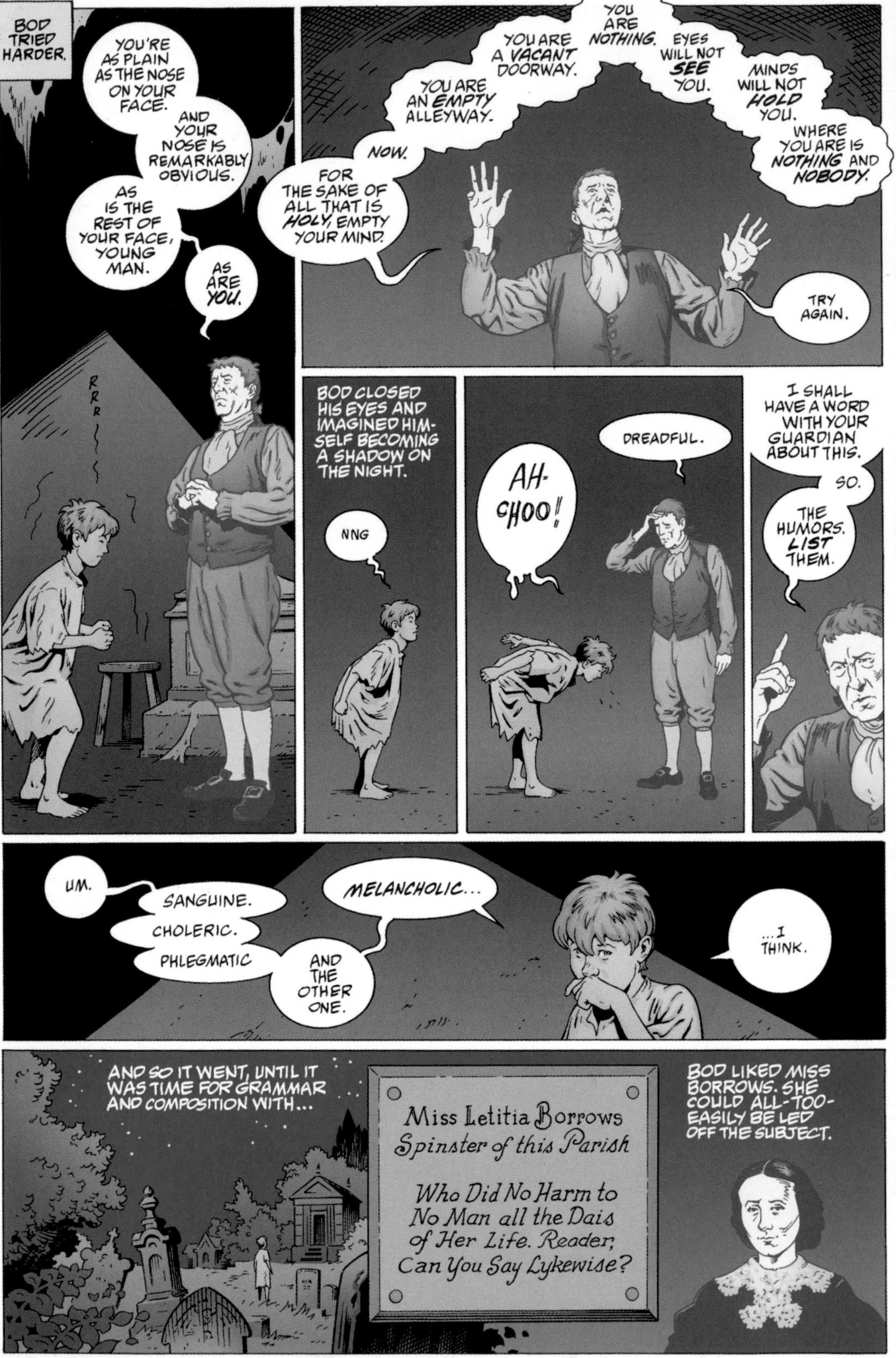
BOD TRIED HARDER.
YOU'RE AS PLAIN AS THE NOSE ON YOUR FACE.
AND YOUR NOSE IS REMARKABLY OBVIOUS.
AS IS THE REST OF YOUR FACE, YOUNG MAN.
AS ARE YOU.
RRR
FOR THE SAKE OF ALL THAT IS HOLY, EMPTY YOUR MIND.
NOW.
YOU ARE AN EMPTY ALLEYWAY.
YOU ARE A VACANT DOORWAY.
YOU ARE NOTHING.
EYES WILL NOT SEE YOU.
MINDS WILL NOT HOLD YOU.
WHERE YOU ARE IS NOTHING AND NOBODY.
TRY AGAIN.
BOD CLOSED HIS EYES AND IMAGINED HIMSELF BECOMING A SHADOW ON THE NIGHT.
NNG
AH-CHOO!
DREADFUL.
I SHALL HAVE A WORD WITH YOUR GUARDIAN ABOUT THIS.
SO.
THE HUMORS. LIST THEM.
UM.
SANGUINE.
CHOLERIC.
PHLEGMATIC
AND THE OTHER ONE.
MELANCHOLIC...
...I THINK.
AND SO IT WENT, UNTIL IT WAS TIME FOR GRAMMAR AND COMPOSITION WITH...
Miss Letitia Borrows
Spinster of this Parish
Who Did No Harm to No Man all the Dais of Her Life. Reader, Can You Say Lykewise?
BOD LIKED MISS BORROWS. SHE COULD ALL-TOO-EASILY BE LED OFF THE SUBJECT.

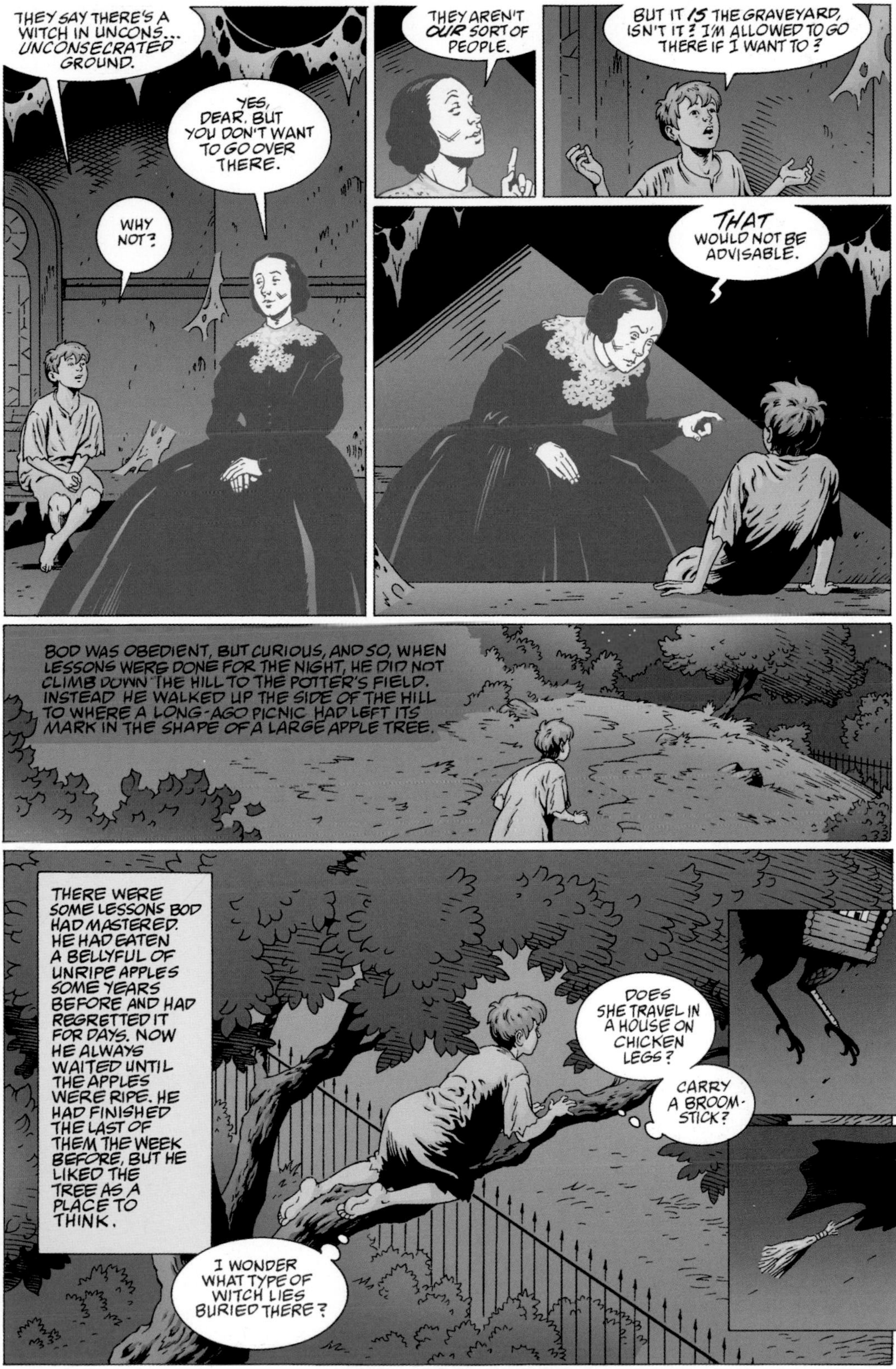
THEY SAY THERE'S A WITCH IN UNCONS... UNCONSECRATED GROUND.
YES, DEAR. BUT YOU DON'T WANT TO GO OVER THERE.
WHY NOT?
THEY AREN'T OUR SORT OF PEOPLE.
BUT IT IS THE GRAVEYARD, ISN'T IT? I'M ALLOWED TO GO THERE IF I WANT TO?
THAT WOULD NOT BE ADVISABLE.
BOD WAS OBEDIENT, BUT CURIOUS, AND SO, WHEN LESSONS WERE DONE FOR THE NIGHT, HE DID NOT CLIMB DOWN THE HILL TO THE POTTER'S FIELD. INSTEAD HE WALKED UP THE SIDE OF THE HILL TO WHERE A LONG-AGO PICNIC HAD LEFT ITS MARK IN THE SHAPE OF A LARGE APPLE TREE.
THERE WERE SOME LESSONS BOD HAD MASTERED. HE HAD EATEN A BELLYFUL OF UNRIPE APPLES SOME YEARS BEFORE AND HAD REGRETTED IT FOR DAYS. NOW HE ALWAYS WAITED UNTIL THE APPLES WERE RIPE. HE HAD FINISHED THE LAST OF THEM THE WEEK BEFORE, BUT HE LIKED THE TREE AS A PLACE TO THINK.
I WONDER WHAT TYPE OF WITCH LIES BURIED THERE?
DOES SHE TRAVEL IN A HOUSE ON CHICKEN LEGS?
CARRY A BROOM-STICK?

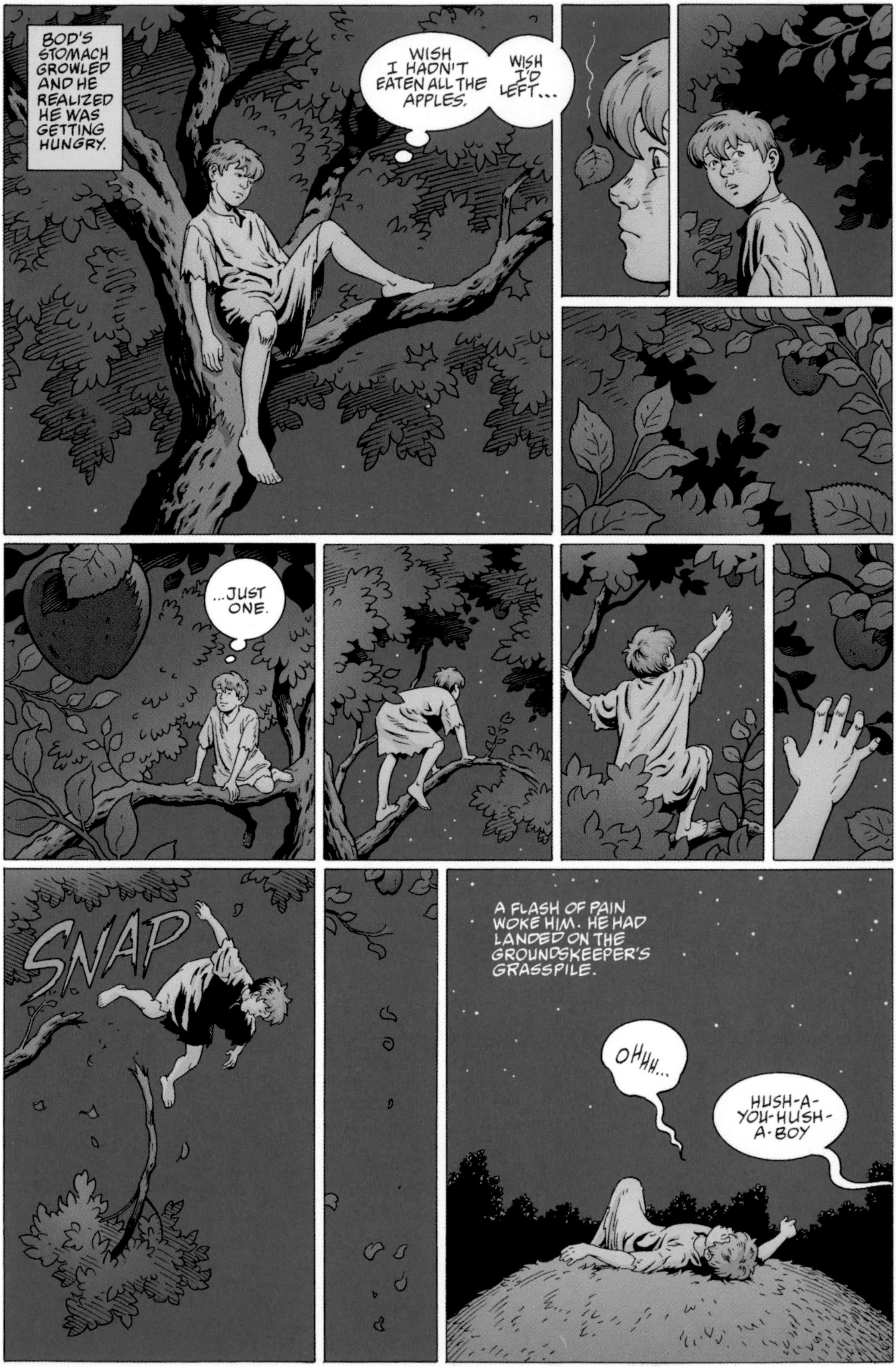
BOD'S STOMACH GROWLED AND HE REALIZED HE WAS GETTING HUNGRY.
WISH I HADN'T EATEN ALL THE APPLES.
WISH I'D LEFT...
...JUST ONE.
SNAP
A FLASH OF PAIN WOKE HIM. HE HAD LANDED ON THE GROUNDSKEEPER'S GRASSPILE.
OHHH...
HUSH-A-YOU-HUSH-A-BOY

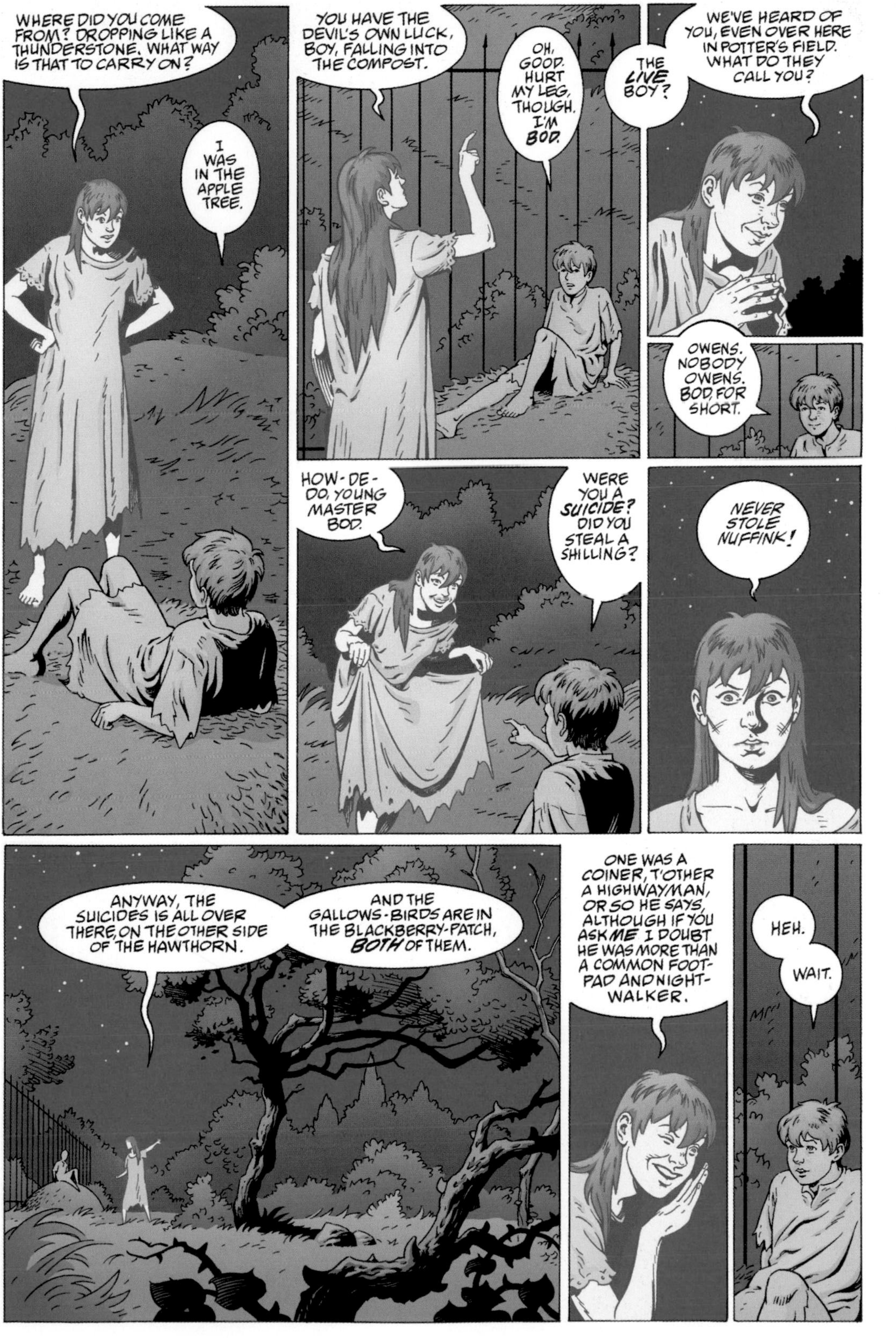

WHERE DID YOU COME FROM? DROPPING LIKE A THUNDERSTONE. WHAT WAY IS THAT TO CARRY ON?
I WAS IN THE APPLE TREE.
YOU HAVE THE DEVIL'S OWN LUCK, BOY, FALLING INTO THE COMPOST.
OH, GOOD. HURT MY LEG, THOUGH. I'M BOD.
WE'VE HEARD OF YOU, EVEN OVER HERE IN POTTER'S FIELD. WHAT DO THEY CALL YOU?
THE LIVE BOY?
OWENS. NOBODY OWENS. BOD, FOR SHORT.
HOW-DE-DO, YOUNG MASTER BOD.
WERE YOU A SUICIDE? DID YOU STEAL A SHILLING?
NEVER STOLE NUFFINK!
ANYWAY, THE SUICIDES IS ALL OVER THERE, ON THE OTHER SIDE OF THE HAWTHORN.
AND THE GALLOWS-BIRDS ARE IN THE BLACKBERRY-PATCH, BOTH OF THEM.
ONE WAS A COINER, T'OTHER A HIGHWAYMAN, OR SO HE SAYS, ALTHOUGH IF YOU ASK ME I DOUBT HE WAS MORE THAN A COMMON FOOT-PAD AND NIGHT-WALKER.
HEH.
WAIT.

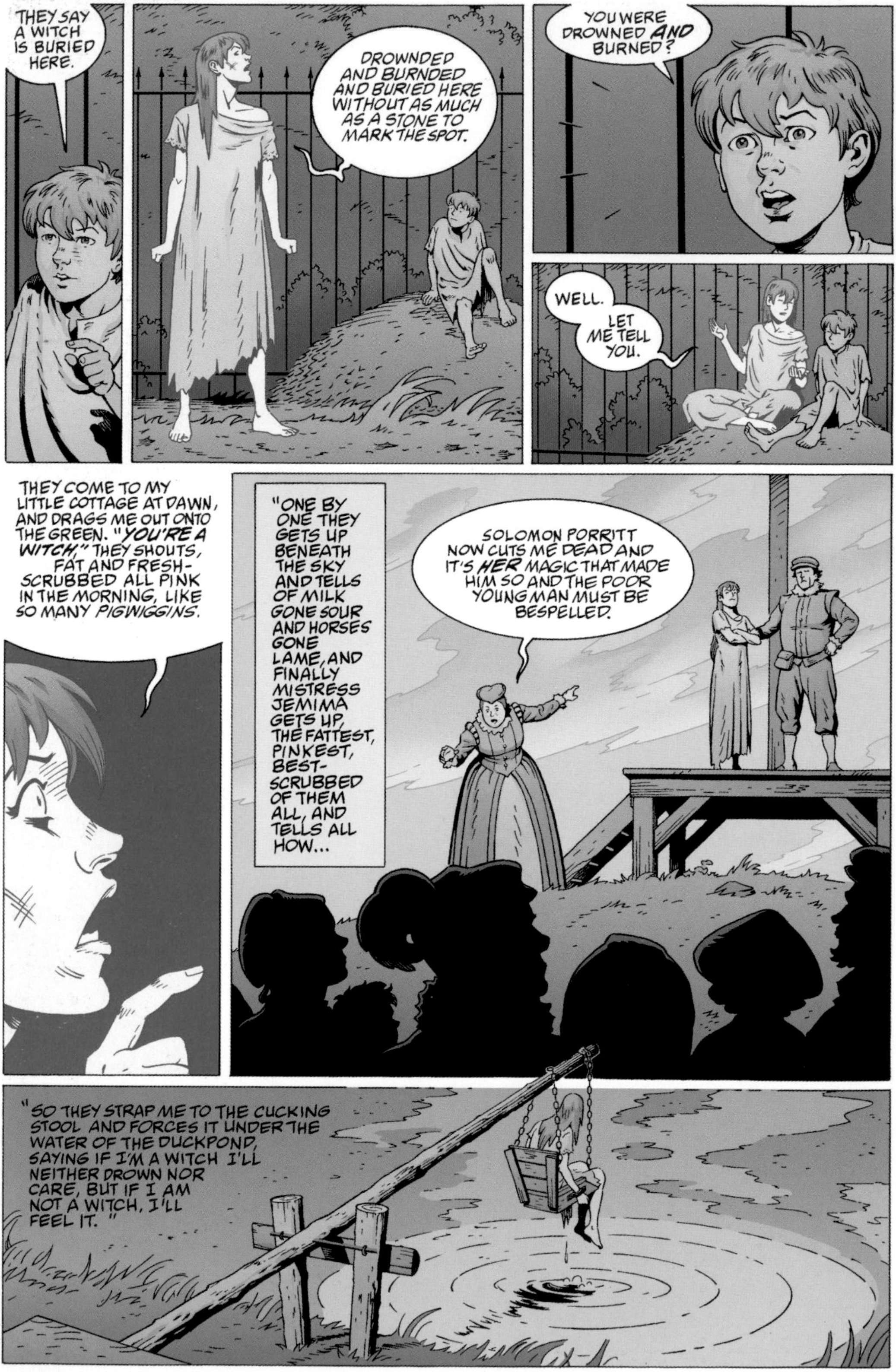

THEY SAY A WITCH IS BURIED HERE.
DROWNDED AND BURNDED AND BURIED HERE WITHOUT AS MUCH AS A STONE TO MARK THE SPOT.
YOU WERE DROWNED AND BURNED?
WELL.
LET ME TELL YOU.
THEY COME TO MY LITTLE COTTAGE AT DAWN, AND DRAGS ME OUT ONTO THE GREEN. "YOU'RE A WITCH," THEY SHOUTS, FAT AND FRESH-SCRUBBED ALL PINK IN THE MORNING, LIKE SO MANY PIGWIGGINS.
"ONE BY ONE THEY GETS UP BENEATH THE SKY AND TELLS OF MILK GONE SOUR AND HORSES GONE LAME, AND FINALLY MISTRESS JEMIMA GETS UP, THE FATTEST, PINKEST, BEST-SCRUBBED OF THEM ALL, AND TELLS ALL HOW...
SOLOMON PORRITT NOW CUTS ME DEAD AND IT'S HER MAGIC THAT MADE HIM SO AND THE POOR YOUNG MAN MUST BE BESPELLED.
"SO THEY STRAP ME TO THE CUCKING STOOL AND FORCES IT UNDER THE WATER OF THE DUCKPOND, SAYING IF I'M A WITCH I'LL NEITHER DROWN NOR CARE, BUT IF I AM NOT A WITCH, I'LL FEEL IT."

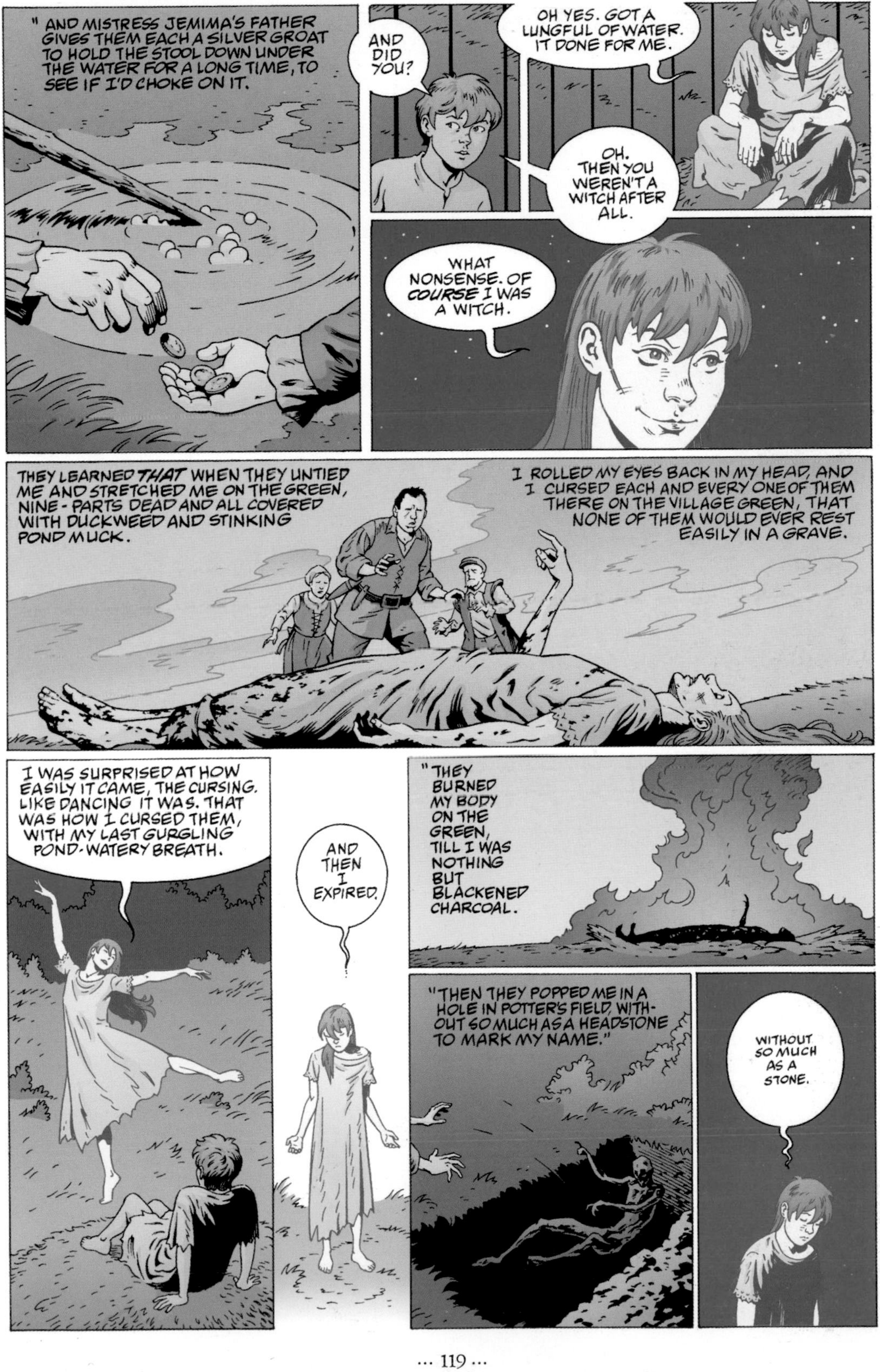
"AND MISTRESS JEMIMA'S FATHER GIVES THEM EACH A SILVER GROAT TO HOLD THE STOOL DOWN UNDER THE WATER FOR A LONG TIME, TO SEE IF I'D CHOKE ON IT.
AND DID YOU?
OH YES. GOT A LUNGFUL OF WATER. IT DONE FOR ME.
OH. THEN YOU WEREN'T A WITCH AFTER ALL.
WHAT NONSENSE. OF COURSE I WAS A WITCH.
THEY LEARNED THAT WHEN THEY UNTIED ME AND STRETCHED ME ON THE GREEN, NINE-PARTS DEAD AND ALL COVERED WITH DUCKWEED AND STINKING POND MUCK.
I ROLLED MY EYES BACK IN MY HEAD, AND I CURSED EACH AND EVERY ONE OF THEM THERE ON THE VILLAGE GREEN, THAT NONE OF THEM WOULD EVER REST EASILY IN A GRAVE.
I WAS SURPRISED AT HOW EASILY IT CAME, THE CURSING. LIKE DANCING IT WAS. THAT WAS HOW I CURSED THEM, WITH MY LAST GURGLING POND-WATERY BREATH.
AND THEN I EXPIRED.
"THEY BURNED MY BODY ON THE GREEN, TILL I WAS NOTHING BUT BLACKENED CHARCOAL.
"THEN THEY POPPED ME IN A HOLE IN POTTER'S FIELD, WITHOUT SO MUCH AS A HEADSTONE TO MARK MY NAME."
WITHOUT SO MUCH AS A STONE.

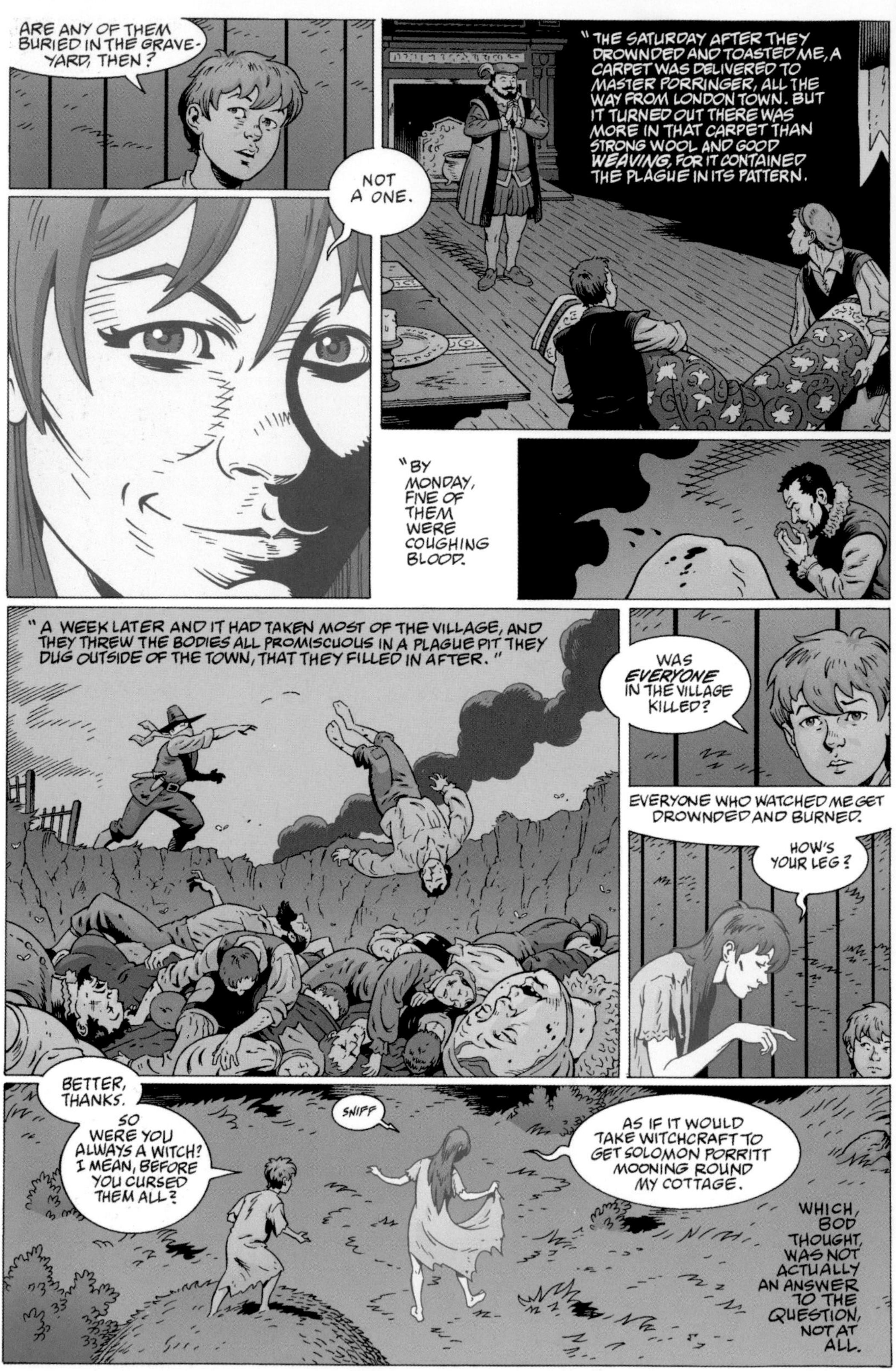
ARE ANY OF THEM BURIED IN THE GRAVE-YARD, THEN?
"THE SATURDAY AFTER THEY DROWNDED AND TOASTED ME, A CARPET WAS DELIVERED TO MASTER PORRINGER, ALL THE WAY FROM LONDON TOWN. BUT IT TURNED OUT THERE WAS MORE IN THAT CARPET THAN STRONG WOOL AND GOOD WEAVING, FOR IT CONTAINED THE PLAGUE IN ITS PATTERN.
NOT A ONE.
"BY MONDAY, FIVE OF THEM WERE COUGHING BLOOD.
"A WEEK LATER AND IT HAD TAKEN MOST OF THE VILLAGE, AND THEY THREW THE BODIES ALL PROMISCUOUS IN A PLAGUE PIT THEY DUG OUTSIDE OF THE TOWN, THAT THEY FILLED IN AFTER."
WAS EVERYONE IN THE VILLAGE KILLED?
EVERYONE WHO WATCHED ME GET DROWNDED AND BURNED.
HOW'S YOUR LEG?
BETTER, THANKS.
SO WERE YOU ALWAYS A WITCH? I MEAN, BEFORE YOU CURSED THEM ALL?
SNIFF
AS IF IT WOULD TAKE WITCHCRAFT TO GET SOLOMON PORRITT MOONING ROUND MY COTTAGE.
WHICH, BOD THOUGHT, WAS NOT ACTUALLY AN ANSWER TO THE QUESTION, NOT AT ALL.

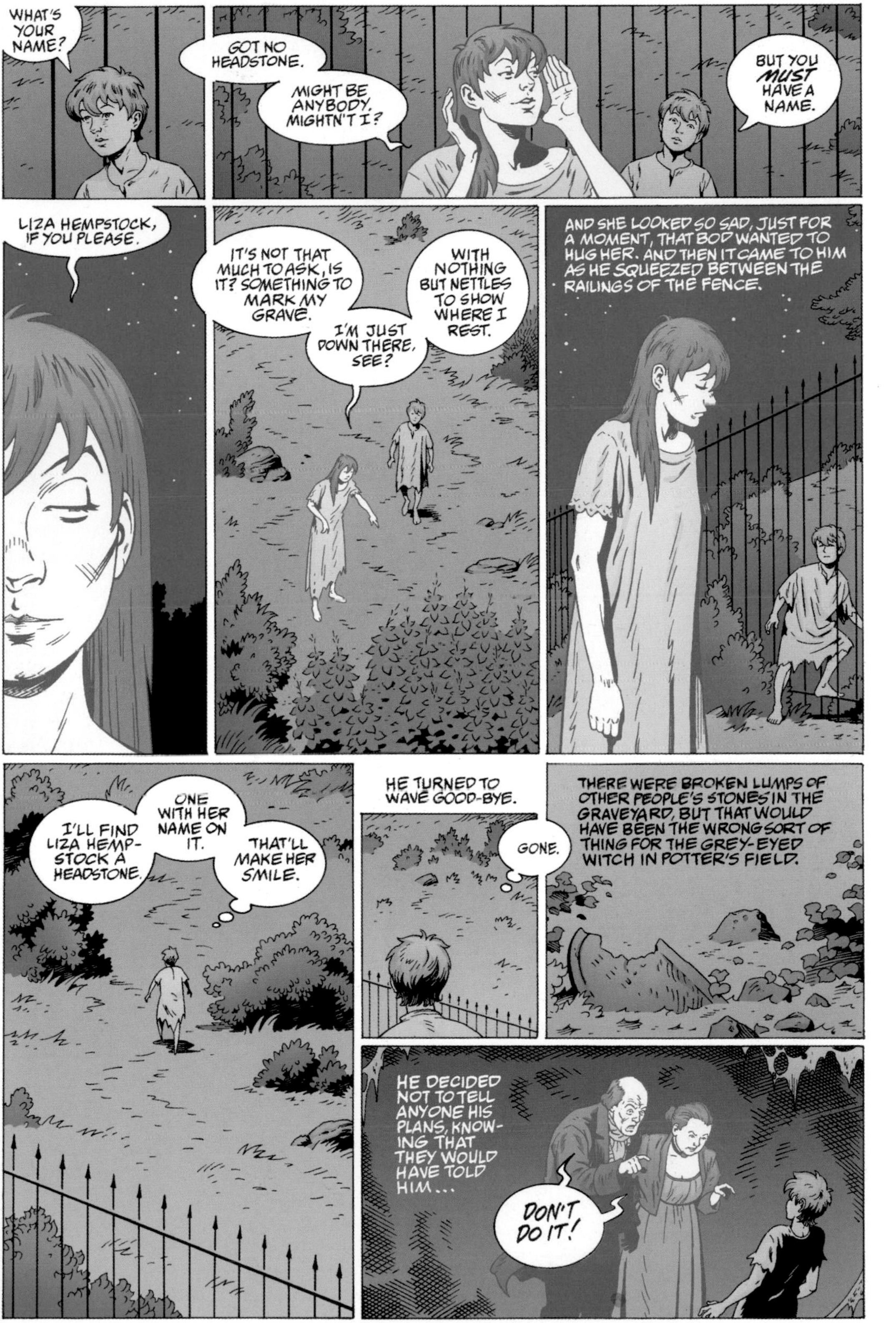
WHAT'S YOUR NAME?
GOT NO HEADSTONE.
MIGHT BE ANYBODY. MIGHTN'T I?
BUT YOU MUST HAVE A NAME.
LIZA HEMPSTOCK, IF YOU PLEASE.
IT'S NOT THAT MUCH TO ASK, IS IT? SOMETHING TO MARK MY GRAVE.
WITH NOTHING BUT NETTLES TO SHOW WHERE I REST.
I'M JUST DOWN THERE, SEE?
AND SHE LOOKED SO SAD, JUST FOR A MOMENT, THAT BOD WANTED TO HUG HER. AND THEN IT CAME TO HIM AS HE SQUEEZED BETWEEN THE RAILINGS OF THE FENCE.
I'LL FIND LIZA HEMPSTOCK A HEADSTONE.
ONE WITH HER NAME ON IT.
THAT'LL MAKE HER SMILE.
HE TURNED TO WAVE GOOD-BYE.
GONE.
THERE WERE BROKEN LUMPS OF OTHER PEOPLE'S STONES IN THE GRAVEYARD, BUT THAT WOULD HAVE BEEN THE WRONG SORT OF THING FOR THE GREY-EYED WITCH IN POTTER'S FIELD.
HE DECIDED NOT TO TELL ANYONE HIS PLANS, KNOWING THAT THEY WOULD HAVE TOLD HIM...
DON'T DO IT!

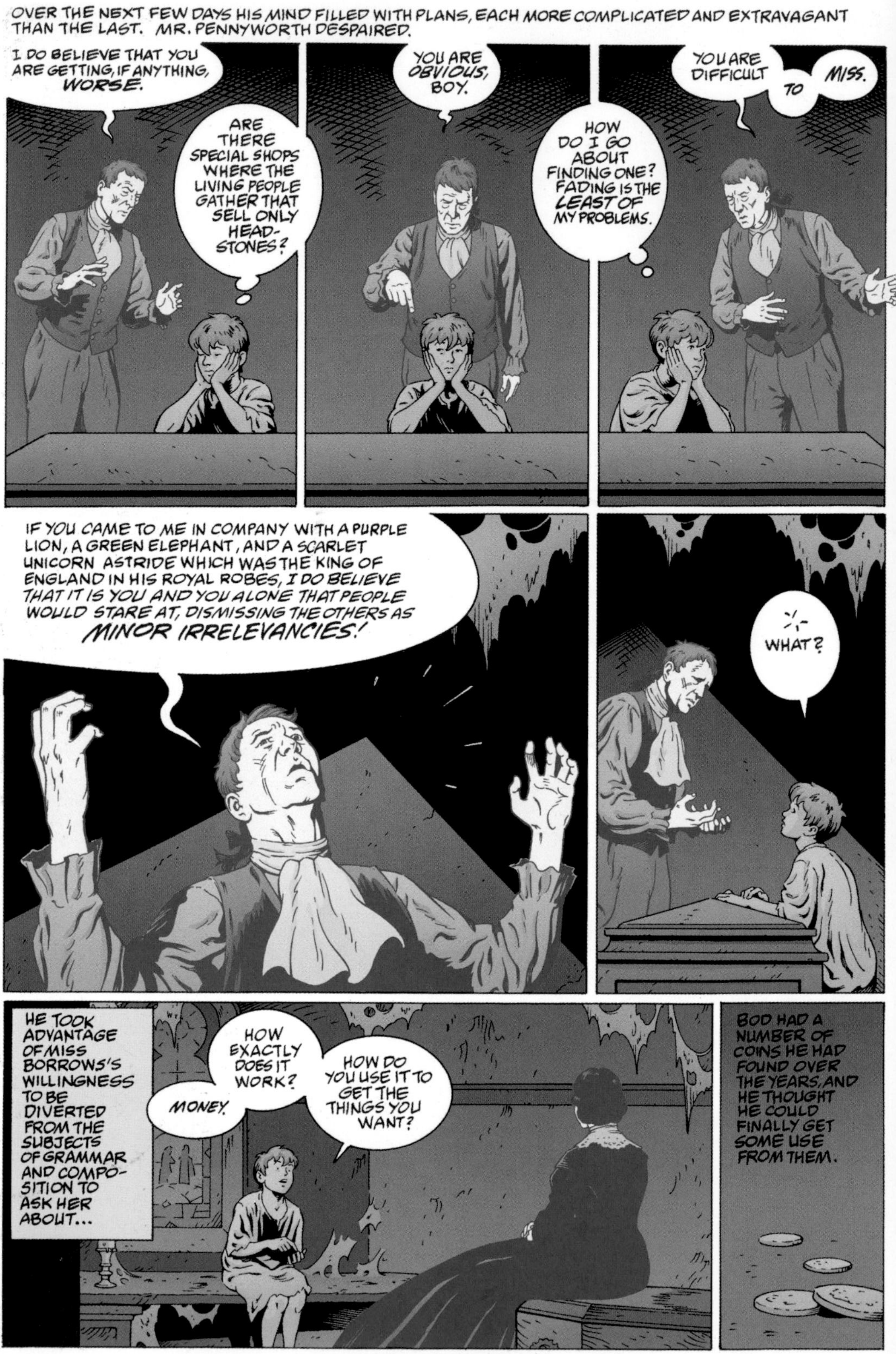

OVER THE NEXT FEW DAYS HIS MIND FILLED WITH PLANS, EACH MORE COMPLICATED AND EXTRAVAGANT THAN THE LAST. MR. PENNYWORTH DESPAIRED.
I DO BELIEVE THAT YOU ARE GETTING, IF ANYTHING, WORSE.
ARE THERE SPECIAL SHOPS WHERE THE LIVING PEOPLE GATHER THAT SELL ONLY HEAD-STONES?
YOU ARE OBVIOUS, BOY.
HOW DO I GO ABOUT FINDING ONE? FADING IS THE LEAST OF MY PROBLEMS.
YOU ARE DIFFICULT
TO
MISS.
IF YOU CAME TO ME IN COMPANY WITH A PURPLE LION, A GREEN ELEPHANT, AND A SCARLET UNICORN ASTRIDE WHICH WAS THE KING OF ENGLAND IN HIS ROYAL ROBES, I DO BELIEVE THAT IT IS YOU AND YOU ALONE THAT PEOPLE WOULD STARE AT, DISMISSING THE OTHERS AS MINOR IRRELEVANCIES!
WHAT?
HE TOOK ADVANTAGE OF MISS BORROWS'S WILLINGNESS TO BE DIVERTED FROM THE SUBJECTS OF GRAMMAR AND COMPO-SITION TO ASK HER ABOUT...
MONEY.
HOW EXACTLY DOES IT WORK?
HOW DO YOU USE IT TO GET THE THINGS YOU WANT?
BOD HAD A NUMBER OF COINS HE HAD FOUND OVER THE YEARS, AND HE THOUGHT HE COULD FINALLY GET SOME USE FROM THEM.

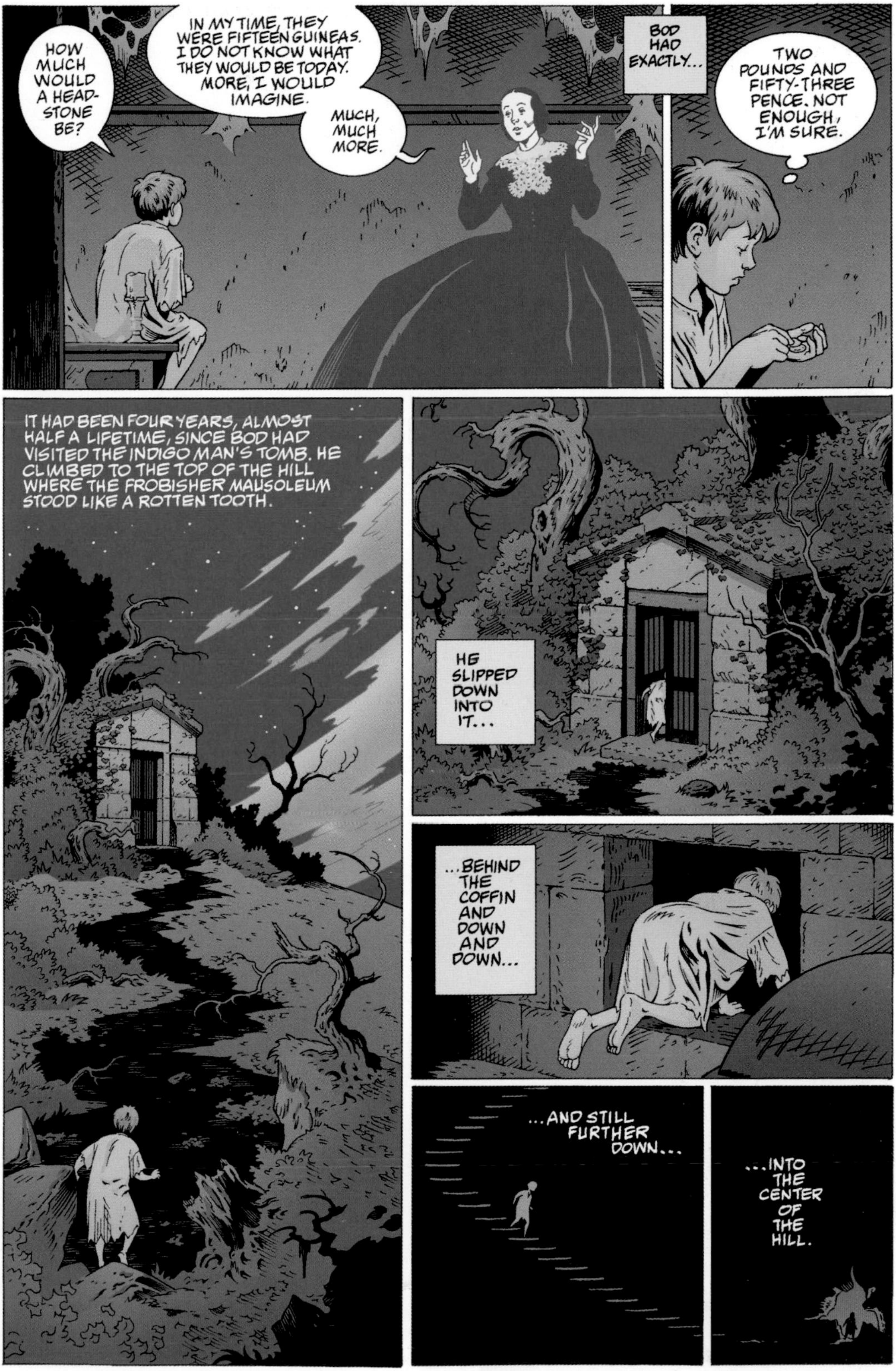
HOW MUCH WOULD A HEAD-STONE BE?
IN MY TIME, THEY WERE FIFTEEN GUINEAS. I DO NOT KNOW WHAT THEY WOULD BE TODAY. MORE, I WOULD IMAGINE.
MUCH, MUCH MORE.
BOD HAD EXACTLY...
TWO POUNDS AND FIFTY-THREE PENCE. NOT ENOUGH, I'M SURE.
IT HAD BEEN FOUR YEARS, ALMOST HALF A LIFETIME, SINCE BOD HAD VISITED THE INDIGO MAN'S TOMB. HE CLIMBED TO THE TOP OF THE HILL WHERE THE FROBISHER MAUSOLEUM STOOD LIKE A ROTTEN TOOTH.
HE SLIPPED DOWN INTO IT...
...BEHIND THE COFFIN AND DOWN AND DOWN...
...AND STILL FURTHER DOWN...
...INTO THE CENTER OF THE HILL.

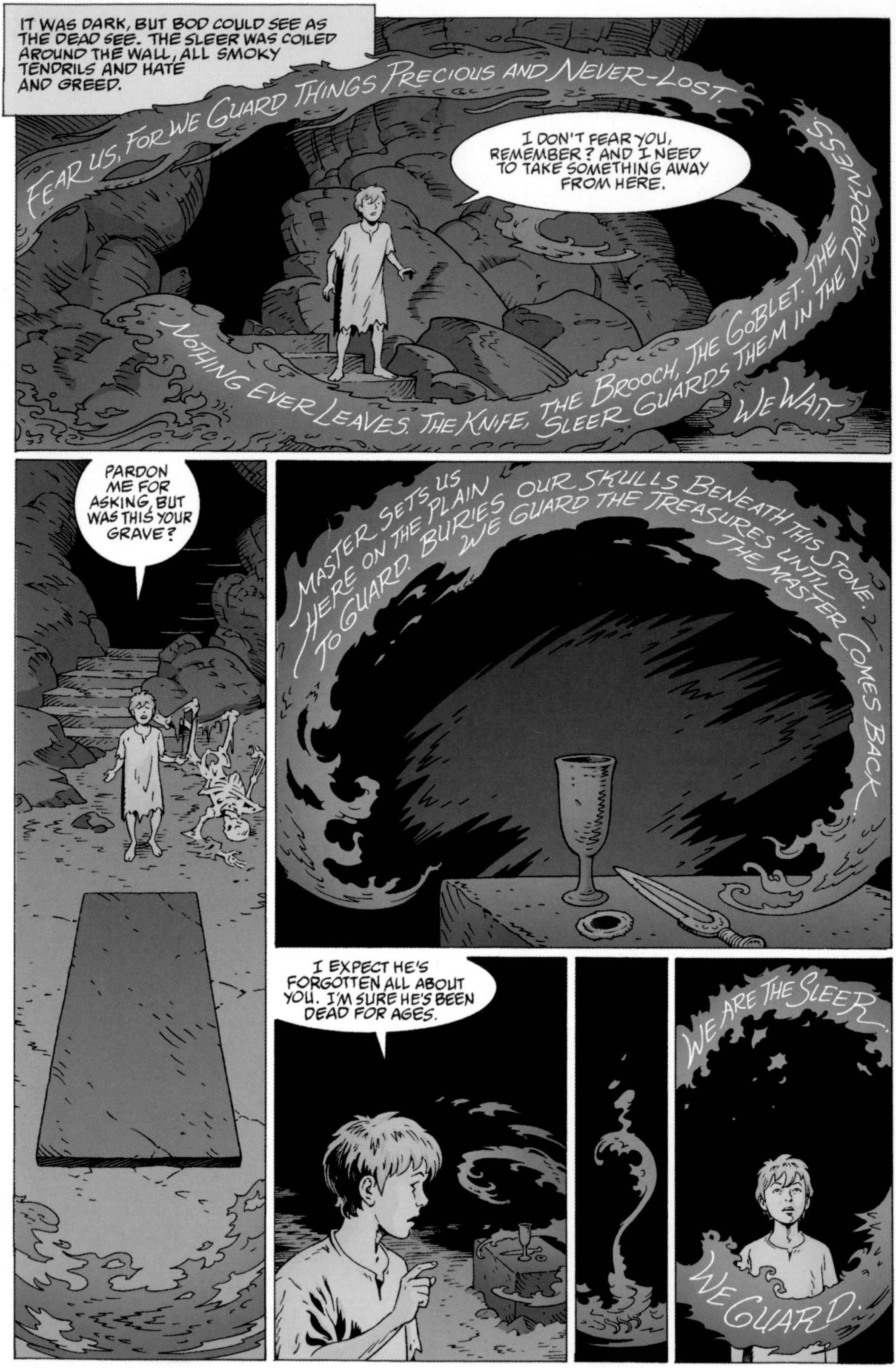
IT WAS DARK, BUT BOD COULD SEE AS THE DEAD SEE. THE SLEER WAS COILED AROUND THE WALL, ALL SMOKY TENDRILS AND HATE AND GREED.
FEAR US, FOR WE GUARD THINGS PRECIOUS AND NEVER-LOST.
I DON'T FEAR YOU, REMEMBER? AND I NEED TO TAKE SOMETHING AWAY FROM HERE.
NOTHING EVER LEAVES. THE KNIFE, THE BROOCH, THE GOBLET. THE SLEER GUARDS THEM IN THE DARKNESS.
WE WAIT.
PARDON ME FOR ASKING, BUT WAS THIS YOUR GRAVE?
MASTER SETS US HERE ON THE PLAIN TO GUARD. BURIES OUR SKULLS BENEATH THIS STONE. WE GUARD THE TREASURES UNTIL THE MASTER COMES BACK.
I EXPECT HE'S FORGOTTEN ALL ABOUT YOU. I'M SURE HE'S BEEN DEAD FOR AGES.
WE ARE THE SLEER.
WE GUARD.

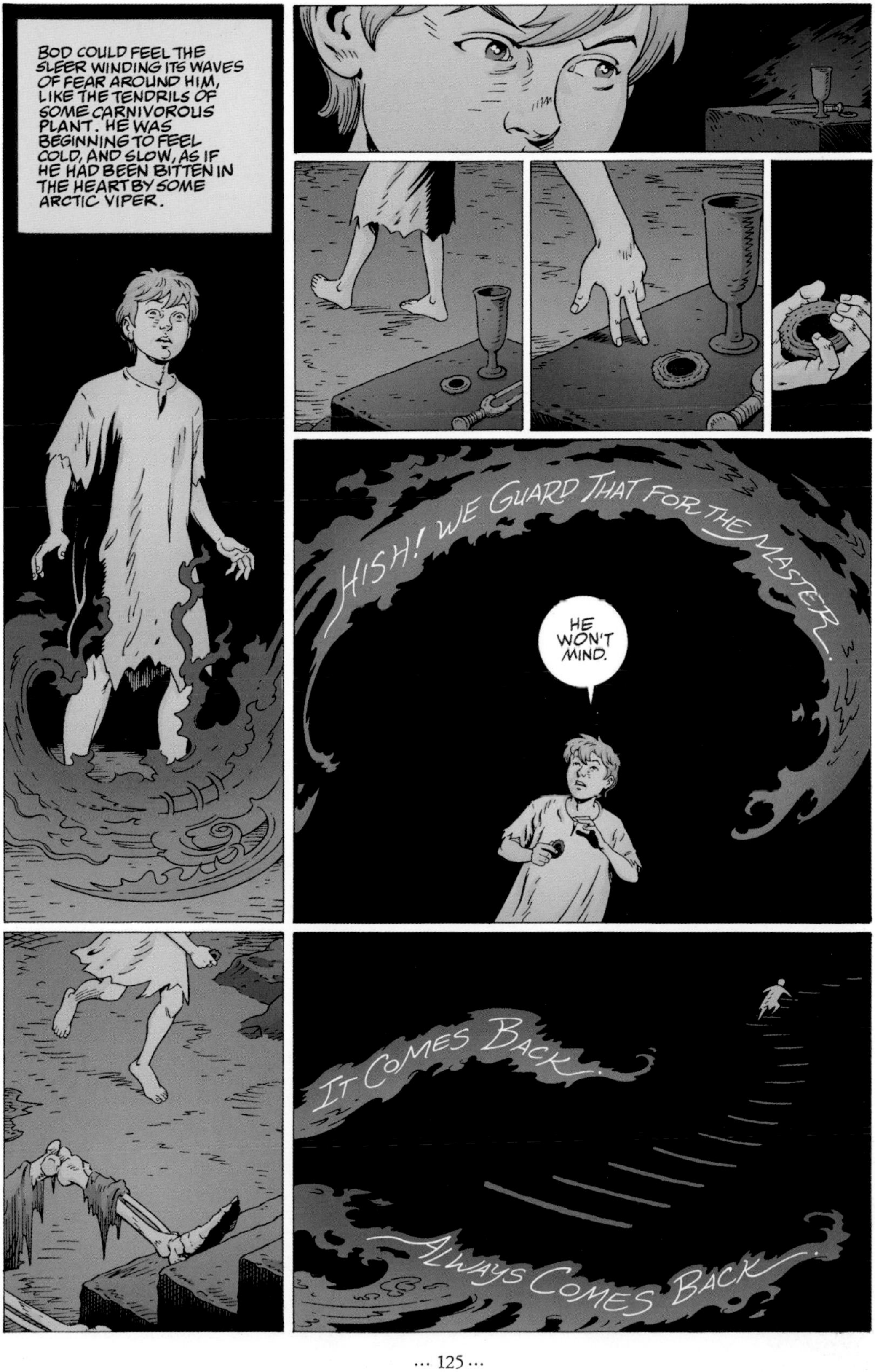
BOD COULD FEEL THE SLEER WINDING ITS WAVES OF FEAR AROUND HIM, LIKE THE TENDRILS OF SOME CARNIVOROUS PLANT. HE WAS BEGINNING TO FEEL COLD, AND SLOW, AS IF HE HAD BEEN BITTEN IN THE HEART BY SOME ARCTIC VIPER.
HISH! WE GUARD THAT FOR THE MASTER.
HE WON'T MIND.
IT COMES BACK.
ALWAYS COMES BACK.

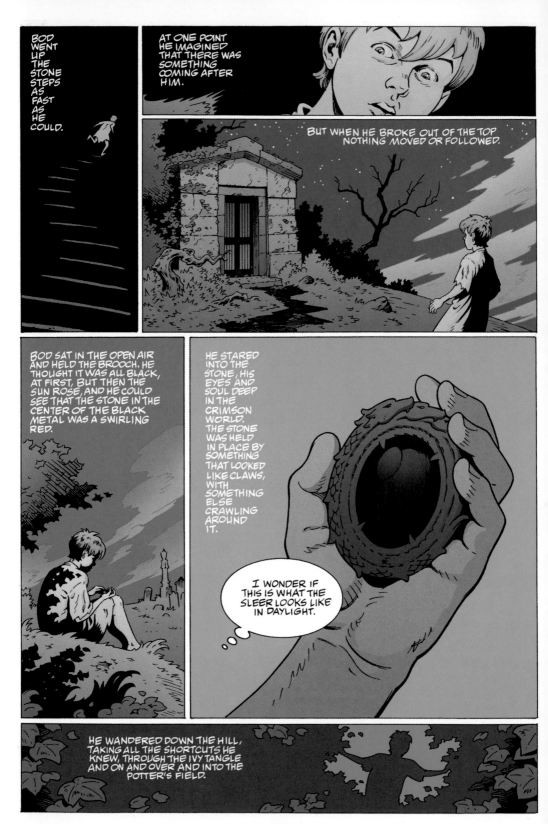

BOD WENT UP THE STONE STEPS AS FAST AS HE COULD.

AT ONE POINT HE IMAGINED THAT THERE WAS SOMETHING COMING AFTER HIM.

BUT WHEN HE BROKE OUT OF THE TOP NOTHING MOVED OR FOLLOWED.

BOD SAT IN THE OPEN AIR AND HELD THE BROOCH. HE THOUGHT IT WAS ALL BLACK, AT FIRST, BUT THEN THE SUN ROSE, AND HE COULD SEE THAT THE STONE IN THE CENTER OF THE BLACK METAL WAS A SWIRLING RED.

HE STARED INTO THE STONE, HIS EYES AND SOUL DEEP IN THE CRIMSON WORLD. THE STONE WAS HELD IN PLACE BY SOMETHING THAT LOOKED LIKE CLAWS, WITH SOMETHING ELSE CRAWLING AROUND IT.

I WONDER IF THIS IS WHAT THE SLEER LOOKS LIKE IN DAYLIGHT.

HE WANDERED DOWN THE HILL, TAKING ALL THE SHORTCUTS HE KNEW, THROUGH THE IVY TANGLE AND ON AND OVER AND INTO THE POTTER'S FIELD.

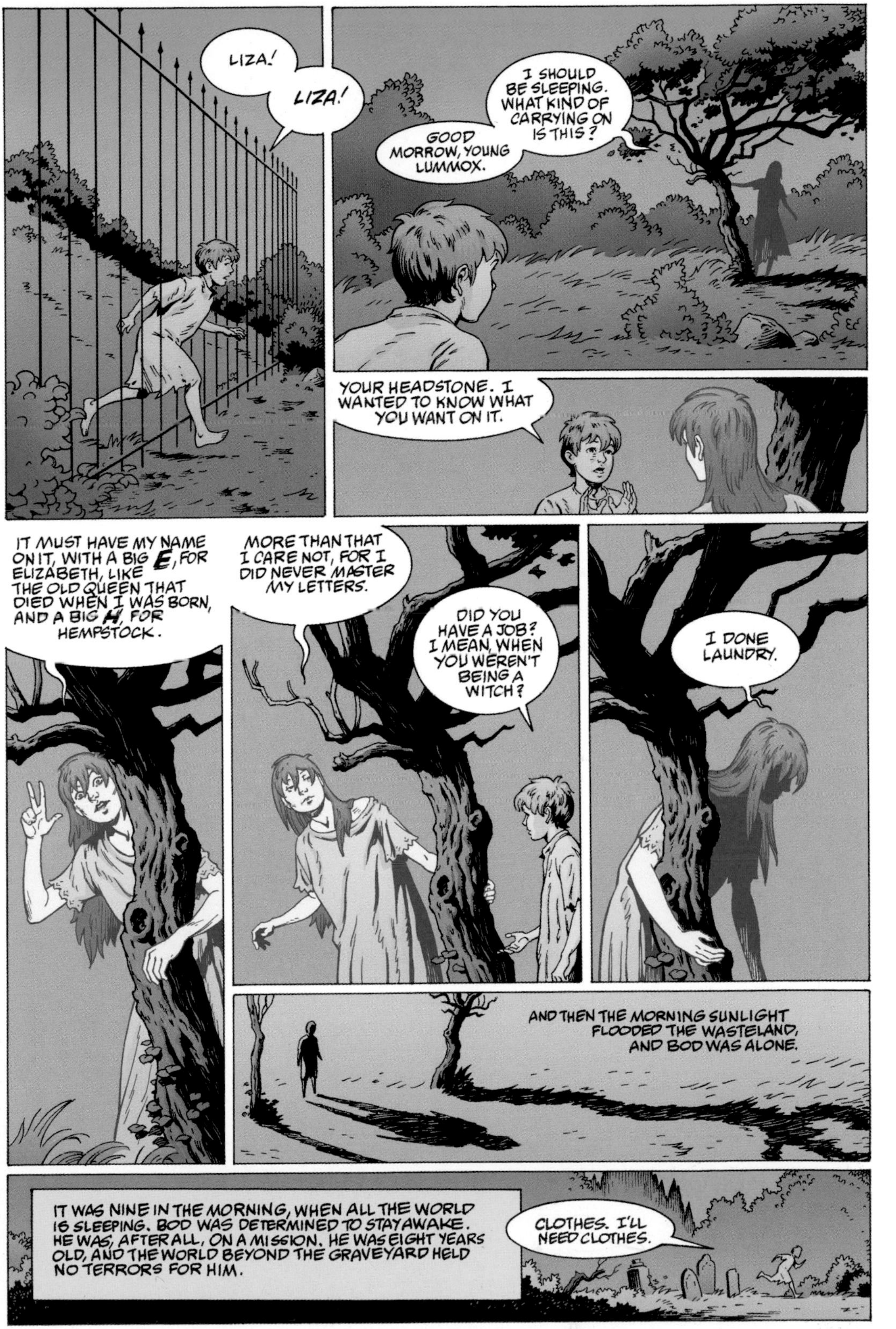
LIZA!
LIZA!
I SHOULD BE SLEEPING. WHAT KIND OF CARRYING ON IS THIS?
GOOD MORROW, YOUNG LUMMOX.
YOUR HEADSTONE. I WANTED TO KNOW WHAT YOU WANT ON IT.
IT MUST HAVE MY NAME ON IT, WITH A BIG E, FOR ELIZABETH, LIKE THE OLD QUEEN THAT DIED WHEN I WAS BORN, AND A BIG H, FOR HEMPSTOCK.
MORE THAN THAT I CARE NOT, FOR I DID NEVER MASTER MY LETTERS.
DID YOU HAVE A JOB? I MEAN, WHEN YOU WEREN'T BEING A WITCH?
I DONE LAUNDRY.
AND THEN THE MORNING SUNLIGHT FLOODED THE WASTELAND, AND BOD WAS ALONE.
IT WAS NINE IN THE MORNING, WHEN ALL THE WORLD IS SLEEPING. BOD WAS DETERMINED TO STAY AWAKE. HE WAS, AFTER ALL, ON A MISSION. HE WAS EIGHT YEARS OLD, AND THE WORLD BEYOND THE GRAVEYARD HELD NO TERRORS FOR HIM.
CLOTHES. I'LL NEED CLOTHES.

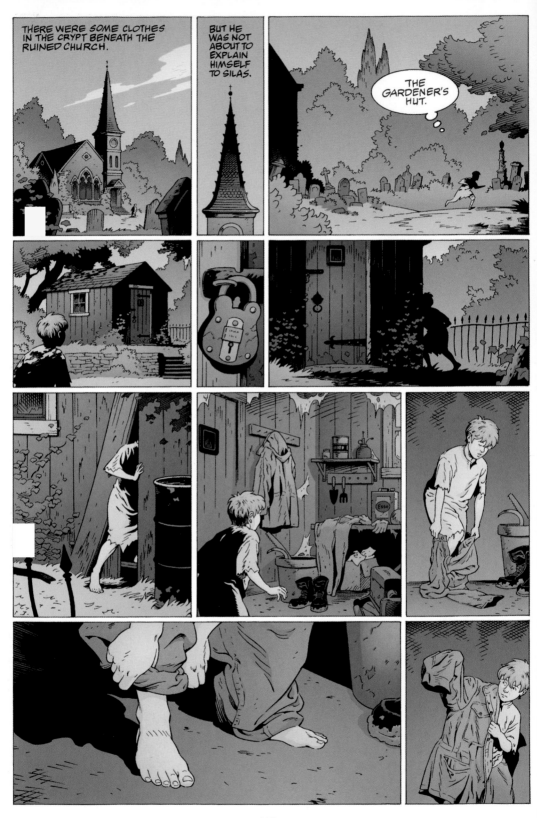

THERE WERE SOME CLOTHES IN THE CRYPT BENEATH THE RUINED CHURCH.

BUT HE WAS NOT ABOUT TO EXPLAIN HIMSELF TO SILAS.

THE GARDENER'S HUT.

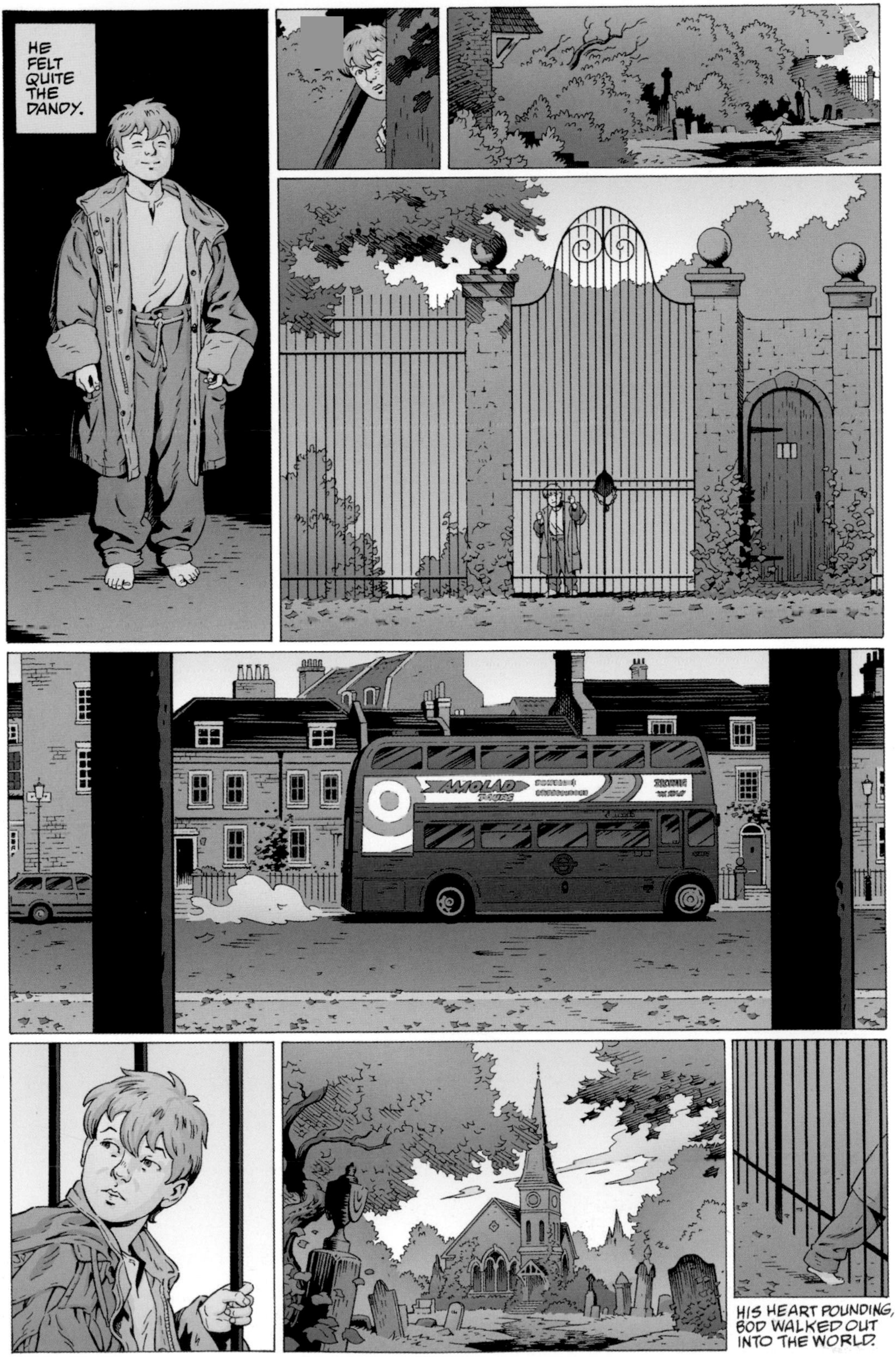
HE FELT QUITE THE DANDY.
HIS HEART POUNDING, BOD WALKED OUT INTO THE WORLD.

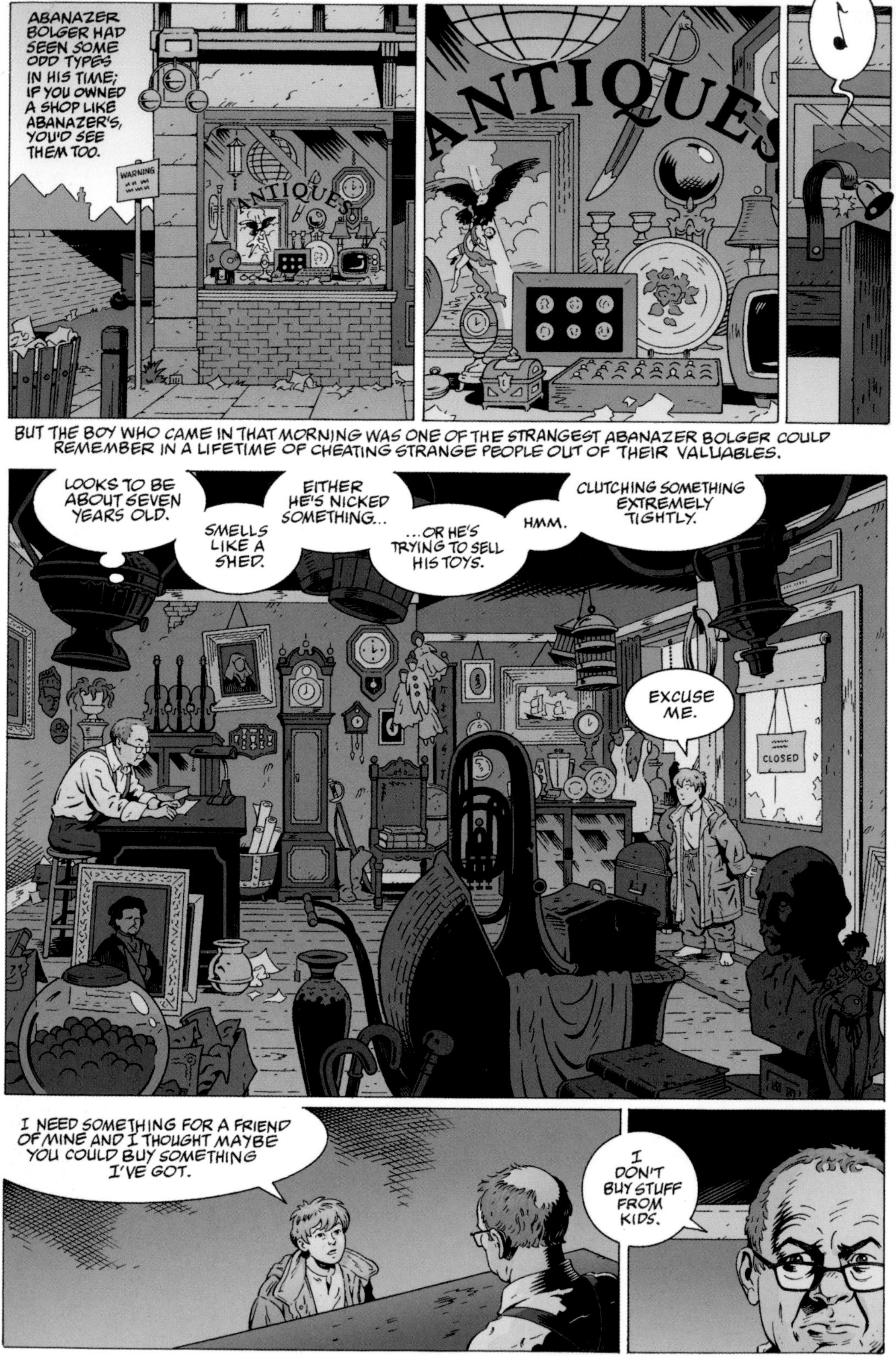
ABANAZER BOLGER HAD SEEN SOME ODD TYPES IN HIS TIME; IF YOU OWNED A SHOP LIKE ABANAZER'S, YOU'D SEE THEM TOO.
WARNING
ANTIQUES
ANTIQUES
BUT THE BOY WHO CAME IN THAT MORNING WAS ONE OF THE STRANGEST ABANAZER BOLGER COULD REMEMBER IN A LIFETIME OF CHEATING STRANGE PEOPLE OUT OF THEIR VALUABLES.
LOOKS TO BE ABOUT SEVEN YEARS OLD.
SMELLS LIKE A SHED.
EITHER HE'S NICKED SOMETHING...
...OR HE'S TRYING TO SELL HIS TOYS.
HMM.
CLUTCHING SOMETHING EXTREMELY TIGHTLY.
EXCUSE ME.
CLOSED
I NEED SOMETHING FOR A FRIEND OF MINE AND I THOUGHT MAYBE YOU COULD BUY SOMETHING I'VE GOT.
I DON'T BUY STUFF FROM KIDS.

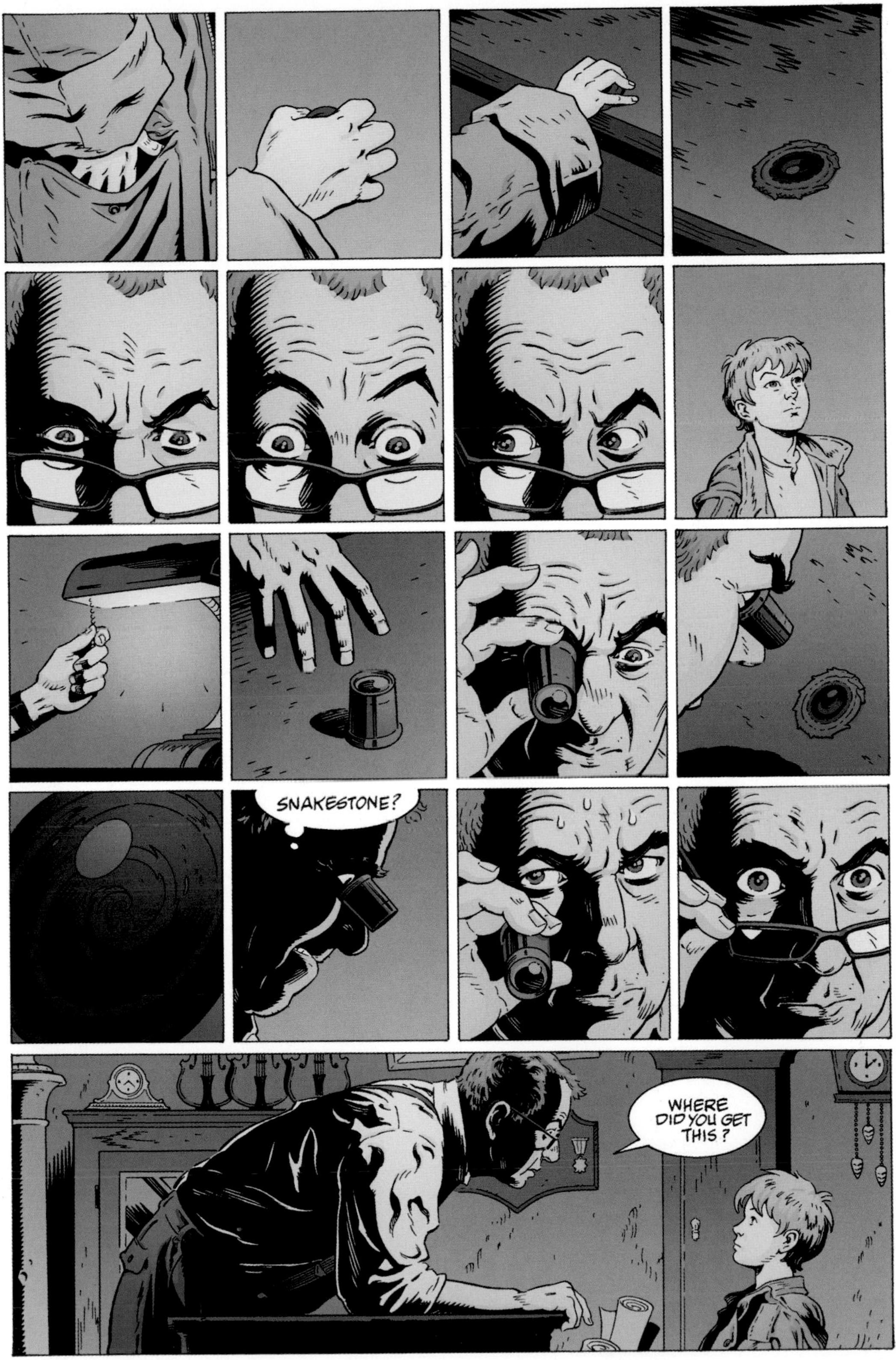
SNAKESTONE?
WHERE DID YOU GET THIS?

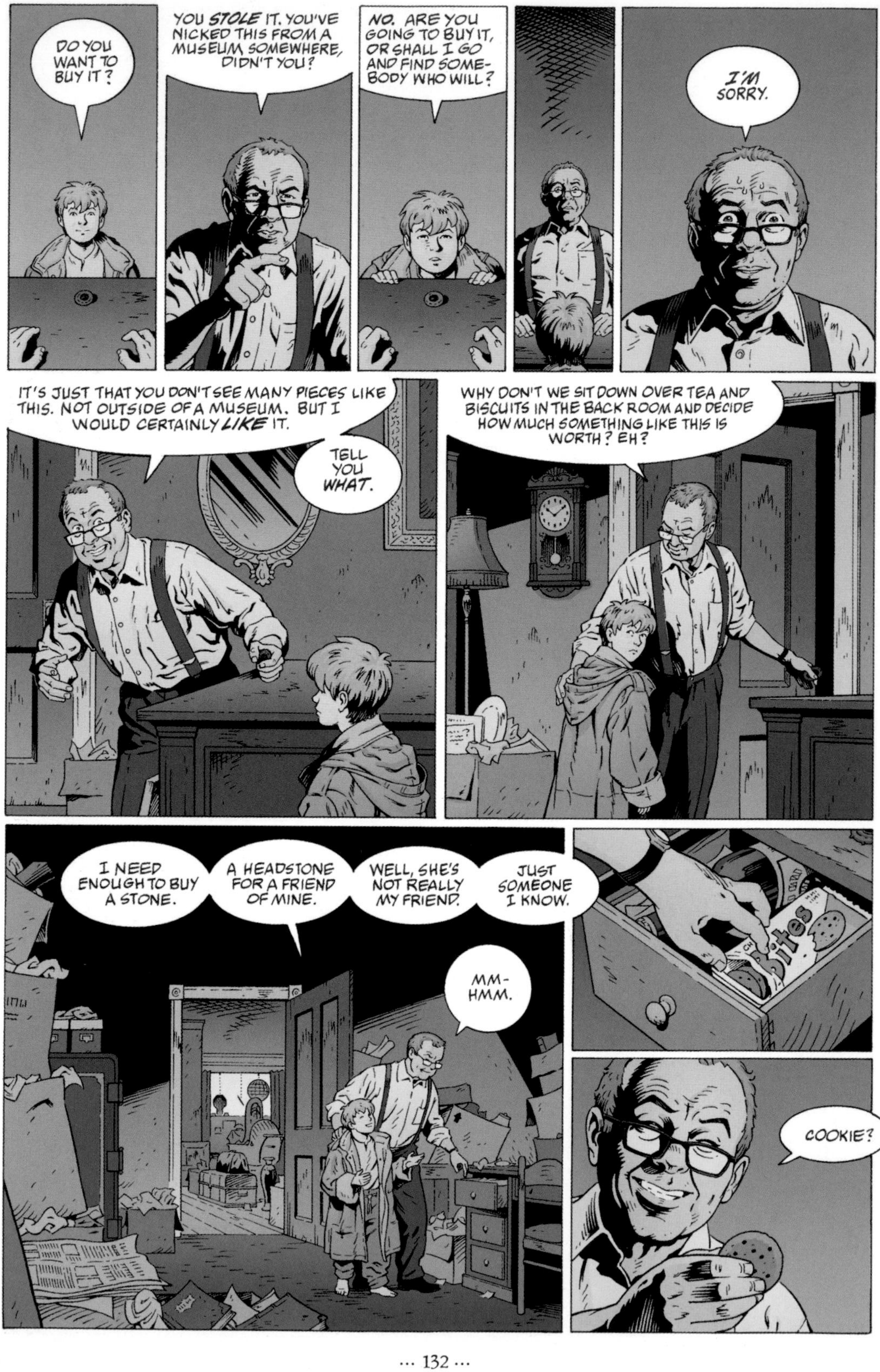
DO YOU WANT TO BUY IT?
YOU STOLE IT. YOU'VE NICKED THIS FROM A MUSEUM SOMEWHERE, DIDN'T YOU?
NO. ARE YOU GOING TO BUY IT, OR SHALL I GO AND FIND SOMEBODY WHO WILL?
I'M SORRY.
IT'S JUST THAT YOU DON'T SEE MANY PIECES LIKE THIS. NOT OUTSIDE OF A MUSEUM. BUT I WOULD CERTAINLY LIKE IT.
TELL YOU WHAT.
WHY DON'T WE SIT DOWN OVER TEA AND BISCUITS IN THE BACK ROOM AND DECIDE HOW MUCH SOMETHING LIKE THIS IS WORTH? EH?
I NEED ENOUGH TO BUY A STONE.
A HEADSTONE FOR A FRIEND OF MINE.
WELL, SHE'S NOT REALLY MY FRIEND.
JUST SOMEONE I KNOW.
MM-HMM.
COOKIE?

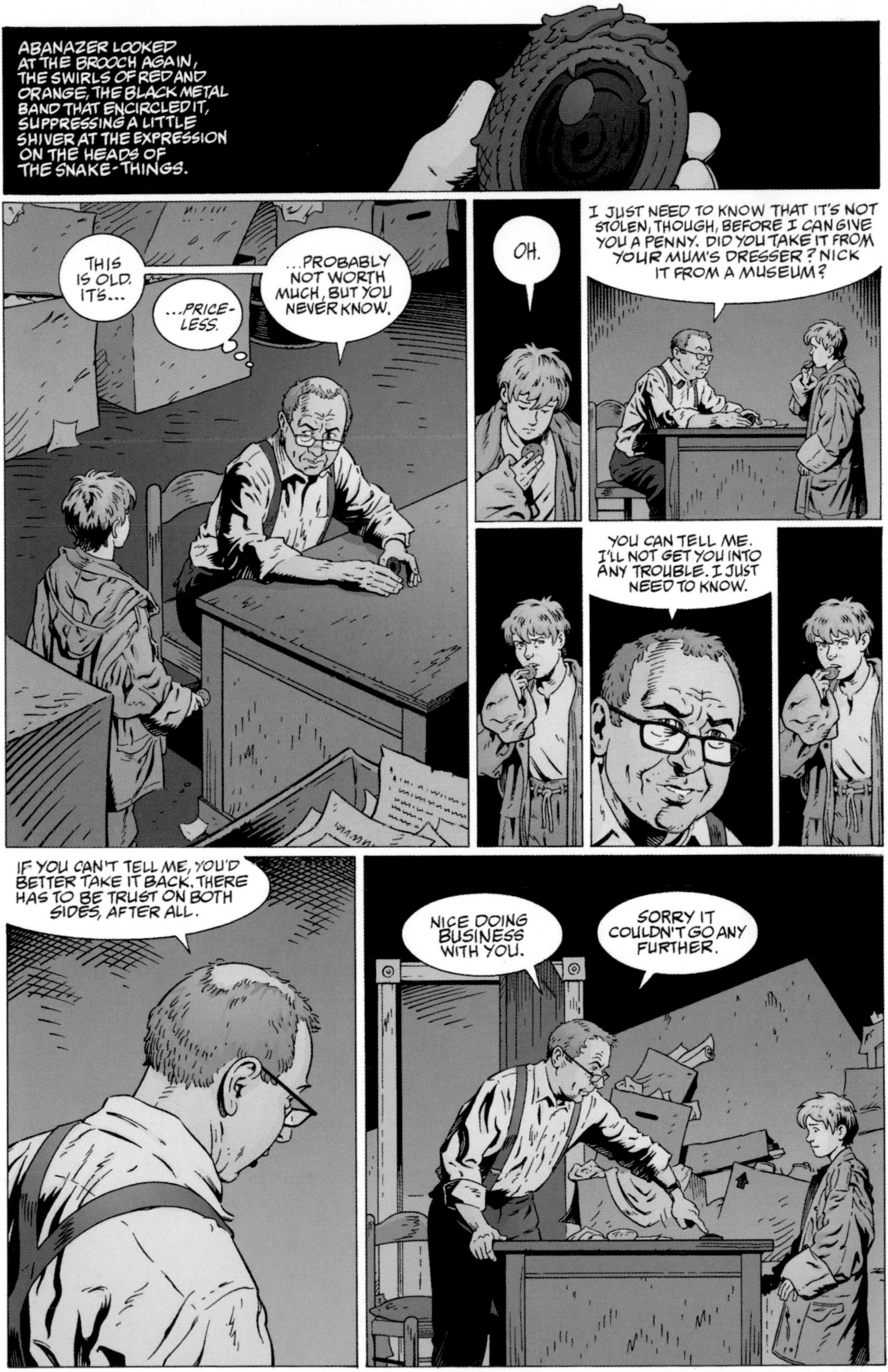
ABANAZER LOOKED AT THE BROOCH AGAIN, THE SWIRLS OF RED AND ORANGE, THE BLACK METAL BAND THAT ENCIRCLED IT, SUPPRESSING A LITTLE SHIVER AT THE EXPRESSION ON THE HEADS OF THE SNAKE-THINGS.
THIS IS OLD. IT'S...
...PRICELESS.
...PROBABLY NOT WORTH MUCH, BUT YOU NEVER KNOW.
OH.
I JUST NEED TO KNOW THAT IT'S NOT STOLEN, THOUGH, BEFORE I CAN GIVE YOU A PENNY. DID YOU TAKE IT FROM YOUR MUM'S DRESSER? NICK IT FROM A MUSEUM?
YOU CAN TELL ME. I'LL NOT GET YOU INTO ANY TROUBLE. I JUST NEED TO KNOW.
IF YOU CAN'T TELL ME, YOU'D BETTER TAKE IT BACK. THERE HAS TO BE TRUST ON BOTH SIDES, AFTER ALL.
NICE DOING BUSINESS WITH YOU.
SORRY IT COULDN'T GO ANY FURTHER.

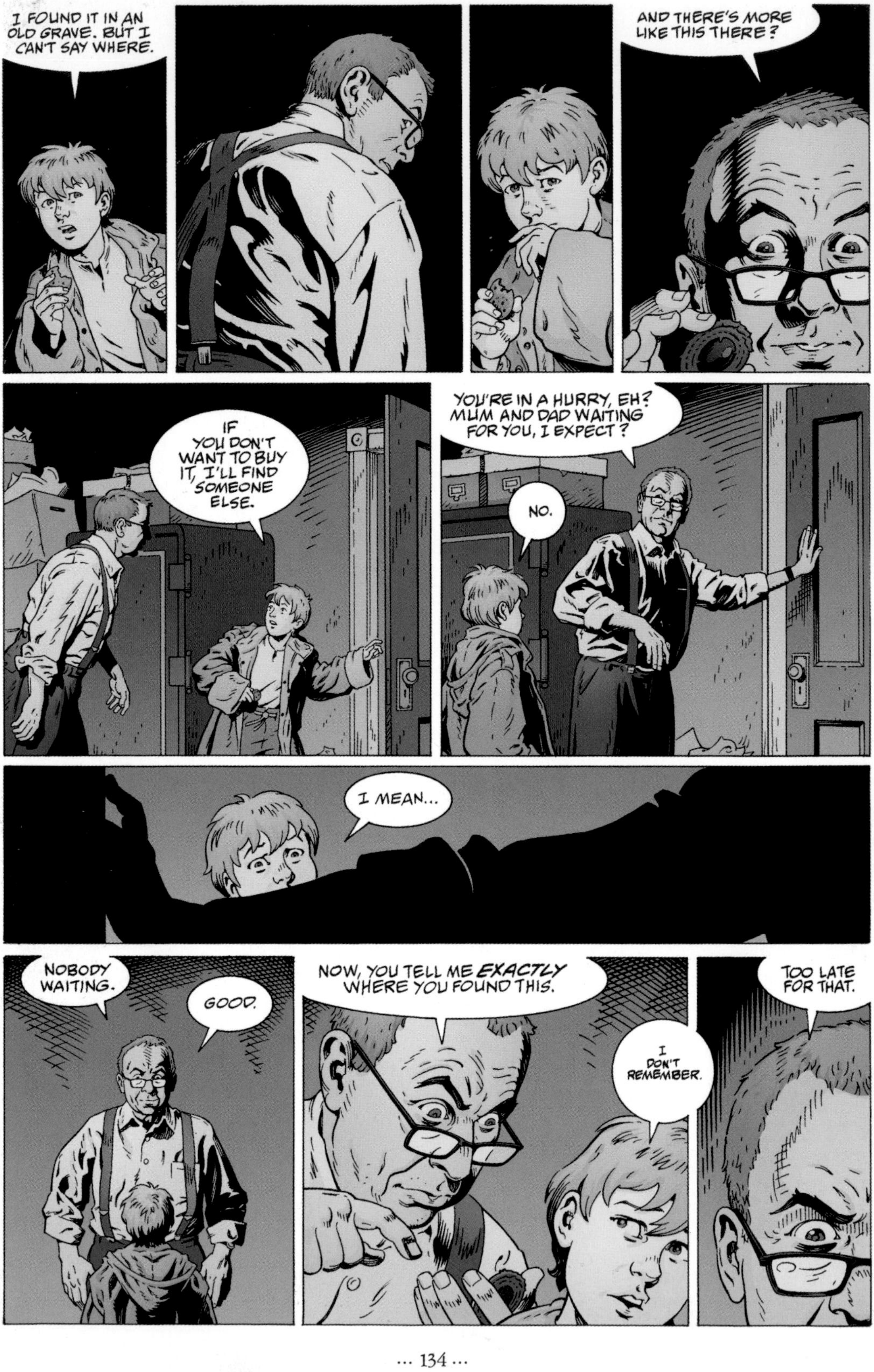
I FOUND IT IN AN OLD GRAVE. BUT I CAN'T SAY WHERE.
AND THERE'S MORE LIKE THIS THERE?
IF YOU DON'T WANT TO BUY IT, I'LL FIND SOMEONE ELSE.
YOU'RE IN A HURRY, EH? MUM AND DAD WAITING FOR YOU, I EXPECT?
NO.
I MEAN...
NOBODY WAITING.
GOOD.
NOW, YOU TELL ME EXACTLY WHERE YOU FOUND THIS.
I DON'T REMEMBER.
TOO LATE FOR THAT.

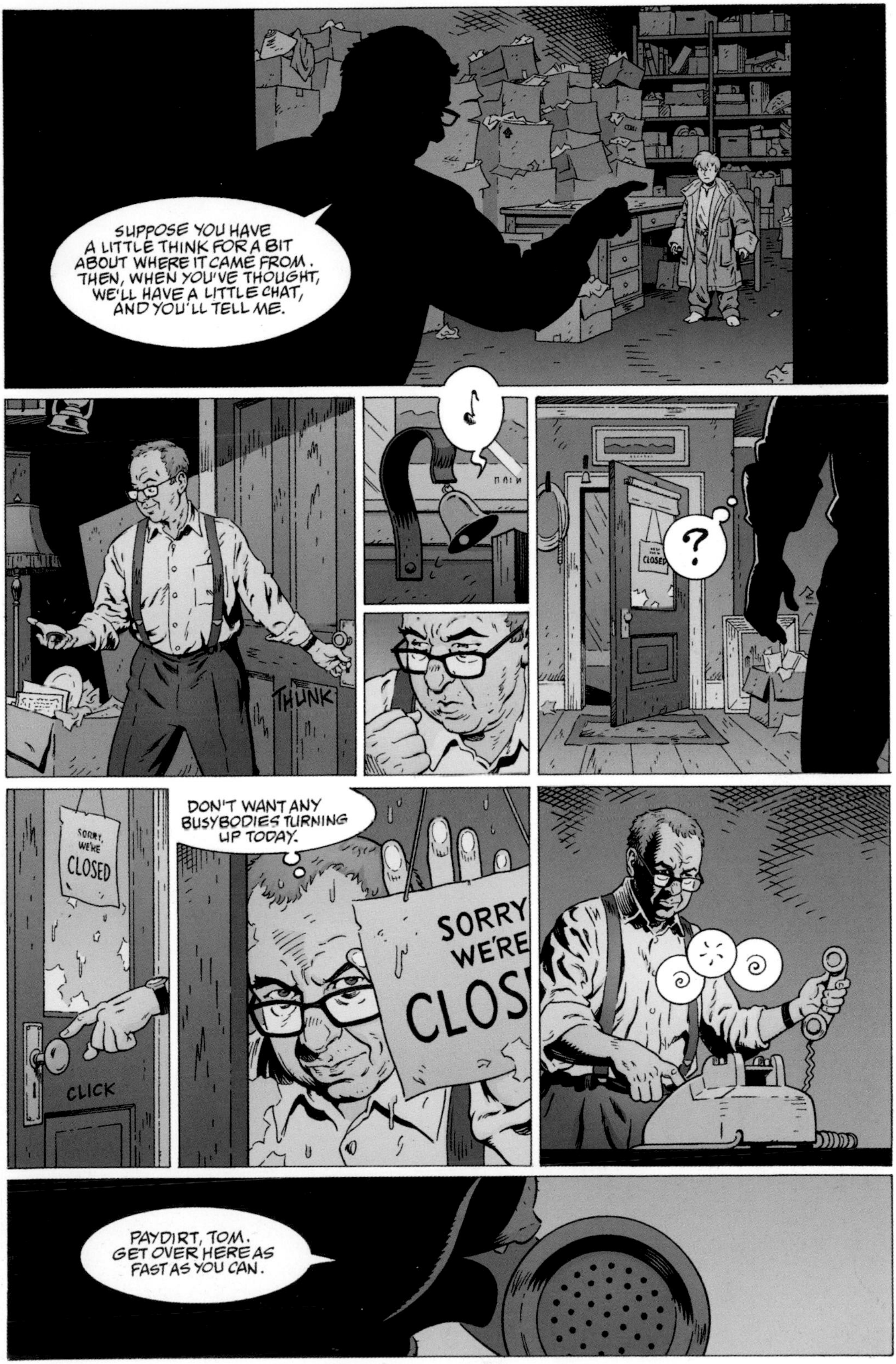
SUPPOSE YOU HAVE A LITTLE THINK FOR A BIT ABOUT WHERE IT CAME FROM. THEN, WHEN YOU'VE THOUGHT, WE'LL HAVE A LITTLE CHAT, AND YOU'LL TELL ME.
THUNK
SORRY, WE'RE CLOSED
CLICK
DON'T WANT ANY BUSYBODIES TURNING UP TODAY.
SORRY WE'RE
PAYDIRT, TOM. GET OVER HERE AS FAST AS YOU CAN.

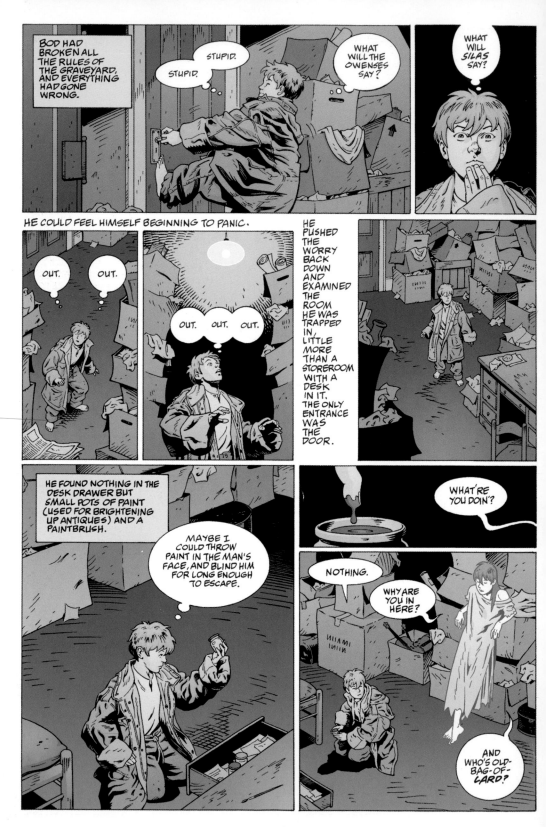

BOD HAD BROKEN ALL THE RULES OF THE GRAVEYARD, AND EVERYTHING HAD GONE WRONG.

STUPID.

STUPID.

WHAT WILL THE OWENSES SAY?

WHAT WILL SILAS SAY?

HE COULD FEEL HIMSELF BEGINNING TO PANIC.

OUT.

OUT.

OUT. OUT. OUT.

HE PUSHED THE WORRY BACK DOWN AND EXAMINED THE ROOM HE WAS TRAPPED IN, LITTLE MORE THAN A STOREROOM WITH A DESK IN IT. THE ONLY ENTRANCE WAS THE DOOR.

HE FOUND NOTHING IN THE DESK DRAWER BUT SMALL POTS OF PAINT (USED FOR BRIGHTENING UP ANTIQUES) AND A PAINTBRUSH.

MAYBE I COULD THROW PAINT IN THE MAN'S FACE, AND BLIND HIM FOR LONG ENOUGH TO ESCAPE.

WHAT'RE YOU DOIN'?

NOTHING.

WHY ARE YOU IN HERE?

AND WHO'S OLD-BAG-OF-LARD?

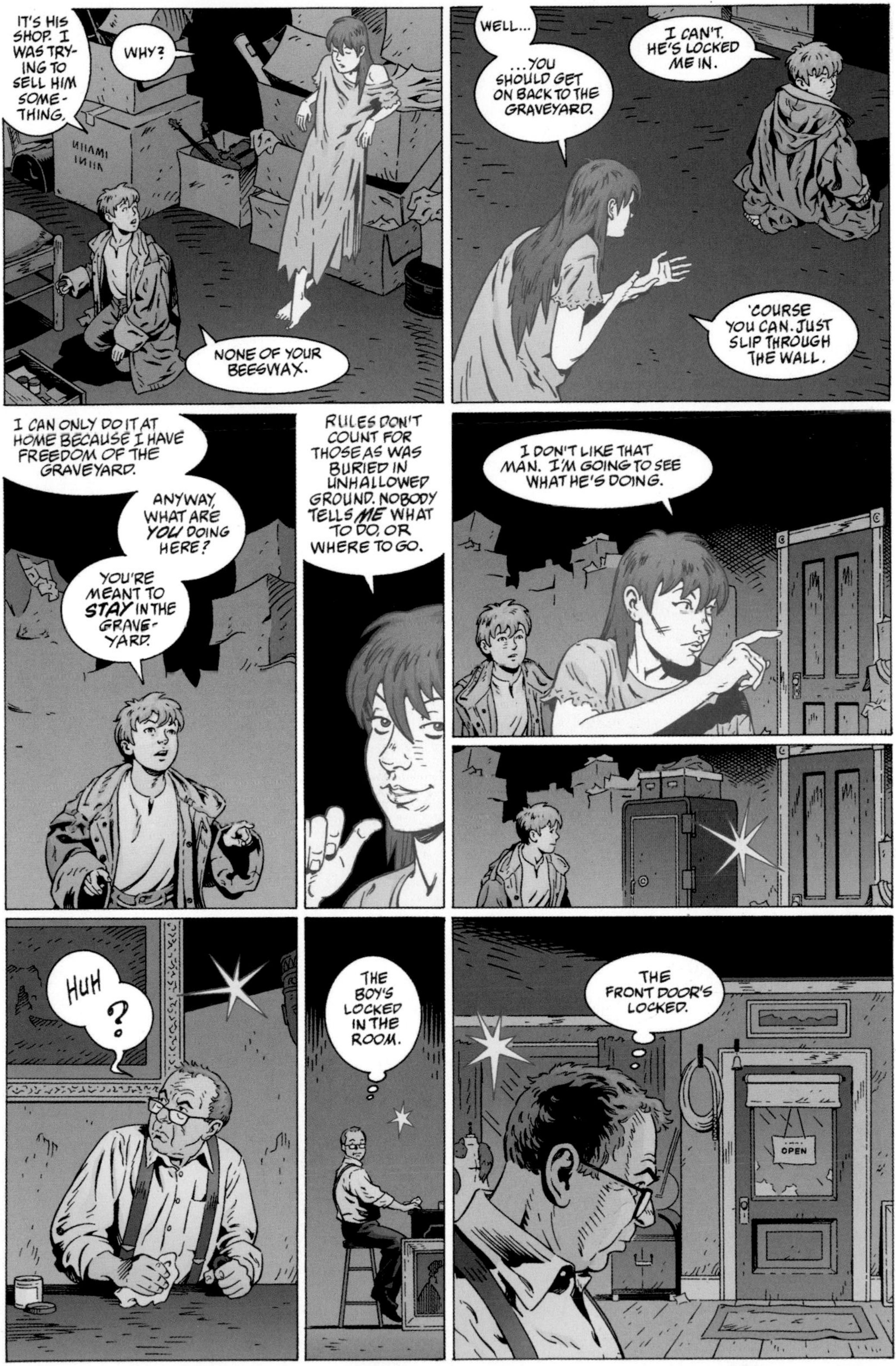
IT'S HIS SHOP. I WAS TRYING TO SELL HIM SOMETHING.
WHY?
NONE OF YOUR BEESWAX.
WELL...
...YOU SHOULD GET ON BACK TO THE GRAVEYARD.
I CAN'T. HE'S LOCKED ME IN.
'COURSE YOU CAN. JUST SLIP THROUGH THE WALL.
I CAN ONLY DO IT AT HOME BECAUSE I HAVE FREEDOM OF THE GRAVEYARD.
ANYWAY, WHAT ARE YOU DOING HERE?
YOU'RE MEANT TO STAY IN THE GRAVEYARD.
RULES DON'T COUNT FOR THOSE AS WAS BURIED IN UNHALLOWED GROUND. NOBODY TELLS ME WHAT TO DO, OR WHERE TO GO.
I DON'T LIKE THAT MAN. I'M GOING TO SEE WHAT HE'S DOING.
HUH ?
THE BOY'S LOCKED IN THE ROOM.
THE FRONT DOOR'S LOCKED.
OPEN

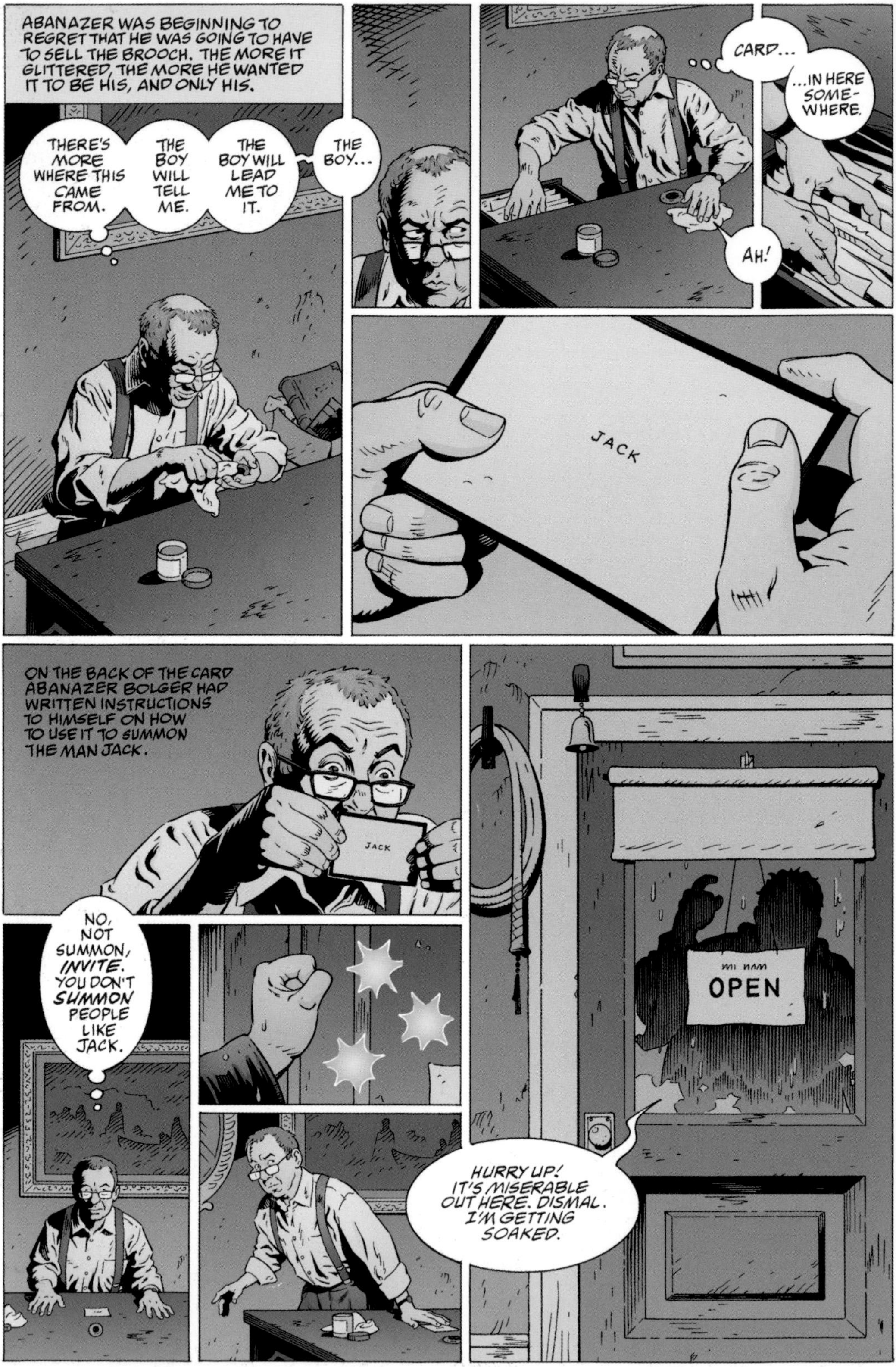
ABANAZER WAS BEGINNING TO REGRET THAT HE WAS GOING TO HAVE TO SELL THE BROOCH. THE MORE IT GLITTERED, THE MORE HE WANTED IT TO BE HIS, AND ONLY HIS.
THERE'S MORE WHERE THIS CAME FROM.
THE BOY WILL TELL ME.
THE BOY WILL LEAD ME TO IT.
THE BOY...
CARD...
...IN HERE SOMEWHERE.
AH!
JACK
ON THE BACK OF THE CARD ABANAZER BOLGER HAD WRITTEN INSTRUCTIONS TO HIMSELF ON HOW TO USE IT TO SUMMON THE MAN JACK.
JACK
NO, NOT SUMMON, INVITE. YOU DON'T SUMMON PEOPLE LIKE JACK.
OPEN
HURRY UP! IT'S MISERABLE OUT HERE. DISMAL. I'M GETTING SOAKED.

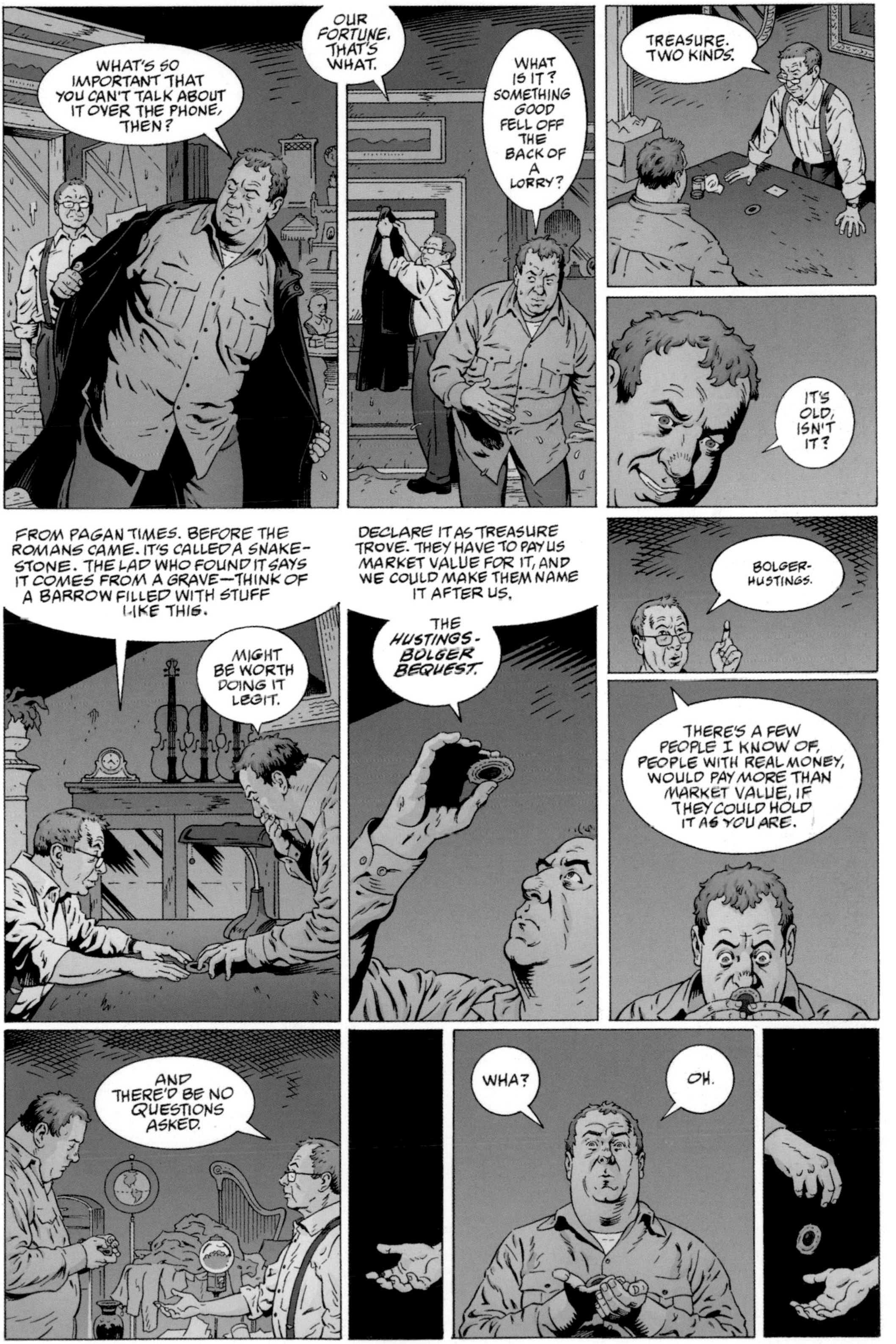
WHAT'S SO IMPORTANT THAT YOU CAN'T TALK ABOUT IT OVER THE PHONE, THEN?
OUR FORTUNE. THAT'S WHAT.
WHAT IS IT? SOMETHING GOOD FELL OFF THE BACK OF A LORRY?
TREASURE. TWO KINDS.
IT'S OLD, ISN'T IT?
FROM PAGAN TIMES. BEFORE THE ROMANS CAME. IT'S CALLED A SNAKE-STONE. THE LAD WHO FOUND IT SAYS IT COMES FROM A GRAVE—THINK OF A BARROW FILLED WITH STUFF LIKE THIS.
MIGHT BE WORTH DOING IT LEGIT.
DECLARE IT AS TREASURE TROVE. THEY HAVE TO PAY US MARKET VALUE FOR IT, AND WE COULD MAKE THEM NAME IT AFTER US.
THE *HUSTINGS-BOLGER BEQUEST.*
BOLGER-HUSTINGS.
THERE'S A FEW PEOPLE I KNOW OF, PEOPLE WITH REAL MONEY, WOULD PAY MORE THAN MARKET VALUE, IF THEY COULD HOLD IT AS YOU ARE.
AND THERE'D BE NO QUESTIONS ASKED.
WHA?
OH.

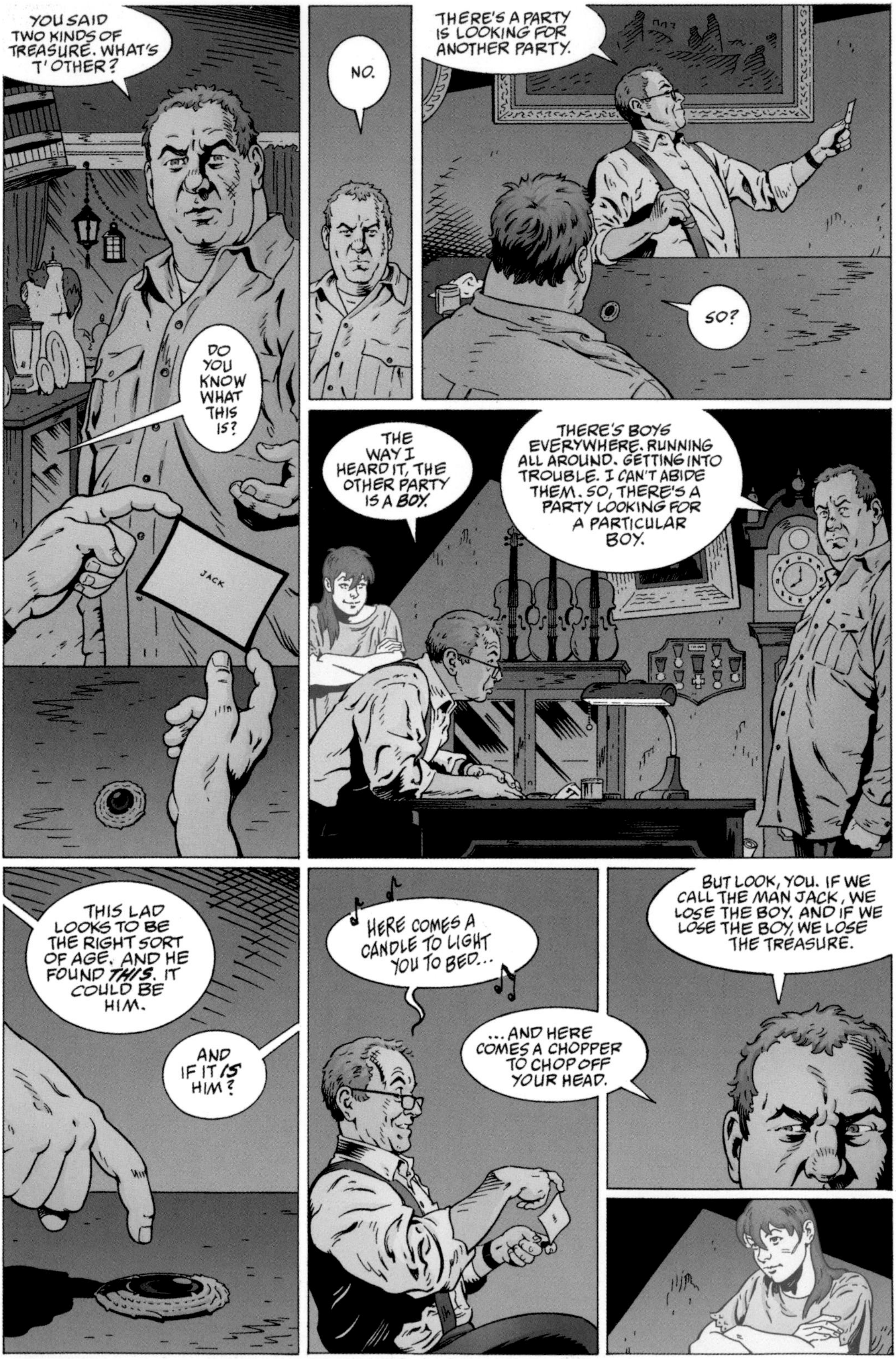
YOU SAID TWO KINDS OF TREASURE. WHAT'S T' OTHER?
DO YOU KNOW WHAT THIS IS?
JACK
NO.
THERE'S A PARTY IS LOOKING FOR ANOTHER PARTY.
SO?
THE WAY I HEARD IT, THE OTHER PARTY IS A BOY.
THERE'S BOYS EVERYWHERE. RUNNING ALL AROUND. GETTING INTO TROUBLE. I CAN'T ABIDE THEM. SO, THERE'S A PARTY LOOKING FOR A PARTICULAR BOY.
THIS LAD LOOKS TO BE THE RIGHT SORT OF AGE. AND HE FOUND THIS. IT COULD BE HIM.
AND IF IT IS HIM?
HERE COMES A CANDLE TO LIGHT YOU TO BED...
...AND HERE COMES A CHOPPER TO CHOP OFF YOUR HEAD.
BUT LOOK, YOU. IF WE CALL THE MAN JACK, WE LOSE THE BOY. AND IF WE LOSE THE BOY, WE LOSE THE TREASURE.

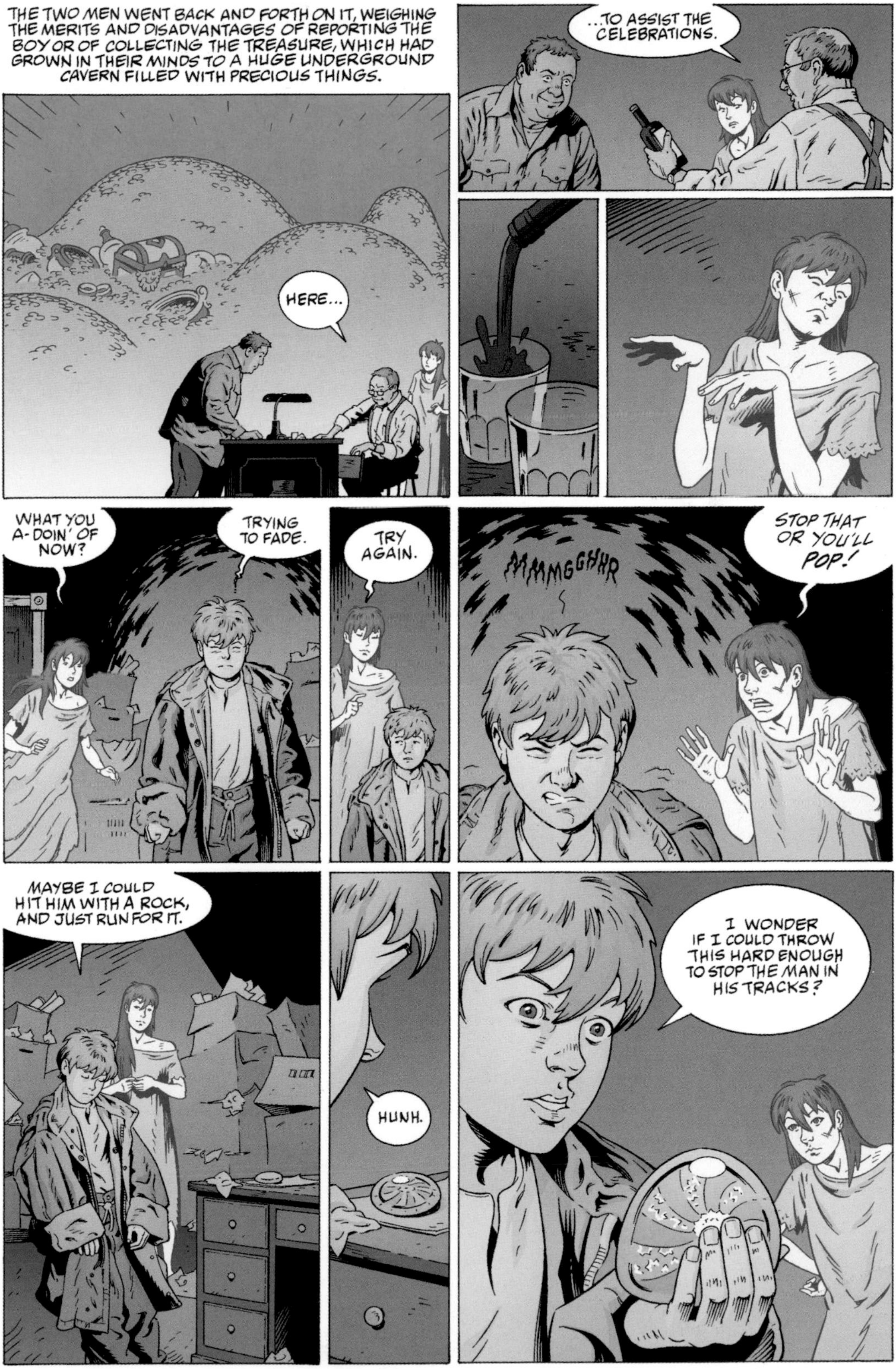
THE TWO MEN WENT BACK AND FORTH ON IT, WEIGHING THE MERITS AND DISADVANTAGES OF REPORTING THE BOY OR OF COLLECTING THE TREASURE, WHICH HAD GROWN IN THEIR MINDS TO A HUGE UNDERGROUND CAVERN FILLED WITH PRECIOUS THINGS.
HERE...
...TO ASSIST THE CELEBRATIONS.
WHAT YOU A-DOIN' OF NOW?
TRYING TO FADE.
TRY AGAIN.
MMMGGHHR
STOP THAT OR YOU'LL POP!
MAYBE I COULD HIT HIM WITH A ROCK, AND JUST RUN FOR IT.
HUNH.
I WONDER IF I COULD THROW THIS HARD ENOUGH TO STOP THE MAN IN HIS TRACKS?

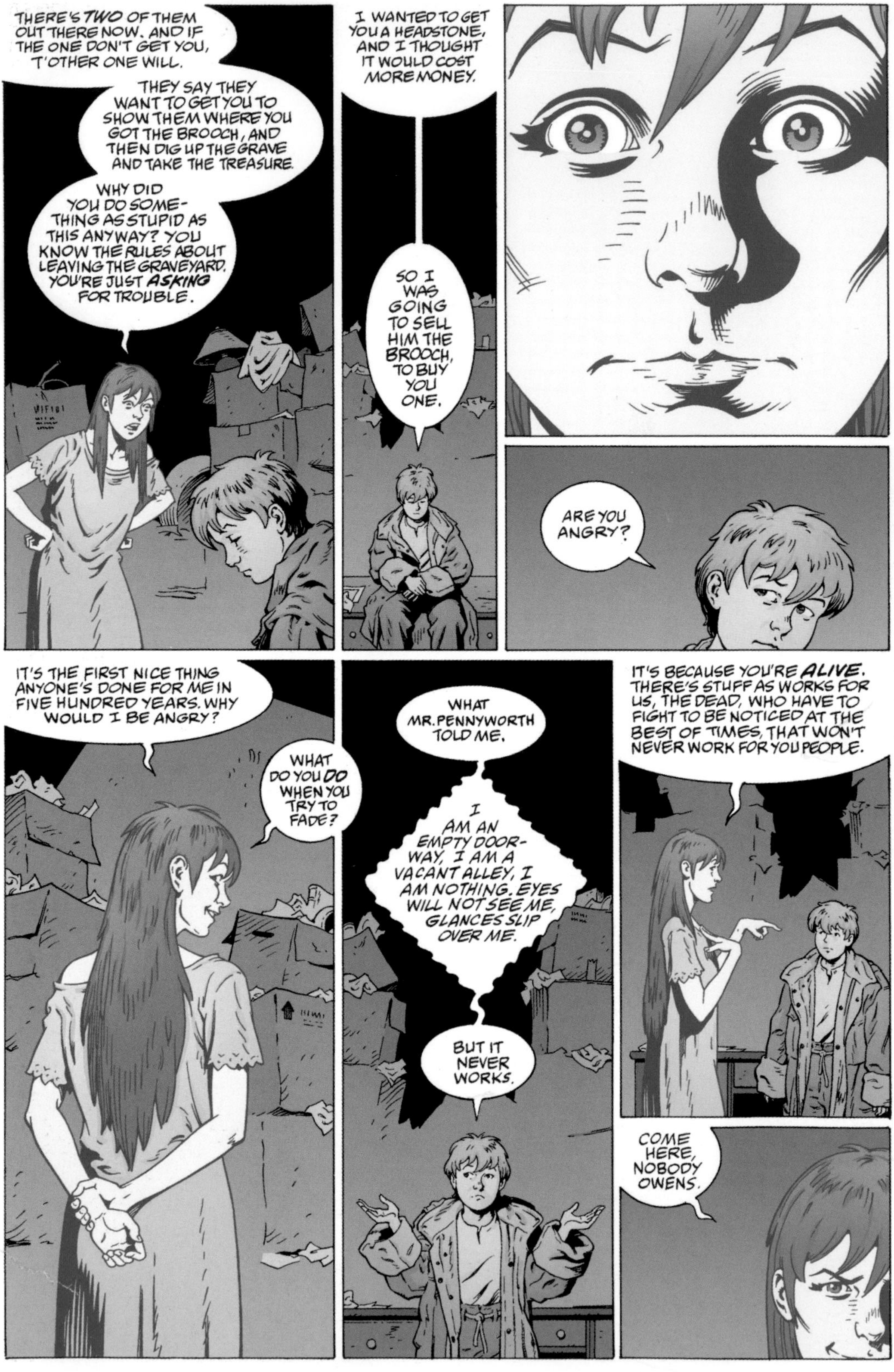

THERE'S TWO OF THEM OUT THERE NOW. AND IF THE ONE DON'T GET YOU, T'OTHER ONE WILL.
THEY SAY THEY WANT TO GET YOU TO SHOW THEM WHERE YOU GOT THE BROOCH, AND THEN DIG UP THE GRAVE AND TAKE THE TREASURE.
WHY DID YOU DO SOMETHING AS STUPID AS THIS ANYWAY? YOU KNOW THE RULES ABOUT LEAVING THE GRAVEYARD. YOU'RE JUST ASKING FOR TROUBLE.
I WANTED TO GET YOU A HEADSTONE, AND I THOUGHT IT WOULD COST MORE MONEY.
SO I WAS GOING TO SELL HIM THE BROOCH, TO BUY YOU ONE.
ARE YOU ANGRY?
IT'S THE FIRST NICE THING ANYONE'S DONE FOR ME IN FIVE HUNDRED YEARS. WHY WOULD I BE ANGRY?
WHAT DO YOU DO WHEN YOU TRY TO FADE?
WHAT MR. PENNYWORTH TOLD ME.
I AM AN EMPTY DOORWAY, I AM A VACANT ALLEY, I AM NOTHING. EYES WILL NOT SEE ME, GLANCES SLIP OVER ME.
BUT IT NEVER WORKS.
IT'S BECAUSE YOU'RE ALIVE. THERE'S STUFF AS WORKS FOR US, THE DEAD, WHO HAVE TO FIGHT TO BE NOTICED AT THE BEST OF TIMES, THAT WON'T NEVER WORK FOR YOU PEOPLE.
COME HERE, NOBODY OWENS.

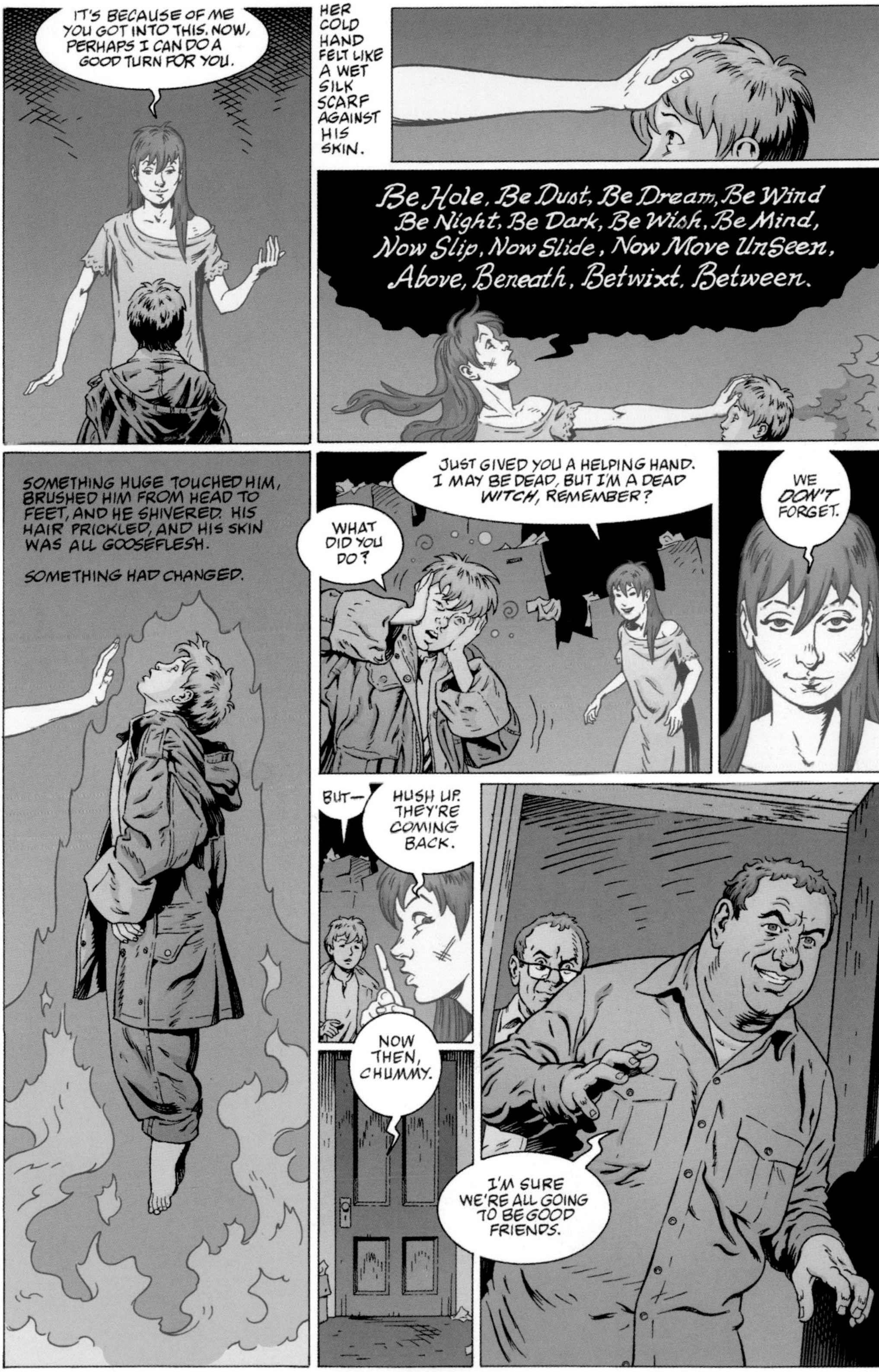
IT'S BECAUSE OF ME YOU GOT INTO THIS. NOW, PERHAPS I CAN DO A GOOD TURN FOR YOU.
HER COLD HAND FELT LIKE A WET SILK SCARF AGAINST HIS SKIN.
Be Hole, Be Dust, Be Dream, Be Wind
Be Night, Be Dark, Be Wish, Be Mind,
Now Slip, Now Slide, Now Move UnSeen,
Above, Beneath, Betwixt, Between.
SOMETHING HUGE TOUCHED HIM, BRUSHED HIM FROM HEAD TO FEET, AND HE SHIVERED. HIS HAIR PRICKLED, AND HIS SKIN WAS ALL GOOSEFLESH.
SOMETHING HAD CHANGED.
WHAT DID YOU DO?
JUST GIVED YOU A HELPING HAND. I MAY BE DEAD, BUT I'M A DEAD WITCH, REMEMBER?
WE DON'T FORGET.
BUT—
HUSH UP. THEY'RE COMING BACK.
NOW THEN, CHUMMY.
I'M SURE WE'RE ALL GOING TO BE GOOD FRIENDS.

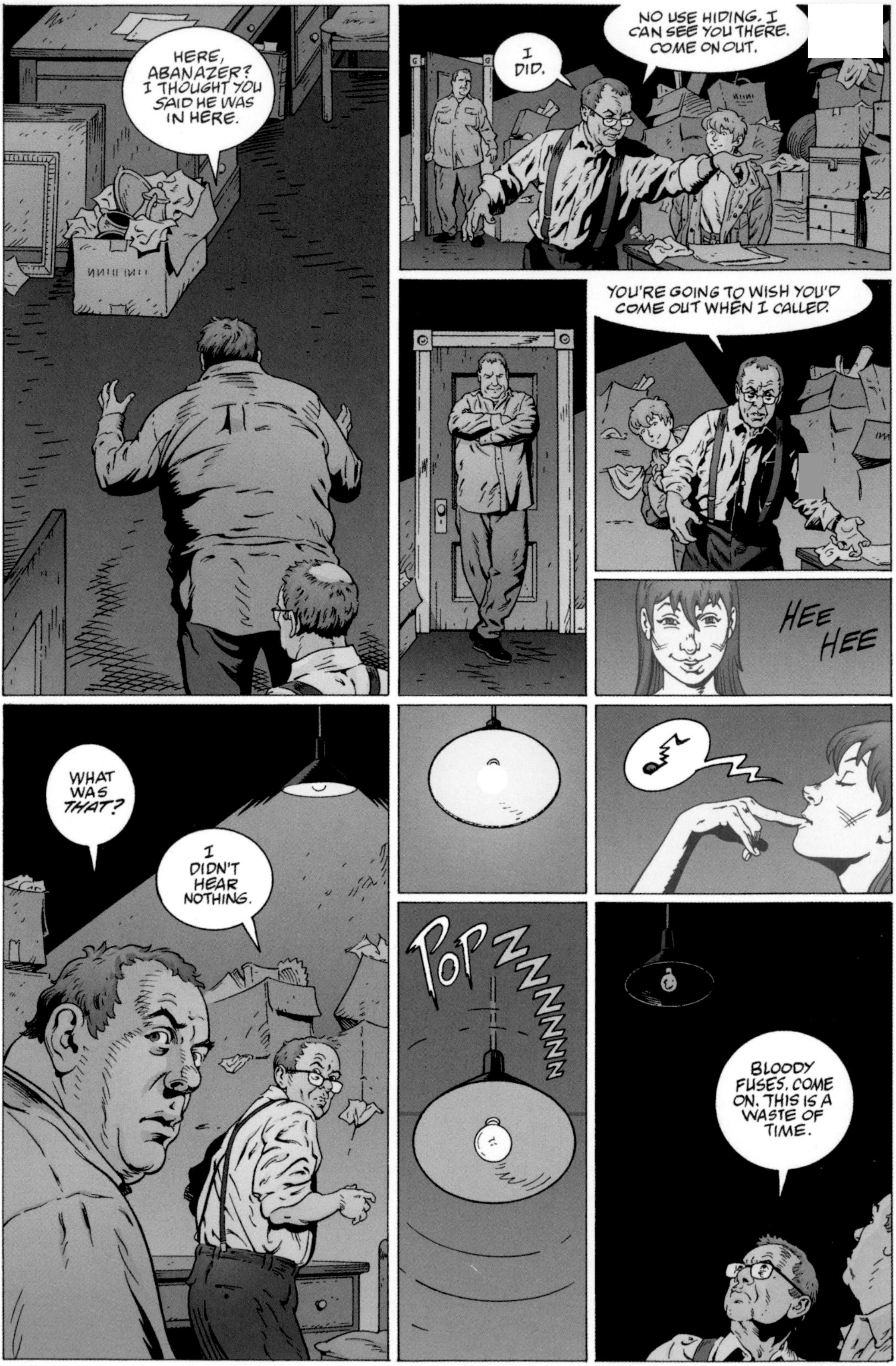
HERE, ABANAZER? I THOUGHT YOU SAID HE WAS IN HERE.
I DID.
NO USE HIDING. I CAN SEE YOU THERE. COME ON OUT.
YOU'RE GOING TO WISH YOU'D COME OUT WHEN I CALLED.
HEE HEE
WHAT WAS THAT?
I DIDN'T HEAR NOTHING.
POP ZZZZZZZ
BLOODY FUSES. COME ON. THIS IS A WASTE OF TIME.

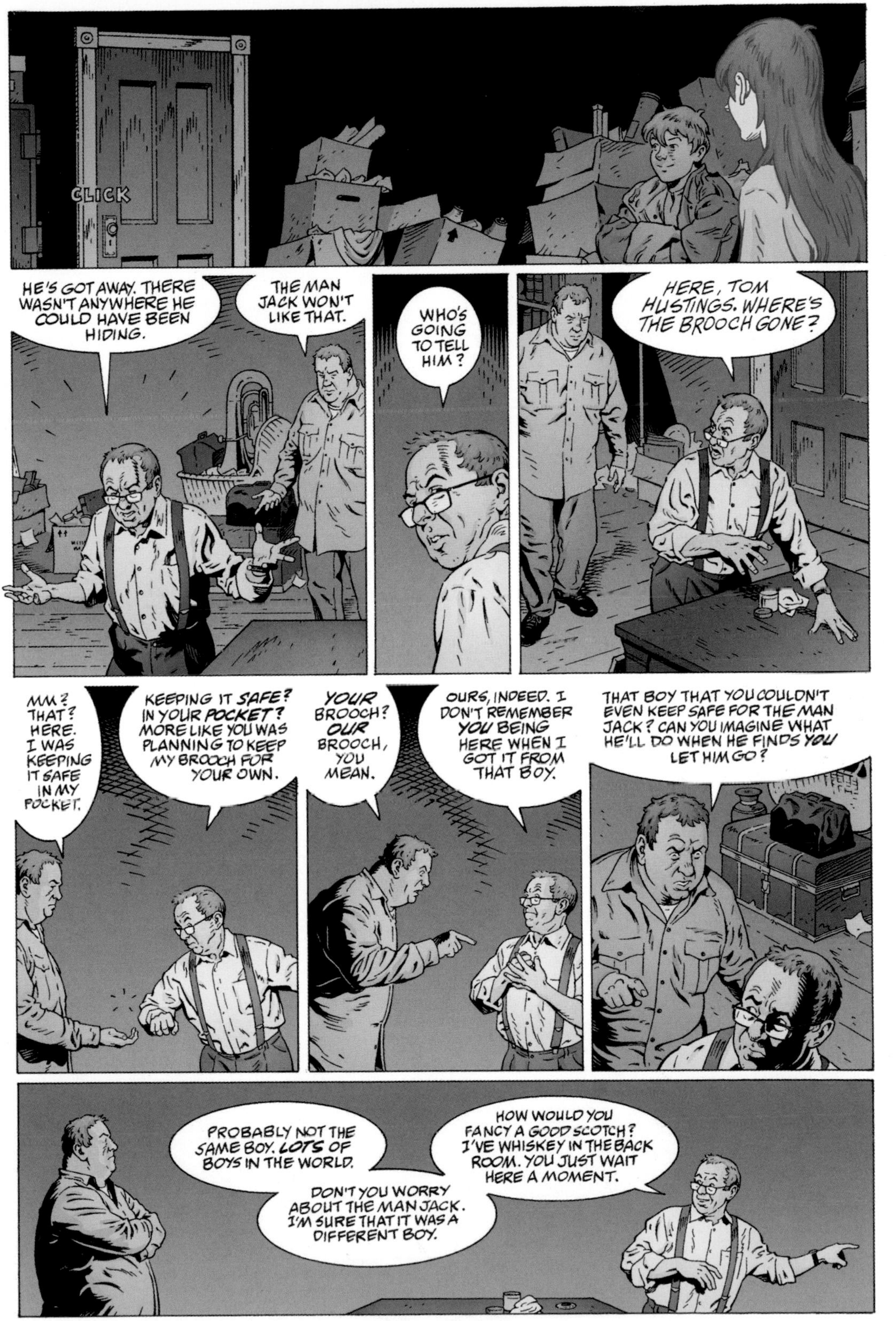
CLICK
HE'S GOT AWAY. THERE WASN'T ANYWHERE HE COULD HAVE BEEN HIDING.
THE MAN JACK WON'T LIKE THAT.
WHO'S GOING TO TELL HIM?
HERE, TOM HUSTINGS. WHERE'S THE BROOCH GONE?
MM? THAT? HERE. I WAS KEEPING IT SAFE IN MY POCKET.
KEEPING IT SAFE? IN YOUR POCKET? MORE LIKE YOU WAS PLANNING TO KEEP MY BROOCH FOR YOUR OWN.
YOUR BROOCH? OUR BROOCH, YOU MEAN.
OURS, INDEED. I DON'T REMEMBER YOU BEING HERE WHEN I GOT IT FROM THAT BOY.
THAT BOY THAT YOU COULDN'T EVEN KEEP SAFE FOR THE MAN JACK? CAN YOU IMAGINE WHAT HE'LL DO WHEN HE FINDS YOU LET HIM GO?
PROBABLY NOT THE SAME BOY. LOTS OF BOYS IN THE WORLD.
DON'T YOU WORRY ABOUT THE MAN JACK. I'M SURE THAT IT WAS A DIFFERENT BOY.
HOW WOULD YOU FANCY A GOOD SCOTCH? I'VE WHISKEY IN THE BACK ROOM. YOU JUST WAIT HERE A MOMENT.

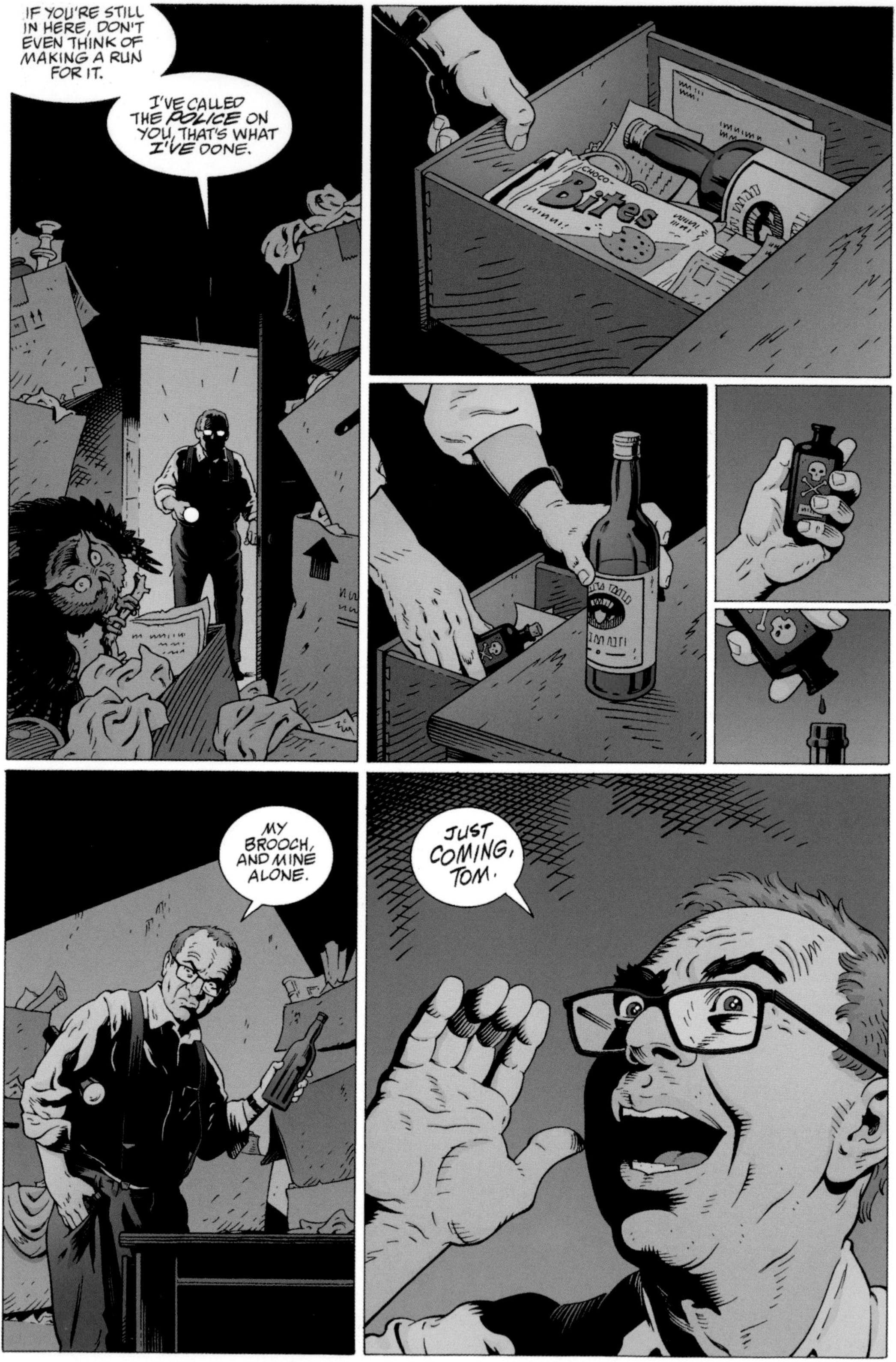
IF YOU'RE STILL IN HERE, DON'T EVEN THINK OF MAKING A RUN FOR IT.
I'VE CALLED THE POLICE ON YOU, THAT'S WHAT I'VE DONE.
CHOCO-Bites
MY BROOCH, AND MINE ALONE.
JUST COMING, TOM.

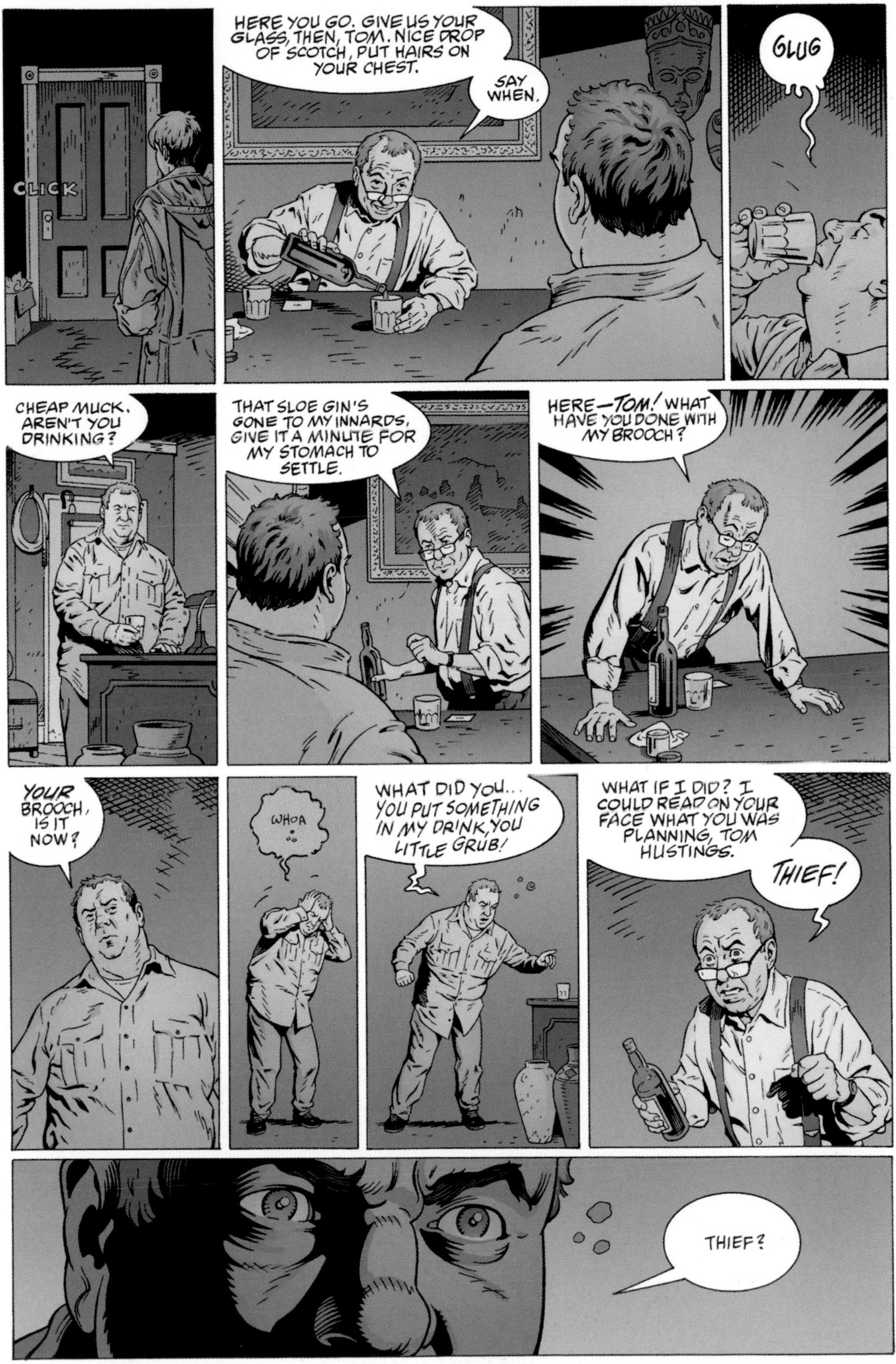
CLICK
HERE YOU GO. GIVE US YOUR GLASS, THEN, TOM. NICE DROP OF SCOTCH, PUT HAIRS ON YOUR CHEST.
SAY WHEN.
GLUG
CHEAP MUCK. AREN'T YOU DRINKING?
THAT SLOE GIN'S GONE TO MY INNARDS, GIVE IT A MINUTE FOR MY STOMACH TO SETTLE.
HERE—TOM! WHAT HAVE YOU DONE WITH MY BROOCH?
YOUR BROOCH, IS IT NOW?
WHOA
WHAT DID YOU... YOU PUT SOMETHING IN MY DRINK, YOU LITTLE GRUB!
WHAT IF I DID? I COULD READ ON YOUR FACE WHAT YOU WAS PLANNING, TOM HUSTINGS.
THIEF!
THIEF?

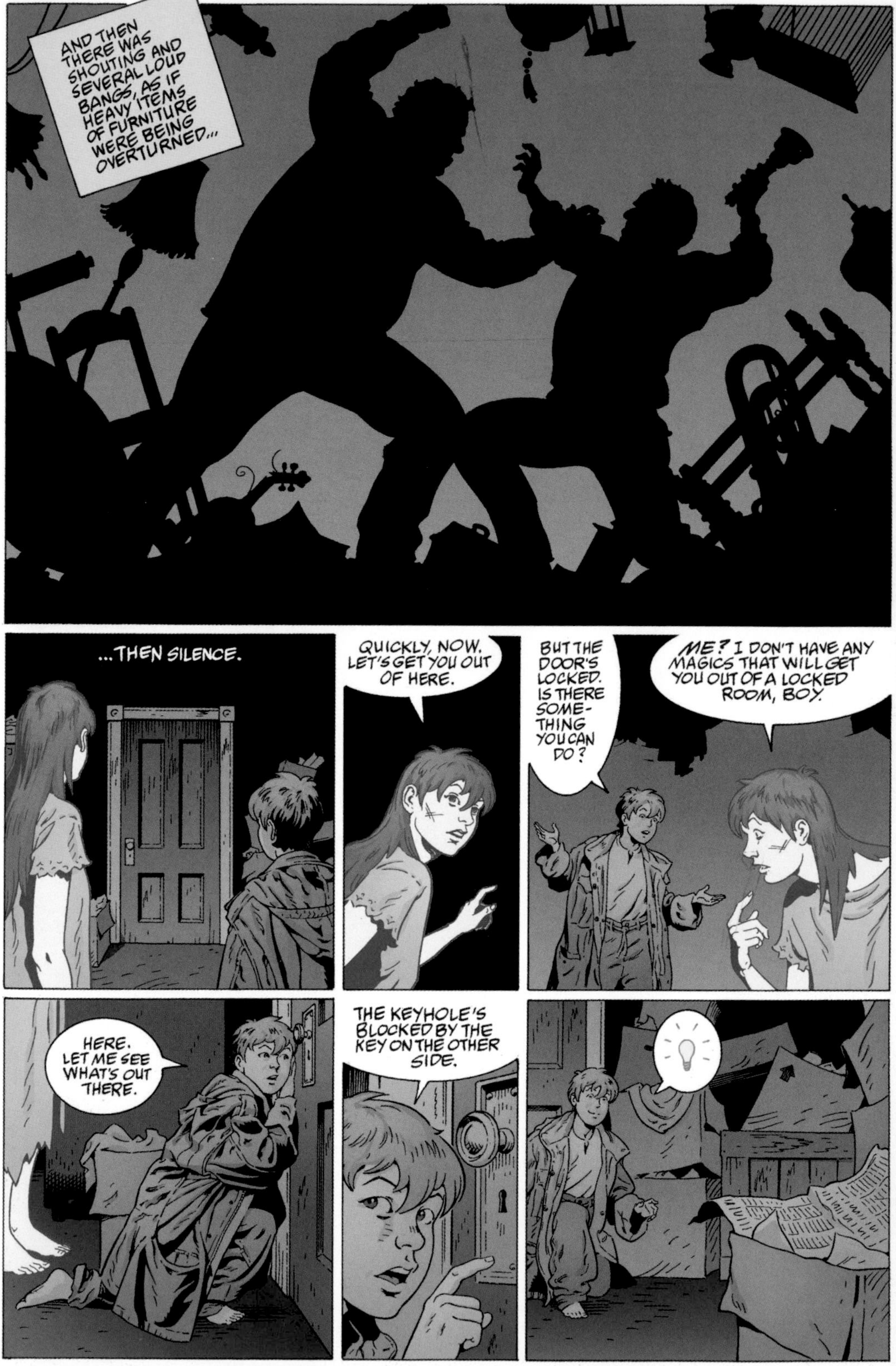
AND THEN THERE WAS SHOUTING AND SEVERAL LOUD BANGS, AS IF HEAVY ITEMS OF FURNITURE WERE BEING OVERTURNED...
...THEN SILENCE.
QUICKLY, NOW. LET'S GET YOU OUT OF HERE.
BUT THE DOOR'S LOCKED. IS THERE SOMETHING YOU CAN DO?
ME? I DON'T HAVE ANY MAGICS THAT WILL GET YOU OUT OF A LOCKED ROOM, BOY.
HERE. LET ME SEE WHAT'S OUT THERE.
THE KEYHOLE'S BLOCKED BY THE KEY ON THE OTHER SIDE.

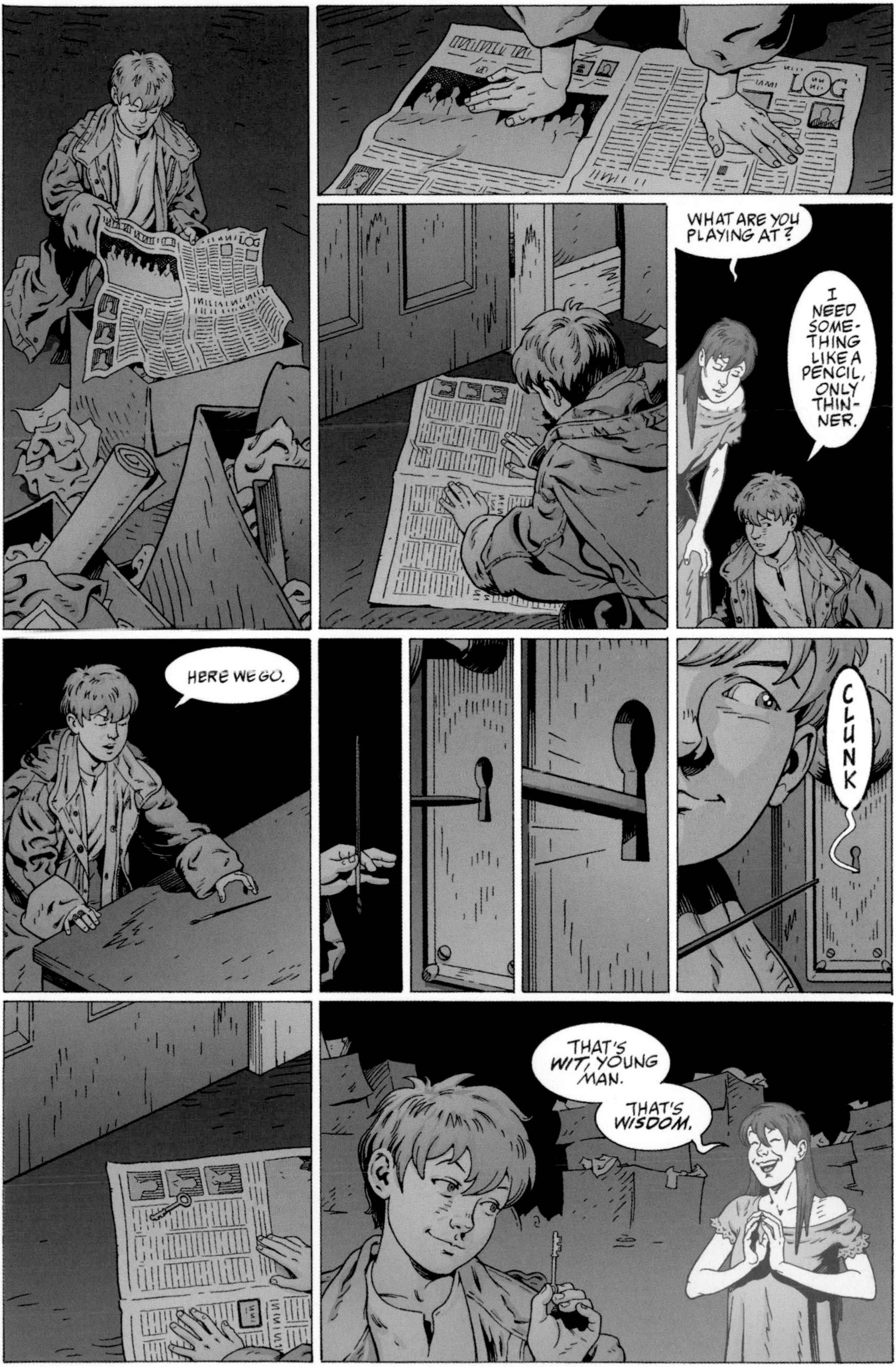
LOG
WHAT ARE YOU PLAYING AT?
I NEED SOME-THING LIKE A PENCIL, ONLY THIN-NER.
HERE WE GO.
CLUNK
THAT'S *WIT*, YOUNG MAN.
THAT'S *WISDOM*.

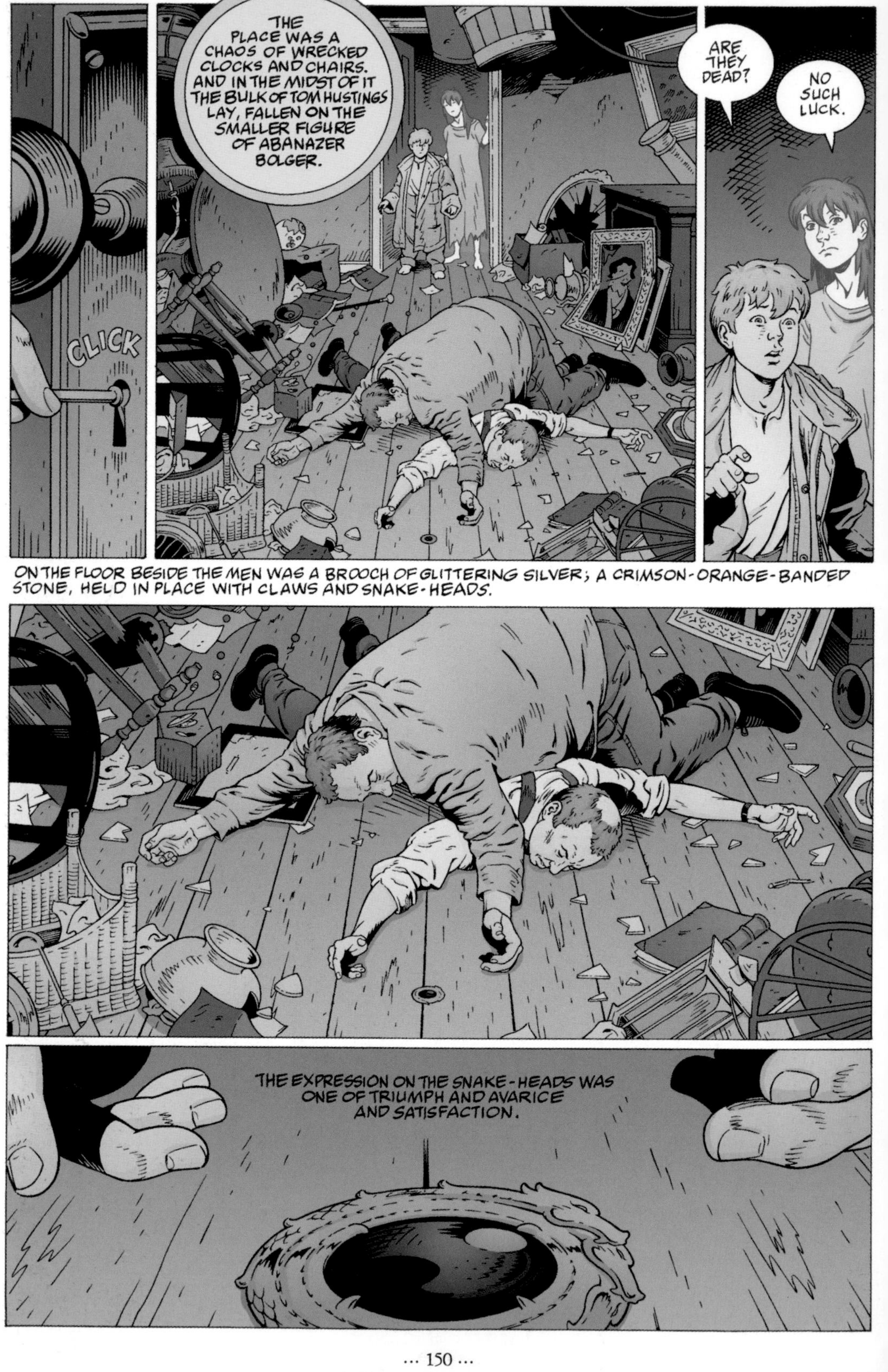
THE PLACE WAS A CHAOS OF WRECKED CLOCKS AND CHAIRS. AND IN THE MIDST OF IT THE BULK OF TOM HUSTINGS LAY, FALLEN ON THE SMALLER FIGURE OF ABANAZER BOLGER.
CLICK
ARE THEY DEAD?
NO SUCH LUCK.
ON THE FLOOR BESIDE THE MEN WAS A BROOCH OF GLITTERING SILVER; A CRIMSON-ORANGE-BANDED STONE, HELD IN PLACE WITH CLAWS AND SNAKE-HEADS.
THE EXPRESSION ON THE SNAKE-HEADS WAS ONE OF TRIUMPH AND AVARICE AND SATISFACTION.

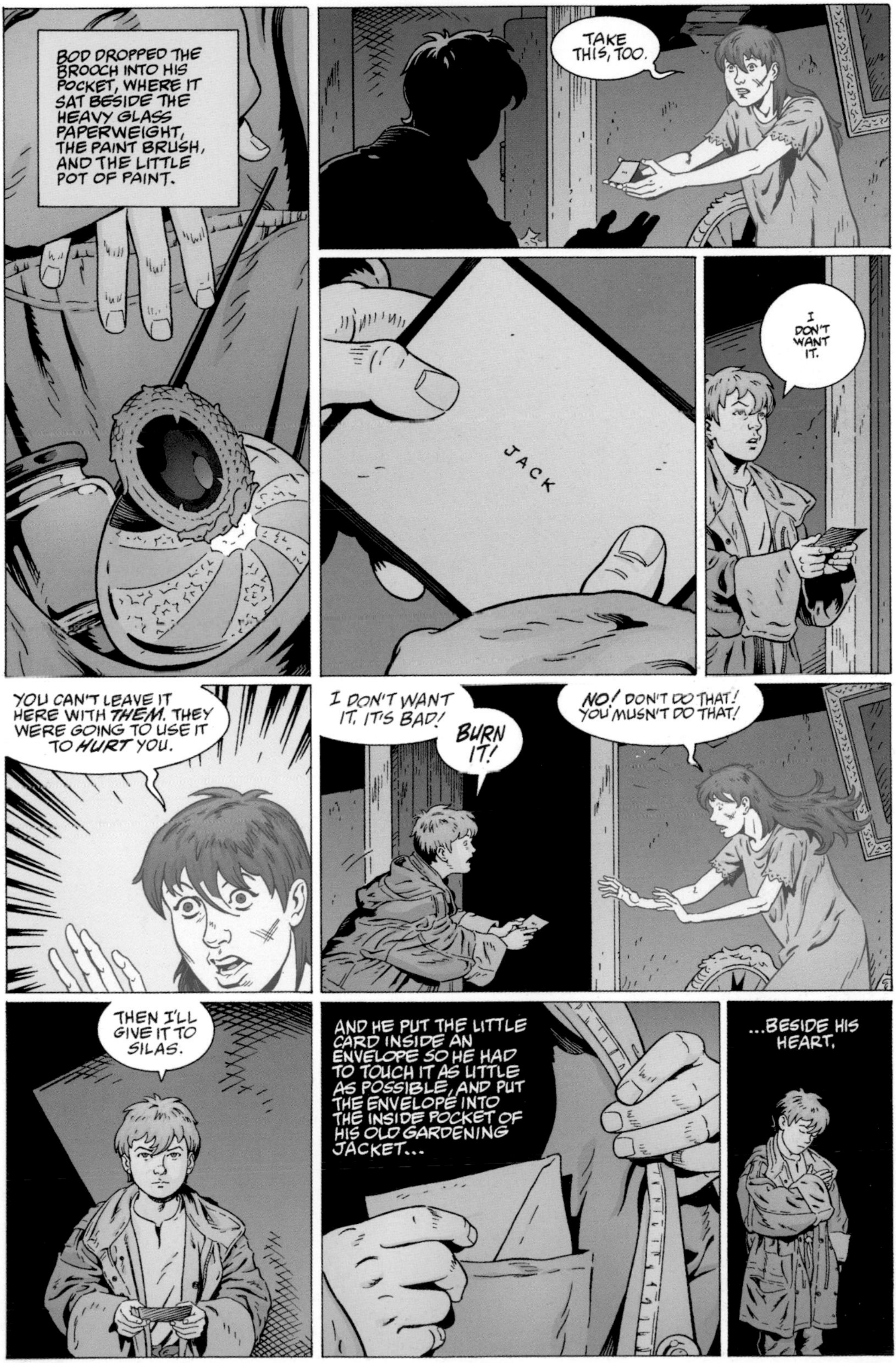
BOD DROPPED THE BROOCH INTO HIS POCKET, WHERE IT SAT BESIDE THE HEAVY GLASS PAPERWEIGHT, THE PAINT BRUSH, AND THE LITTLE POT OF PAINT.
TAKE THIS, TOO.
JACK
I DON'T WANT IT.
YOU CAN'T LEAVE IT HERE WITH THEM. THEY WERE GOING TO USE IT TO HURT YOU.
I DON'T WANT IT. IT'S BAD!
BURN IT!
NO! DON'T DO THAT! YOU MUSN'T DO THAT!
THEN I'LL GIVE IT TO SILAS.
AND HE PUT THE LITTLE CARD INSIDE AN ENVELOPE SO HE HAD TO TOUCH IT AS LITTLE AS POSSIBLE, AND PUT THE ENVELOPE INTO THE INSIDE POCKET OF HIS OLD GARDENING JACKET...
...BESIDE HIS HEART.

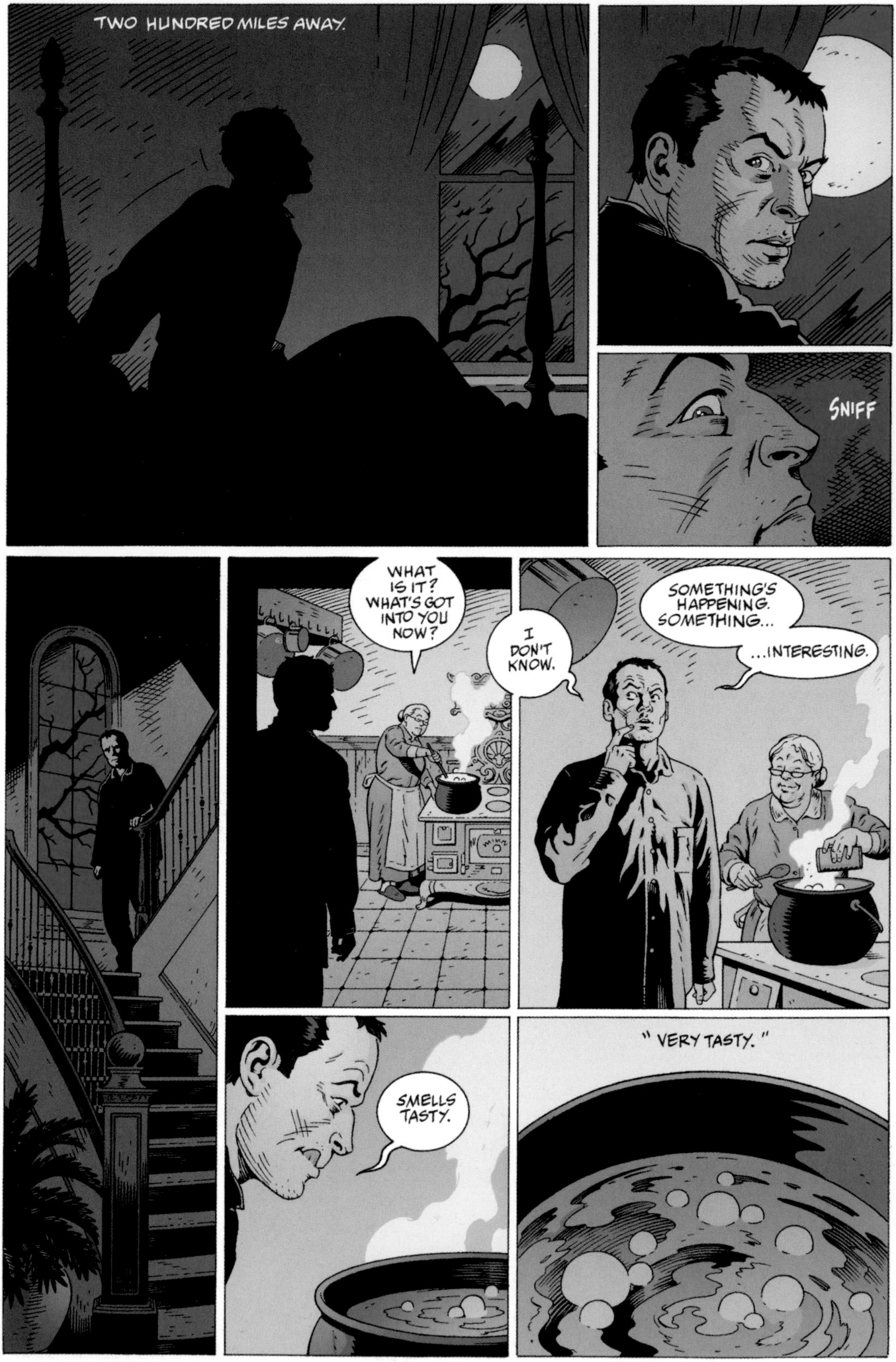

TWO HUNDRED MILES AWAY.
SNIFF
WHAT IS IT? WHAT'S GOT INTO YOU NOW?
I DON'T KNOW.
SOMETHING'S HAPPENING. SOMETHING...
...INTERESTING.
SMELLS TASTY.
"VERY TASTY."

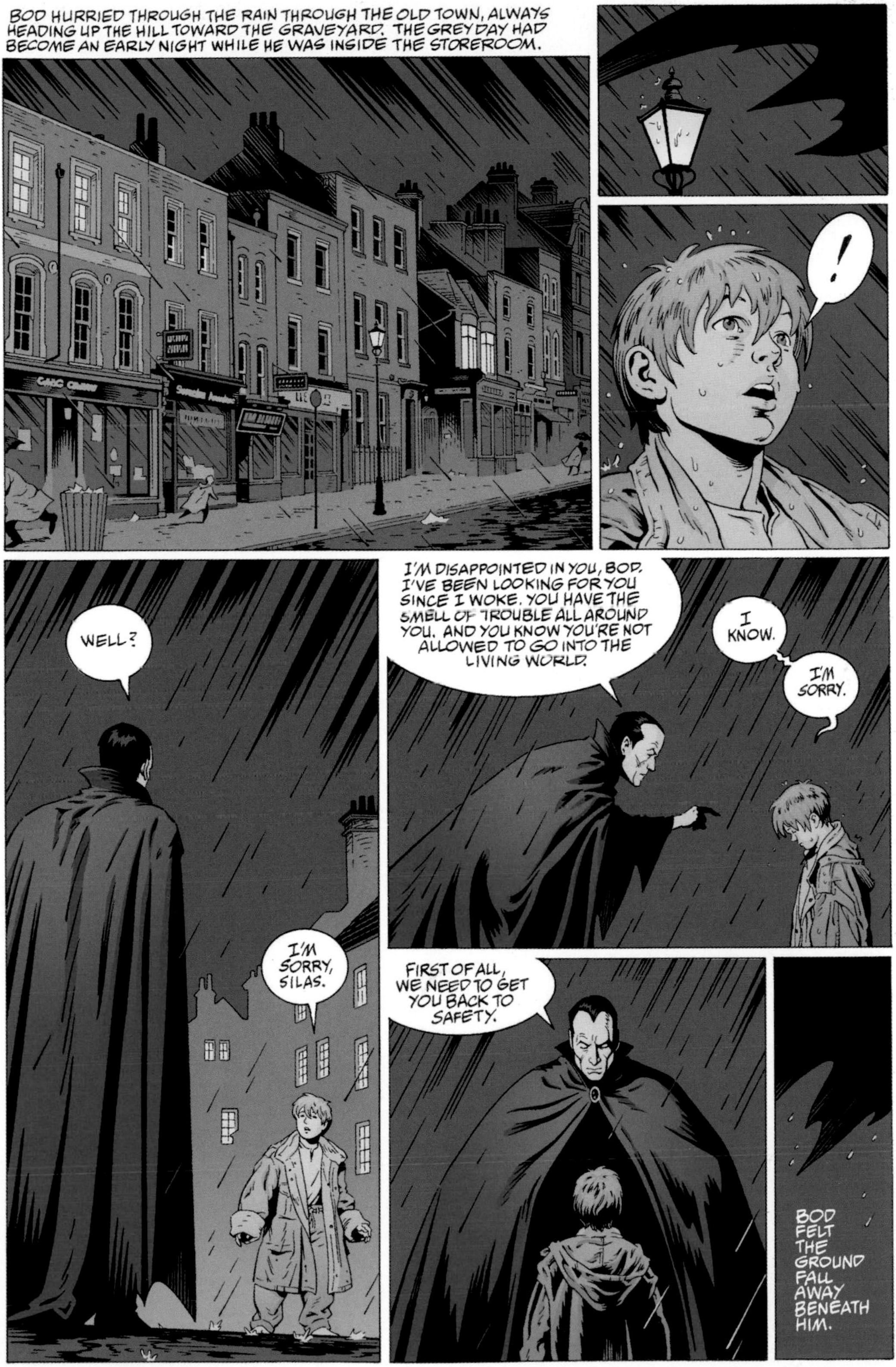

BOD HURRIED THROUGH THE RAIN THROUGH THE OLD TOWN, ALWAYS HEADING UP THE HILL TOWARD THE GRAVEYARD. THE GREY DAY HAD BECOME AN EARLY NIGHT WHILE HE WAS INSIDE THE STOREROOM.
!
WELL?
I'M SORRY, SILAS.
I'M DISAPPOINTED IN YOU, BOD. I'VE BEEN LOOKING FOR YOU SINCE I WOKE. YOU HAVE THE SMELL OF TROUBLE ALL AROUND YOU. AND YOU KNOW YOU'RE NOT ALLOWED TO GO INTO THE LIVING WORLD.
I KNOW.
I'M SORRY.
FIRST OF ALL, WE NEED TO GET YOU BACK TO SAFETY.
BOD FELT THE GROUND FALL AWAY BENEATH HIM.

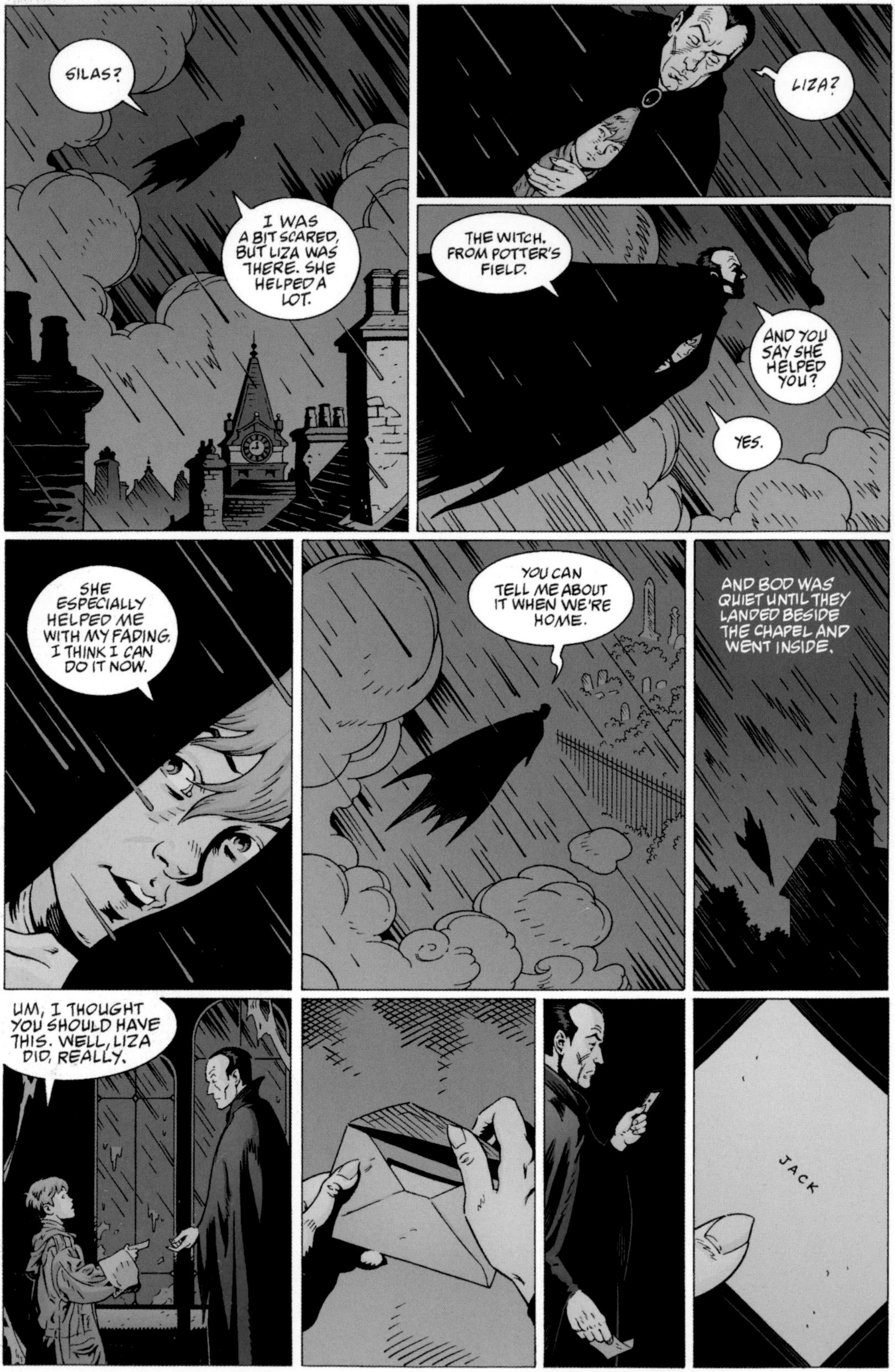
SILAS?
LIZA?
I WAS A BIT SCARED, BUT LIZA WAS THERE. SHE HELPED A LOT.
THE WITCH. FROM POTTER'S FIELD.
AND YOU SAY SHE HELPED YOU?
YES.
SHE ESPECIALLY HELPED ME WITH MY FADING. I THINK I CAN DO IT NOW.
YOU CAN TELL ME ABOUT IT WHEN WE'RE HOME.
AND BOD WAS QUIET UNTIL THEY LANDED BESIDE THE CHAPEL AND WENT INSIDE.
UM, I THOUGHT YOU SHOULD HAVE THIS. WELL, LIZA DID, REALLY.
JACK

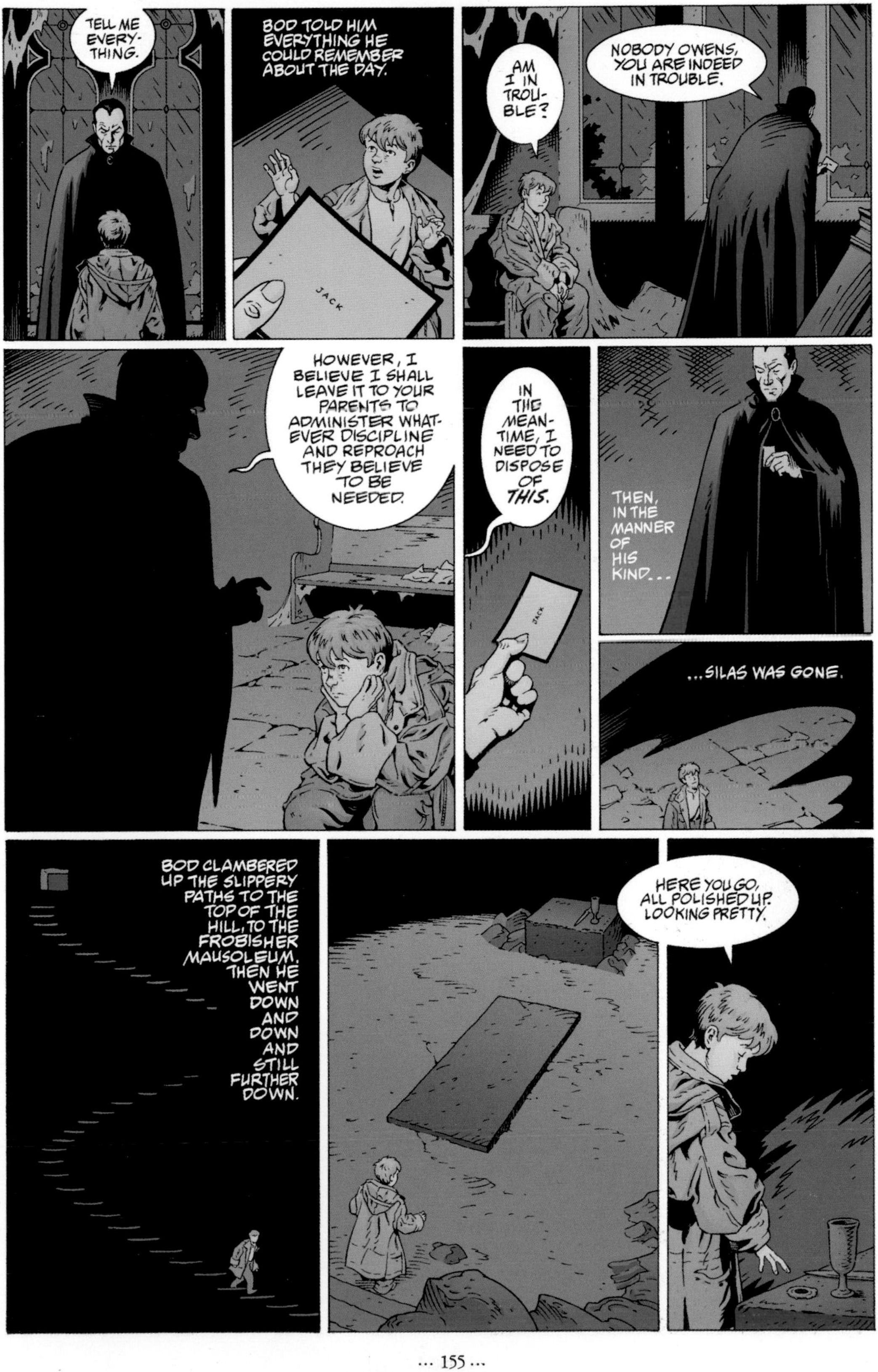
TELL ME EVERY-THING.
BOD TOLD HIM EVERYTHING HE COULD REMEMBER ABOUT THE DAY.
JACK
AM I IN TROU-BLE?
NOBODY OWENS, YOU ARE INDEED IN TROUBLE.
HOWEVER, I BELIEVE I SHALL LEAVE IT TO YOUR PARENTS TO ADMINISTER WHAT-EVER DISCIPLINE AND REPROACH THEY BELIEVE TO BE NEEDED.
IN THE MEAN-TIME, I NEED TO DISPOSE OF THIS.
JACK
THEN, IN THE MANNER OF HIS KIND...
...SILAS WAS GONE.
BOD CLAMBERED UP THE SLIPPERY PATHS TO THE TOP OF THE HILL, TO THE FROBISHER MAUSOLEUM. THEN HE WENT DOWN AND DOWN AND STILL FURTHER DOWN.
HERE YOU GO, ALL POLISHED UP. LOOKING PRETTY.

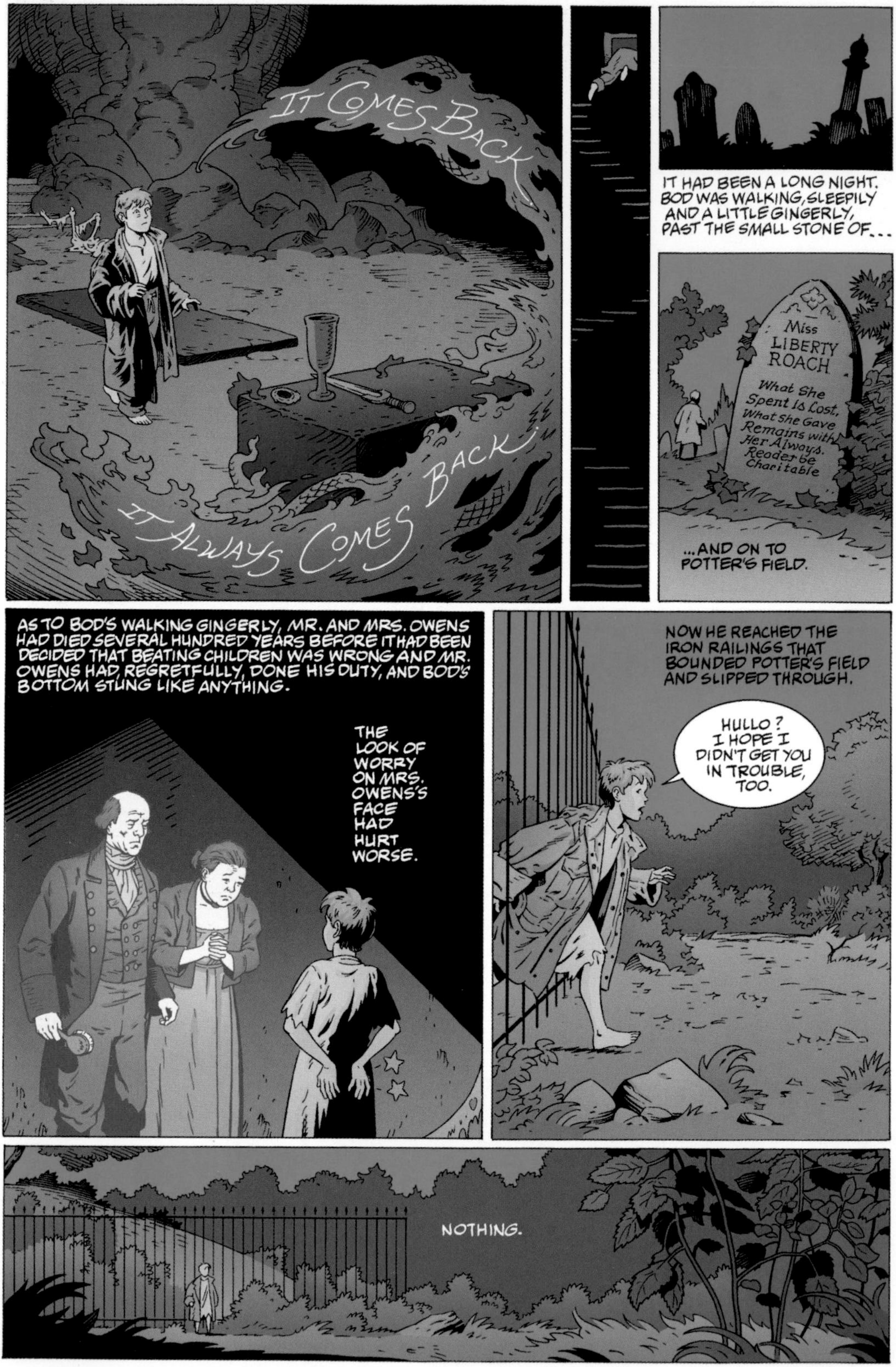
IT COMES BACK.
IT ALWAYS COMES BACK.
IT HAD BEEN A LONG NIGHT. BOD WAS WALKING, SLEEPILY AND A LITTLE GINGERLY, PAST THE SMALL STONE OF...
Miss LIBERTY ROACH What She Spent is Lost, What She Gave Remains with Her Always. Reader be Charitable
...AND ON TO POTTER'S FIELD.
AS TO BOD'S WALKING GINGERLY, MR. AND MRS. OWENS HAD DIED SEVERAL HUNDRED YEARS BEFORE IT HAD BEEN DECIDED THAT BEATING CHILDREN WAS WRONG AND MR. OWENS HAD, REGRETFULLY, DONE HIS DUTY, AND BOD'S BOTTOM STUNG LIKE ANYTHING.
THE LOOK OF WORRY ON MRS. OWENS'S FACE HAD HURT WORSE.
NOW HE REACHED THE IRON RAILINGS THAT BOUNDED POTTER'S FIELD AND SLIPPED THROUGH.
HULLO? I HOPE I DIDN'T GET YOU IN TROUBLE, TOO.
NOTHING.

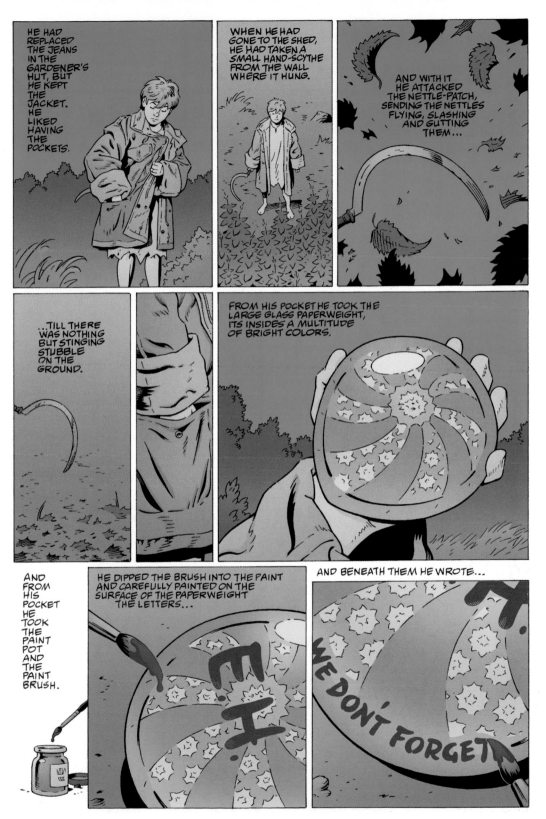

HE HAD REPLACED THE JEANS IN THE GARDENER'S HUT, BUT HE KEPT THE JACKET. HE LIKED HAVING THE POCKETS.

WHEN HE HAD GONE TO THE SHED, HE HAD TAKEN A SMALL HAND-SCYTHE FROM THE WALL WHERE IT HUNG.

AND WITH IT HE ATTACKED THE NETTLE-PATCH, SENDING THE NETTLES FLYING, SLASHING AND GUTTING THEM...

...TILL THERE WAS NOTHING BUT STINGING STUBBLE ON THE GROUND.

FROM HIS POCKET HE TOOK THE LARGE GLASS PAPERWEIGHT, ITS INSIDES A MULTITUDE OF BRIGHT COLORS.

AND FROM HIS POCKET HE TOOK THE PAINT POT AND THE PAINT BRUSH.

HE DIPPED THE BRUSH INTO THE PAINT AND CAREFULLY PAINTED ON THE SURFACE OF THE PAPERWEIGHT THE LETTERS...

E.H.

AND BENEATH THEM HE WROTE...

WE DON'T FORGET

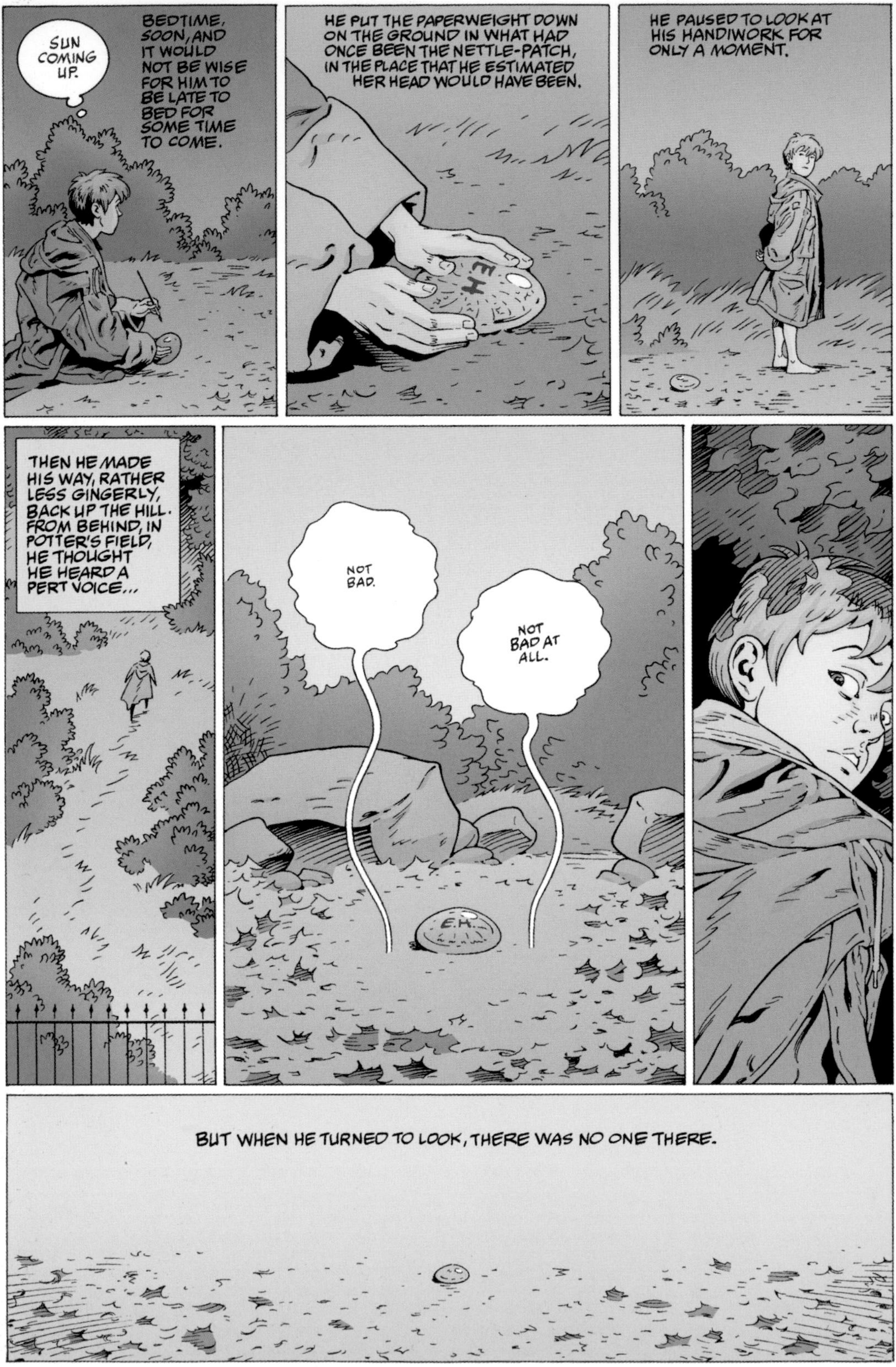
SUN COMING UP.
BEDTIME, SOON, AND IT WOULD NOT BE WISE FOR HIM TO BE LATE TO BED FOR SOME TIME TO COME.
HE PUT THE PAPERWEIGHT DOWN ON THE GROUND IN WHAT HAD ONCE BEEN THE NETTLE-PATCH, IN THE PLACE THAT HE ESTIMATED HER HEAD WOULD HAVE BEEN.
E H
HE PAUSED TO LOOK AT HIS HANDIWORK FOR ONLY A MOMENT.
THEN HE MADE HIS WAY, RATHER LESS GINGERLY, BACK UP THE HILL. FROM BEHIND, IN POTTER'S FIELD, HE THOUGHT HE HEARD A PERT VOICE...
NOT BAD.
NOT BAD AT ALL.
E.H.
BUT WHEN HE TURNED TO LOOK, THERE WAS NO ONE THERE.

5

Danse Macabre

Illustrated by Jill Thompson

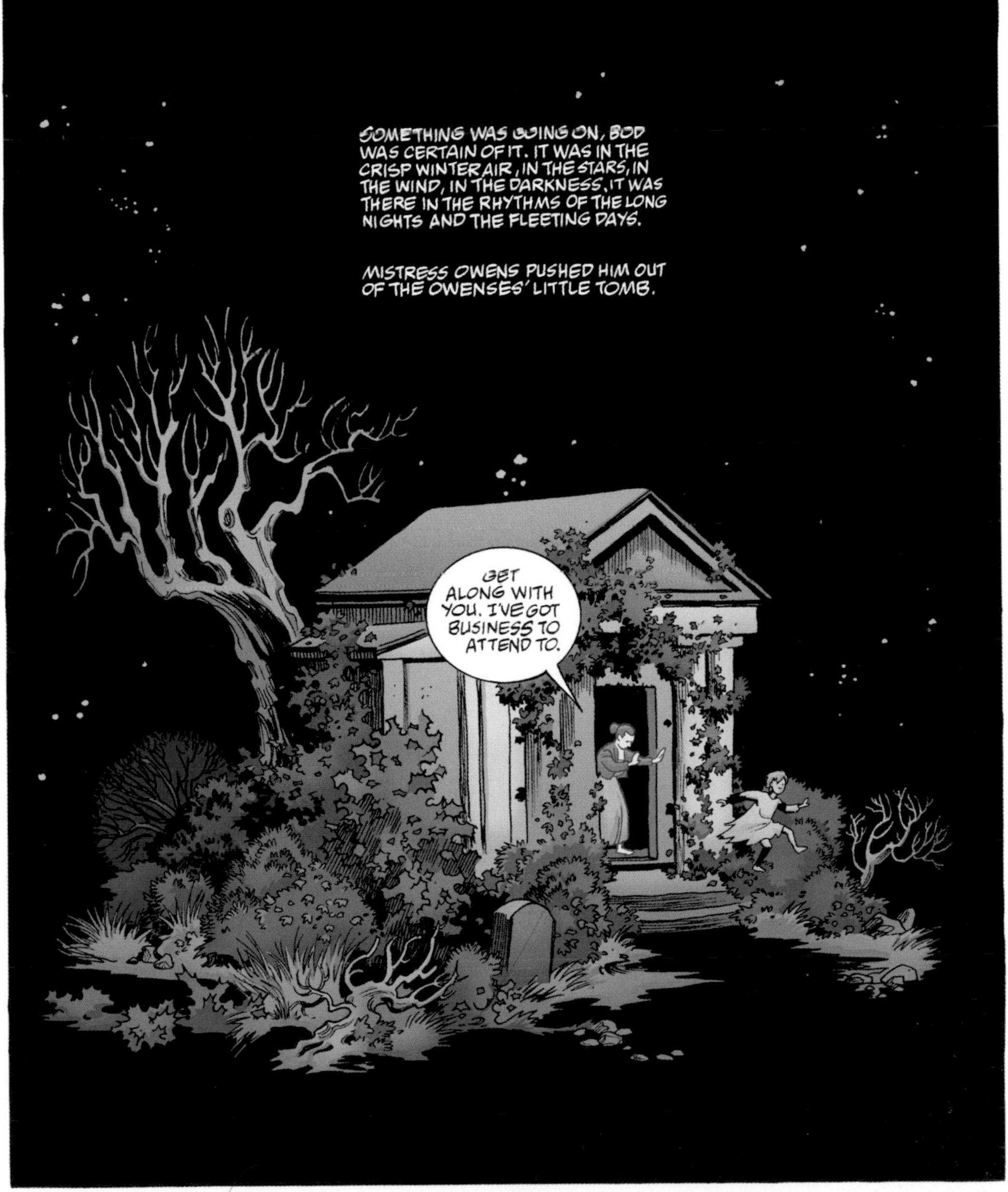
SOMETHING WAS GOING ON, BOD WAS CERTAIN OF IT. IT WAS IN THE CRISP WINTER AIR, IN THE STARS, IN THE WIND, IN THE DARKNESS, IT WAS THERE IN THE RHYTHMS OF THE LONG NIGHTS AND THE FLEETING DAYS.
MISTRESS OWENS PUSHED HIM OUT OF THE OWENSES' LITTLE TOMB.
GET ALONG WITH YOU. I'VE GOT BUSINESS TO ATTEND TO.

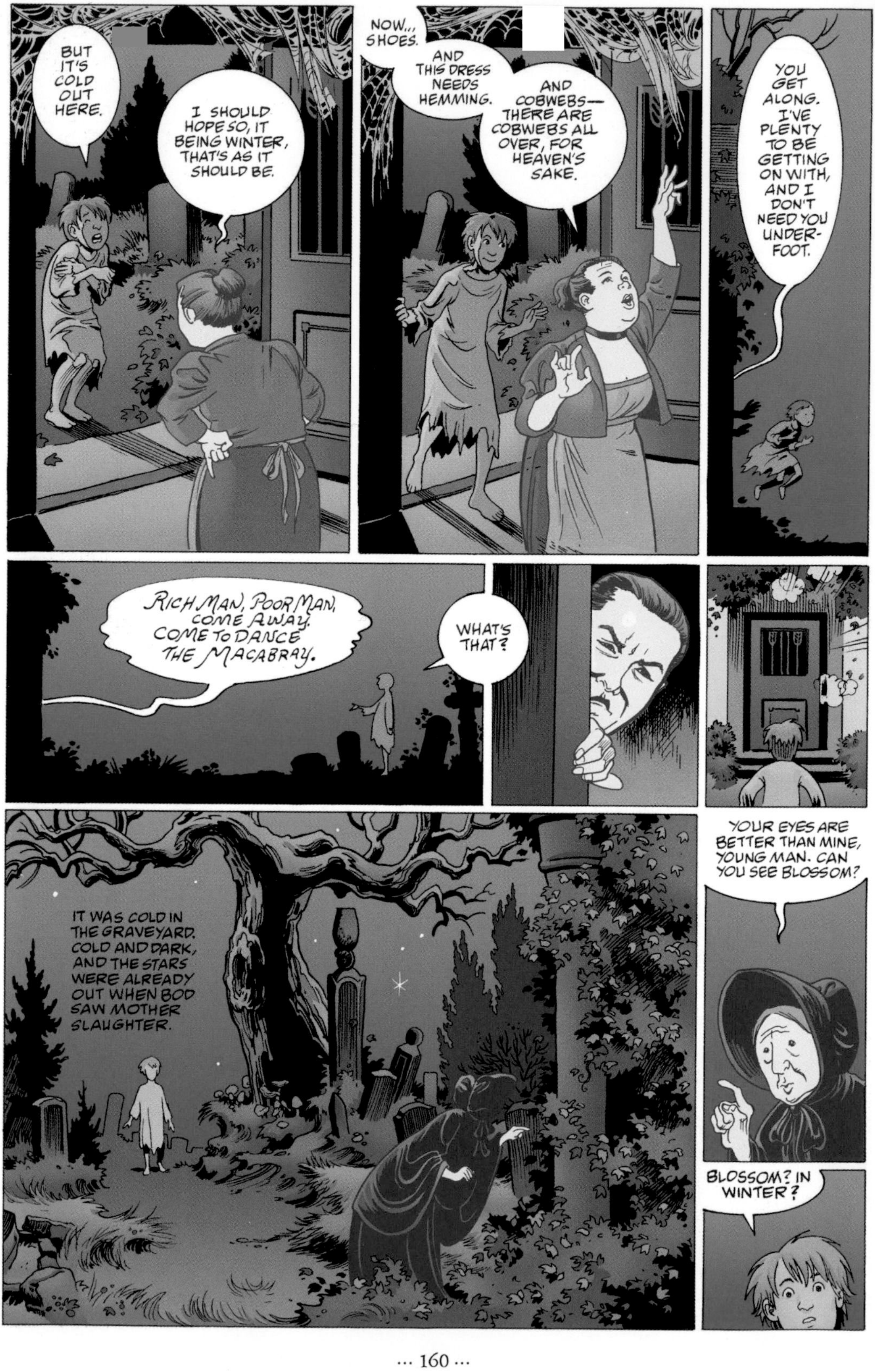
BUT IT'S COLD OUT HERE.
I SHOULD HOPE SO, IT BEING WINTER, THAT'S AS IT SHOULD BE.
NOW... SHOES.
AND THIS DRESS NEEDS HEMMING.
AND COBWEBS— THERE ARE COBWEBS ALL OVER, FOR HEAVEN'S SAKE.
YOU GET ALONG. I'VE PLENTY TO BE GETTING ON WITH, AND I DON'T NEED YOU UNDER-FOOT.
RICH MAN, POOR MAN, COME AWAY. COME TO DANCE THE MACABRAY.
WHAT'S THAT?
IT WAS COLD IN THE GRAVEYARD. COLD AND DARK, AND THE STARS WERE ALREADY OUT WHEN BOD SAW MOTHER SLAUGHTER.
YOUR EYES ARE BETTER THAN MINE, YOUNG MAN. CAN YOU SEE BLOSSOM?
BLOSSOM? IN WINTER?

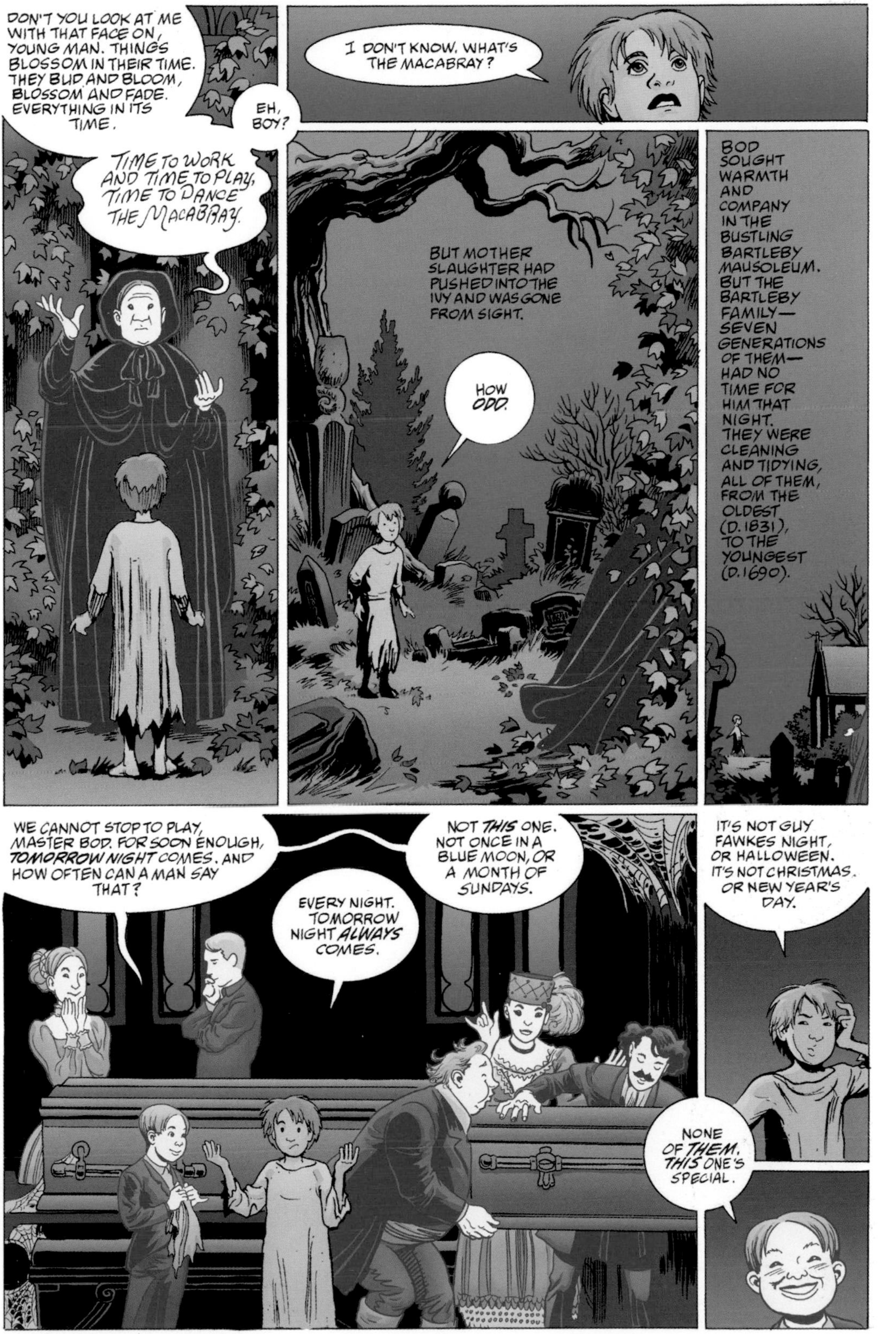
DON'T YOU LOOK AT ME WITH THAT FACE ON, YOUNG MAN. THINGS BLOSSOM IN THEIR TIME. THEY BUD AND BLOOM, BLOSSOM AND FADE. EVERYTHING IN ITS TIME.
EH, BOY?
TIME TO WORK AND TIME TO PLAY, TIME TO DANCE THE MACABRAY.
I DON'T KNOW. WHAT'S THE MACABRAY?
BUT MOTHER SLAUGHTER HAD PUSHED INTO THE IVY AND WAS GONE FROM SIGHT.
HOW ODD.
BOD SOUGHT WARMTH AND COMPANY IN THE BUSTLING BARTLEBY MAUSOLEUM. BUT THE BARTLEBY FAMILY— SEVEN GENERATIONS OF THEM— HAD NO TIME FOR HIM THAT NIGHT. THEY WERE CLEANING AND TIDYING, ALL OF THEM, FROM THE OLDEST (D.1831), TO THE YOUNGEST (D.1690).
WE CANNOT STOP TO PLAY, MASTER BOD. FOR SOON ENOUGH, TOMORROW NIGHT COMES. AND HOW OFTEN CAN A MAN SAY THAT?
EVERY NIGHT. TOMORROW NIGHT ALWAYS COMES.
NOT THIS ONE. NOT ONCE IN A BLUE MOON, OR A MONTH OF SUNDAYS.
IT'S NOT GUY FAWKES NIGHT, OR HALLOWEEN. IT'S NOT CHRISTMAS. OR NEW YEAR'S DAY.
NONE OF THEM. THIS ONE'S SPECIAL.

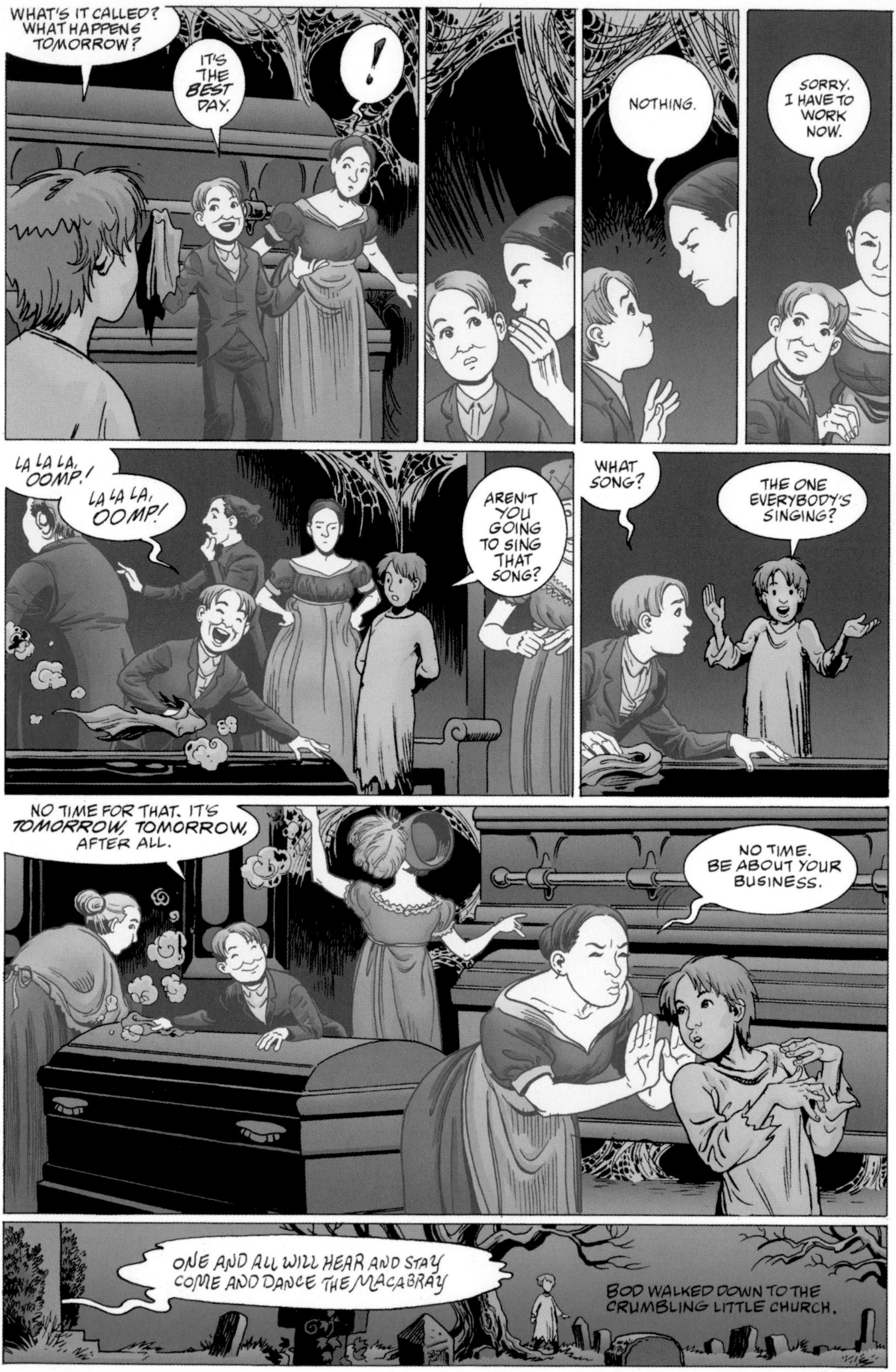
WHAT'S IT CALLED? WHAT HAPPENS TOMORROW?
IT'S THE BEST DAY.
!
NOTHING.
SORRY. I HAVE TO WORK NOW.
LA LA LA, OOMP!
LA LA LA, OOMP!
AREN'T YOU GOING TO SING THAT SONG?
WHAT SONG?
THE ONE EVERYBODY'S SINGING?
NO TIME FOR THAT. IT'S TOMORROW, TOMORROW, AFTER ALL.
NO TIME. BE ABOUT YOUR BUSINESS.
ONE AND ALL WILL HEAR AND STAY
COME AND DANCE THE MACABRAY
BOD WALKED DOWN TO THE CRUMBLING LITTLE CHURCH.

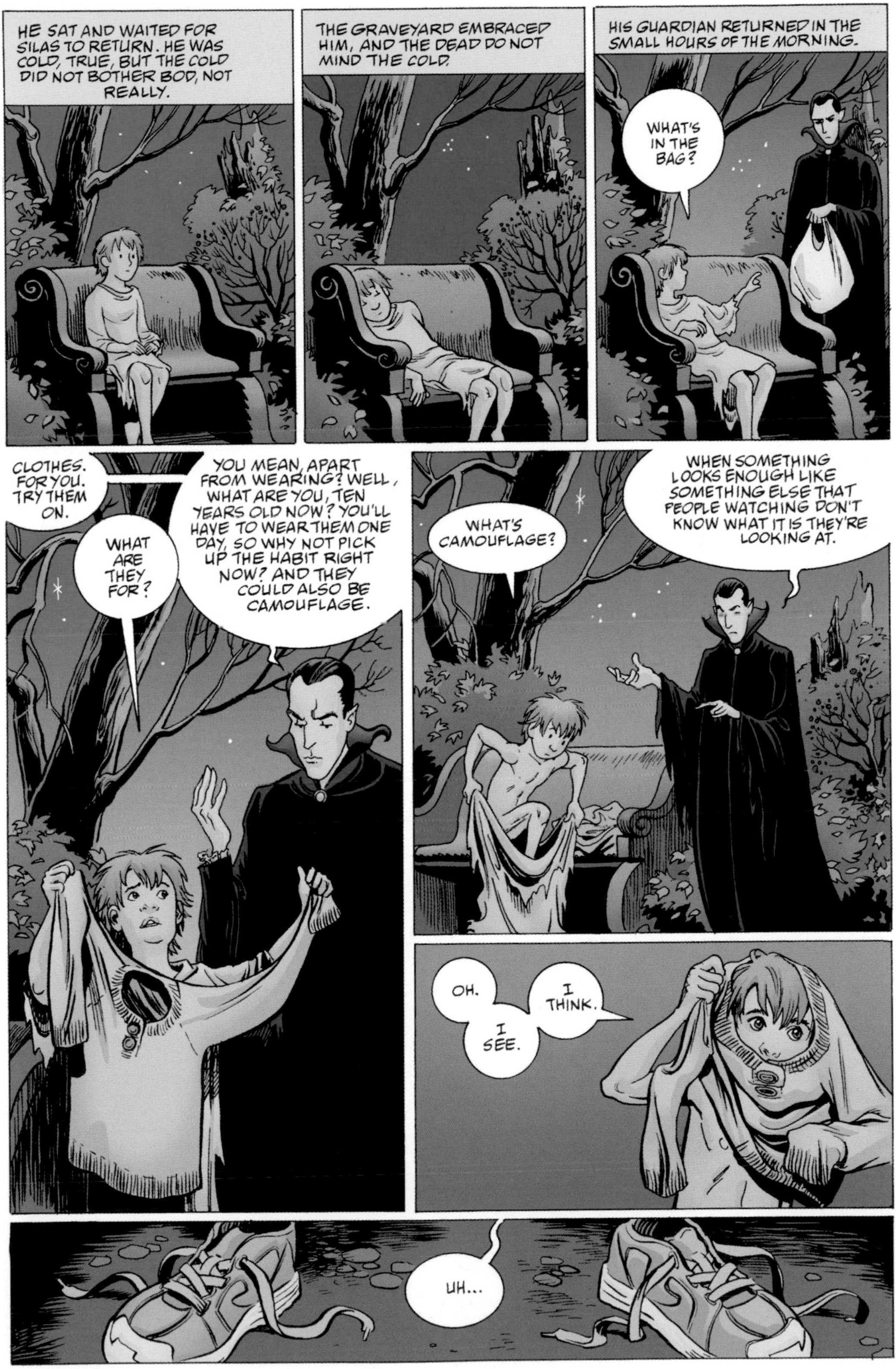
HE SAT AND WAITED FOR SILAS TO RETURN. HE WAS COLD, TRUE, BUT THE COLD DID NOT BOTHER BOD, NOT REALLY.
THE GRAVEYARD EMBRACED HIM, AND THE DEAD DO NOT MIND THE COLD.
HIS GUARDIAN RETURNED IN THE SMALL HOURS OF THE MORNING.
WHAT'S IN THE BAG?
CLOTHES. FOR YOU. TRY THEM ON.
WHAT ARE THEY FOR?
YOU MEAN, APART FROM WEARING? WELL, WHAT ARE YOU, TEN YEARS OLD NOW? YOU'LL HAVE TO WEAR THEM ONE DAY, SO WHY NOT PICK UP THE HABIT RIGHT NOW? AND THEY COULD ALSO BE CAMOUFLAGE.
WHAT'S CAMOUFLAGE?
WHEN SOMETHING LOOKS ENOUGH LIKE SOMETHING ELSE THAT PEOPLE WATCHING DON'T KNOW WHAT IT IS THEY'RE LOOKING AT.
OH.
I SEE.
I THINK.
UH...

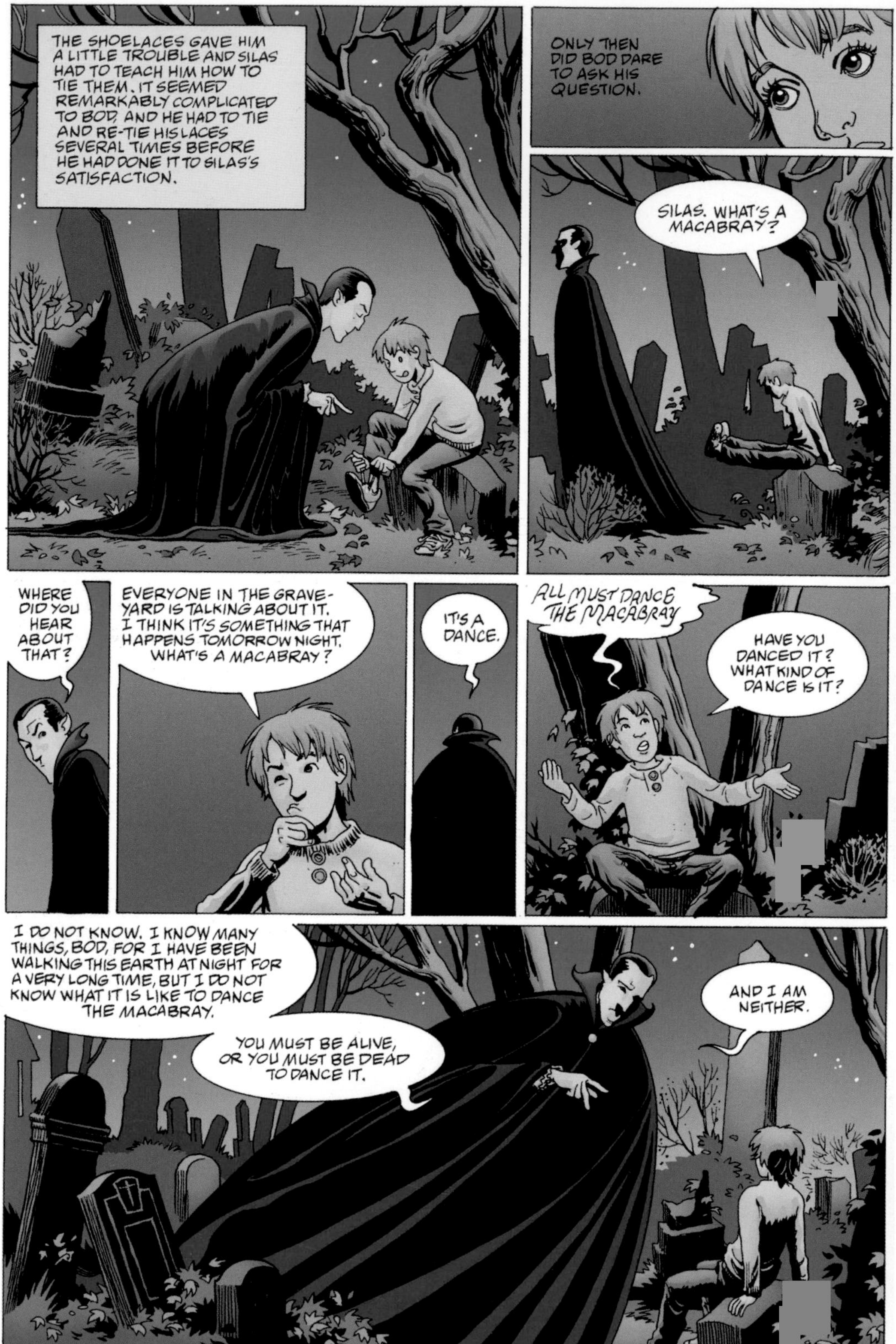

THE SHOELACES GAVE HIM A LITTLE TROUBLE AND SILAS HAD TO TEACH HIM HOW TO TIE THEM. IT SEEMED REMARKABLY COMPLICATED TO BOD, AND HE HAD TO TIE AND RE-TIE HIS LACES SEVERAL TIMES BEFORE HE HAD DONE IT TO SILAS'S SATISFACTION.
ONLY THEN DID BOD DARE TO ASK HIS QUESTION.
SILAS. WHAT'S A MACABRAY?
WHERE DID YOU HEAR ABOUT THAT?
EVERYONE IN THE GRAVEYARD IS TALKING ABOUT IT. I THINK IT'S SOMETHING THAT HAPPENS TOMORROW NIGHT. WHAT'S A MACABRAY?
IT'S A DANCE.
ALL MUST DANCE THE MACABRAY
HAVE YOU DANCED IT? WHAT KIND OF DANCE IS IT?
I DO NOT KNOW. I KNOW MANY THINGS, BOD, FOR I HAVE BEEN WALKING THIS EARTH AT NIGHT FOR A VERY LONG TIME, BUT I DO NOT KNOW WHAT IT IS LIKE TO DANCE THE MACABRAY.
YOU MUST BE ALIVE, OR YOU MUST BE DEAD TO DANCE IT.
AND I AM NEITHER.

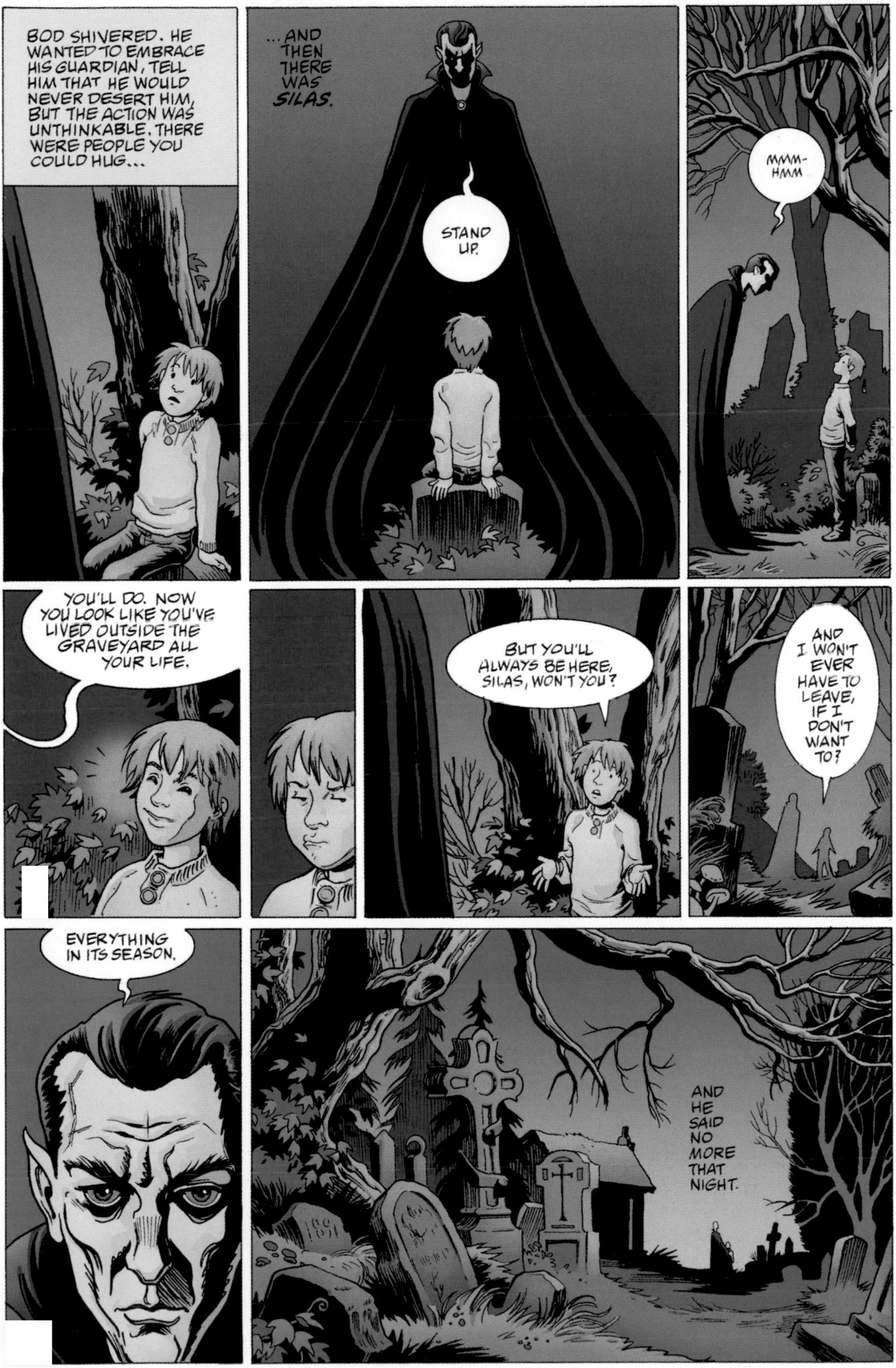
BOD SHIVERED. HE WANTED TO EMBRACE HIS GUARDIAN, TELL HIM THAT HE WOULD NEVER DESERT HIM, BUT THE ACTION WAS UNTHINKABLE. THERE WERE PEOPLE YOU COULD HUG...
...AND THEN THERE WAS SILAS.
STAND UP.
MMM-HMM
YOU'LL DO. NOW YOU LOOK LIKE YOU'VE LIVED OUTSIDE THE GRAVEYARD ALL YOUR LIFE.
BUT YOU'LL ALWAYS BE HERE, SILAS, WON'T YOU?
AND I WON'T EVER HAVE TO LEAVE, IF I DON'T WANT TO?
EVERYTHING IN ITS SEASON.
AND HE SAID NO MORE THAT NIGHT.

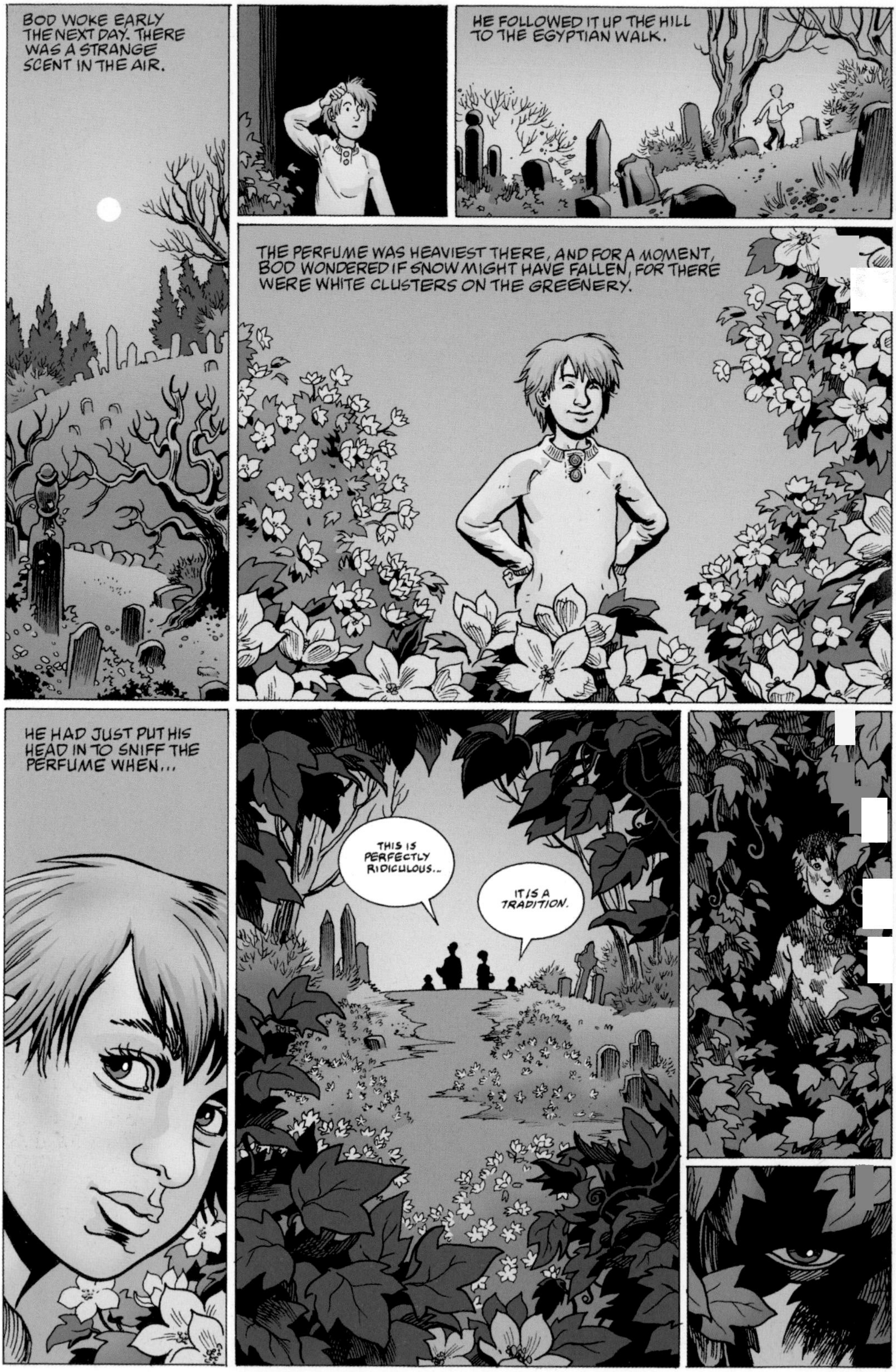
BOD WOKE EARLY THE NEXT DAY. THERE WAS A STRANGE SCENT IN THE AIR.
HE FOLLOWED IT UP THE HILL TO THE EGYPTIAN WALK.
THE PERFUME WAS HEAVIEST THERE, AND FOR A MOMENT, BOD WONDERED IF SNOW MIGHT HAVE FALLEN, FOR THERE WERE WHITE CLUSTERS ON THE GREENERY.
HE HAD JUST PUT HIS HEAD IN TO SNIFF THE PERFUME WHEN...
THIS IS PERFECTLY RIDICULOUS...
IT IS A TRADITION.

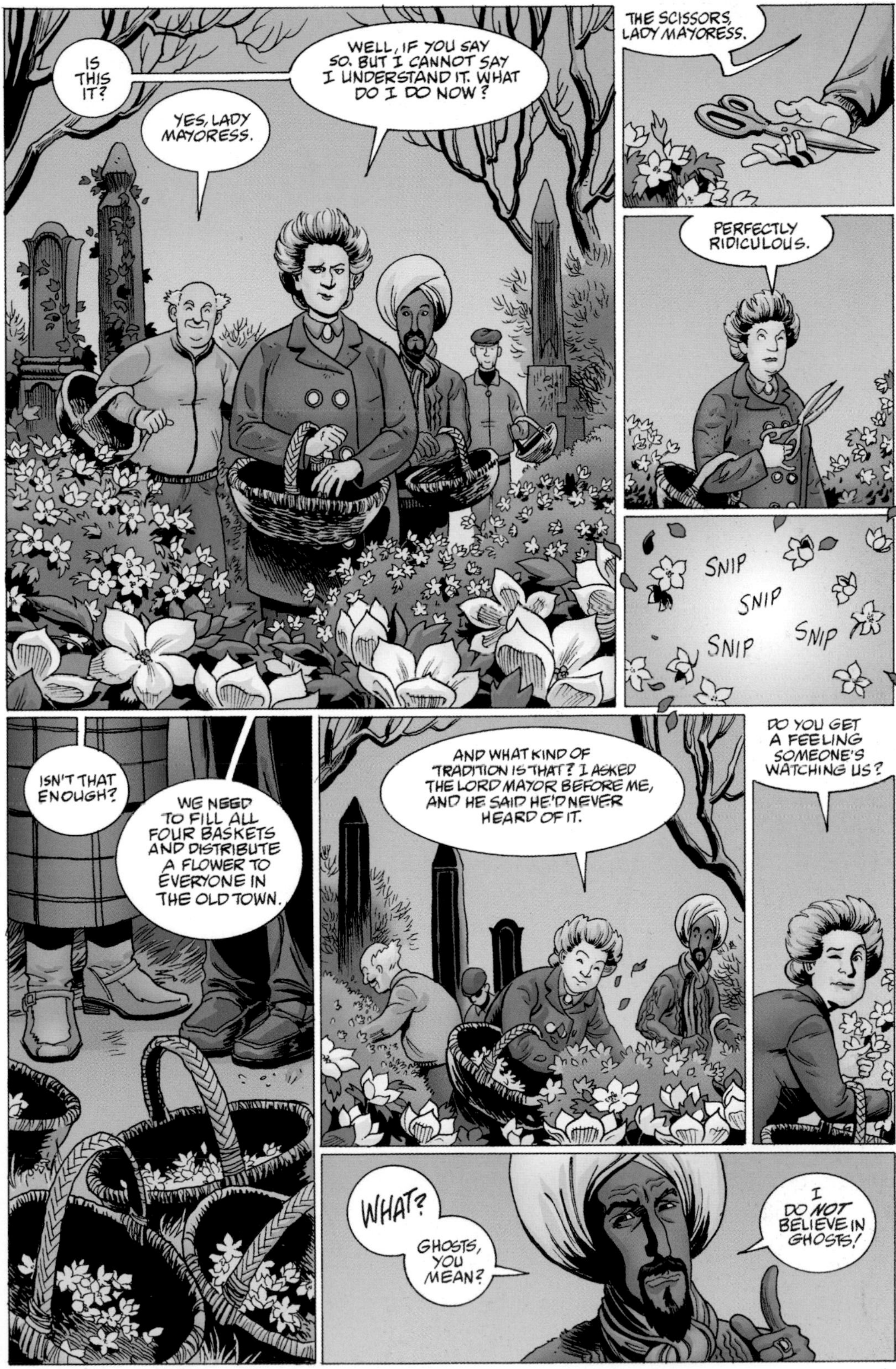
IS THIS IT?
YES, LADY MAYORESS.
WELL, IF YOU SAY SO. BUT I CANNOT SAY I UNDERSTAND IT. WHAT DO I DO NOW?
THE SCISSORS, LADY MAYORESS.
PERFECTLY RIDICULOUS.
SNIP
SNIP
SNIP
SNIP
ISN'T THAT ENOUGH?
WE NEED TO FILL ALL FOUR BASKETS AND DISTRIBUTE A FLOWER TO EVERYONE IN THE OLD TOWN.
AND WHAT KIND OF TRADITION IS THAT? I ASKED THE LORD MAYOR BEFORE ME, AND HE SAID HE'D NEVER HEARD OF IT.
DO YOU GET A FEELING SOMEONE'S WATCHING US?
WHAT?
GHOSTS, YOU MEAN?
I DO NOT BELIEVE IN GHOSTS!

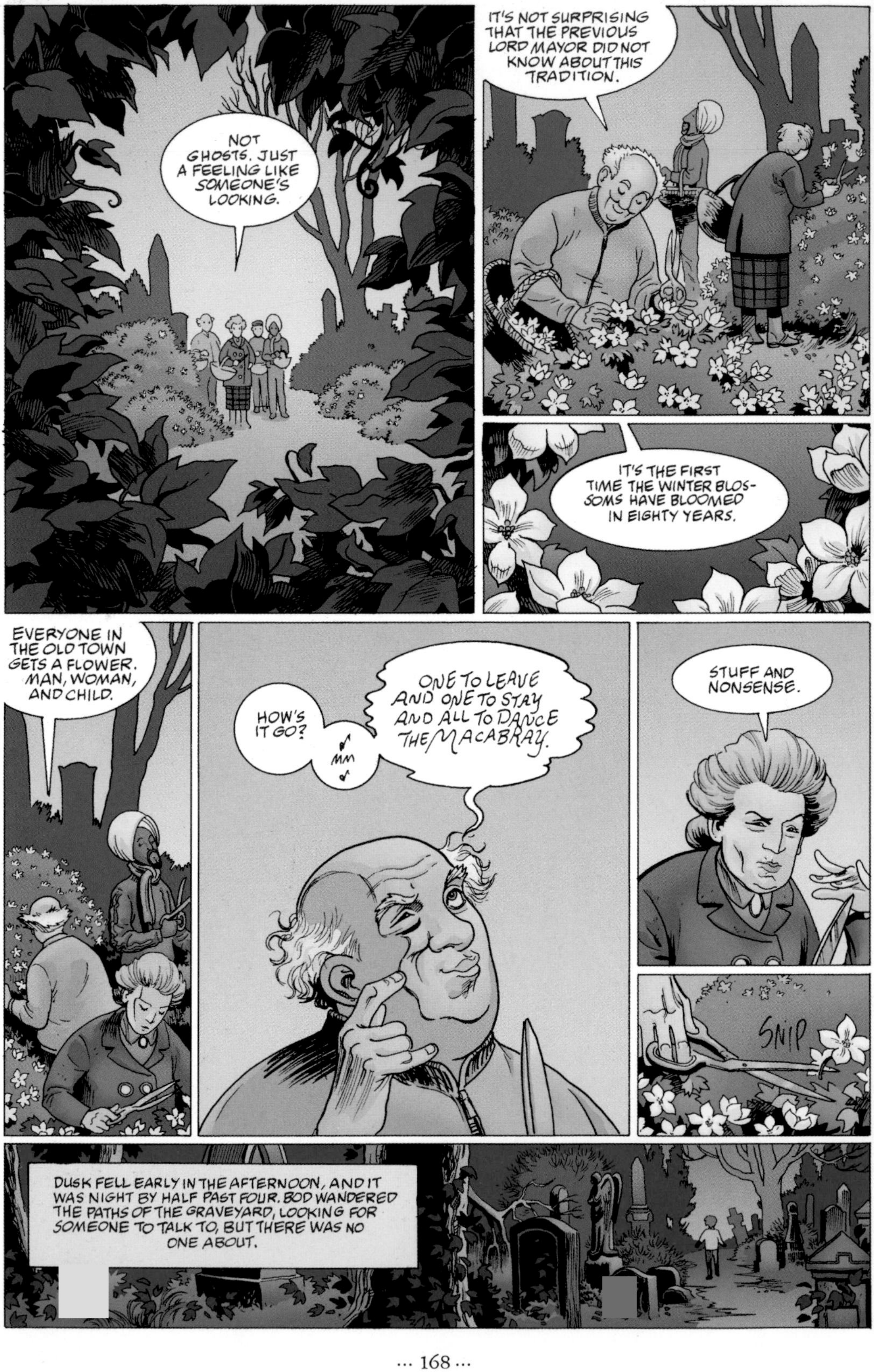
NOT GHOSTS. JUST A FEELING LIKE SOMEONE'S LOOKING.
IT'S NOT SURPRISING THAT THE PREVIOUS LORD MAYOR DID NOT KNOW ABOUT THIS TRADITION.
IT'S THE FIRST TIME THE WINTER BLOSSOMS HAVE BLOOMED IN EIGHTY YEARS.
EVERYONE IN THE OLD TOWN GETS A FLOWER. MAN, WOMAN, AND CHILD.
HOW'S IT GO?
MM
ONE TO LEAVE AND ONE TO STAY AND ALL TO DANCE THE MACABRAY.
STUFF AND NONSENSE.
SNIP
DUSK FELL EARLY IN THE AFTERNOON, AND IT WAS NIGHT BY HALF PAST FOUR. BOD WANDERED THE PATHS OF THE GRAVEYARD, LOOKING FOR SOMEONE TO TALK TO, BUT THERE WAS NO ONE ABOUT.

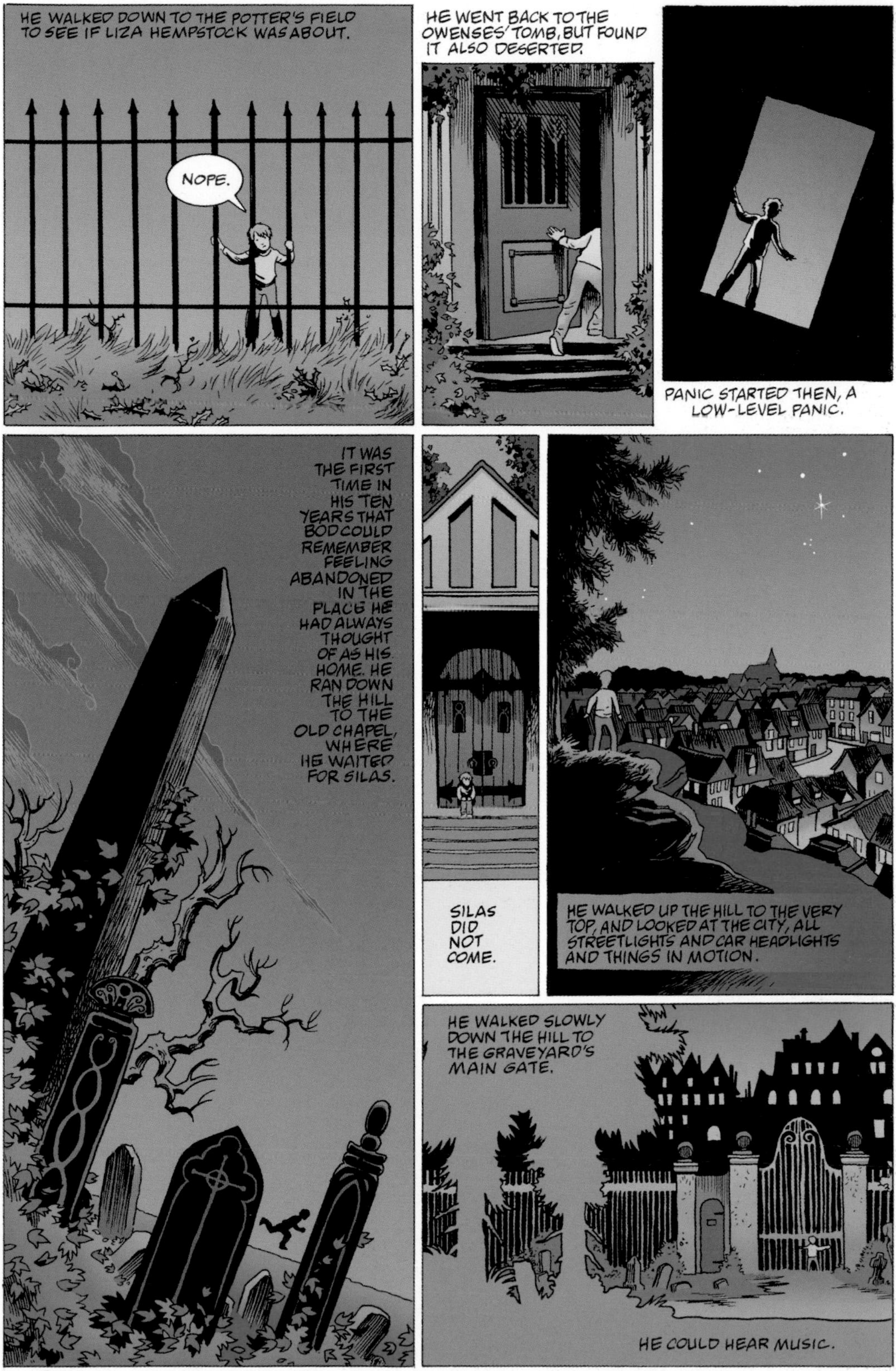
HE WALKED DOWN TO THE POTTER'S FIELD TO SEE IF LIZA HEMPSTOCK WAS ABOUT.
NOPE.
HE WENT BACK TO THE OWENSES' TOMB, BUT FOUND IT ALSO DESERTED.
PANIC STARTED THEN, A LOW-LEVEL PANIC.
IT WAS THE FIRST TIME IN HIS TEN YEARS THAT BOD COULD REMEMBER FEELING ABANDONED IN THE PLACE HE HAD ALWAYS THOUGHT OF AS HIS HOME. HE RAN DOWN THE HILL TO THE OLD CHAPEL, WHERE HE WAITED FOR SILAS.
SILAS DID NOT COME.
HE WALKED UP THE HILL TO THE VERY TOP, AND LOOKED AT THE CITY, ALL STREETLIGHTS AND CAR HEADLIGHTS AND THINGS IN MOTION.
HE WALKED SLOWLY DOWN THE HILL TO THE GRAVEYARD'S MAIN GATE.
HE COULD HEAR MUSIC.

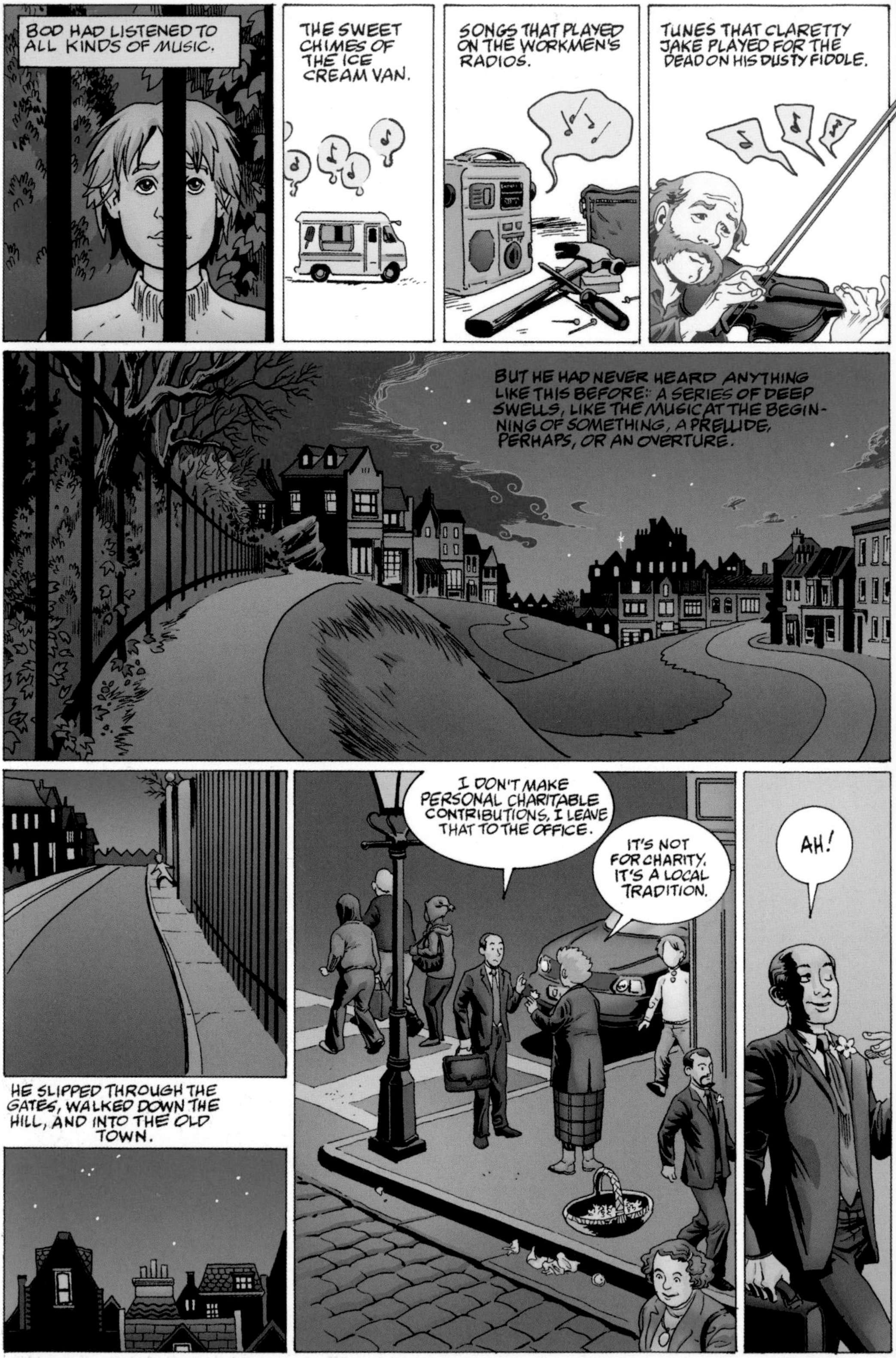

BOD HAD LISTENED TO ALL KINDS OF MUSIC.
THE SWEET CHIMES OF THE ICE CREAM VAN.
SONGS THAT PLAYED ON THE WORKMEN'S RADIOS.
TUNES THAT CLARETTY JAKE PLAYED FOR THE DEAD ON HIS DUSTY FIDDLE.
BUT HE HAD NEVER HEARD ANYTHING LIKE THIS BEFORE: A SERIES OF DEEP SWELLS, LIKE THE MUSIC AT THE BEGINNING OF SOMETHING, A PRELUDE, PERHAPS, OR AN OVERTURE.
HE SLIPPED THROUGH THE GATES, WALKED DOWN THE HILL, AND INTO THE OLD TOWN.
I DON'T MAKE PERSONAL CHARITABLE CONTRIBUTIONS, I LEAVE THAT TO THE OFFICE.
IT'S NOT FOR CHARITY. IT'S A LOCAL TRADITION.
AH!

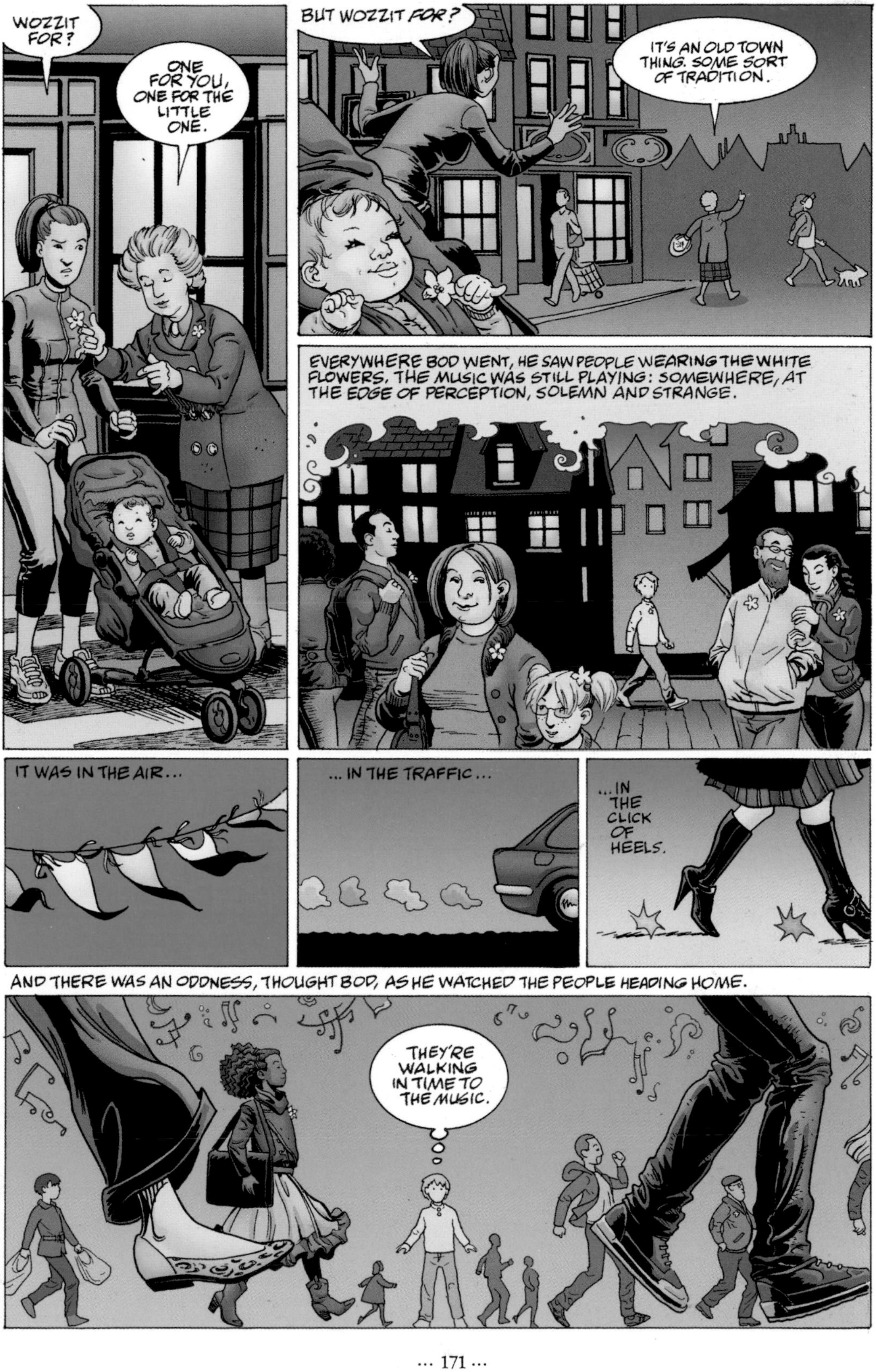
WOZZIT FOR?
ONE FOR YOU, ONE FOR THE LITTLE ONE.
BUT WOZZIT FOR?
IT'S AN OLD TOWN THING. SOME SORT OF TRADITION.
EVERYWHERE BOD WENT, HE SAW PEOPLE WEARING THE WHITE FLOWERS. THE MUSIC WAS STILL PLAYING: SOMEWHERE, AT THE EDGE OF PERCEPTION, SOLEMN AND STRANGE.
IT WAS IN THE AIR...
... IN THE TRAFFIC ...
...IN THE CLICK OF HEELS.
AND THERE WAS AN ODDNESS, THOUGHT BOD, AS HE WATCHED THE PEOPLE HEADING HOME.
THEY'RE WALKING IN TIME TO THE MUSIC.

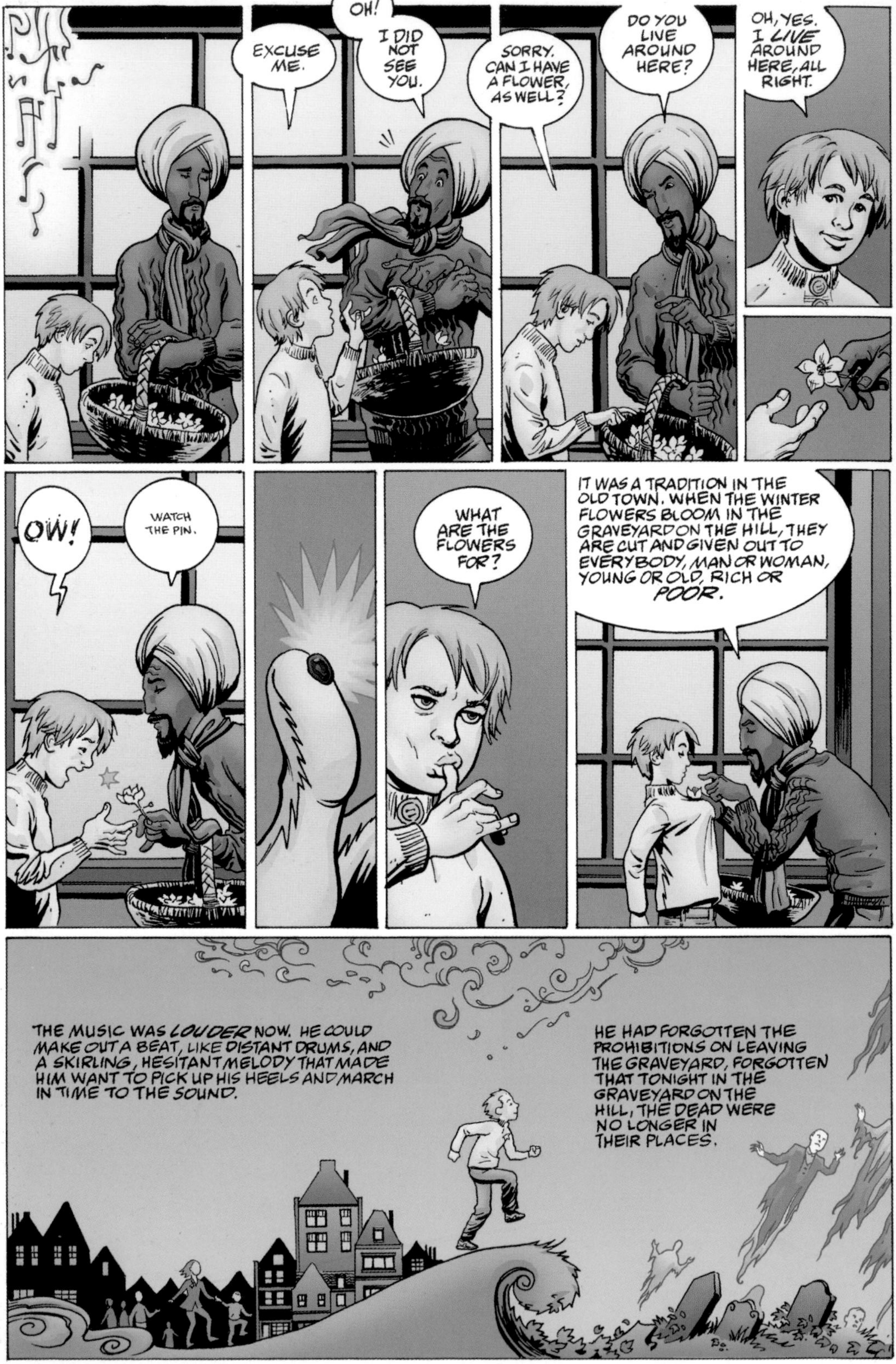
EXCUSE ME.
OH!
I DID NOT SEE YOU.
SORRY. CAN I HAVE A FLOWER, AS WELL?
DO YOU LIVE AROUND HERE?
OH, YES. I LIVE AROUND HERE, ALL RIGHT.
OW!
WATCH THE PIN.
WHAT ARE THE FLOWERS FOR?
IT WAS A TRADITION IN THE OLD TOWN. WHEN THE WINTER FLOWERS BLOOM IN THE GRAVEYARD ON THE HILL, THEY ARE CUT AND GIVEN OUT TO EVERYBODY, MAN OR WOMAN, YOUNG OR OLD, RICH OR POOR.
THE MUSIC WAS LOUDER NOW. HE COULD MAKE OUT A BEAT, LIKE DISTANT DRUMS, AND A SKIRLING, HESITANT MELODY THAT MADE HIM WANT TO PICK UP HIS HEELS AND MARCH IN TIME TO THE SOUND.
HE HAD FORGOTTEN THE PROHIBITIONS ON LEAVING THE GRAVEYARD, FORGOTTEN THAT TONIGHT IN THE GRAVEYARD ON THE HILL, THE DEAD WERE NO LONGER IN THEIR PLACES.

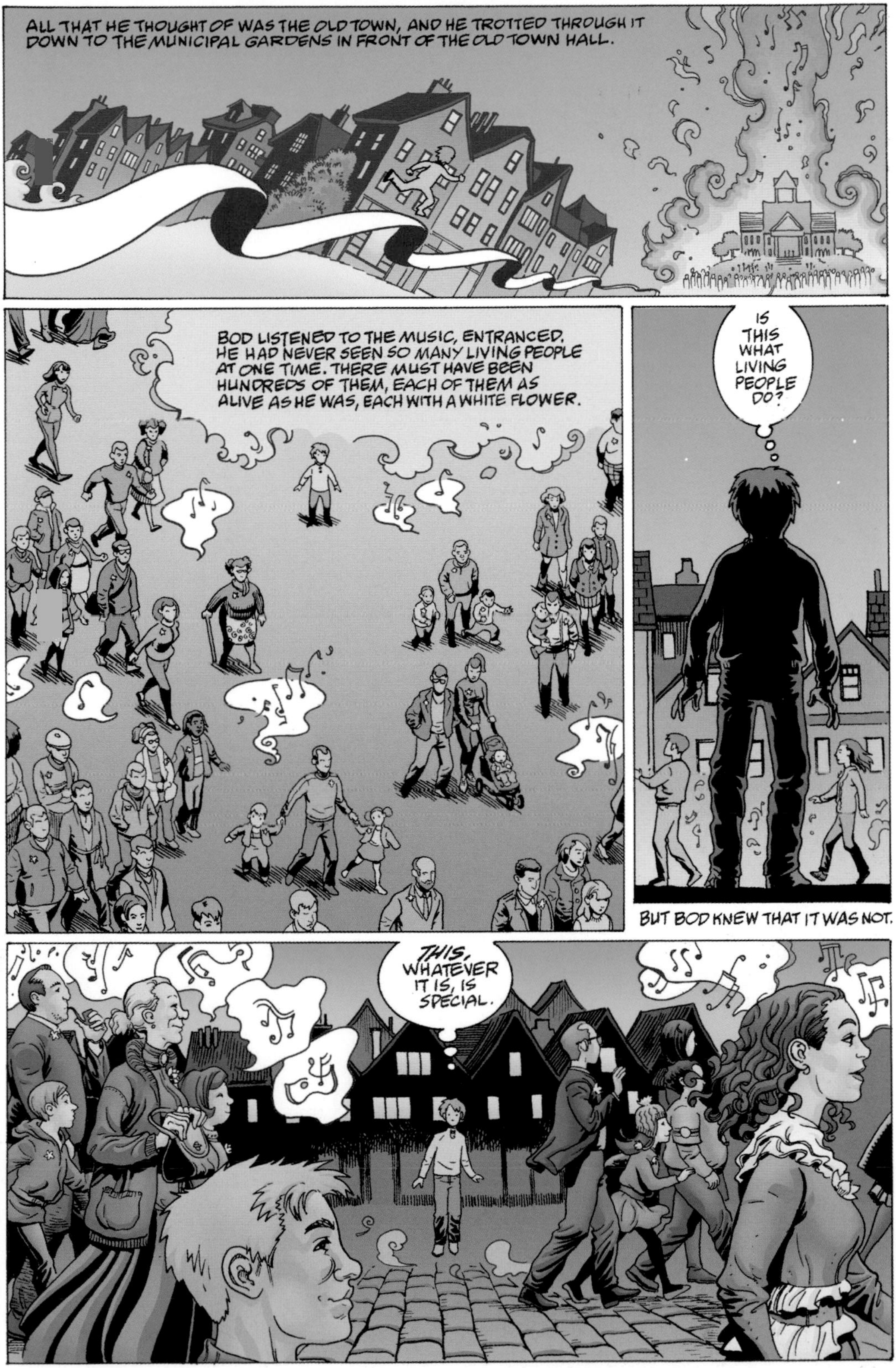
ALL THAT HE THOUGHT OF WAS THE OLD TOWN, AND HE TROTTED THROUGH IT DOWN TO THE MUNICIPAL GARDENS IN FRONT OF THE OLD TOWN HALL.
BOD LISTENED TO THE MUSIC, ENTRANCED. HE HAD NEVER SEEN SO MANY LIVING PEOPLE AT ONE TIME. THERE MUST HAVE BEEN HUNDREDS OF THEM, EACH OF THEM AS ALIVE AS HE WAS, EACH WITH A WHITE FLOWER.
IS THIS WHAT LIVING PEOPLE DO?
BUT BOD KNEW THAT IT WAS NOT.
THIS, WHATEVER IT IS, IS SPECIAL.

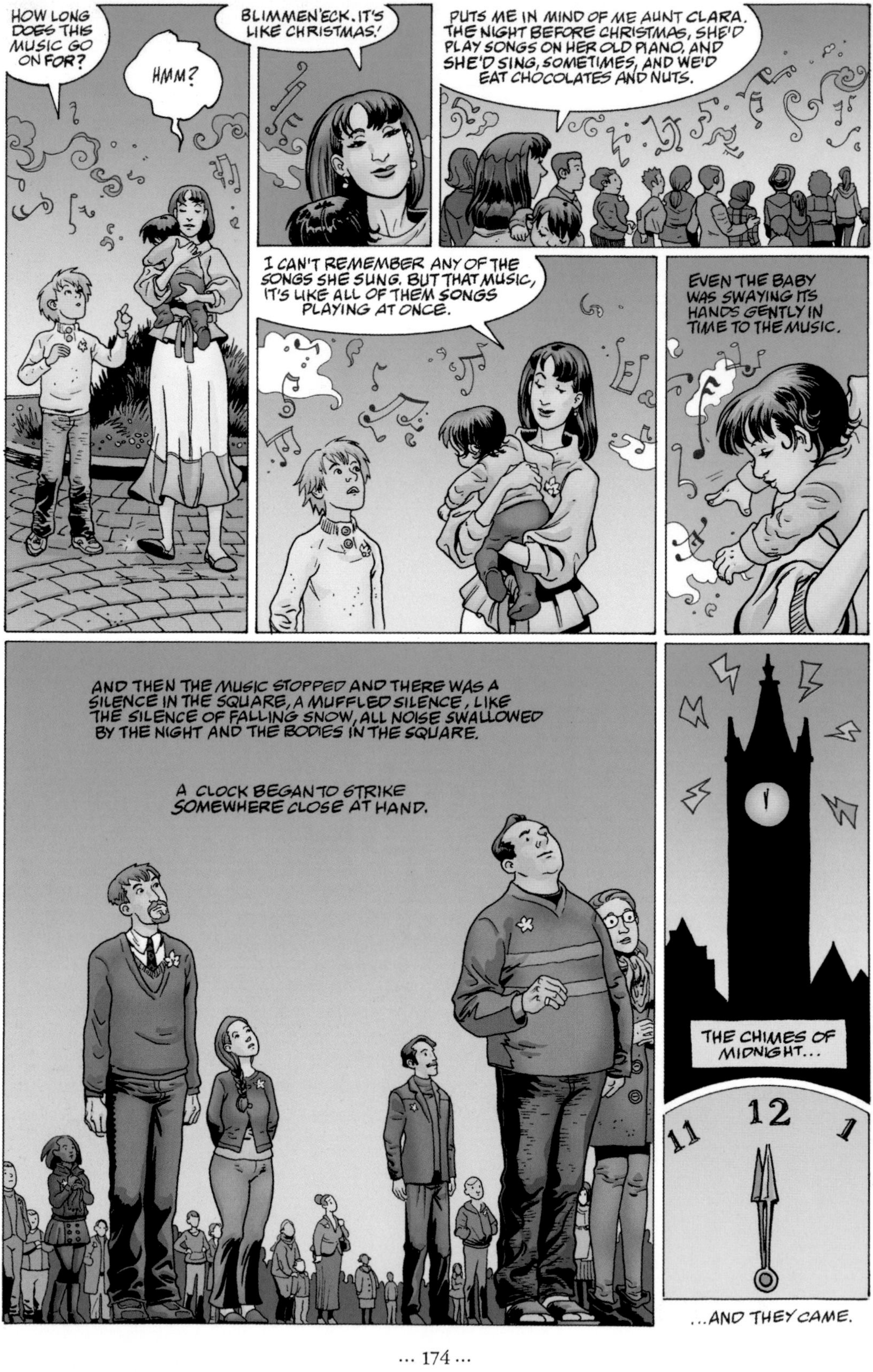
HOW LONG DOES THIS MUSIC GO ON FOR?
HMM?
BLIMMEN'ECK. IT'S LIKE CHRISTMAS!
PUTS ME IN MIND OF ME AUNT CLARA. THE NIGHT BEFORE CHRISTMAS, SHE'D PLAY SONGS ON HER OLD PIANO, AND SHE'D SING, SOMETIMES, AND WE'D EAT CHOCOLATES AND NUTS.
I CAN'T REMEMBER ANY OF THE SONGS SHE SUNG. BUT THAT MUSIC, IT'S LIKE ALL OF THEM SONGS PLAYING AT ONCE.
EVEN THE BABY WAS SWAYING ITS HANDS GENTLY IN TIME TO THE MUSIC.
AND THEN THE MUSIC STOPPED AND THERE WAS A SILENCE IN THE SQUARE, A MUFFLED SILENCE, LIKE THE SILENCE OF FALLING SNOW, ALL NOISE SWALLOWED BY THE NIGHT AND THE BODIES IN THE SQUARE.
A CLOCK BEGAN TO STRIKE SOMEWHERE CLOSE AT HAND.
THE CHIMES OF MIDNIGHT...
11 12 1
...AND THEY CAME.

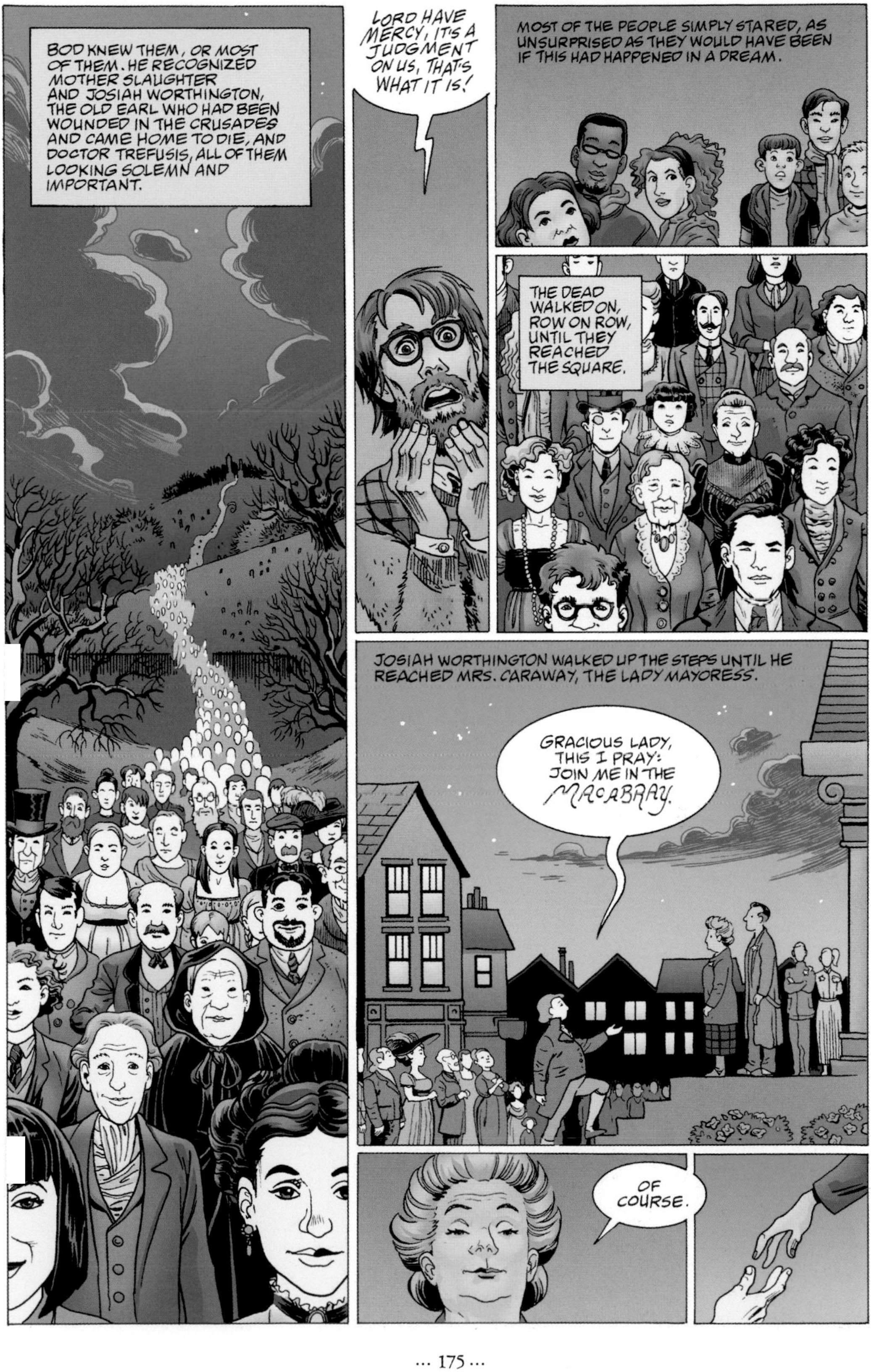
BOD KNEW THEM, OR MOST OF THEM. HE RECOGNIZED MOTHER SLAUGHTER AND JOSIAH WORTHINGTON, THE OLD EARL WHO HAD BEEN WOUNDED IN THE CRUSADES AND CAME HOME TO DIE, AND DOCTOR TREFUSIS, ALL OF THEM LOOKING SOLEMN AND IMPORTANT.
LORD HAVE MERCY, IT'S A JUDGMENT ON US, THAT'S WHAT IT IS!
MOST OF THE PEOPLE SIMPLY STARED, AS UNSURPRISED AS THEY WOULD HAVE BEEN IF THIS HAD HAPPENED IN A DREAM.
THE DEAD WALKED ON, ROW ON ROW, UNTIL THEY REACHED THE SQUARE.
JOSIAH WORTHINGTON WALKED UP THE STEPS UNTIL HE REACHED MRS. CARAWAY, THE LADY MAYORESS.
GRACIOUS LADY, THIS I PRAY: JOIN ME IN THE MACABRAY.
OF COURSE.

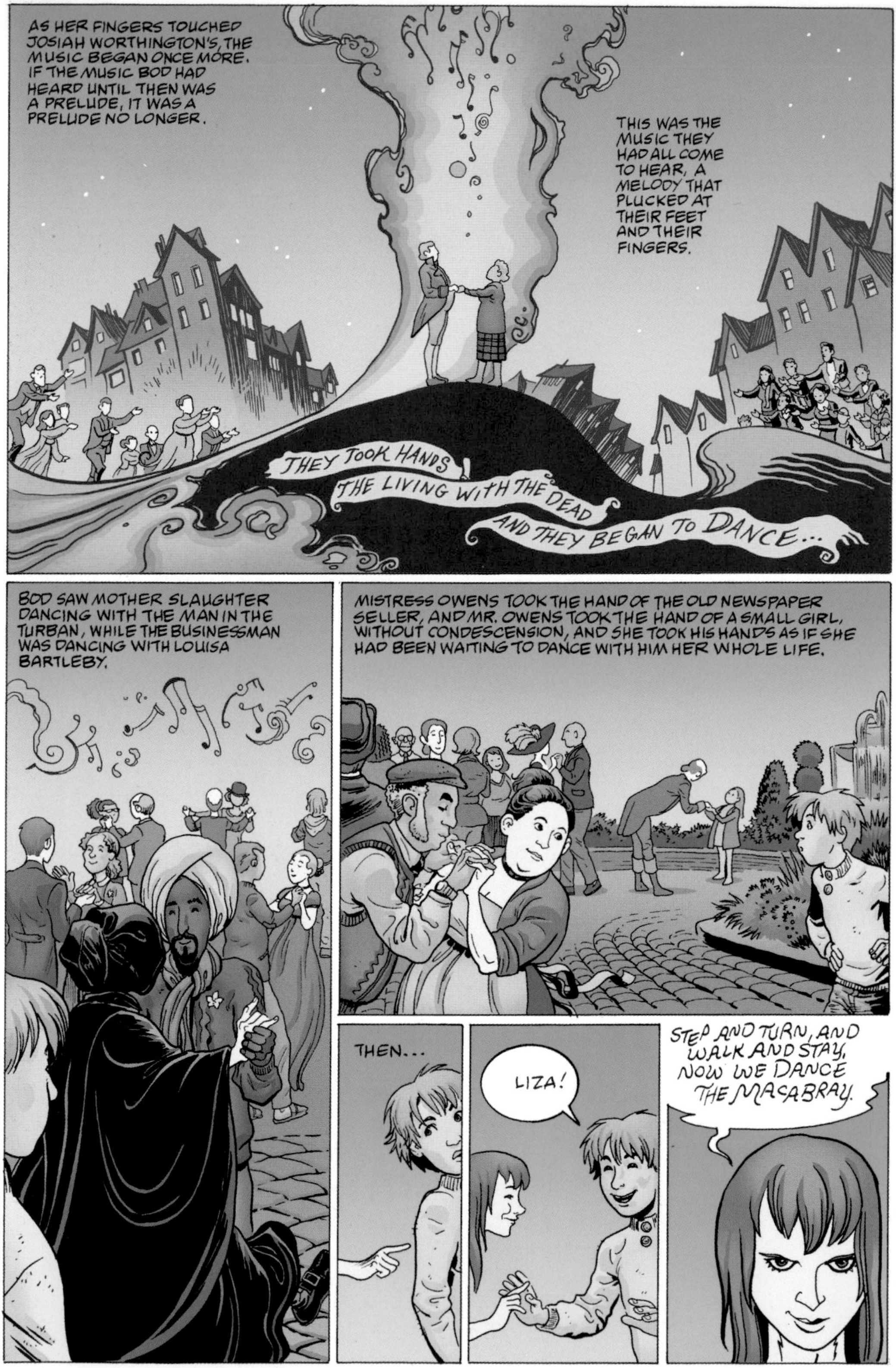
AS HER FINGERS TOUCHED JOSIAH WORTHINGTON'S, THE MUSIC BEGAN ONCE MORE. IF THE MUSIC BOD HAD HEARD UNTIL THEN WAS A PRELUDE, IT WAS A PRELUDE NO LONGER.
THIS WAS THE MUSIC THEY HAD ALL COME TO HEAR, A MELODY THAT PLUCKED AT THEIR FEET AND THEIR FINGERS.
THEY TOOK HANDS
THE LIVING WITH THE DEAD
AND THEY BEGAN TO DANCE...
BOD SAW MOTHER SLAUGHTER DANCING WITH THE MAN IN THE TURBAN, WHILE THE BUSINESSMAN WAS DANCING WITH LOUISA BARTLEBY.
MISTRESS OWENS TOOK THE HAND OF THE OLD NEWSPAPER SELLER, AND MR. OWENS TOOK THE HAND OF A SMALL GIRL, WITHOUT CONDESCENSION, AND SHE TOOK HIS HANDS AS IF SHE HAD BEEN WAITING TO DANCE WITH HIM HER WHOLE LIFE.
THEN...
LIZA!
STEP AND TURN, AND WALK AND STAY, NOW WE DANCE THE MACABRAY.

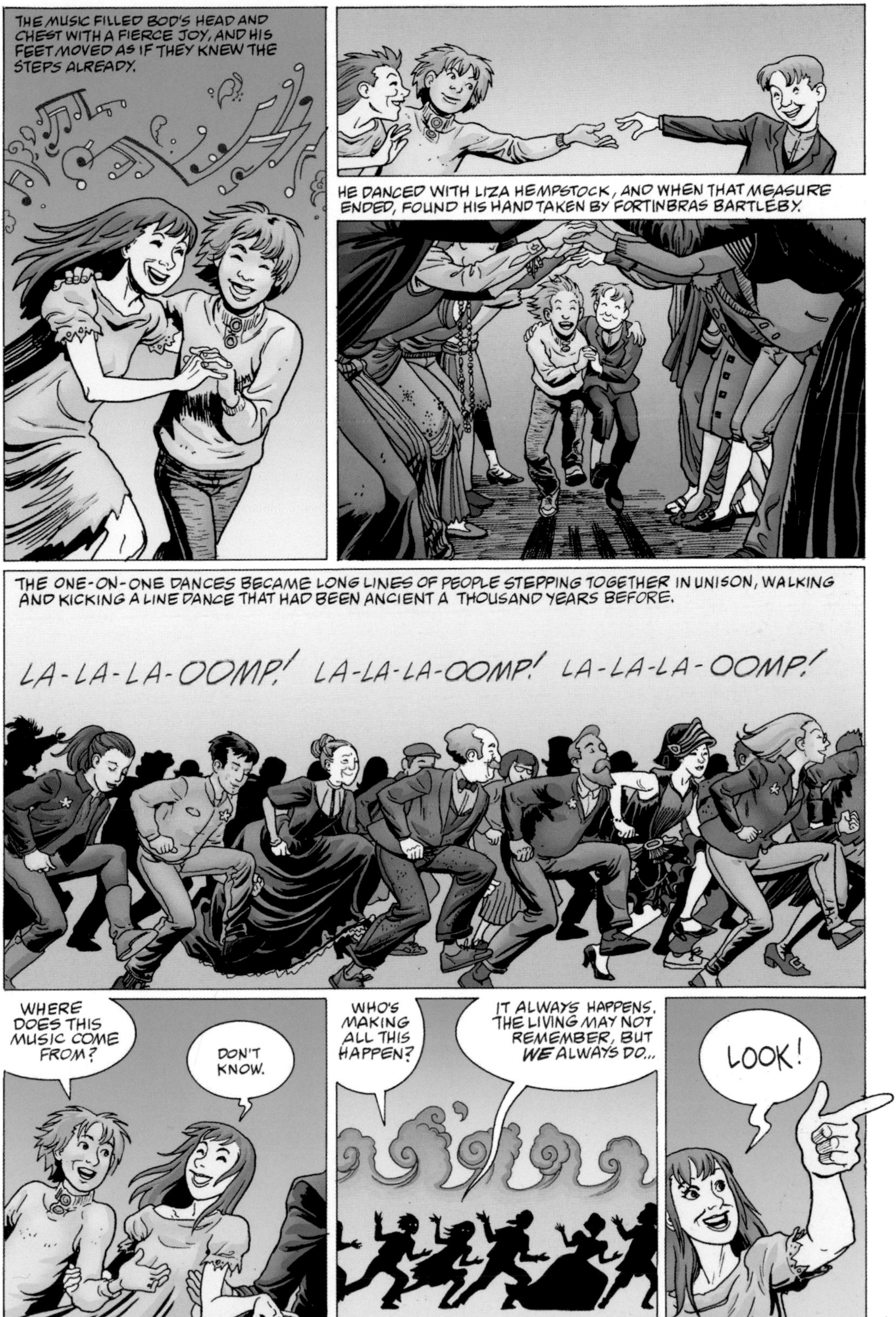
THE MUSIC FILLED BOD'S HEAD AND CHEST WITH A FIERCE JOY, AND HIS FEET MOVED AS IF THEY KNEW THE STEPS ALREADY.
HE DANCED WITH LIZA HEMPSTOCK, AND WHEN THAT MEASURE ENDED, FOUND HIS HAND TAKEN BY FORTINBRAS BARTLEBY.
THE ONE-ON-ONE DANCES BECAME LONG LINES OF PEOPLE STEPPING TOGETHER IN UNISON, WALKING AND KICKING A LINE DANCE THAT HAD BEEN ANCIENT A THOUSAND YEARS BEFORE.
LA-LA-LA-OOMP! LA-LA-LA-OOMP! LA-LA-LA-OOMP!
WHERE DOES THIS MUSIC COME FROM?
DON'T KNOW.
WHO'S MAKING ALL THIS HAPPEN?
IT ALWAYS HAPPENS. THE LIVING MAY NOT REMEMBER, BUT WE ALWAYS DO...
LOOK!

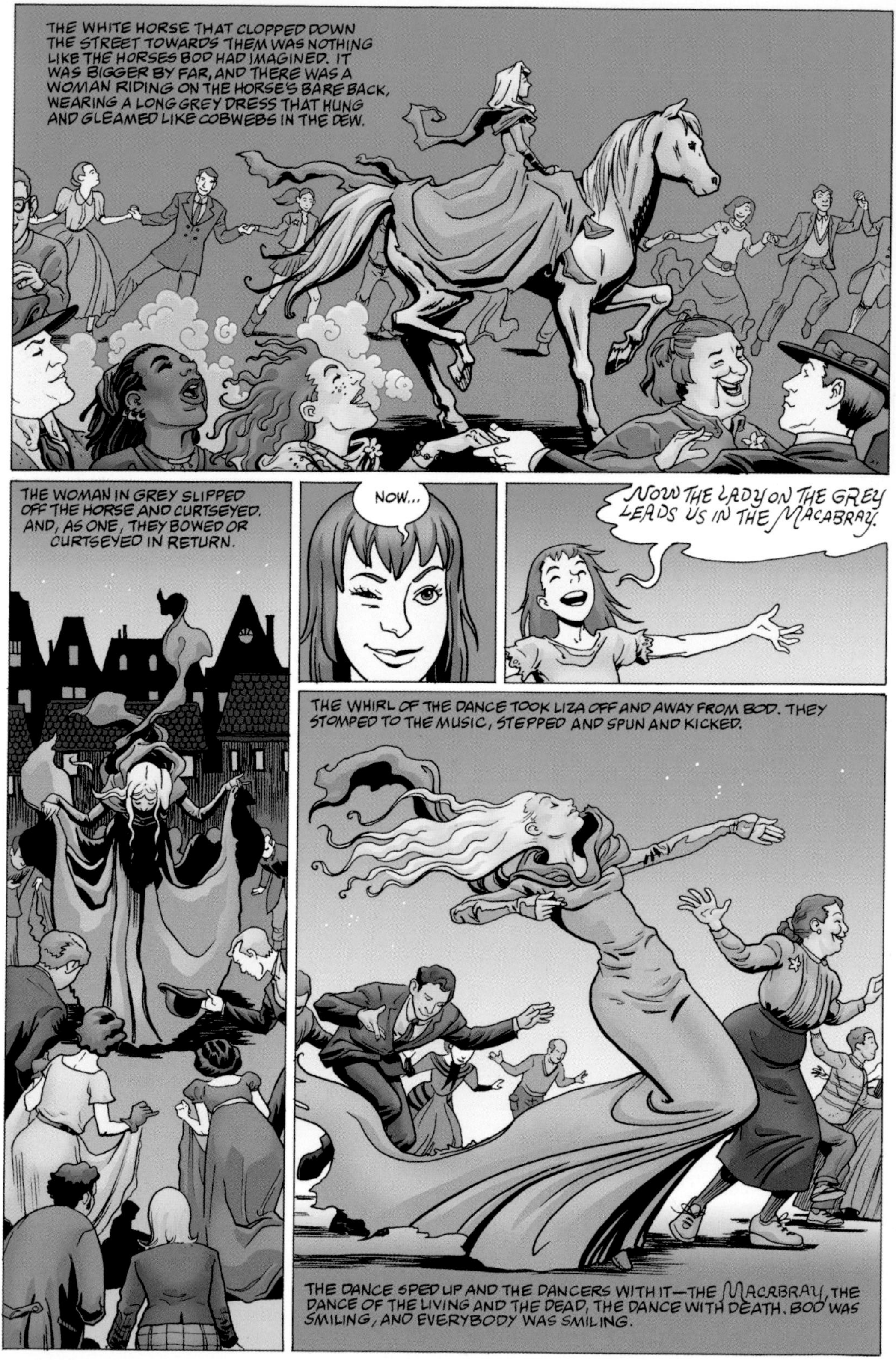
THE WHITE HORSE THAT CLOPPED DOWN THE STREET TOWARDS THEM WAS NOTHING LIKE THE HORSES BOD HAD IMAGINED. IT WAS BIGGER BY FAR, AND THERE WAS A WOMAN RIDING ON THE HORSE'S BARE BACK, WEARING A LONG GREY DRESS THAT HUNG AND GLEAMED LIKE COBWEBS IN THE DEW.
THE WOMAN IN GREY SLIPPED OFF THE HORSE AND CURTSEYED. AND, AS ONE, THEY BOWED OR CURTSEYED IN RETURN.
NOW...
NOW THE LADY ON THE GREY LEADS US IN THE MACABRAY.
THE WHIRL OF THE DANCE TOOK LIZA OFF AND AWAY FROM BOD. THEY STOMPED TO THE MUSIC, STEPPED AND SPUN AND KICKED.
THE DANCE SPED UP AND THE DANCERS WITH IT—THE MACRBRAY, THE DANCE OF THE LIVING AND THE DEAD, THE DANCE WITH DEATH. BOD WAS SMILING, AND EVERYBODY WAS SMILING.

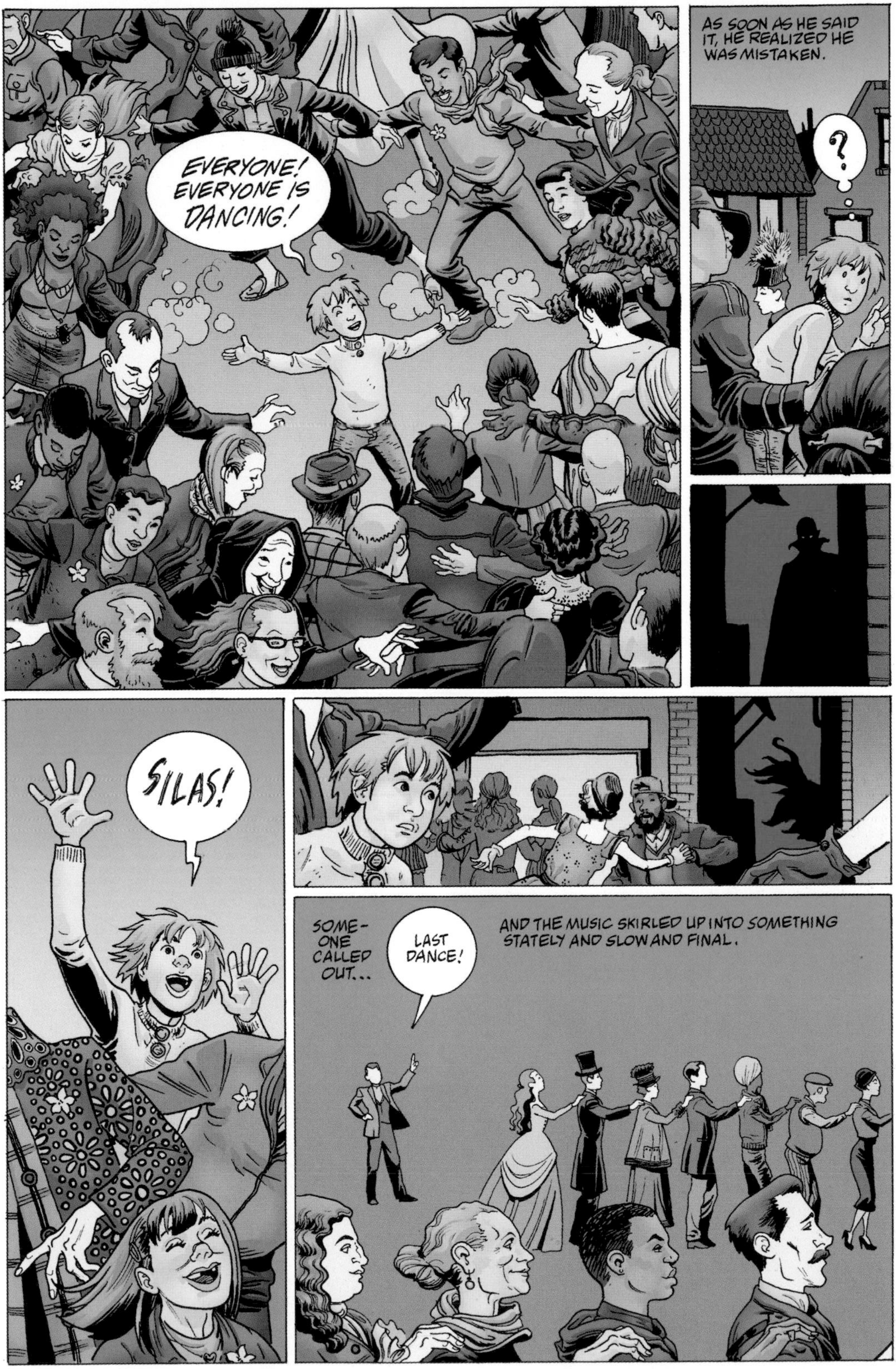
EVERYONE! EVERYONE IS DANCING!
AS SOON AS HE SAID IT, HE REALIZED HE WAS MISTAKEN.
?
SILAS!
SOME-ONE CALLED OUT...
LAST DANCE!
AND THE MUSIC SKIRLED UP INTO SOMETHING STATELY AND SLOW AND FINAL.

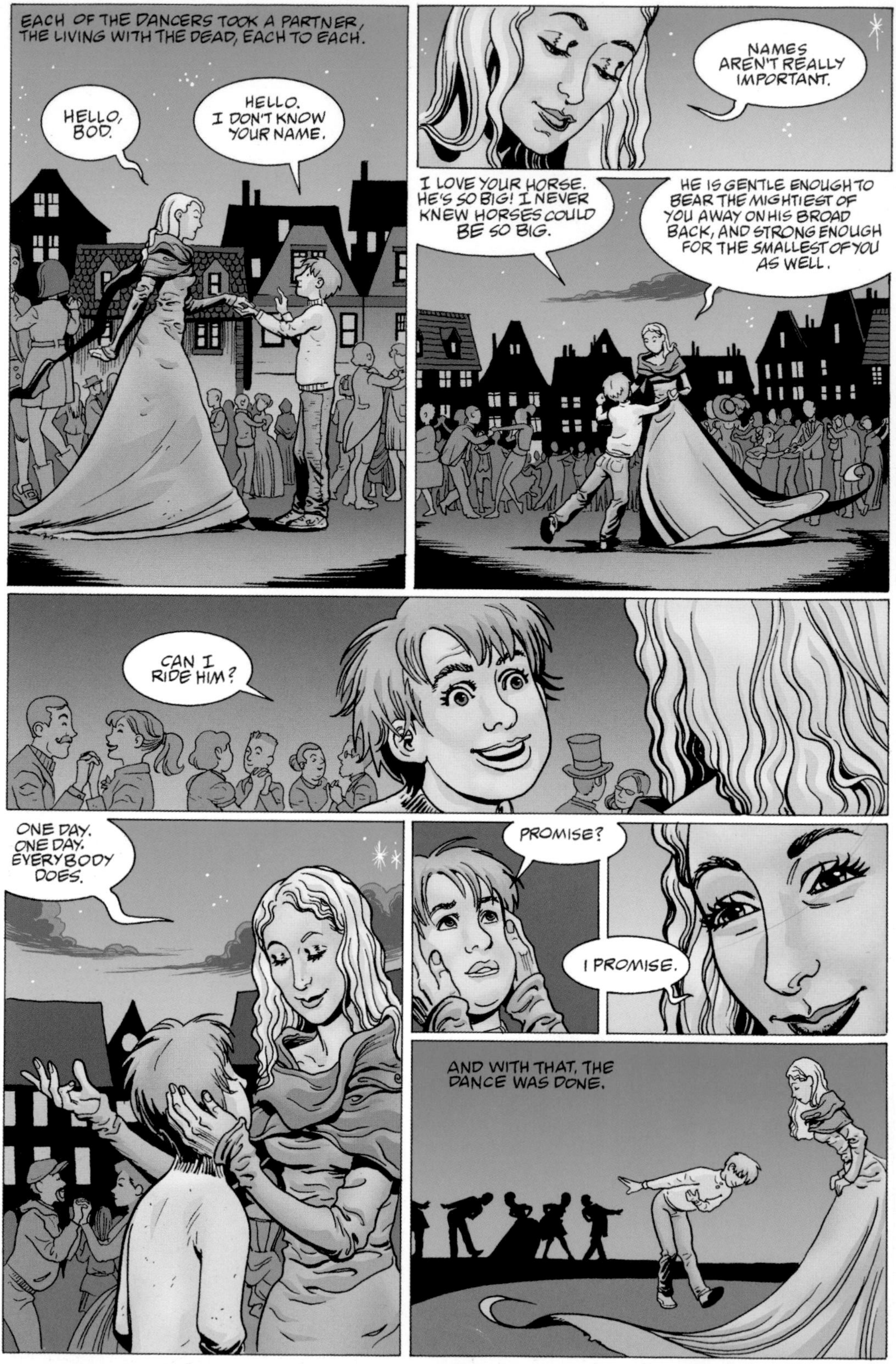
EACH OF THE DANCERS TOOK A PARTNER, THE LIVING WITH THE DEAD, EACH TO EACH.
HELLO, BOD.
HELLO. I DON'T KNOW YOUR NAME.
NAMES AREN'T REALLY IMPORTANT.
I LOVE YOUR HORSE. HE'S SO BIG! I NEVER KNEW HORSES COULD BE SO BIG.
HE IS GENTLE ENOUGH TO BEAR THE MIGHTIEST OF YOU AWAY ON HIS BROAD BACK, AND STRONG ENOUGH FOR THE SMALLEST OF YOU AS WELL.
CAN I RIDE HIM?
ONE DAY. ONE DAY. EVERYBODY DOES.
PROMISE?
I PROMISE.
AND WITH THAT, THE DANCE WAS DONE.

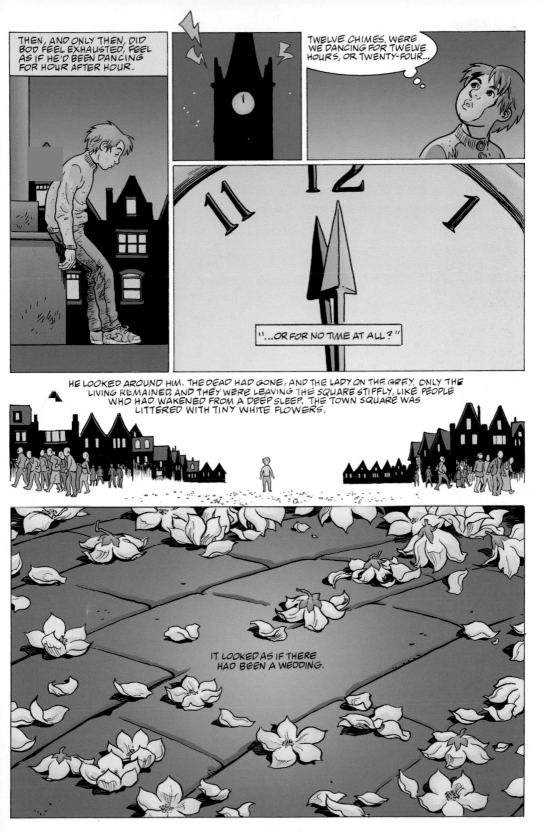

THEN, AND ONLY THEN, DID BOD FEEL EXHAUSTED, FEEL AS IF HE'D BEEN DANCING FOR HOUR AFTER HOUR.

TWELVE CHIMES. WERE WE DANCING FOR TWELVE HOURS, OR TWENTY-FOUR...

"...OR FOR NO TIME AT ALL?"

HE LOOKED AROUND HIM. THE DEAD HAD GONE, AND THE LADY ON THE GREY. ONLY THE LIVING REMAINED, AND THEY WERE LEAVING THE SQUARE STIFFLY, LIKE PEOPLE WHO HAD WAKENED FROM A DEEP SLEEP. THE TOWN SQUARE WAS LITTERED WITH TINY WHITE FLOWERS.

IT LOOKED AS IF THERE HAD BEEN A WEDDING.

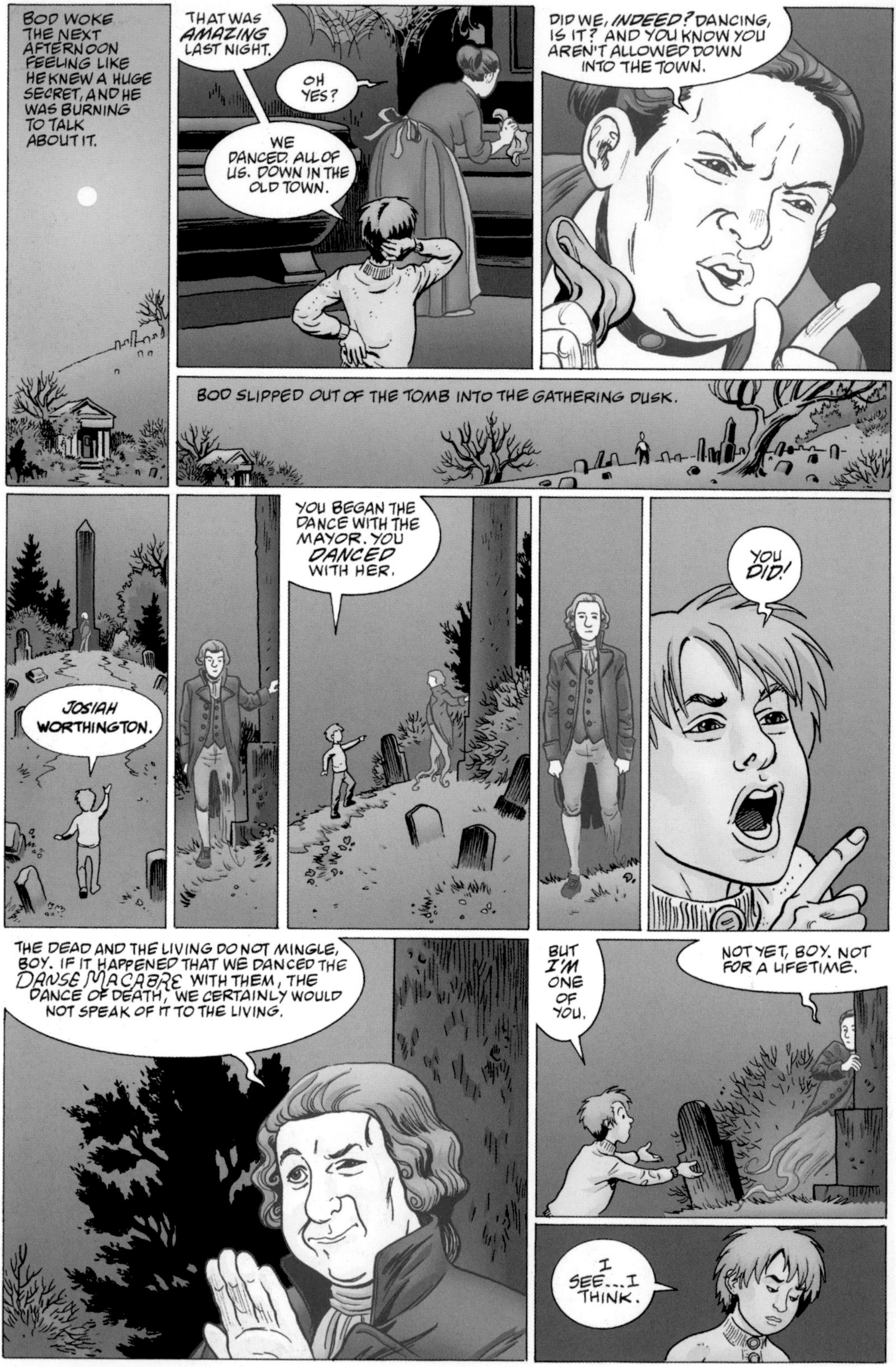
BOD WOKE THE NEXT AFTERNOON FEELING LIKE HE KNEW A HUGE SECRET, AND HE WAS BURNING TO TALK ABOUT IT.
THAT WAS AMAZING LAST NIGHT.
OH YES?
WE DANCED. ALL OF US. DOWN IN THE OLD TOWN.
DID WE, INDEED? DANCING, IS IT? AND YOU KNOW YOU AREN'T ALLOWED DOWN INTO THE TOWN.
BOD SLIPPED OUT OF THE TOMB INTO THE GATHERING DUSK.
JOSIAH WORTHINGTON.
YOU BEGAN THE DANCE WITH THE MAYOR. YOU DANCED WITH HER.
YOU DID!
THE DEAD AND THE LIVING DO NOT MINGLE, BOY. IF IT HAPPENED THAT WE DANCED THE DANSE MACABRE WITH THEM, THE DANCE OF DEATH, WE CERTAINLY WOULD NOT SPEAK OF IT TO THE LIVING.
BUT I'M ONE OF YOU.
NOT YET, BOY. NOT FOR A LIFETIME.
I SEE... I THINK.

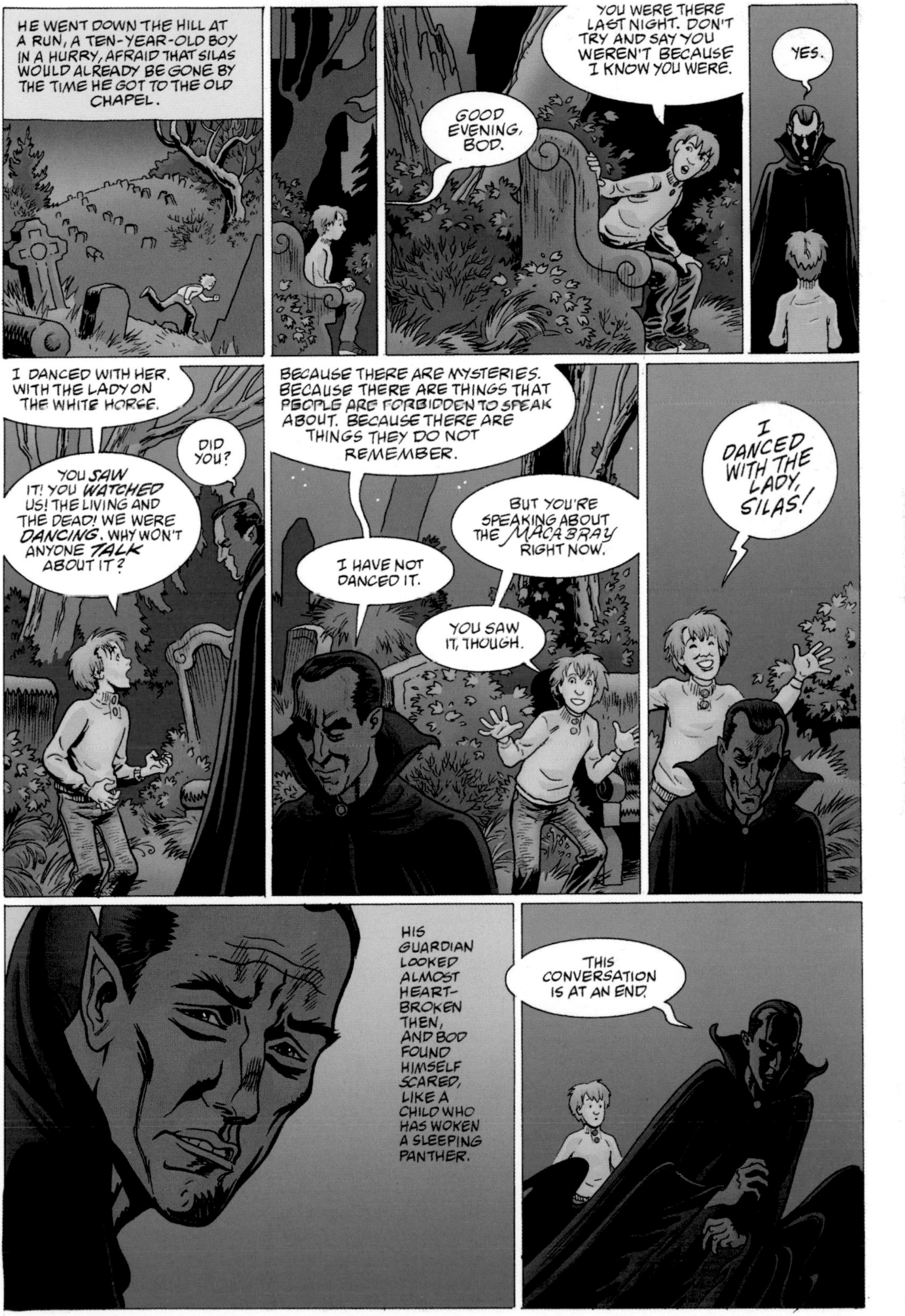
HE WENT DOWN THE HILL AT A RUN, A TEN-YEAR-OLD BOY IN A HURRY, AFRAID THAT SILAS WOULD ALREADY BE GONE BY THE TIME HE GOT TO THE OLD CHAPEL.
GOOD EVENING, BOD.
YOU WERE THERE LAST NIGHT. DON'T TRY AND SAY YOU WEREN'T BECAUSE I KNOW YOU WERE.
YES.
I DANCED WITH HER. WITH THE LADY ON THE WHITE HORSE.
DID YOU?
YOU SAW IT! YOU WATCHED US! THE LIVING AND THE DEAD! WE WERE DANCING. WHY WON'T ANYONE TALK ABOUT IT?
BECAUSE THERE ARE MYSTERIES. BECAUSE THERE ARE THINGS THAT PEOPLE ARE FORBIDDEN TO SPEAK ABOUT. BECAUSE THERE ARE THINGS THEY DO NOT REMEMBER.
BUT YOU'RE SPEAKING ABOUT THE MACABRAY RIGHT NOW.
I HAVE NOT DANCED IT.
YOU SAW IT, THOUGH.
I DANCED WITH THE LADY, SILAS!
HIS GUARDIAN LOOKED ALMOST HEART-BROKEN THEN, AND BOD FOUND HIMSELF SCARED, LIKE A CHILD WHO HAS WOKEN A SLEEPING PANTHER.
THIS CONVERSATION IS AT AN END.

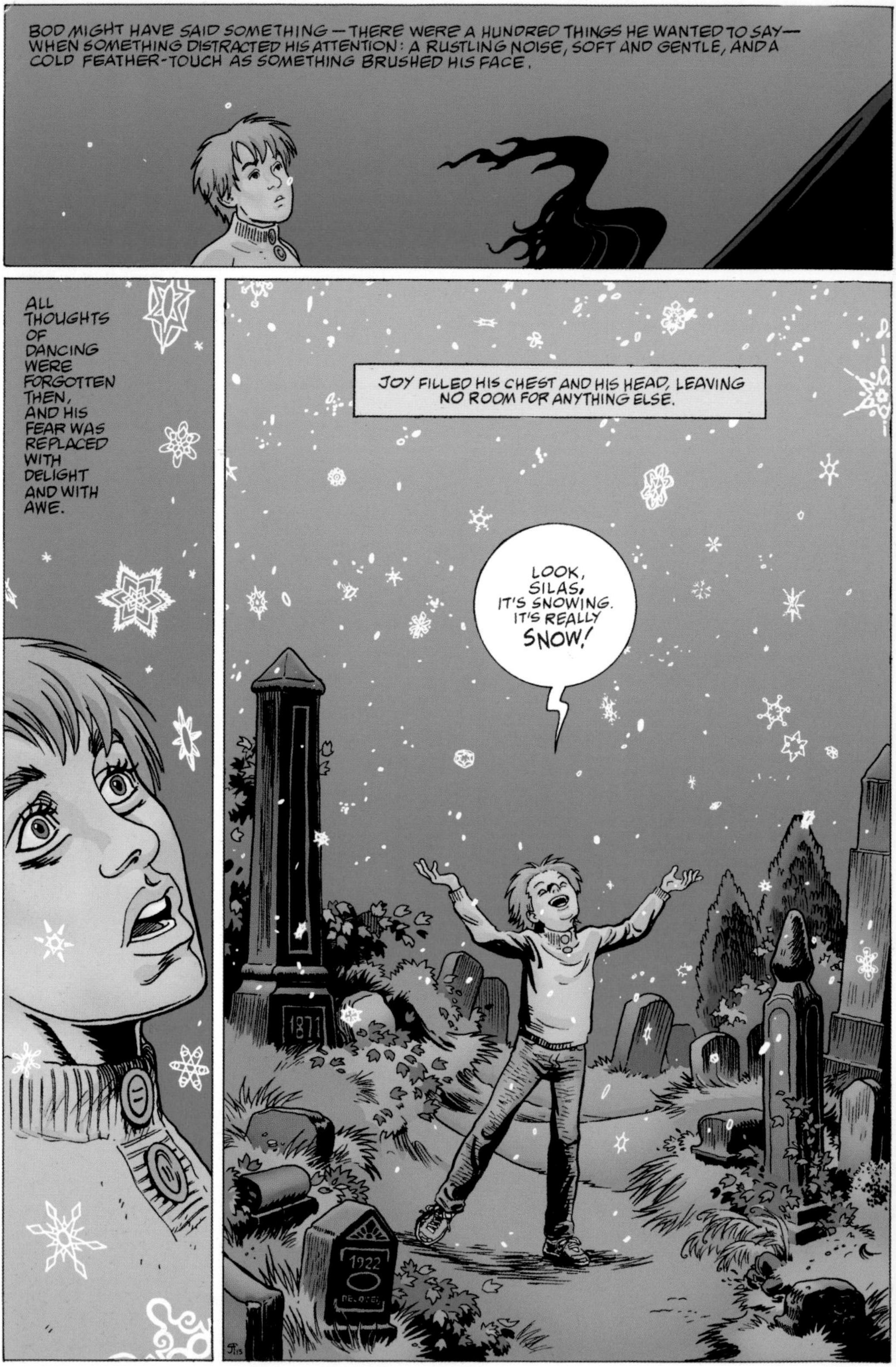
BOD MIGHT HAVE SAID SOMETHING — THERE WERE A HUNDRED THINGS HE WANTED TO SAY — WHEN SOMETHING DISTRACTED HIS ATTENTION: A RUSTLING NOISE, SOFT AND GENTLE, AND A COLD FEATHER-TOUCH AS SOMETHING BRUSHED HIS FACE.
ALL THOUGHTS OF DANCING WERE FORGOTTEN THEN, AND HIS FEAR WAS REPLACED WITH DELIGHT AND WITH AWE.
JOY FILLED HIS CHEST AND HIS HEAD, LEAVING NO ROOM FOR ANYTHING ELSE.
LOOK, SILAS, IT'S SNOWING. IT'S REALLY SNOW!
1871
1922

INTERLUDE

Illustrated by Stephen B. Scott

THE WASHINGTON ROOM
PRIVATE FUNCTION
IF YOU WERE TO LOOK AT THE INHABITANTS OF THE WASHINGTON ROOM THAT NIGHT, YOU WOULD HAVE NO CLEAR IDEA OF WHAT WAS HAPPENING, ALTHOUGH A RAPID GLANCE WOULD TELL YOU THAT THERE WERE NO WOMEN IN THERE. THEY WERE ALL MEN, THAT MUCH WAS CLEAR, AND THEY ALL SPOKE ENGLISH, BUT THEIR ACCENTS WERE AS DIVERSE AS THE GENTLEMEN.
SO MANY GOOD DEEDS. FOR THE CHILDREN AND FOR THOSE IN SUCH... DES-PERATE NEED...
GUT.
YA-YA.
YAAS.
HEAR, HEAR.
BRA-VO.

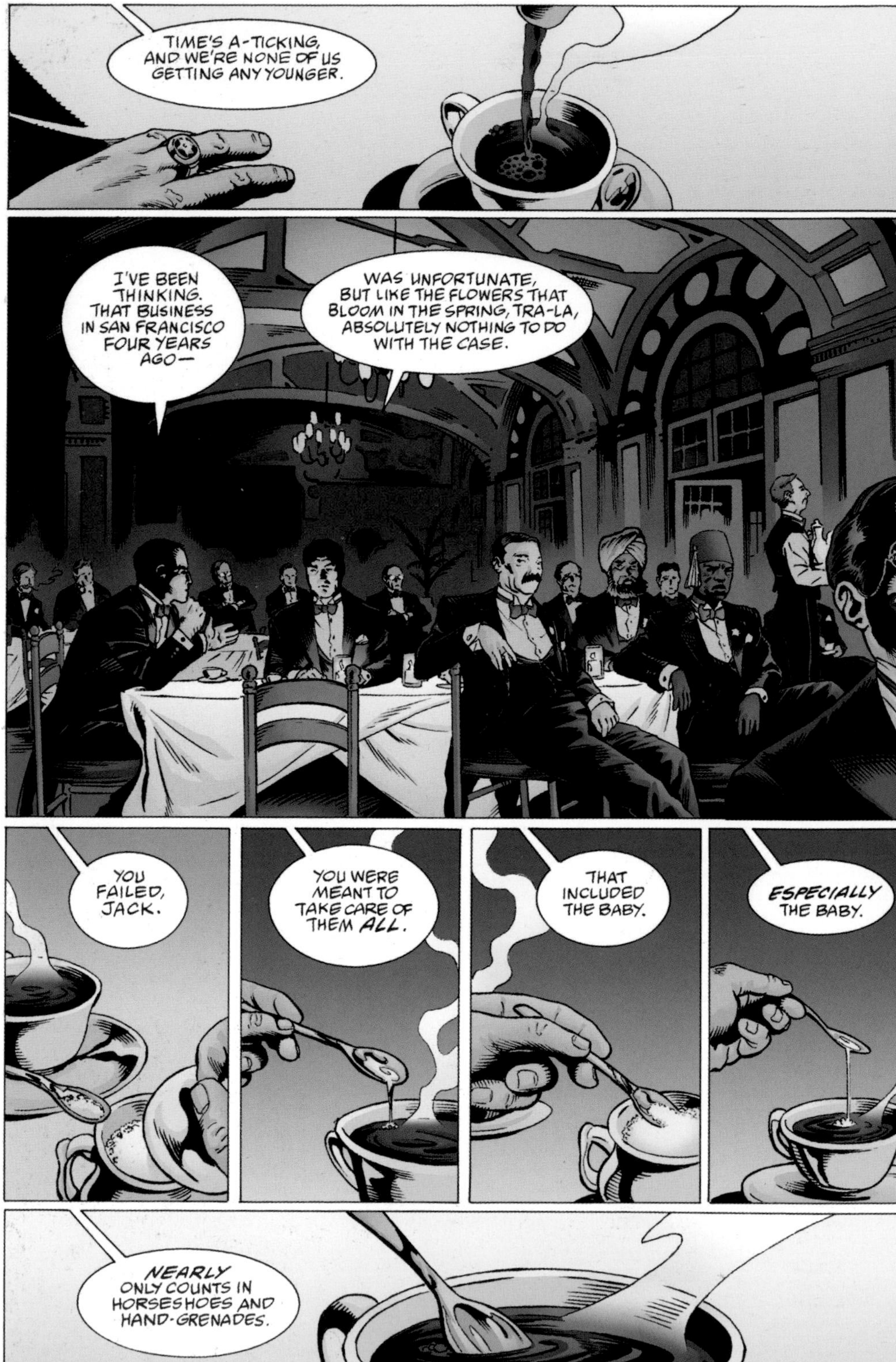
TIME'S A-TICKING, AND WE'RE NONE OF US GETTING ANY YOUNGER.
I'VE BEEN THINKING. THAT BUSINESS IN SAN FRANCISCO FOUR YEARS AGO—
WAS UNFORTUNATE, BUT LIKE THE FLOWERS THAT BLOOM IN THE SPRING, TRA-LA, ABSOLUTELY NOTHING TO DO WITH THE CASE.
YOU FAILED, JACK.
YOU WERE MEANT TO TAKE CARE OF THEM *ALL*.
THAT INCLUDED THE BABY.
ESPECIALLY THE BABY.
NEARLY ONLY COUNTS IN HORSESHOES AND HAND-GRENADES.

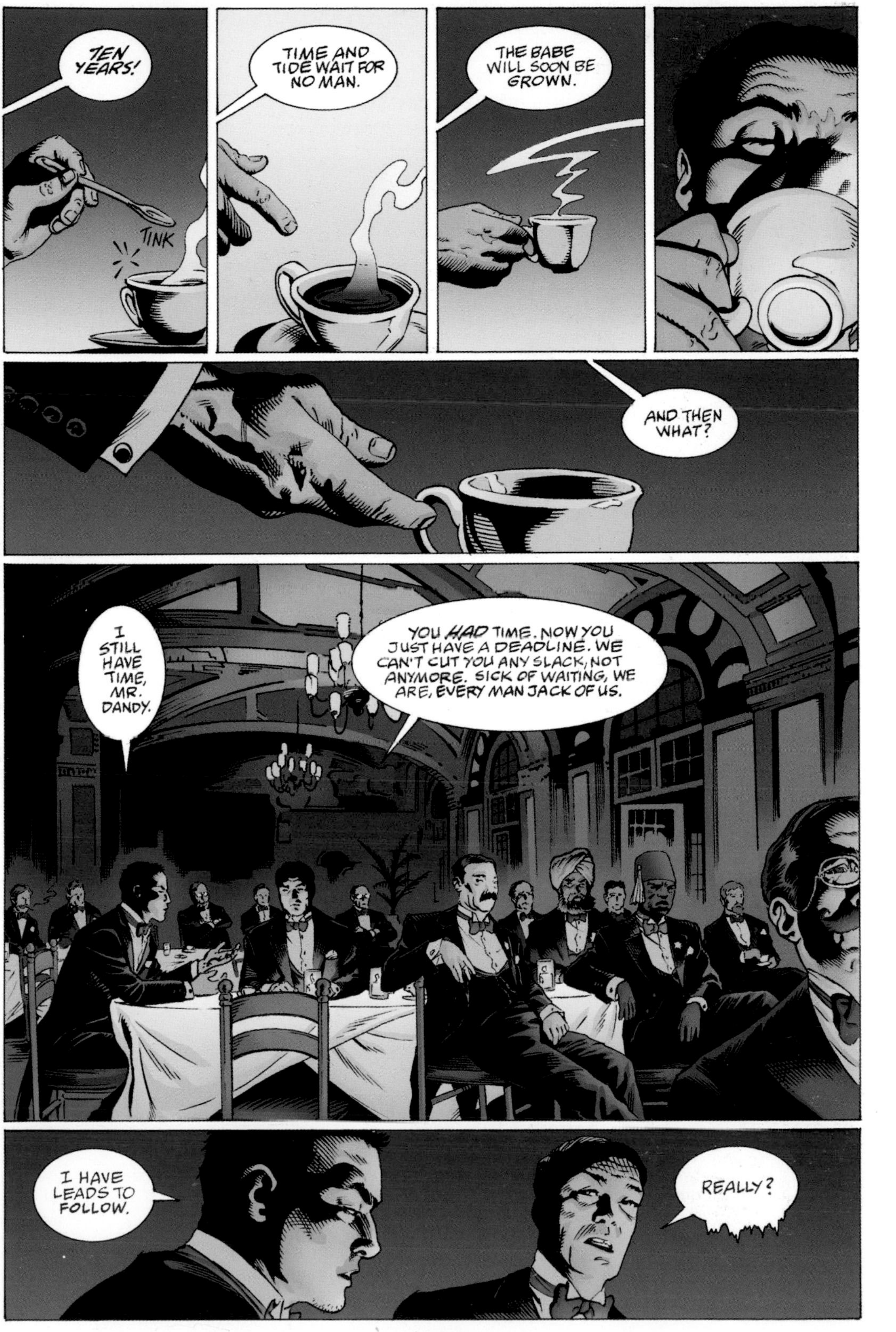
TEN YEARS!
TINK
TIME AND TIDE WAIT FOR NO MAN.
THE BABE WILL SOON BE GROWN.
AND THEN WHAT?
I STILL HAVE TIME, MR. DANDY.
YOU HAD TIME. NOW YOU JUST HAVE A DEADLINE. WE CAN'T CUT YOU ANY SLACK, NOT ANYMORE. SICK OF WAITING, WE ARE, EVERY MAN JACK OF US.
I HAVE LEADS TO FOLLOW.
REALLY?

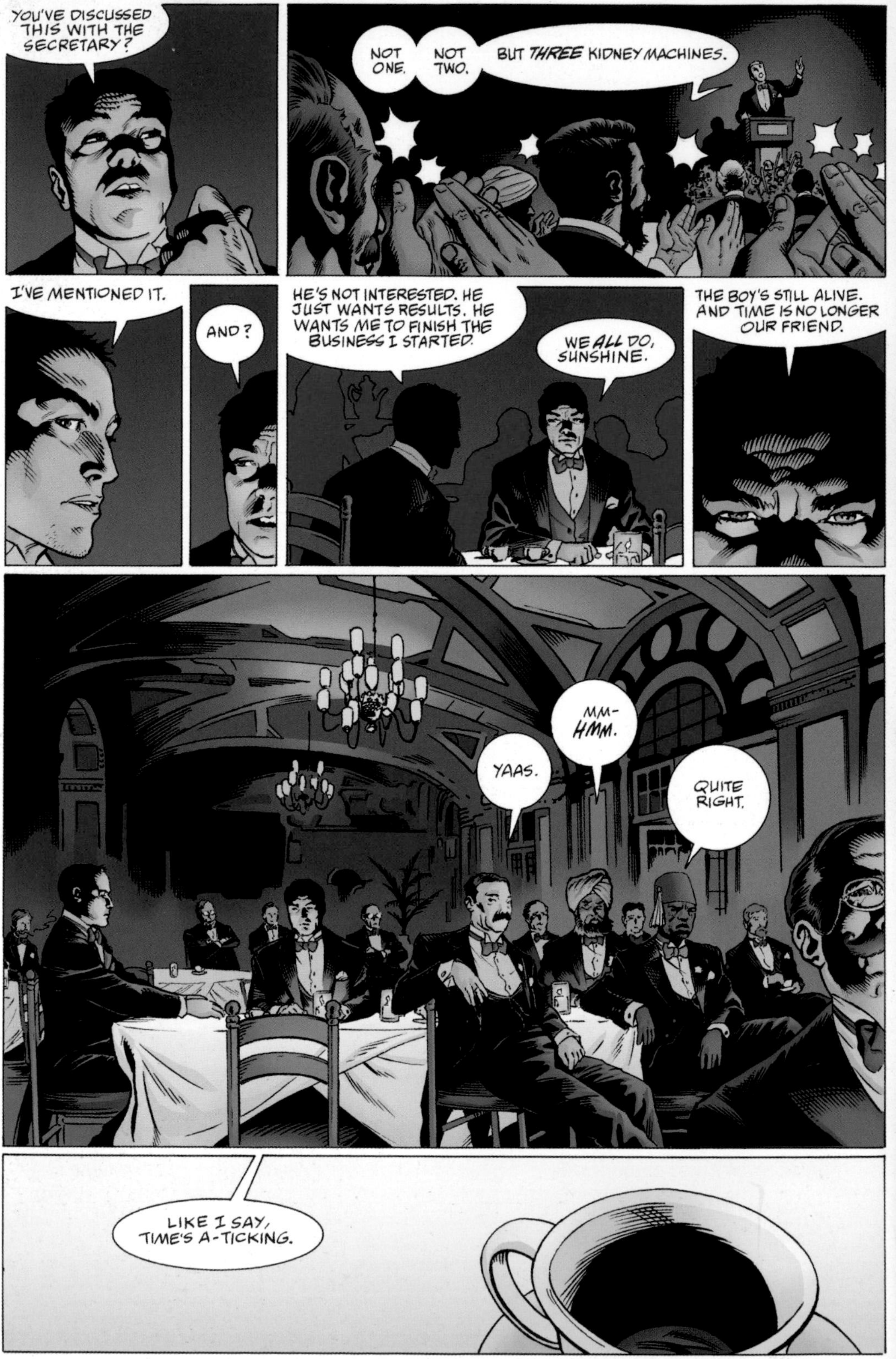
YOU'VE DISCUSSED THIS WITH THE SECRETARY?
NOT ONE.
NOT TWO.
BUT THREE KIDNEY MACHINES.
I'VE MENTIONED IT.
AND?
HE'S NOT INTERESTED. HE JUST WANTS RESULTS. HE WANTS ME TO FINISH THE BUSINESS I STARTED.
WE ALL DO, SUNSHINE.
THE BOY'S STILL ALIVE. AND TIME IS NO LONGER OUR FRIEND.
YAAS.
MM-HMM.
QUITE RIGHT.
LIKE I SAY, TIME'S A-TICKING.

THE GRAVEYARD BOOK

VOLUME 2

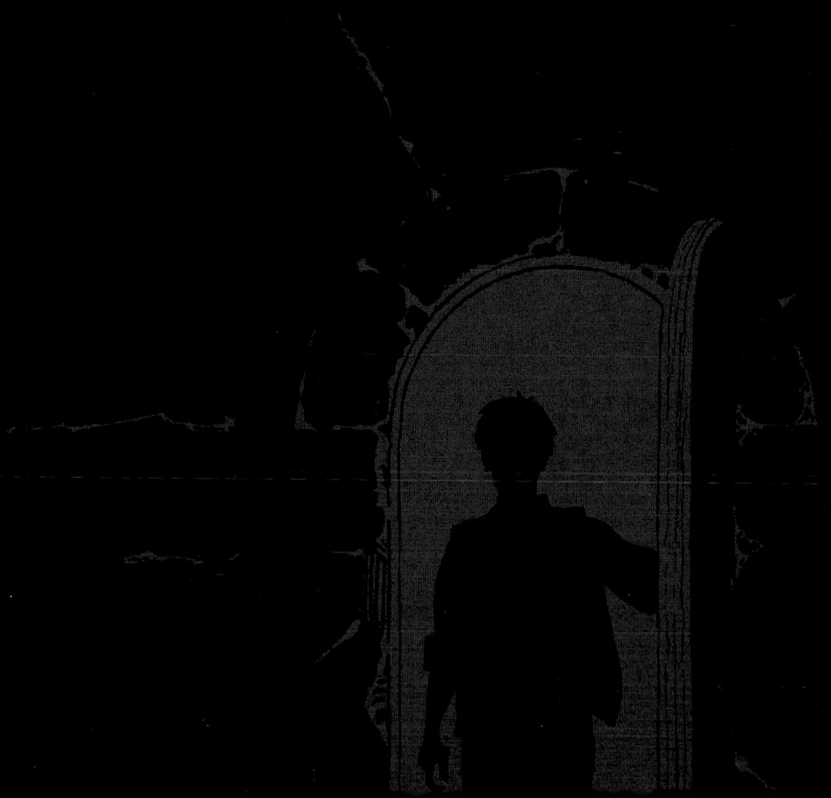

6
Nobody Owens' School Days

Illustrated by David Lafuente

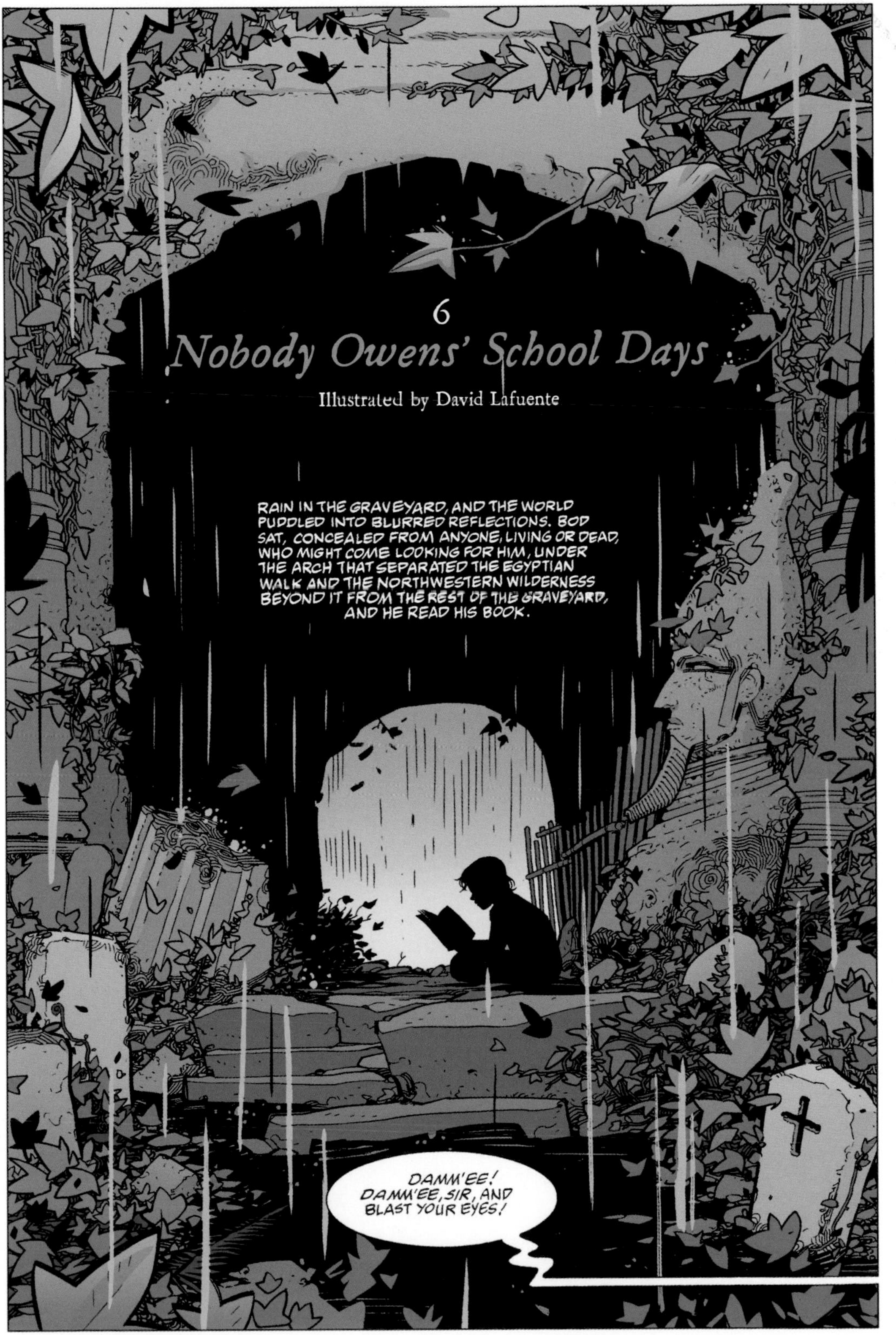
RAIN IN THE GRAVEYARD, AND THE WORLD PUDDLED INTO BLURRED REFLECTIONS. BOD SAT, CONCEALED FROM ANYONE, LIVING OR DEAD, WHO MIGHT COME LOOKING FOR HIM, UNDER THE ARCH THAT SEPARATED THE EGYPTIAN WALK AND THE NORTHWESTERN WILDERNESS BEYOND IT FROM THE REST OF THE GRAVEYARD, AND HE READ HIS BOOK.
DAMM'EE! DAMM'EE, SIR, AND BLAST YOUR EYES!

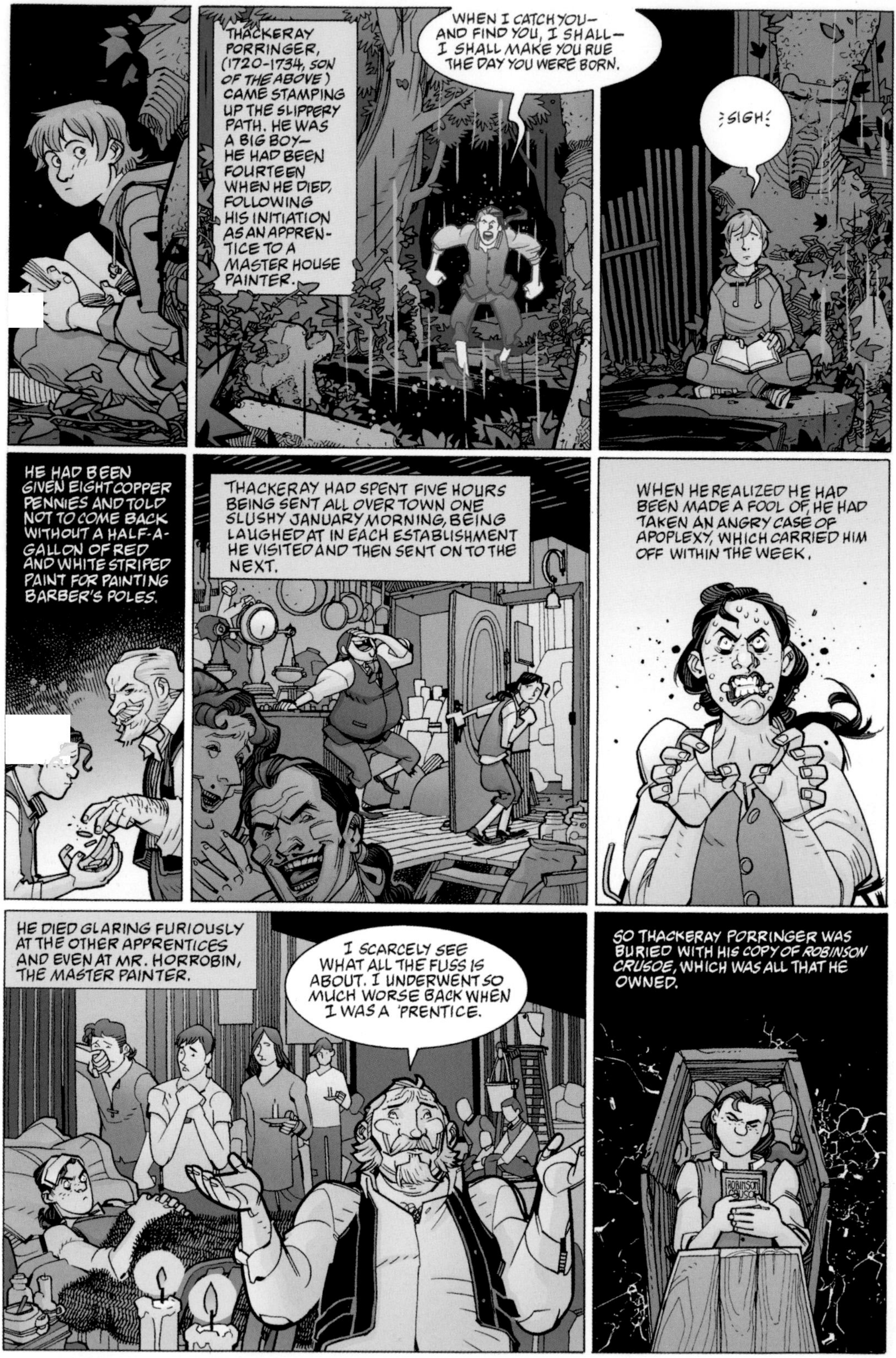
THACKERAY PORRINGER, (1720-1734, SON OF THE ABOVE) CAME STAMPING UP THE SLIPPERY PATH. HE WAS A BIG BOY— HE HAD BEEN FOURTEEN WHEN HE DIED, FOLLOWING HIS INITIATION AS AN APPRENTICE TO A MASTER HOUSE PAINTER.
WHEN I CATCH YOU— AND FIND YOU, I SHALL— I SHALL MAKE YOU RUE THE DAY YOU WERE BORN.
SIGH
HE HAD BEEN GIVEN EIGHT COPPER PENNIES AND TOLD NOT TO COME BACK WITHOUT A HALF-A-GALLON OF RED AND WHITE STRIPED PAINT FOR PAINTING BARBER'S POLES.
THACKERAY HAD SPENT FIVE HOURS BEING SENT ALL OVER TOWN ONE SLUSHY JANUARY MORNING, BEING LAUGHED AT IN EACH ESTABLISHMENT HE VISITED AND THEN SENT ON TO THE NEXT.
WHEN HE REALIZED HE HAD BEEN MADE A FOOL OF, HE HAD TAKEN AN ANGRY CASE OF APOPLEXY, WHICH CARRIED HIM OFF WITHIN THE WEEK.
HE DIED GLARING FURIOUSLY AT THE OTHER APPRENTICES AND EVEN AT MR. HORROBIN, THE MASTER PAINTER.
I SCARCELY SEE WHAT ALL THE FUSS IS ABOUT. I UNDERWENT SO MUCH WORSE BACK WHEN I WAS A 'PRENTICE.
SO THACKERAY PORRINGER WAS BURIED WITH HIS COPY OF ROBINSON CRUSOE, WHICH WAS ALL THAT HE OWNED.
ROBINSON CRUSOE

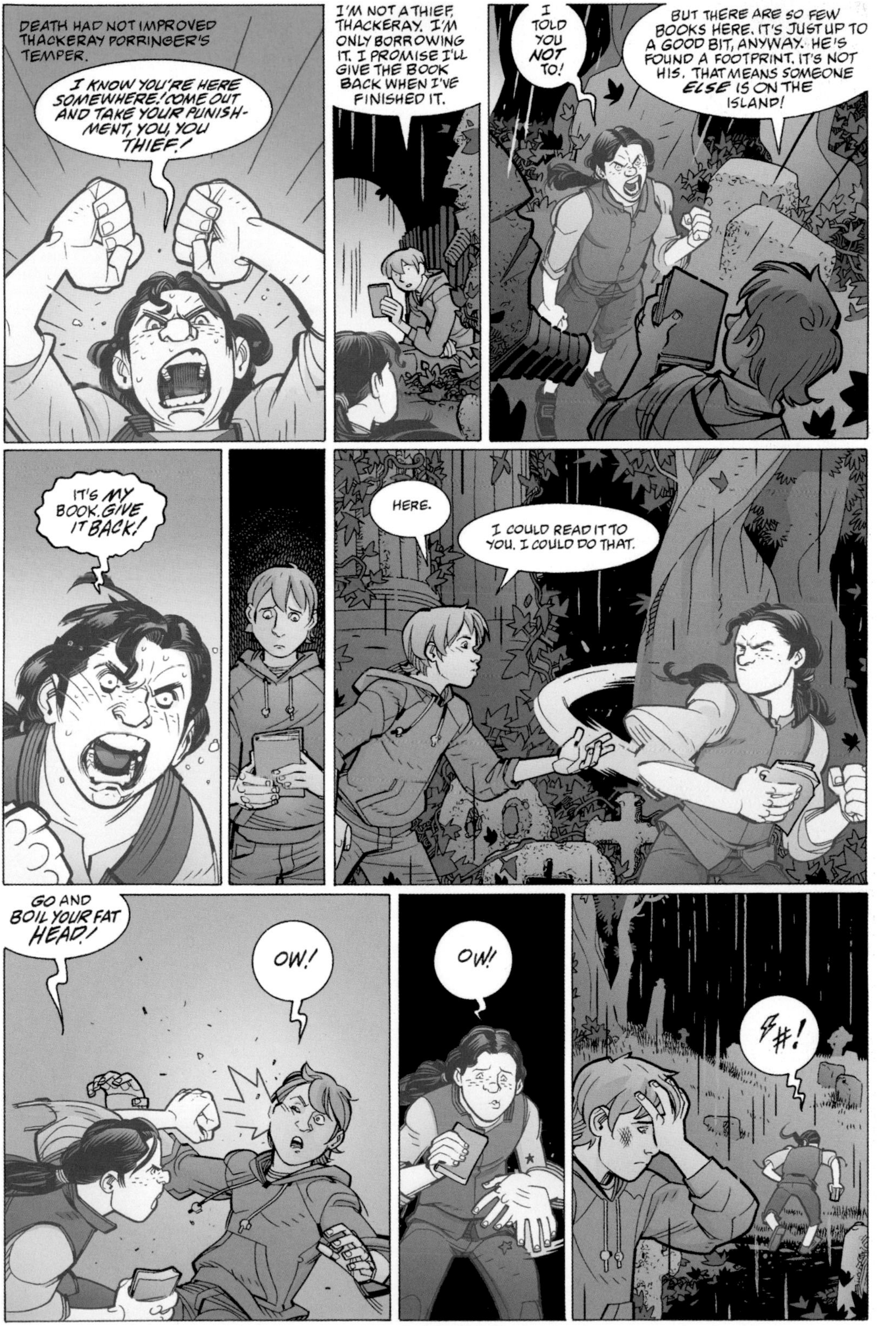
DEATH HAD NOT IMPROVED THACKERAY PORRINGER'S TEMPER.
I KNOW YOU'RE HERE SOMEWHERE! COME OUT AND TAKE YOUR PUNISHMENT, YOU, YOU THIEF!
I'M NOT A THIEF, THACKERAY. I'M ONLY BORROWING IT. I PROMISE I'LL GIVE THE BOOK BACK WHEN I'VE FINISHED IT.
I TOLD YOU NOT TO!
BUT THERE ARE SO FEW BOOKS HERE. IT'S JUST UP TO A GOOD BIT, ANYWAY. HE'S FOUND A FOOTPRINT. IT'S NOT HIS. THAT MEANS SOMEONE ELSE IS ON THE ISLAND!
IT'S MY BOOK. GIVE IT BACK!
HERE.
I COULD READ IT TO YOU. I COULD DO THAT.
GO AND BOIL YOUR FAT HEAD!
OW!
OW!
#!

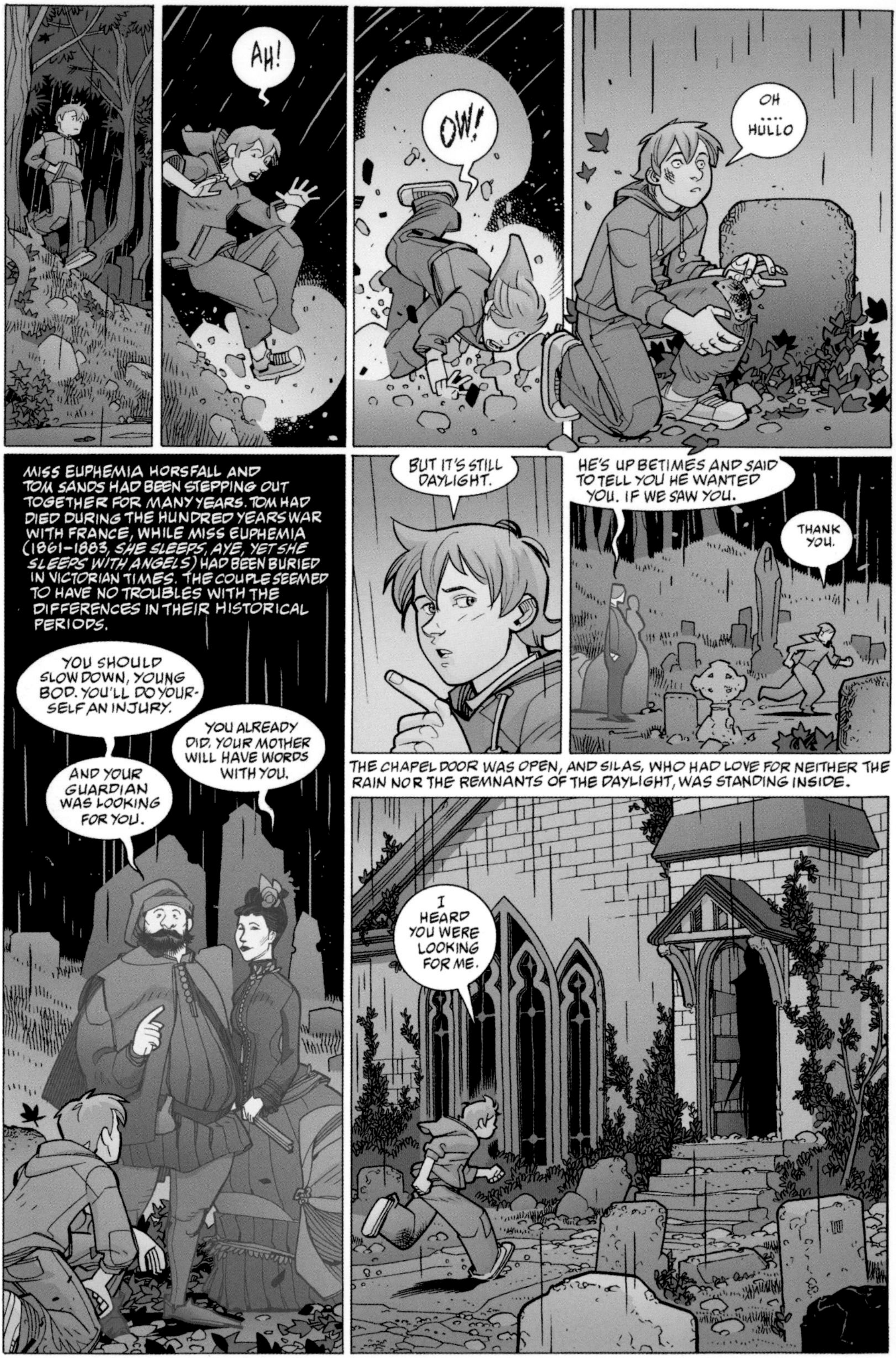
AH!
OW!
OH .... HULLO
MISS EUPHEMIA HORSFALL AND TOM SANDS HAD BEEN STEPPING OUT TOGETHER FOR MANY YEARS. TOM HAD DIED DURING THE HUNDRED YEARS WAR WITH FRANCE, WHILE MISS EUPHEMIA (1861–1883, SHE SLEEPS, AYE, YET SHE SLEEPS WITH ANGELS) HAD BEEN BURIED IN VICTORIAN TIMES. THE COUPLE SEEMED TO HAVE NO TROUBLES WITH THE DIFFERENCES IN THEIR HISTORICAL PERIODS.
YOU SHOULD SLOW DOWN, YOUNG BOD. YOU'LL DO YOURSELF AN INJURY.
YOU ALREADY DID. YOUR MOTHER WILL HAVE WORDS WITH YOU.
AND YOUR GUARDIAN WAS LOOKING FOR YOU.
BUT IT'S STILL DAYLIGHT.
HE'S UP BETIMES AND SAID TO TELL YOU HE WANTED YOU. IF WE SAW YOU.
THANK YOU.
THE CHAPEL DOOR WAS OPEN, AND SILAS, WHO HAD LOVE FOR NEITHER THE RAIN NOR THE REMNANTS OF THE DAYLIGHT, WAS STANDING INSIDE.
I HEARD YOU WERE LOOKING FOR ME.

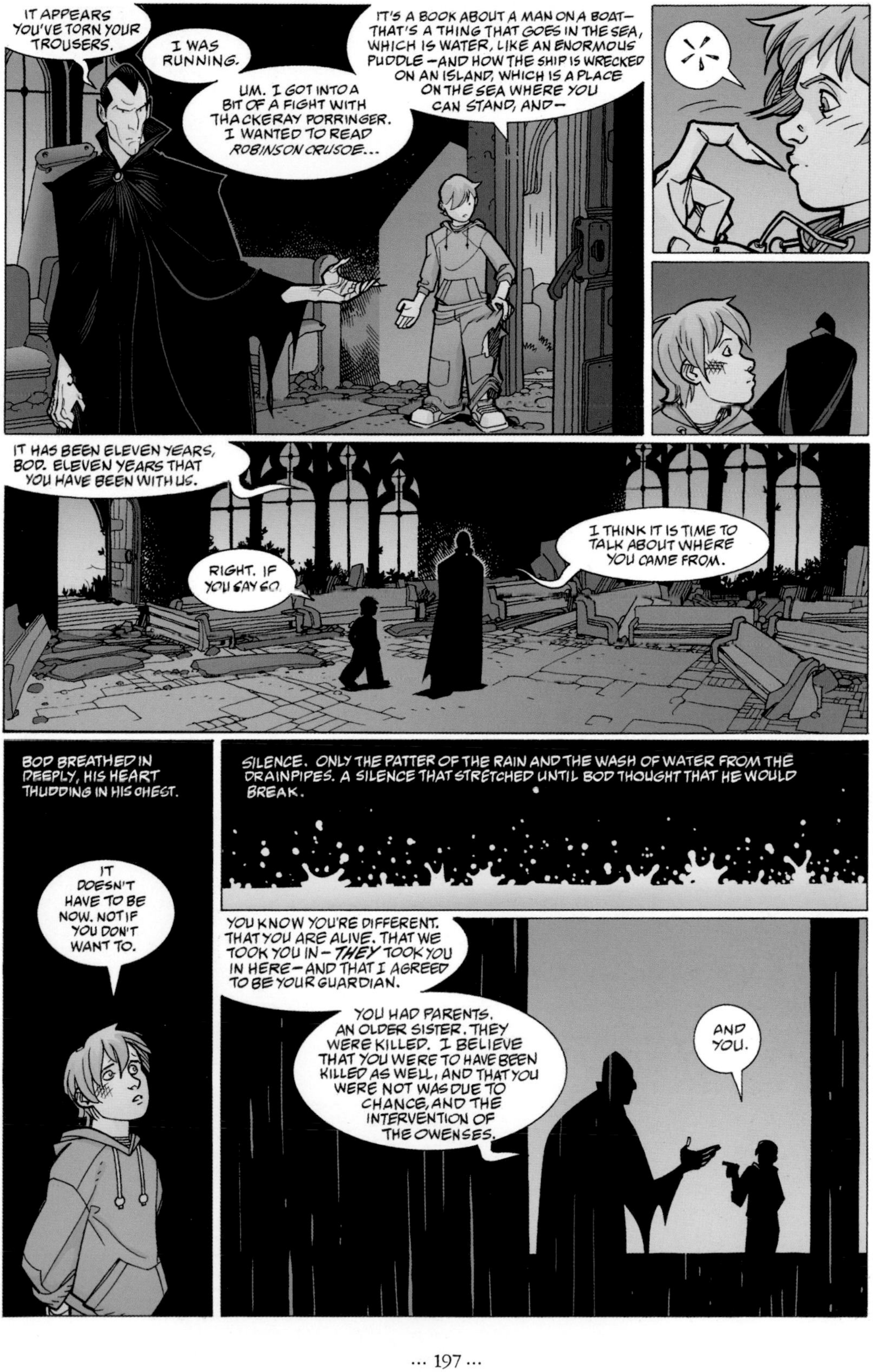
IT APPEARS YOU'VE TORN YOUR TROUSERS.
I WAS RUNNING.
UM. I GOT INTO A BIT OF A FIGHT WITH THACKERAY PORRINGER. I WANTED TO READ ROBINSON CRUSOE...
IT'S A BOOK ABOUT A MAN ON A BOAT— THAT'S A THING THAT GOES IN THE SEA, WHICH IS WATER, LIKE AN ENORMOUS PUDDLE—AND HOW THE SHIP IS WRECKED ON AN ISLAND, WHICH IS A PLACE ON THE SEA WHERE YOU CAN STAND, AND—
IT HAS BEEN ELEVEN YEARS, BOD. ELEVEN YEARS THAT YOU HAVE BEEN WITH US.
RIGHT. IF YOU SAY SO.
I THINK IT IS TIME TO TALK ABOUT WHERE YOU CAME FROM.
BOD BREATHED IN DEEPLY, HIS HEART THUDDING IN HIS CHEST.
IT DOESN'T HAVE TO BE NOW. NOT IF YOU DON'T WANT TO.
SILENCE. ONLY THE PATTER OF THE RAIN AND THE WASH OF WATER FROM THE DRAINPIPES. A SILENCE THAT STRETCHED UNTIL BOD THOUGHT THAT HE WOULD BREAK.
YOU KNOW YOU'RE DIFFERENT. THAT YOU ARE ALIVE. THAT WE TOOK YOU IN—THEY TOOK YOU IN HERE—AND THAT I AGREED TO BE YOUR GUARDIAN.
YOU HAD PARENTS. AN OLDER SISTER. THEY WERE KILLED. I BELIEVE THAT YOU WERE TO HAVE BEEN KILLED AS WELL, AND THAT YOU WERE NOT WAS DUE TO CHANCE, AND THE INTERVENTION OF THE OWENSES.
AND YOU.

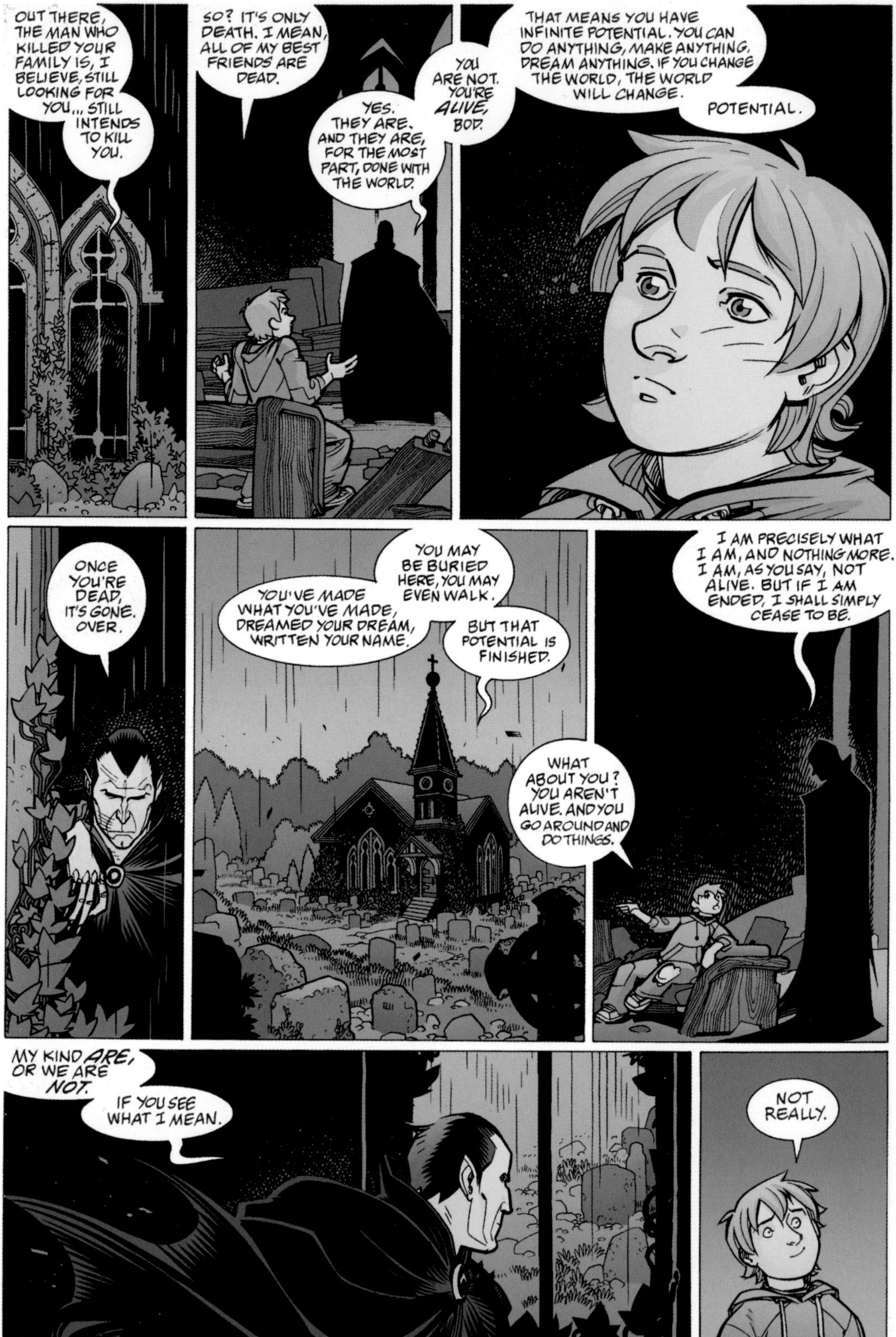
OUT THERE, THE MAN WHO KILLED YOUR FAMILY IS, I BELIEVE, STILL LOOKING FOR YOU... STILL INTENDS TO KILL YOU.
SO? IT'S ONLY DEATH. I MEAN, ALL OF MY BEST FRIENDS ARE DEAD.
YOU ARE NOT. YOU'RE ALIVE, BOD.
YES. THEY ARE. AND THEY ARE, FOR THE MOST PART, DONE WITH THE WORLD.
THAT MEANS YOU HAVE INFINITE POTENTIAL. YOU CAN DO ANYTHING, MAKE ANYTHING, DREAM ANYTHING. IF YOU CHANGE THE WORLD, THE WORLD WILL CHANGE.
POTENTIAL.
ONCE YOU'RE DEAD, IT'S GONE. OVER.
YOU MAY BE BURIED HERE, YOU MAY EVEN WALK.
YOU'VE MADE WHAT YOU'VE MADE, DREAMED YOUR DREAM, WRITTEN YOUR NAME.
BUT THAT POTENTIAL IS FINISHED.
WHAT ABOUT YOU? YOU AREN'T ALIVE. AND YOU GO AROUND AND DO THINGS.
I AM PRECISELY WHAT I AM, AND NOTHING MORE. I AM, AS YOU SAY, NOT ALIVE. BUT IF I AM ENDED, I SHALL SIMPLY CEASE TO BE.
MY KIND ARE, OR WE ARE NOT.
IF YOU SEE WHAT I MEAN.
NOT REALLY.

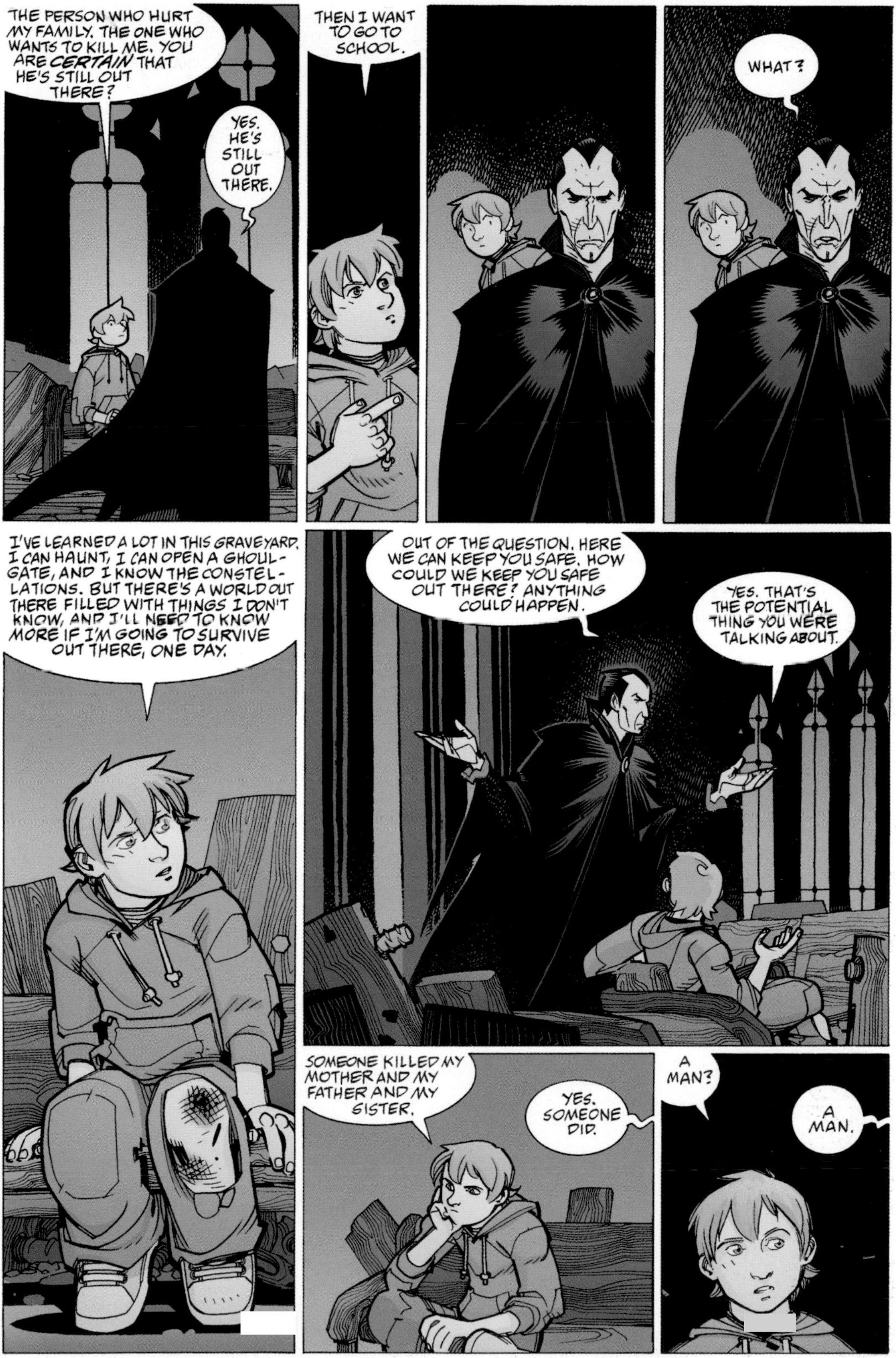

THE PERSON WHO HURT MY FAMILY. THE ONE WHO WANTS TO KILL ME. YOU ARE CERTAIN THAT HE'S STILL OUT THERE?
YES. HE'S STILL OUT THERE.
THEN I WANT TO GO TO SCHOOL.
WHAT?
I'VE LEARNED A LOT IN THIS GRAVEYARD. I CAN HAUNT, I CAN OPEN A GHOUL-GATE, AND I KNOW THE CONSTEL-LATIONS. BUT THERE'S A WORLD OUT THERE FILLED WITH THINGS I DON'T KNOW, AND I'LL NEED TO KNOW MORE IF I'M GOING TO SURVIVE OUT THERE, ONE DAY.
OUT OF THE QUESTION. HERE WE CAN KEEP YOU SAFE. HOW COULD WE KEEP YOU SAFE OUT THERE? ANYTHING COULD HAPPEN.
YES. THAT'S THE POTENTIAL THING YOU WERE TALKING ABOUT.
SOMEONE KILLED MY MOTHER AND MY FATHER AND MY SISTER.
YES. SOMEONE DID.
A MAN?
A MAN.

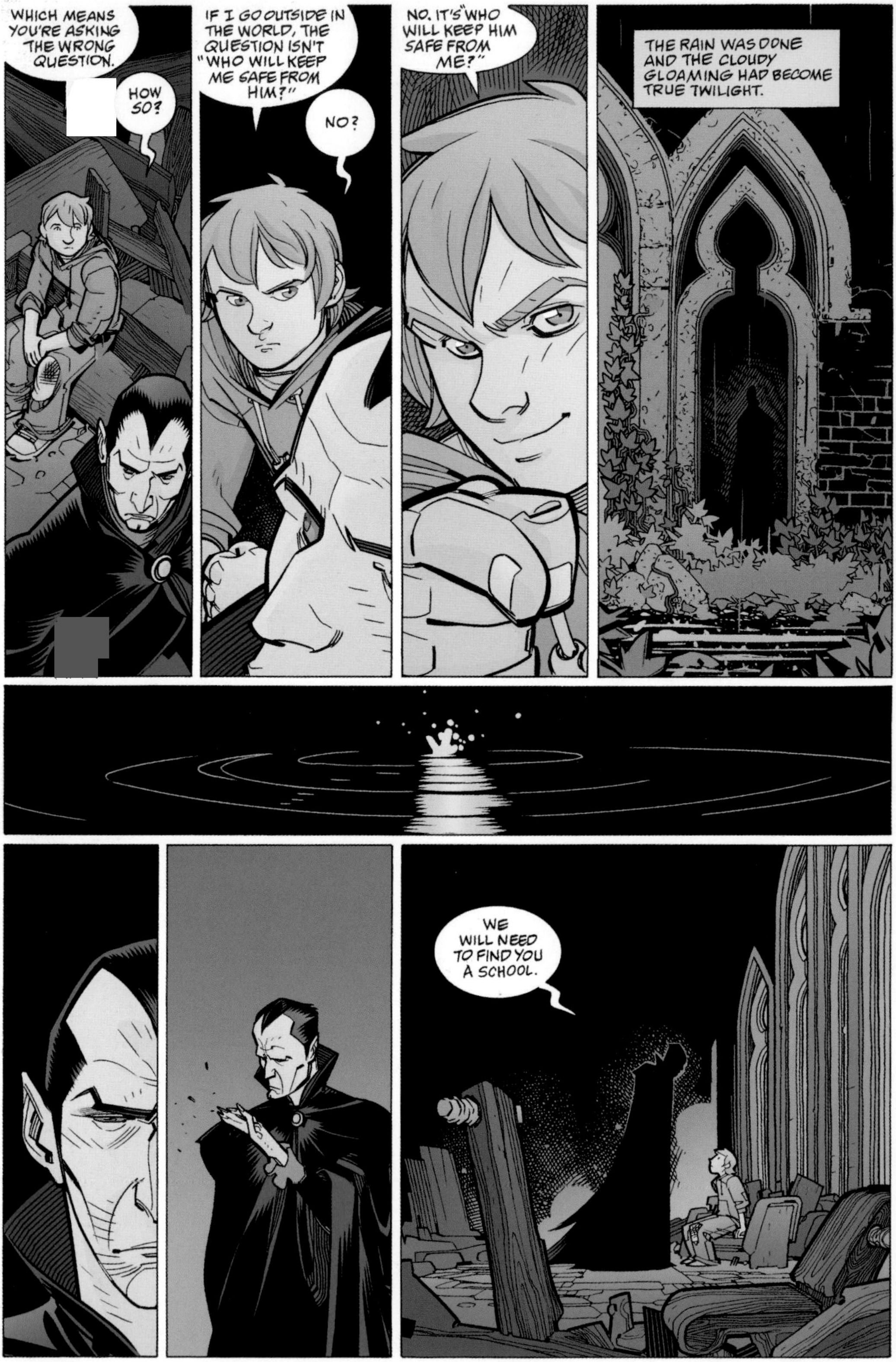
WHICH MEANS YOU'RE ASKING THE WRONG QUESTION.
HOW SO?
IF I GO OUTSIDE IN THE WORLD, THE QUESTION ISN'T "WHO WILL KEEP ME SAFE FROM HIM?"
NO?
NO. IT'S "WHO WILL KEEP HIM SAFE FROM ME?"
THE RAIN WAS DONE AND THE CLOUDY GLOAMING HAD BECOME TRUE TWILIGHT.
WE WILL NEED TO FIND YOU A SCHOOL.

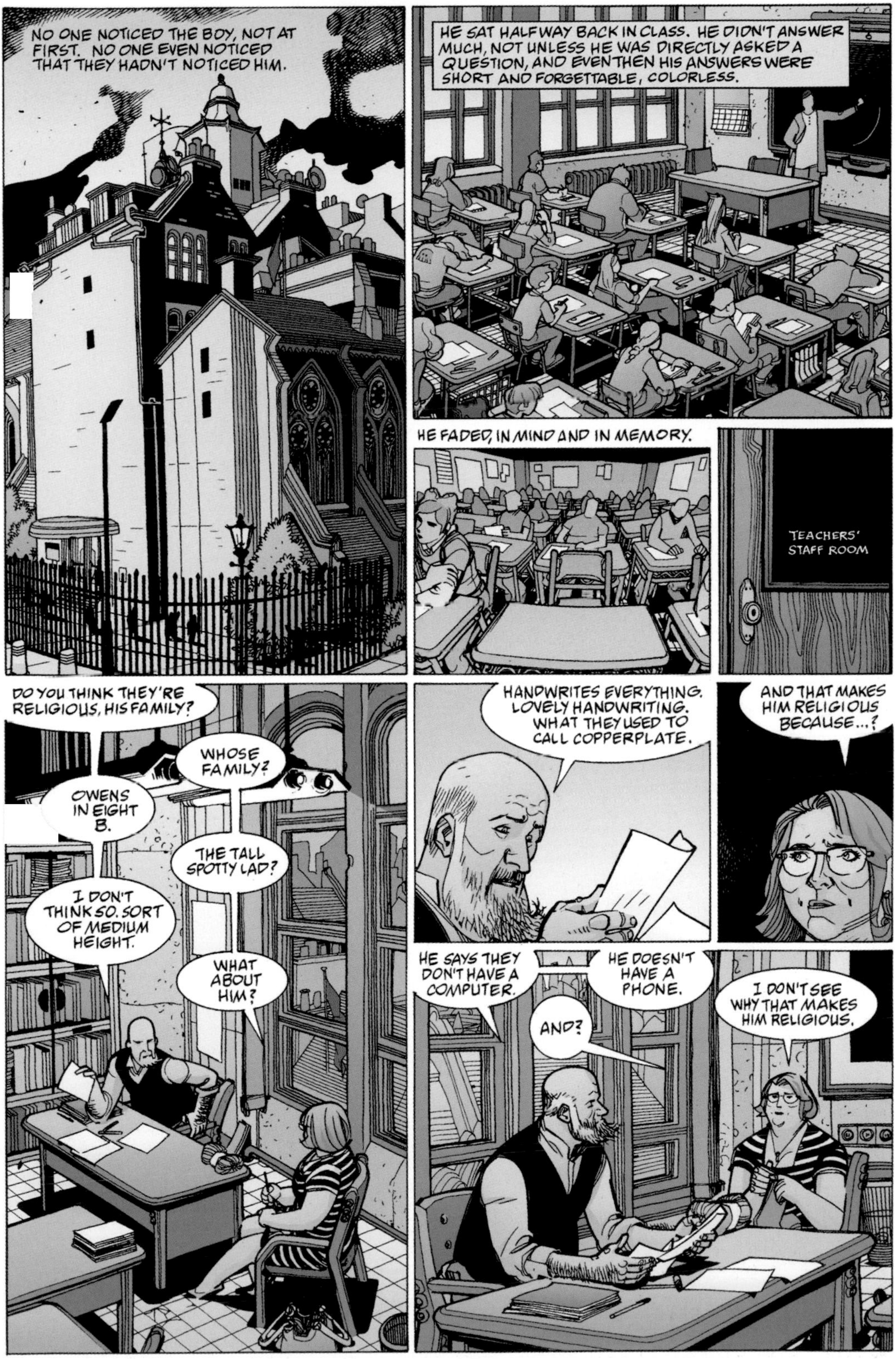

NO ONE NOTICED THE BOY, NOT AT FIRST. NO ONE EVEN NOTICED THAT THEY HADN'T NOTICED HIM.
HE SAT HALFWAY BACK IN CLASS. HE DIDN'T ANSWER MUCH, NOT UNLESS HE WAS DIRECTLY ASKED A QUESTION, AND EVEN THEN HIS ANSWERS WERE SHORT AND FORGETTABLE, COLORLESS.
HE FADED, IN MIND AND IN MEMORY.
TEACHERS' STAFF ROOM
DO YOU THINK THEY'RE RELIGIOUS, HIS FAMILY?
WHOSE FAMILY?
OWENS IN EIGHT B.
THE TALL SPOTTY LAD?
I DON'T THINK SO. SORT OF MEDIUM HEIGHT.
WHAT ABOUT HIM?
HANDWRITES EVERYTHING. LOVELY HANDWRITING. WHAT THEY USED TO CALL COPPERPLATE.
AND THAT MAKES HIM RELIGIOUS BECAUSE...?
HE SAYS THEY DON'T HAVE A COMPUTER.
HE DOESN'T HAVE A PHONE.
AND?
I DON'T SEE WHY THAT MAKES HIM RELIGIOUS.

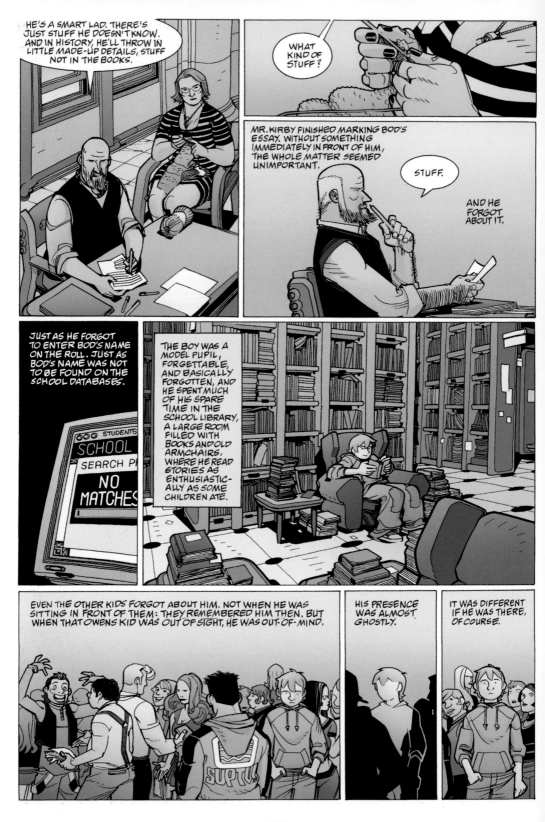

HE'S A SMART LAD. THERE'S JUST STUFF HE DOESN'T KNOW. AND IN HISTORY, HE'LL THROW IN LITTLE MADE-UP DETAILS, STUFF NOT IN THE BOOKS.

WHAT KIND OF STUFF?

MR. KIRBY FINISHED MARKING BOD'S ESSAY. WITHOUT SOMETHING IMMEDIATELY IN FRONT OF HIM, THE WHOLE MATTER SEEMED UNIMPORTANT.

STUFF.

AND HE FORGOT ABOUT IT.

JUST AS HE FORGOT TO ENTER BOD'S NAME ON THE ROLL. JUST AS BOD'S NAME WAS NOT TO BE FOUND ON THE SCHOOL DATABASES.

STUDENTS
SCHOOL
SEARCH P
NO MATCHES

THE BOY WAS A MODEL PUPIL, FORGETTABLE, AND BASICALLY FORGOTTEN, AND HE SPENT MUCH OF HIS SPARE TIME IN THE SCHOOL LIBRARY, A LARGE ROOM FILLED WITH BOOKS AND OLD ARMCHAIRS, WHERE HE READ STORIES AS ENTHUSIASTIC-ALLY AS SOME CHILDREN ATE.

EVEN THE OTHER KIDS FORGOT ABOUT HIM. NOT WHEN HE WAS SITTING IN FRONT OF THEM: THEY REMEMBERED HIM THEN, BUT WHEN THAT OWENS KID WAS OUT OF SIGHT, HE WAS OUT-OF-MIND.

HIS PRESENCE WAS ALMOST GHOSTLY.

IT WAS DIFFERENT IF HE WAS THERE, OF COURSE.

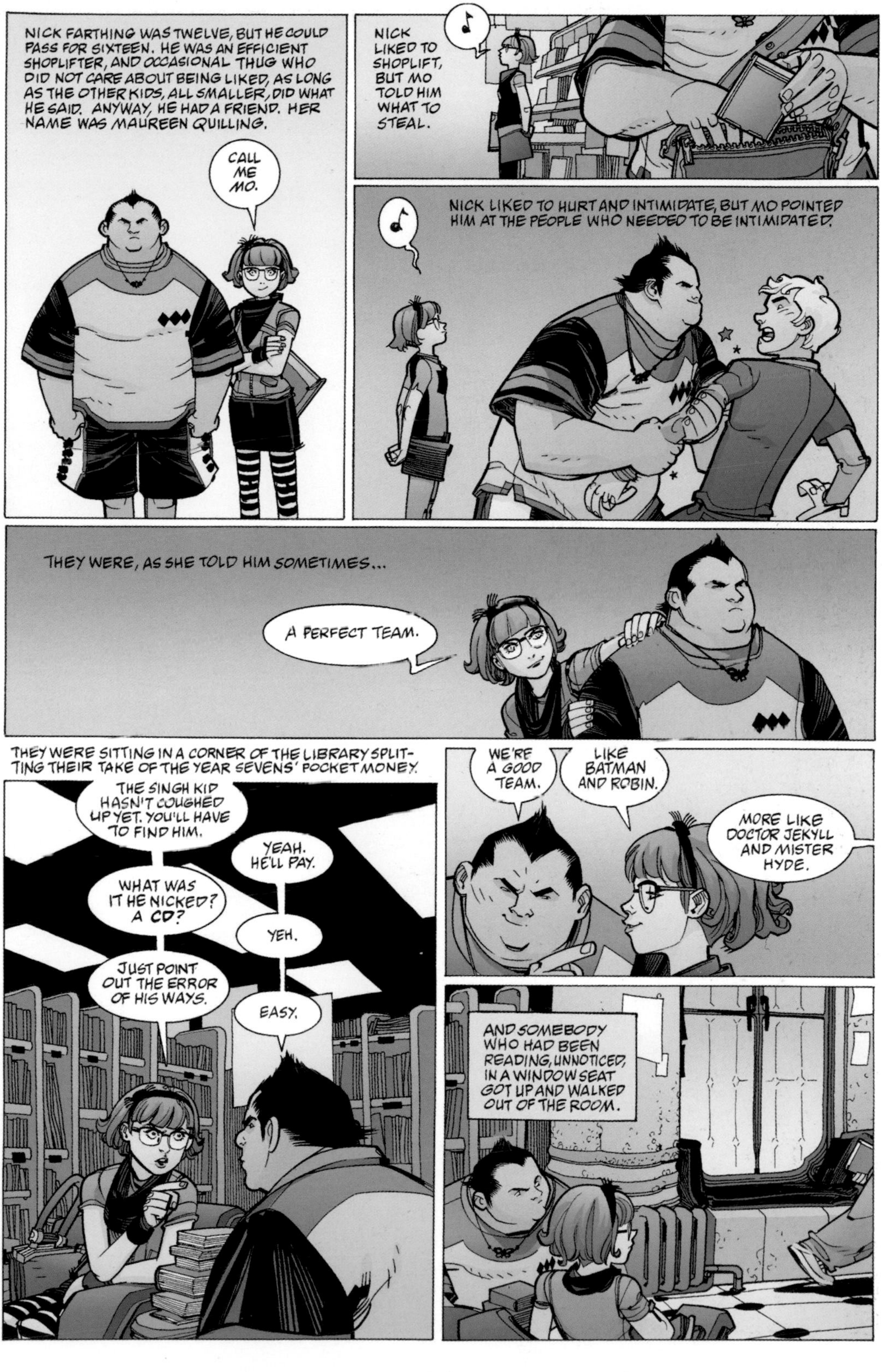

NICK FARTHING WAS TWELVE, BUT HE COULD PASS FOR SIXTEEN. HE WAS AN EFFICIENT SHOPLIFTER, AND OCCASIONAL THUG WHO DID NOT CARE ABOUT BEING LIKED, AS LONG AS THE OTHER KIDS, ALL SMALLER, DID WHAT HE SAID. ANYWAY, HE HAD A FRIEND. HER NAME WAS MAUREEN QUILLING.
CALL ME MO.
NICK LIKED TO SHOPLIFT, BUT MO TOLD HIM WHAT TO STEAL.
NICK LIKED TO HURT AND INTIMIDATE, BUT MO POINTED HIM AT THE PEOPLE WHO NEEDED TO BE INTIMIDATED.
THEY WERE, AS SHE TOLD HIM SOMETIMES...
A PERFECT TEAM.
THEY WERE SITTING IN A CORNER OF THE LIBRARY SPLITTING THEIR TAKE OF THE YEAR SEVENS' POCKET MONEY.
THE SINGH KID HASN'T COUGHED UP YET. YOU'LL HAVE TO FIND HIM.
YEAH. HE'LL PAY.
WHAT WAS IT HE NICKED? A CD?
YEH.
JUST POINT OUT THE ERROR OF HIS WAYS.
EASY.
WE'RE A GOOD TEAM.
LIKE BATMAN AND ROBIN.
MORE LIKE DOCTOR JEKYLL AND MISTER HYDE.
AND SOMEBODY WHO HAD BEEN READING, UNNOTICED, IN A WINDOW SEAT GOT UP AND WALKED OUT OF THE ROOM.

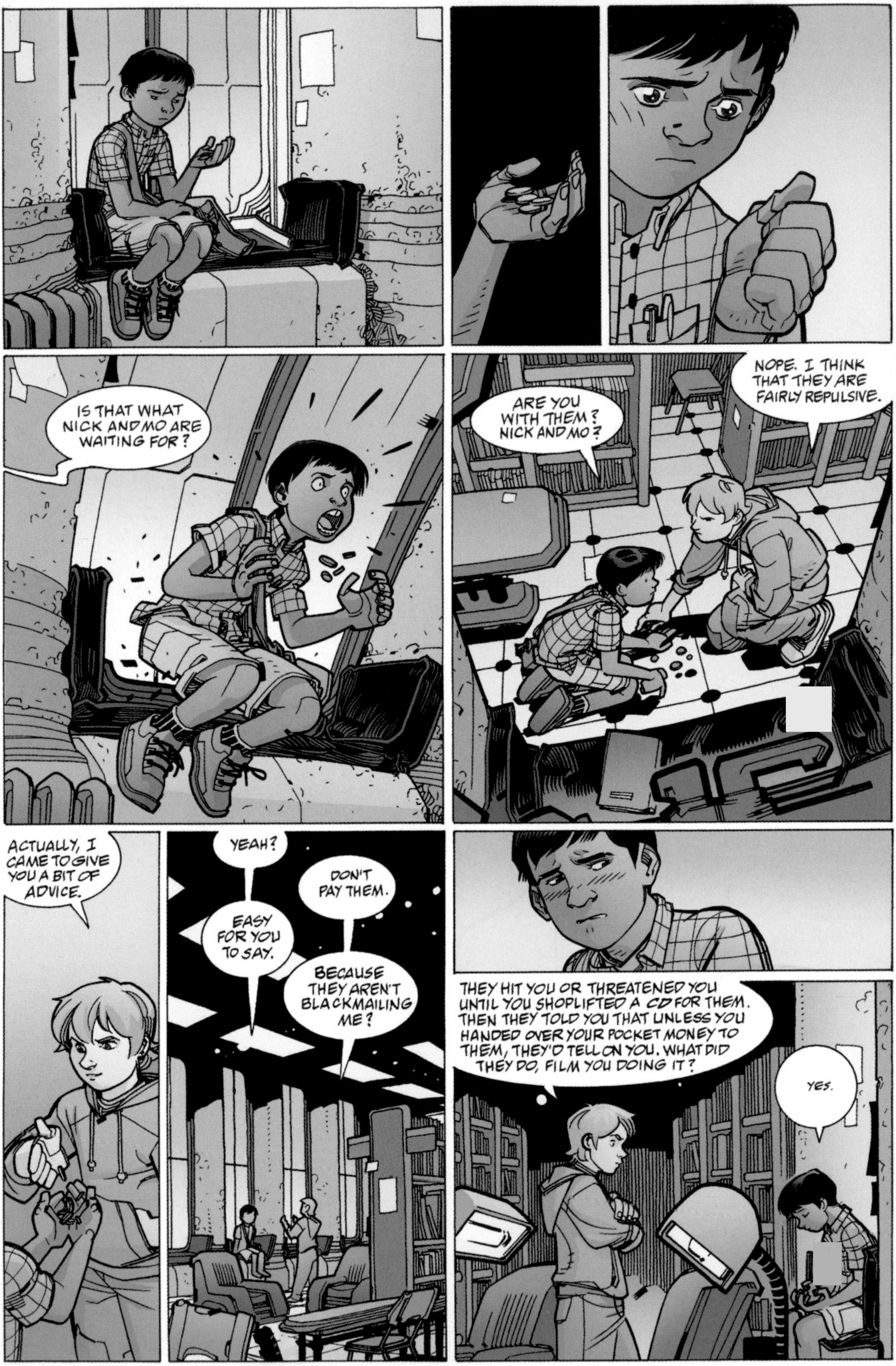

IS THAT WHAT NICK AND MO ARE WAITING FOR?
ARE YOU WITH THEM? NICK AND MO?
NOPE. I THINK THAT THEY ARE FAIRLY REPULSIVE.
ACTUALLY, I CAME TO GIVE YOU A BIT OF ADVICE.
YEAH?
DON'T PAY THEM.
EASY FOR YOU TO SAY.
BECAUSE THEY AREN'T BLACKMAILING ME?
THEY HIT YOU OR THREATENED YOU UNTIL YOU SHOPLIFTED A CD FOR THEM. THEN THEY TOLD YOU THAT UNLESS YOU HANDED OVER YOUR POCKET MONEY TO THEM, THEY'D TELL ON YOU. WHAT DID THEY DO, FILM YOU DOING IT?
YES.

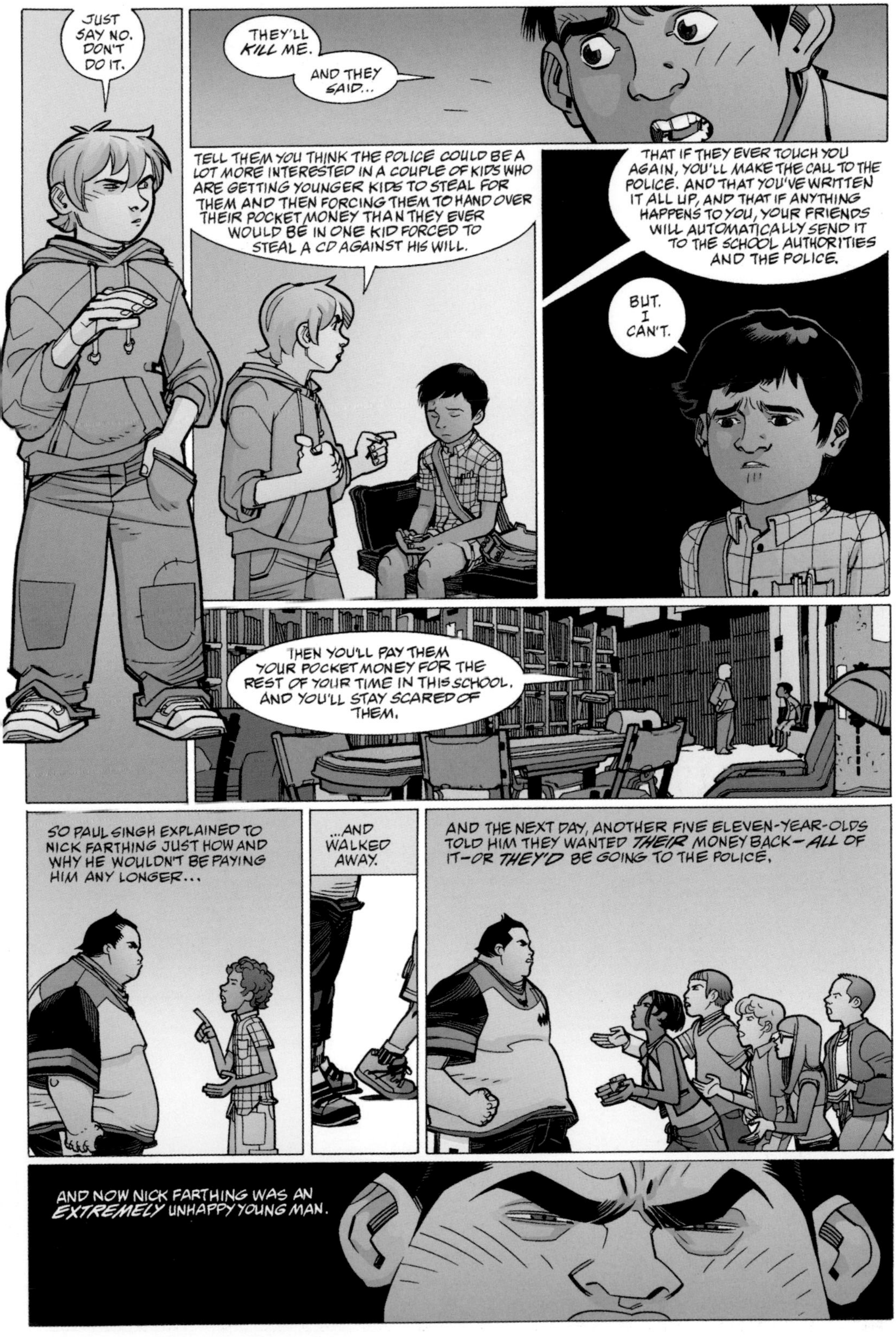
JUST SAY NO. DON'T DO IT.
THEY'LL KILL ME.
AND THEY SAID...
TELL THEM YOU THINK THE POLICE COULD BE A LOT MORE INTERESTED IN A COUPLE OF KIDS WHO ARE GETTING YOUNGER KIDS TO STEAL FOR THEM AND THEN FORCING THEM TO HAND OVER THEIR POCKET MONEY THAN THEY EVER WOULD BE IN ONE KID FORCED TO STEAL A CD AGAINST HIS WILL.
THAT IF THEY EVER TOUCH YOU AGAIN, YOU'LL MAKE THE CALL TO THE POLICE. AND THAT YOU'VE WRITTEN IT ALL UP, AND THAT IF ANYTHING HAPPENS TO YOU, YOUR FRIENDS WILL AUTOMATICALLY SEND IT TO THE SCHOOL AUTHORITIES AND THE POLICE.
BUT. I CAN'T.
THEN YOU'LL PAY THEM YOUR POCKET MONEY FOR THE REST OF YOUR TIME IN THIS SCHOOL. AND YOU'LL STAY SCARED OF THEM.
SO PAUL SINGH EXPLAINED TO NICK FARTHING JUST HOW AND WHY HE WOULDN'T BE PAYING HIM ANY LONGER...
...AND WALKED AWAY.
AND THE NEXT DAY, ANOTHER FIVE ELEVEN-YEAR-OLDS TOLD HIM THEY WANTED THEIR MONEY BACK—ALL OF IT—OR THEY'D BE GOING TO THE POLICE.
AND NOW NICK FARTHING WAS AN EXTREMELY UNHAPPY YOUNG MAN.

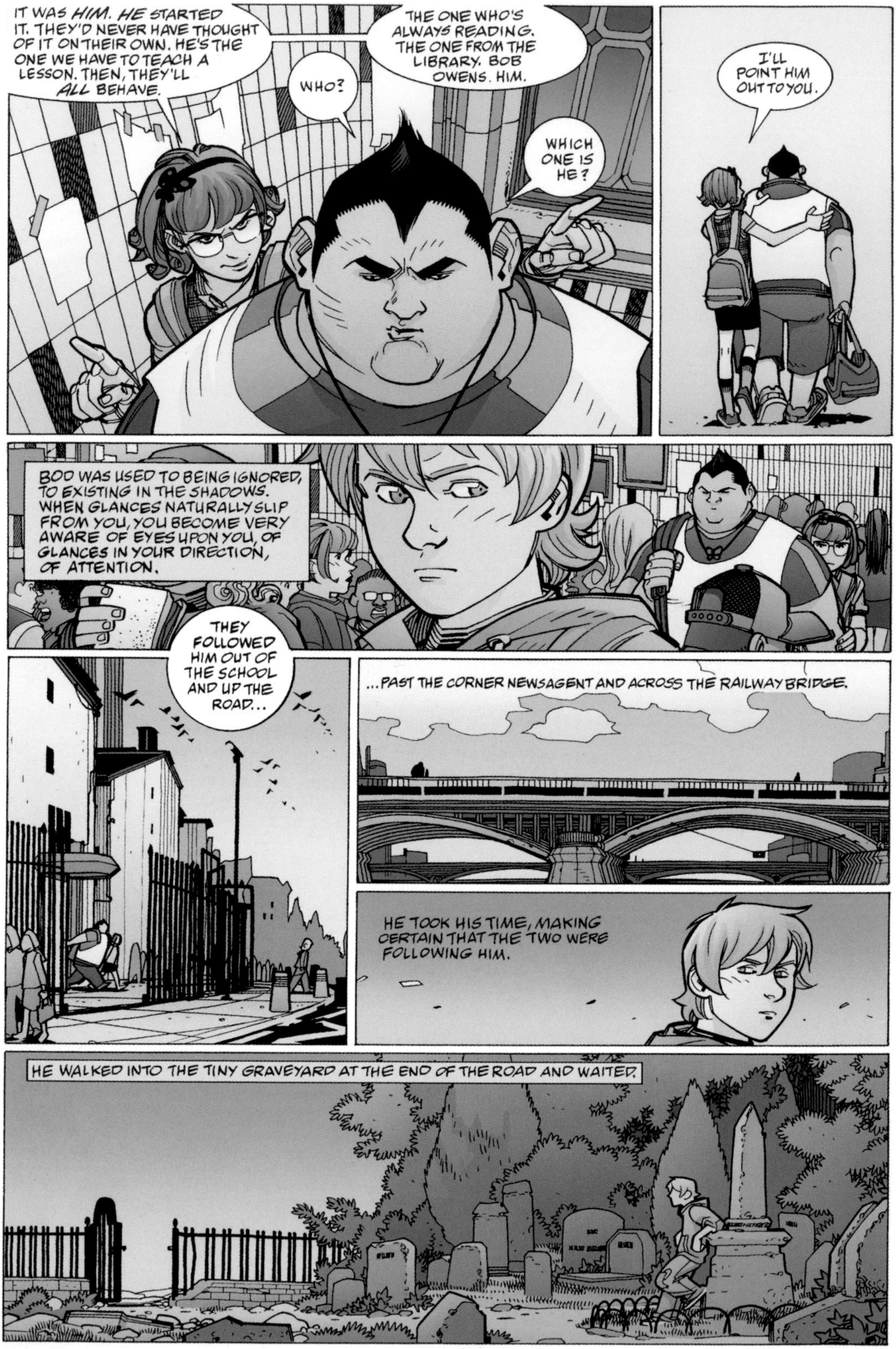
IT WAS HIM. HE STARTED IT. THEY'D NEVER HAVE THOUGHT OF IT ON THEIR OWN. HE'S THE ONE WE HAVE TO TEACH A LESSON. THEN, THEY'LL ALL BEHAVE.
WHO?
THE ONE WHO'S ALWAYS READING. THE ONE FROM THE LIBRARY. BOB OWENS. HIM.
WHICH ONE IS HE?
I'LL POINT HIM OUT TO YOU.
BOD WAS USED TO BEING IGNORED, TO EXISTING IN THE SHADOWS. WHEN GLANCES NATURALLY SLIP FROM YOU, YOU BECOME VERY AWARE OF EYES UPON YOU, OF GLANCES IN YOUR DIRECTION, OF ATTENTION.
THEY FOLLOWED HIM OUT OF THE SCHOOL AND UP THE ROAD...
...PAST THE CORNER NEWSAGENT AND ACROSS THE RAILWAY BRIDGE.
HE TOOK HIS TIME, MAKING CERTAIN THAT THE TWO WERE FOLLOWING HIM.
HE WALKED INTO THE TINY GRAVEYARD AT THE END OF THE ROAD AND WAITED.

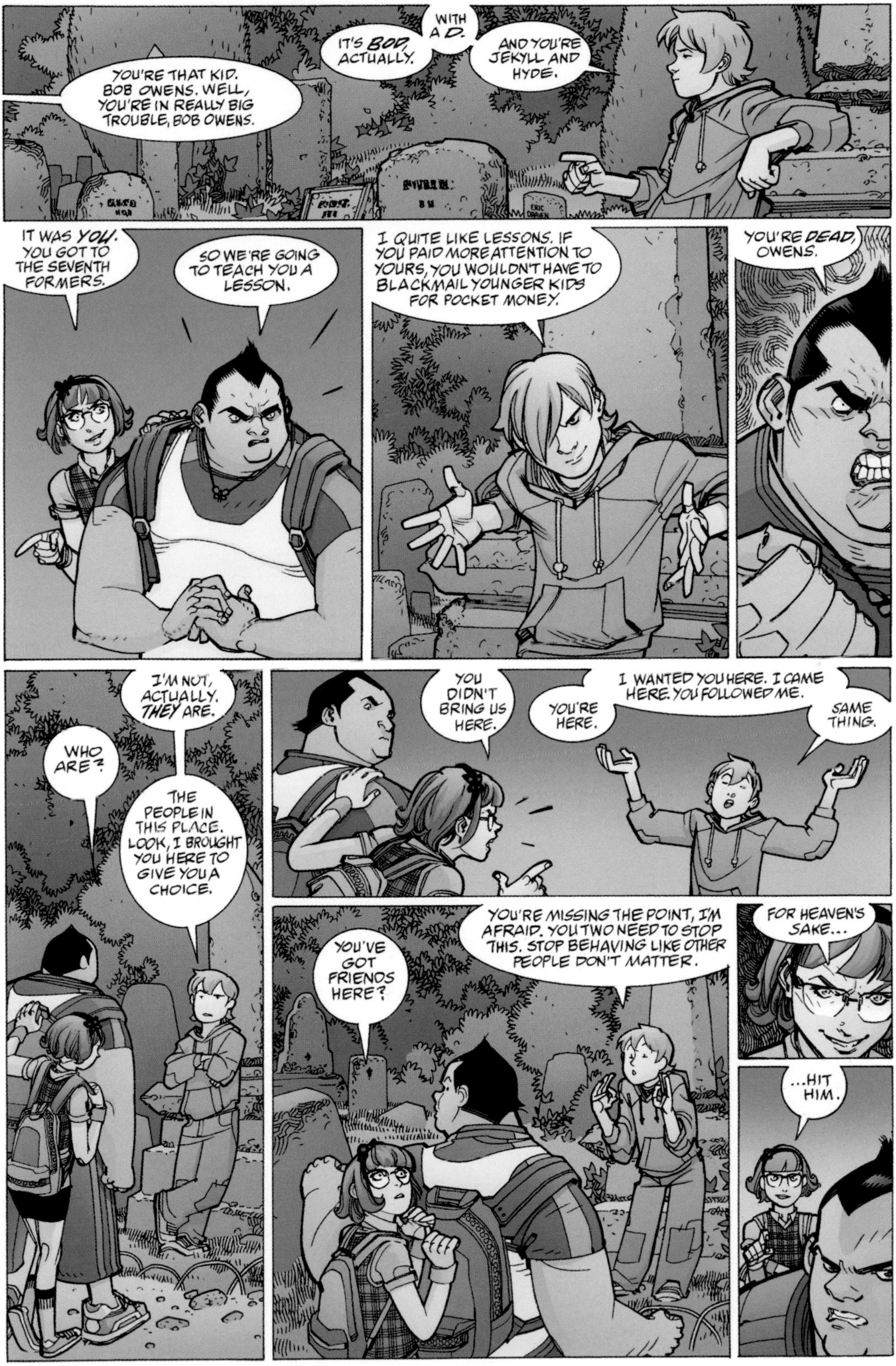
YOU'RE THAT KID. BOB OWENS. WELL, YOU'RE IN REALLY BIG TROUBLE, BOB OWENS.
IT'S BOD, ACTUALLY.
WITH A D.
AND YOU'RE JEKYLL AND HYDE.
IT WAS YOU. YOU GOT TO THE SEVENTH FORMERS.
SO WE'RE GOING TO TEACH YOU A LESSON.
I QUITE LIKE LESSONS. IF YOU PAID MORE ATTENTION TO YOURS, YOU WOULDN'T HAVE TO BLACKMAIL YOUNGER KIDS FOR POCKET MONEY.
YOU'RE DEAD, OWENS.
I'M NOT, ACTUALLY. THEY ARE.
WHO ARE?
THE PEOPLE IN THIS PLACE. LOOK, I BROUGHT YOU HERE TO GIVE YOU A CHOICE.
YOU DIDN'T BRING US HERE.
YOU'RE HERE.
I WANTED YOU HERE. I CAME HERE. YOU FOLLOWED ME.
SAME THING.
YOU'VE GOT FRIENDS HERE?
YOU'RE MISSING THE POINT, I'M AFRAID. YOU TWO NEED TO STOP THIS. STOP BEHAVING LIKE OTHER PEOPLE DON'T MATTER.
FOR HEAVEN'S SAKE...
...HIT HIM.

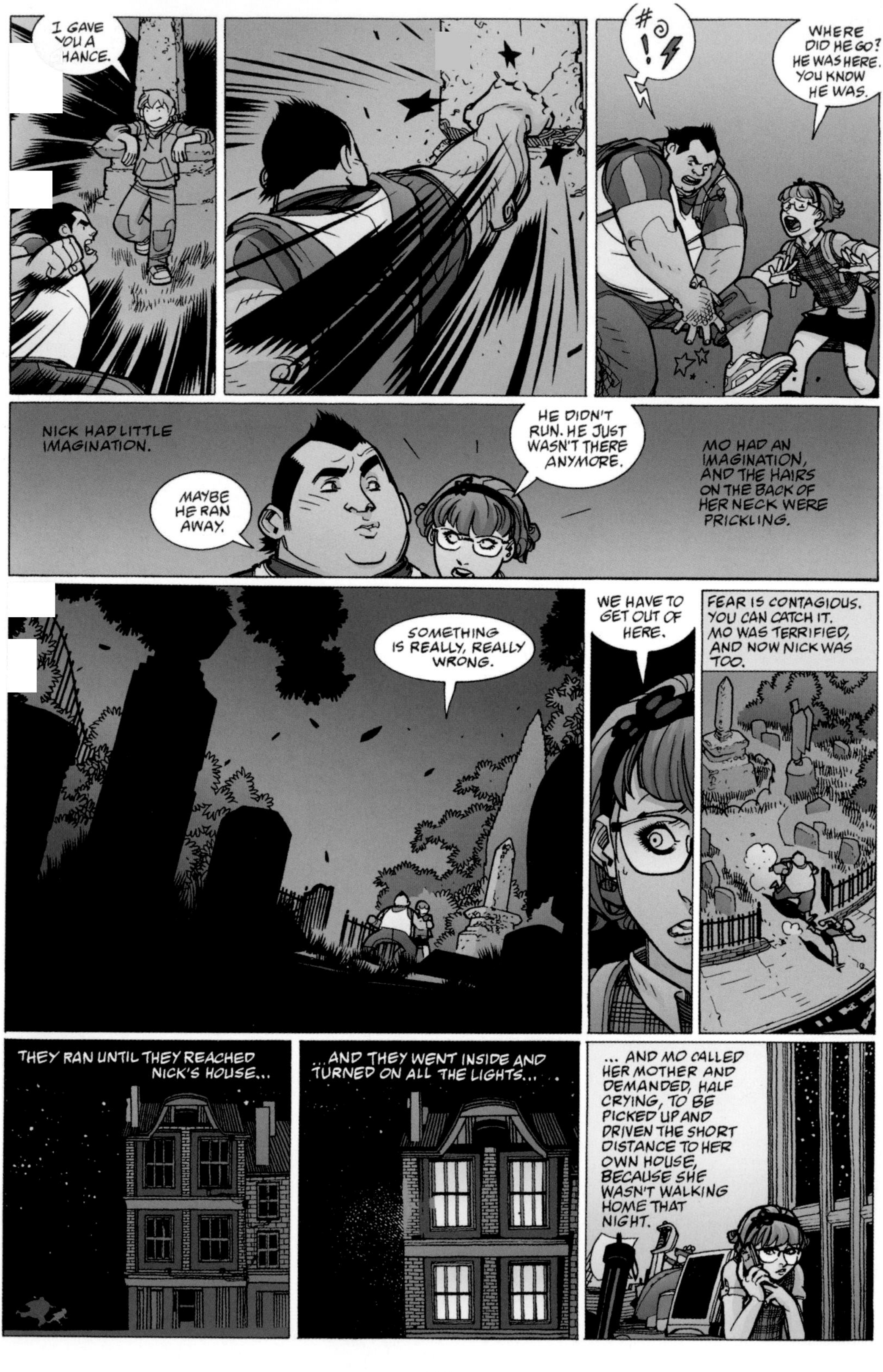

I GAVE YOU A CHANCE.
@ ! ⚡
WHERE DID HE GO? HE WAS HERE. YOU KNOW HE WAS.
NICK HAD LITTLE IMAGINATION.
MAYBE HE RAN AWAY.
HE DIDN'T RUN. HE JUST WASN'T THERE ANYMORE.
MO HAD AN IMAGINATION, AND THE HAIRS ON THE BACK OF HER NECK WERE PRICKLING.
SOMETHING IS REALLY, REALLY WRONG.
WE HAVE TO GET OUT OF HERE.
FEAR IS CONTAGIOUS. YOU CAN CATCH IT. MO WAS TERRIFIED, AND NOW NICK WAS TOO.
THEY RAN UNTIL THEY REACHED NICK'S HOUSE...
...AND THEY WENT INSIDE AND TURNED ON ALL THE LIGHTS...
... AND MO CALLED HER MOTHER AND DEMANDED, HALF CRYING, TO BE PICKED UP AND DRIVEN THE SHORT DISTANCE TO HER OWN HOUSE, BECAUSE SHE WASN'T WALKING HOME THAT NIGHT.

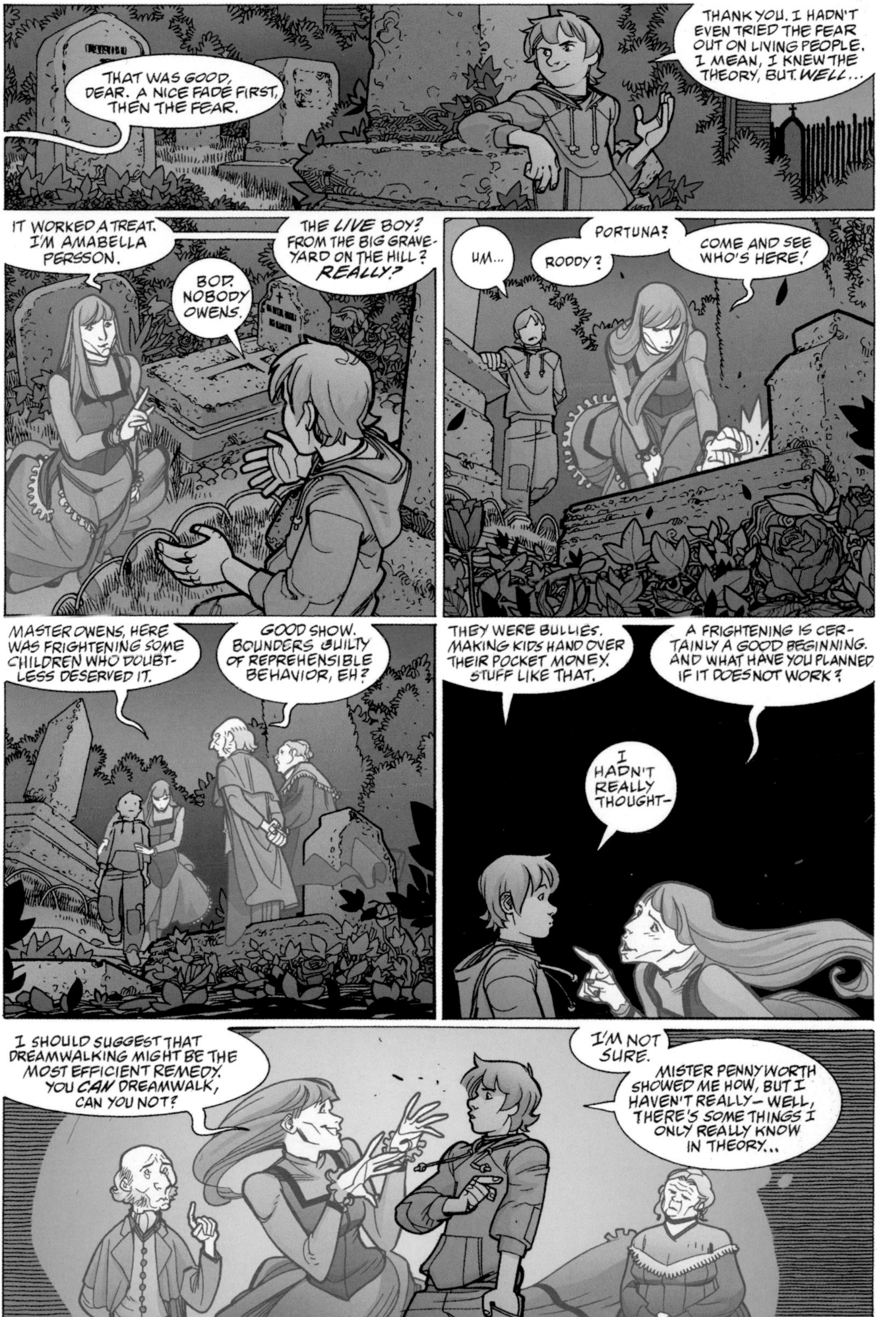

THAT WAS GOOD, DEAR. A NICE FADE FIRST, THEN THE FEAR.
THANK YOU. I HADN'T EVEN TRIED THE FEAR OUT ON LIVING PEOPLE. I MEAN, I KNEW THE THEORY, BUT. WELL...
IT WORKED A TREAT. I'M AMABELLA PERSSON.
BOD. NOBODY OWENS.
THE LIVE BOY? FROM THE BIG GRAVEYARD ON THE HILL? REALLY?
UM...
PORTUNA?
RODDY?
COME AND SEE WHO'S HERE!
MASTER OWENS, HERE WAS FRIGHTENING SOME CHILDREN WHO DOUBTLESS DESERVED IT.
GOOD SHOW. BOUNDERS GUILTY OF REPREHENSIBLE BEHAVIOR, EH?
THEY WERE BULLIES. MAKING KIDS HAND OVER THEIR POCKET MONEY. STUFF LIKE THAT.
A FRIGHTENING IS CERTAINLY A GOOD BEGINNING. AND WHAT HAVE YOU PLANNED IF IT DOES NOT WORK?
I HADN'T REALLY THOUGHT-
I SHOULD SUGGEST THAT DREAMWALKING MIGHT BE THE MOST EFFICIENT REMEDY. YOU CAN DREAMWALK, CAN YOU NOT?
I'M NOT SURE.
MISTER PENNYWORTH SHOWED ME HOW, BUT I HAVEN'T REALLY- WELL, THERE'S SOME THINGS I ONLY REALLY KNOW IN THEORY...

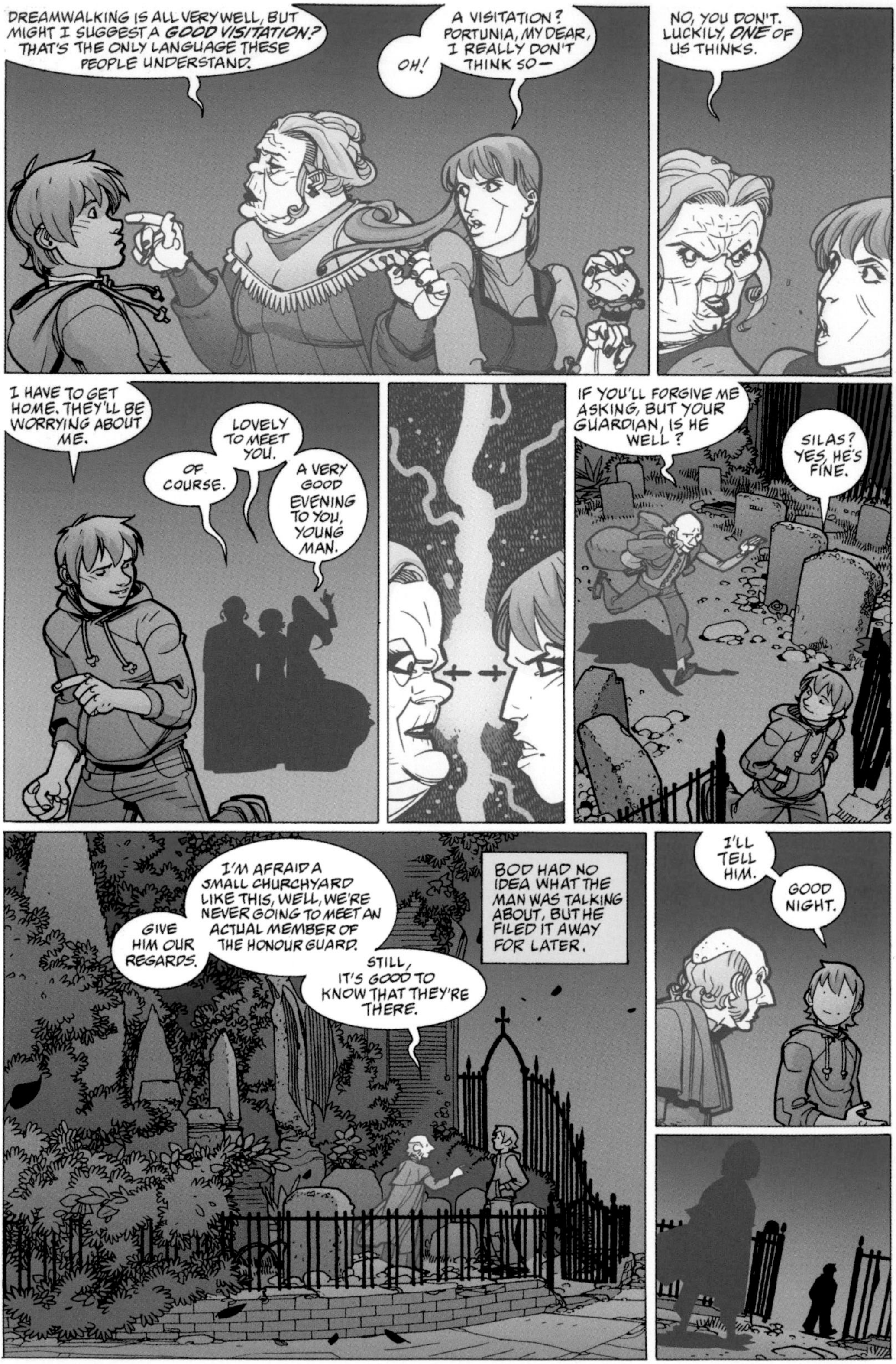
DREAMWALKING IS ALL VERY WELL, BUT MIGHT I SUGGEST A GOOD VISITATION? THAT'S THE ONLY LANGUAGE THESE PEOPLE UNDERSTAND.
OH!
A VISITATION? PORTUNIA, MY DEAR, I REALLY DON'T THINK SO—
NO, YOU DON'T. LUCKILY, ONE OF US THINKS.
I HAVE TO GET HOME. THEY'LL BE WORRYING ABOUT ME.
OF COURSE.
LOVELY TO MEET YOU.
A VERY GOOD EVENING TO YOU, YOUNG MAN.
IF YOU'LL FORGIVE ME ASKING, BUT YOUR GUARDIAN, IS HE WELL?
SILAS? YES, HE'S FINE.
GIVE HIM OUR REGARDS.
I'M AFRAID A SMALL CHURCHYARD LIKE THIS, WELL, WE'RE NEVER GOING TO MEET AN ACTUAL MEMBER OF THE HONOUR GUARD.
STILL, IT'S GOOD TO KNOW THAT THEY'RE THERE.
BOD HAD NO IDEA WHAT THE MAN WAS TALKING ABOUT, BUT HE FILED IT AWAY FOR LATER.
I'LL TELL HIM.
GOOD NIGHT.

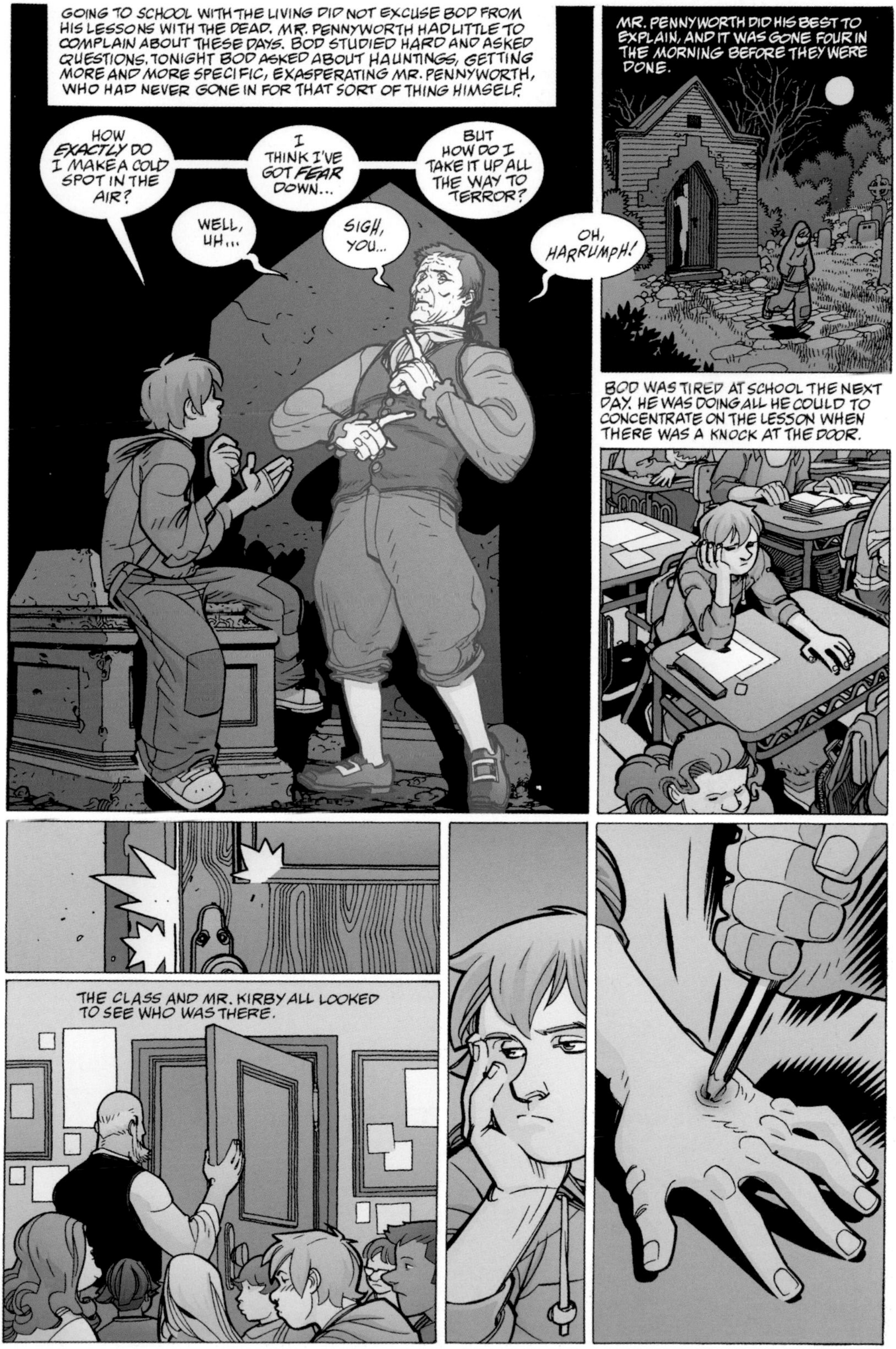
GOING TO SCHOOL WITH THE LIVING DID NOT EXCUSE BOD FROM HIS LESSONS WITH THE DEAD. MR. PENNYWORTH HAD LITTLE TO COMPLAIN ABOUT THESE DAYS. BOD STUDIED HARD AND ASKED QUESTIONS. TONIGHT BOD ASKED ABOUT HAUNTINGS, GETTING MORE AND MORE SPECIFIC, EXASPERATING MR. PENNYWORTH, WHO HAD NEVER GONE IN FOR THAT SORT OF THING HIMSELF.
HOW EXACTLY DO I MAKE A COLD SPOT IN THE AIR?
WELL, UH...
I THINK I'VE GOT FEAR DOWN...
SIGH, YOU...
BUT HOW DO I TAKE IT UP ALL THE WAY TO TERROR?
OH, HARRUMPH!
MR. PENNYWORTH DID HIS BEST TO EXPLAIN, AND IT WAS GONE FOUR IN THE MORNING BEFORE THEY WERE DONE.
BOD WAS TIRED AT SCHOOL THE NEXT DAY. HE WAS DOING ALL HE COULD TO CONCENTRATE ON THE LESSON WHEN THERE WAS A KNOCK AT THE DOOR.
THE CLASS AND MR. KIRBY ALL LOOKED TO SEE WHO WAS THERE.

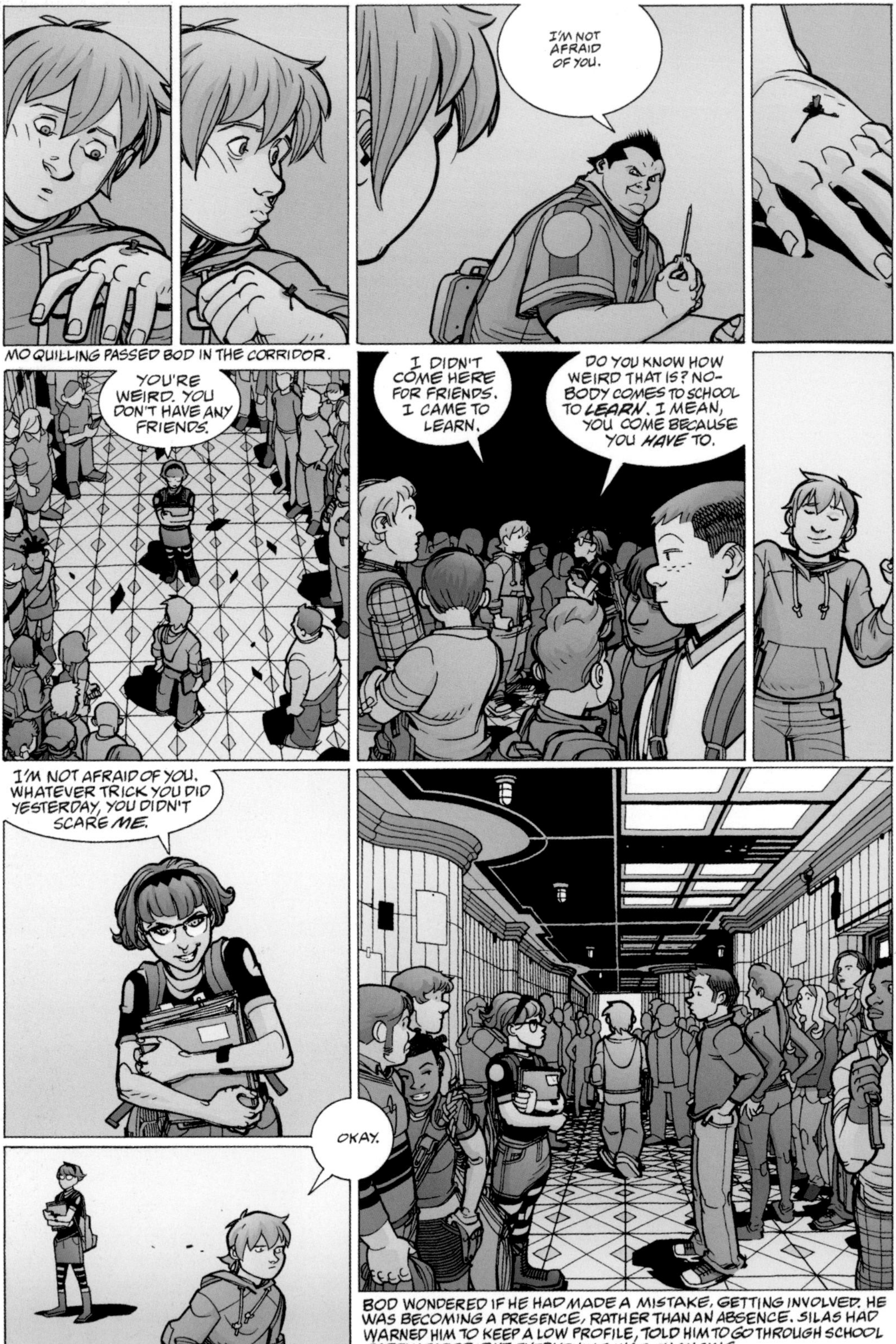
I'M NOT AFRAID OF YOU.
MO QUILLING PASSED BOD IN THE CORRIDOR.
YOU'RE WEIRD. YOU DON'T HAVE ANY FRIENDS.
I DIDN'T COME HERE FOR FRIENDS. I CAME TO LEARN.
DO YOU KNOW HOW WEIRD THAT IS? NO-BODY COMES TO SCHOOL TO LEARN. I MEAN, YOU COME BECAUSE YOU HAVE TO.
I'M NOT AFRAID OF YOU. WHATEVER TRICK YOU DID YESTERDAY, YOU DIDN'T SCARE ME.
OKAY.
BOD WONDERED IF HE HAD MADE A MISTAKE, GETTING INVOLVED. HE WAS BECOMING A PRESENCE, RATHER THAN AN ABSENCE. SILAS HAD WARNED HIM TO KEEP A LOW PROFILE, TOLD HIM TO GO THROUGH SCHOOL PARTLY FADED, BUT EVERYTHING WAS CHANGING.

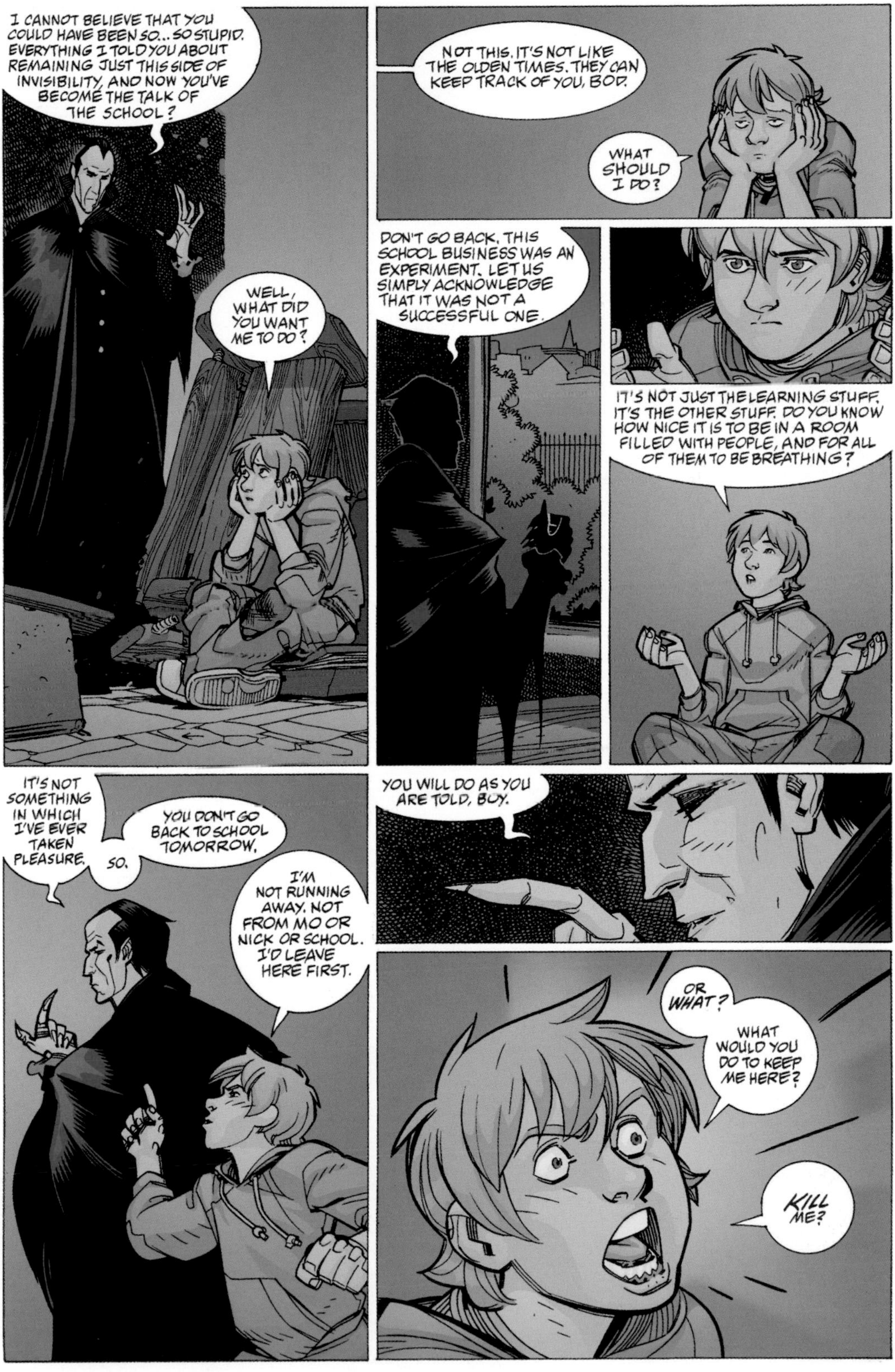

I CANNOT BELIEVE THAT YOU COULD HAVE BEEN SO... SO STUPID. EVERYTHING I TOLD YOU ABOUT REMAINING JUST THIS SIDE OF INVISIBILITY, AND NOW YOU'VE BECOME THE TALK OF THE SCHOOL?
WELL, WHAT DID YOU WANT ME TO DO?
NOT THIS. IT'S NOT LIKE THE OLDEN TIMES. THEY CAN KEEP TRACK OF YOU, BOD.
WHAT SHOULD I DO?
DON'T GO BACK. THIS SCHOOL BUSINESS WAS AN EXPERIMENT. LET US SIMPLY ACKNOWLEDGE THAT IT WAS NOT A SUCCESSFUL ONE.
IT'S NOT JUST THE LEARNING STUFF. IT'S THE OTHER STUFF. DO YOU KNOW HOW NICE IT IS TO BE IN A ROOM FILLED WITH PEOPLE, AND FOR ALL OF THEM TO BE BREATHING?
IT'S NOT SOMETHING IN WHICH I'VE EVER TAKEN PLEASURE.
SO.
YOU DON'T GO BACK TO SCHOOL TOMORROW.
I'M NOT RUNNING AWAY. NOT FROM MO OR NICK OR SCHOOL. I'D LEAVE HERE FIRST.
YOU WILL DO AS YOU ARE TOLD, BOY.
OR WHAT?
WHAT WOULD YOU DO TO KEEP ME HERE?
KILL ME?

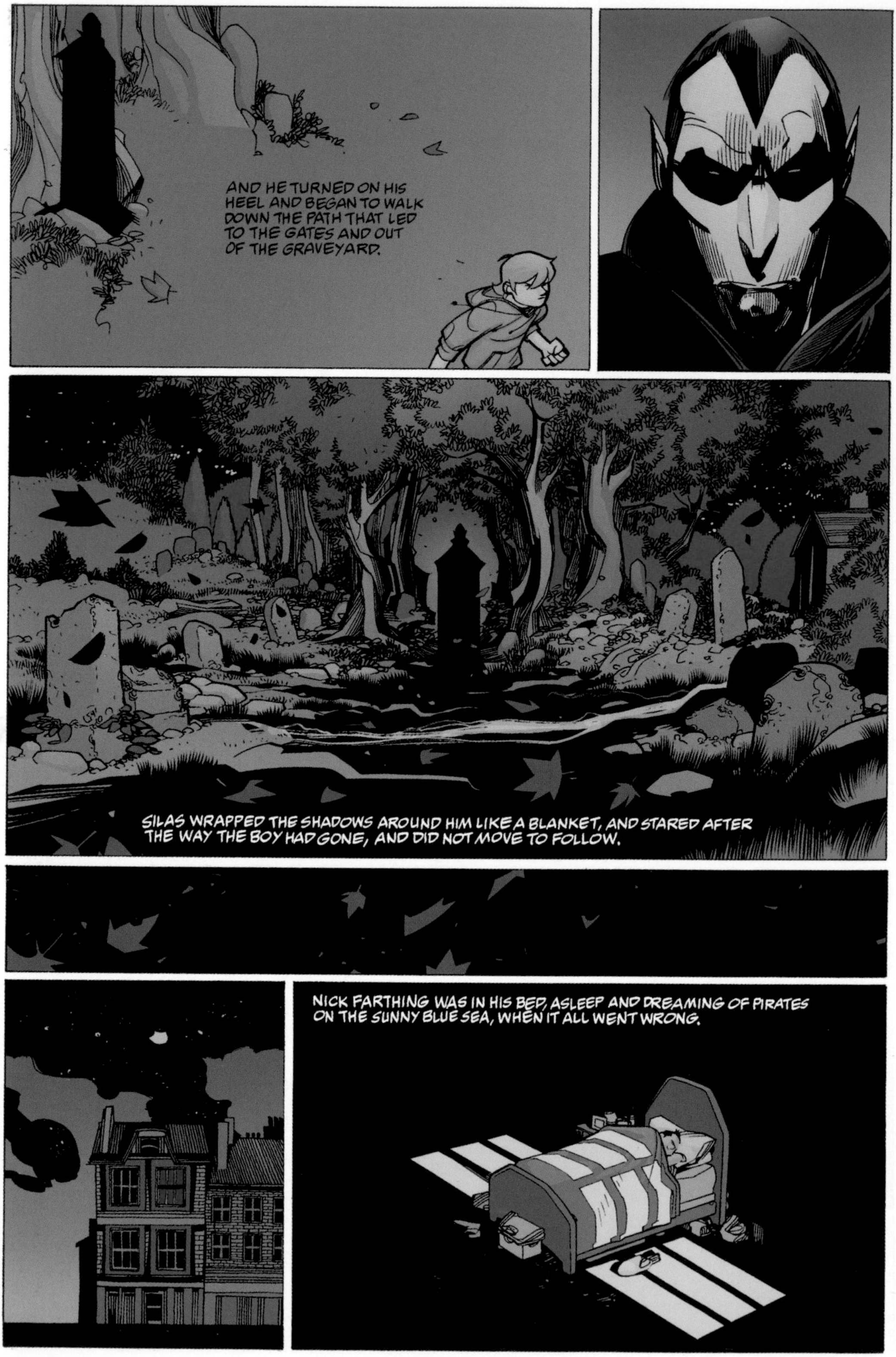
AND HE TURNED ON HIS HEEL AND BEGAN TO WALK DOWN THE PATH THAT LED TO THE GATES AND OUT OF THE GRAVEYARD.
SILAS WRAPPED THE SHADOWS AROUND HIM LIKE A BLANKET, AND STARED AFTER THE WAY THE BOY HAD GONE, AND DID NOT MOVE TO FOLLOW.
NICK FARTHING WAS IN HIS BED, ASLEEP AND DREAMING OF PIRATES ON THE SUNNY BLUE SEA, WHEN IT ALL WENT WRONG.

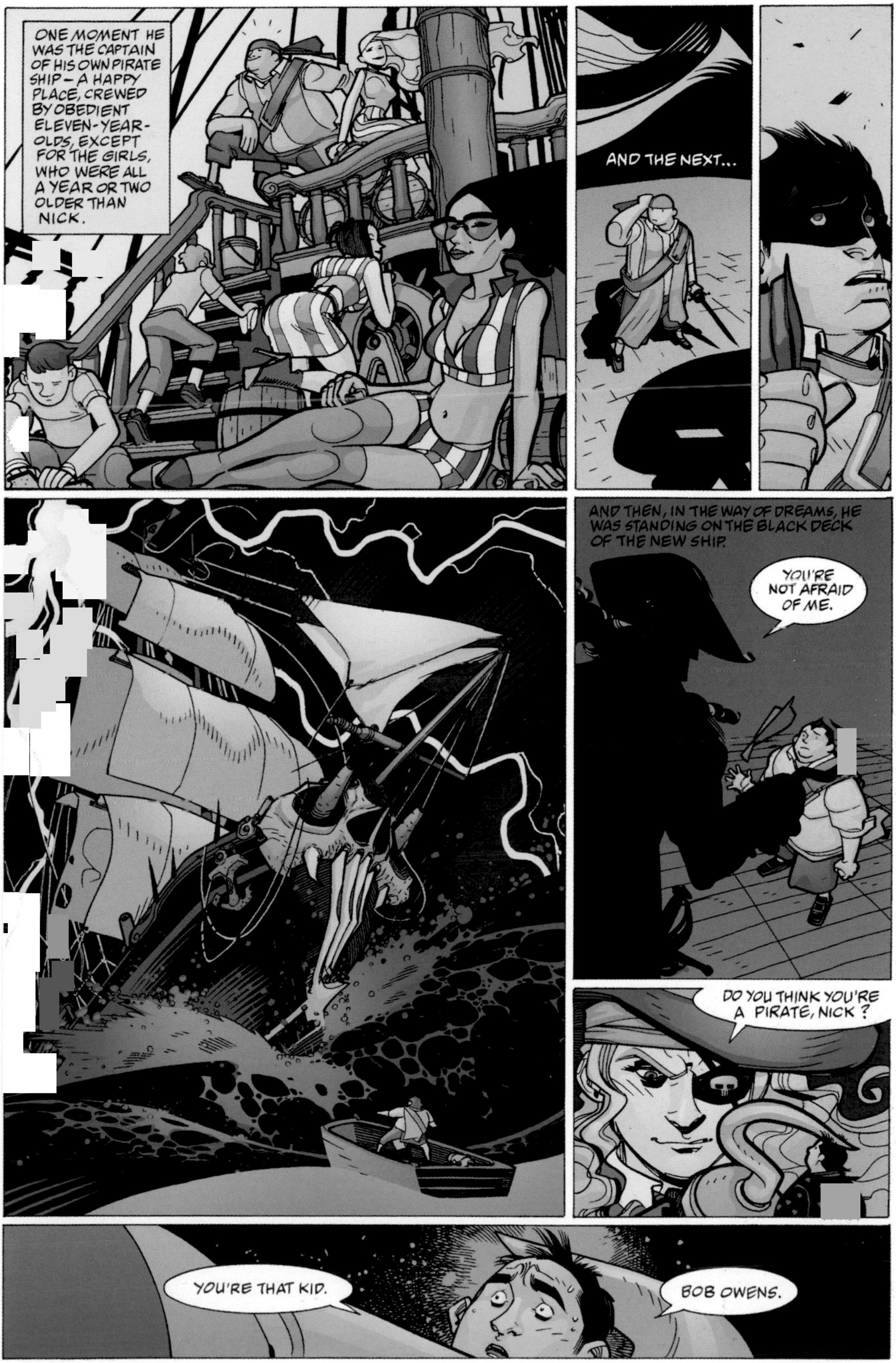
ONE MOMENT HE WAS THE CAPTAIN OF HIS OWN PIRATE SHIP – A HAPPY PLACE, CREWED BY OBEDIENT ELEVEN-YEAR-OLDS, EXCEPT FOR THE GIRLS, WHO WERE ALL A YEAR OR TWO OLDER THAN NICK.
AND THE NEXT...
AND THEN, IN THE WAY OF DREAMS, HE WAS STANDING ON THE BLACK DECK OF THE NEW SHIP.
YOU'RE NOT AFRAID OF ME.
DO YOU THINK YOU'RE A PIRATE, NICK?
YOU'RE THAT KID.
BOB OWENS.

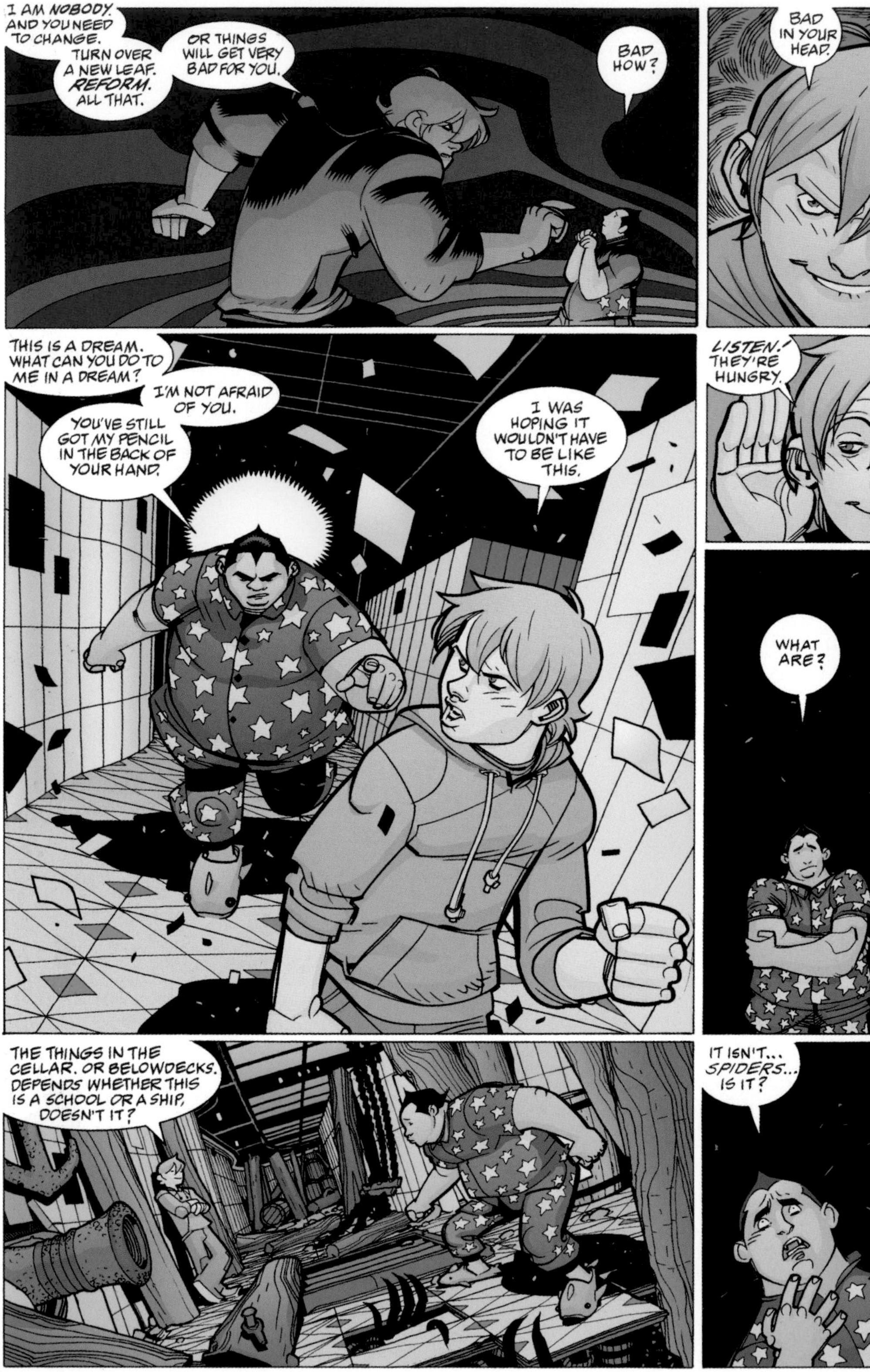
I AM NOBODY. AND YOU NEED TO CHANGE. TURN OVER A NEW LEAF. REFORM. ALL THAT.
OR THINGS WILL GET VERY BAD FOR YOU.
BAD HOW?
BAD IN YOUR HEAD.
THIS IS A DREAM. WHAT CAN YOU DO TO ME IN A DREAM?
I'M NOT AFRAID OF YOU.
YOU'VE STILL GOT MY PENCIL IN THE BACK OF YOUR HAND.
I WAS HOPING IT WOULDN'T HAVE TO BE LIKE THIS.
LISTEN! THEY'RE HUNGRY.
WHAT ARE?
THE THINGS IN THE CELLAR. OR BELOWDECKS. DEPENDS WHETHER THIS IS A SCHOOL OR A SHIP, DOESN'T IT?
IT ISN'T... SPIDERS... IS IT?

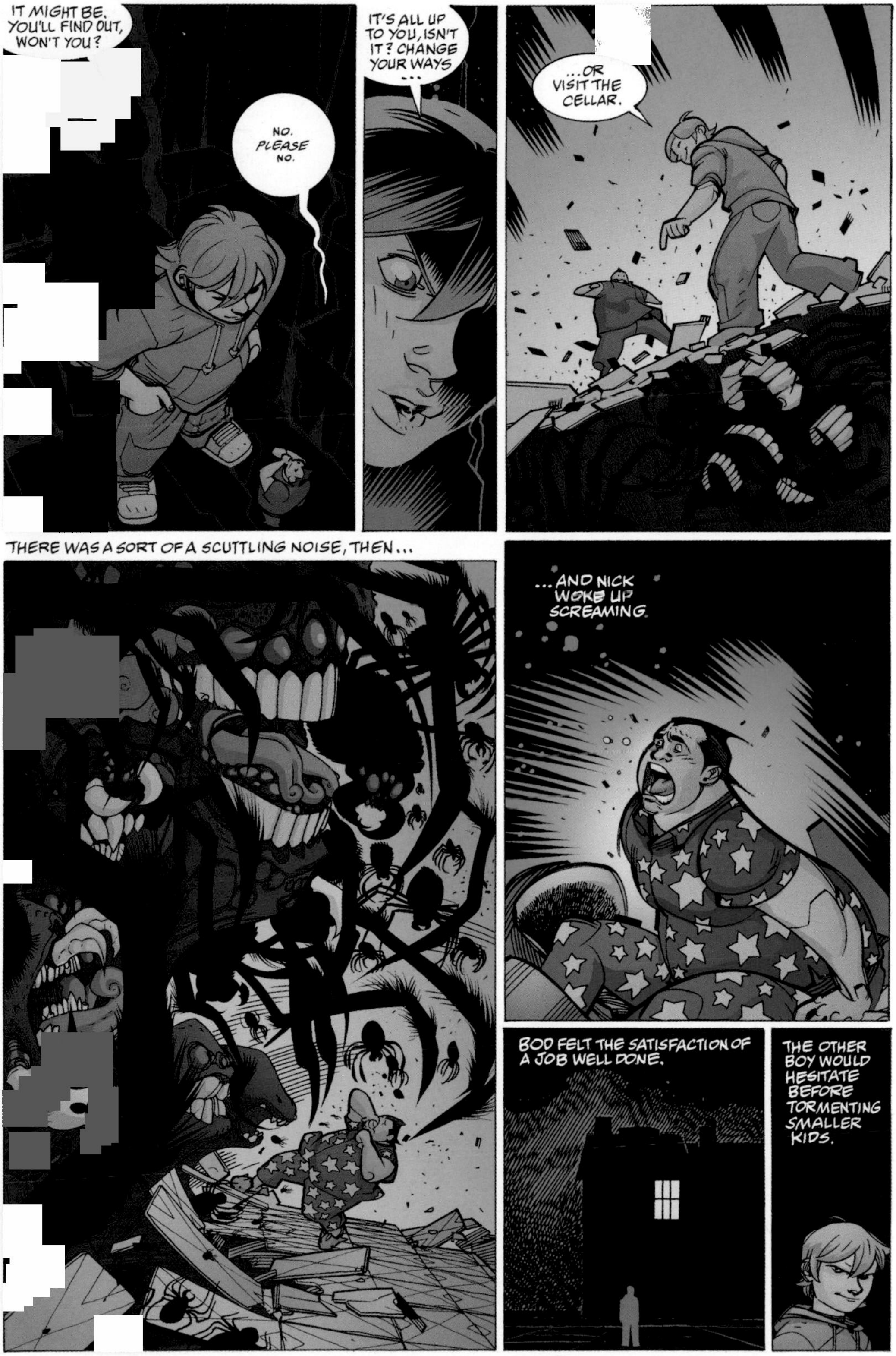
IT MIGHT BE. YOU'LL FIND OUT, WON'T YOU?
NO. PLEASE NO.
IT'S ALL UP TO YOU, ISN'T IT? CHANGE YOUR WAYS ...
...OR VISIT THE CELLAR.
THERE WAS A SORT OF A SCUTTLING NOISE, THEN...
...AND NICK WOKE UP SCREAMING.
BOD FELT THE SATISFACTION OF A JOB WELL DONE.
THE OTHER BOY WOULD HESITATE BEFORE TORMENTING SMALLER KIDS.

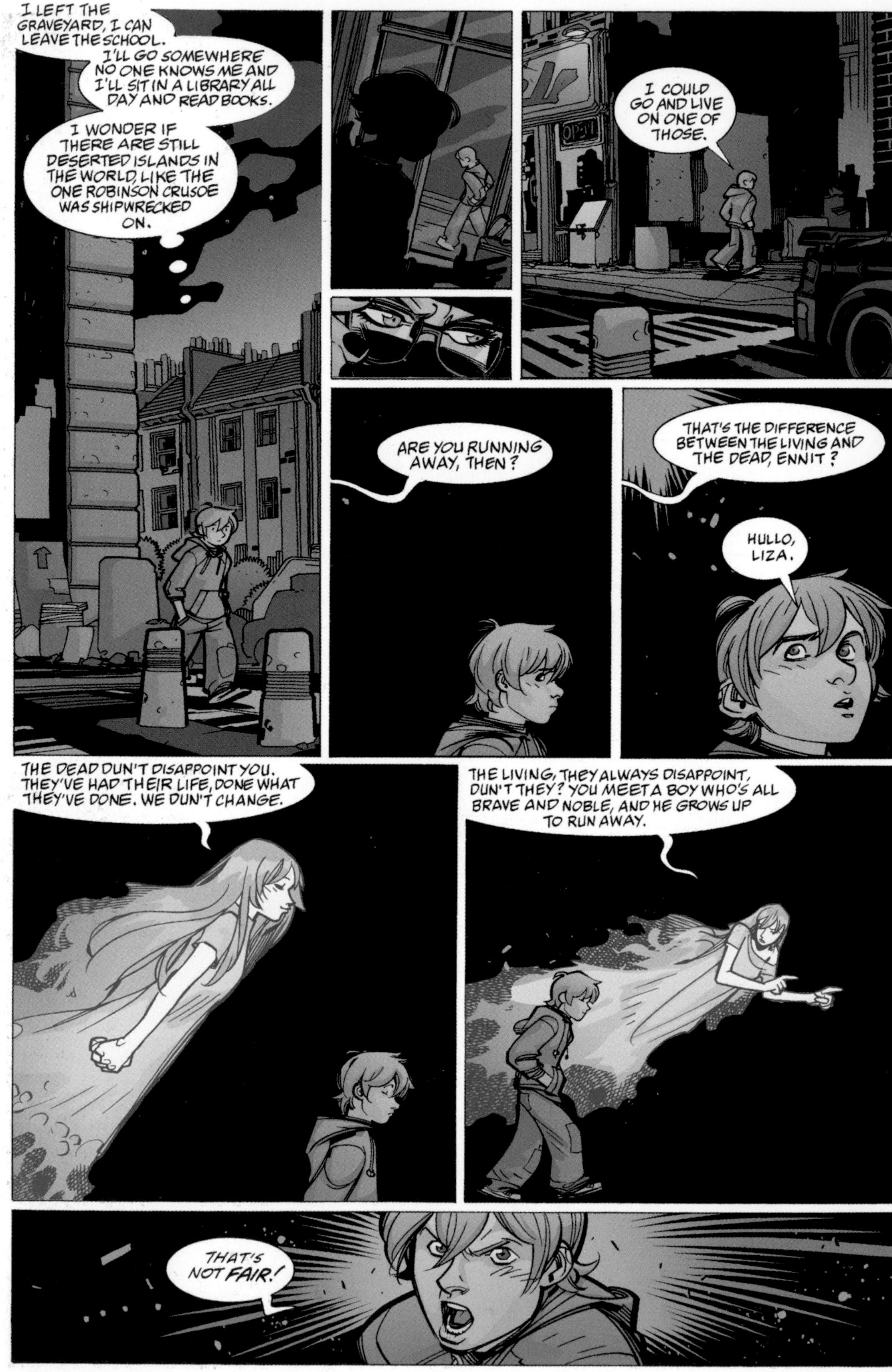
I LEFT THE GRAVEYARD, I CAN LEAVE THE SCHOOL.
I'LL GO SOMEWHERE NO ONE KNOWS ME AND I'LL SIT IN A LIBRARY ALL DAY AND READ BOOKS.
I WONDER IF THERE ARE STILL DESERTED ISLANDS IN THE WORLD, LIKE THE ONE ROBINSON CRUSOE WAS SHIPWRECKED ON.
I COULD GO AND LIVE ON ONE OF THOSE.
OPEN
ARE YOU RUNNING AWAY, THEN?
THAT'S THE DIFFERENCE BETWEEN THE LIVING AND THE DEAD, ENNIT?
HULLO, LIZA.
THE DEAD DUN'T DISAPPOINT YOU. THEY'VE HAD THEIR LIFE, DONE WHAT THEY'VE DONE. WE DUN'T CHANGE.
THE LIVING, THEY ALWAYS DISAPPOINT, DUN'T THEY? YOU MEET A BOY WHO'S ALL BRAVE AND NOBLE, AND HE GROWS UP TO RUN AWAY.
THAT'S NOT FAIR!

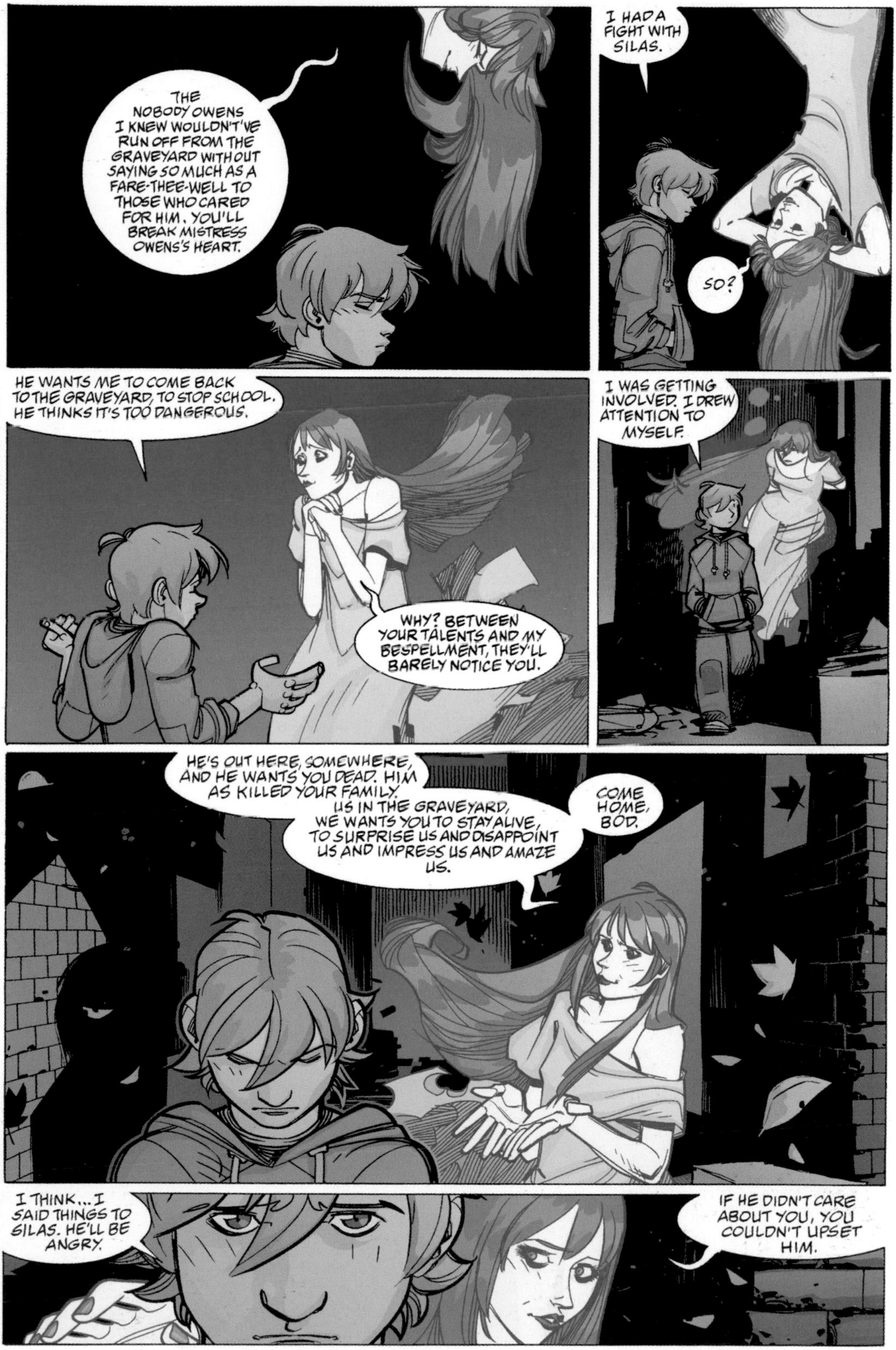
THE NOBODY OWENS I KNEW WOULDN'T'VE RUN OFF FROM THE GRAVEYARD WITHOUT SAYING SO MUCH AS A FARE-THEE-WELL TO THOSE WHO CARED FOR HIM. YOU'LL BREAK MISTRESS OWENS'S HEART.
I HAD A FIGHT WITH SILAS.
SO?
HE WANTS ME TO COME BACK TO THE GRAVEYARD, TO STOP SCHOOL. HE THINKS IT'S TOO DANGEROUS.
WHY? BETWEEN YOUR TALENTS AND MY BESPELLMENT, THEY'LL BARELY NOTICE YOU.
I WAS GETTING INVOLVED. I DREW ATTENTION TO MYSELF.
HE'S OUT HERE, SOMEWHERE, AND HE WANTS YOU DEAD. HIM AS KILLED YOUR FAMILY.
US IN THE GRAVEYARD, WE WANTS YOU TO STAY ALIVE, TO SURPRISE US AND DISAPPOINT US AND IMPRESS US AND AMAZE US.
COME HOME, BOD.
I THINK... I SAID THINGS TO SILAS. HE'LL BE ANGRY.
IF HE DIDN'T CARE ABOUT YOU, YOU COULDN'T UPSET HIM.

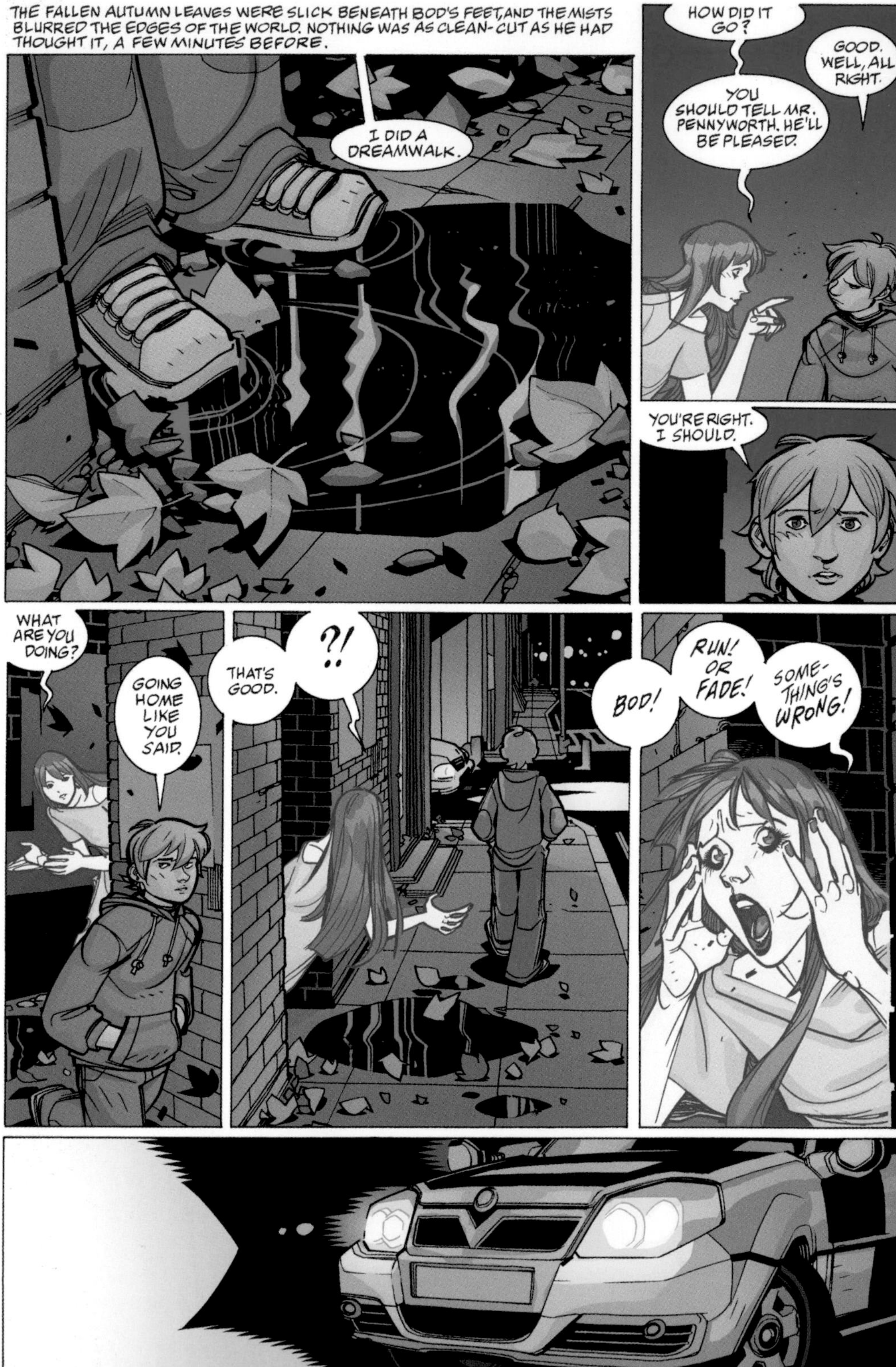
THE FALLEN AUTUMN LEAVES WERE SLICK BENEATH BOD'S FEET, AND THE MISTS BLURRED THE EDGES OF THE WORLD. NOTHING WAS AS CLEAN-CUT AS HE HAD THOUGHT IT, A FEW MINUTES BEFORE.
I DID A DREAMWALK.
HOW DID IT GO?
GOOD. WELL, ALL RIGHT.
YOU SHOULD TELL MR. PENNYWORTH. HE'LL BE PLEASED.
YOU'RE RIGHT. I SHOULD.
WHAT ARE YOU DOING?
GOING HOME LIKE YOU SAID.
THAT'S GOOD.
?!
BOD!
RUN! OR FADE!
SOME-THING'S WRONG!

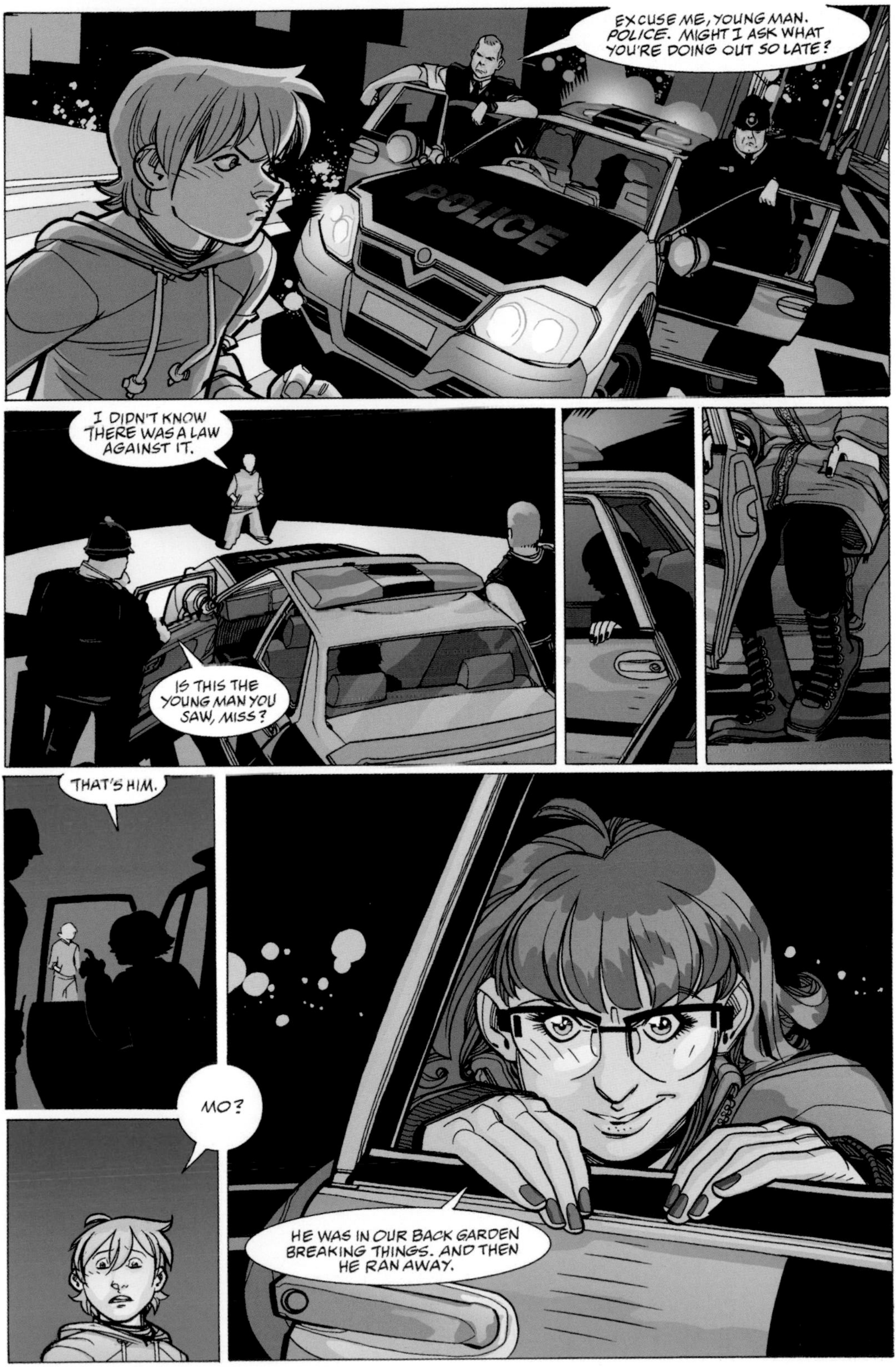
EXCUSE ME, YOUNG MAN. POLICE. MIGHT I ASK WHAT YOU'RE DOING OUT SO LATE?
POLICE
I DIDN'T KNOW THERE WAS A LAW AGAINST IT.
IS THIS THE YOUNG MAN YOU SAW, MISS?
THAT'S HIM.
MO?
HE WAS IN OUR BACK GARDEN BREAKING THINGS. AND THEN HE RAN AWAY.

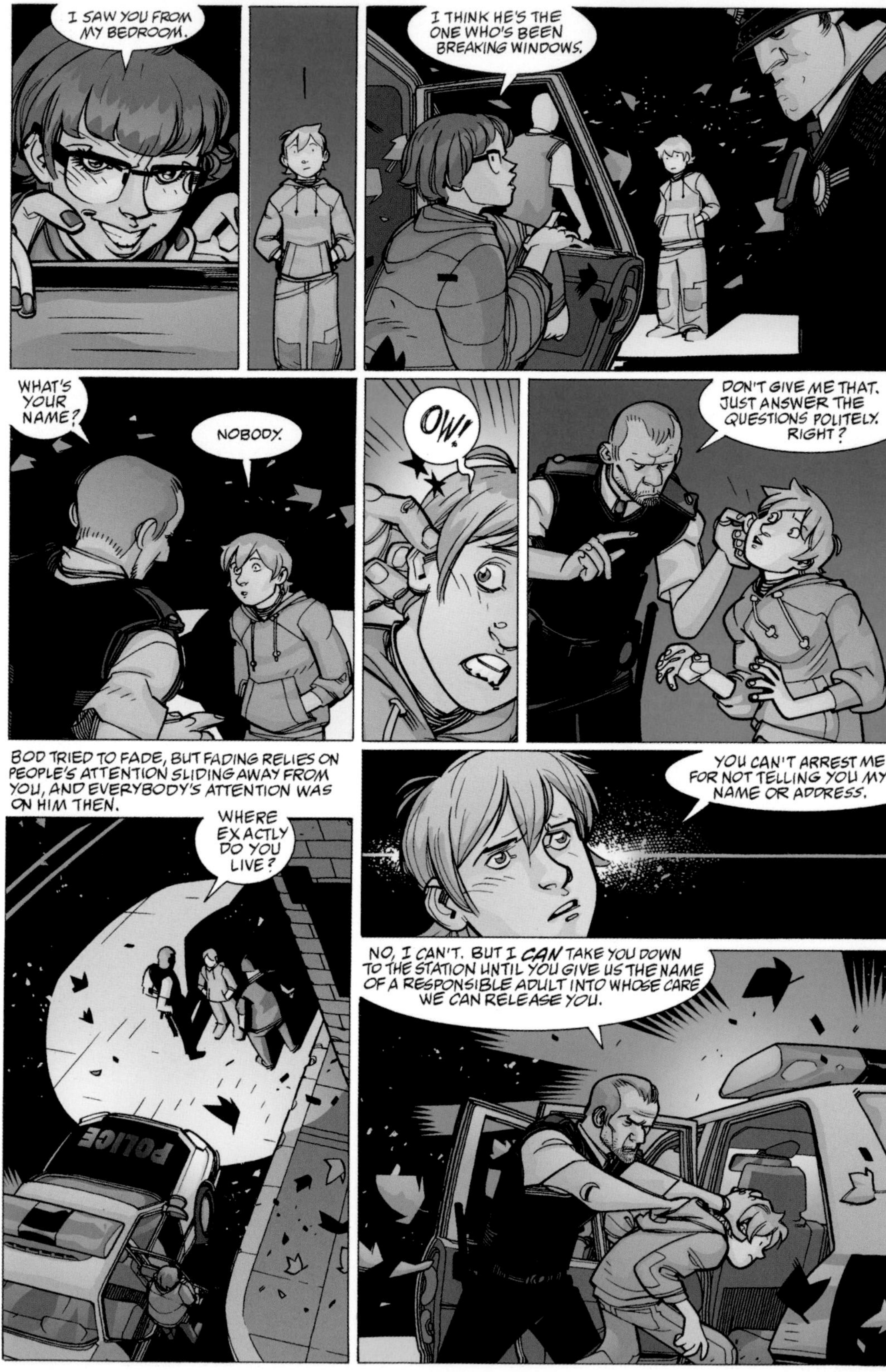
I SAW YOU FROM MY BEDROOM.
I THINK HE'S THE ONE WHO'S BEEN BREAKING WINDOWS.
WHAT'S YOUR NAME?
NOBODY.
OW!
DON'T GIVE ME THAT. JUST ANSWER THE QUESTIONS POLITELY. RIGHT?
BOD TRIED TO FADE, BUT FADING RELIES ON PEOPLE'S ATTENTION SLIDING AWAY FROM YOU, AND EVERYBODY'S ATTENTION WAS ON HIM THEN.
WHERE EXACTLY DO YOU LIVE?
POLICE
YOU CAN'T ARREST ME FOR NOT TELLING YOU MY NAME OR ADDRESS.
NO, I CAN'T. BUT I CAN TAKE YOU DOWN TO THE STATION UNTIL YOU GIVE US THE NAME OF A RESPONSIBLE ADULT INTO WHOSE CARE WE CAN RELEASE YOU.

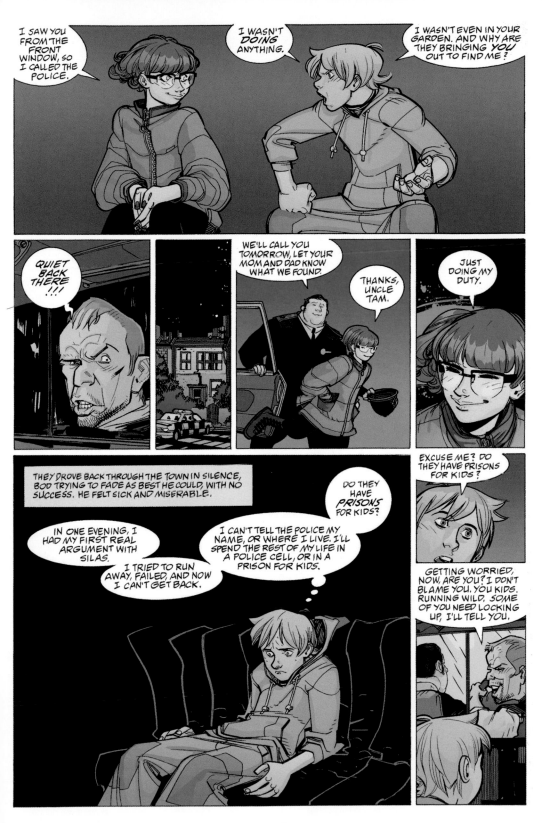

I SAW YOU FROM THE FRONT WINDOW, SO I CALLED THE POLICE.

I WASN'T *DOING* ANYTHING.

I WASN'T EVEN IN YOUR GARDEN. AND WHY ARE THEY BRINGING *YOU* OUT TO FIND ME?

QUIET BACK THERE !!!

WE'LL CALL YOU TOMORROW, LET YOUR MOM AND DAD KNOW WHAT WE FOUND.

THANKS, UNCLE TAM.

JUST DOING MY DUTY.

THEY DROVE BACK THROUGH THE TOWN IN SILENCE, BOD TRYING TO FADE AS BEST HE COULD, WITH NO SUCCESS. HE FELT SICK AND MISERABLE.

EXCUSE ME? DO THEY HAVE PRISONS FOR KIDS?

DO THEY HAVE *PRISONS* FOR KIDS?

IN ONE EVENING, I HAD MY FIRST REAL ARGUMENT WITH SILAS.

I CAN'T TELL THE POLICE MY NAME, OR WHERE I LIVE. I'LL SPEND THE REST OF MY LIFE IN A POLICE CELL, OR IN A PRISON FOR KIDS.

I TRIED TO RUN AWAY, FAILED, AND NOW I CAN'T GET BACK.

GETTING WORRIED, NOW, ARE YOU? I DON'T BLAME YOU. YOU KIDS. RUNNING WILD. SOME OF YOU NEED LOCKING UP, I'LL TELL YOU.

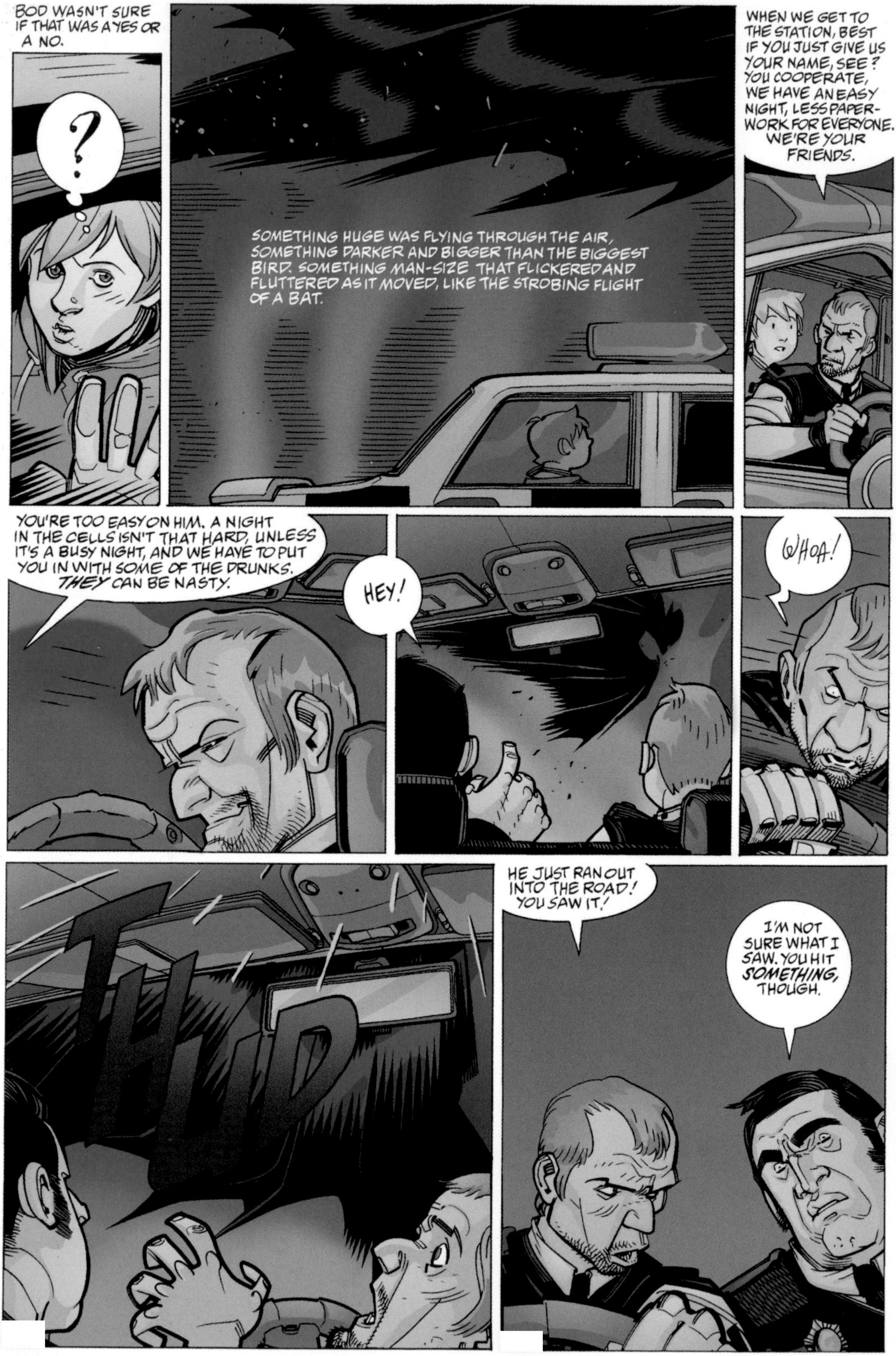
BOD WASN'T SURE IF THAT WAS A YES OR A NO.
?
SOMETHING HUGE WAS FLYING THROUGH THE AIR, SOMETHING DARKER AND BIGGER THAN THE BIGGEST BIRD. SOMETHING MAN-SIZE THAT FLICKERED AND FLUTTERED AS IT MOVED, LIKE THE STROBING FLIGHT OF A BAT.
WHEN WE GET TO THE STATION, BEST IF YOU JUST GIVE US YOUR NAME, SEE? YOU COOPERATE, WE HAVE AN EASY NIGHT, LESS PAPER-WORK FOR EVERYONE. WE'RE YOUR FRIENDS.
YOU'RE TOO EASY ON HIM. A NIGHT IN THE CELLS ISN'T THAT HARD, UNLESS IT'S A BUSY NIGHT, AND WE HAVE TO PUT YOU IN WITH SOME OF THE DRUNKS. THEY CAN BE NASTY.
HEY!
WHOA!
THUD
HE JUST RAN OUT INTO THE ROAD! YOU SAW IT!
I'M NOT SURE WHAT I SAW. YOU HIT SOMETHING, THOUGH.

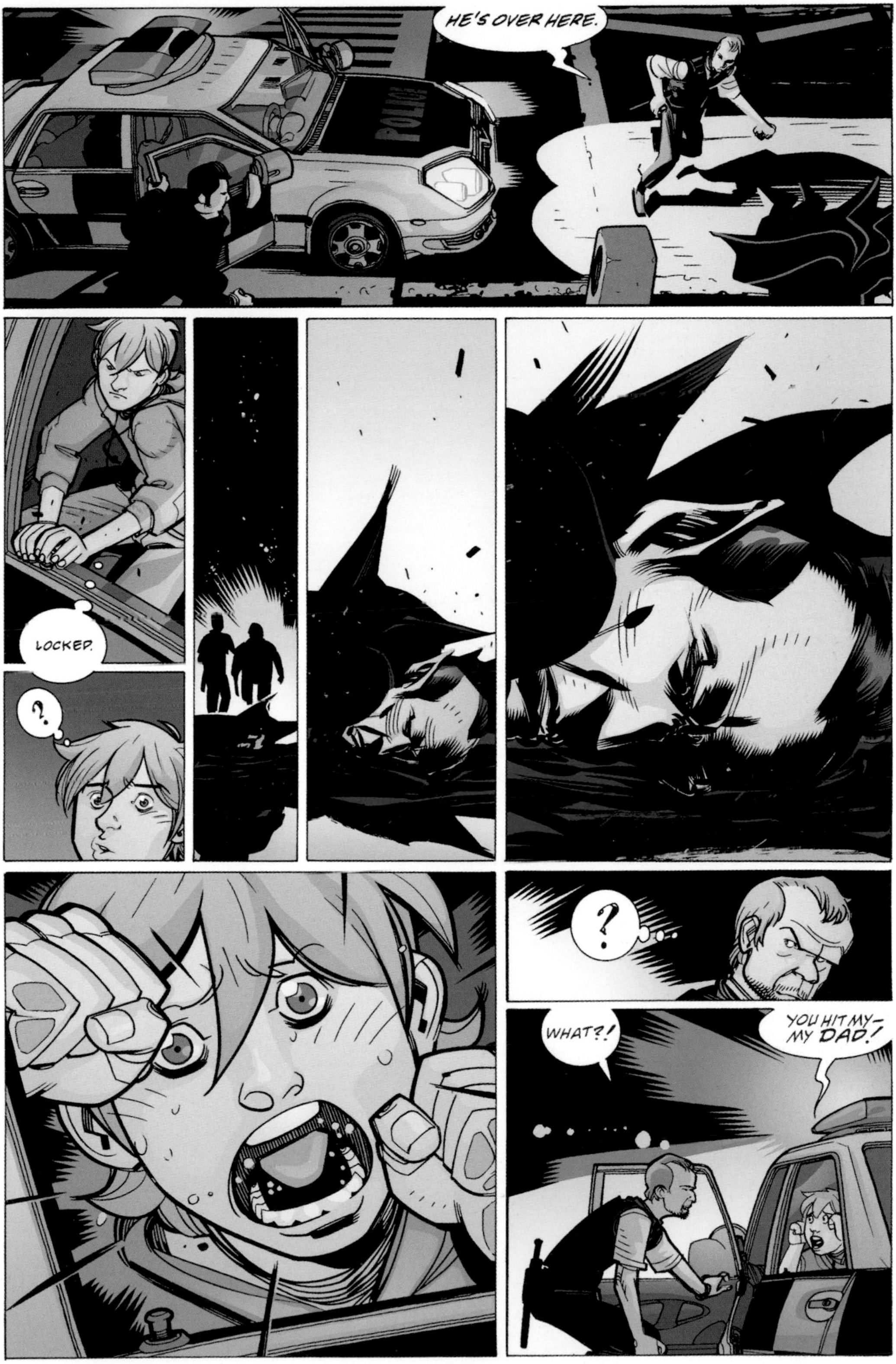
HE'S OVER HERE.
LOCKED.
?
?
WHAT?!
YOU HIT MY—
MY DAD!

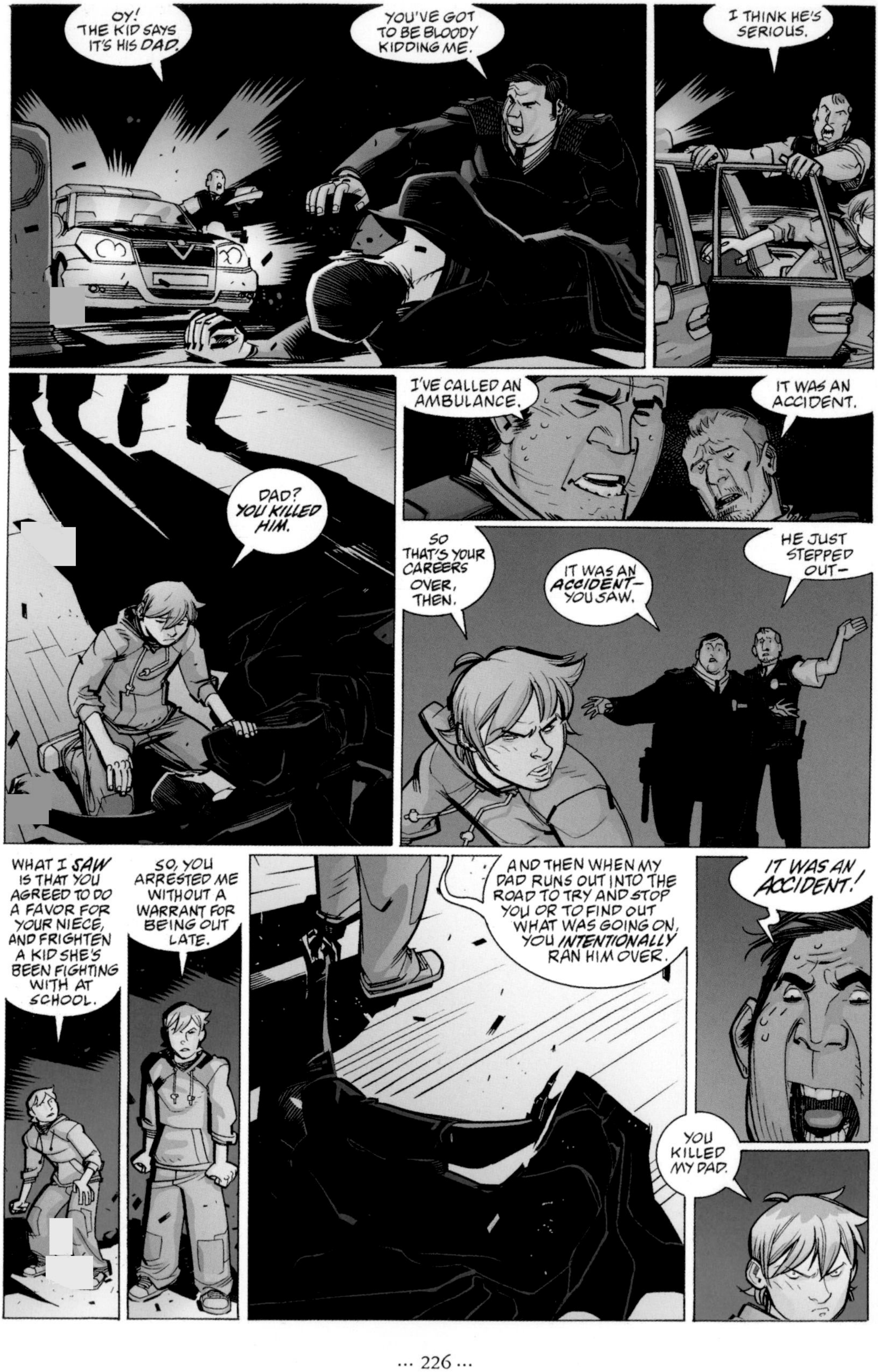
OY! THE KID SAYS IT'S HIS DAD.
YOU'VE GOT TO BE BLOODY KIDDING ME.
I THINK HE'S SERIOUS.
DAD? YOU KILLED HIM.
I'VE CALLED AN AMBULANCE.
IT WAS AN ACCIDENT.
SO THAT'S YOUR CAREERS OVER, THEN.
IT WAS AN ACCIDENT— YOU SAW.
HE JUST STEPPED OUT—
WHAT I SAW IS THAT YOU AGREED TO DO A FAVOR FOR YOUR NIECE, AND FRIGHTEN A KID SHE'S BEEN FIGHTING WITH AT SCHOOL.
SO, YOU ARRESTED ME WITHOUT A WARRANT FOR BEING OUT LATE.
AND THEN WHEN MY DAD RUNS OUT INTO THE ROAD TO TRY AND STOP YOU OR TO FIND OUT WHAT WAS GOING ON, YOU INTENTIONALLY RAN HIM OVER.
IT WAS AN ACCIDENT!
YOU KILLED MY DAD.

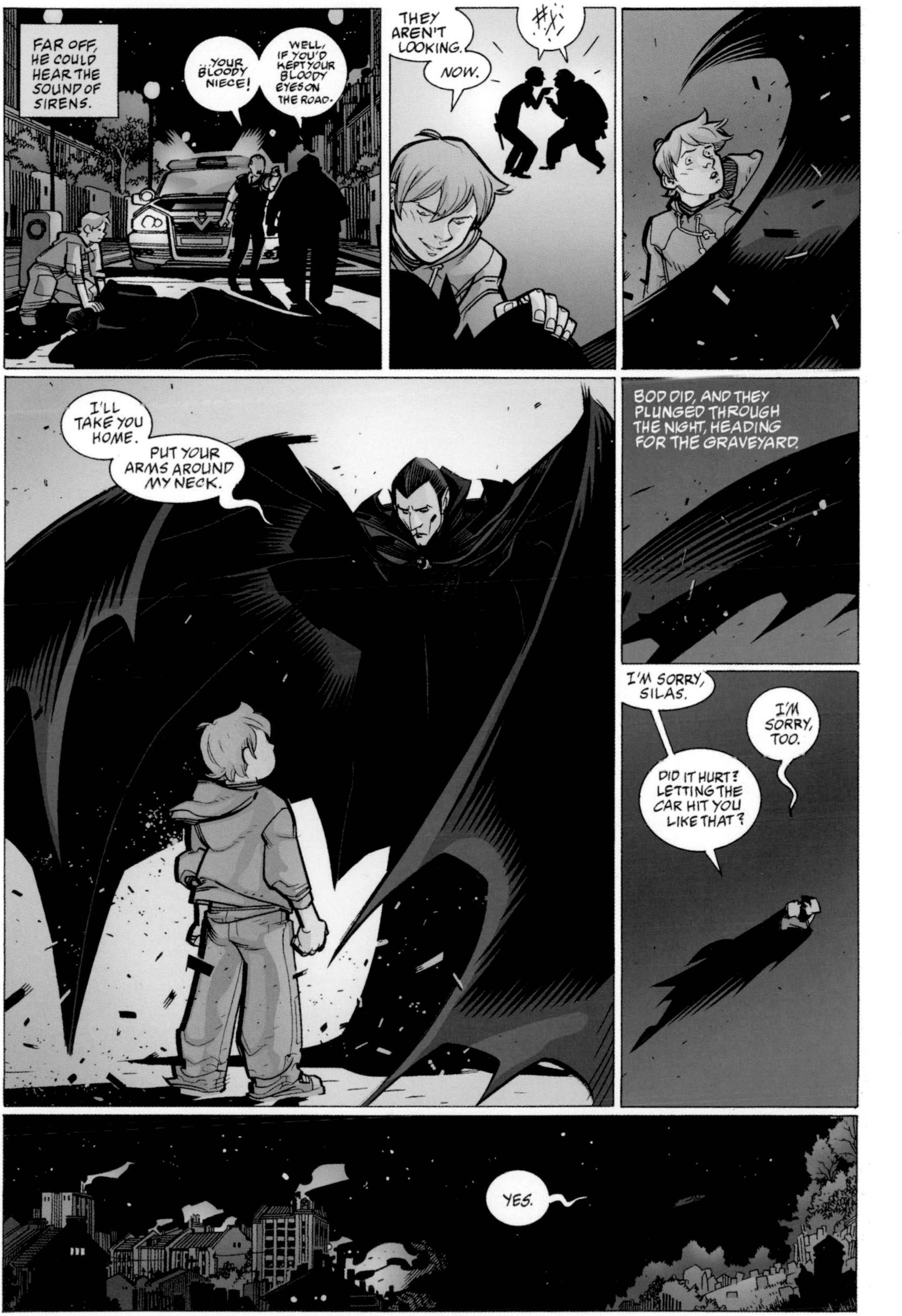
FAR OFF, HE COULD HEAR THE SOUND OF SIRENS.
...YOUR BLOODY NIECE!
WELL, IF YOU'D KEPT YOUR BLOODY EYES ON THE ROAD.
THEY AREN'T LOOKING.
NOW.
I'LL TAKE YOU HOME.
PUT YOUR ARMS AROUND MY NECK.
BOD DID, AND THEY PLUNGED THROUGH THE NIGHT, HEADING FOR THE GRAVEYARD.
I'M SORRY, SILAS.
I'M SORRY, TOO.
DID IT HURT? LETTING THE CAR HIT YOU LIKE THAT?
YES.

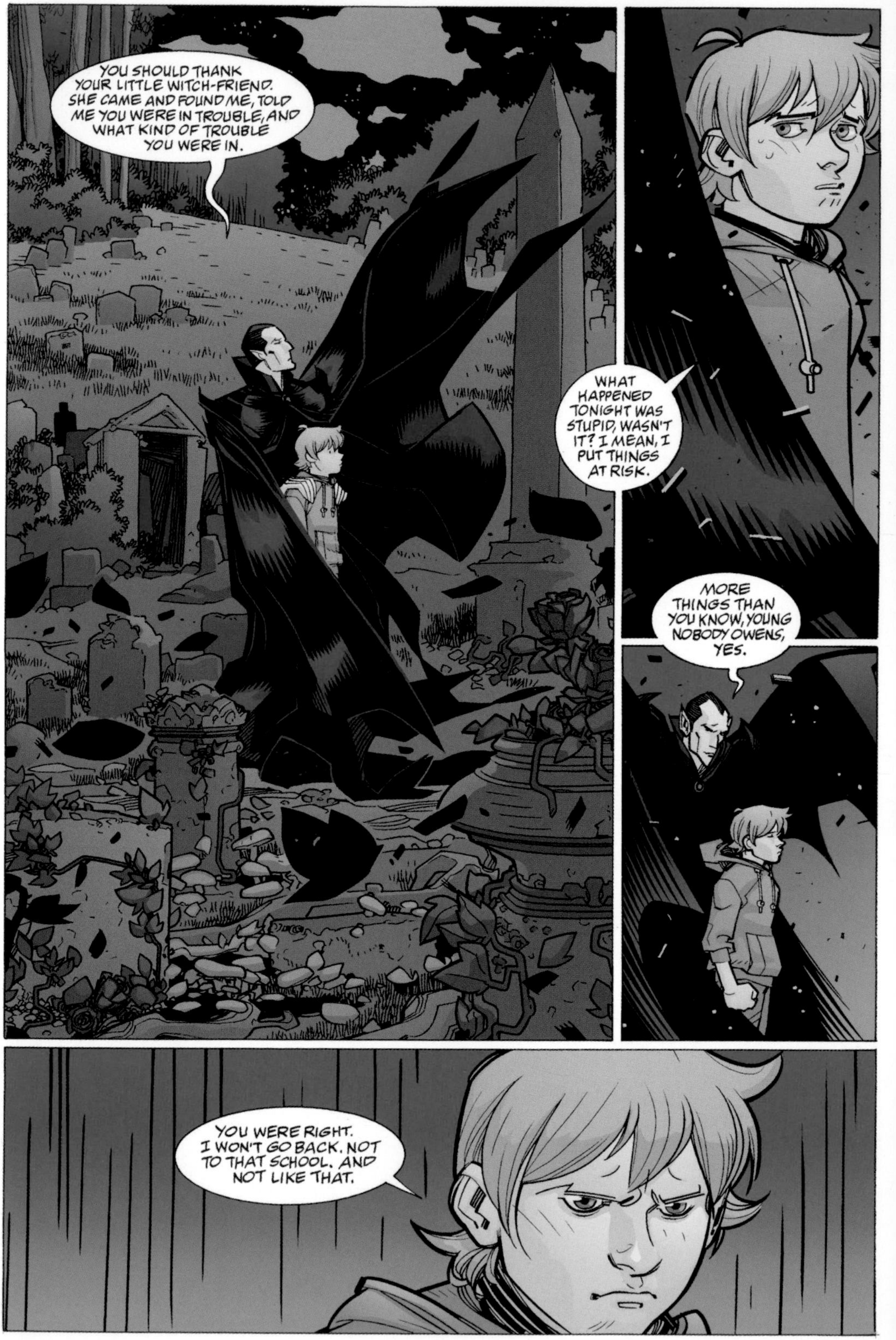
YOU SHOULD THANK YOUR LITTLE WITCH-FRIEND. SHE CAME AND FOUND ME, TOLD ME YOU WERE IN TROUBLE, AND WHAT KIND OF TROUBLE YOU WERE IN.
WHAT HAPPENED TONIGHT WAS STUPID, WASN'T IT? I MEAN, I PUT THINGS AT RISK.
MORE THINGS THAN YOU KNOW, YOUNG NOBODY OWENS, YES.
YOU WERE RIGHT. I WON'T GO BACK. NOT TO THAT SCHOOL. AND NOT LIKE THAT.

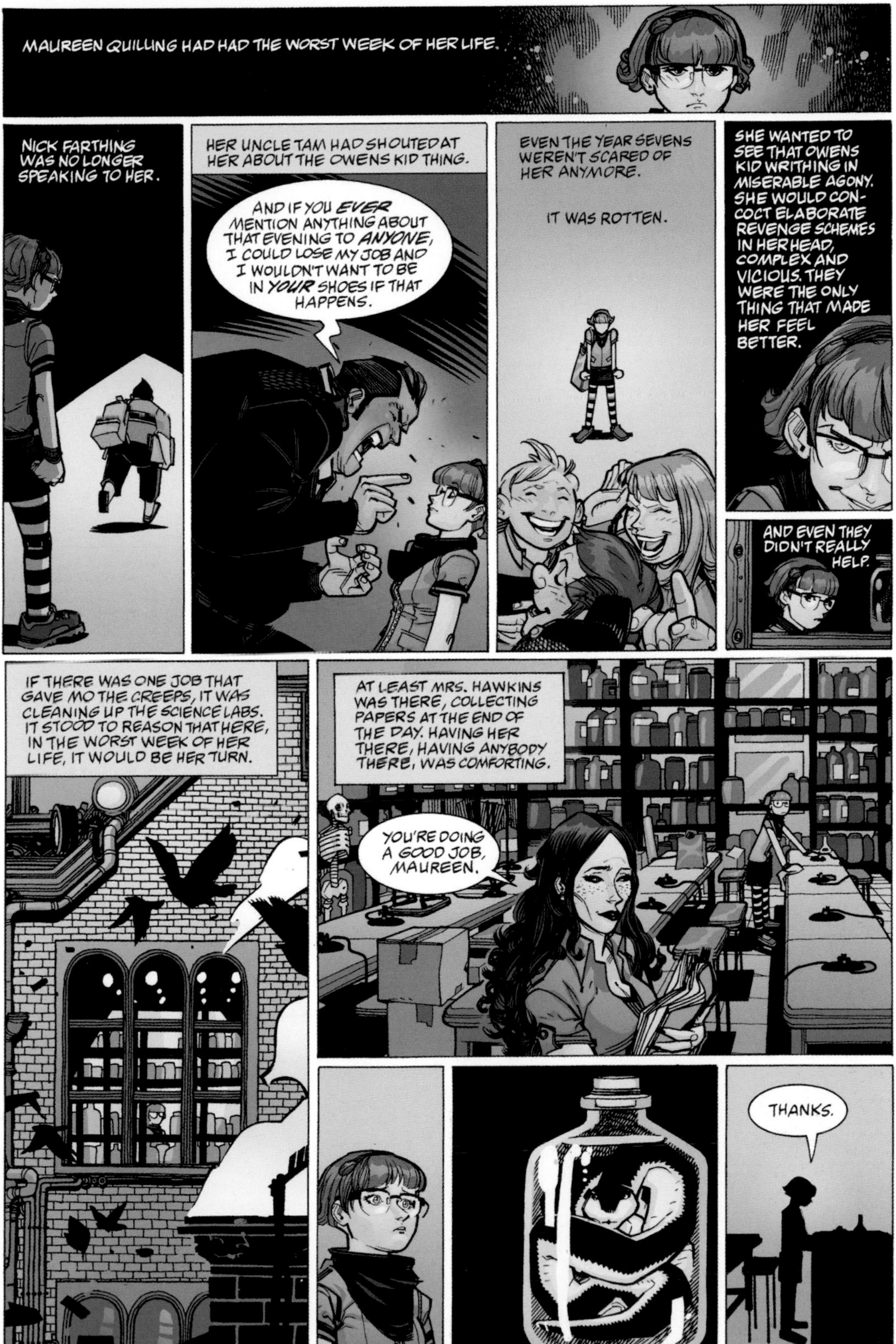
MAUREEN QUILLING HAD HAD THE WORST WEEK OF HER LIFE. . .
NICK FARTHING WAS NO LONGER SPEAKING TO HER.
HER UNCLE TAM HAD SHOUTED AT HER ABOUT THE OWENS KID THING.
AND IF YOU EVER MENTION ANYTHING ABOUT THAT EVENING TO ANYONE, I COULD LOSE MY JOB AND I WOULDN'T WANT TO BE IN YOUR SHOES IF THAT HAPPENS.
EVEN THE YEAR SEVENS WEREN'T SCARED OF HER ANYMORE.
IT WAS ROTTEN.
SHE WANTED TO SEE THAT OWENS KID WRITHING IN MISERABLE AGONY. SHE WOULD CONCOCT ELABORATE REVENGE SCHEMES IN HER HEAD, COMPLEX AND VICIOUS. THEY WERE THE ONLY THING THAT MADE HER FEEL BETTER.
AND EVEN THEY DIDN'T REALLY HELP.
IF THERE WAS ONE JOB THAT GAVE MO THE CREEPS, IT WAS CLEANING UP THE SCIENCE LABS. IT STOOD TO REASON THAT HERE, IN THE WORST WEEK OF HER LIFE, IT WOULD BE HER TURN.
AT LEAST MRS. HAWKINS WAS THERE, COLLECTING PAPERS AT THE END OF THE DAY. HAVING HER THERE, HAVING ANYBODY THERE, WAS COMFORTING.
YOU'RE DOING A GOOD JOB, MAUREEN.
THANKS.

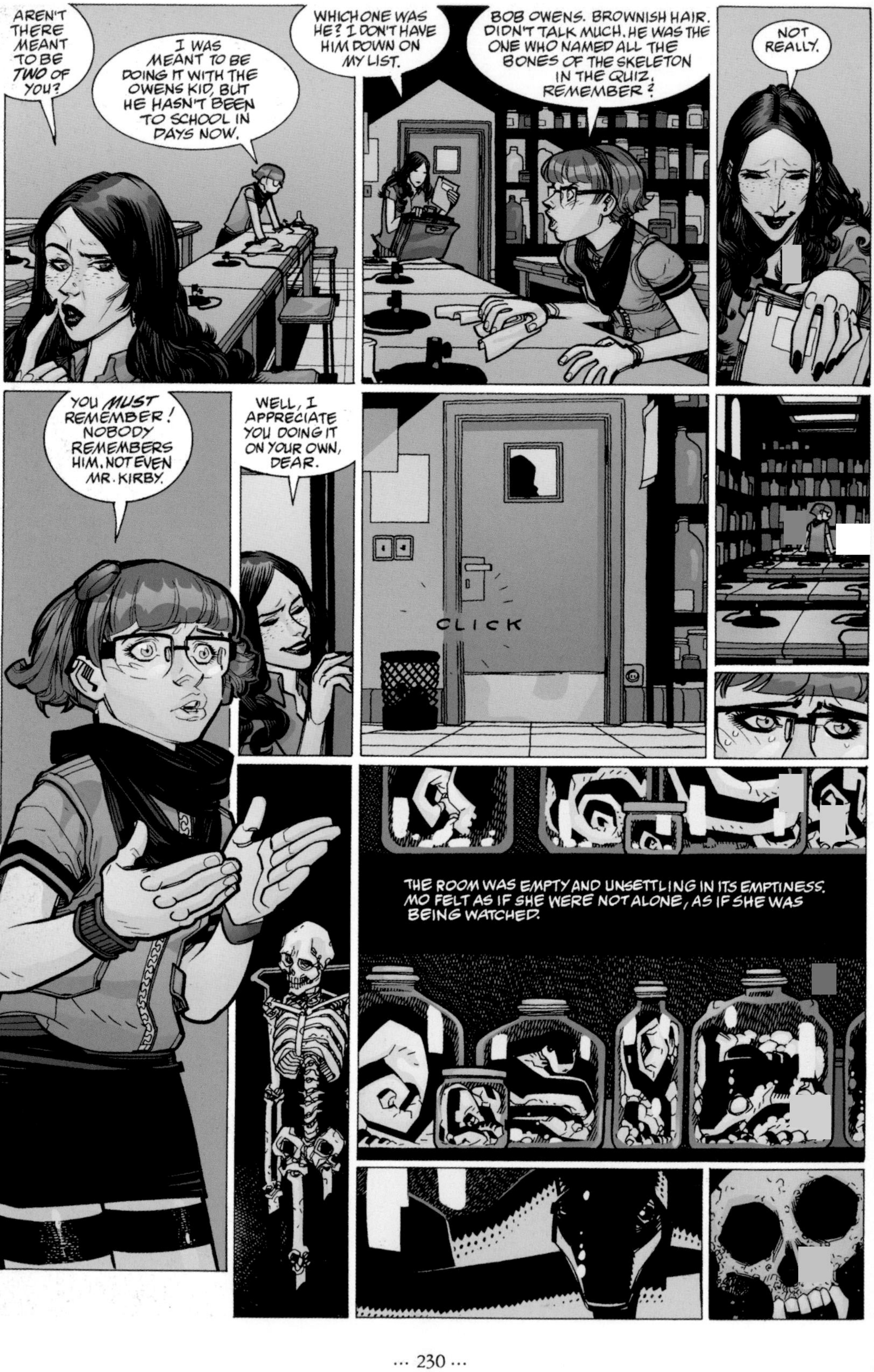

AREN'T THERE MEANT TO BE TWO OF YOU?
I WAS MEANT TO BE DOING IT WITH THE OWENS KID, BUT HE HASN'T BEEN TO SCHOOL IN DAYS NOW.
WHICH ONE WAS HE? I DON'T HAVE HIM DOWN ON MY LIST.
BOB OWENS. BROWNISH HAIR. DIDN'T TALK MUCH. HE WAS THE ONE WHO NAMED ALL THE BONES OF THE SKELETON IN THE QUIZ, REMEMBER?
NOT REALLY.
YOU MUST REMEMBER! NOBODY REMEMBERS HIM. NOT EVEN MR. KIRBY.
WELL, I APPRECIATE YOU DOING IT ON YOUR OWN, DEAR.
CLICK
THE ROOM WAS EMPTY AND UNSETTLING IN ITS EMPTINESS. MO FELT AS IF SHE WERE NOT ALONE, AS IF SHE WAS BEING WATCHED.

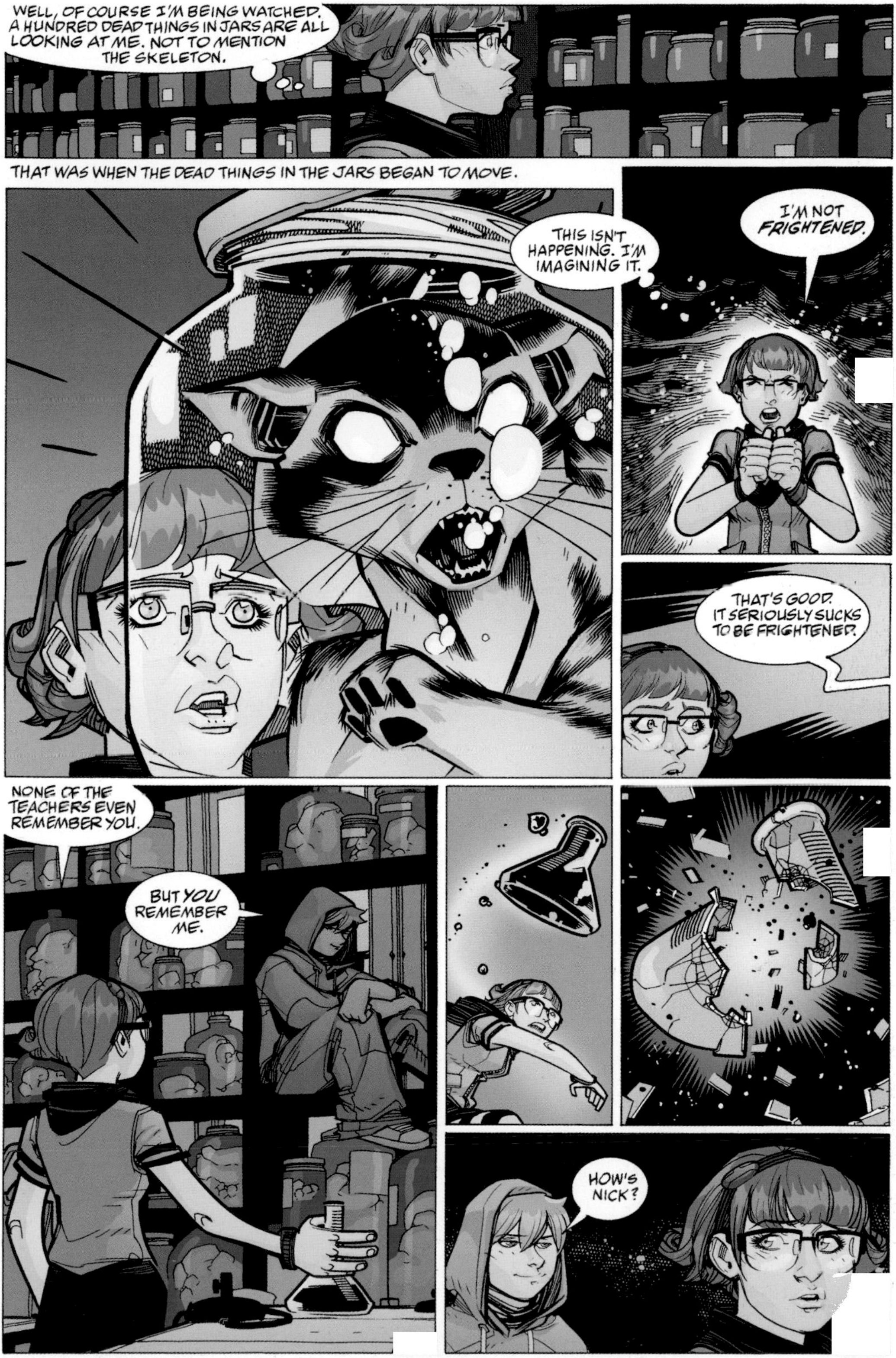

WELL, OF COURSE I'M BEING WATCHED. A HUNDRED DEAD THINGS IN JARS ARE ALL LOOKING AT ME. NOT TO MENTION THE SKELETON.
THAT WAS WHEN THE DEAD THINGS IN THE JARS BEGAN TO MOVE.
THIS ISN'T HAPPENING. I'M IMAGINING IT.
I'M NOT FRIGHTENED.
THAT'S GOOD. IT SERIOUSLY SUCKS TO BE FRIGHTENED.
NONE OF THE TEACHERS EVEN REMEMBER YOU.
BUT YOU REMEMBER ME.
HOW'S NICK?

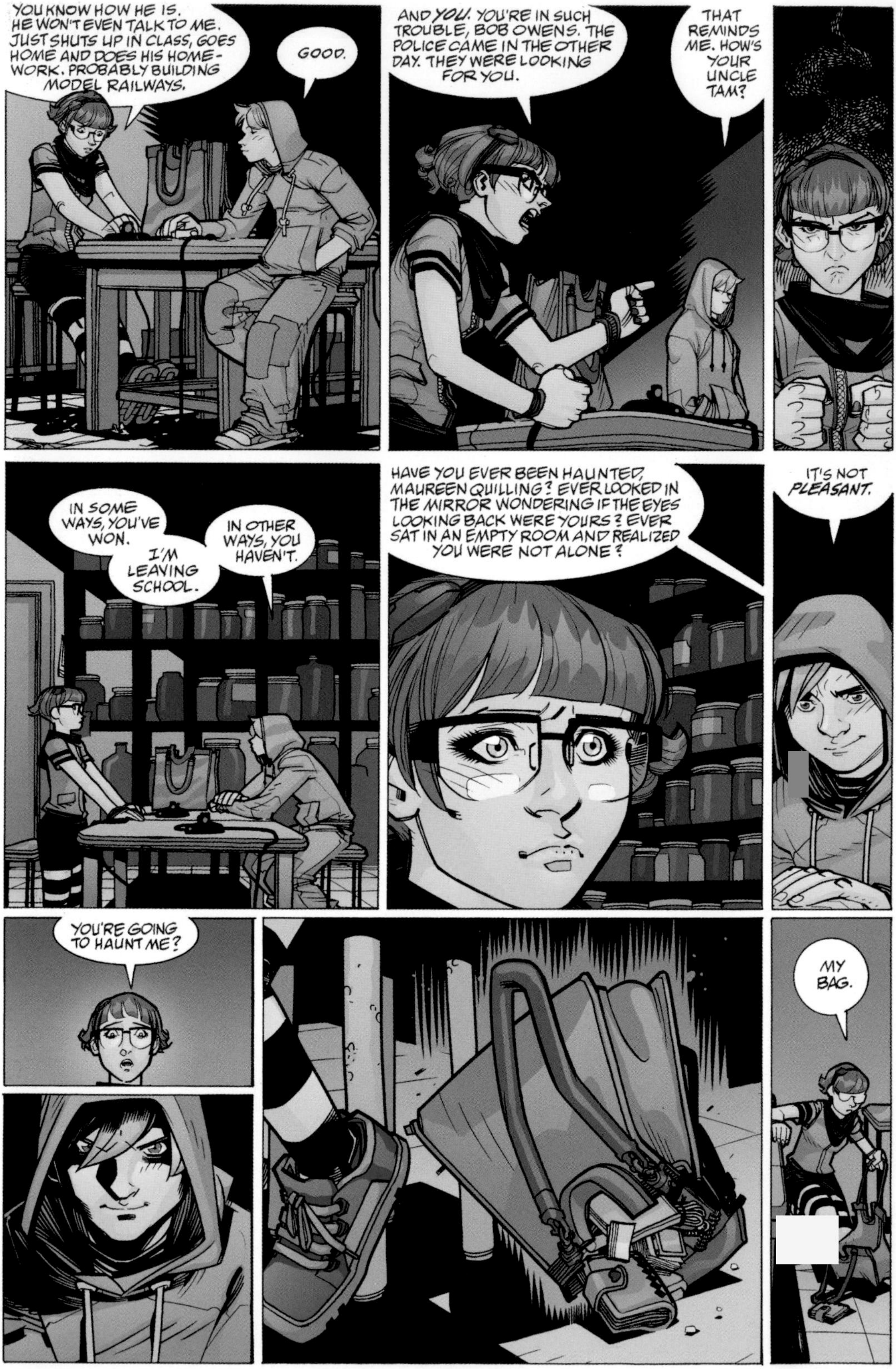
YOU KNOW HOW HE IS. HE WON'T EVEN TALK TO ME. JUST SHUTS UP IN CLASS, GOES HOME AND DOES HIS HOME-WORK. PROBABLY BUILDING MODEL RAILWAYS.
GOOD.
AND YOU. YOU'RE IN SUCH TROUBLE, BOB OWENS. THE POLICE CAME IN THE OTHER DAY. THEY WERE LOOKING FOR YOU.
THAT REMINDS ME. HOW'S YOUR UNCLE TAM?
IN SOME WAYS, YOU'VE WON.
I'M LEAVING SCHOOL.
IN OTHER WAYS, YOU HAVEN'T.
HAVE YOU EVER BEEN HAUNTED, MAUREEN QUILLING? EVER LOOKED IN THE MIRROR WONDERING IF THE EYES LOOKING BACK WERE YOURS? EVER SAT IN AN EMPTY ROOM AND REALIZED YOU WERE NOT ALONE?
IT'S NOT PLEASANT.
YOU'RE GOING TO HAUNT ME?
MY BAG.

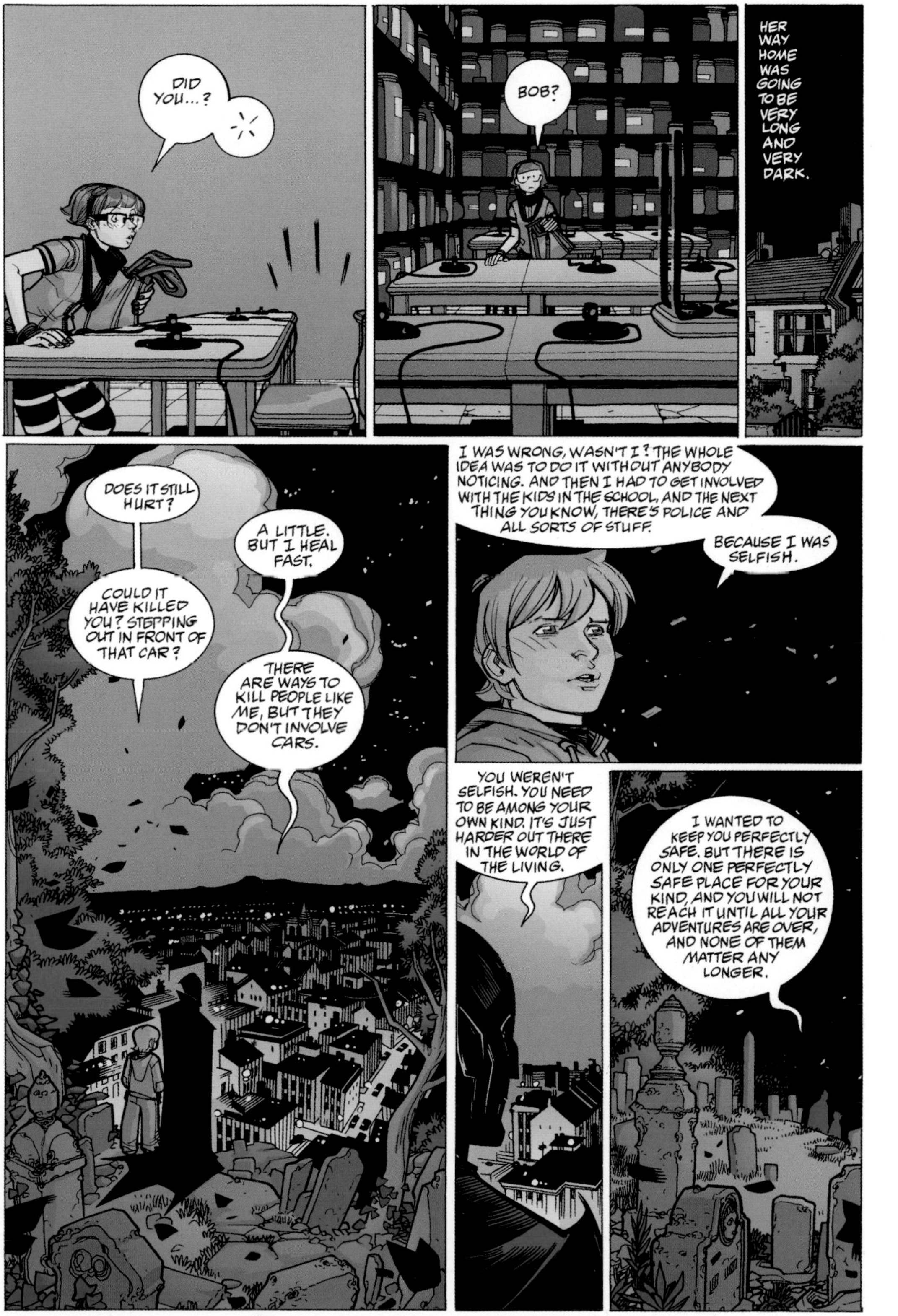
DID YOU...?
HER WAY HOME WAS GOING TO BE VERY LONG AND VERY DARK.
DOES IT STILL HURT?
A LITTLE. BUT I HEAL FAST.
COULD IT HAVE KILLED YOU? STEPPING OUT IN FRONT OF THAT CAR?
THERE ARE WAYS TO KILL PEOPLE LIKE ME, BUT THEY DON'T INVOLVE CARS.
I WAS WRONG, WASN'T I? THE WHOLE IDEA WAS TO DO IT WITHOUT ANYBODY NOTICING. AND THEN I HAD TO GET INVOLVED WITH THE KIDS IN THE SCHOOL, AND THE NEXT THING YOU KNOW, THERE'S POLICE AND ALL SORTS OF STUFF.
BECAUSE I WAS SELFISH.
YOU WEREN'T SELFISH. YOU NEED TO BE AMONG YOUR OWN KIND. IT'S JUST HARDER OUT THERE IN THE WORLD OF THE LIVING.
I WANTED TO KEEP YOU PERFECTLY SAFE. BUT THERE IS ONLY ONE PERFECTLY SAFE PLACE FOR YOUR KIND, AND YOU WILL NOT REACH IT UNTIL ALL YOUR ADVENTURES ARE OVER, AND NONE OF THEM MATTER ANY LONGER.

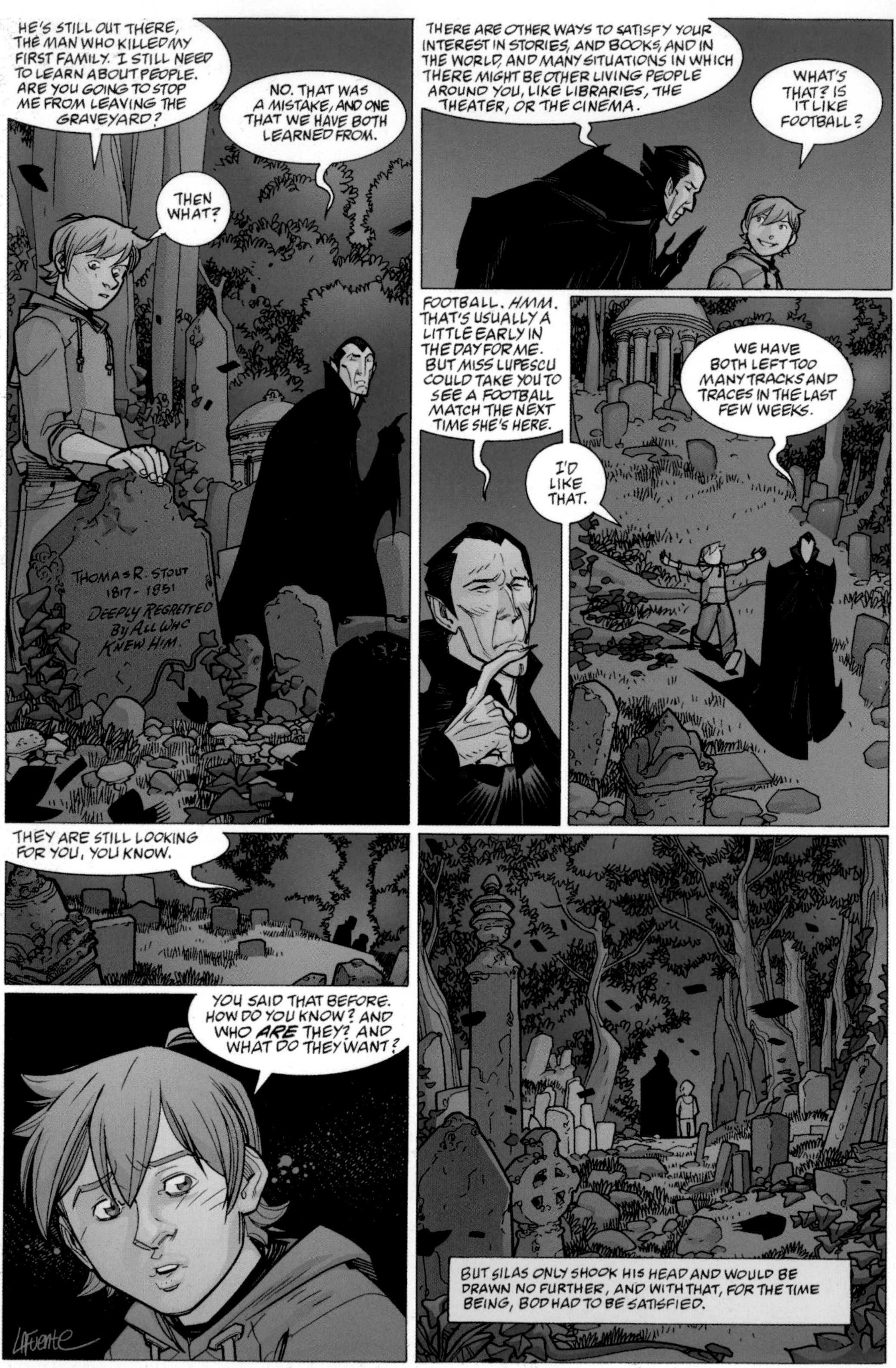

HE'S STILL OUT THERE, THE MAN WHO KILLED MY FIRST FAMILY. I STILL NEED TO LEARN ABOUT PEOPLE. ARE YOU GOING TO STOP ME FROM LEAVING THE GRAVEYARD?
NO. THAT WAS A MISTAKE, AND ONE THAT WE HAVE BOTH LEARNED FROM.
THEN WHAT?
THOMAS R. STOUT 1817 - 1851 DEEPLY REGRETTED BY ALL WHO KNEW HIM.
THERE ARE OTHER WAYS TO SATISFY YOUR INTEREST IN STORIES, AND BOOKS, AND IN THE WORLD, AND MANY SITUATIONS IN WHICH THERE MIGHT BE OTHER LIVING PEOPLE AROUND YOU, LIKE LIBRARIES, THE THEATER, OR THE CINEMA.
WHAT'S THAT? IS IT LIKE FOOTBALL?
FOOTBALL. HMM. THAT'S USUALLY A LITTLE EARLY IN THE DAY FOR ME. BUT MISS LUPESCU COULD TAKE YOU TO SEE A FOOTBALL MATCH THE NEXT TIME SHE'S HERE.
I'D LIKE THAT.
WE HAVE BOTH LEFT TOO MANY TRACKS AND TRACES IN THE LAST FEW WEEKS.
THEY ARE STILL LOOKING FOR YOU, YOU KNOW.
YOU SAID THAT BEFORE. HOW DO YOU KNOW? AND WHO ARE THEY? AND WHAT DO THEY WANT?
BUT SILAS ONLY SHOOK HIS HEAD AND WOULD BE DRAWN NO FURTHER, AND WITH THAT, FOR THE TIME BEING, BOD HAD TO BE SATISFIED.
LAFUENTE

7
Every Man Jack

Illustrated by Scott Hampton

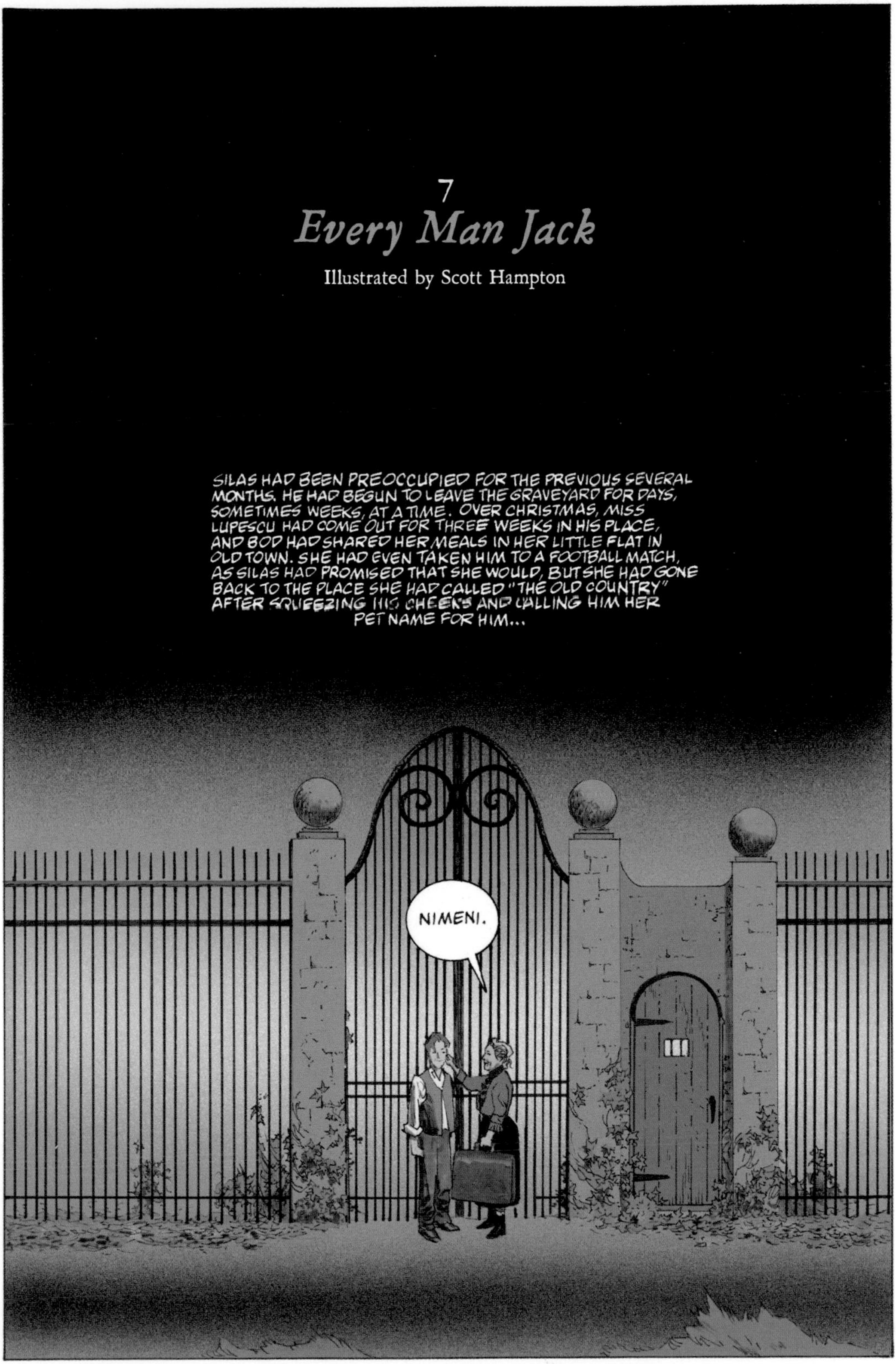
SILAS HAD BEEN PREOCCUPIED FOR THE PREVIOUS SEVERAL MONTHS. HE HAD BEGUN TO LEAVE THE GRAVEYARD FOR DAYS, SOMETIMES WEEKS, AT A TIME. OVER CHRISTMAS, MISS LUPESCU HAD COME OUT FOR THREE WEEKS IN HIS PLACE, AND BOD HAD SHARED HER MEALS IN HER LITTLE FLAT IN OLD TOWN. SHE HAD EVEN TAKEN HIM TO A FOOTBALL MATCH, AS SILAS HAD PROMISED THAT SHE WOULD, BUT SHE HAD GONE BACK TO THE PLACE SHE HAD CALLED "THE OLD COUNTRY" AFTER SQUEEZING HIS CHEEKS AND CALLING HIM HER PET NAME FOR HIM...
NIMENI.

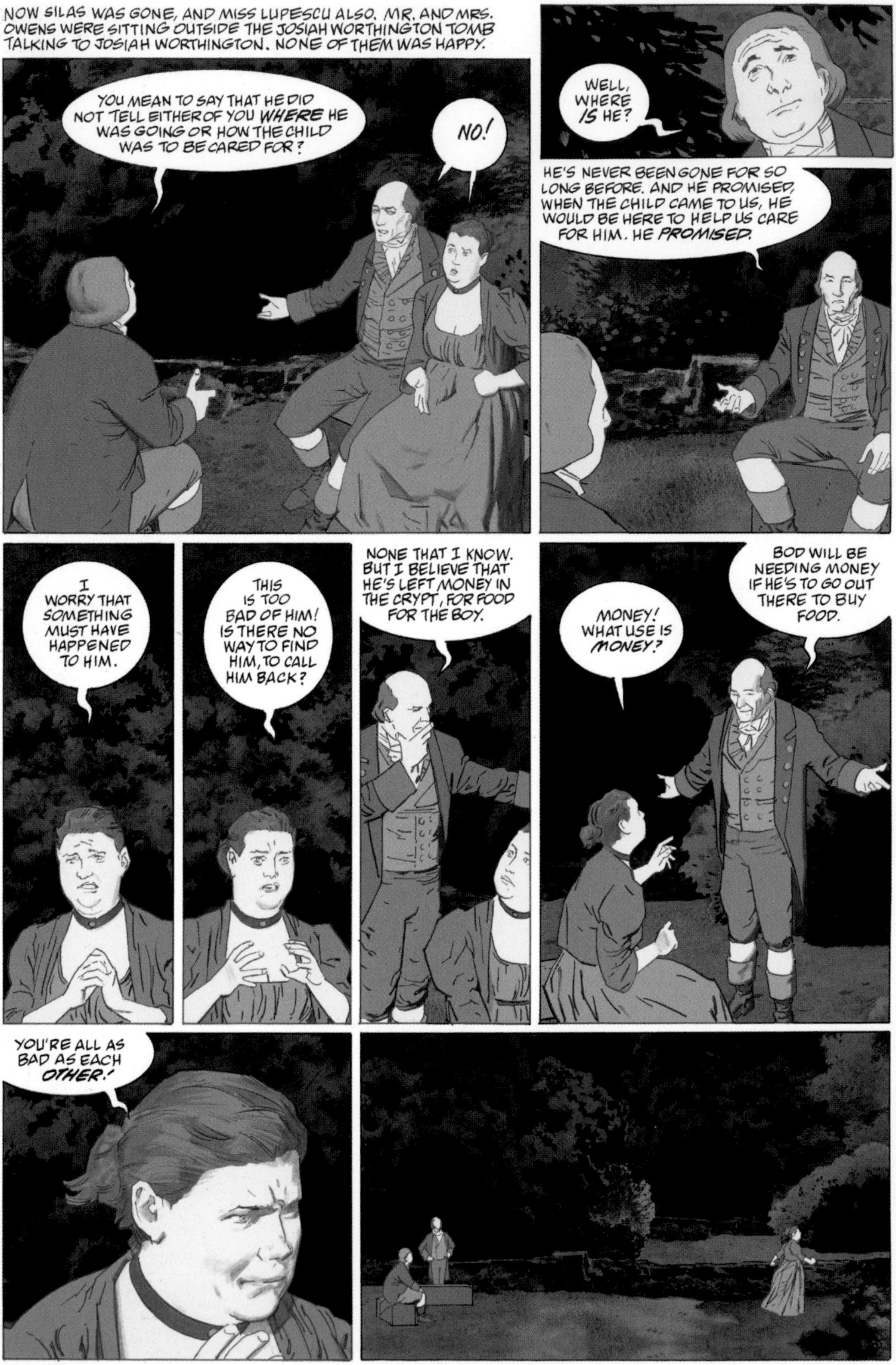
NOW SILAS WAS GONE, AND MISS LUPESCU ALSO. MR. AND MRS. OWENS WERE SITTING OUTSIDE THE JOSIAH WORTHINGTON TOMB TALKING TO JOSIAH WORTHINGTON. NONE OF THEM WAS HAPPY.
YOU MEAN TO SAY THAT HE DID NOT TELL EITHER OF YOU WHERE HE WAS GOING OR HOW THE CHILD WAS TO BE CARED FOR?
NO!
WELL, WHERE IS HE?
HE'S NEVER BEEN GONE FOR SO LONG BEFORE. AND HE PROMISED, WHEN THE CHILD CAME TO US, HE WOULD BE HERE TO HELP US CARE FOR HIM. HE PROMISED.
I WORRY THAT SOMETHING MUST HAVE HAPPENED TO HIM.
THIS IS TOO BAD OF HIM! IS THERE NO WAY TO FIND HIM, TO CALL HIM BACK?
NONE THAT I KNOW. BUT I BELIEVE THAT HE'S LEFT MONEY IN THE CRYPT, FOR FOOD FOR THE BOY.
MONEY! WHAT USE IS MONEY?
BOD WILL BE NEEDING MONEY IF HE'S TO GO OUT THERE TO BUY FOOD.
YOU'RE ALL AS BAD AS EACH OTHER!

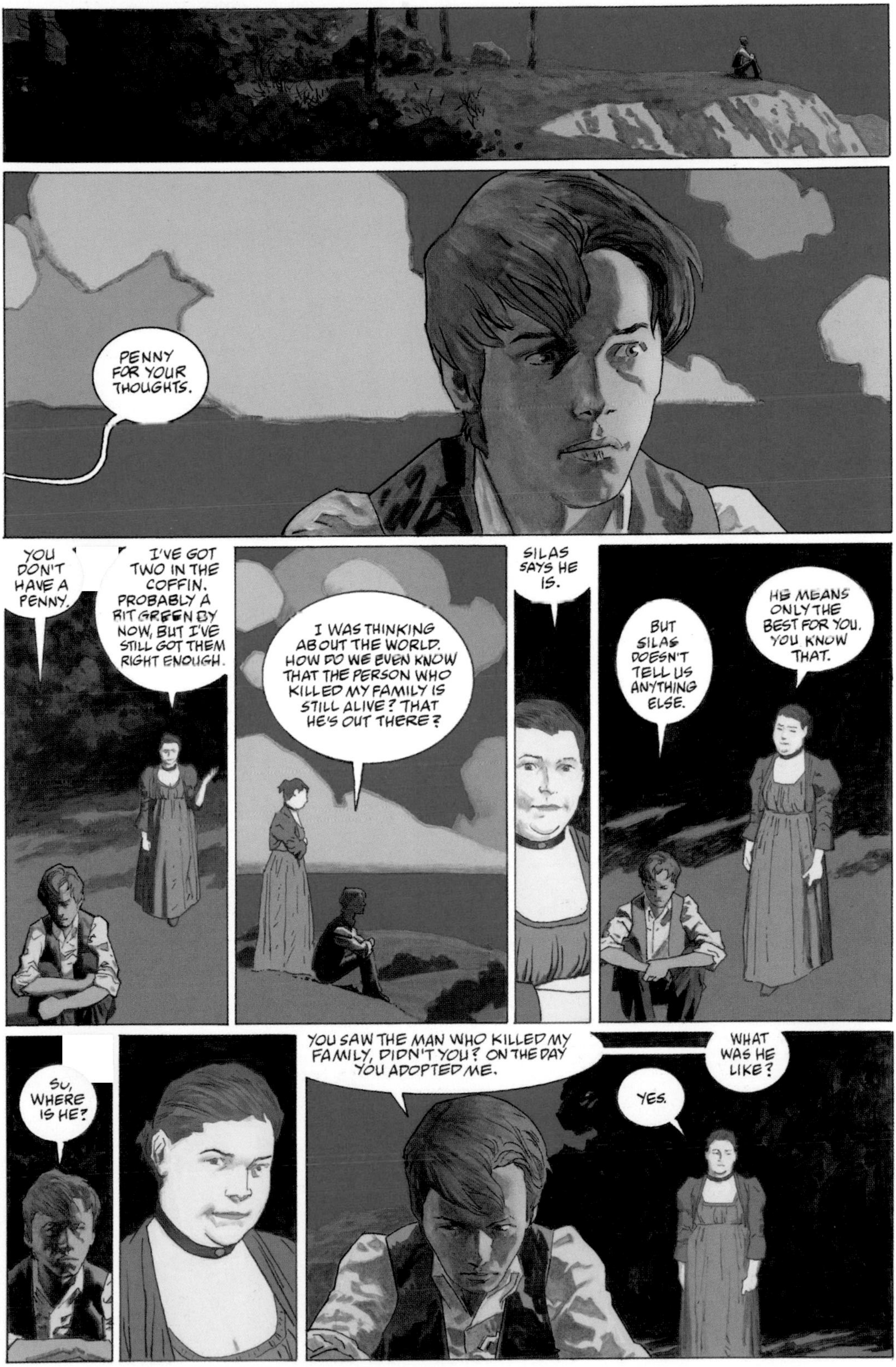
PENNY FOR YOUR THOUGHTS.
YOU DON'T HAVE A PENNY.
I'VE GOT TWO IN THE COFFIN. PROBABLY A BIT GREEN BY NOW, BUT I'VE STILL GOT THEM RIGHT ENOUGH.
I WAS THINKING ABOUT THE WORLD. HOW DO WE EVEN KNOW THAT THE PERSON WHO KILLED MY FAMILY IS STILL ALIVE? THAT HE'S OUT THERE?
SILAS SAYS HE IS.
BUT SILAS DOESN'T TELL US ANYTHING ELSE.
HE MEANS ONLY THE BEST FOR YOU. YOU KNOW THAT.
SO, WHERE IS HE?
YOU SAW THE MAN WHO KILLED MY FAMILY, DIDN'T YOU? ON THE DAY YOU ADOPTED ME.
YES.
WHAT WAS HE LIKE?

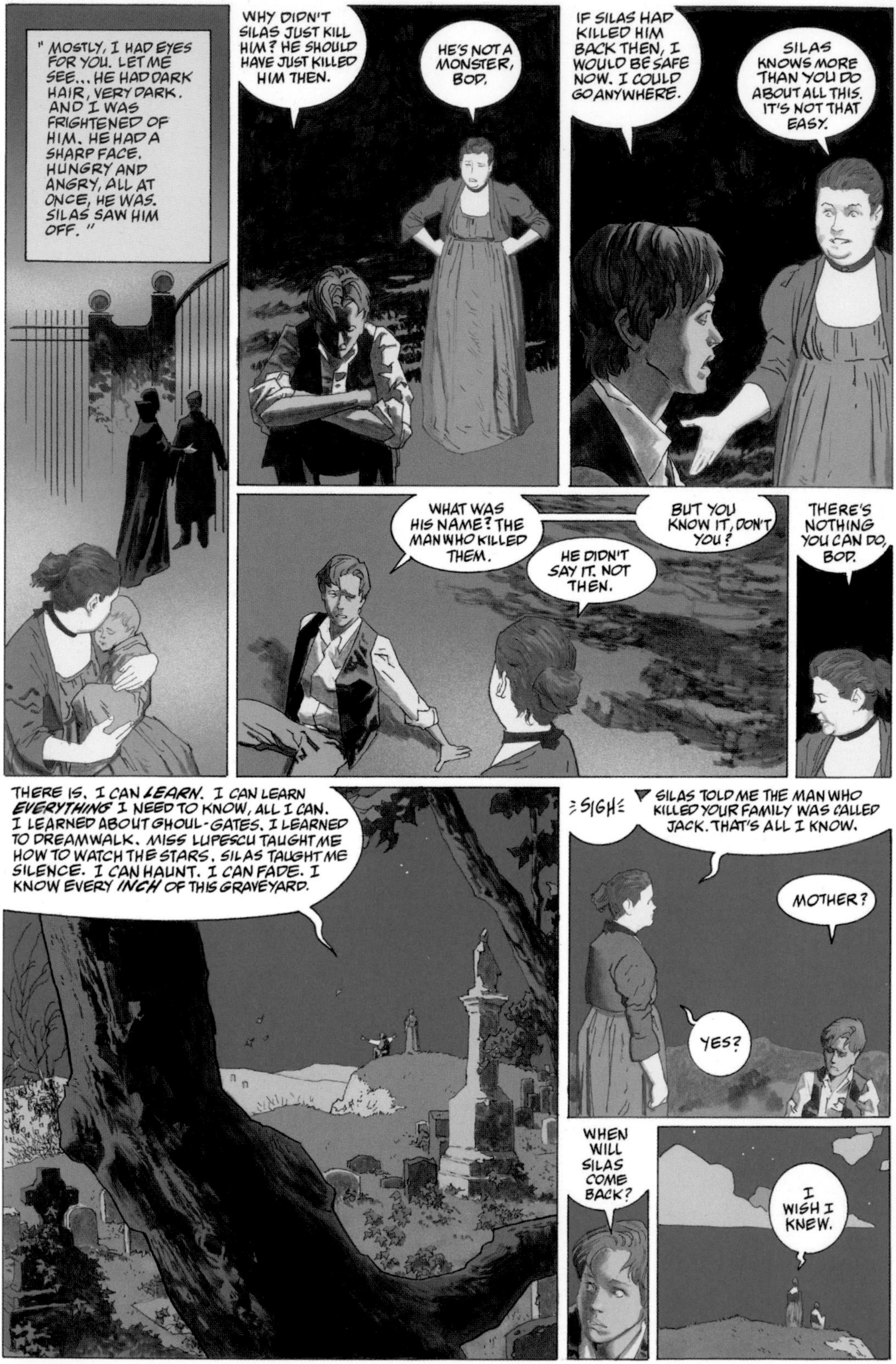

" MOSTLY, I HAD EYES FOR YOU. LET ME SEE... HE HAD DARK HAIR, VERY DARK. AND I WAS FRIGHTENED OF HIM. HE HAD A SHARP FACE. HUNGRY AND ANGRY, ALL AT ONCE, HE WAS. SILAS SAW HIM OFF. "
WHY DIDN'T SILAS JUST KILL HIM? HE SHOULD HAVE JUST KILLED HIM THEN.
HE'S NOT A MONSTER, BOD.
IF SILAS HAD KILLED HIM BACK THEN, I WOULD BE SAFE NOW. I COULD GO ANYWHERE.
SILAS KNOWS MORE THAN YOU DO ABOUT ALL THIS. IT'S NOT THAT EASY.
WHAT WAS HIS NAME? THE MAN WHO KILLED THEM.
HE DIDN'T SAY IT. NOT THEN.
BUT YOU KNOW IT, DON'T YOU?
THERE'S NOTHING YOU CAN DO, BOD.
THERE IS. I CAN LEARN. I CAN LEARN EVERYTHING I NEED TO KNOW, ALL I CAN. I LEARNED ABOUT GHOUL-GATES. I LEARNED TO DREAMWALK. MISS LUPESCU TAUGHT ME HOW TO WATCH THE STARS. SILAS TAUGHT ME SILENCE. I CAN HAUNT. I CAN FADE. I KNOW EVERY INCH OF THIS GRAVEYARD.
SIGH
SILAS TOLD ME THE MAN WHO KILLED YOUR FAMILY WAS CALLED JACK. THAT'S ALL I KNOW.
MOTHER?
YES?
WHEN WILL SILAS COME BACK?
I WISH I KNEW.

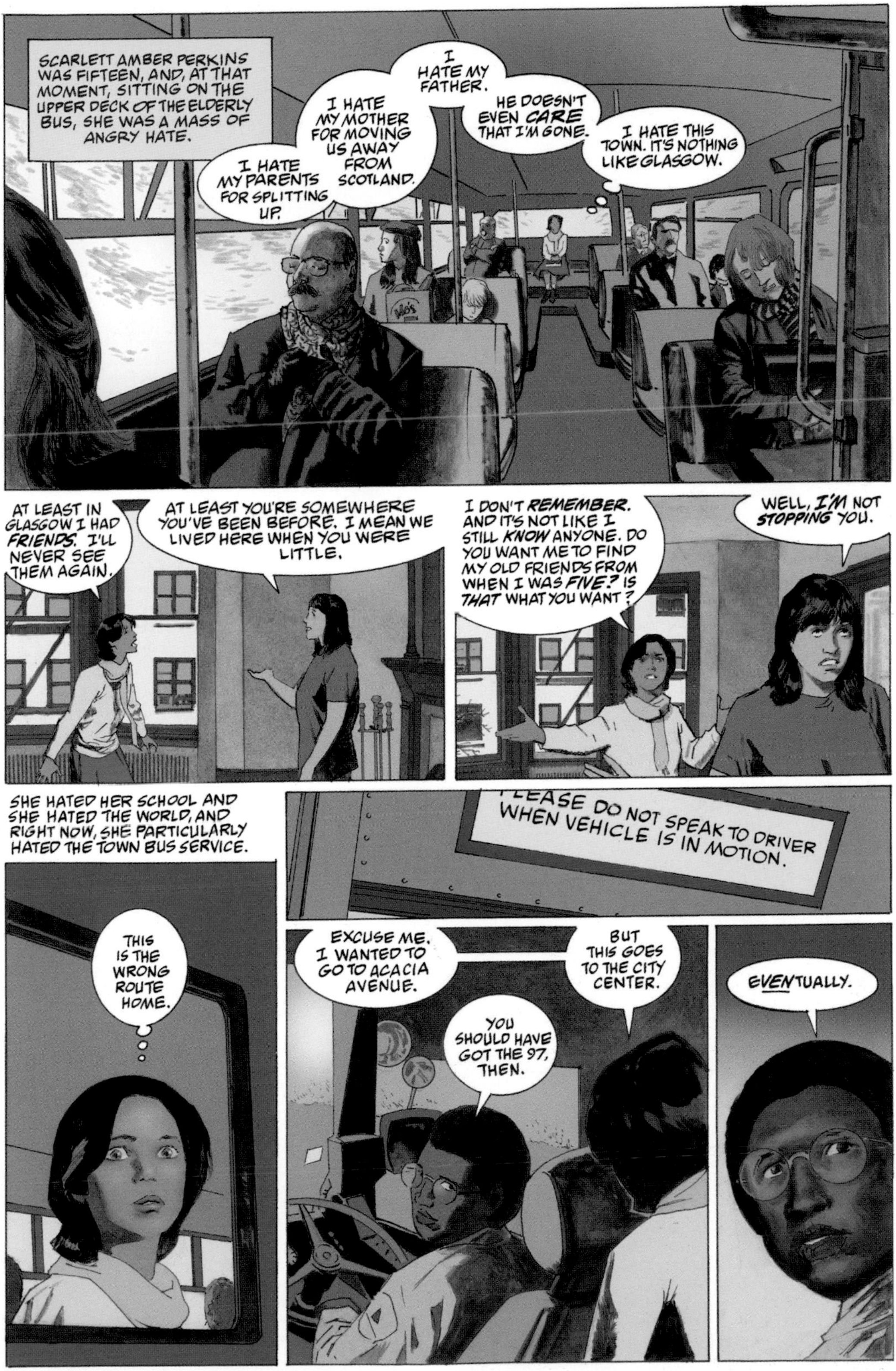
SCARLETT AMBER PERKINS WAS FIFTEEN, AND, AT THAT MOMENT, SITTING ON THE UPPER DECK OF THE ELDERLY BUS, SHE WAS A MASS OF ANGRY HATE.
I HATE MY PARENTS FOR SPLITTING UP.
I HATE MY MOTHER FOR MOVING US AWAY FROM SCOTLAND.
I HATE MY FATHER.
HE DOESN'T EVEN CARE THAT I'M GONE.
I HATE THIS TOWN. IT'S NOTHING LIKE GLASGOW.
AT LEAST IN GLASGOW I HAD FRIENDS. I'LL NEVER SEE THEM AGAIN.
AT LEAST YOU'RE SOMEWHERE YOU'VE BEEN BEFORE. I MEAN WE LIVED HERE WHEN YOU WERE LITTLE.
I DON'T REMEMBER. AND IT'S NOT LIKE I STILL KNOW ANYONE. DO YOU WANT ME TO FIND MY OLD FRIENDS FROM WHEN I WAS FIVE? IS THAT WHAT YOU WANT?
WELL, I'M NOT STOPPING YOU.
SHE HATED HER SCHOOL AND SHE HATED THE WORLD, AND RIGHT NOW, SHE PARTICULARLY HATED THE TOWN BUS SERVICE.
PLEASE DO NOT SPEAK TO DRIVER WHEN VEHICLE IS IN MOTION.
THIS IS THE WRONG ROUTE HOME.
EXCUSE ME. I WANTED TO GO TO ACACIA AVENUE.
YOU SHOULD HAVE GOT THE 97, THEN.
BUT THIS GOES TO THE CITY CENTER.
EVENTUALLY.

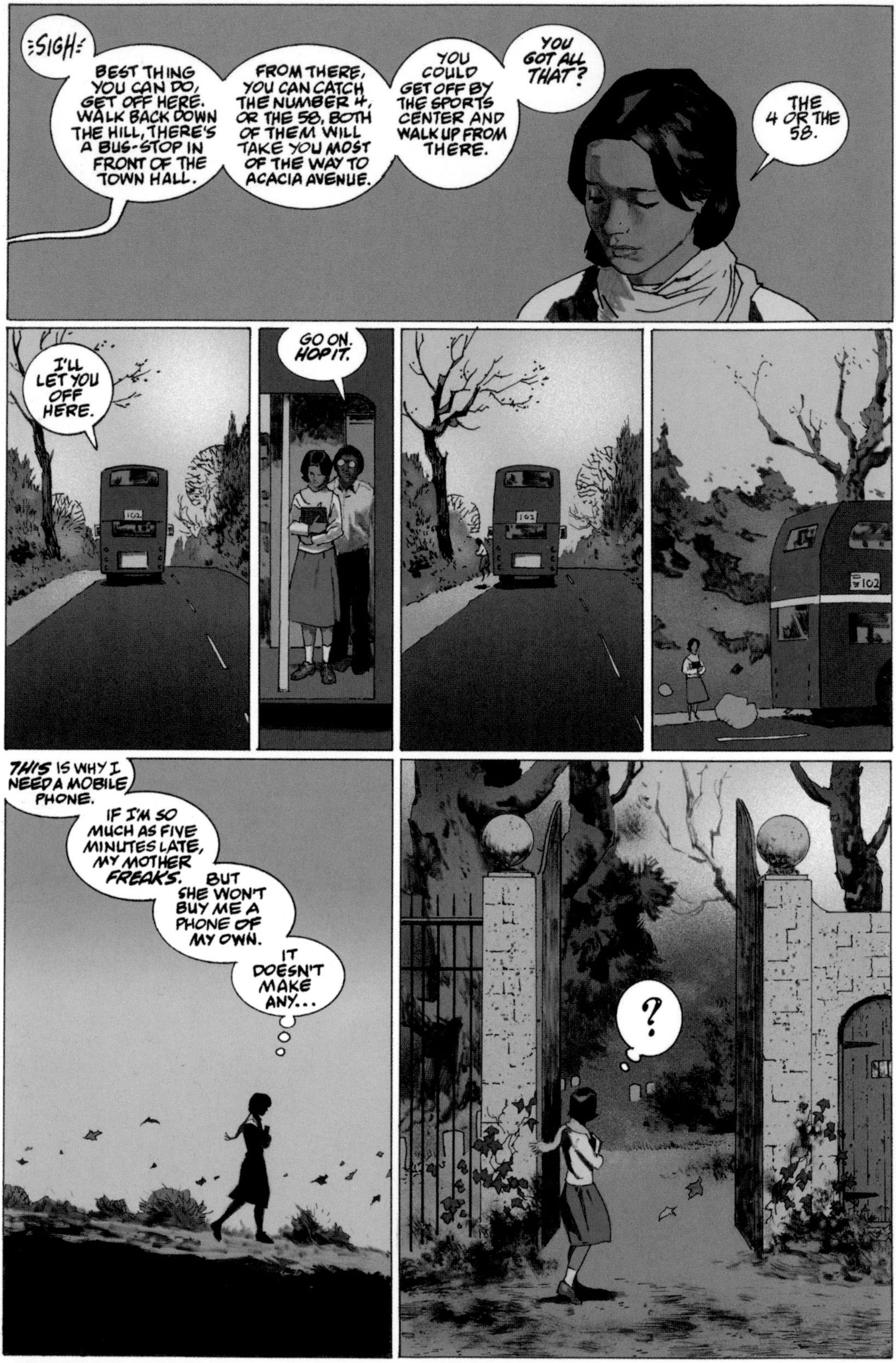
SIGH
BEST THING YOU CAN DO, GET OFF HERE. WALK BACK DOWN THE HILL, THERE'S A BUS-STOP IN FRONT OF THE TOWN HALL.
FROM THERE, YOU CAN CATCH THE NUMBER 4, OR THE 58, BOTH OF THEM WILL TAKE YOU MOST OF THE WAY TO ACACIA AVENUE.
YOU COULD GET OFF BY THE SPORTS CENTER AND WALK UP FROM THERE.
YOU GOT ALL THAT?
THE 4 OR THE 58.
I'LL LET YOU OFF HERE.
102
GO ON. HOP IT.
102
102
THIS IS WHY I NEED A MOBILE PHONE.
IF I'M SO MUCH AS FIVE MINUTES LATE, MY MOTHER FREAKS.
BUT SHE WON'T BUY ME A PHONE OF MY OWN.
IT DOESN'T MAKE ANY...
?

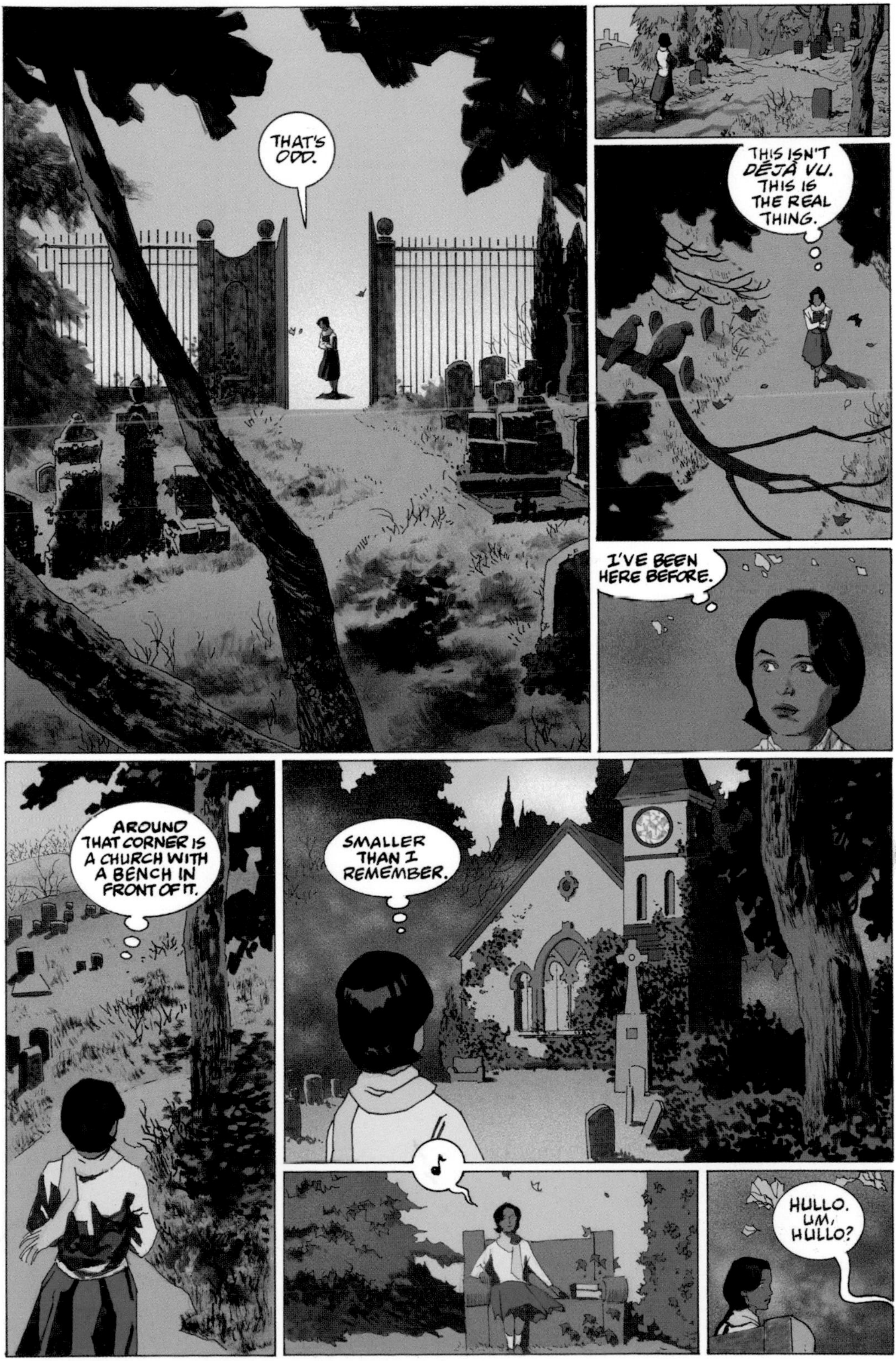
THAT'S ODD.
THIS ISN'T DÉJÀ VU. THIS IS THE REAL THING.
I'VE BEEN HERE BEFORE.
AROUND THAT CORNER IS A CHURCH WITH A BENCH IN FRONT OF IT.
SMALLER THAN I REMEMBER.
♪
HULLO. UM, HULLO?

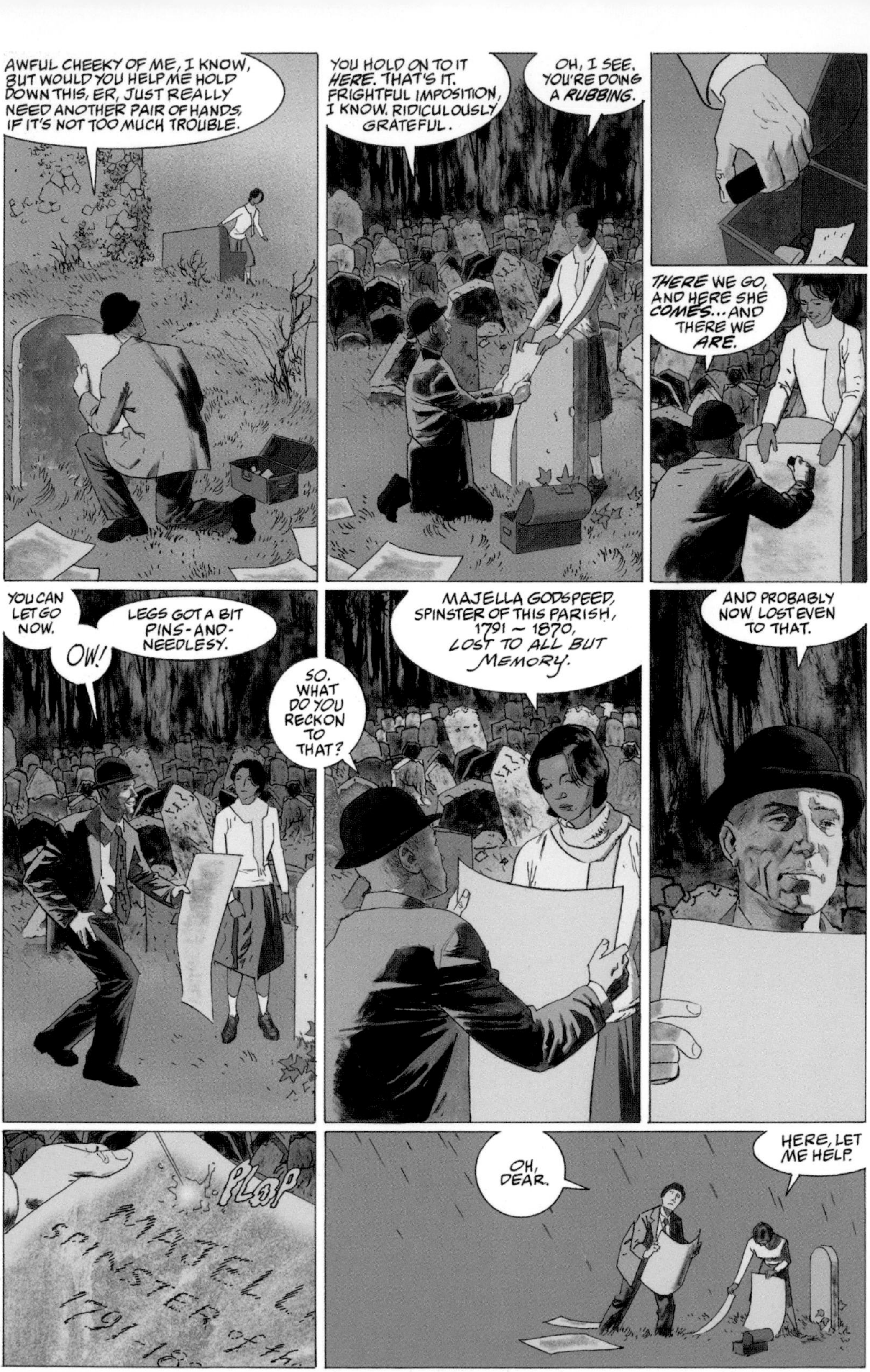
AWFUL CHEEKY OF ME, I KNOW, BUT WOULD YOU HELP ME HOLD DOWN THIS, ER, JUST REALLY NEED ANOTHER PAIR OF HANDS, IF IT'S NOT TOO MUCH TROUBLE.
YOU HOLD ON TO IT HERE. THAT'S IT. FRIGHTFUL IMPOSITION, I KNOW. RIDICULOUSLY GRATEFUL.
OH, I SEE. YOU'RE DOING A RUBBING.
THERE WE GO, AND HERE SHE COMES... AND THERE WE ARE.
YOU CAN LET GO NOW.
OW!
LEGS GOT A BIT PINS-AND-NEEDLESY.
SO. WHAT DO YOU RECKON TO THAT?
MAJELLA GODSPEED, SPINSTER OF THIS PARISH, 1791 ~ 1870, LOST TO ALL BUT MEMORY.
AND PROBABLY NOW LOST EVEN TO THAT.
PLOP
OH, DEAR.
HERE, LET ME HELP.

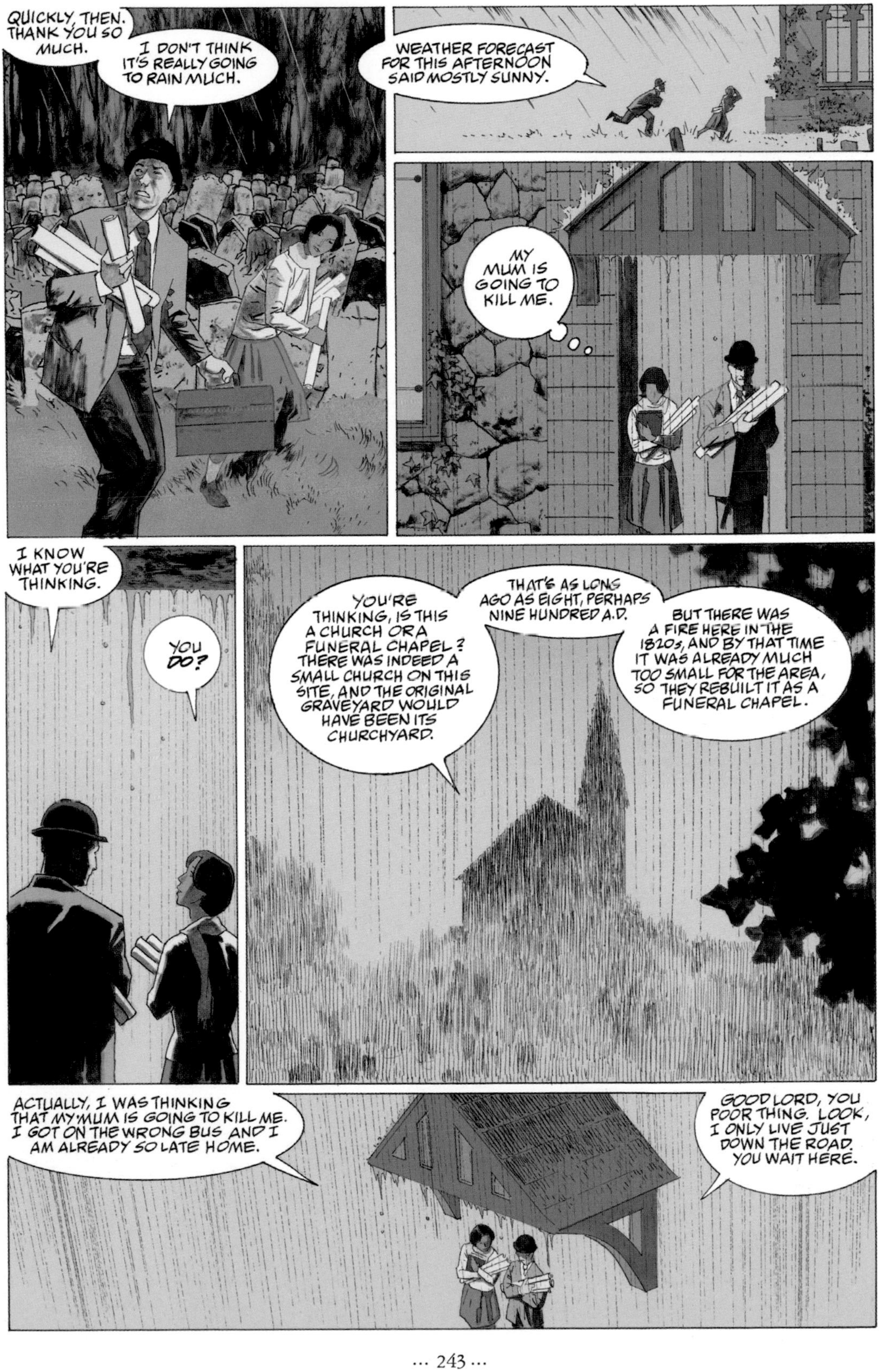

QUICKLY, THEN. THANK YOU SO MUCH.
I DON'T THINK IT'S REALLY GOING TO RAIN MUCH.
WEATHER FORECAST FOR THIS AFTERNOON SAID MOSTLY SUNNY.
MY MUM IS GOING TO KILL ME.
I KNOW WHAT YOU'RE THINKING.
YOU *DO*?
YOU'RE THINKING, IS THIS A CHURCH OR A FUNERAL CHAPEL? THERE WAS INDEED A SMALL CHURCH ON THIS SITE, AND THE ORIGINAL GRAVEYARD WOULD HAVE BEEN ITS CHURCHYARD.
THAT'S AS LONG AGO AS EIGHT, PERHAPS NINE HUNDRED A.D.
BUT THERE WAS A FIRE HERE IN THE 1820s, AND BY THAT TIME IT WAS ALREADY MUCH TOO SMALL FOR THE AREA, SO THEY REBUILT IT AS A FUNERAL CHAPEL.
ACTUALLY, I WAS THINKING THAT MY MUM IS GOING TO KILL ME. I GOT ON THE WRONG BUS AND I AM ALREADY SO LATE HOME.
GOOD LORD, YOU POOR THING. LOOK, I ONLY LIVE JUST DOWN THE ROAD. YOU WAIT HERE.

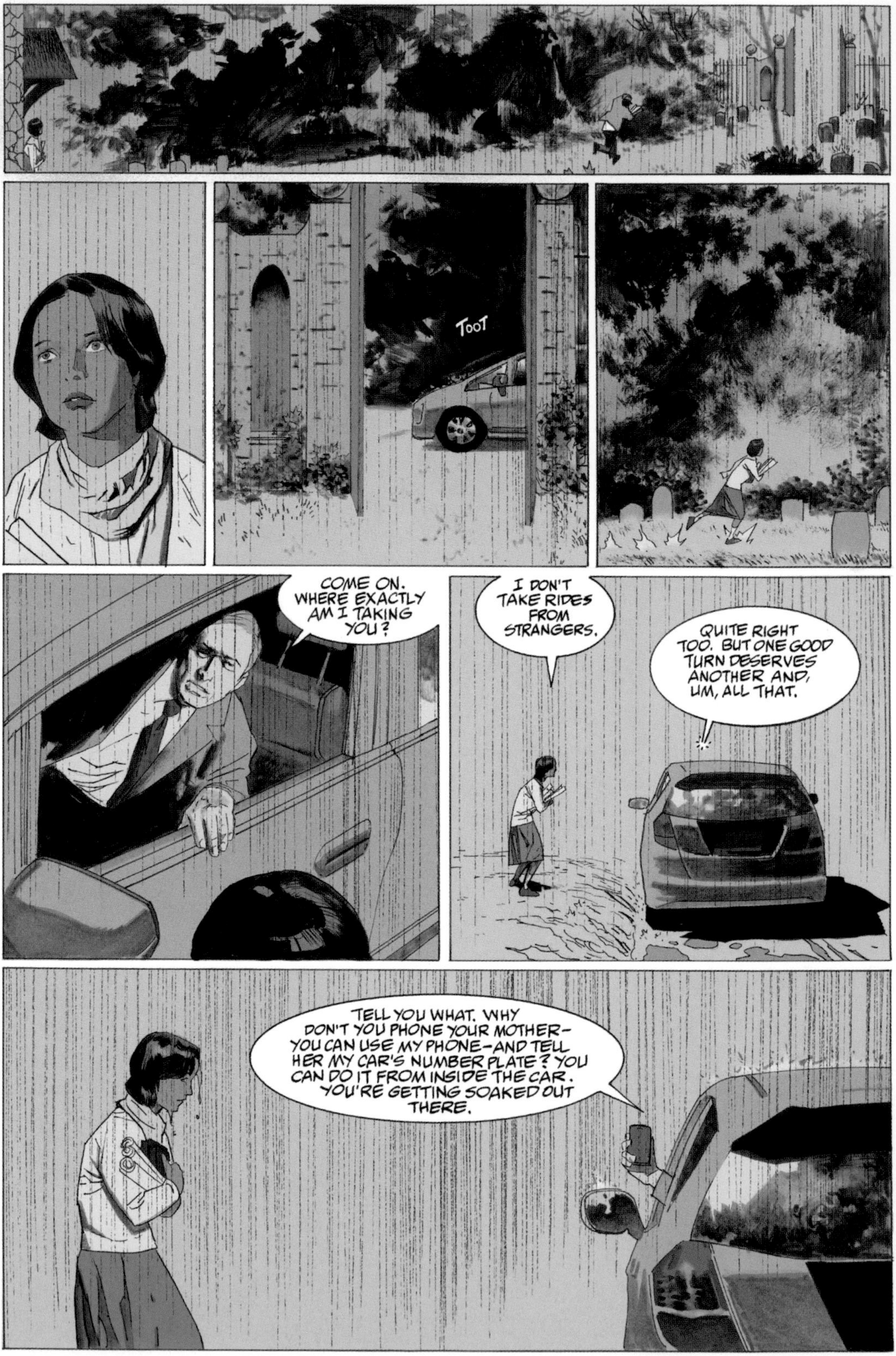
TOOT
COME ON. WHERE EXACTLY AM I TAKING YOU?
I DON'T TAKE RIDES FROM STRANGERS.
QUITE RIGHT TOO. BUT ONE GOOD TURN DESERVES ANOTHER AND, UM, ALL THAT.
TELL YOU WHAT. WHY DON'T YOU PHONE YOUR MOTHER- YOU CAN USE MY PHONE-AND TELL HER MY CAR'S NUMBER PLATE? YOU CAN DO IT FROM INSIDE THE CAR. YOU'RE GETTING SOAKED OUT THERE.

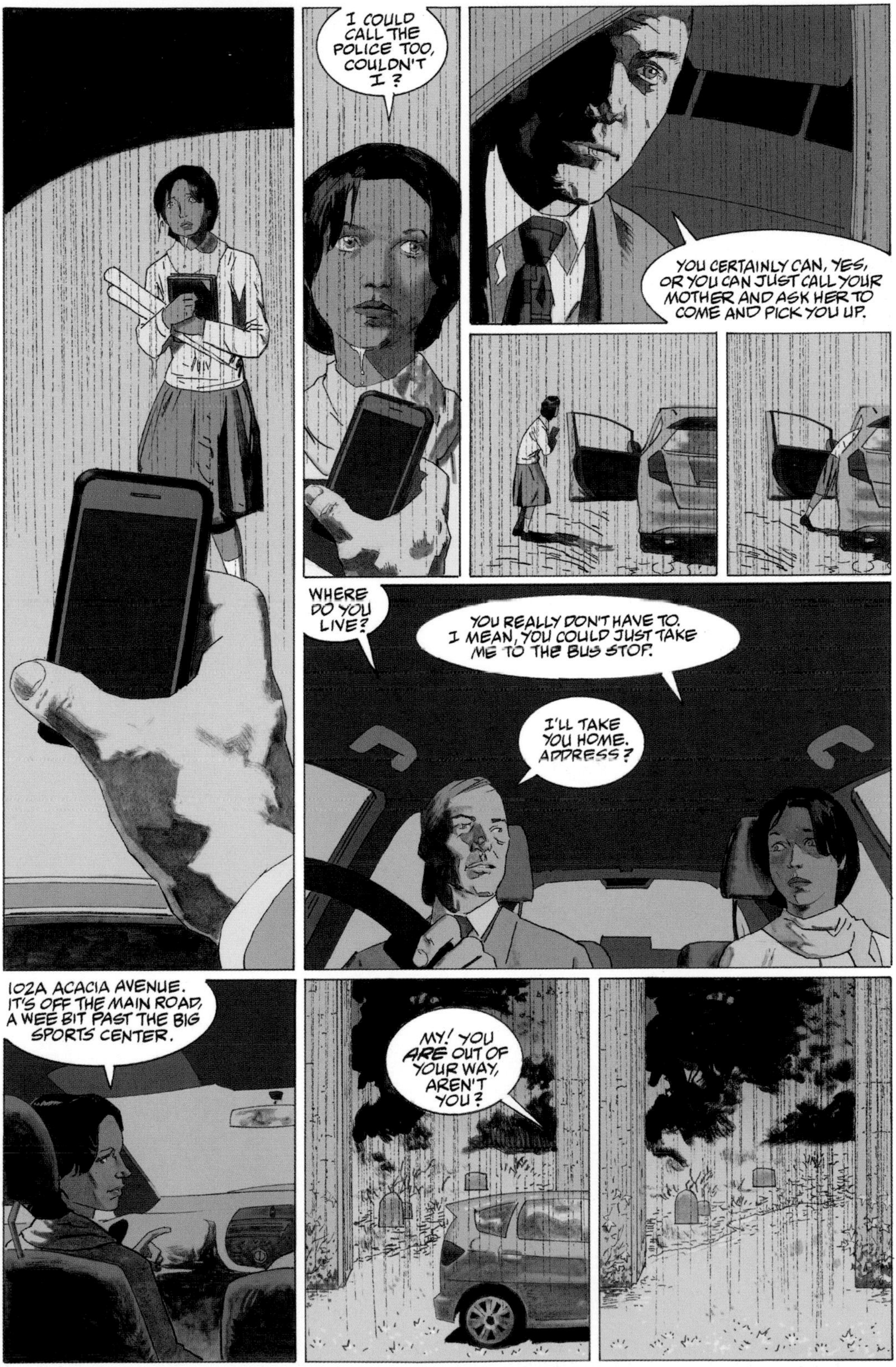
I COULD CALL THE POLICE TOO, COULDN'T I?
YOU CERTAINLY CAN, YES, OR YOU CAN JUST CALL YOUR MOTHER AND ASK HER TO COME AND PICK YOU UP.
WHERE DO YOU LIVE?
YOU REALLY DON'T HAVE TO. I MEAN, YOU COULD JUST TAKE ME TO THE BUS STOP.
I'LL TAKE YOU HOME. ADDRESS?
102A ACACIA AVENUE. IT'S OFF THE MAIN ROAD, A WEE BIT PAST THE BIG SPORTS CENTER.
MY! YOU ARE OUT OF YOUR WAY, AREN'T YOU?

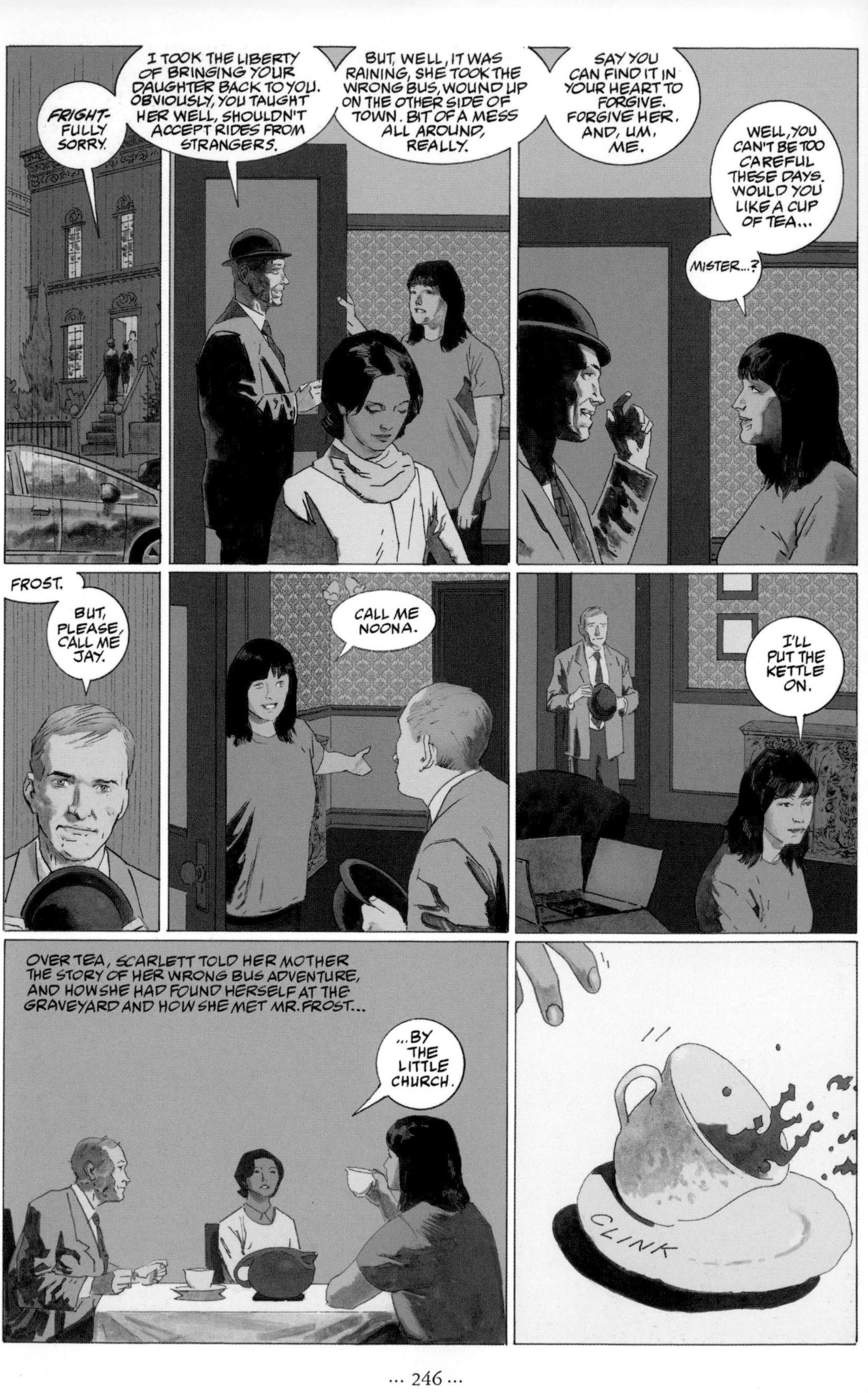
FRIGHT-FULLY SORRY.
I TOOK THE LIBERTY OF BRINGING YOUR DAUGHTER BACK TO YOU. OBVIOUSLY, YOU TAUGHT HER WELL, SHOULDN'T ACCEPT RIDES FROM STRANGERS.
BUT, WELL, IT WAS RAINING, SHE TOOK THE WRONG BUS, WOUND UP ON THE OTHER SIDE OF TOWN. BIT OF A MESS ALL AROUND, REALLY.
SAY YOU CAN FIND IT IN YOUR HEART TO FORGIVE. FORGIVE HER. AND, UM, ME.
WELL, YOU CAN'T BE TOO CAREFUL THESE DAYS. WOULD YOU LIKE A CUP OF TEA...
MISTER...?
FROST.
BUT, PLEASE, CALL ME JAY.
CALL ME NOONA.
I'LL PUT THE KETTLE ON.
OVER TEA, SCARLETT TOLD HER MOTHER THE STORY OF HER WRONG BUS ADVENTURE, AND HOW SHE HAD FOUND HERSELF AT THE GRAVEYARD AND HOW SHE MET MR. FROST...
...BY THE LITTLE CHURCH.
CLINK

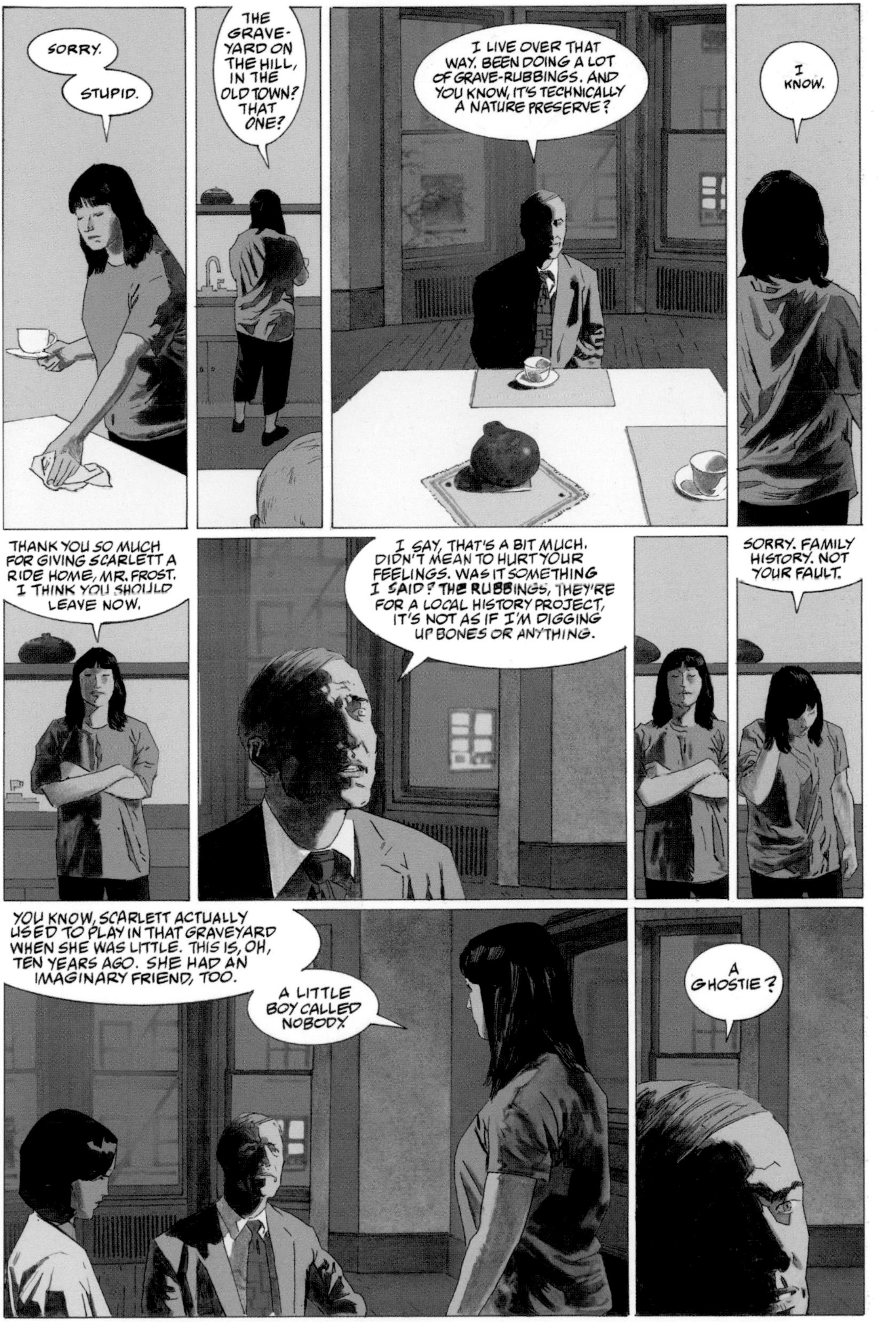
SORRY.
STUPID.
THE GRAVE-YARD ON THE HILL, IN THE OLD TOWN? THAT ONE?
I LIVE OVER THAT WAY. BEEN DOING A LOT OF GRAVE-RUBBINGS. AND YOU KNOW, IT'S TECHNICALLY A NATURE PRESERVE?
I KNOW.
THANK YOU SO MUCH FOR GIVING SCARLETT A RIDE HOME, MR. FROST. I THINK YOU SHOULD LEAVE NOW.
I SAY, THAT'S A BIT MUCH. DIDN'T MEAN TO HURT YOUR FEELINGS. WAS IT SOMETHING I SAID? THE RUBBINGS, THEY'RE FOR A LOCAL HISTORY PROJECT, IT'S NOT AS IF I'M DIGGING UP BONES OR ANYTHING.
SORRY. FAMILY HISTORY. NOT YOUR FAULT.
YOU KNOW, SCARLETT ACTUALLY USED TO PLAY IN THAT GRAVEYARD WHEN SHE WAS LITTLE. THIS IS, OH, TEN YEARS AGO. SHE HAD AN IMAGINARY FRIEND, TOO.
A LITTLE BOY CALLED NOBODY.
A GHOSTIE?

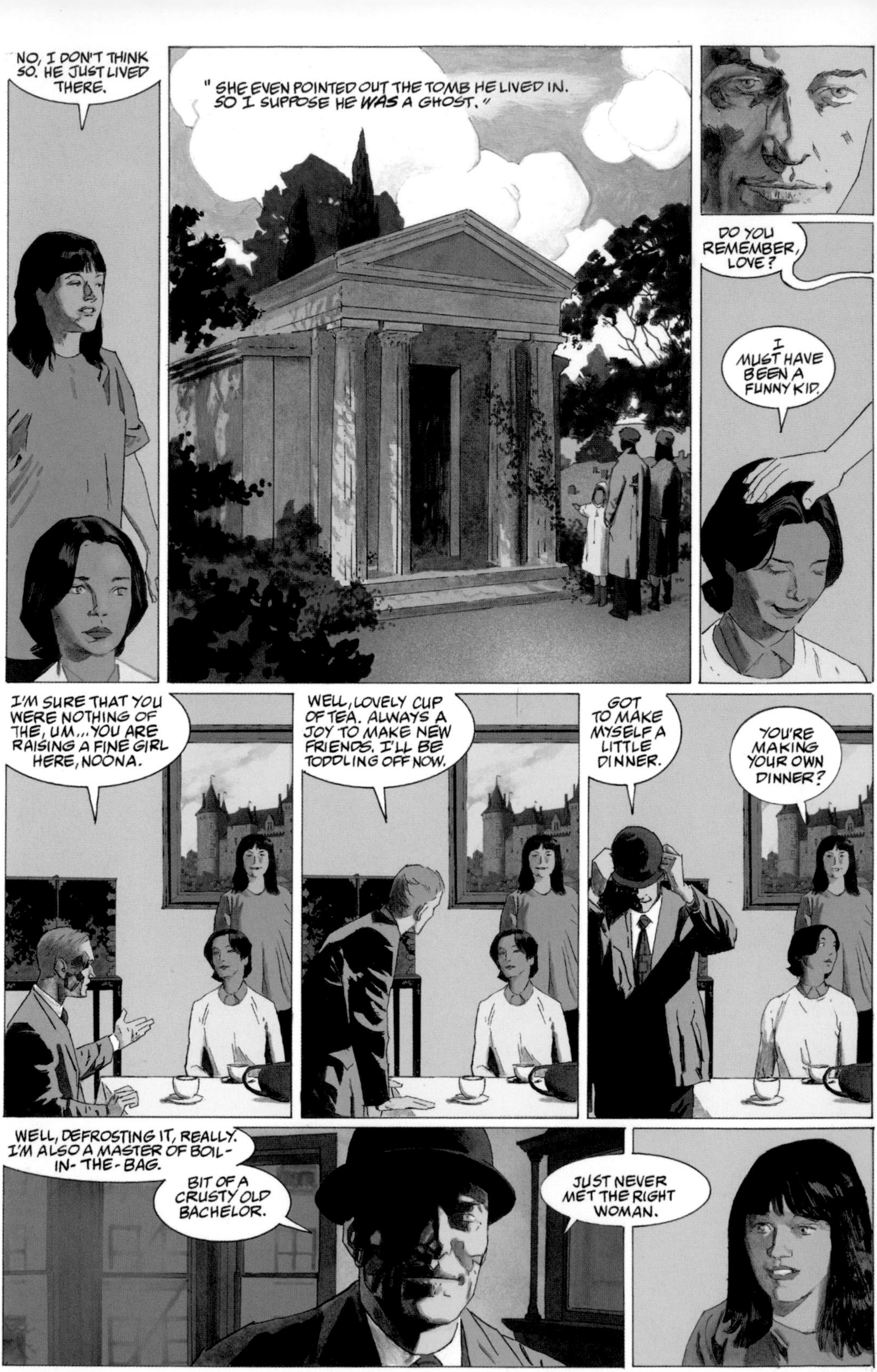
NO, I DON'T THINK SO. HE JUST LIVED THERE.
"SHE EVEN POINTED OUT THE TOMB HE LIVED IN. SO I SUPPOSE HE WAS A GHOST."
DO YOU REMEMBER, LOVE?
I MUST HAVE BEEN A FUNNY KID.
I'M SURE THAT YOU WERE NOTHING OF THE, UM... YOU ARE RAISING A FINE GIRL HERE, NOONA.
WELL, LOVELY CUP OF TEA. ALWAYS A JOY TO MAKE NEW FRIENDS. I'LL BE TODDLING OFF NOW.
GOT TO MAKE MYSELF A LITTLE DINNER.
YOU'RE MAKING YOUR OWN DINNER?
WELL, DEFROSTING IT, REALLY. I'M ALSO A MASTER OF BOIL-IN-THE-BAG.
BIT OF A CRUSTY OLD BACHELOR.
JUST NEVER MET THE RIGHT WOMAN.

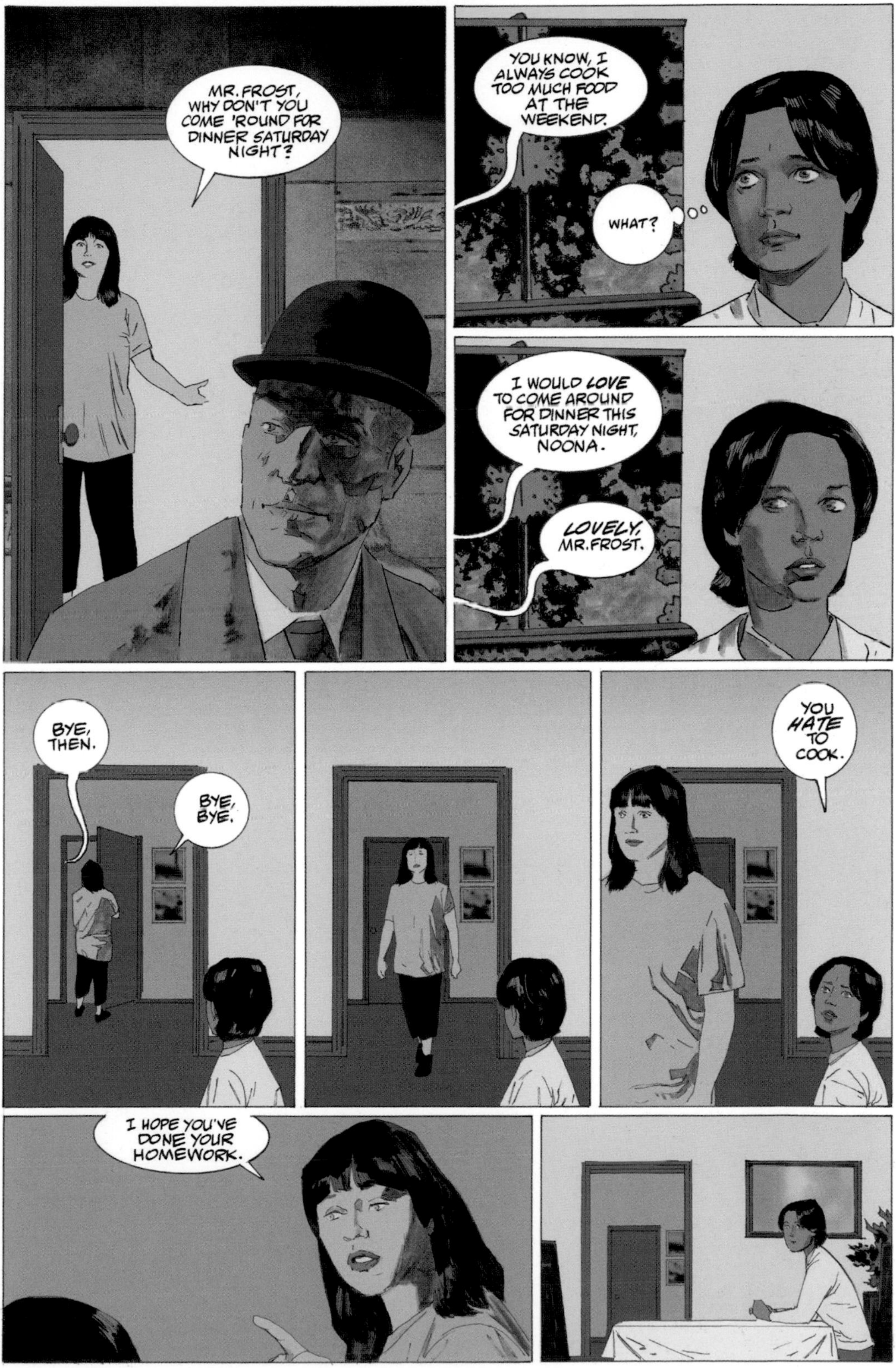
MR. FROST, WHY DON'T YOU COME 'ROUND FOR DINNER SATURDAY NIGHT?
YOU KNOW, I ALWAYS COOK TOO MUCH FOOD AT THE WEEKEND.
WHAT?
I WOULD *LOVE* TO COME AROUND FOR DINNER THIS SATURDAY NIGHT, NOONA.
LOVELY, MR. FROST.
BYE, THEN.
BYE, BYE.
YOU *HATE* TO COOK.
I HOPE YOU'VE DONE YOUR HOMEWORK.

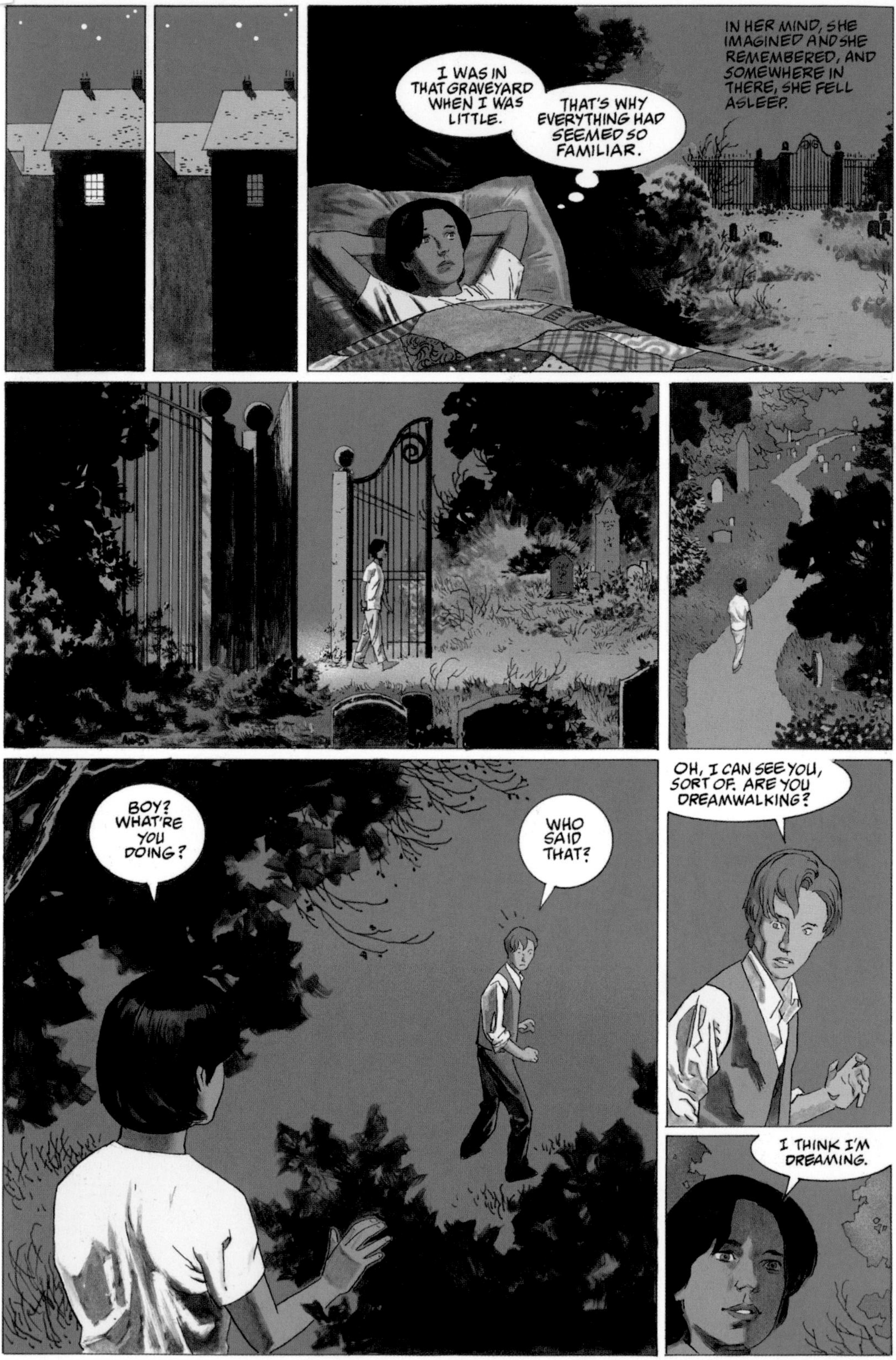
I WAS IN THAT GRAVEYARD WHEN I WAS LITTLE.
THAT'S WHY EVERYTHING HAD SEEMED SO FAMILIAR.
IN HER MIND, SHE IMAGINED AND SHE REMEMBERED, AND SOMEWHERE IN THERE, SHE FELL ASLEEP.
BOY? WHAT'RE YOU DOING?
WHO SAID THAT?
OH, I CAN SEE YOU, SORT OF. ARE YOU DREAMWALKING?
I THINK I'M DREAMING.

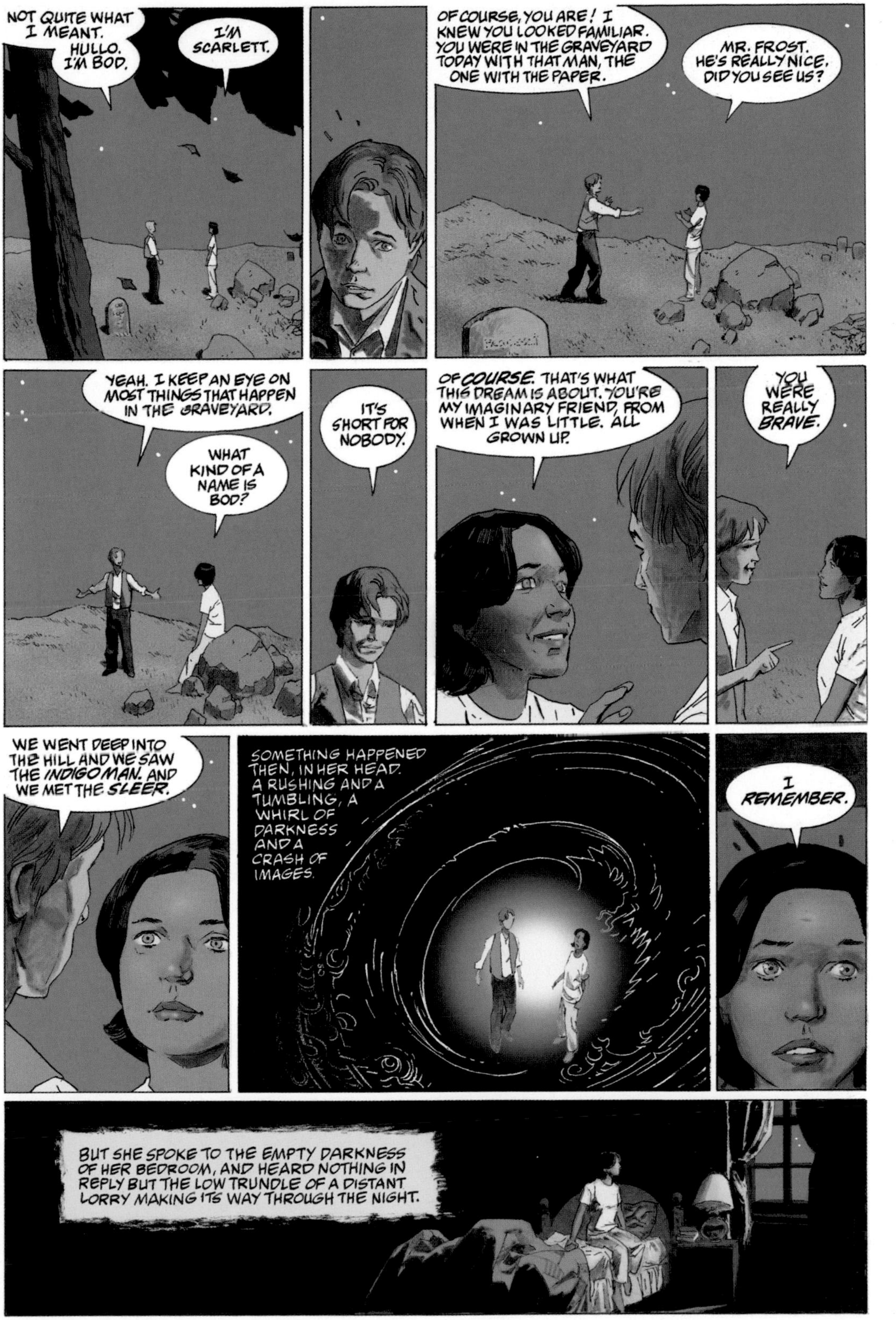

NOT QUITE WHAT I MEANT. HULLO. I'M BOD.
I'M SCARLETT.
OF COURSE, YOU ARE! I KNEW YOU LOOKED FAMILIAR. YOU WERE IN THE GRAVEYARD TODAY WITH THAT MAN, THE ONE WITH THE PAPER.
MR. FROST. HE'S REALLY NICE. DID YOU SEE US?
YEAH. I KEEP AN EYE ON MOST THINGS THAT HAPPEN IN THE GRAVEYARD.
WHAT KIND OF A NAME IS BOD?
IT'S SHORT FOR NOBODY.
OF COURSE. THAT'S WHAT THIS DREAM IS ABOUT. YOU'RE MY IMAGINARY FRIEND, FROM WHEN I WAS LITTLE. ALL GROWN UP.
YOU WERE REALLY BRAVE.
WE WENT DEEP INTO THE HILL AND WE SAW THE INDIGO MAN. AND WE MET THE SLEER.
SOMETHING HAPPENED THEN, IN HER HEAD. A RUSHING AND A TUMBLING, A WHIRL OF DARKNESS AND A CRASH OF IMAGES.
I REMEMBER.
BUT SHE SPOKE TO THE EMPTY DARKNESS OF HER BEDROOM, AND HEARD NOTHING IN REPLY BUT THE LOW TRUNDLE OF A DISTANT LORRY MAKING ITS WAY THROUGH THE NIGHT.

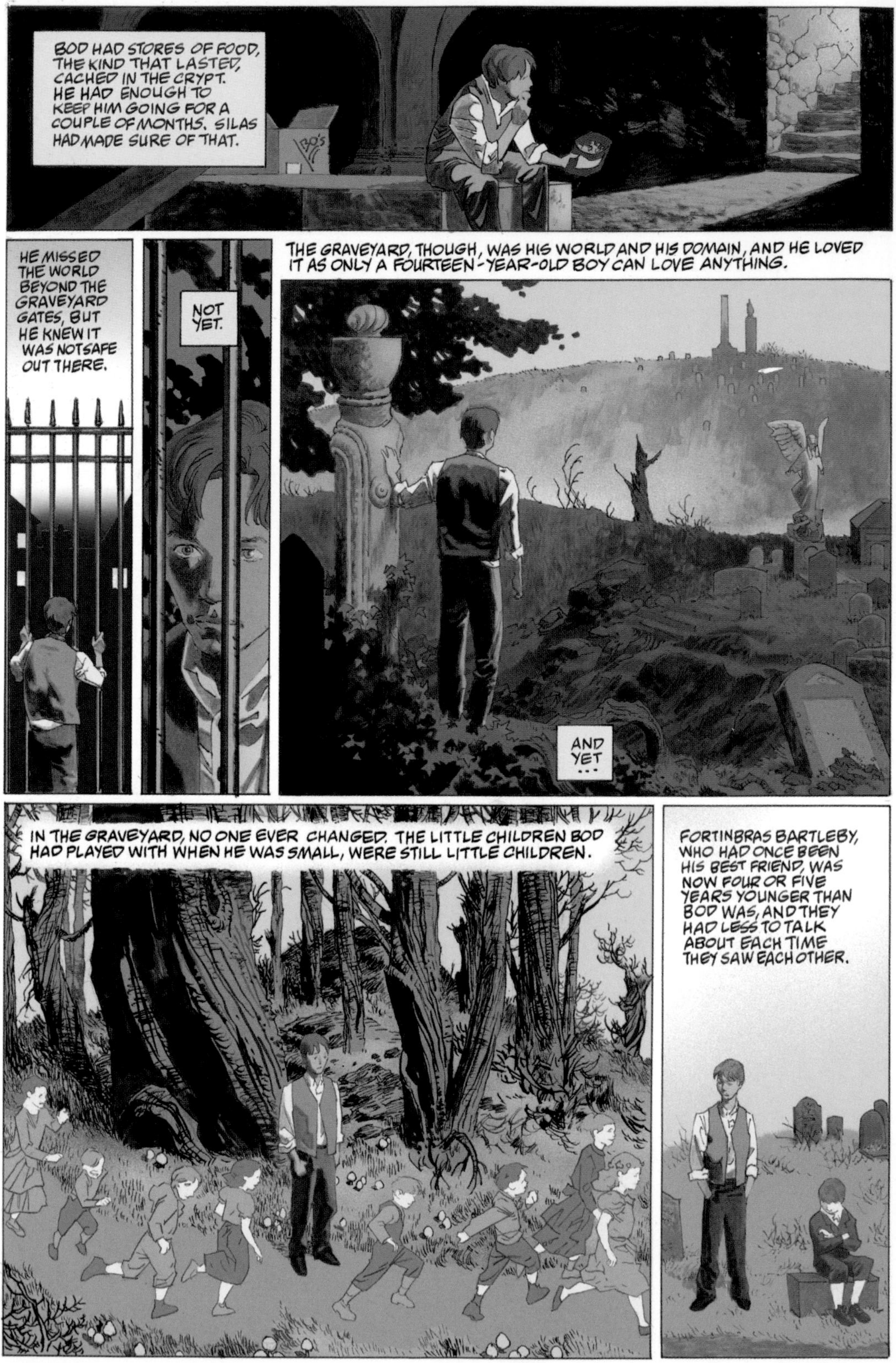
BOD HAD STORES OF FOOD, THE KIND THAT LASTED, CACHED IN THE CRYPT. HE HAD ENOUGH TO KEEP HIM GOING FOR A COUPLE OF MONTHS. SILAS HAD MADE SURE OF THAT.
BOD'S
HE MISSED THE WORLD BEYOND THE GRAVEYARD GATES, BUT HE KNEW IT WAS NOT SAFE OUT THERE.
NOT YET.
THE GRAVEYARD, THOUGH, WAS HIS WORLD AND HIS DOMAIN, AND HE LOVED IT AS ONLY A FOURTEEN-YEAR-OLD BOY CAN LOVE ANYTHING.
AND YET ...
IN THE GRAVEYARD, NO ONE EVER CHANGED. THE LITTLE CHILDREN BOD HAD PLAYED WITH WHEN HE WAS SMALL, WERE STILL LITTLE CHILDREN.
FORTINBRAS BARTLEBY, WHO HAD ONCE BEEN HIS BEST FRIEND, WAS NOW FOUR OR FIVE YEARS YOUNGER THAN BOD WAS, AND THEY HAD LESS TO TALK ABOUT EACH TIME THEY SAW EACH OTHER.

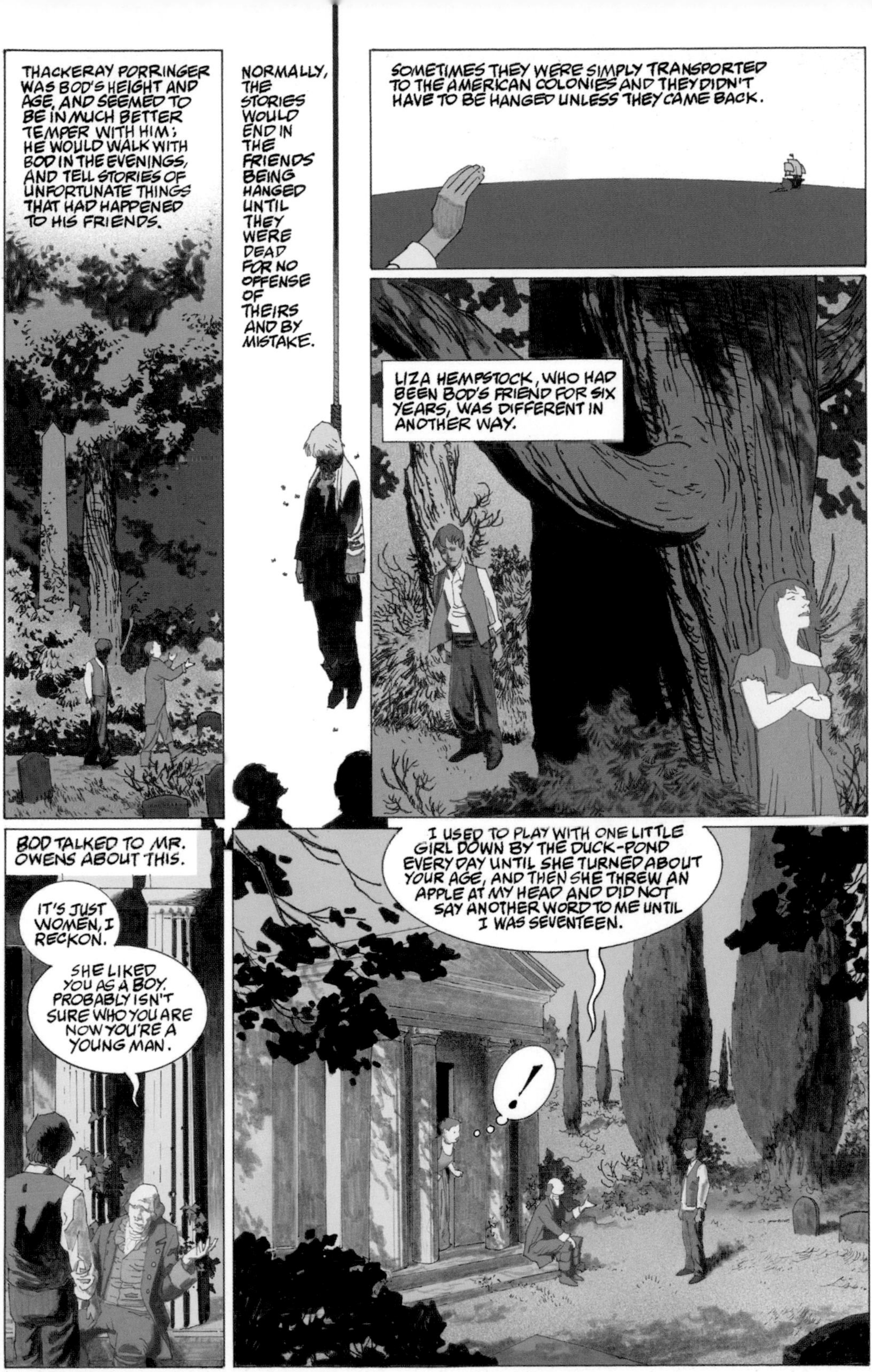

THACKERAY PORRINGER WAS BOD'S HEIGHT AND AGE, AND SEEMED TO BE IN MUCH BETTER TEMPER WITH HIM; HE WOULD WALK WITH BOD IN THE EVENINGS, AND TELL STORIES OF UNFORTUNATE THINGS THAT HAD HAPPENED TO HIS FRIENDS.
NORMALLY, THE STORIES WOULD END IN THE FRIENDS BEING HANGED UNTIL THEY WERE DEAD FOR NO OFFENSE OF THEIRS AND BY MISTAKE.
SOMETIMES THEY WERE SIMPLY TRANSPORTED TO THE AMERICAN COLONIES AND THEY DIDN'T HAVE TO BE HANGED UNLESS THEY CAME BACK.
LIZA HEMPSTOCK, WHO HAD BEEN BOD'S FRIEND FOR SIX YEARS, WAS DIFFERENT IN ANOTHER WAY.
BOD TALKED TO MR. OWENS ABOUT THIS.
IT'S JUST WOMEN, I RECKON.
SHE LIKED YOU AS A BOY. PROBABLY ISN'T SURE WHO YOU ARE NOW YOU'RE A YOUNG MAN.
I USED TO PLAY WITH ONE LITTLE GIRL DOWN BY THE DUCK-POND EVERY DAY UNTIL SHE TURNED ABOUT YOUR AGE, AND THEN SHE THREW AN APPLE AT MY HEAD AND DID NOT SAY ANOTHER WORD TO ME UNTIL I WAS SEVENTEEN.
!

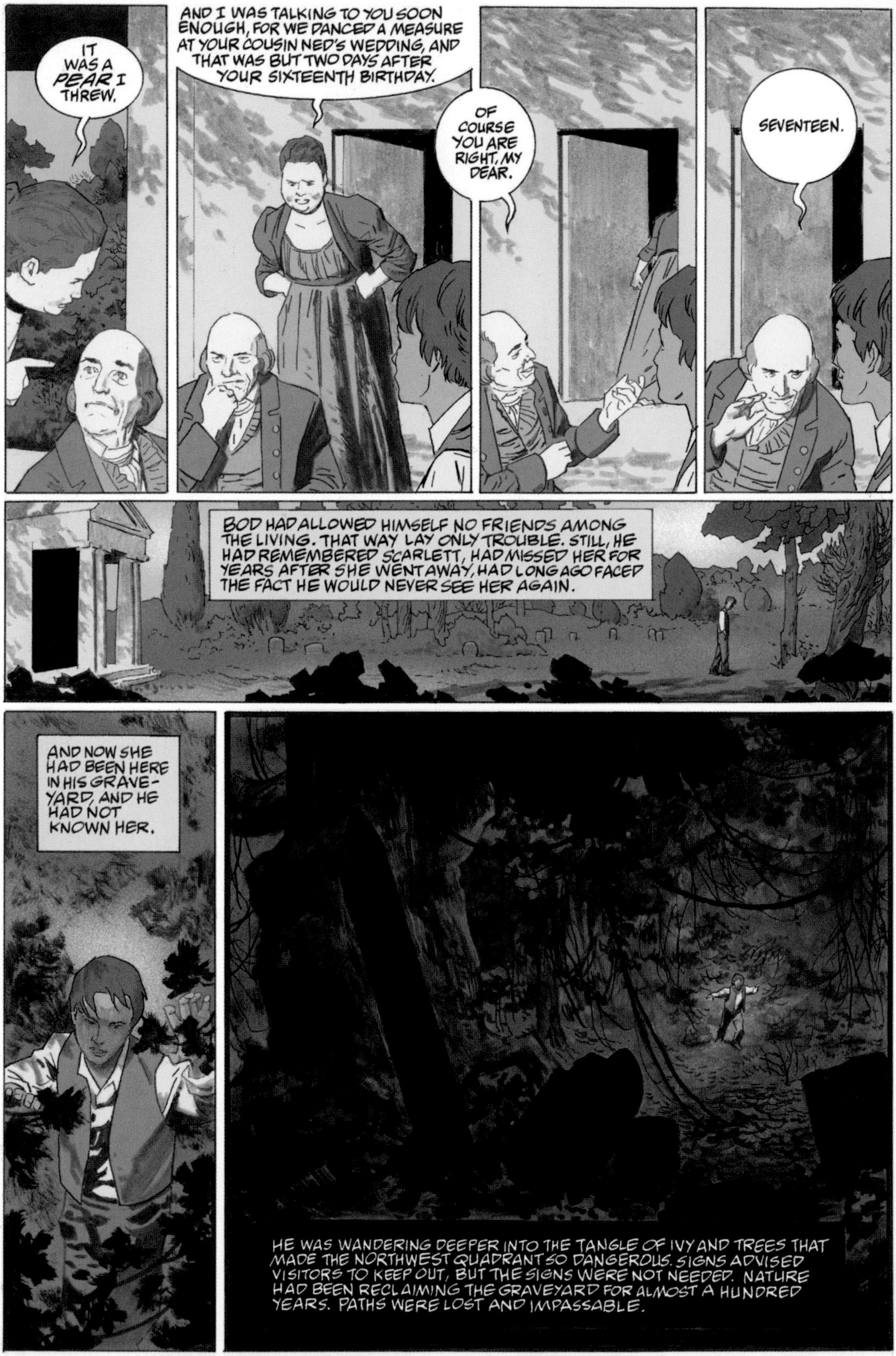
IT WAS A PEAR I THREW.
AND I WAS TALKING TO YOU SOON ENOUGH, FOR WE DANCED A MEASURE AT YOUR COUSIN NED'S WEDDING, AND THAT WAS BUT TWO DAYS AFTER YOUR SIXTEENTH BIRTHDAY.
OF COURSE YOU ARE RIGHT, MY DEAR.
SEVENTEEN.
BOD HAD ALLOWED HIMSELF NO FRIENDS AMONG THE LIVING. THAT WAY LAY ONLY TROUBLE. STILL, HE HAD REMEMBERED SCARLETT, HAD MISSED HER FOR YEARS AFTER SHE WENT AWAY, HAD LONG AGO FACED THE FACT HE WOULD NEVER SEE HER AGAIN.
AND NOW SHE HAD BEEN HERE IN HIS GRAVEYARD, AND HE HAD NOT KNOWN HER.
HE WAS WANDERING DEEPER INTO THE TANGLE OF IVY AND TREES THAT MADE THE NORTHWEST QUADRANT SO DANGEROUS. SIGNS ADVISED VISITORS TO KEEP OUT, BUT THE SIGNS WERE NOT NEEDED. NATURE HAD BEEN RECLAIMING THE GRAVEYARD FOR ALMOST A HUNDRED YEARS. PATHS WERE LOST AND IMPASSABLE.

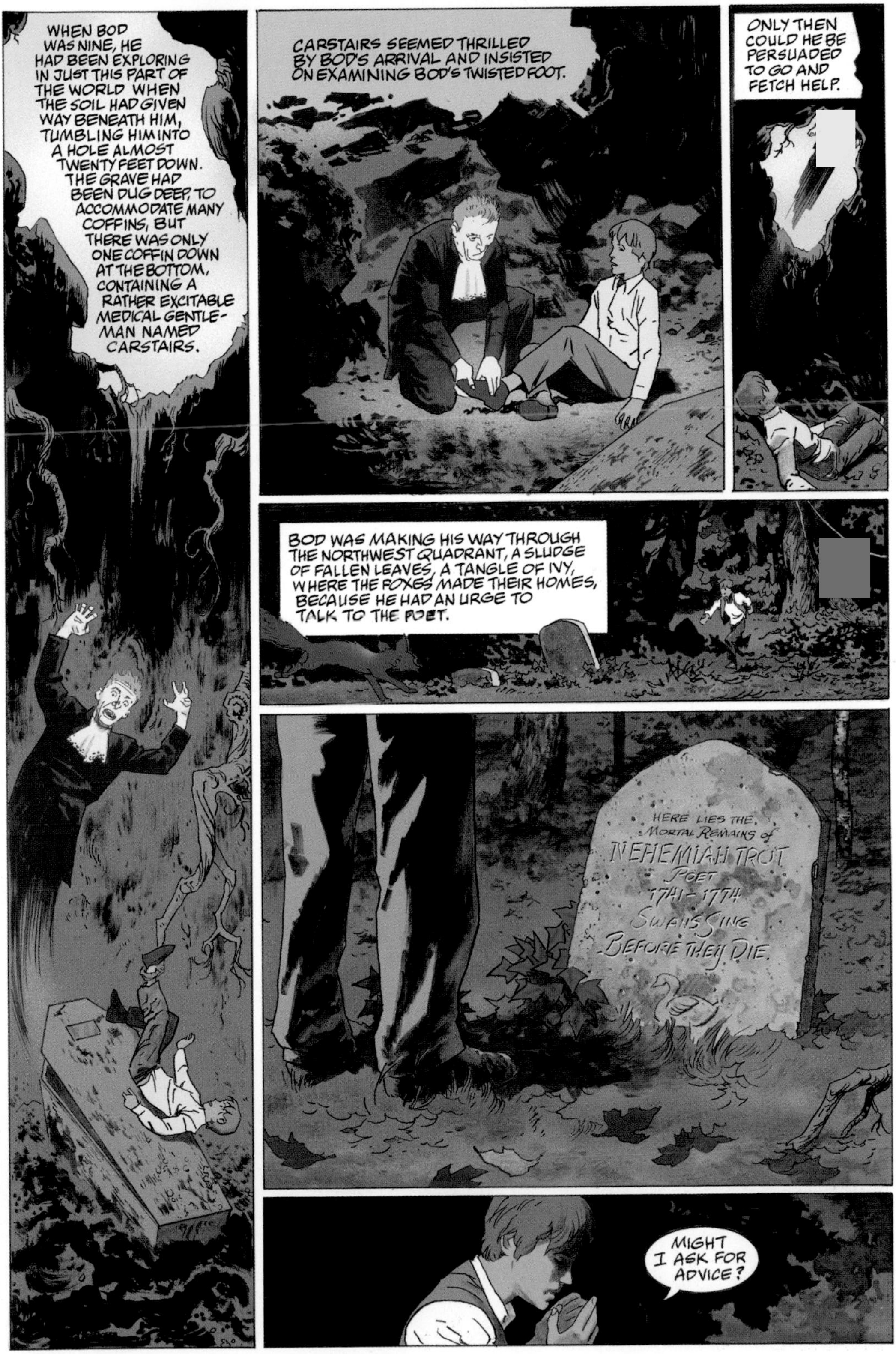
WHEN BOD WAS NINE, HE HAD BEEN EXPLORING IN JUST THIS PART OF THE WORLD WHEN THE SOIL HAD GIVEN WAY BENEATH HIM, TUMBLING HIM INTO A HOLE ALMOST TWENTY FEET DOWN. THE GRAVE HAD BEEN DUG DEEP, TO ACCOMMODATE MANY COFFINS, BUT THERE WAS ONLY ONE COFFIN DOWN AT THE BOTTOM, CONTAINING A RATHER EXCITABLE MEDICAL GENTLE-MAN NAMED CARSTAIRS.
CARSTAIRS SEEMED THRILLED BY BOD'S ARRIVAL AND INSISTED ON EXAMINING BOD'S TWISTED FOOT.
ONLY THEN COULD HE BE PERSUADED TO GO AND FETCH HELP.
BOD WAS MAKING HIS WAY THROUGH THE NORTHWEST QUADRANT, A SLUDGE OF FALLEN LEAVES, A TANGLE OF IVY, WHERE THE FOXES MADE THEIR HOMES, BECAUSE HE HAD AN URGE TO TALK TO THE POET.
HERE LIES THE MORTAL REMAINS of NEHEMIAH TROT POET 1741 - 1774 SWANS SING BEFORE THEY DIE.
MIGHT I ASK FOR ADVICE?

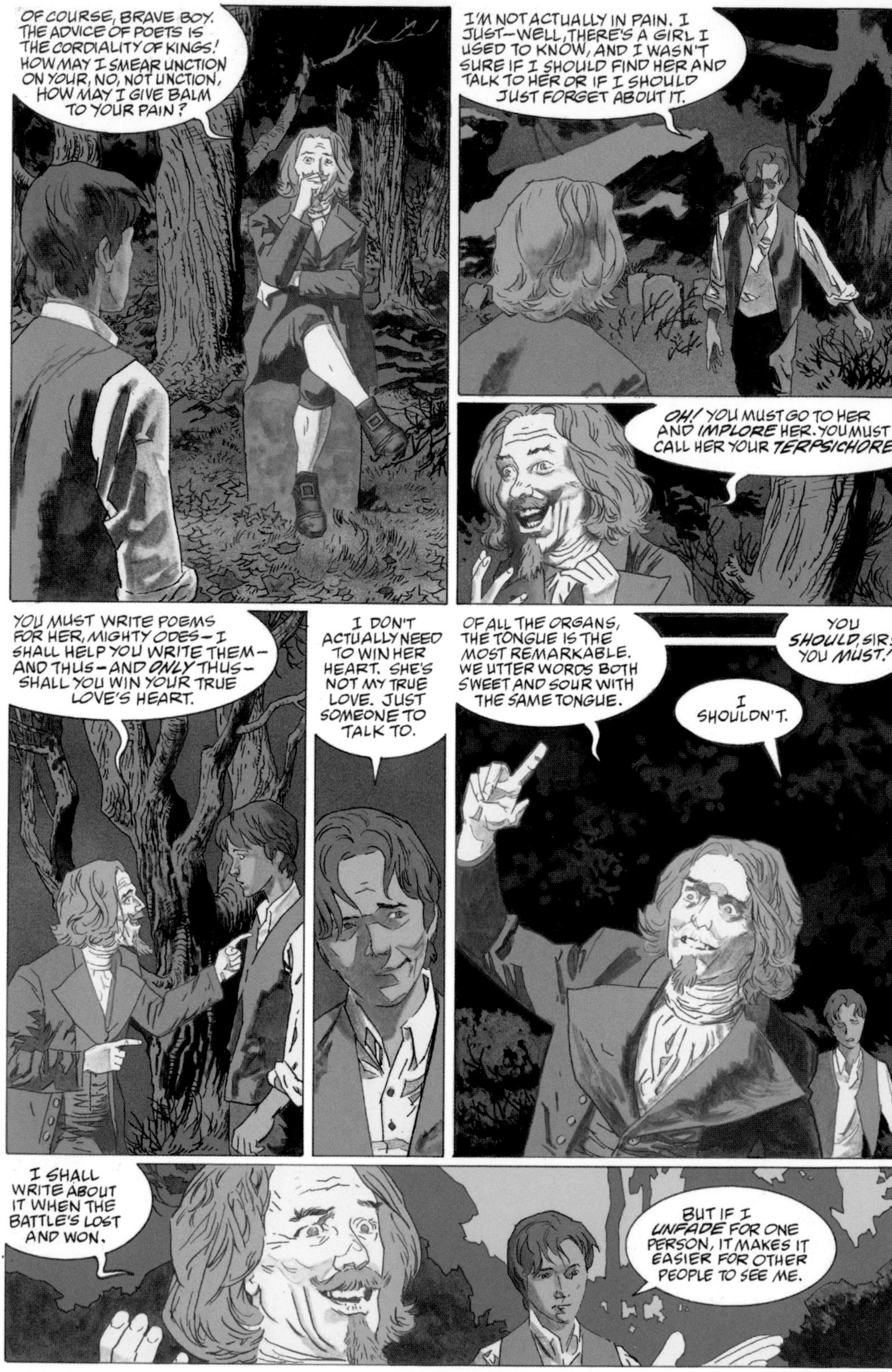
OF COURSE, BRAVE BOY. THE ADVICE OF POETS IS THE CORDIALITY OF KINGS! HOW MAY I SMEAR UNCTION ON YOUR, NO, NOT UNCTION, HOW MAY I GIVE BALM TO YOUR PAIN?
I'M NOT ACTUALLY IN PAIN. I JUST—WELL, THERE'S A GIRL I USED TO KNOW, AND I WASN'T SURE IF I SHOULD FIND HER AND TALK TO HER OR IF I SHOULD JUST FORGET ABOUT IT.
OH! YOU MUST GO TO HER AND IMPLORE HER. YOU MUST CALL HER YOUR TERPSICHORE.
YOU MUST WRITE POEMS FOR HER, MIGHTY ODES—I SHALL HELP YOU WRITE THEM—AND THUS—AND ONLY THUS—SHALL YOU WIN YOUR TRUE LOVE'S HEART.
I DON'T ACTUALLY NEED TO WIN HER HEART. SHE'S NOT MY TRUE LOVE. JUST SOMEONE TO TALK TO.
OF ALL THE ORGANS, THE TONGUE IS THE MOST REMARKABLE. WE UTTER WORDS BOTH SWEET AND SOUR WITH THE SAME TONGUE.
YOU SHOULD, SIR! YOU MUST!
I SHOULDN'T.
I SHALL WRITE ABOUT IT WHEN THE BATTLE'S LOST AND WON.
BUT IF I UNFADE FOR ONE PERSON, IT MAKES IT EASIER FOR OTHER PEOPLE TO SEE ME.

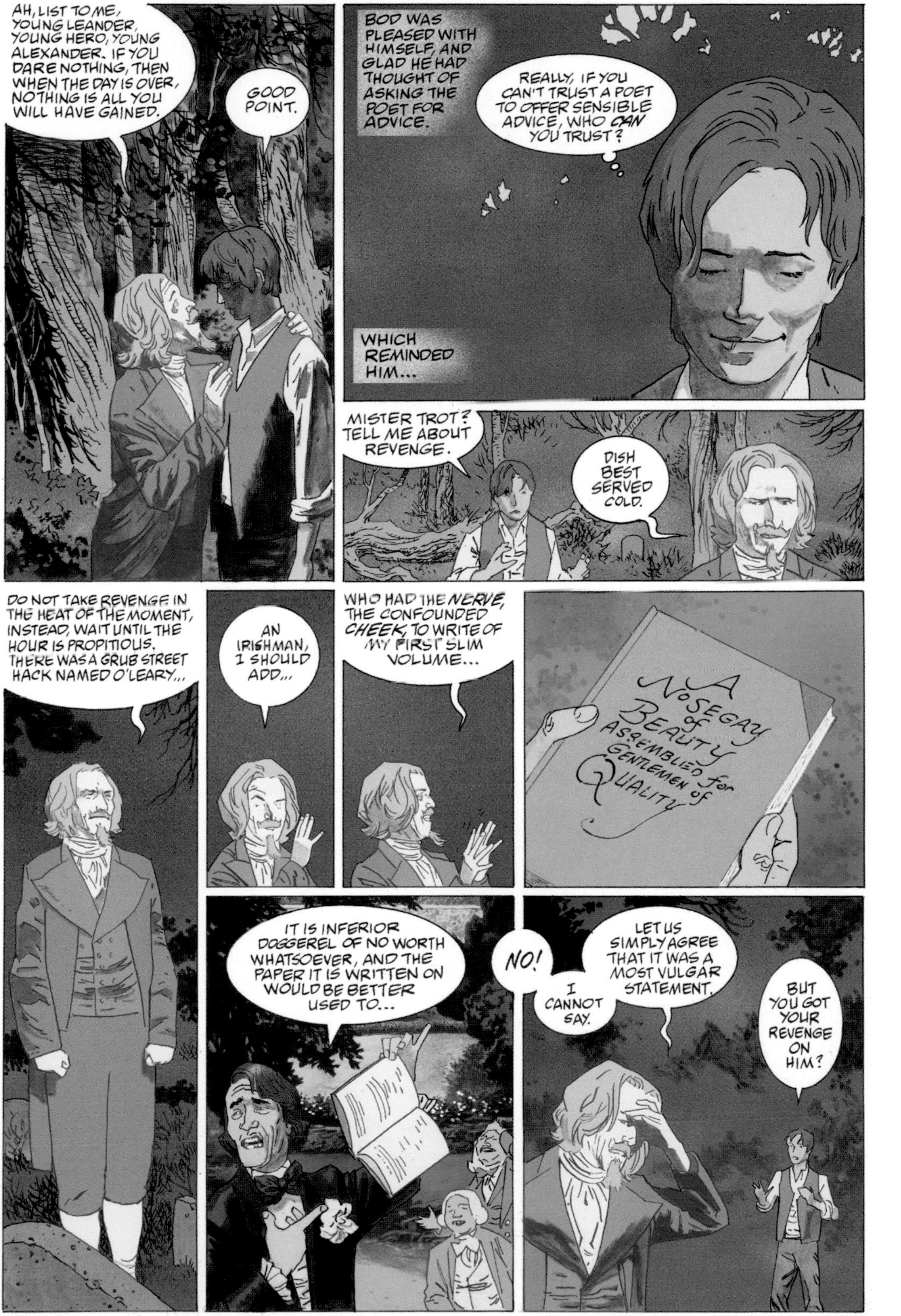
AH, LIST TO ME, YOUNG LEANDER, YOUNG HERO, YOUNG ALEXANDER. IF YOU DARE NOTHING, THEN WHEN THE DAY IS OVER, NOTHING IS ALL YOU WILL HAVE GAINED.
GOOD POINT.
BOD WAS PLEASED WITH HIMSELF, AND GLAD HE HAD THOUGHT OF ASKING THE POET FOR ADVICE.
REALLY, IF YOU CAN'T TRUST A POET TO OFFER SENSIBLE ADVICE, WHO CAN YOU TRUST?
WHICH REMINDED HIM...
MISTER TROT? TELL ME ABOUT REVENGE.
DISH BEST SERVED COLD.
DO NOT TAKE REVENGE IN THE HEAT OF THE MOMENT, INSTEAD, WAIT UNTIL THE HOUR IS PROPITIOUS. THERE WAS A GRUB STREET HACK NAMED O'LEARY...
AN IRISHMAN, I SHOULD ADD...
WHO HAD THE NERVE, THE CONFOUNDED CHEEK, TO WRITE OF MY FIRST SLIM VOLUME...
A Nosegay of Beauty Assembled for Gentlemen of Quality
IT IS INFERIOR DOGGEREL OF NO WORTH WHATSOEVER, AND THE PAPER IT IS WRITTEN ON WOULD BE BETTER USED TO...
NO!
I CANNOT SAY.
LET US SIMPLY AGREE THAT IT WAS A MOST VULGAR STATEMENT.
BUT YOU GOT YOUR REVENGE ON HIM?

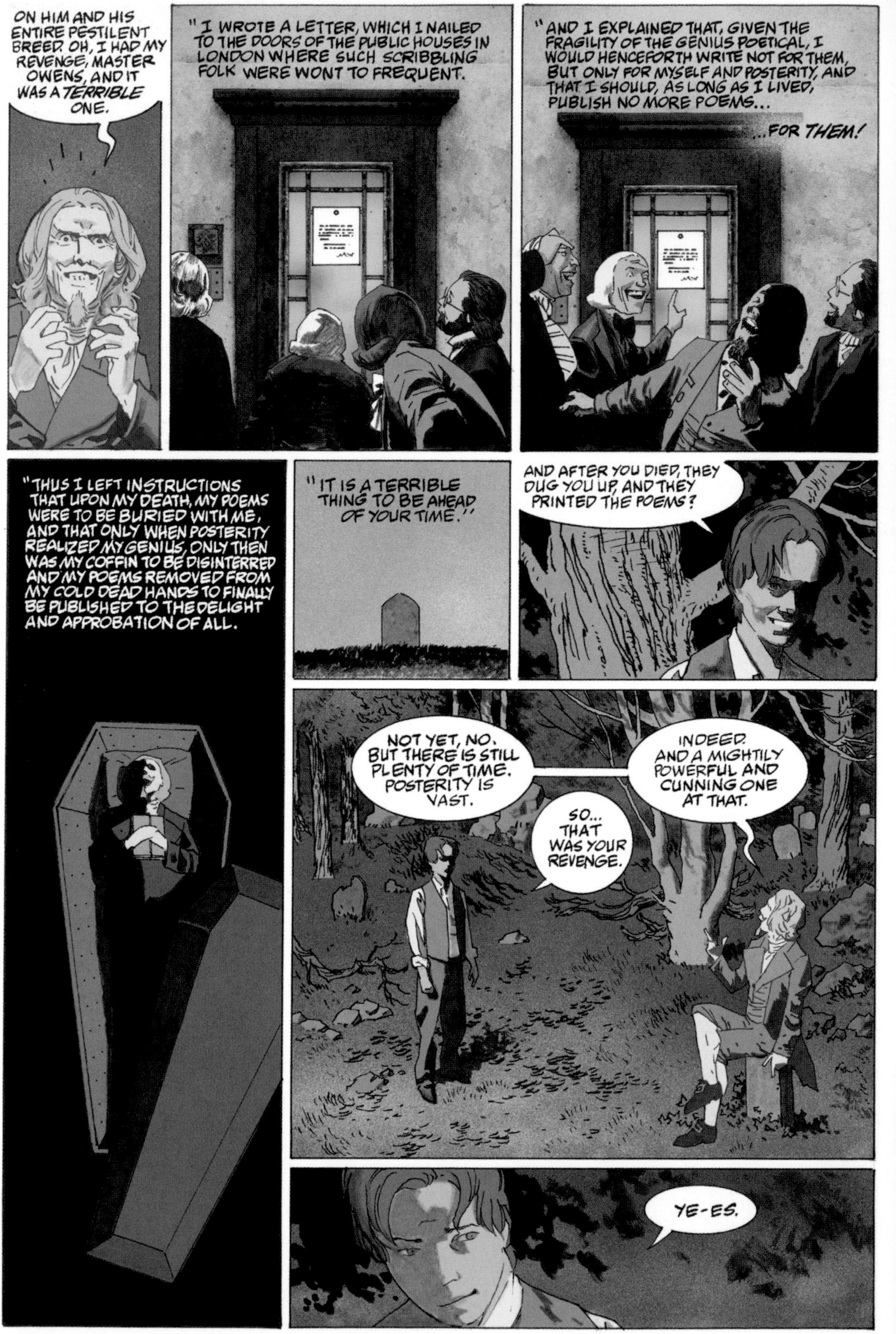
ON HIM AND HIS ENTIRE PESTILENT BREED. OH, I HAD MY REVENGE, MASTER OWENS, AND IT WAS A TERRIBLE ONE.
"I WROTE A LETTER, WHICH I NAILED TO THE DOORS OF THE PUBLIC HOUSES IN LONDON WHERE SUCH SCRIBBLING FOLK WERE WONT TO FREQUENT.
"AND I EXPLAINED THAT, GIVEN THE FRAGILITY OF THE GENIUS POETICAL, I WOULD HENCEFORTH WRITE NOT FOR THEM, BUT ONLY FOR MYSELF AND POSTERITY, AND THAT I SHOULD, AS LONG AS I LIVED, PUBLISH NO MORE POEMS...
...FOR THEM!
"THUS I LEFT INSTRUCTIONS THAT UPON MY DEATH, MY POEMS WERE TO BE BURIED WITH ME, AND THAT ONLY WHEN POSTERITY REALIZED MY GENIUS, ONLY THEN WAS MY COFFIN TO BE DISINTERRED AND MY POEMS REMOVED FROM MY COLD DEAD HANDS TO FINALLY BE PUBLISHED TO THE DELIGHT AND APPROBATION OF ALL.
"IT IS A TERRIBLE THING TO BE AHEAD OF YOUR TIME."
AND AFTER YOU DIED, THEY DUG YOU UP, AND THEY PRINTED THE POEMS?
NOT YET, NO. BUT THERE IS STILL PLENTY OF TIME. POSTERITY IS VAST.
SO... THAT WAS YOUR REVENGE.
INDEED. AND A MIGHTILY POWERFUL AND CUNNING ONE AT THAT.
YE-ES.

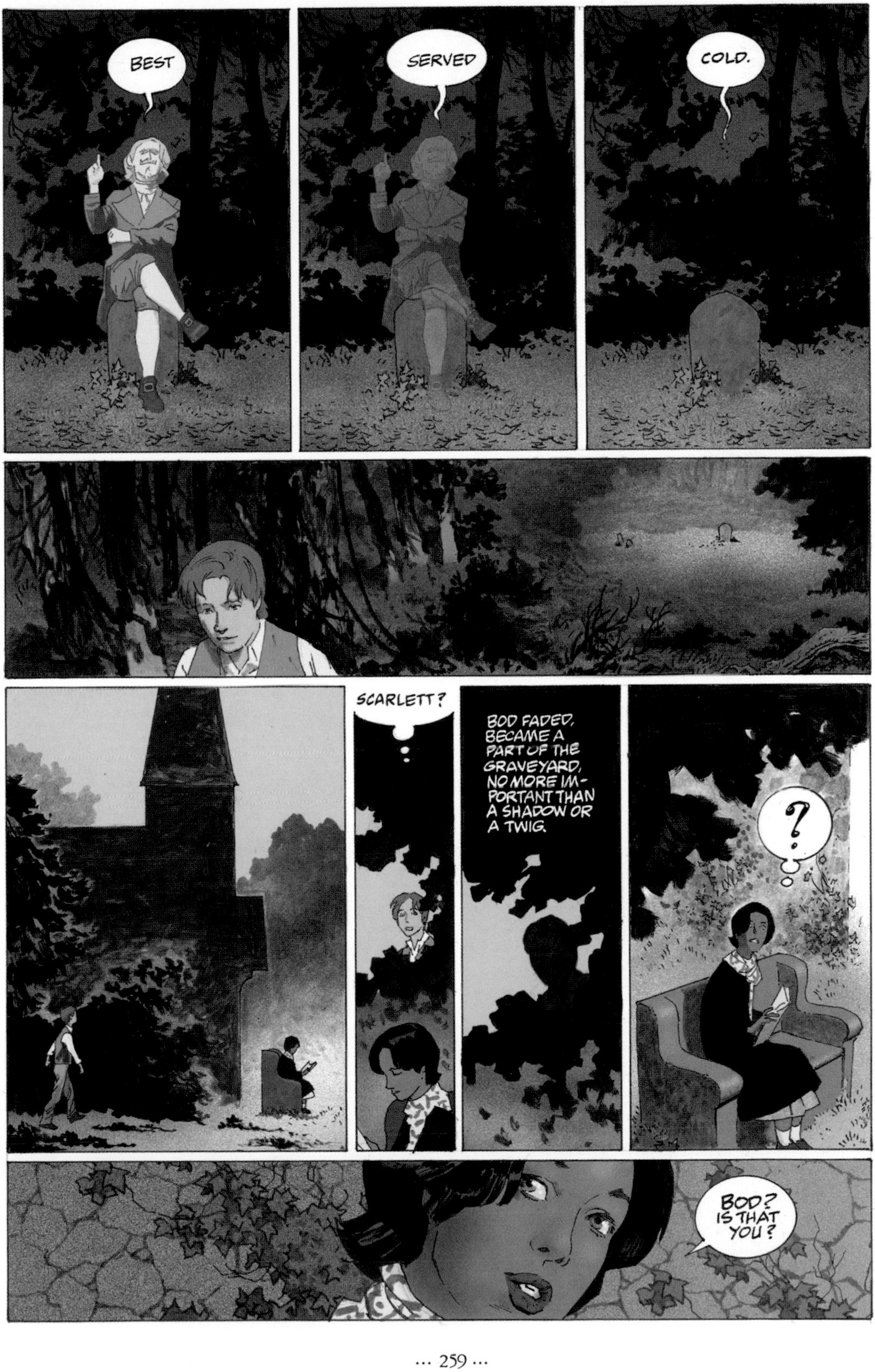
BEST
SERVED
COLD.
SCARLETT?
BOD FADED, BECAME A PART OF THE GRAVEYARD, NO MORE IM-PORTANT THAN A SHADOW OR A TWIG.
?
BOD? IS THAT YOU?

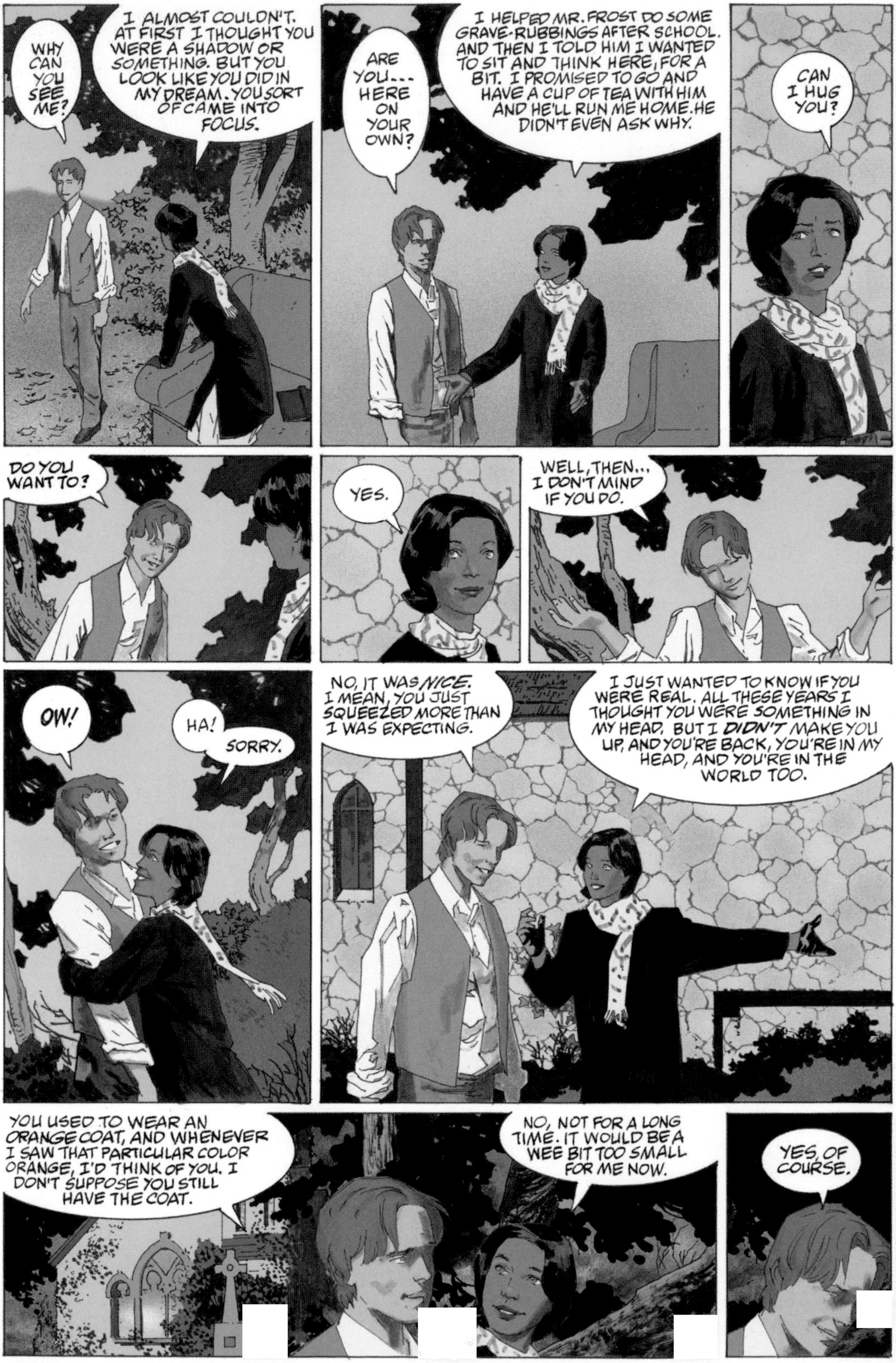
WHY CAN YOU SEE ME?
I ALMOST COULDN'T. AT FIRST I THOUGHT YOU WERE A SHADOW OR SOMETHING. BUT YOU LOOK LIKE YOU DID IN MY DREAM. YOU SORT OF CAME INTO FOCUS.
ARE YOU... HERE ON YOUR OWN?
I HELPED MR. FROST DO SOME GRAVE-RUBBINGS AFTER SCHOOL. AND THEN I TOLD HIM I WANTED TO SIT AND THINK HERE, FOR A BIT. I PROMISED TO GO AND HAVE A CUP OF TEA WITH HIM AND HE'LL RUN ME HOME. HE DIDN'T EVEN ASK WHY.
CAN I HUG YOU?
DO YOU WANT TO?
YES.
WELL, THEN... I DON'T MIND IF YOU DO.
OW!
HA!
SORRY.
NO, IT WAS NICE. I MEAN, YOU JUST SQUEEZED MORE THAN I WAS EXPECTING.
I JUST WANTED TO KNOW IF YOU WERE REAL. ALL THESE YEARS I THOUGHT YOU WERE SOMETHING IN MY HEAD. BUT I DIDN'T MAKE YOU UP, AND YOU'RE BACK, YOU'RE IN MY HEAD, AND YOU'RE IN THE WORLD TOO.
YOU USED TO WEAR AN ORANGE COAT, AND WHENEVER I SAW THAT PARTICULAR COLOR ORANGE, I'D THINK OF YOU. I DON'T SUPPOSE YOU STILL HAVE THE COAT.
NO, NOT FOR A LONG TIME. IT WOULD BE A WEE BIT TOO SMALL FOR ME NOW.
YES, OF COURSE.

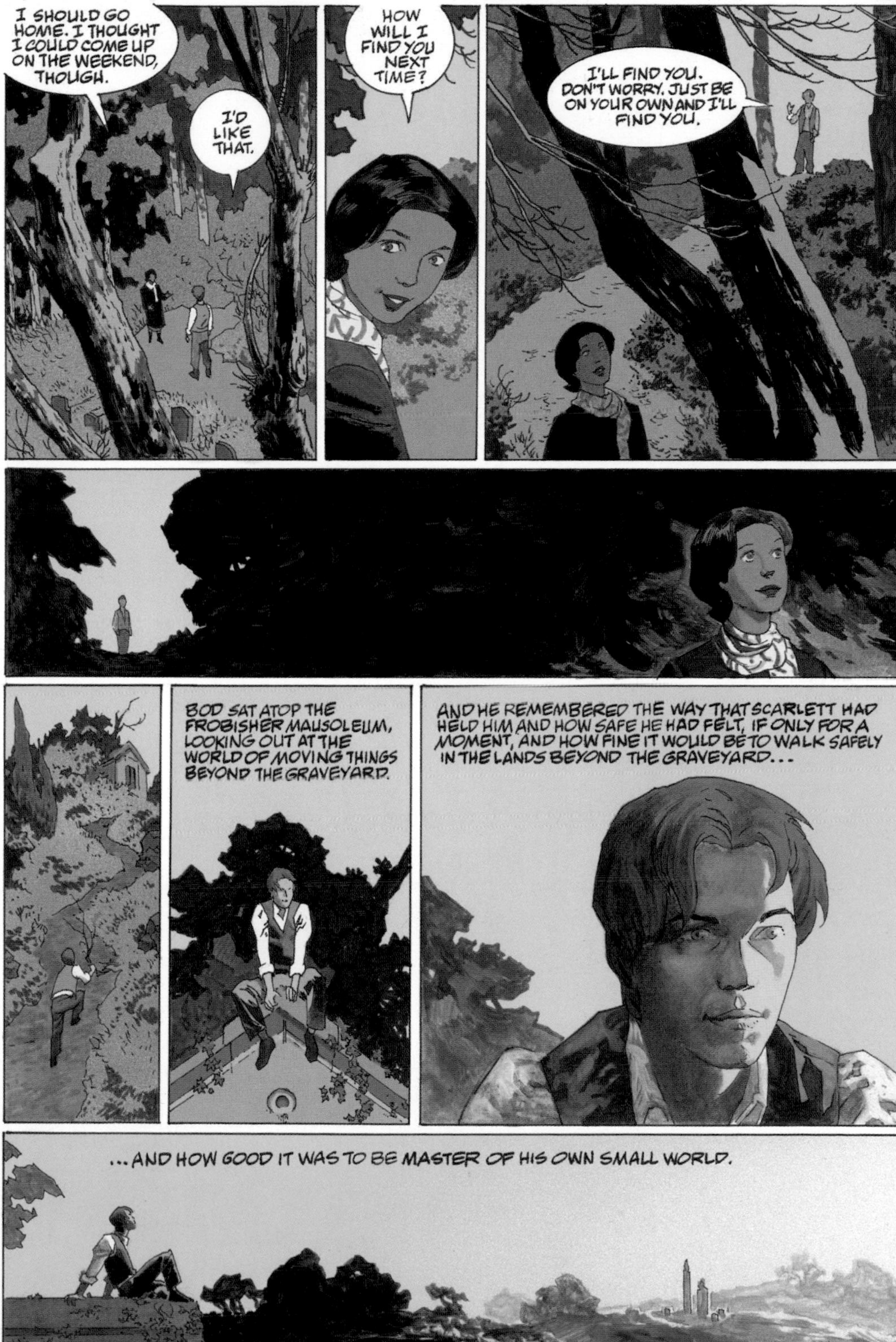
I SHOULD GO HOME. I THOUGHT I COULD COME UP ON THE WEEKEND, THOUGH.
I'D LIKE THAT.
HOW WILL I FIND YOU NEXT TIME?
I'LL FIND YOU. DON'T WORRY. JUST BE ON YOUR OWN AND I'LL FIND YOU.
BOD SAT ATOP THE FROBISHER MAUSOLEUM, LOOKING OUT AT THE WORLD OF MOVING THINGS BEYOND THE GRAVEYARD.
AND HE REMEMBERED THE WAY THAT SCARLETT HAD HELD HIM AND HOW SAFE HE HAD FELT, IF ONLY FOR A MOMENT, AND HOW FINE IT WOULD BE TO WALK SAFELY IN THE LANDS BEYOND THE GRAVEYARD...
...AND HOW GOOD IT WAS TO BE MASTER OF HIS OWN SMALL WORLD.

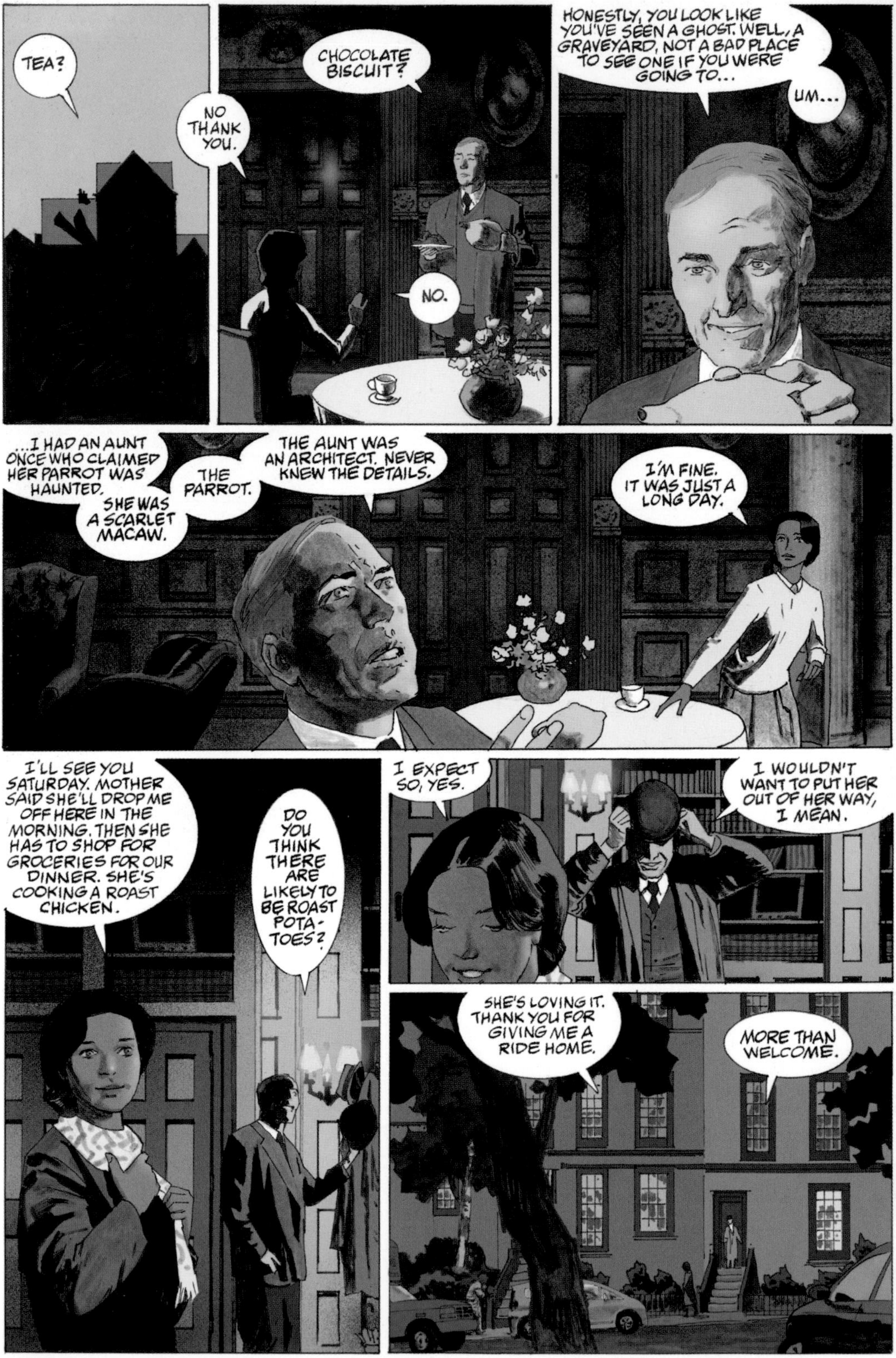
TEA?
CHOCOLATE BISCUIT?
NO THANK YOU.
NO.
HONESTLY, YOU LOOK LIKE YOU'VE SEEN A GHOST. WELL, A GRAVEYARD, NOT A BAD PLACE TO SEE ONE IF YOU WERE GOING TO...
UM...
...I HAD AN AUNT ONCE WHO CLAIMED HER PARROT WAS HAUNTED.
SHE WAS A SCARLET MACAW.
THE PARROT.
THE AUNT WAS AN ARCHITECT. NEVER KNEW THE DETAILS.
I'M FINE. IT WAS JUST A LONG DAY.
I'LL SEE YOU SATURDAY. MOTHER SAID SHE'LL DROP ME OFF HERE IN THE MORNING. THEN SHE HAS TO SHOP FOR GROCERIES FOR OUR DINNER. SHE'S COOKING A ROAST CHICKEN.
DO YOU THINK THERE ARE LIKELY TO BE ROAST POTA-TOES?
I EXPECT SO, YES.
I WOULDN'T WANT TO PUT HER OUT OF HER WAY, I MEAN.
SHE'S LOVING IT. THANK YOU FOR GIVING ME A RIDE HOME.
MORE THAN WELCOME.

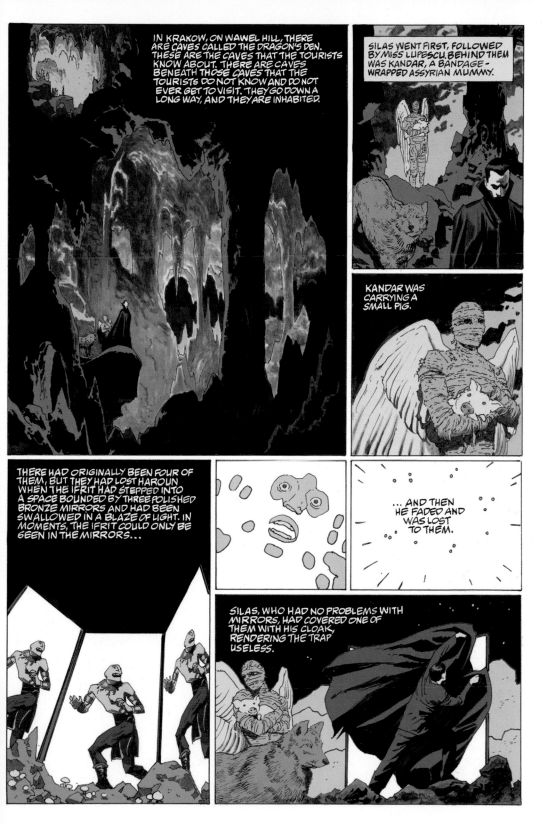

IN KRAKOW, ON WAWEL HILL, THERE ARE CAVES CALLED THE DRAGON'S DEN. THESE ARE THE CAVES THAT THE TOURISTS KNOW ABOUT. THERE ARE CAVES BENEATH THOSE CAVES THAT THE TOURISTS DO NOT KNOW AND DO NOT EVER GET TO VISIT. THEY GO DOWN A LONG WAY, AND THEY ARE INHABITED.

SILAS WENT FIRST, FOLLOWED BY MISS LUPESCU. BEHIND THEM WAS KANDAR, A BANDAGE-WRAPPED ASSYRIAN MUMMY.

KANDAR WAS CARRYING A SMALL PIG.

THERE HAD ORIGINALLY BEEN FOUR OF THEM, BUT THEY HAD LOST HAROUN WHEN THE IFRIT HAD STEPPED INTO A SPACE BOUNDED BY THREE POLISHED BRONZE MIRRORS AND HAD BEEN SWALLOWED IN A BLAZE OF LIGHT. IN MOMENTS, THE IFRIT COULD ONLY BE SEEN IN THE MIRRORS...

... AND THEN HE FADED AND WAS LOST TO THEM.

SILAS, WHO HAD NO PROBLEMS WITH MIRRORS, HAD COVERED ONE OF THEM WITH HIS CLOAK, RENDERING THE TRAP USELESS.

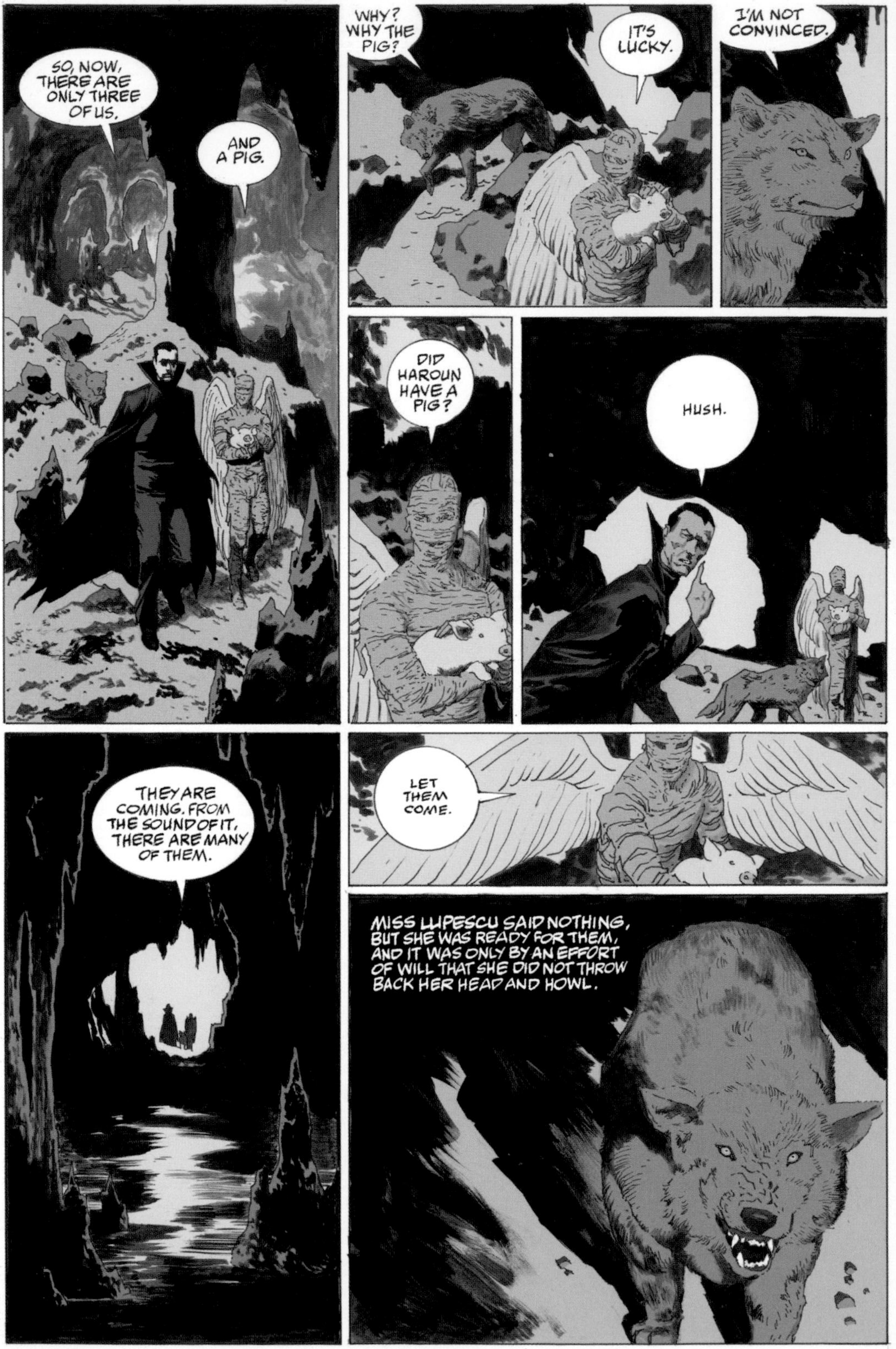
SO, NOW, THERE ARE ONLY THREE OF US.
AND A PIG.
WHY? WHY THE PIG?
IT'S LUCKY.
I'M NOT CONVINCED.
DID HAROUN HAVE A PIG?
HUSH.
THEY ARE COMING. FROM THE SOUND OF IT, THERE ARE MANY OF THEM.
LET THEM COME.
MISS LUPESCU SAID NOTHING, BUT SHE WAS READY FOR THEM, AND IT WAS ONLY BY AN EFFORT OF WILL THAT SHE DID NOT THROW BACK HER HEAD AND HOWL.

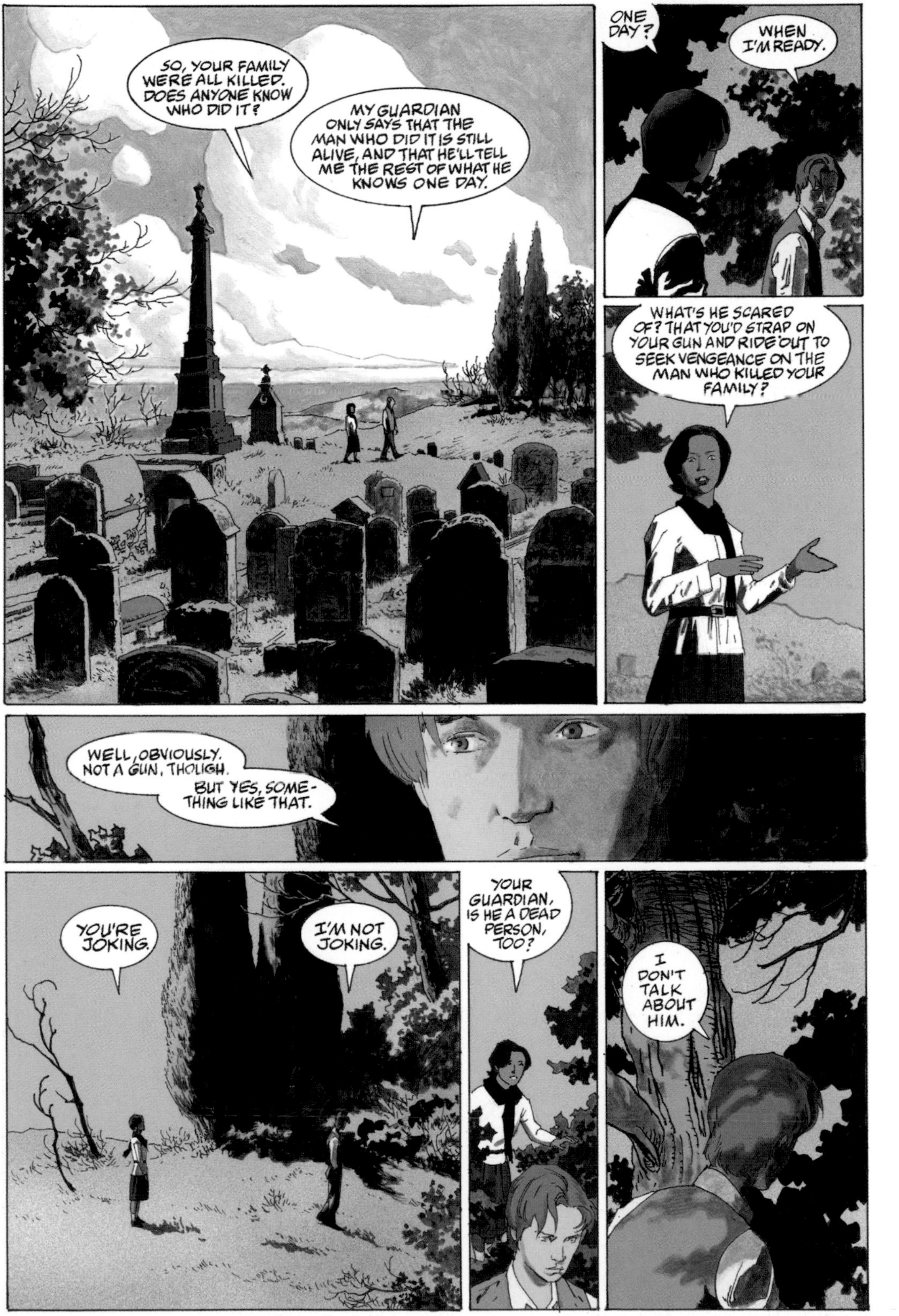
SO, YOUR FAMILY WERE ALL KILLED. DOES ANYONE KNOW WHO DID IT?
MY GUARDIAN ONLY SAYS THAT THE MAN WHO DID IT IS STILL ALIVE, AND THAT HE'LL TELL ME THE REST OF WHAT HE KNOWS ONE DAY.
ONE DAY?
WHEN I'M READY.
WHAT'S HE SCARED OF? THAT YOU'D STRAP ON YOUR GUN AND RIDE OUT TO SEEK VENGEANCE ON THE MAN WHO KILLED YOUR FAMILY?
WELL, OBVIOUSLY. NOT A GUN, THOUGH.
BUT YES, SOMETHING LIKE THAT.
YOU'RE JOKING.
I'M NOT JOKING.
YOUR GUARDIAN, IS HE A DEAD PERSON, TOO?
I DON'T TALK ABOUT HIM.

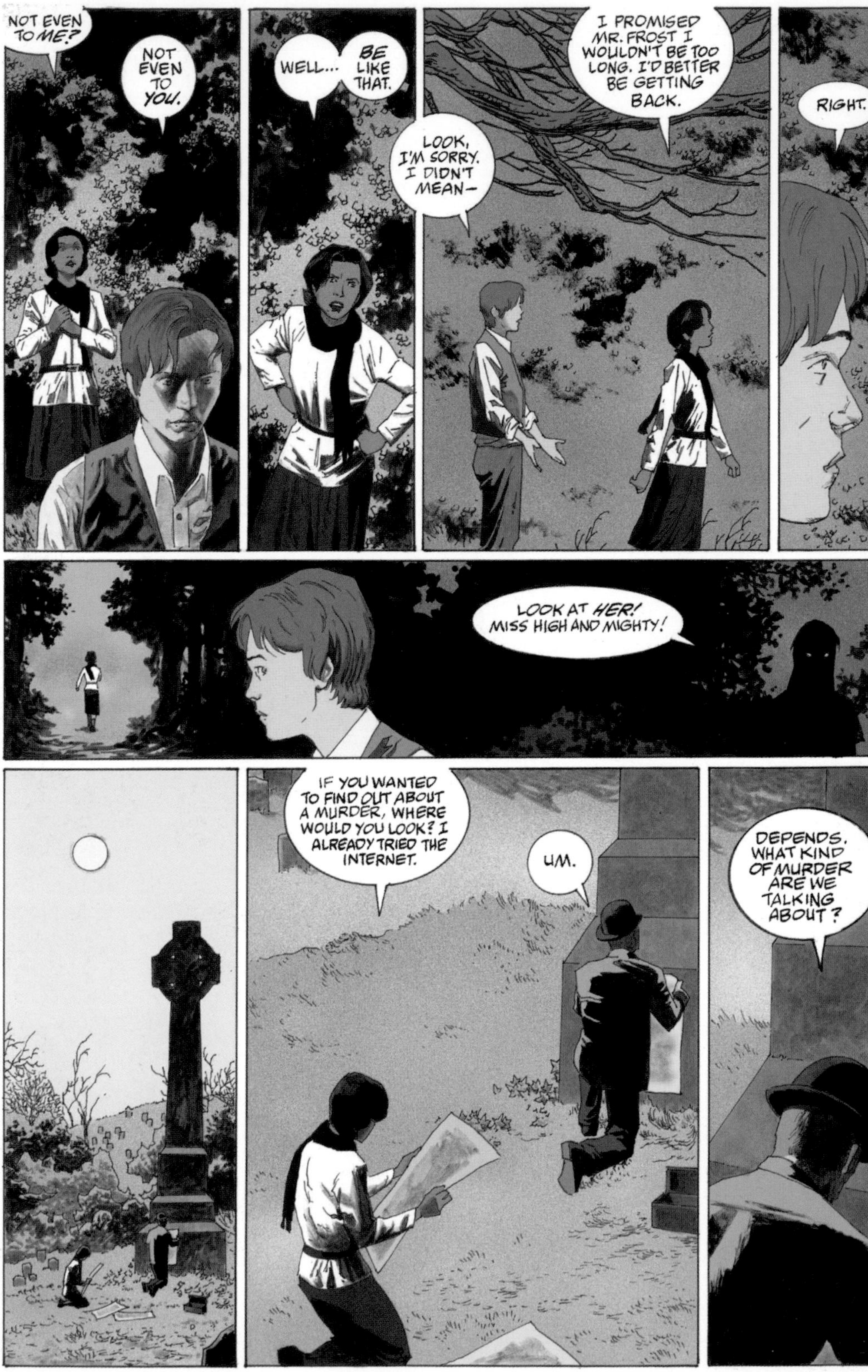
NOT EVEN TO ME?
NOT EVEN TO YOU.
WELL...
BE LIKE THAT.
LOOK, I'M SORRY. I DIDN'T MEAN—
I PROMISED MR. FROST I WOULDN'T BE TOO LONG. I'D BETTER BE GETTING BACK.
RIGHT.
LOOK AT HER! MISS HIGH AND MIGHTY!
IF YOU WANTED TO FIND OUT ABOUT A MURDER, WHERE WOULD YOU LOOK? I ALREADY TRIED THE INTERNET.
UM.
DEPENDS. WHAT KIND OF MURDER ARE WE TALKING ABOUT?

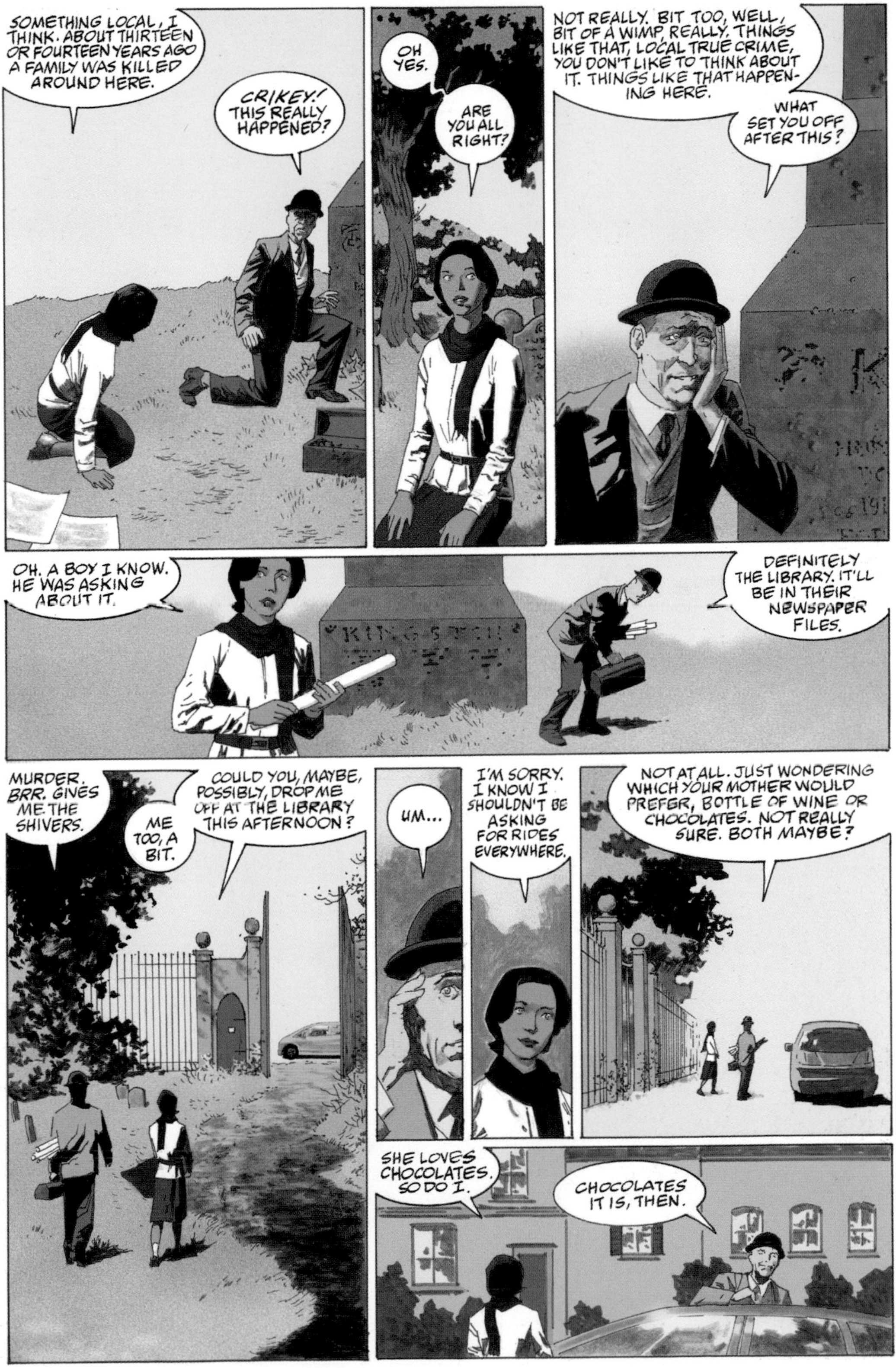
SOMETHING LOCAL, I THINK. ABOUT THIRTEEN OR FOURTEEN YEARS AGO A FAMILY WAS KILLED AROUND HERE.
CRIKEY! THIS REALLY HAPPENED?
OH YES.
ARE YOU ALL RIGHT?
NOT REALLY. BIT TOO, WELL, BIT OF A WIMP, REALLY. THINGS LIKE THAT, LOCAL TRUE CRIME, YOU DON'T LIKE TO THINK ABOUT IT. THINGS LIKE THAT HAPPENING HERE.
WHAT SET YOU OFF AFTER THIS?
OH. A BOY I KNOW. HE WAS ASKING ABOUT IT.
DEFINITELY THE LIBRARY. IT'LL BE IN THEIR NEWSPAPER FILES.
MURDER. BRR. GIVES ME THE SHIVERS.
ME TOO, A BIT.
COULD YOU, MAYBE, POSSIBLY, DROP ME OFF AT THE LIBRARY THIS AFTERNOON?
UM...
I'M SORRY. I KNOW I SHOULDN'T BE ASKING FOR RIDES EVERYWHERE.
NOT AT ALL. JUST WONDERING WHICH YOUR MOTHER WOULD PREFER, BOTTLE OF WINE OR CHOCOLATES. NOT REALLY SURE. BOTH MAYBE?
SHE LOVES CHOCOLATES. SO DO I.
CHOCOLATES IT IS, THEN.

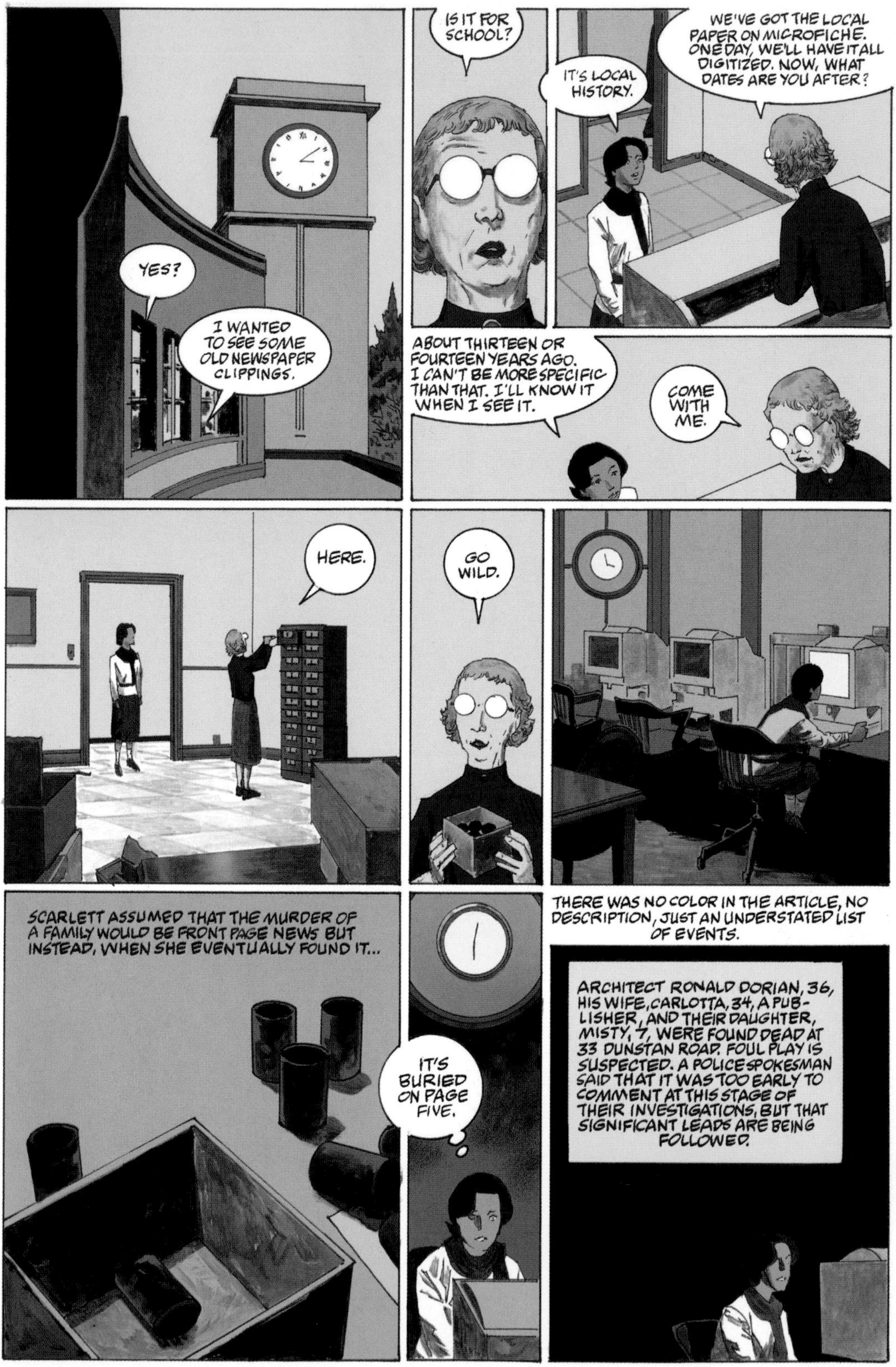
YES?
I WANTED TO SEE SOME OLD NEWSPAPER CLIPPINGS.
IS IT FOR SCHOOL?
IT'S LOCAL HISTORY.
WE'VE GOT THE LOCAL PAPER ON MICROFICHE. ONE DAY, WE'LL HAVE IT ALL DIGITIZED. NOW, WHAT DATES ARE YOU AFTER?
ABOUT THIRTEEN OR FOURTEEN YEARS AGO. I CAN'T BE MORE SPECIFIC THAN THAT. I'LL KNOW IT WHEN I SEE IT.
COME WITH ME.
HERE.
GO WILD.
SCARLETT ASSUMED THAT THE MURDER OF A FAMILY WOULD BE FRONT PAGE NEWS BUT INSTEAD, WHEN SHE EVENTUALLY FOUND IT...
IT'S BURIED ON PAGE FIVE.
THERE WAS NO COLOR IN THE ARTICLE, NO DESCRIPTION, JUST AN UNDERSTATED LIST OF EVENTS.
ARCHITECT RONALD DORIAN, 36, HIS WIFE, CARLOTTA, 34, A PUBLISHER, AND THEIR DAUGHTER, MISTY, 7, WERE FOUND DEAD AT 33 DUNSTAN ROAD. FOUL PLAY IS SUSPECTED. A POLICE SPOKESMAN SAID THAT IT WAS TOO EARLY TO COMMENT AT THIS STAGE OF THEIR INVESTIGATIONS, BUT THAT SIGNIFICANT LEADS ARE BEING FOLLOWED.

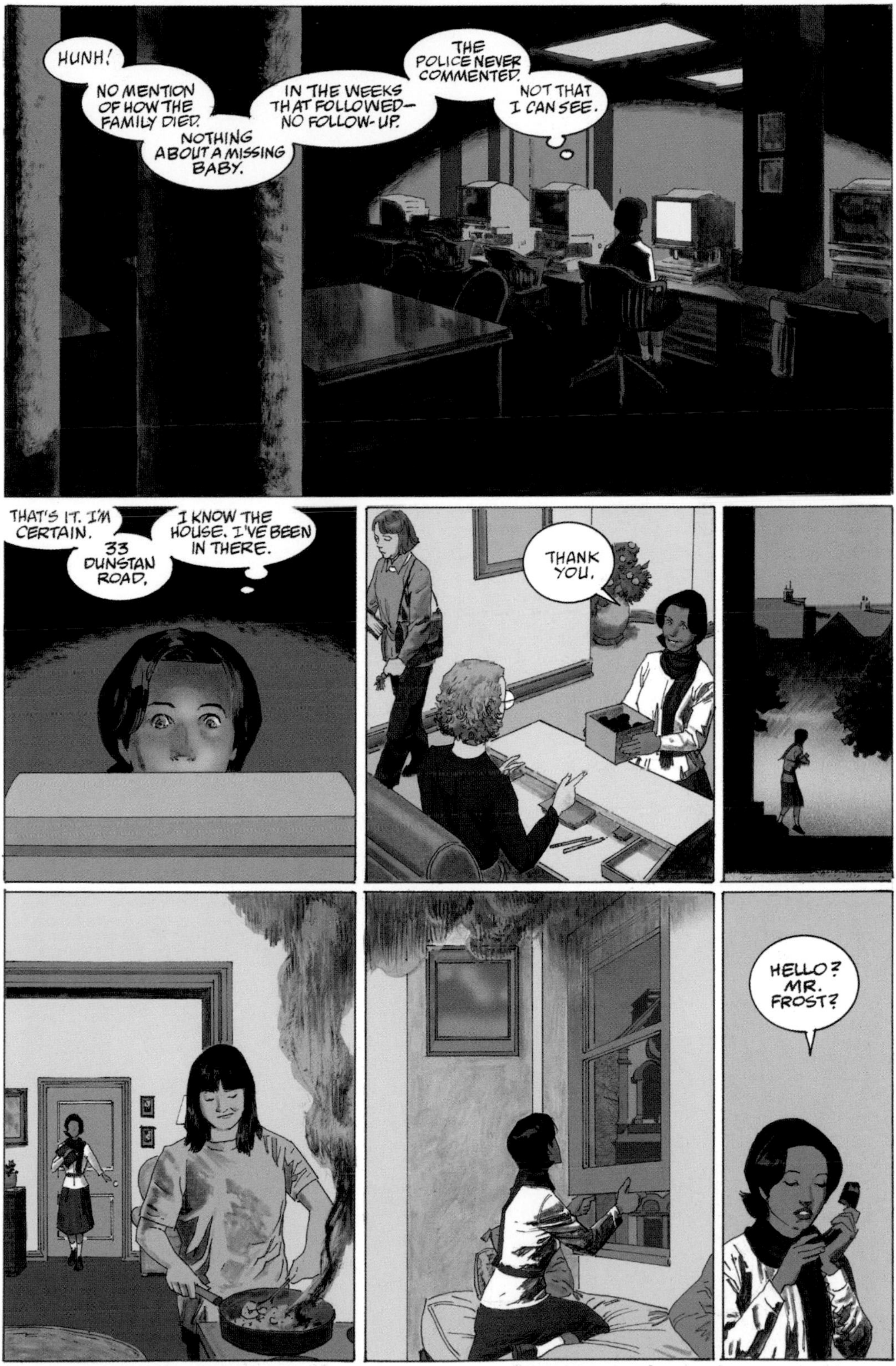
HUNH!
NO MENTION OF HOW THE FAMILY DIED.
NOTHING ABOUT A MISSING BABY.
IN THE WEEKS THAT FOLLOWED— NO FOLLOW-UP.
THE POLICE NEVER COMMENTED.
NOT THAT I CAN SEE.
THAT'S IT. I'M CERTAIN.
33 DUNSTAN ROAD.
I KNOW THE HOUSE. I'VE BEEN IN THERE.
THANK YOU.
HELLO? MR. FROST?

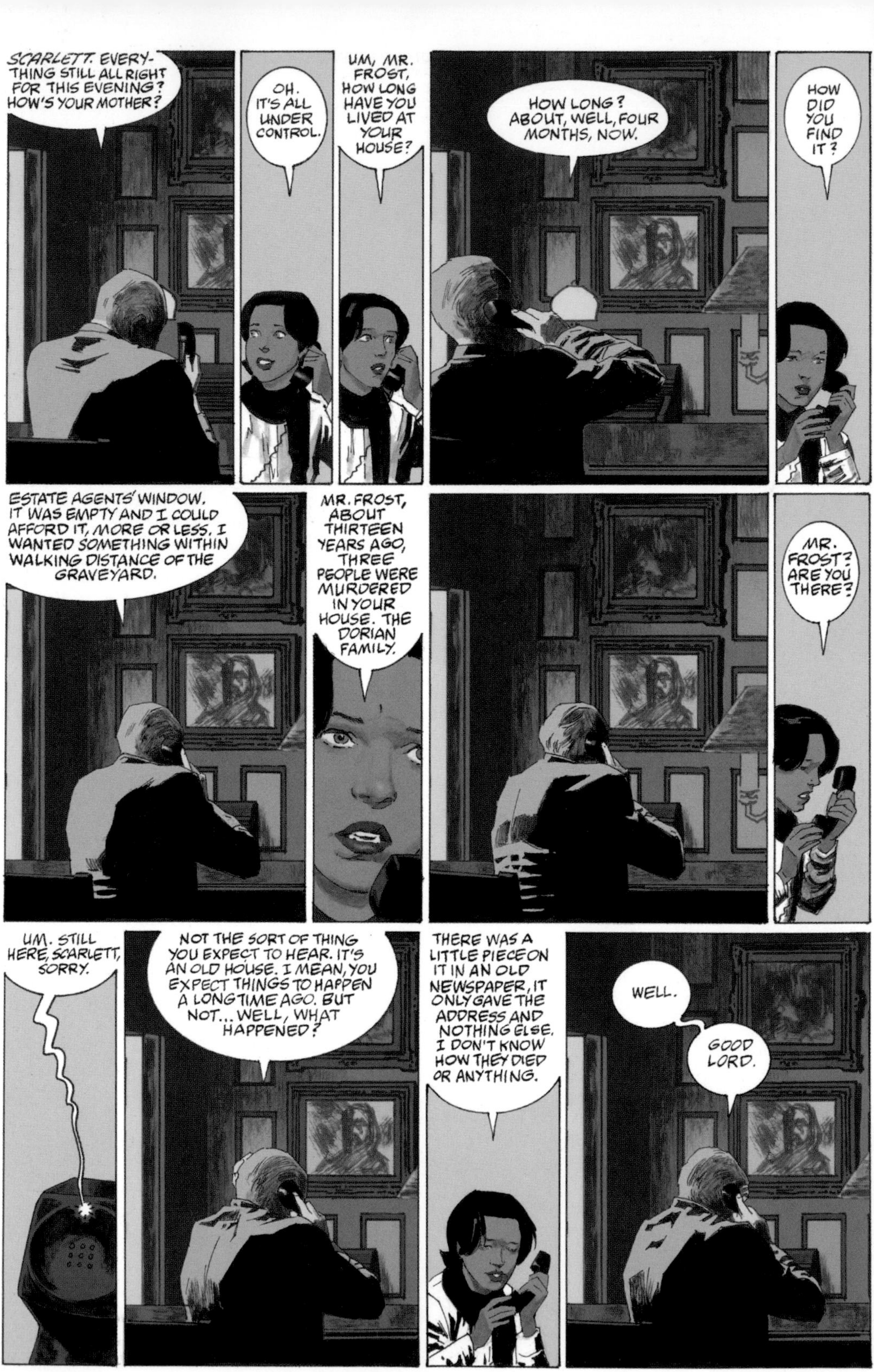
SCARLETT. EVERYTHING STILL ALL RIGHT FOR THIS EVENING? HOW'S YOUR MOTHER?
OH. IT'S ALL UNDER CONTROL.
UM, MR. FROST, HOW LONG HAVE YOU LIVED AT YOUR HOUSE?
HOW LONG? ABOUT, WELL, FOUR MONTHS, NOW.
HOW DID YOU FIND IT?
ESTATE AGENTS' WINDOW. IT WAS EMPTY AND I COULD AFFORD IT, MORE OR LESS. I WANTED SOMETHING WITHIN WALKING DISTANCE OF THE GRAVEYARD.
MR. FROST, ABOUT THIRTEEN YEARS AGO, THREE PEOPLE WERE MURDERED IN YOUR HOUSE. THE DORIAN FAMILY.
MR. FROST? ARE YOU THERE?
UM. STILL HERE, SCARLETT, SORRY.
NOT THE SORT OF THING YOU EXPECT TO HEAR. IT'S AN OLD HOUSE. I MEAN, YOU EXPECT THINGS TO HAPPEN A LONG TIME AGO. BUT NOT... WELL, WHAT HAPPENED?
THERE WAS A LITTLE PIECE ON IT IN AN OLD NEWSPAPER, IT ONLY GAVE THE ADDRESS AND NOTHING ELSE. I DON'T KNOW HOW THEY DIED OR ANYTHING.
WELL.
GOOD LORD.

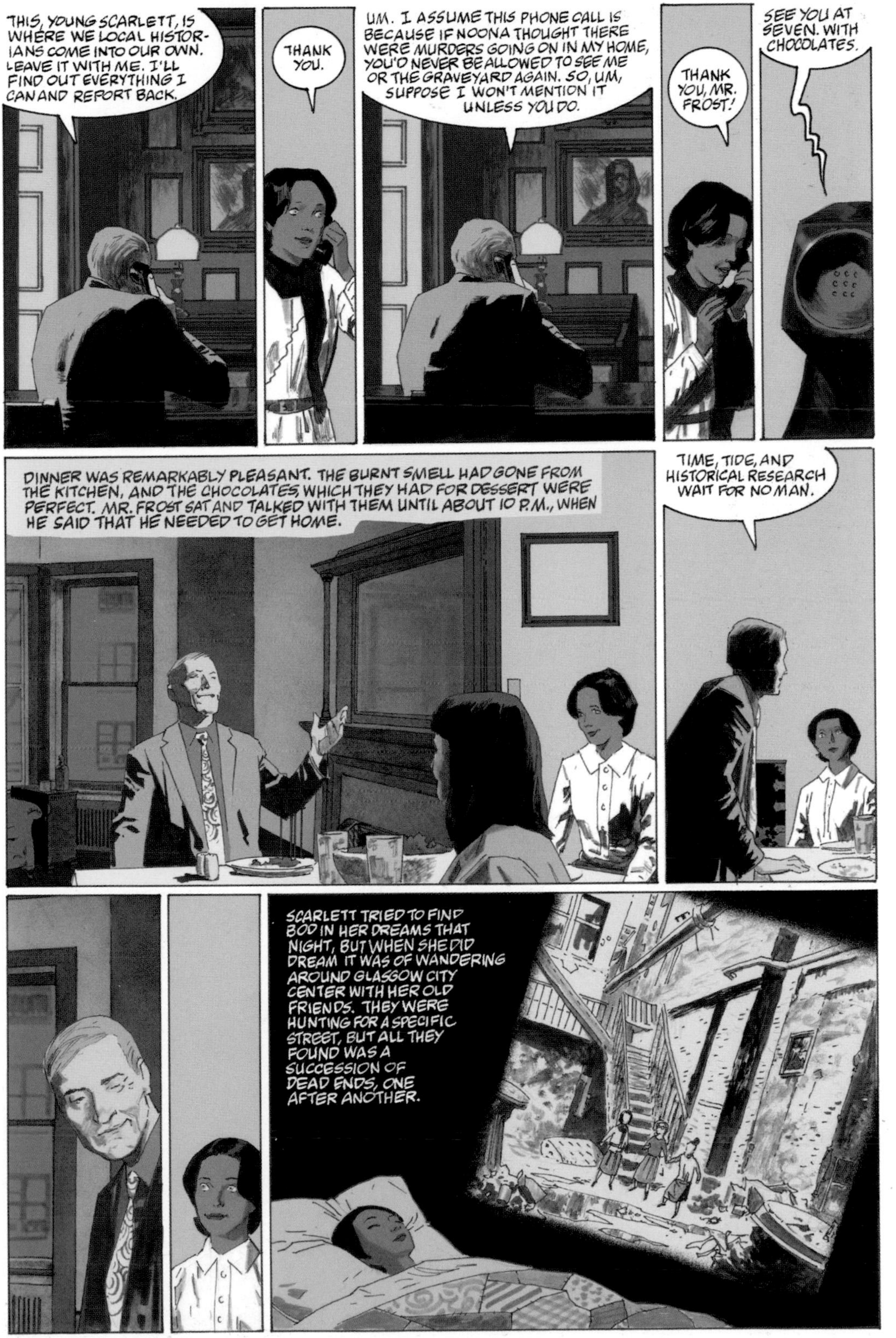
THIS, YOUNG SCARLETT, IS WHERE WE LOCAL HISTORIANS COME INTO OUR OWN. LEAVE IT WITH ME. I'LL FIND OUT EVERYTHING I CAN AND REPORT BACK.
THANK YOU.
UM. I ASSUME THIS PHONE CALL IS BECAUSE IF NOONA THOUGHT THERE WERE MURDERS GOING ON IN MY HOME, YOU'D NEVER BE ALLOWED TO SEE ME OR THE GRAVEYARD AGAIN. SO, UM, SUPPOSE I WON'T MENTION IT UNLESS YOU DO.
THANK YOU, MR. FROST!
SEE YOU AT SEVEN. WITH CHOCOLATES.
DINNER WAS REMARKABLY PLEASANT. THE BURNT SMELL HAD GONE FROM THE KITCHEN, AND THE CHOCOLATES, WHICH THEY HAD FOR DESSERT WERE PERFECT. MR. FROST SAT AND TALKED WITH THEM UNTIL ABOUT 10 P.M., WHEN HE SAID THAT HE NEEDED TO GET HOME.
TIME, TIDE, AND HISTORICAL RESEARCH WAIT FOR NO MAN.
SCARLETT TRIED TO FIND BOD IN HER DREAMS THAT NIGHT, BUT WHEN SHE DID DREAM IT WAS OF WANDERING AROUND GLASGOW CITY CENTER WITH HER OLD FRIENDS. THEY WERE HUNTING FOR A SPECIFIC STREET, BUT ALL THEY FOUND WAS A SUCCESSION OF DEAD ENDS, ONE AFTER ANOTHER.

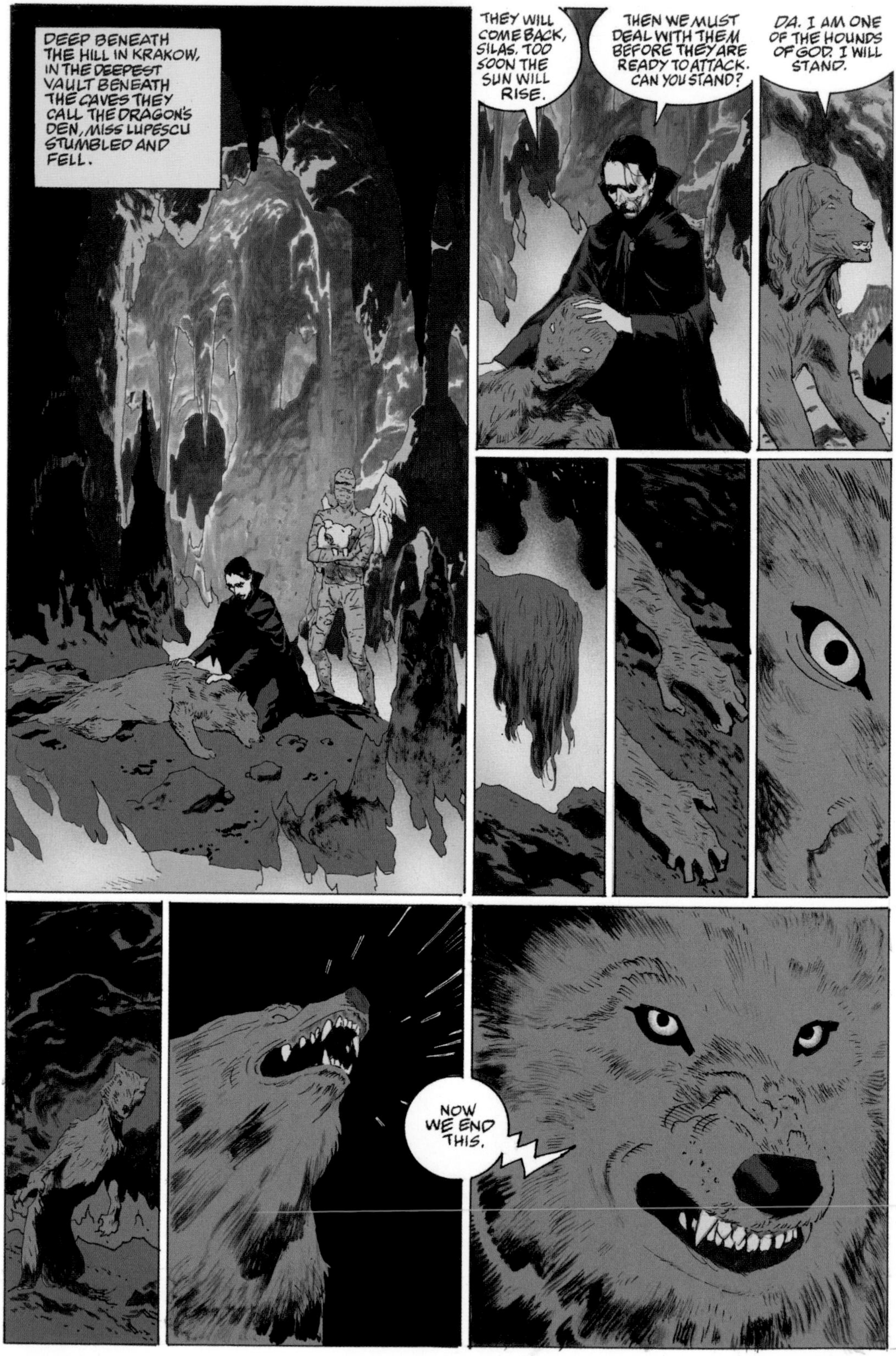
DEEP BENEATH THE HILL IN KRAKOW, IN THE DEEPEST VAULT BENEATH THE CAVES THEY CALL THE DRAGON'S DEN, MISS LUPESCU STUMBLED AND FELL.
THEY WILL COME BACK, SILAS. TOO SOON THE SUN WILL RISE.
THEN WE MUST DEAL WITH THEM BEFORE THEY ARE READY TO ATTACK. CAN YOU STAND?
DA. I AM ONE OF THE HOUNDS OF GOD. I WILL STAND.
NOW WE END THIS.

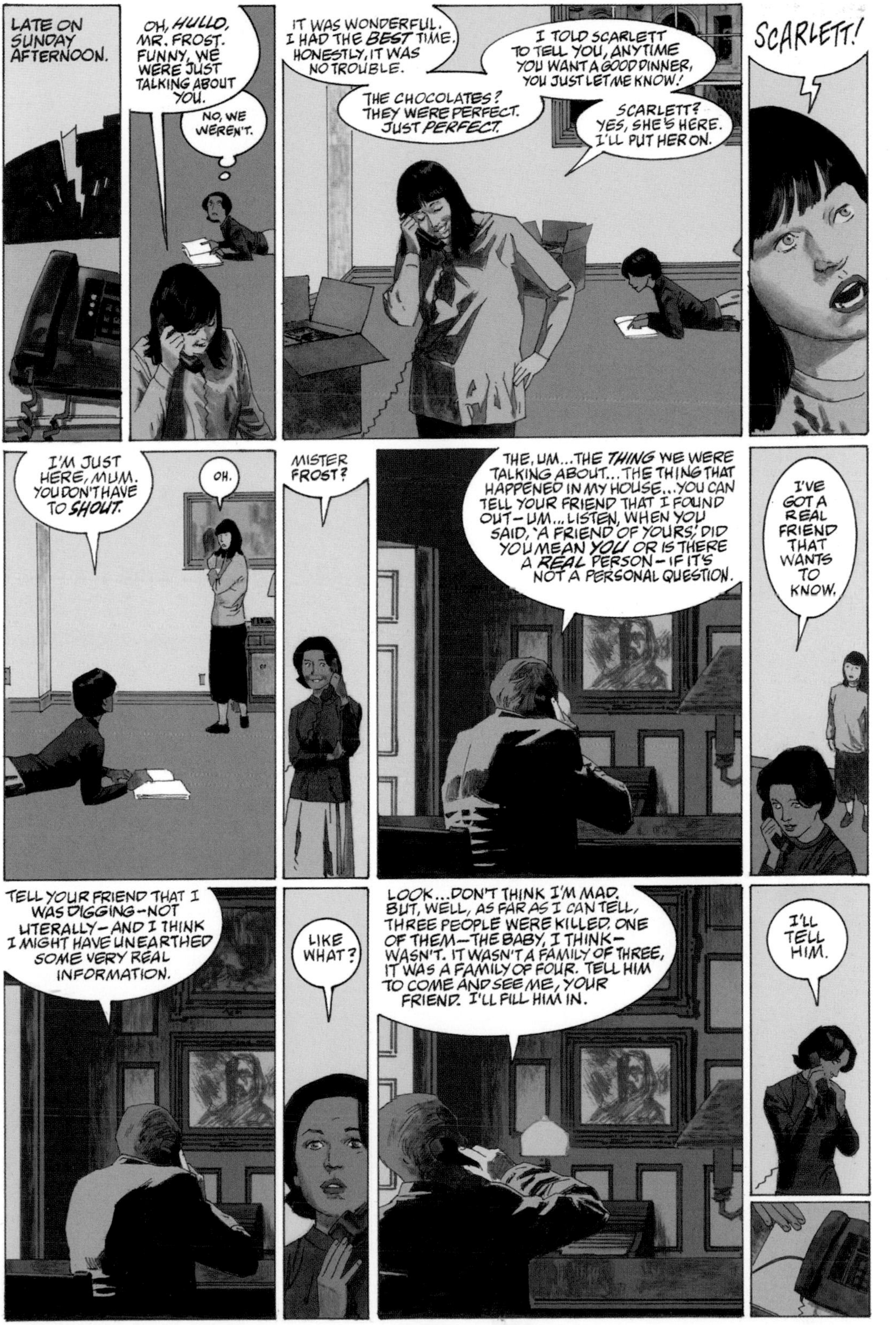

LATE ON SUNDAY AFTERNOON.
OH, HULLO, MR. FROST. FUNNY, WE WERE JUST TALKING ABOUT YOU.
NO, WE WEREN'T.
IT WAS WONDERFUL. I HAD THE BEST TIME. HONESTLY, IT WAS NO TROUBLE.
THE CHOCOLATES? THEY WERE PERFECT. JUST PERFECT.
I TOLD SCARLETT TO TELL YOU, ANYTIME YOU WANT A GOOD DINNER, YOU JUST LET ME KNOW!
SCARLETT? YES, SHE'S HERE. I'LL PUT HER ON.
SCARLETT!
I'M JUST HERE, MUM. YOU DON'T HAVE TO SHOUT.
OH.
MISTER FROST?
THE, UM... THE THING WE WERE TALKING ABOUT... THE THING THAT HAPPENED IN MY HOUSE... YOU CAN TELL YOUR FRIEND THAT I FOUND OUT – UM... LISTEN, WHEN YOU SAID, 'A FRIEND OF YOURS,' DID YOU MEAN YOU OR IS THERE A REAL PERSON – IF IT'S NOT A PERSONAL QUESTION.
I'VE GOT A REAL FRIEND THAT WANTS TO KNOW.
TELL YOUR FRIEND THAT I WAS DIGGING – NOT LITERALLY – AND I THINK I MIGHT HAVE UNEARTHED SOME VERY REAL INFORMATION.
LIKE WHAT?
LOOK... DON'T THINK I'M MAD. BUT, WELL, AS FAR AS I CAN TELL, THREE PEOPLE WERE KILLED. ONE OF THEM – THE BABY, I THINK – WASN'T. IT WASN'T A FAMILY OF THREE, IT WAS A FAMILY OF FOUR. TELL HIM TO COME AND SEE ME, YOUR FRIEND. I'LL FILL HIM IN.
I'LL TELL HIM.

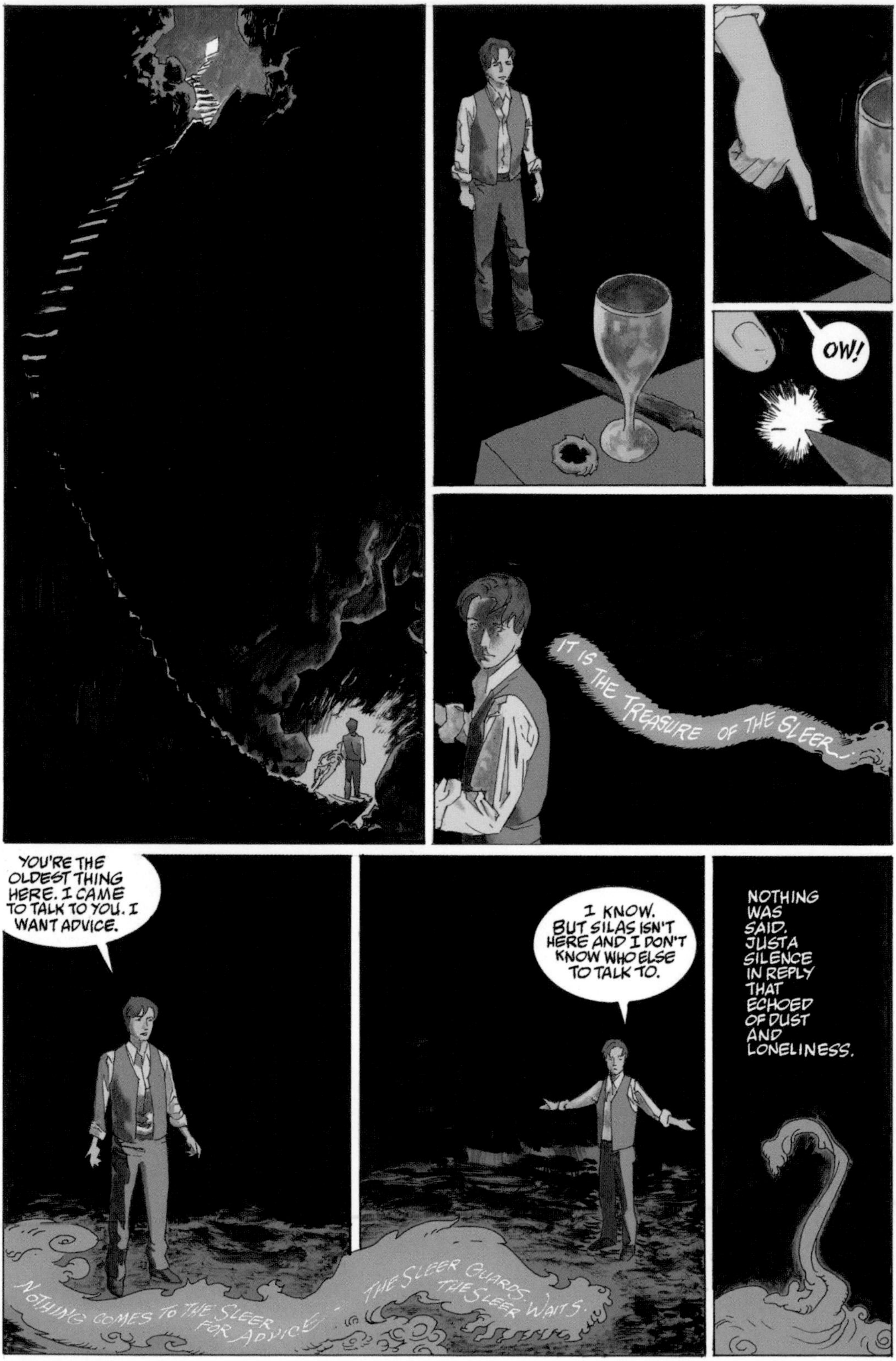
OW!
IT IS THE TREASURE OF THE SLEER...
YOU'RE THE OLDEST THING HERE. I CAME TO TALK TO YOU. I WANT ADVICE.
NOTHING COMES TO THE SLEER FOR ADVICE.
THE SLEER GUARDS. THE SLEER WAITS.
I KNOW. BUT SILAS ISN'T HERE AND I DON'T KNOW WHO ELSE TO TALK TO.
NOTHING WAS SAID. JUST A SILENCE IN REPLY THAT ECHOED OF DUST AND LONELINESS.

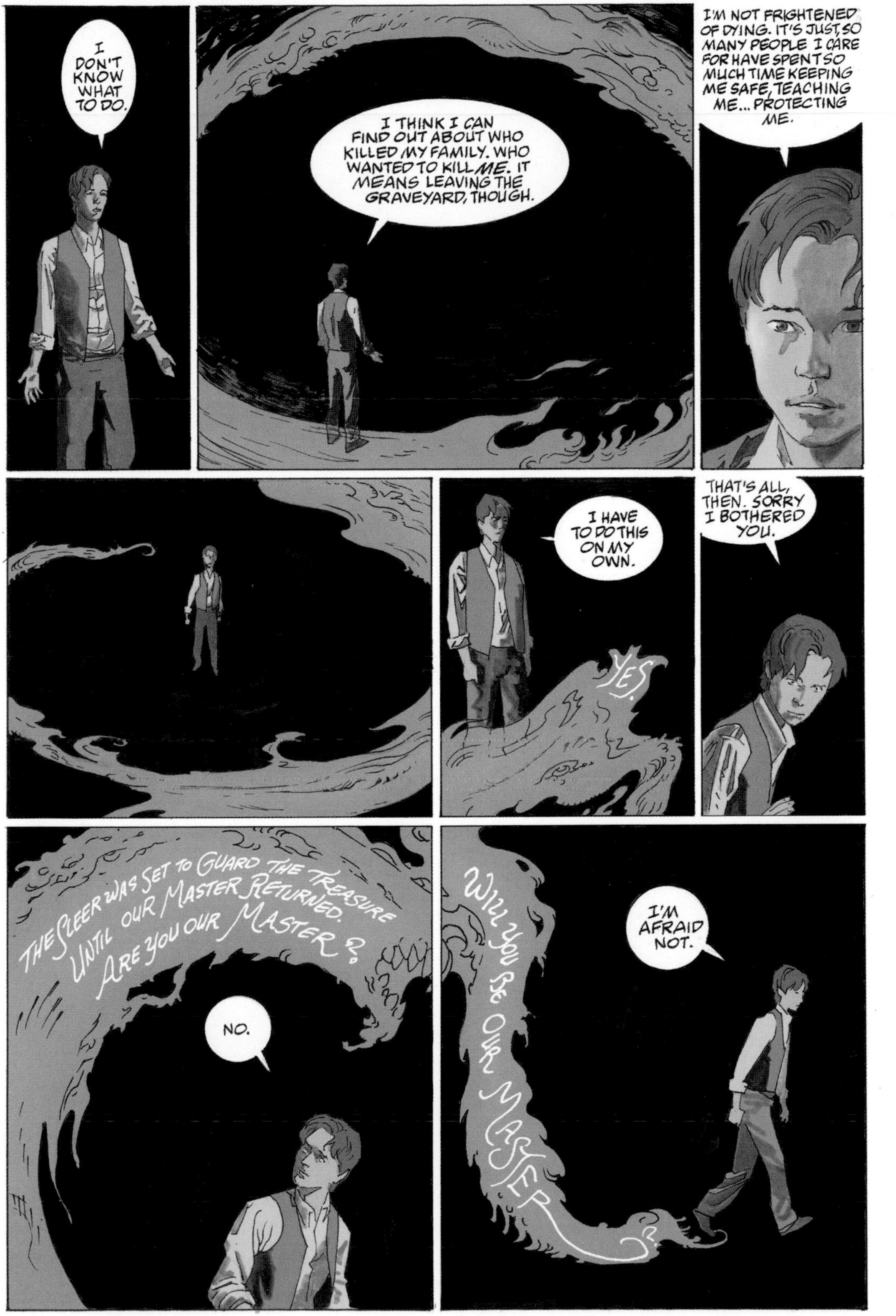
I DON'T KNOW WHAT TO DO.
I THINK I CAN FIND OUT ABOUT WHO KILLED MY FAMILY. WHO WANTED TO KILL *ME*. IT MEANS LEAVING THE GRAVEYARD, THOUGH.
I'M NOT FRIGHTENED OF DYING. IT'S JUST, SO MANY PEOPLE I CARE FOR HAVE SPENT SO MUCH TIME KEEPING ME SAFE, TEACHING ME... PROTECTING ME.
I HAVE TO DO THIS ON MY OWN.
YES.
THAT'S ALL, THEN. SORRY I BOTHERED YOU.
THE SLEER WAS SET TO GUARD THE TREASURE UNTIL OUR MASTER RETURNED. ARE YOU OUR MASTER?
NO.
WILL YOU BE OUR MASTER?
I'M AFRAID NOT.

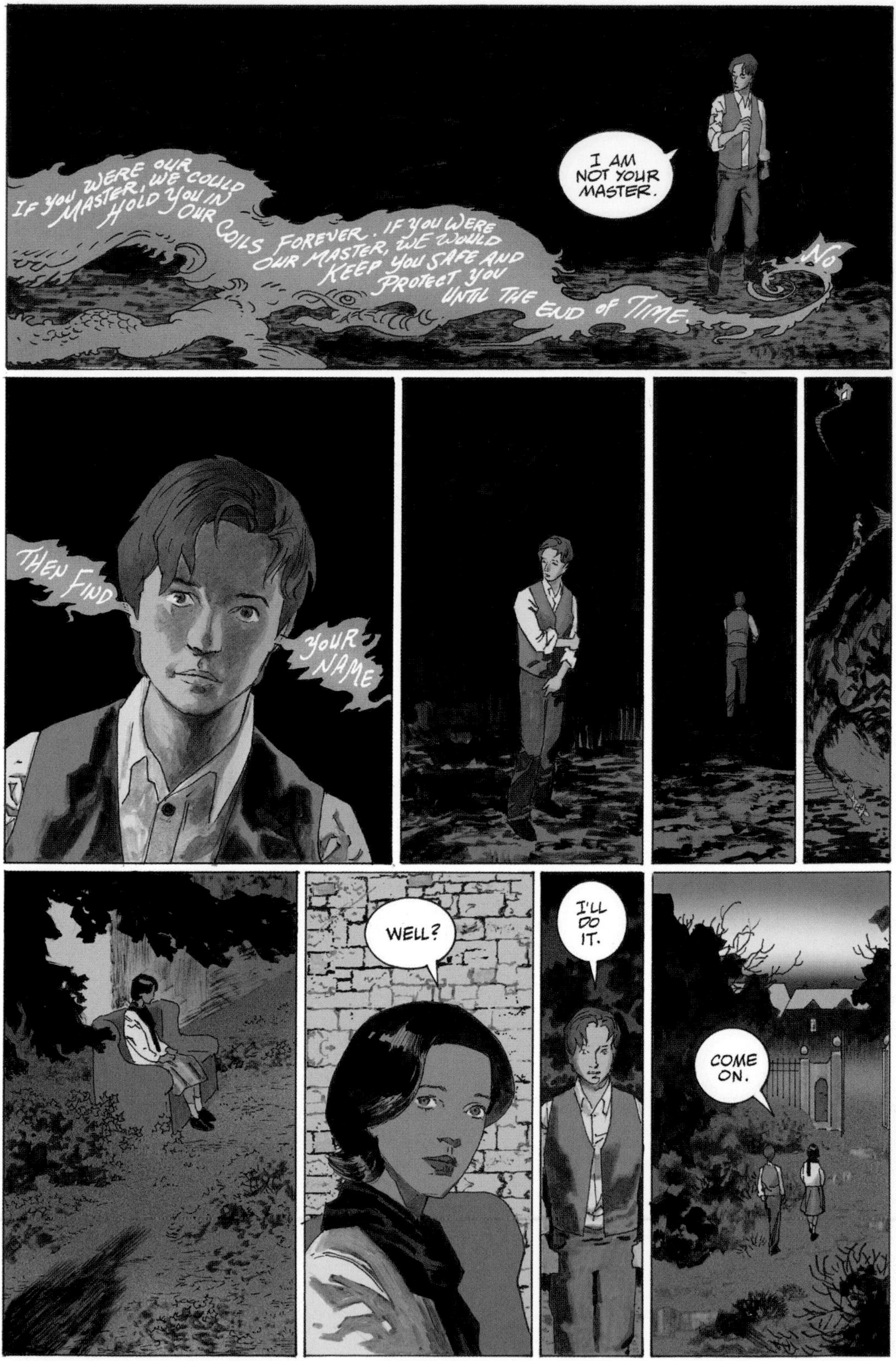
IF YOU WERE OUR MASTER, WE COULD HOLD YOU IN OUR COILS FOREVER. IF YOU WERE OUR MASTER, WE WOULD KEEP YOU SAFE AND PROTECT YOU UNTIL THE END OF TIME.
I AM NOT YOUR MASTER.
NO
THEN FIND
YOUR NAME
WELL?
I'LL DO IT.
COME ON.

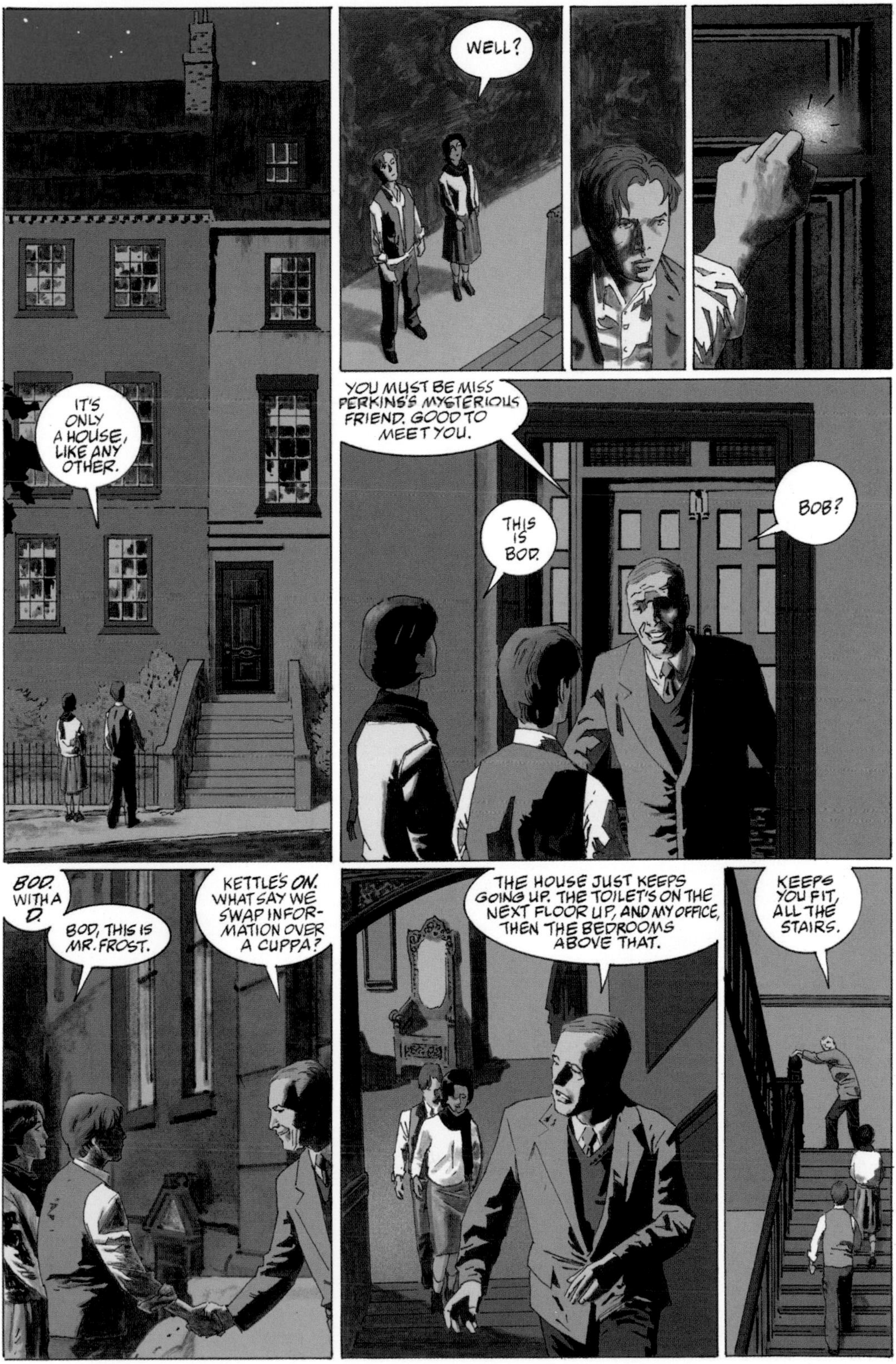
IT'S ONLY A HOUSE, LIKE ANY OTHER.
WELL?
YOU MUST BE MISS PERKINS'S MYSTERIOUS FRIEND. GOOD TO MEET YOU.
THIS IS BOD.
BOB?
BOD. WITH A D.
BOD, THIS IS MR. FROST.
KETTLE'S ON. WHAT SAY WE SWAP INFORMATION OVER A CUPPA?
THE HOUSE JUST KEEPS GOING UP. THE TOILET'S ON THE NEXT FLOOR UP, AND MY OFFICE, THEN THE BEDROOMS ABOVE THAT.
KEEPS YOU FIT, ALL THE STAIRS.

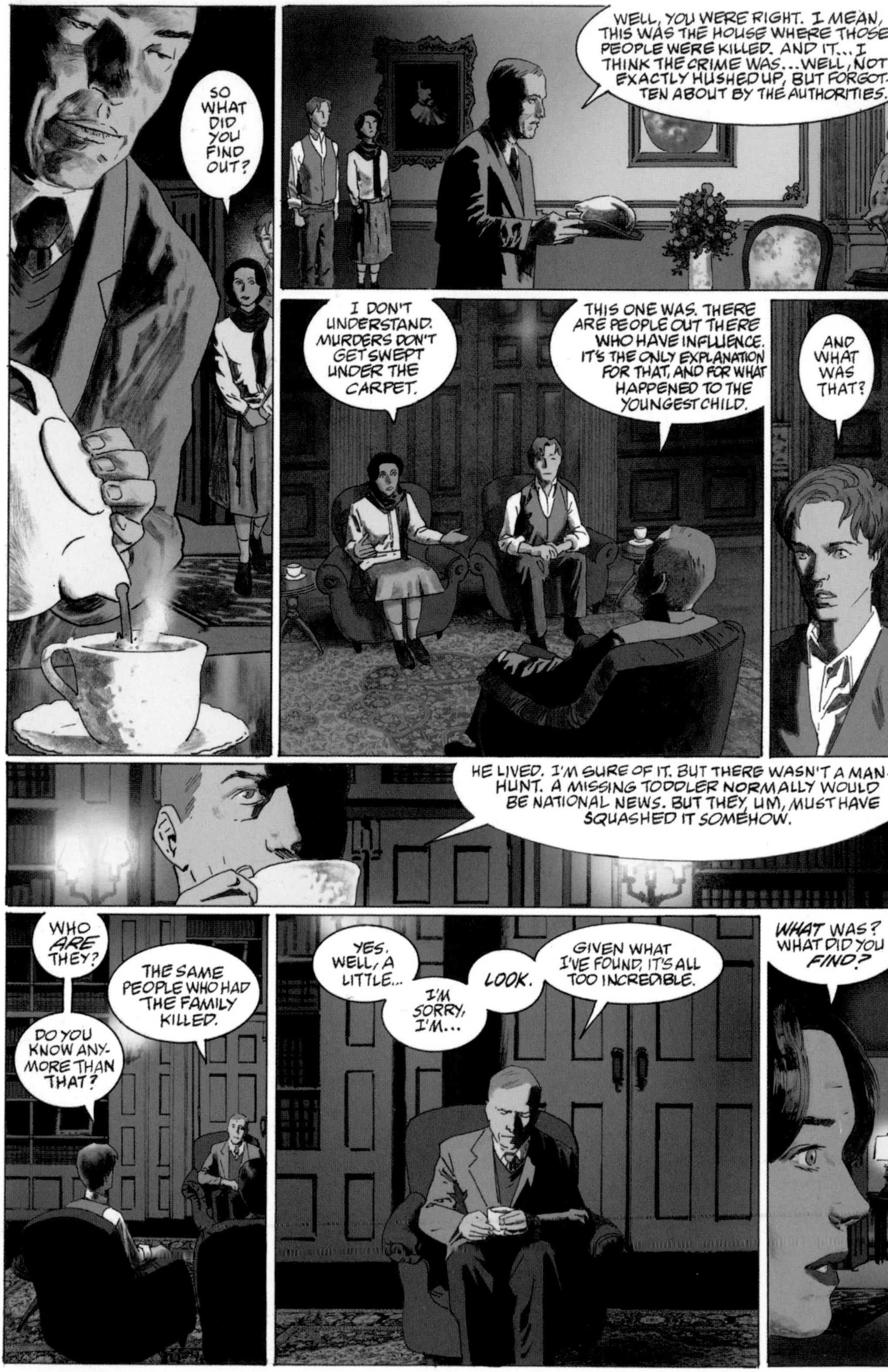
SO WHAT DID YOU FIND OUT?
WELL, YOU WERE RIGHT. I MEAN, THIS WAS THE HOUSE WHERE THOSE PEOPLE WERE KILLED. AND IT... I THINK THE CRIME WAS... WELL, NOT EXACTLY HUSHED UP, BUT FORGOTTEN ABOUT BY THE AUTHORITIES.
I DON'T UNDERSTAND. MURDERS DON'T GET SWEPT UNDER THE CARPET.
THIS ONE WAS. THERE ARE PEOPLE OUT THERE WHO HAVE INFLUENCE. IT'S THE ONLY EXPLANATION FOR THAT, AND FOR WHAT HAPPENED TO THE YOUNGEST CHILD.
AND WHAT WAS THAT?
HE LIVED. I'M SURE OF IT. BUT THERE WASN'T A MANHUNT. A MISSING TODDLER NORMALLY WOULD BE NATIONAL NEWS. BUT THEY, UM, MUST HAVE SQUASHED IT *SOMEHOW*.
WHO *ARE* THEY?
THE SAME PEOPLE WHO HAD THE FAMILY KILLED.
DO YOU KNOW ANYMORE THAN THAT?
YES. WELL, A LITTLE...
I'M SORRY, I'M...
LOOK.
GIVEN WHAT I'VE FOUND, IT'S ALL TOO INCREDIBLE.
WHAT WAS? WHAT DID YOU *FIND?*

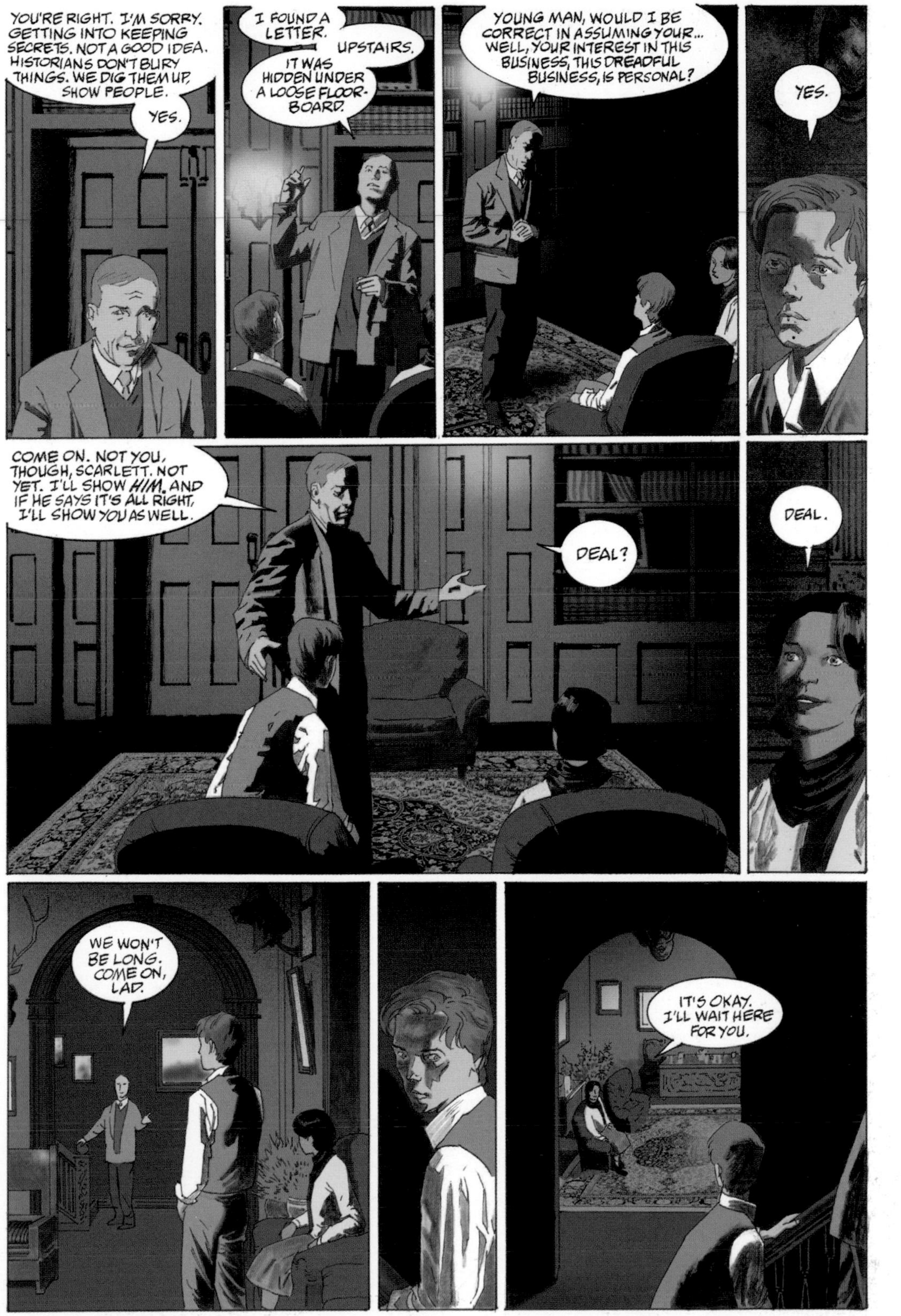
YOU'RE RIGHT. I'M SORRY. GETTING INTO KEEPING SECRETS. NOT A GOOD IDEA. HISTORIANS DON'T BURY THINGS. WE DIG THEM UP, SHOW PEOPLE.
YES.
I FOUND A LETTER.
UPSTAIRS.
IT WAS HIDDEN UNDER A LOOSE FLOOR-BOARD.
YOUNG MAN, WOULD I BE CORRECT IN ASSUMING YOUR... WELL, YOUR INTEREST IN THIS BUSINESS, THIS DREADFUL BUSINESS, IS PERSONAL?
YES.
COME ON. NOT YOU, THOUGH, SCARLETT. NOT YET. I'LL SHOW *HIM*. AND IF HE SAYS IT'S ALL RIGHT, I'LL SHOW YOU AS WELL.
DEAL?
DEAL.
WE WON'T BE LONG. COME ON, LAD.
IT'S OKAY. I'LL WAIT HERE FOR YOU.

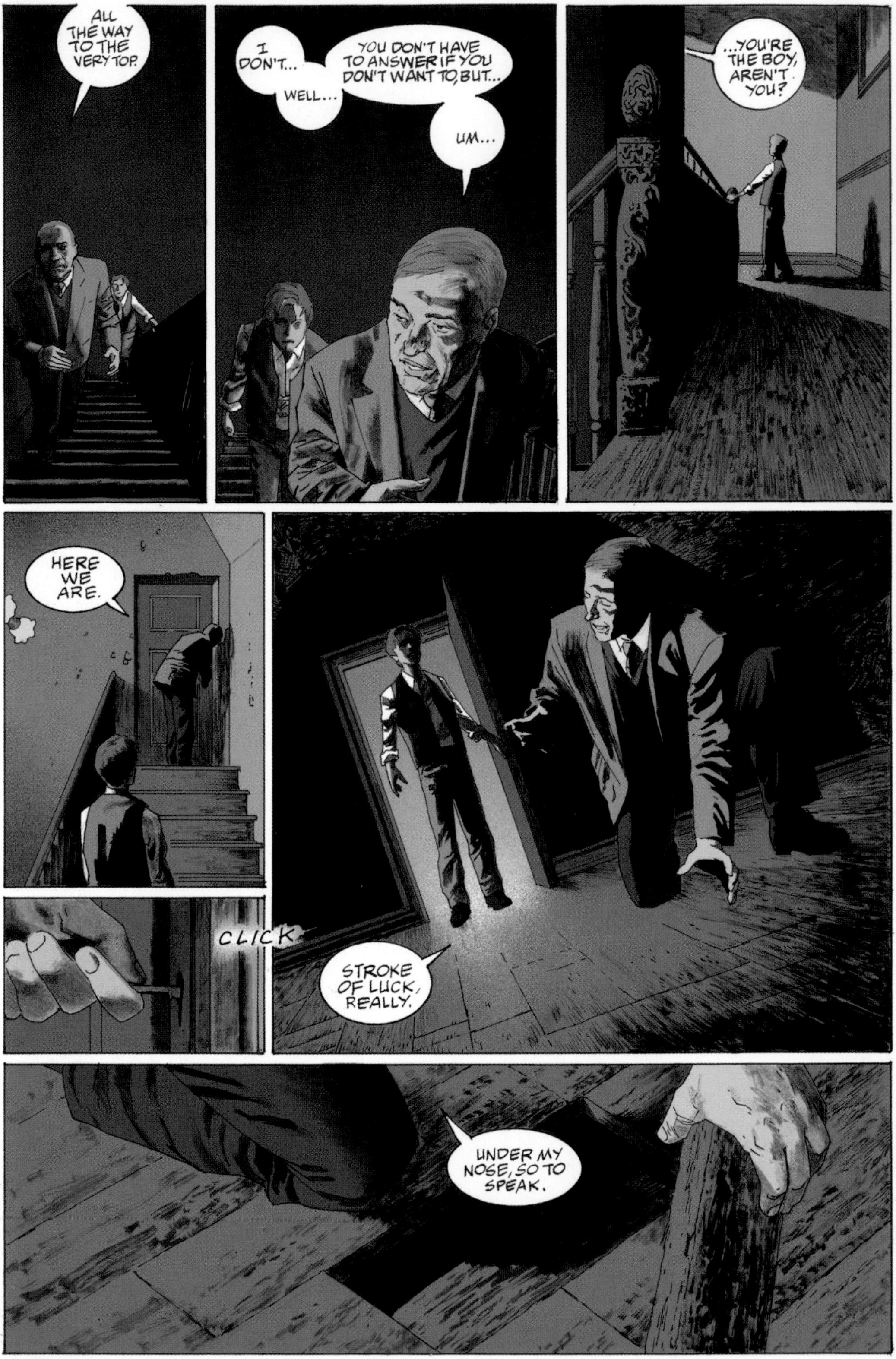
ALL THE WAY TO THE VERY TOP.
I DON'T...
WELL...
YOU DON'T HAVE TO ANSWER IF YOU DON'T WANT TO, BUT...
UM...
...YOU'RE THE BOY, AREN'T YOU?
HERE WE ARE.
CLICK
STROKE OF LUCK, REALLY.
UNDER MY NOSE, SO TO SPEAK.

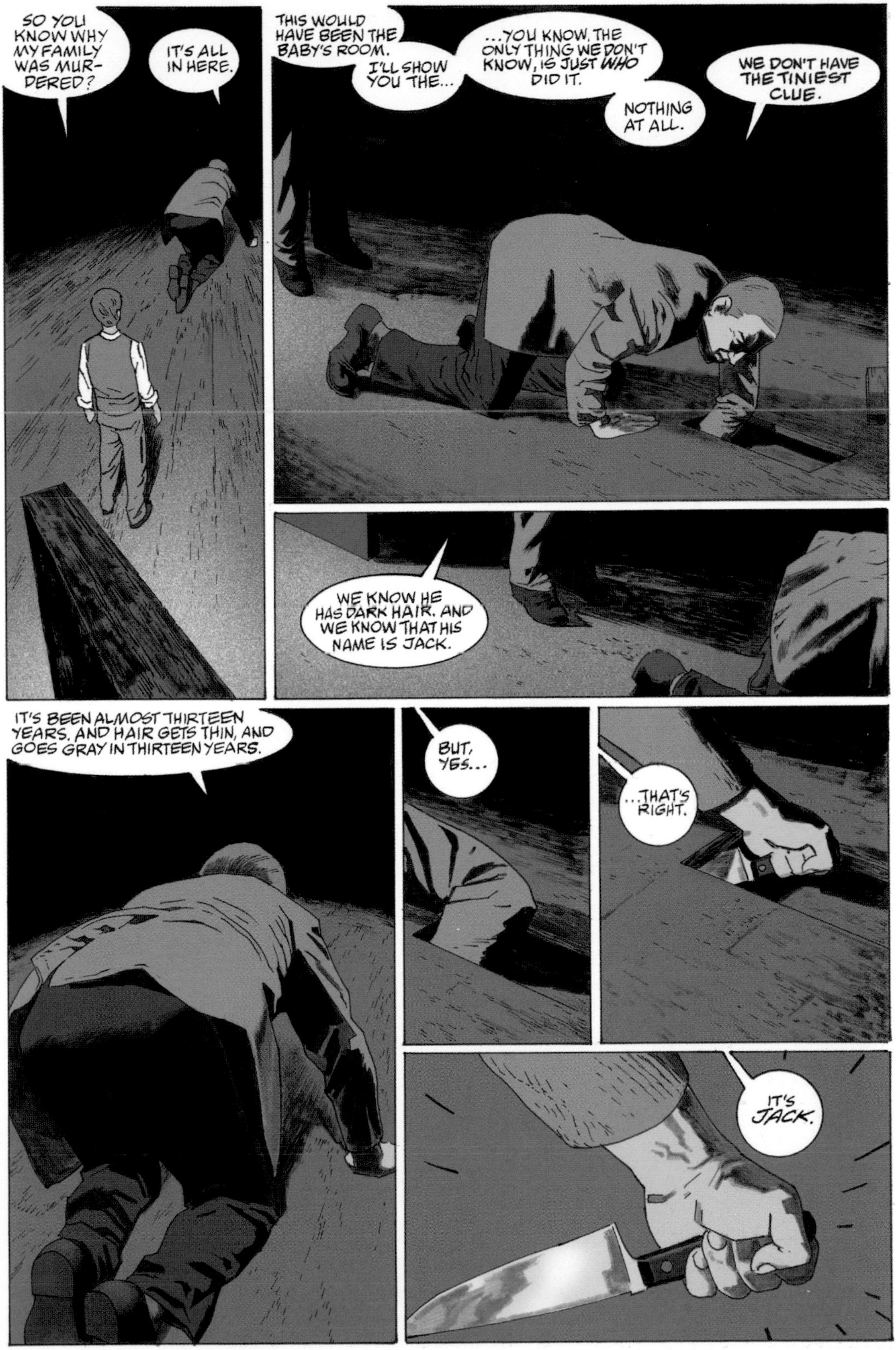
SO YOU KNOW WHY MY FAMILY WAS MURDERED?
IT'S ALL IN HERE.
THIS WOULD HAVE BEEN THE BABY'S ROOM.
I'LL SHOW YOU THE...
...YOU KNOW, THE ONLY THING WE DON'T KNOW, IS JUST WHO DID IT.
NOTHING AT ALL.
WE DON'T HAVE THE TINIEST CLUE.
WE KNOW HE HAS DARK HAIR. AND WE KNOW THAT HIS NAME IS JACK.
IT'S BEEN ALMOST THIRTEEN YEARS. AND HAIR GETS THIN, AND GOES GRAY IN THIRTEEN YEARS.
BUT, YES...
...THAT'S RIGHT.
IT'S JACK.

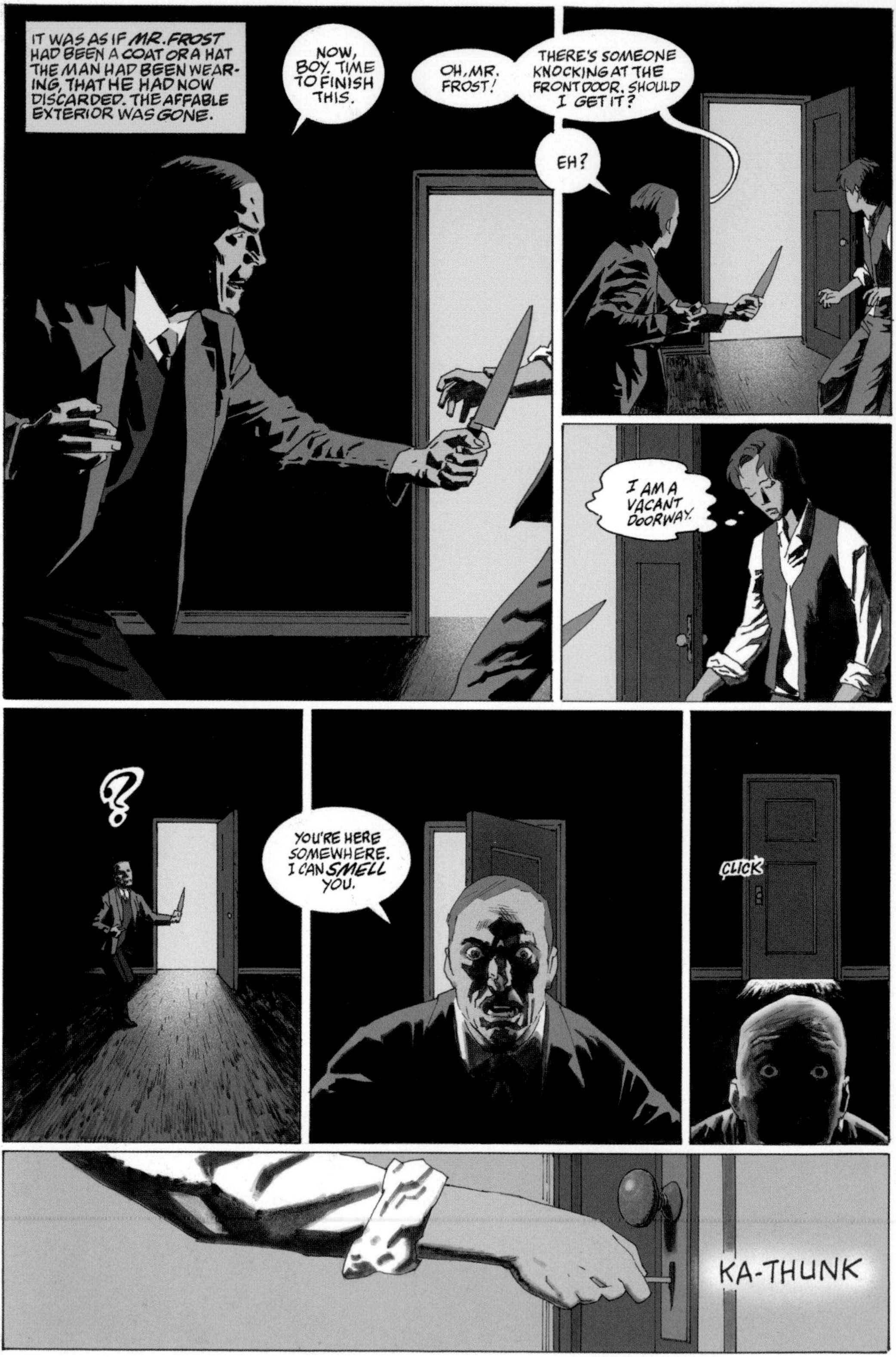
IT WAS AS IF MR. FROST HAD BEEN A COAT OR A HAT THE MAN HAD BEEN WEARING, THAT HE HAD NOW DISCARDED. THE AFFABLE EXTERIOR WAS GONE.
NOW, BOY. TIME TO FINISH THIS.
OH, MR. FROST!
THERE'S SOMEONE KNOCKING AT THE FRONT DOOR. SHOULD I GET IT?
EH?
I AM A VACANT DOORWAY.
?
YOU'RE HERE SOMEWHERE. I CAN SMELL YOU.
CLICK
KA-THUNK

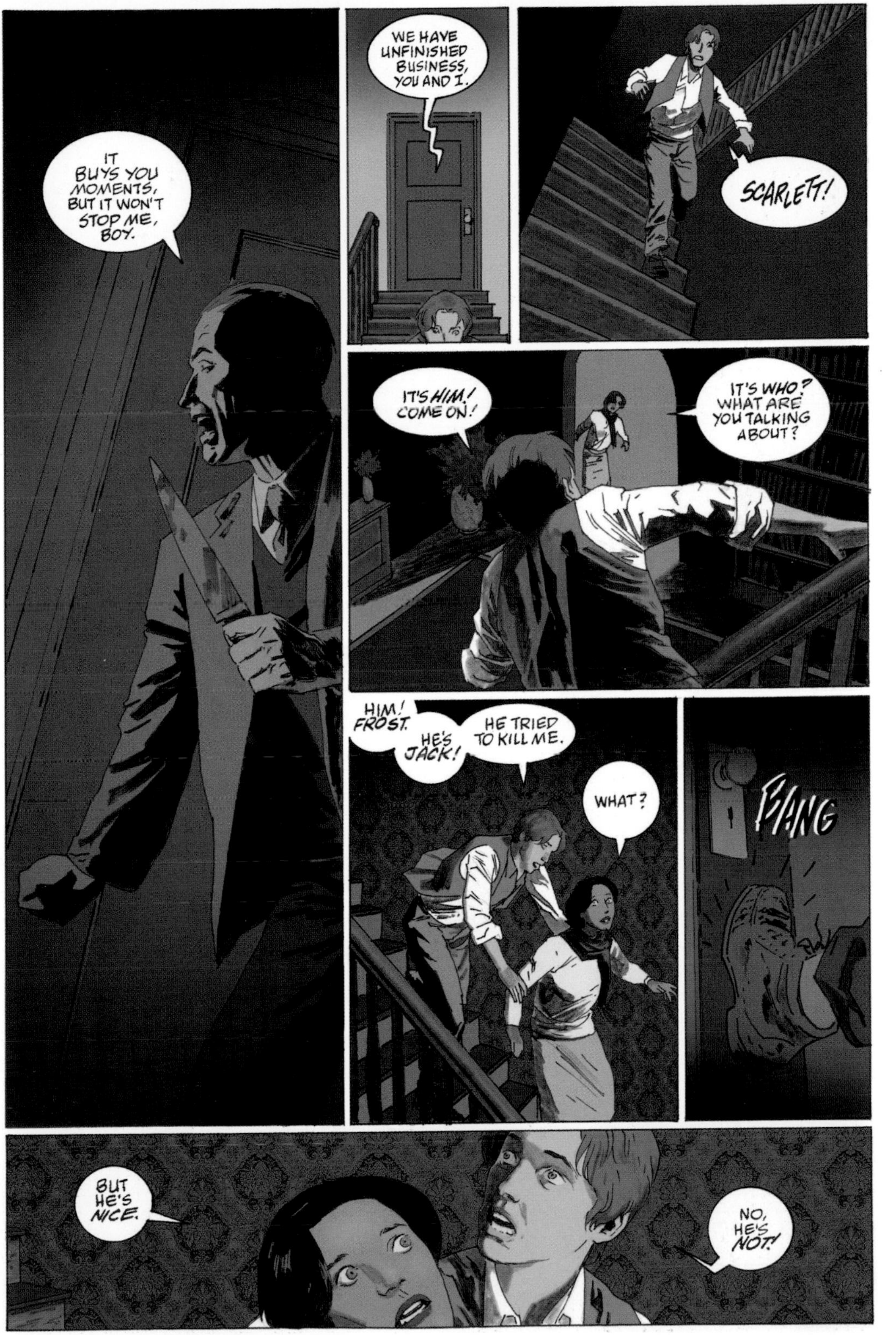
IT BUYS YOU MOMENTS, BUT IT WON'T STOP ME, BOY.
WE HAVE UNFINISHED BUSINESS, YOU AND I.
SCARLETT!
IT'S HIM! COME ON!
IT'S WHO? WHAT ARE YOU TALKING ABOUT?
HIM! FROST.
HE'S JACK!
HE TRIED TO KILL ME.
WHAT?
BANG
BUT HE'S NICE.
NO, HE'S NOT!

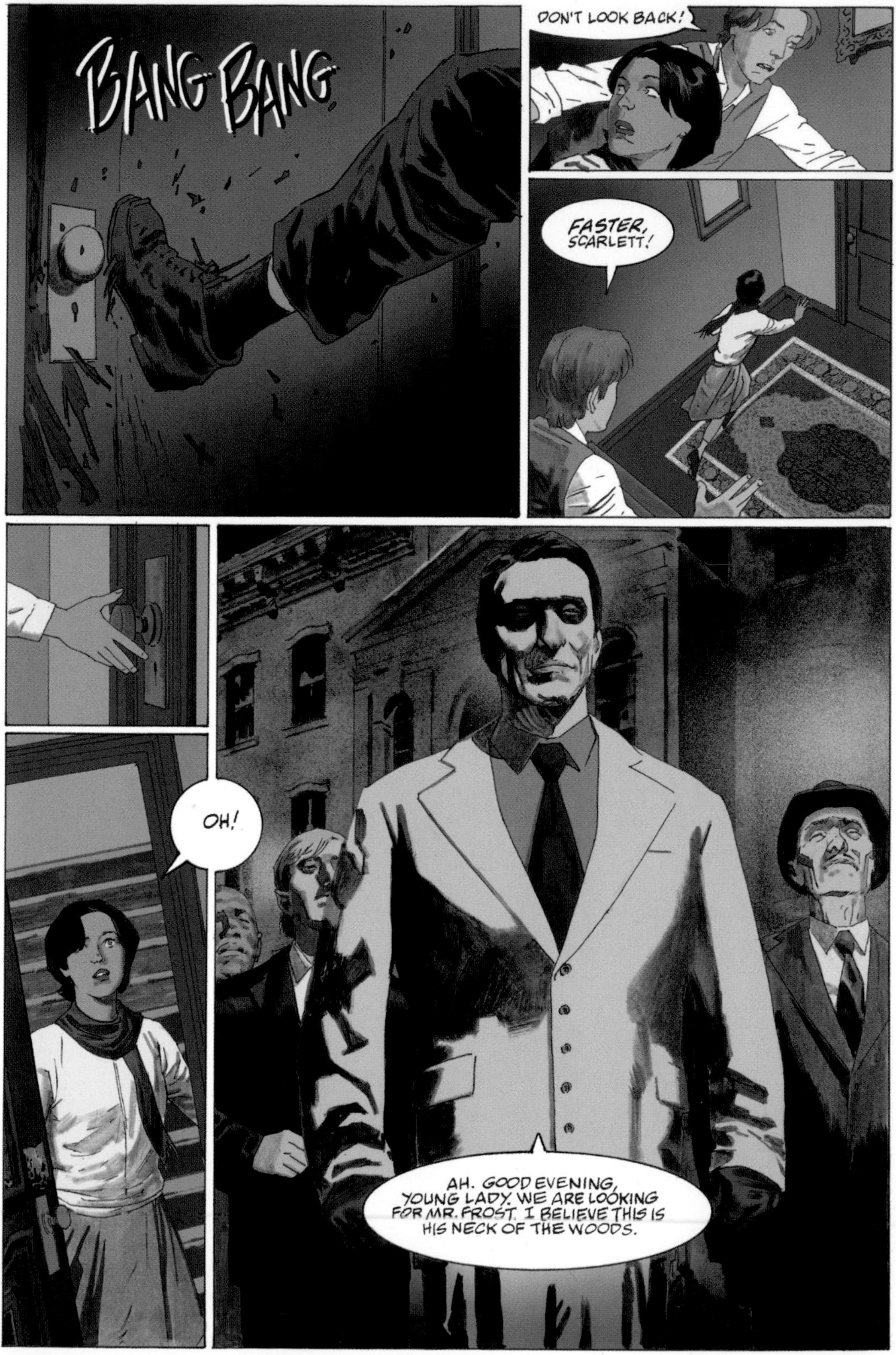
BANG BANG
DON'T LOOK BACK!
FASTER, SCARLETT!
OH!
AH. GOOD EVENING, YOUNG LADY. WE ARE LOOKING FOR MR. FROST. I BELIEVE THIS IS HIS NECK OF THE WOODS.

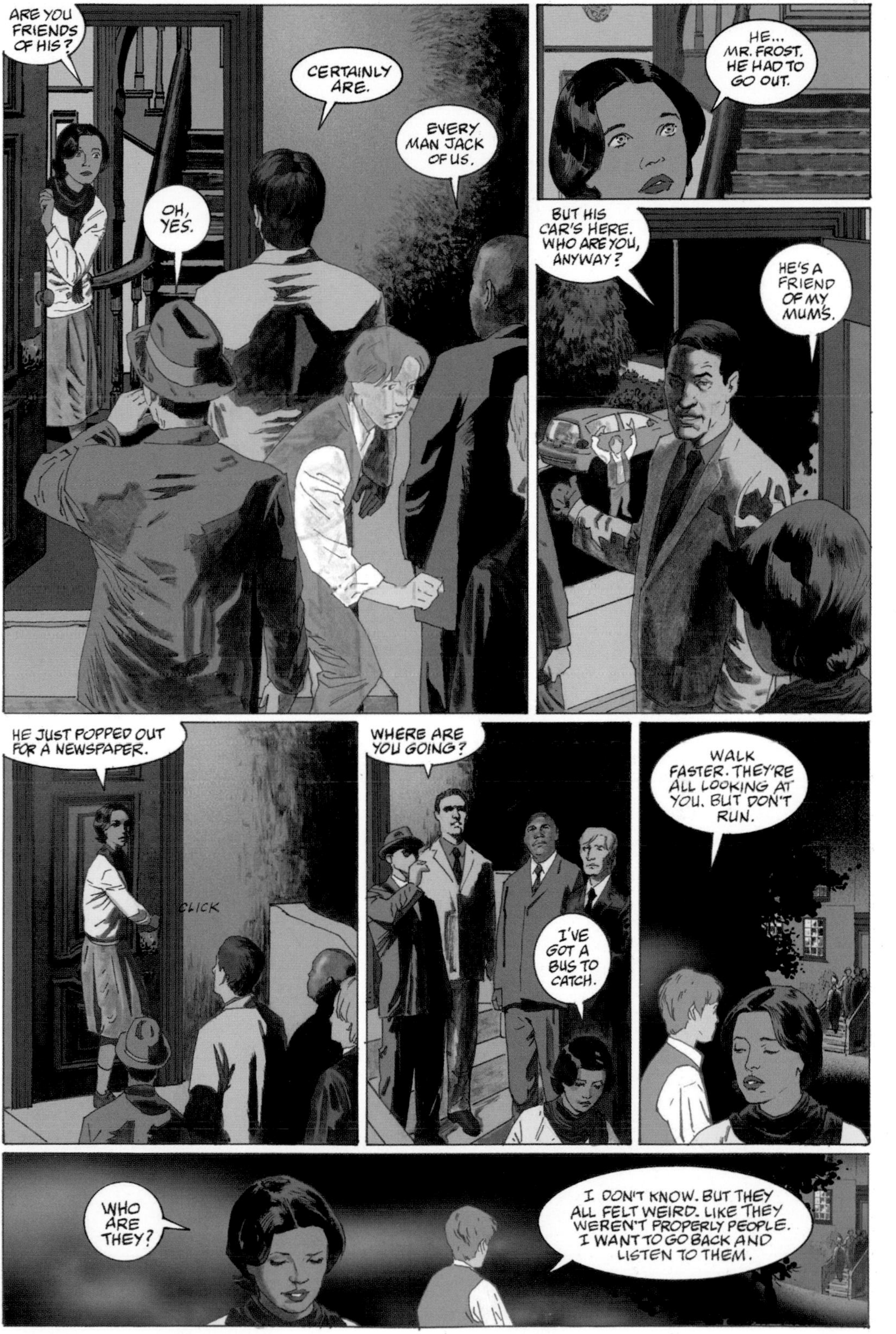
ARE YOU FRIENDS OF HIS?
CERTAINLY ARE.
EVERY MAN JACK OF US.
OH, YES.
HE... MR. FROST. HE HAD TO GO OUT.
BUT HIS CAR'S HERE. WHO ARE YOU, ANYWAY?
HE'S A FRIEND OF MY MUM'S.
HE JUST POPPED OUT FOR A NEWSPAPER.
CLICK
WHERE ARE YOU GOING?
I'VE GOT A BUS TO CATCH.
WALK FASTER. THEY'RE ALL LOOKING AT YOU. BUT DON'T RUN.
WHO ARE THEY?
I DON'T KNOW. BUT THEY ALL FELT WEIRD. LIKE THEY WEREN'T PROPERLY PEOPLE. I WANT TO GO BACK AND LISTEN TO THEM.

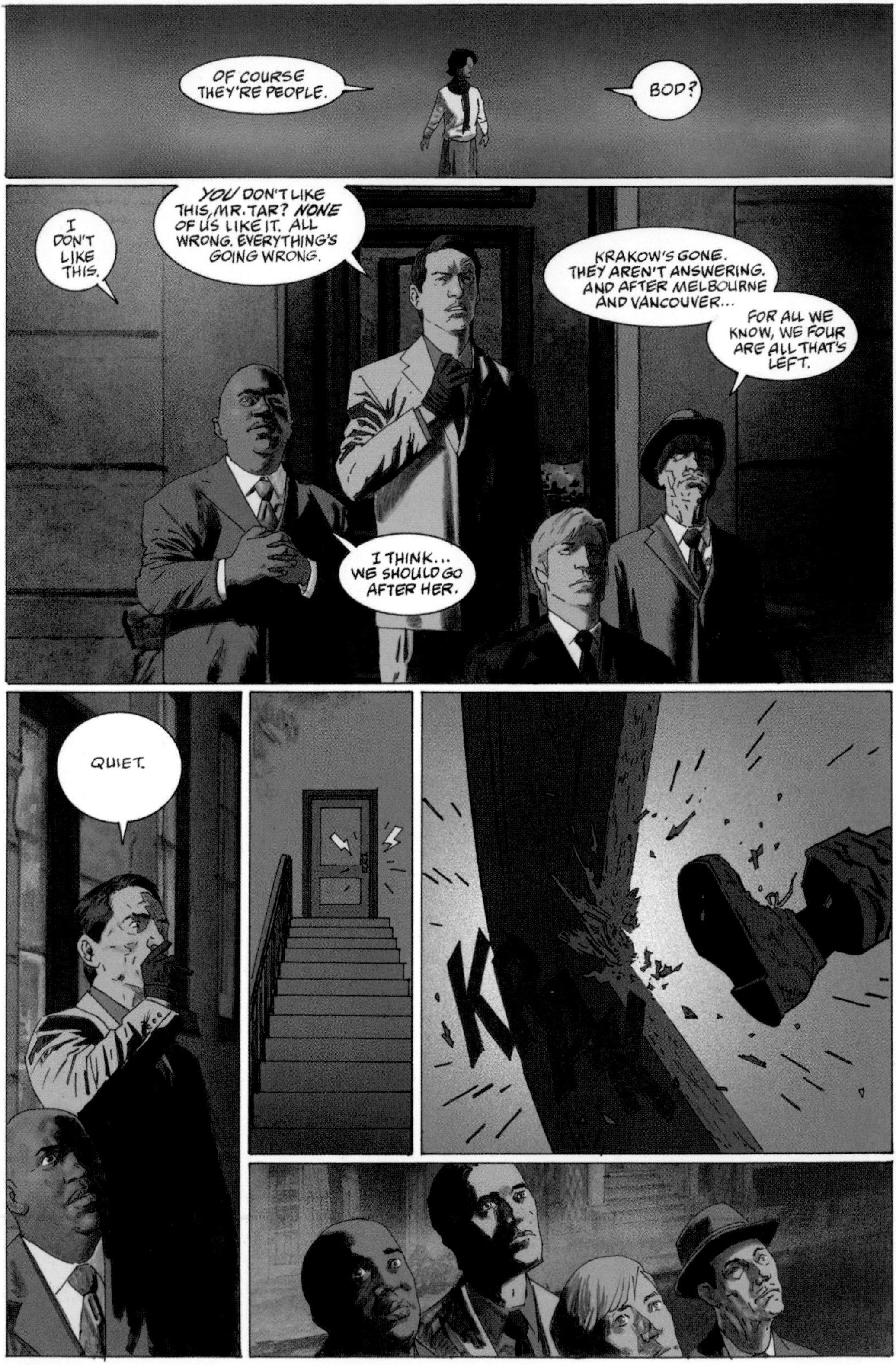
OF COURSE THEY'RE PEOPLE.
BOD?
I DON'T LIKE THIS.
YOU DON'T LIKE THIS, MR. TAR? NONE OF US LIKE IT. ALL WRONG. EVERYTHING'S GOING WRONG.
KRAKOW'S GONE. THEY AREN'T ANSWERING. AND AFTER MELBOURNE AND VANCOUVER...
FOR ALL WE KNOW, WE FOUR ARE ALL THAT'S LEFT.
I THINK... WE SHOULD GO AFTER HER.
QUIET.

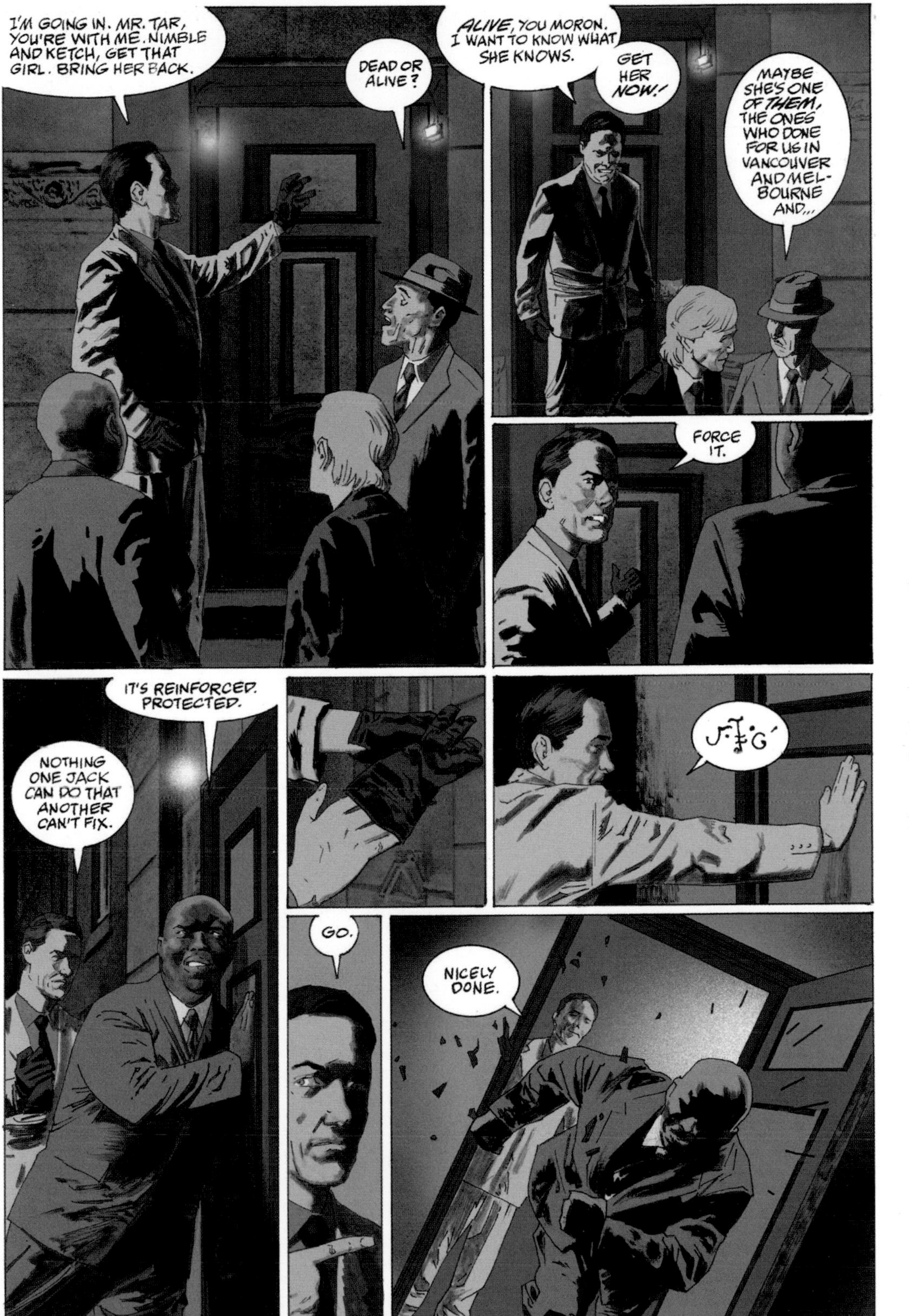
I'M GOING IN. MR. TAR, YOU'RE WITH ME. NIMBLE AND KETCH, GET THAT GIRL. BRING HER BACK.
DEAD OR ALIVE?
ALIVE, YOU MORON. I WANT TO KNOW WHAT SHE KNOWS.
GET HER NOW!
MAYBE SHE'S ONE OF THEM, THE ONES WHO DONE FOR US IN VANCOUVER AND MEL-BOURNE AND...
FORCE IT.
IT'S REINFORCED. PROTECTED.
NOTHING ONE JACK CAN DO THAT ANOTHER CAN'T FIX.
GO.
NICELY DONE.

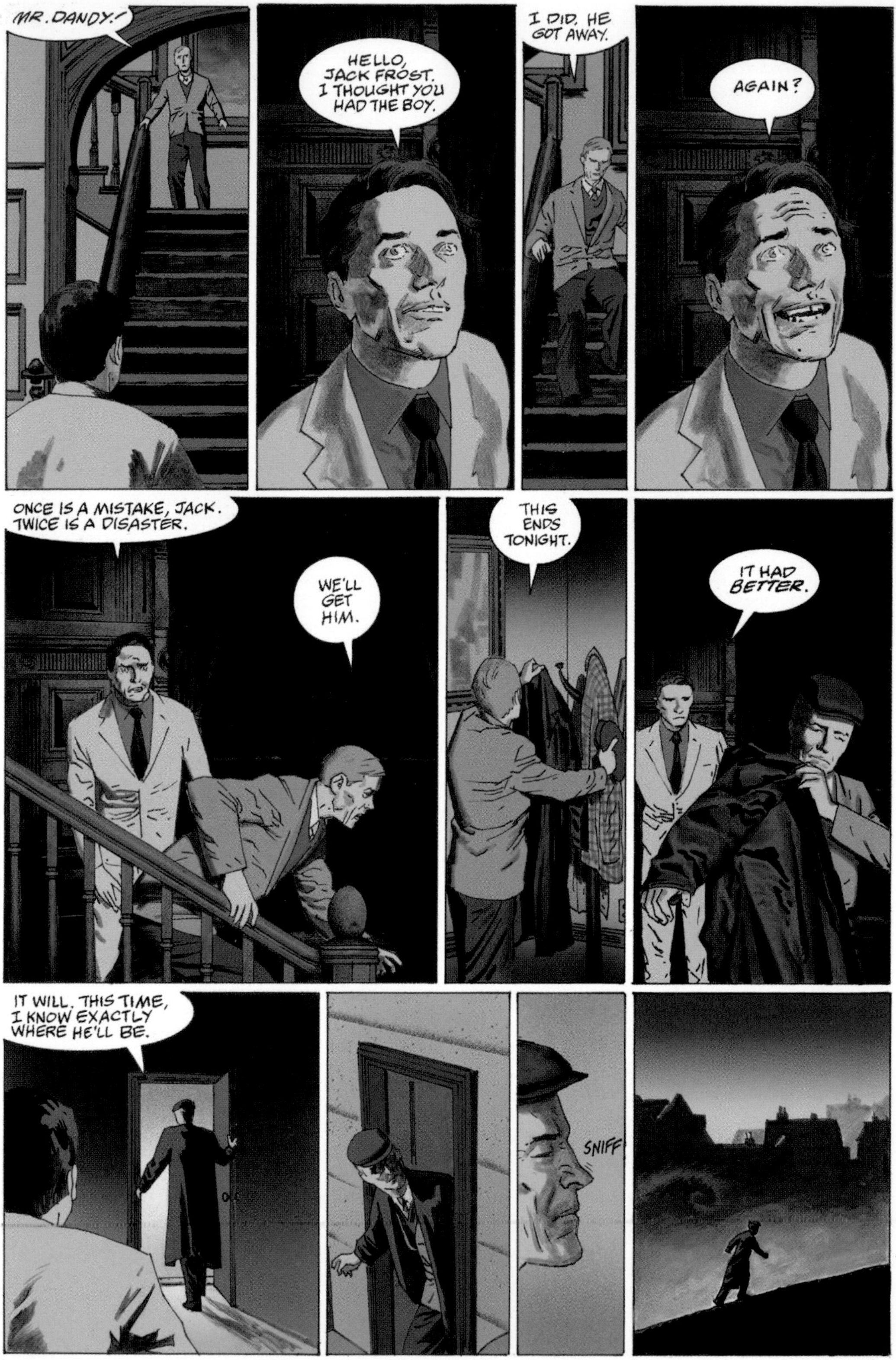
MR. DANDY!
HELLO, JACK FROST. I THOUGHT YOU HAD THE BOY.
I DID. HE GOT AWAY.
AGAIN?
ONCE IS A MISTAKE, JACK. TWICE IS A DISASTER.
WE'LL GET HIM.
THIS ENDS TONIGHT.
IT HAD BETTER.
IT WILL. THIS TIME, I KNOW EXACTLY WHERE HE'LL BE.
SNIFF

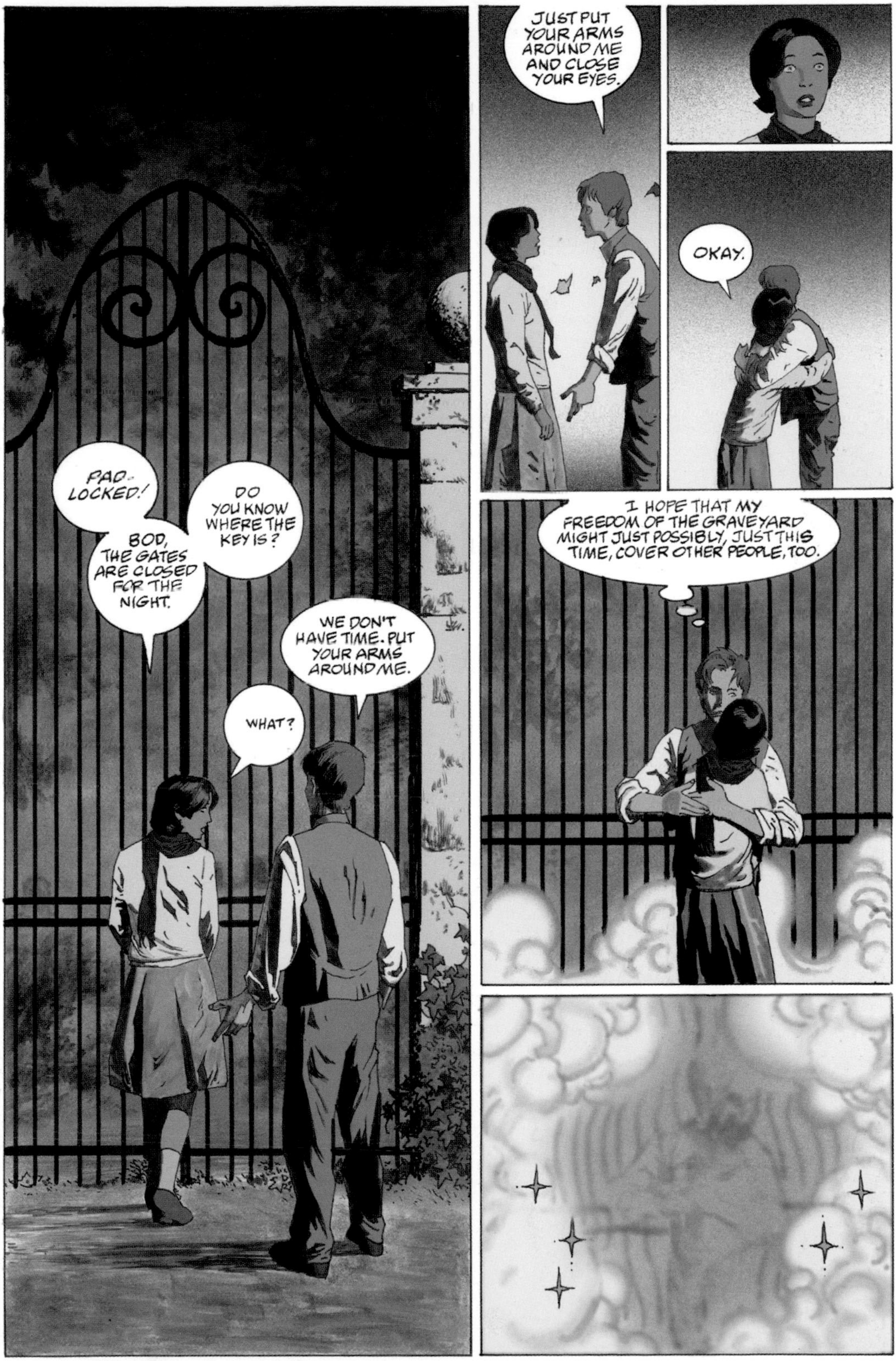
PAD-LOCKED!
BOD, THE GATES ARE CLOSED FOR THE NIGHT.
DO YOU KNOW WHERE THE KEY IS?
WE DON'T HAVE TIME. PUT YOUR ARMS AROUND ME.
WHAT?
JUST PUT YOUR ARMS AROUND ME AND CLOSE YOUR EYES.
OKAY.
I HOPE THAT MY FREEDOM OF THE GRAVEYARD MIGHT JUST POSSIBLY, JUST THIS TIME, COVER OTHER PEOPLE, TOO.

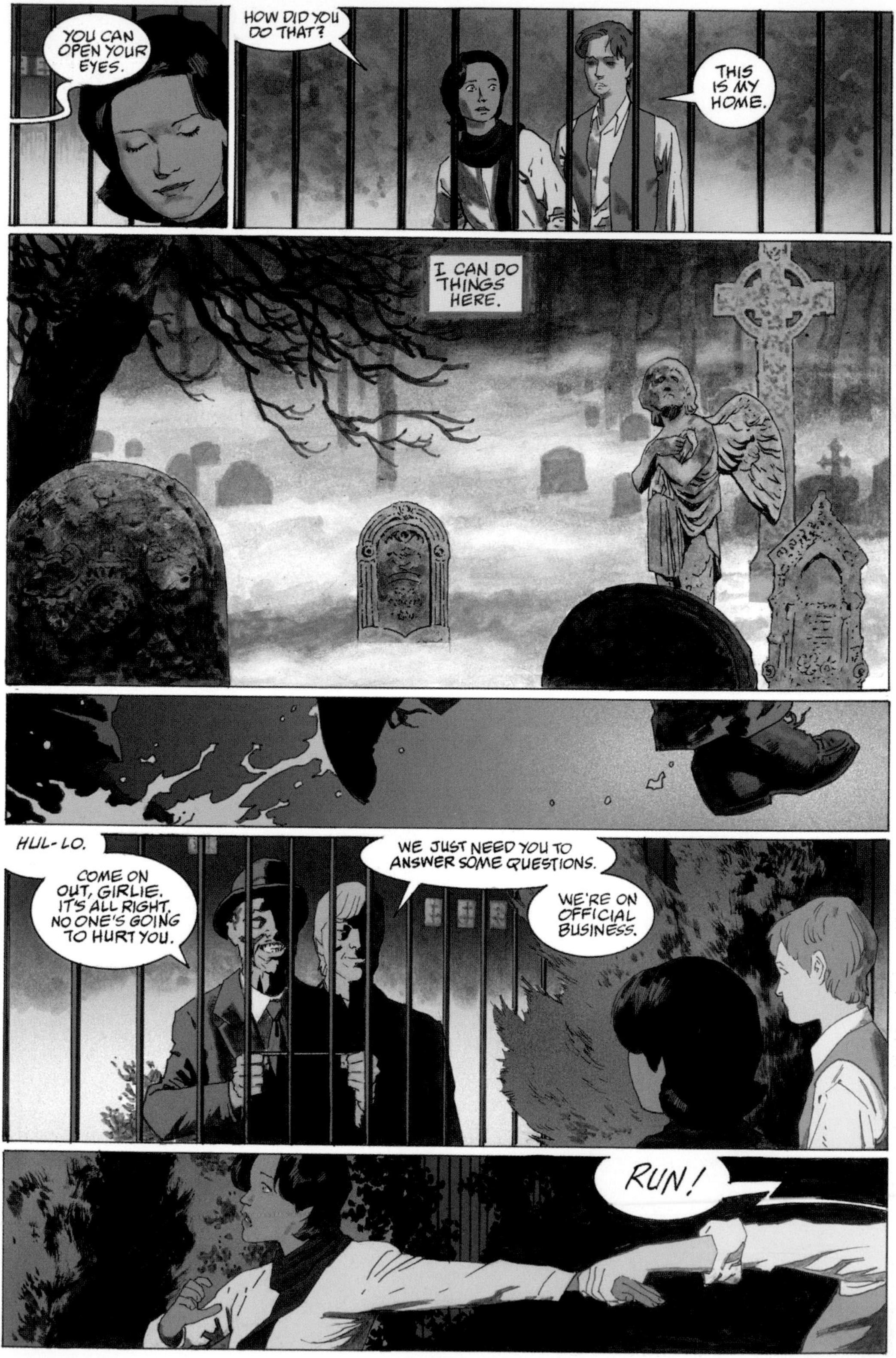
YOU CAN OPEN YOUR EYES.
HOW DID YOU DO THAT?
THIS IS MY HOME.
I CAN DO THINGS HERE.
HUL-LO.
COME ON OUT, GIRLIE. IT'S ALL RIGHT. NO ONE'S GOING TO HURT YOU.
WE JUST NEED YOU TO ANSWER SOME QUESTIONS.
WE'RE ON OFFICIAL BUSINESS.
RUN!

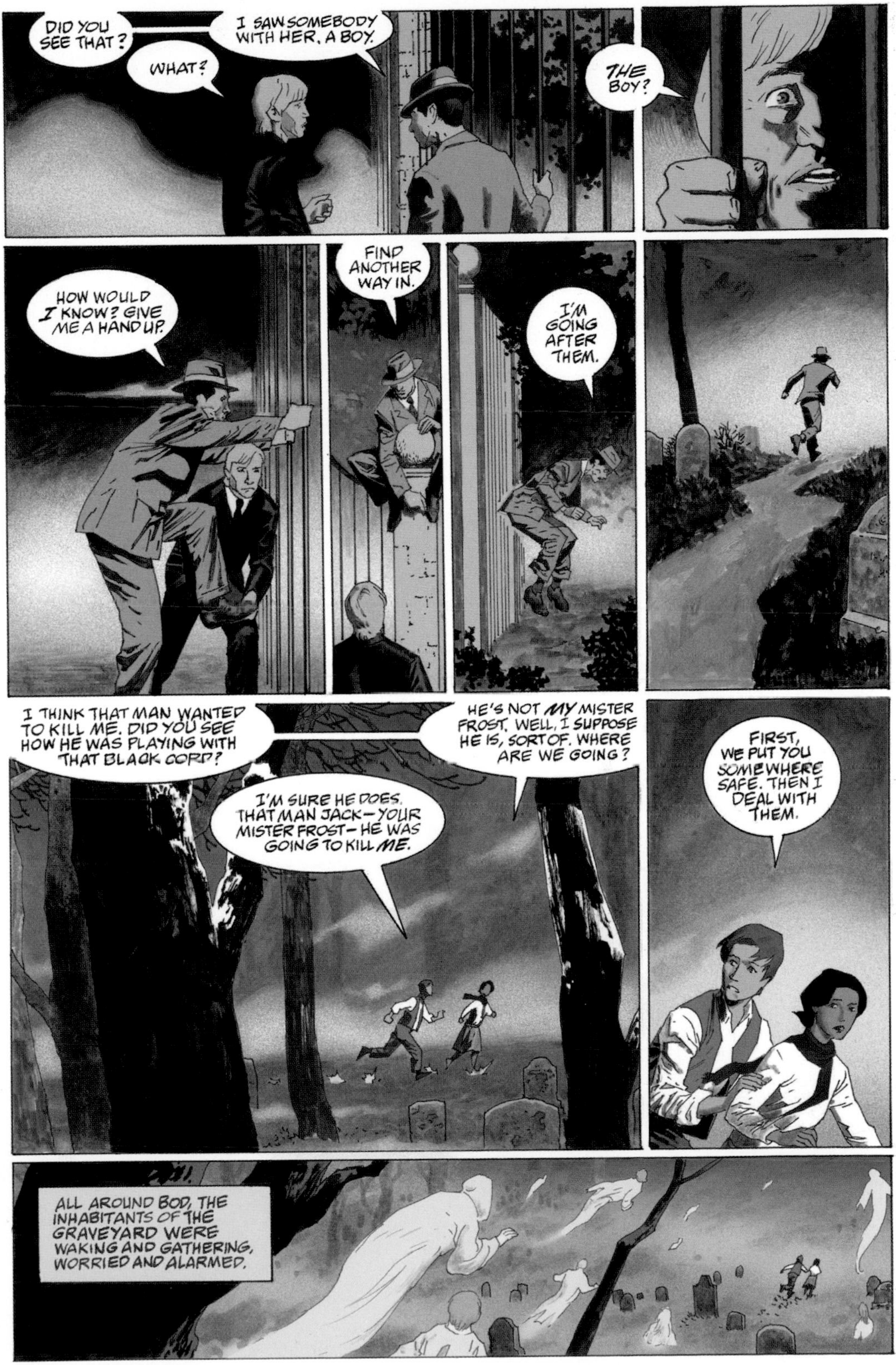
DID YOU SEE THAT?
I SAW SOMEBODY WITH HER, A BOY.
WHAT?
THE BOY?
HOW WOULD I KNOW? GIVE ME A HAND UP.
FIND ANOTHER WAY IN.
I'M GOING AFTER THEM.
I THINK THAT MAN WANTED TO KILL ME. DID YOU SEE HOW HE WAS PLAYING WITH THAT BLACK CORD?
I'M SURE HE DOES. THAT MAN JACK—YOUR MISTER FROST—HE WAS GOING TO KILL ME.
HE'S NOT MY MISTER FROST. WELL, I SUPPOSE HE IS, SORT OF. WHERE ARE WE GOING?
FIRST, WE PUT YOU SOMEWHERE SAFE. THEN I DEAL WITH THEM.
ALL AROUND BOD, THE INHABITANTS OF THE GRAVEYARD WERE WAKING AND GATHERING, WORRIED AND ALARMED.

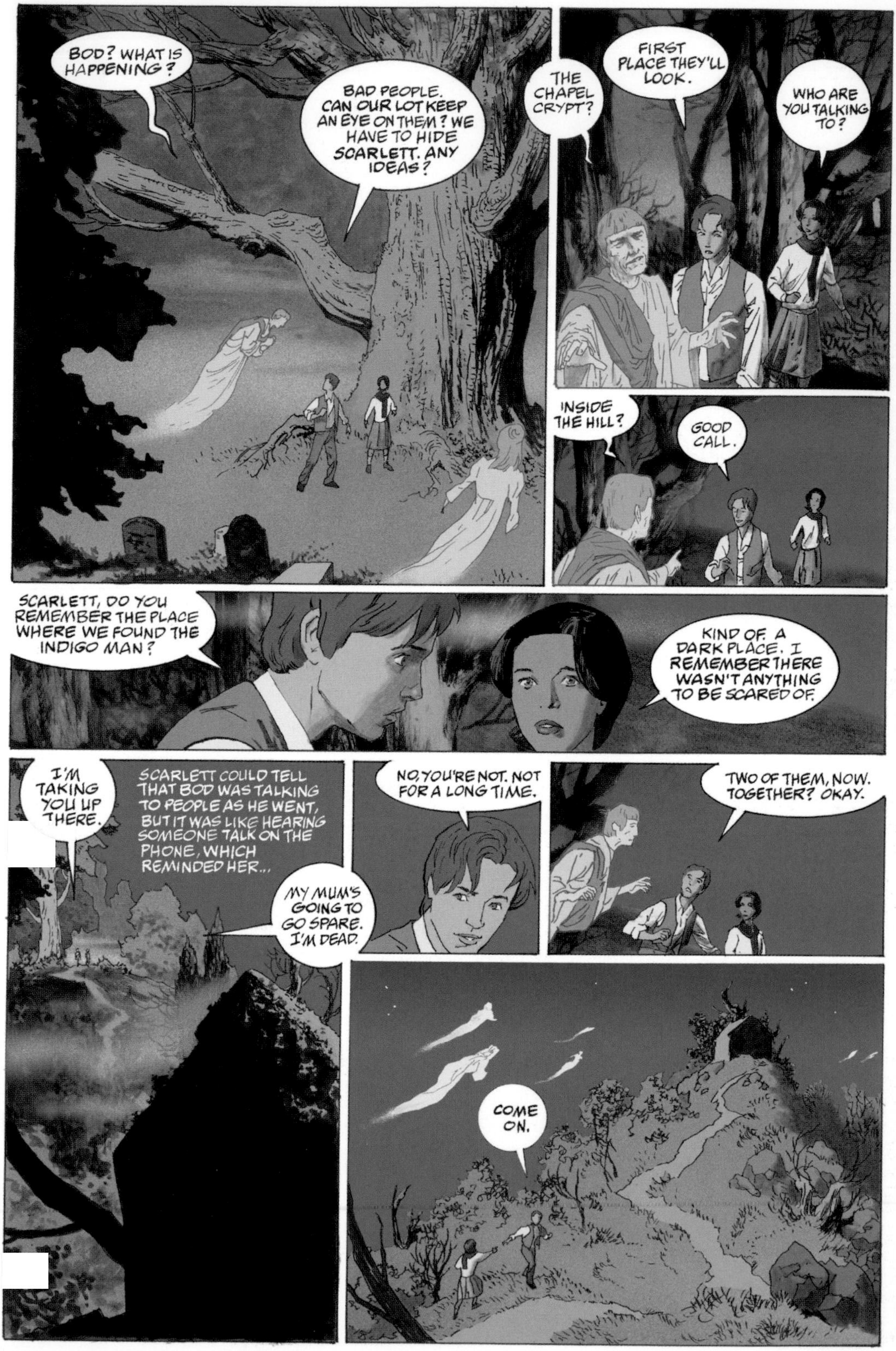
BOD? WHAT IS HAPPENING?
BAD PEOPLE. CAN OUR LOT KEEP AN EYE ON THEM? WE HAVE TO HIDE SCARLETT. ANY IDEAS?
THE CHAPEL CRYPT?
FIRST PLACE THEY'LL LOOK.
WHO ARE YOU TALKING TO?
INSIDE THE HILL?
GOOD CALL.
SCARLETT, DO YOU REMEMBER THE PLACE WHERE WE FOUND THE INDIGO MAN?
KIND OF. A DARK PLACE. I REMEMBER THERE WASN'T ANYTHING TO BE SCARED OF.
I'M TAKING YOU UP THERE.
SCARLETT COULD TELL THAT BOD WAS TALKING TO PEOPLE AS HE WENT, BUT IT WAS LIKE HEARING SOMEONE TALK ON THE PHONE, WHICH REMINDED HER...
MY MUM'S GOING TO GO SPARE. I'M DEAD.
NO, YOU'RE NOT. NOT FOR A LONG TIME.
TWO OF THEM, NOW. TOGETHER? OKAY.
COME ON.

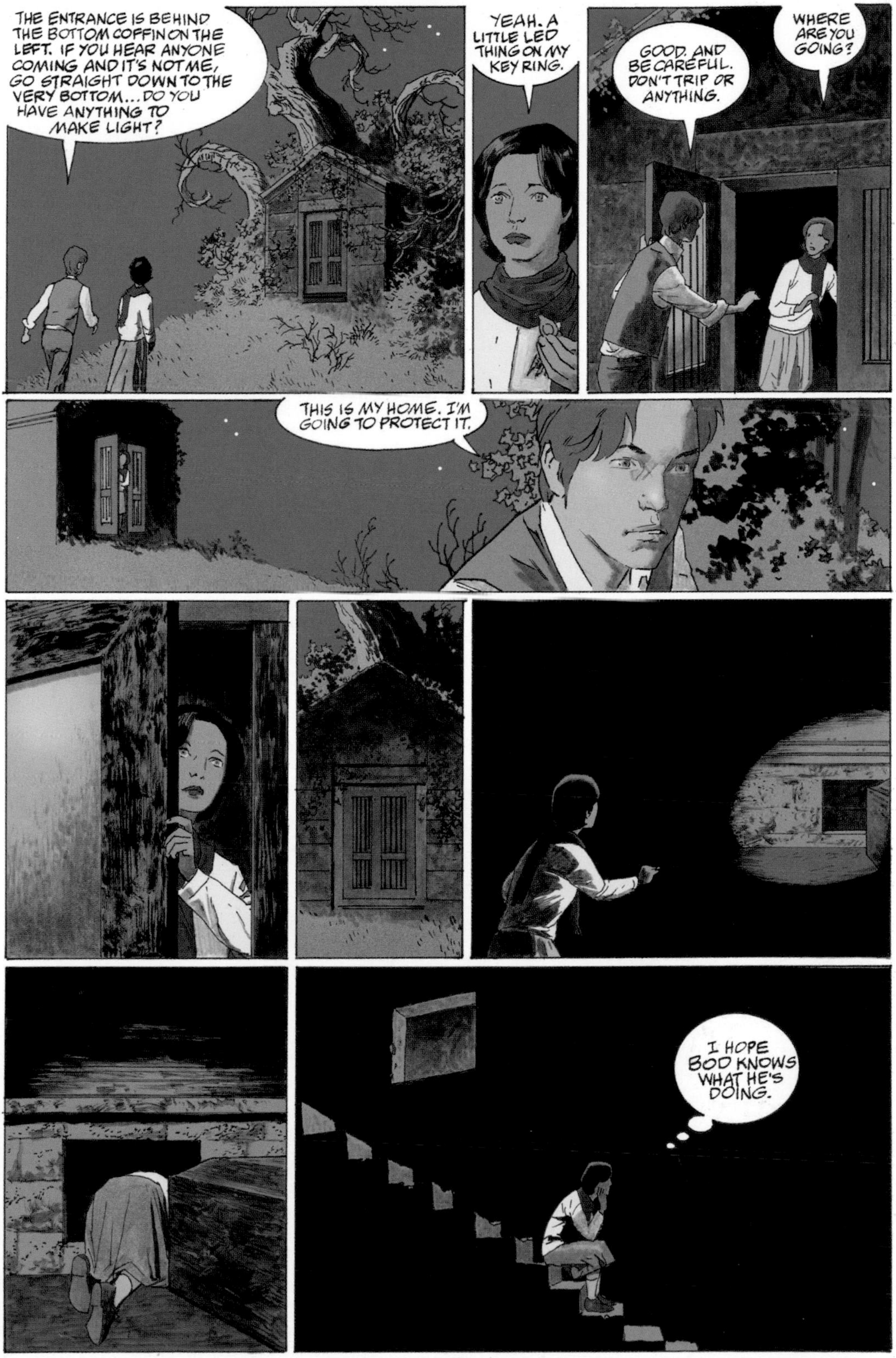
THE ENTRANCE IS BEHIND THE BOTTOM COFFIN ON THE LEFT. IF YOU HEAR ANYONE COMING AND IT'S NOT ME, GO STRAIGHT DOWN TO THE VERY BOTTOM... DO YOU HAVE ANYTHING TO MAKE LIGHT?
YEAH. A LITTLE LED THING ON MY KEY RING.
GOOD. AND BE CAREFUL. DON'T TRIP OR ANYTHING.
WHERE ARE YOU GOING?
THIS IS MY HOME. I'M GOING TO PROTECT IT.
I HOPE BOD KNOWS WHAT HE'S DOING.

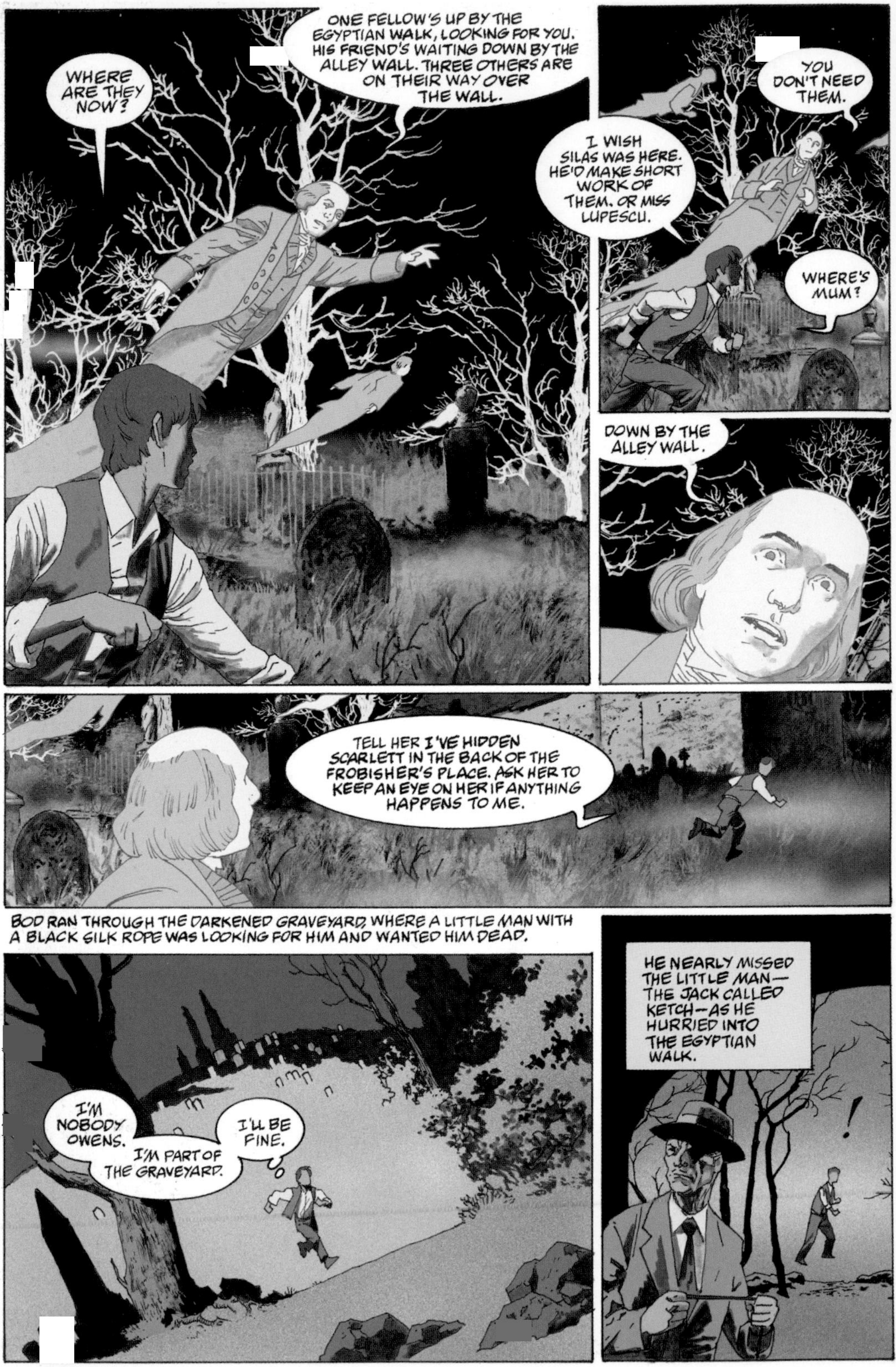
WHERE ARE THEY NOW?
ONE FELLOW'S UP BY THE EGYPTIAN WALK, LOOKING FOR YOU. HIS FRIEND'S WAITING DOWN BY THE ALLEY WALL. THREE OTHERS ARE ON THEIR WAY OVER THE WALL.
YOU DON'T NEED THEM.
I WISH SILAS WAS HERE. HE'D MAKE SHORT WORK OF THEM. OR MISS LUPESCU.
WHERE'S MUM?
DOWN BY THE ALLEY WALL.
TELL HER I'VE HIDDEN SCARLETT IN THE BACK OF THE FROBISHER'S PLACE. ASK HER TO KEEP AN EYE ON HER IF ANYTHING HAPPENS TO ME.
BOD RAN THROUGH THE DARKENED GRAVEYARD, WHERE A LITTLE MAN WITH A BLACK SILK ROPE WAS LOOKING FOR HIM AND WANTED HIM DEAD.
I'M NOBODY OWENS.
I'M PART OF THE GRAVEYARD.
I'LL BE FINE.
HE NEARLY MISSED THE LITTLE MAN— THE JACK CALLED KETCH—AS HE HURRIED INTO THE EGYPTIAN WALK.
!

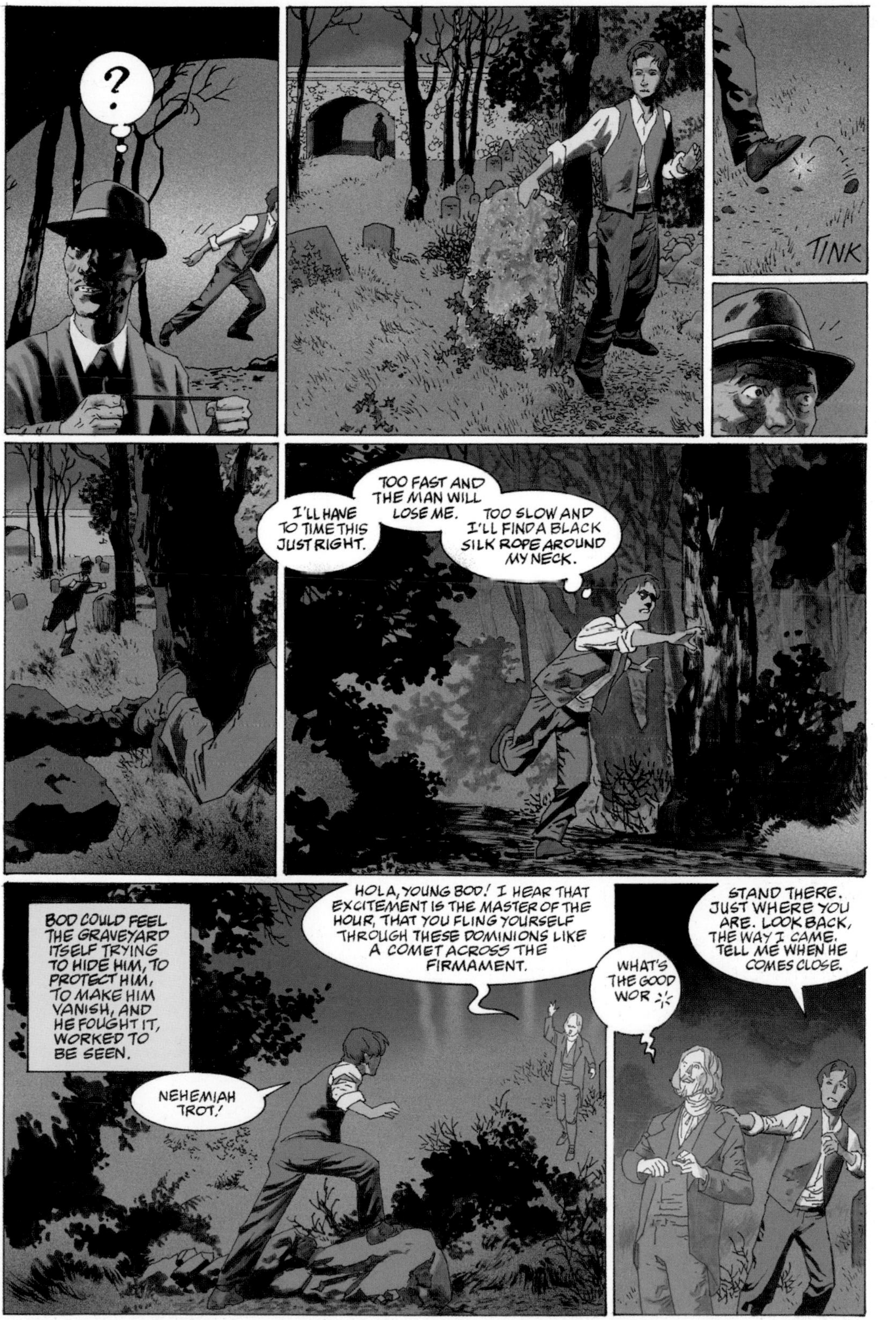
?
TINK
I'LL HAVE TO TIME THIS JUST RIGHT.
TOO FAST AND THE MAN WILL LOSE ME.
TOO SLOW AND I'LL FIND A BLACK SILK ROPE AROUND MY NECK.
BOD COULD FEEL THE GRAVEYARD ITSELF TRYING TO HIDE HIM, TO PROTECT HIM, TO MAKE HIM VANISH, AND HE FOUGHT IT, WORKED TO BE SEEN.
HOLA, YOUNG BOD! I HEAR THAT EXCITEMENT IS THE MASTER OF THE HOUR, THAT YOU FLING YOURSELF THROUGH THESE DOMINIONS LIKE A COMET ACROSS THE FIRMAMENT.
NEHEMIAH TROT!
WHAT'S THE GOOD WOR
STAND THERE. JUST WHERE YOU ARE. LOOK BACK, THE WAY I CAME. TELL ME WHEN HE COMES CLOSE.

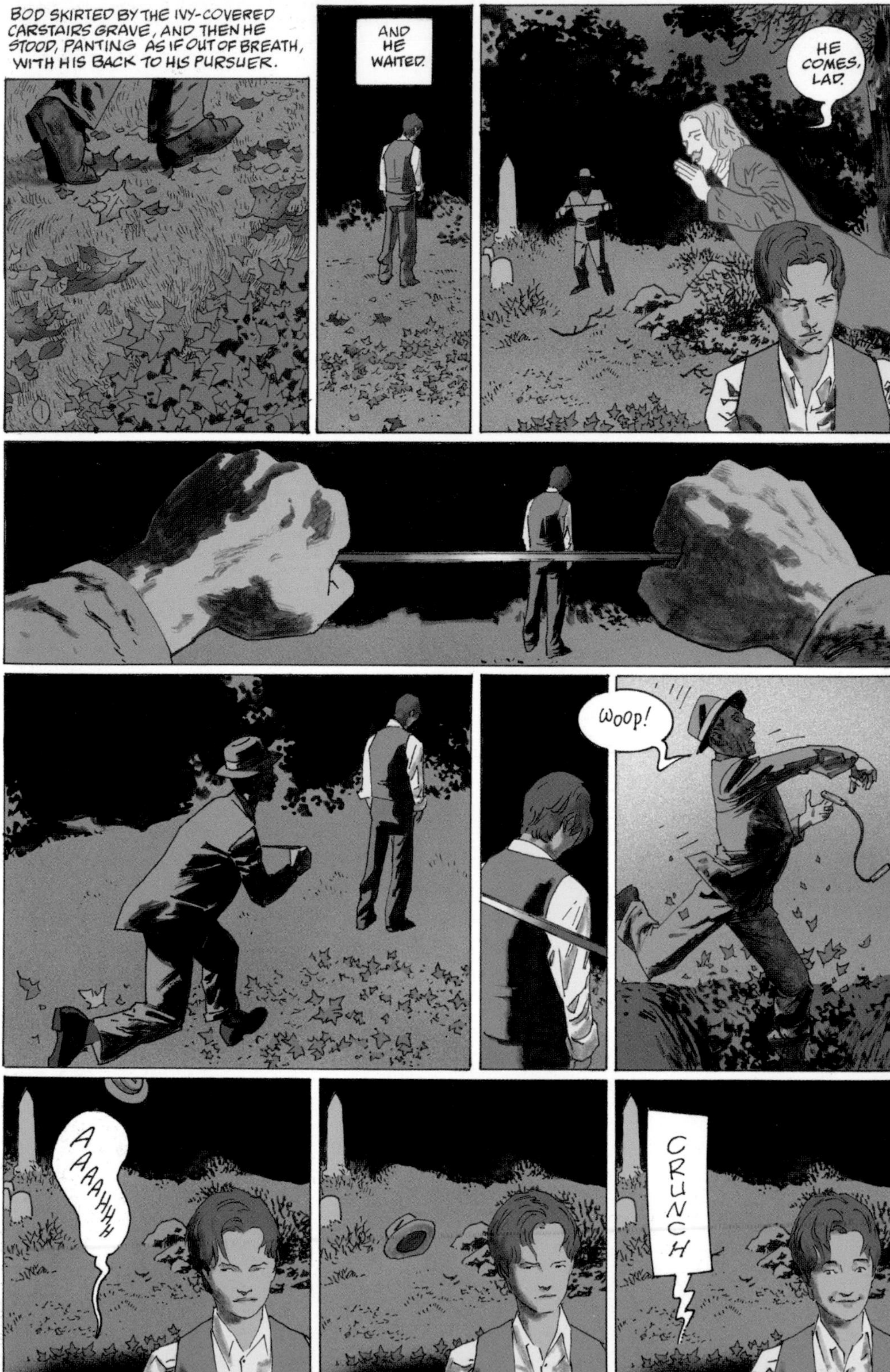
BOD SKIRTED BY THE IVY-COVERED CARSTAIRS GRAVE, AND THEN HE STOOD, PANTING AS IF OUT OF BREATH, WITH HIS BACK TO HIS PURSUER.
AND HE WAITED.
HE COMES, LAD.
WOOP!
AAAAHHH
CRUNCH

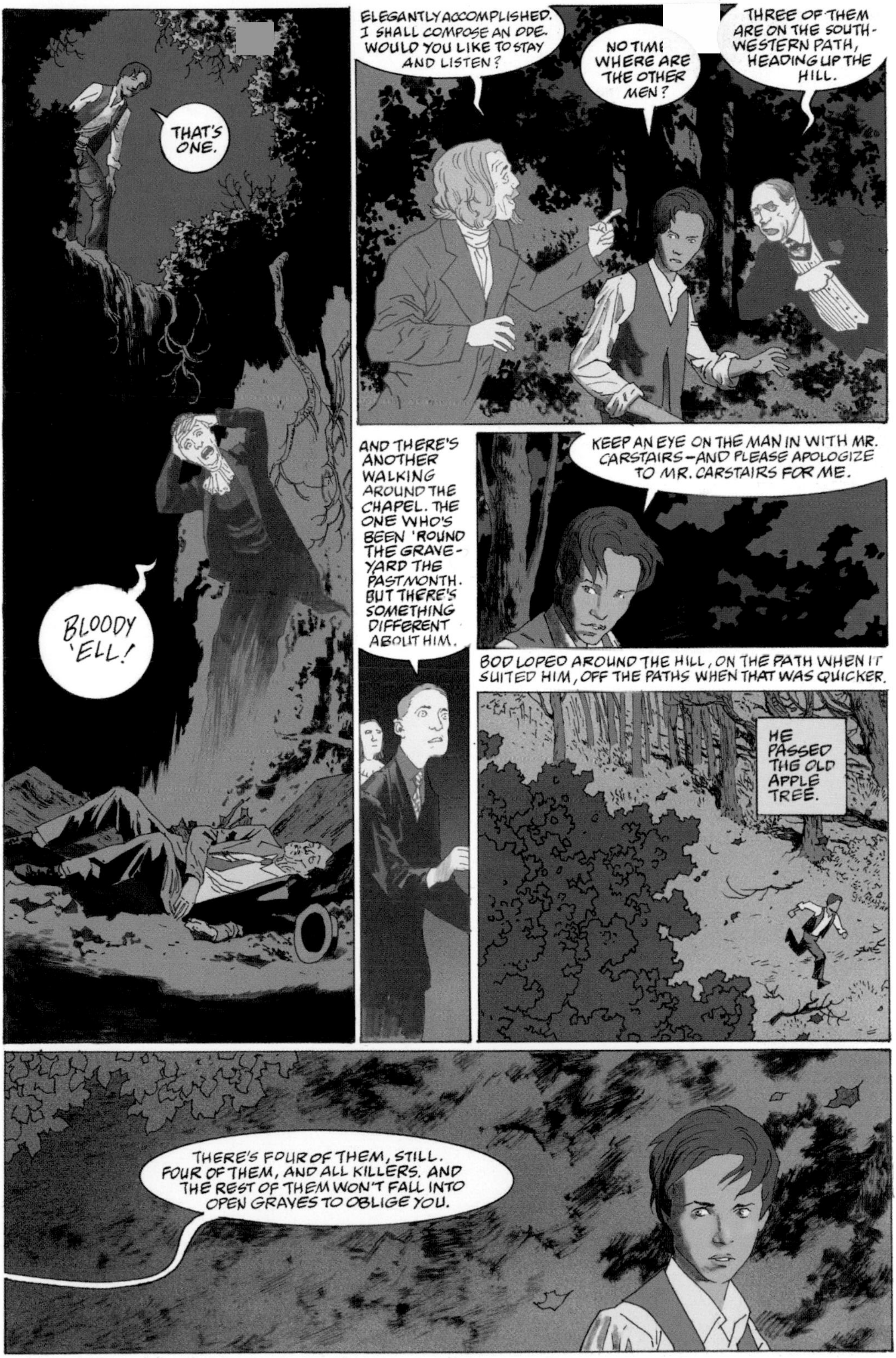
THAT'S ONE.
BLOODY 'ELL!
ELEGANTLY ACCOMPLISHED. I SHALL COMPOSE AN ODE. WOULD YOU LIKE TO STAY AND LISTEN?
NO TIME. WHERE ARE THE OTHER MEN?
THREE OF THEM ARE ON THE SOUTH-WESTERN PATH, HEADING UP THE HILL.
AND THERE'S ANOTHER WALKING AROUND THE CHAPEL. THE ONE WHO'S BEEN 'ROUND THE GRAVEYARD THE PAST MONTH. BUT THERE'S SOMETHING DIFFERENT ABOUT HIM.
KEEP AN EYE ON THE MAN IN WITH MR. CARSTAIRS—AND PLEASE APOLOGIZE TO MR. CARSTAIRS FOR ME.
BOD LOPED AROUND THE HILL, ON THE PATH WHEN IT SUITED HIM, OFF THE PATHS WHEN THAT WAS QUICKER.
HE PASSED THE OLD APPLE TREE.
THERE'S FOUR OF THEM, STILL. FOUR OF THEM, AND ALL KILLERS. AND THE REST OF THEM WON'T FALL INTO OPEN GRAVES TO OBLIGE YOU.

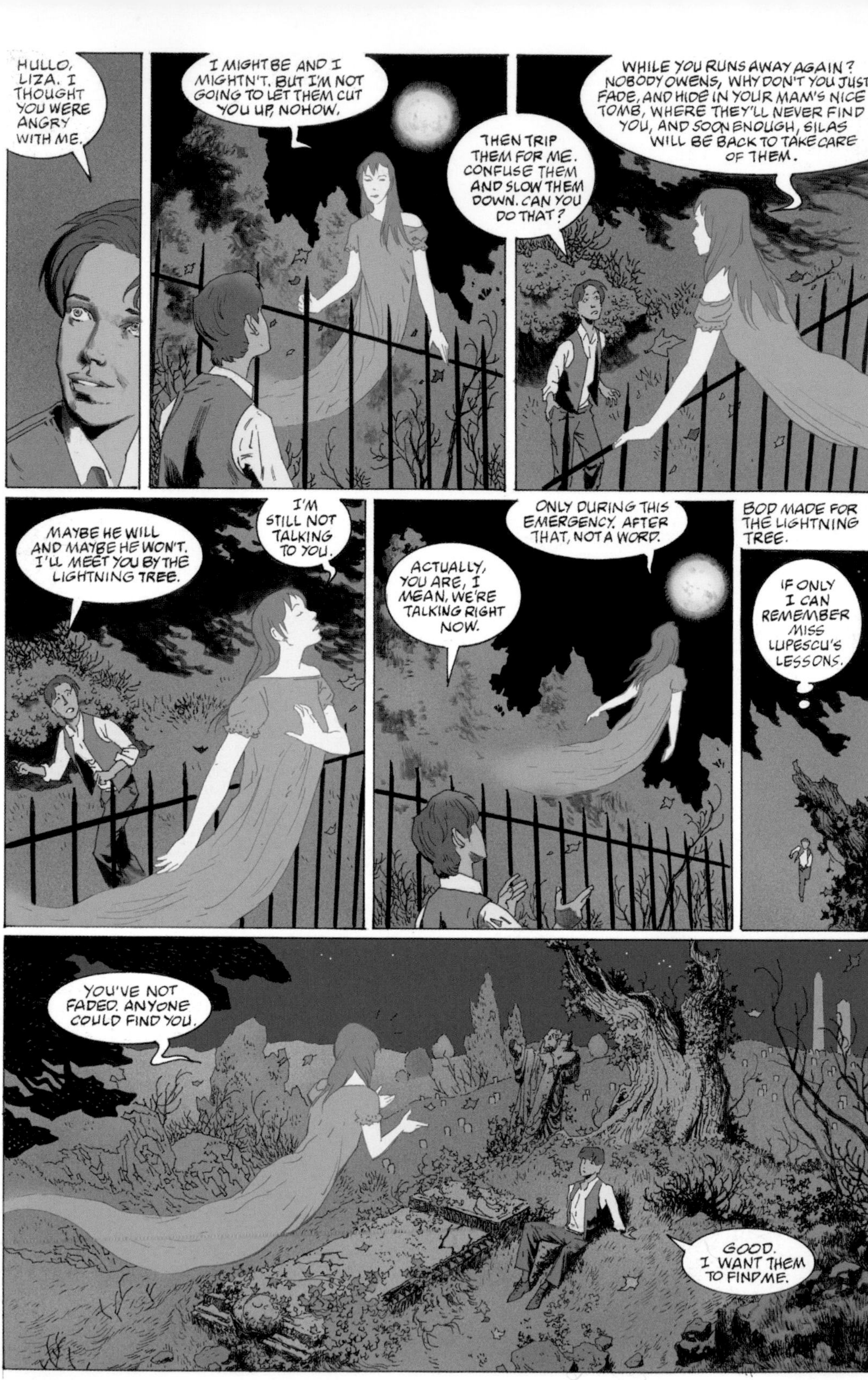
HULLO, LIZA. I THOUGHT YOU WERE ANGRY WITH ME.
I MIGHT BE AND I MIGHTN'T. BUT I'M NOT GOING TO LET THEM CUT YOU UP, NOHOW.
THEN TRIP THEM FOR ME. CONFUSE THEM AND SLOW THEM DOWN. CAN YOU DO THAT?
WHILE YOU RUNS AWAY AGAIN? NOBODY OWENS, WHY DON'T YOU JUST FADE, AND HIDE IN YOUR MAM'S NICE TOMB, WHERE THEY'LL NEVER FIND YOU, AND SOON ENOUGH, SILAS WILL BE BACK TO TAKE CARE OF THEM.
MAYBE HE WILL AND MAYBE HE WON'T. I'LL MEET YOU BY THE LIGHTNING TREE.
I'M STILL NOT TALKING TO YOU.
ACTUALLY, YOU ARE, I MEAN, WE'RE TALKING RIGHT NOW.
ONLY DURING THIS EMERGENCY. AFTER THAT, NOT A WORD.
BOD MADE FOR THE LIGHTNING TREE.
IF ONLY I CAN REMEMBER MISS LUPESCU'S LESSONS.
YOU'VE NOT FADED. ANYONE COULD FIND YOU.
GOOD. I WANT THEM TO FIND ME.

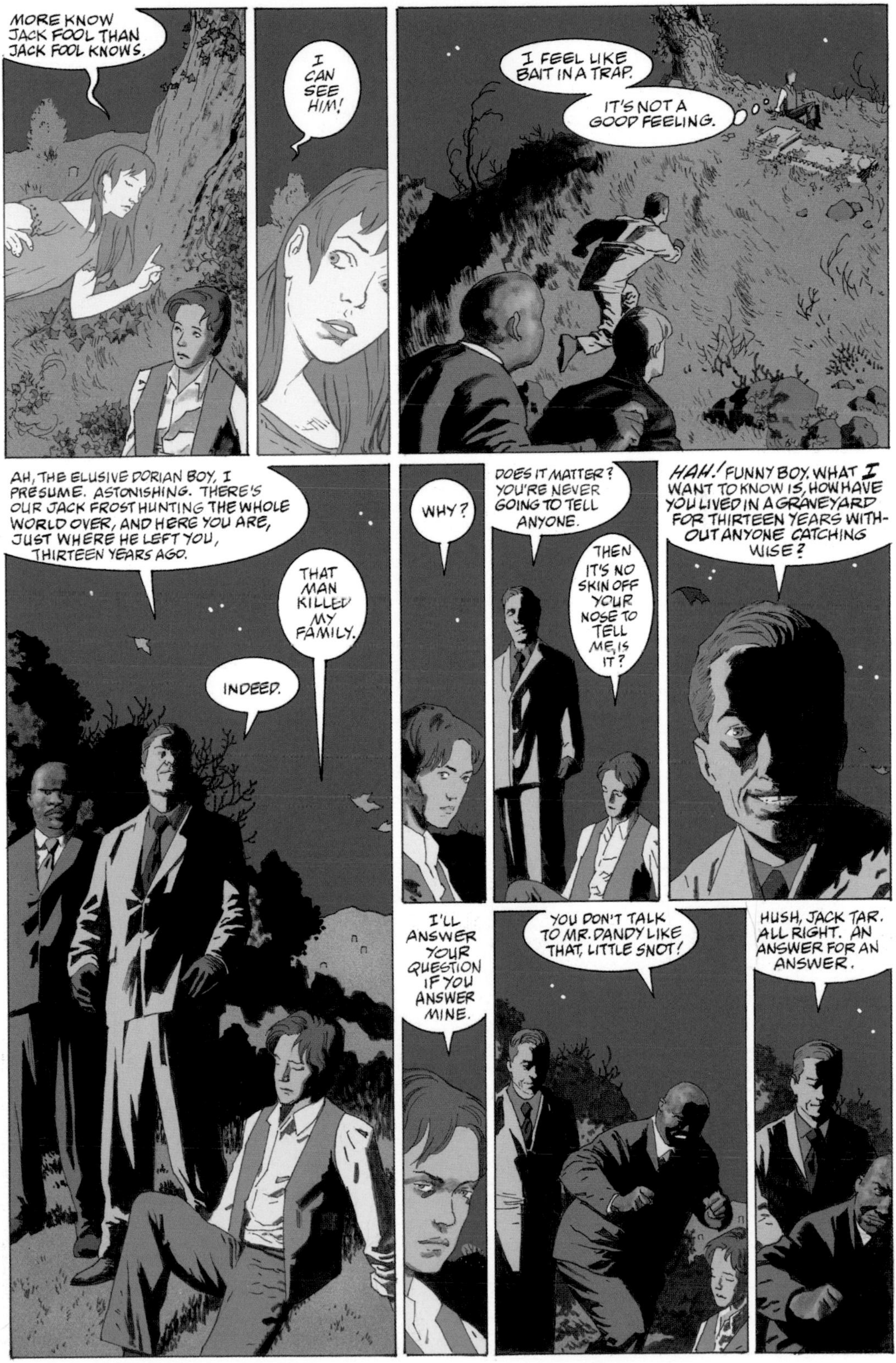
MORE KNOW JACK FOOL THAN JACK FOOL KNOWS.
I CAN SEE HIM!
I FEEL LIKE BAIT IN A TRAP.
IT'S NOT A GOOD FEELING.
AH, THE ELUSIVE DORIAN BOY, I PRESUME. ASTONISHING. THERE'S OUR JACK FROST HUNTING THE WHOLE WORLD OVER, AND HERE YOU ARE, JUST WHERE HE LEFT YOU, THIRTEEN YEARS AGO.
THAT MAN KILLED MY FAMILY.
INDEED.
WHY?
DOES IT MATTER? YOU'RE NEVER GOING TO TELL ANYONE.
THEN IT'S NO SKIN OFF YOUR NOSE TO TELL ME, IS IT?
HAH! FUNNY BOY. WHAT I WANT TO KNOW IS, HOW HAVE YOU LIVED IN A GRAVEYARD FOR THIRTEEN YEARS WITHOUT ANYONE CATCHING WISE?
I'LL ANSWER YOUR QUESTION IF YOU ANSWER MINE.
YOU DON'T TALK TO MR. DANDY LIKE THAT, LITTLE SNOT!
HUSH, JACK TAR. ALL RIGHT. AN ANSWER FOR AN ANSWER.

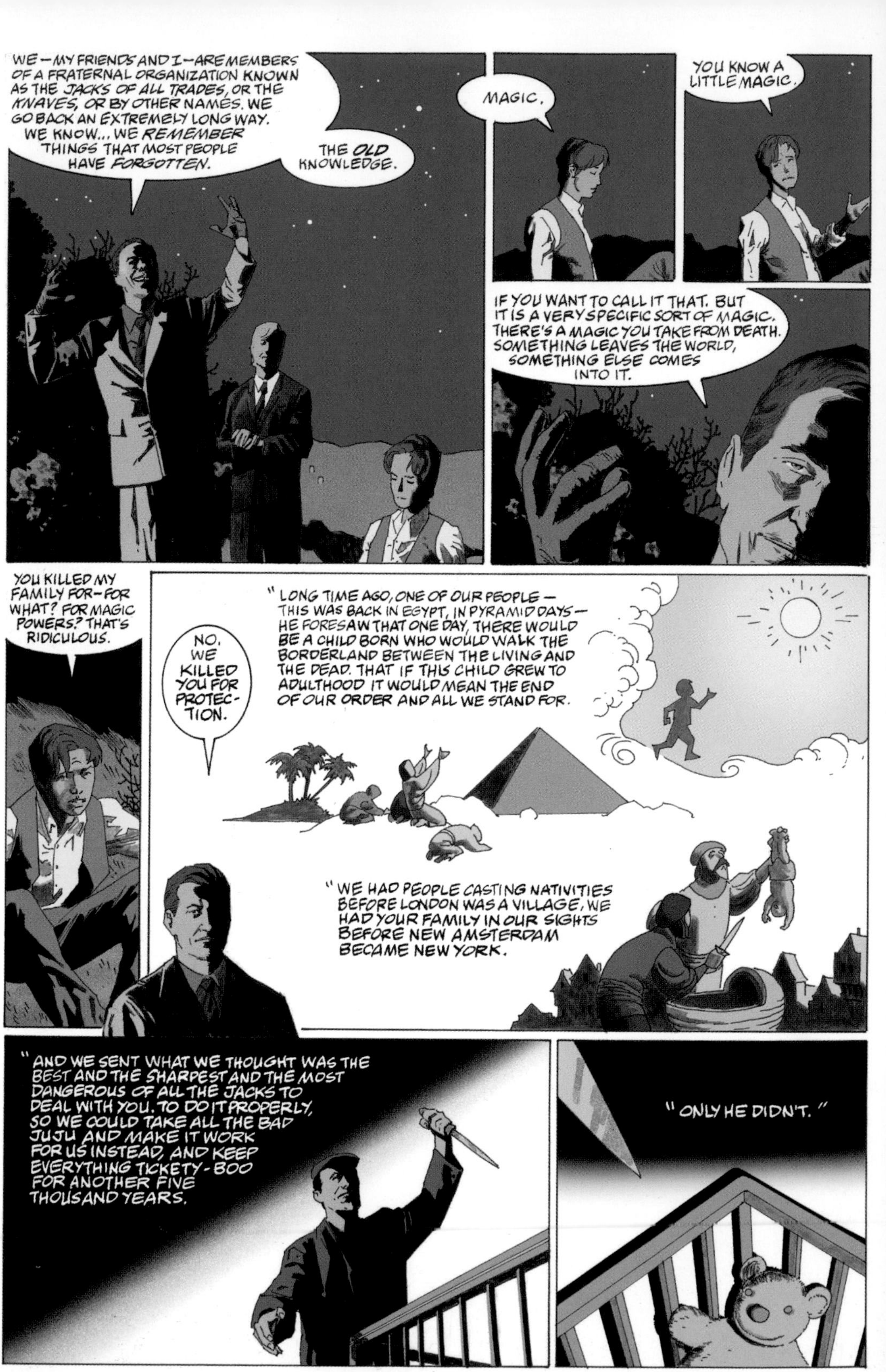
WE—MY FRIENDS AND I—ARE MEMBERS OF A FRATERNAL ORGANIZATION KNOWN AS THE JACKS OF ALL TRADES, OR THE KNAVES, OR BY OTHER NAMES. WE GO BACK AN EXTREMELY LONG WAY. WE KNOW... WE REMEMBER THINGS THAT MOST PEOPLE HAVE FORGOTTEN.
THE OLD KNOWLEDGE.
MAGIC.
YOU KNOW A LITTLE MAGIC.
IF YOU WANT TO CALL IT THAT. BUT IT IS A VERY SPECIFIC SORT OF MAGIC. THERE'S A MAGIC YOU TAKE FROM DEATH. SOMETHING LEAVES THE WORLD, SOMETHING ELSE COMES INTO IT.
YOU KILLED MY FAMILY FOR—FOR WHAT? FOR MAGIC POWERS? THAT'S RIDICULOUS.
NO. WE KILLED YOU FOR PROTECTION.
"LONG TIME AGO, ONE OF OUR PEOPLE—THIS WAS BACK IN EGYPT, IN PYRAMID DAYS—HE FORESAW THAT ONE DAY, THERE WOULD BE A CHILD BORN WHO WOULD WALK THE BORDERLAND BETWEEN THE LIVING AND THE DEAD. THAT IF THIS CHILD GREW TO ADULTHOOD IT WOULD MEAN THE END OF OUR ORDER AND ALL WE STAND FOR.
"WE HAD PEOPLE CASTING NATIVITIES BEFORE LONDON WAS A VILLAGE, WE HAD YOUR FAMILY IN OUR SIGHTS BEFORE NEW AMSTERDAM BECAME NEW YORK.
"AND WE SENT WHAT WE THOUGHT WAS THE BEST AND THE SHARPEST AND THE MOST DANGEROUS OF ALL THE JACKS TO DEAL WITH YOU. TO DO IT PROPERLY, SO WE COULD TAKE ALL THE BAD JUJU AND MAKE IT WORK FOR US INSTEAD, AND KEEP EVERYTHING TICKETY-BOO FOR ANOTHER FIVE THOUSAND YEARS.
"ONLY HE DIDN'T."

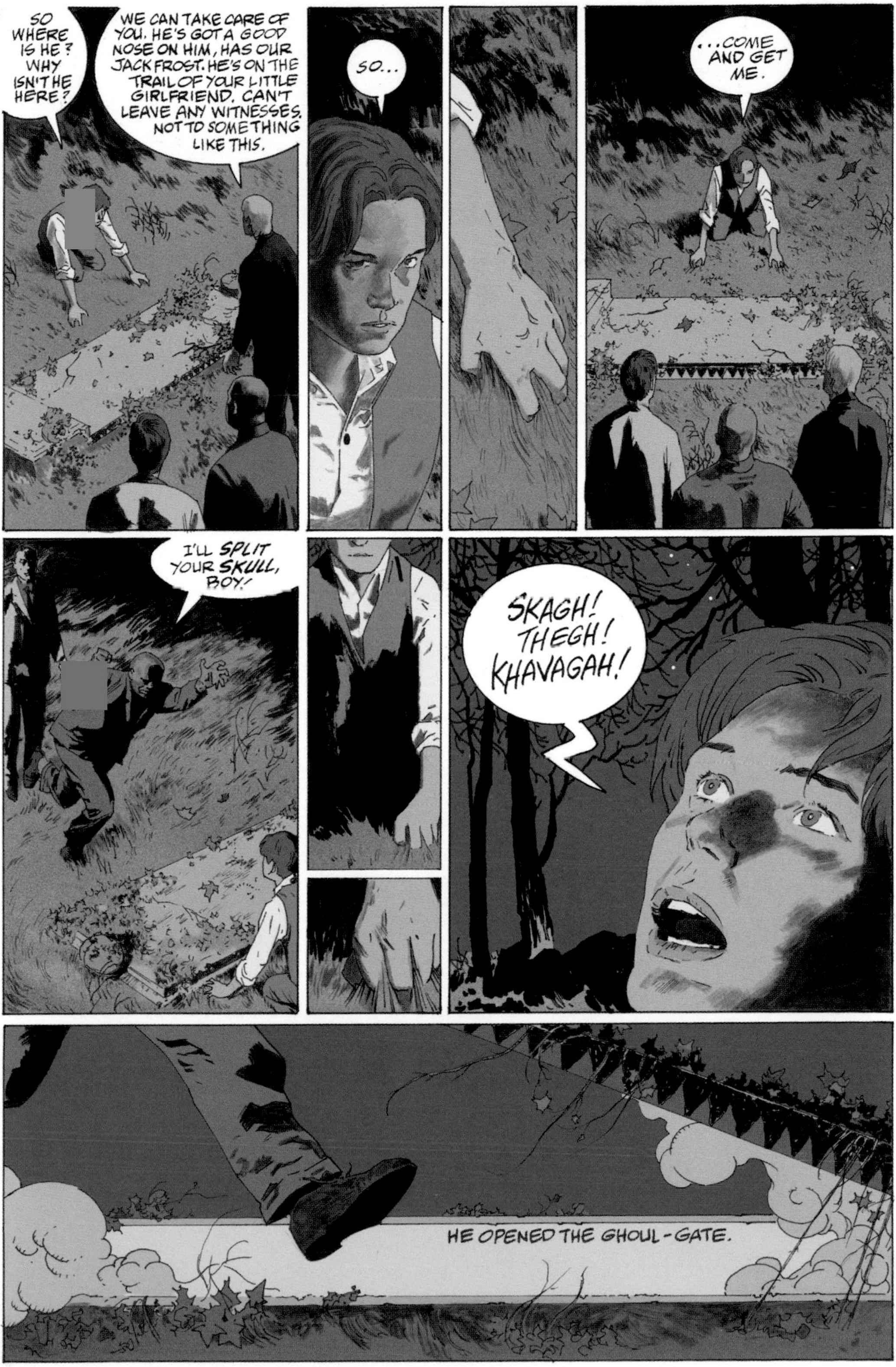
SO WHERE IS HE? WHY ISN'T HE HERE?
WE CAN TAKE CARE OF YOU. HE'S GOT A GOOD NOSE ON HIM, HAS OUR JACK FROST. HE'S ON THE TRAIL OF YOUR LITTLE GIRLFRIEND. CAN'T LEAVE ANY WITNESSES. NOT TO SOMETHING LIKE THIS.
SO...
...COME AND GET ME.
I'LL SPLIT YOUR SKULL, BOY!
SKAGH! THEGH! KHAVAGAH!
HE OPENED THE GHOUL-GATE.

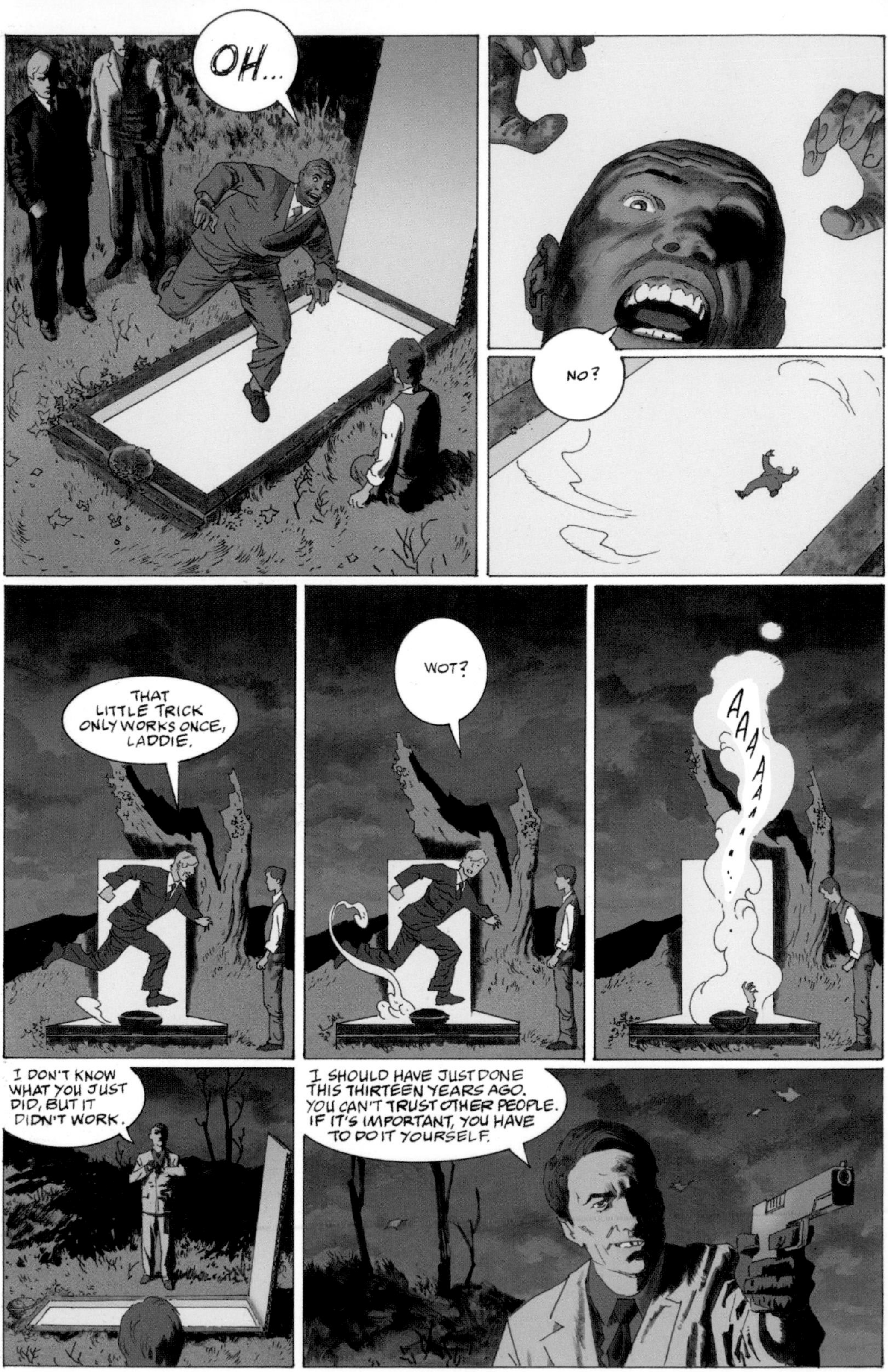
OH...
NO?
THAT LITTLE TRICK ONLY WORKS ONCE, LADDIE.
WOT?
AAAAAA...
I DON'T KNOW WHAT YOU JUST DID, BUT IT DIDN'T WORK.
I SHOULD HAVE JUST DONE THIS THIRTEEN YEARS AGO. YOU CAN'T TRUST OTHER PEOPLE. IF IT'S IMPORTANT, YOU HAVE TO DO IT YOURSELF.

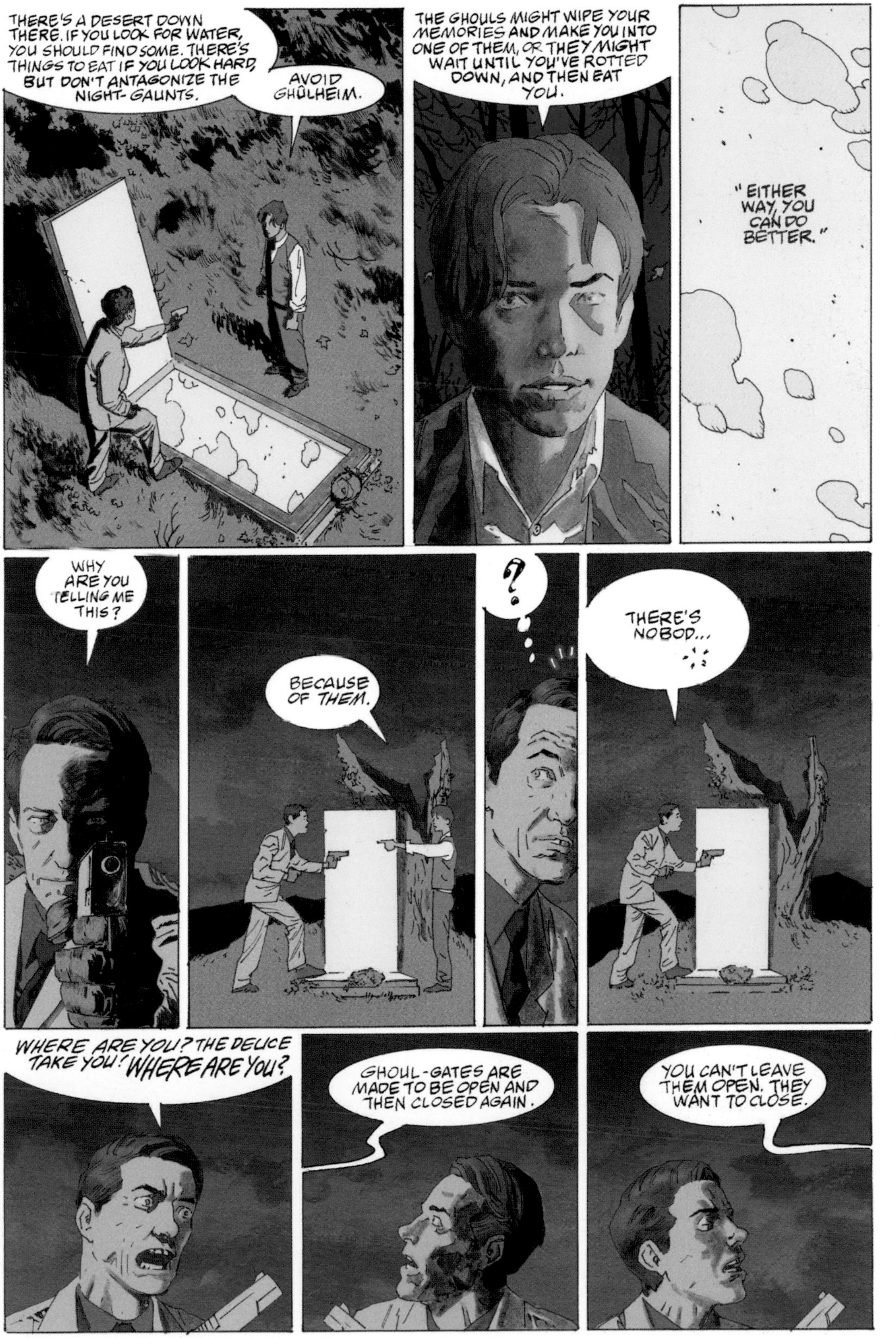
THERE'S A DESERT DOWN THERE. IF YOU LOOK FOR WATER, YOU SHOULD FIND SOME. THERE'S THINGS TO EAT IF YOU LOOK HARD, BUT DON'T ANTAGONIZE THE NIGHT-GAUNTS.
AVOID GHÛLHEIM.
THE GHOULS MIGHT WIPE YOUR MEMORIES AND MAKE YOU INTO ONE OF THEM, OR THEY MIGHT WAIT UNTIL YOU'VE ROTTED DOWN, AND THEN EAT YOU.
"EITHER WAY, YOU CAN DO BETTER."
WHY ARE YOU TELLING ME THIS?
BECAUSE OF THEM.
?
THERE'S NOBOD...
WHERE ARE YOU? THE DEUCE TAKE YOU! WHERE ARE YOU?
GHOUL-GATES ARE MADE TO BE OPEN AND THEN CLOSED AGAIN.
YOU CAN'T LEAVE THEM OPEN. THEY WANT TO CLOSE.

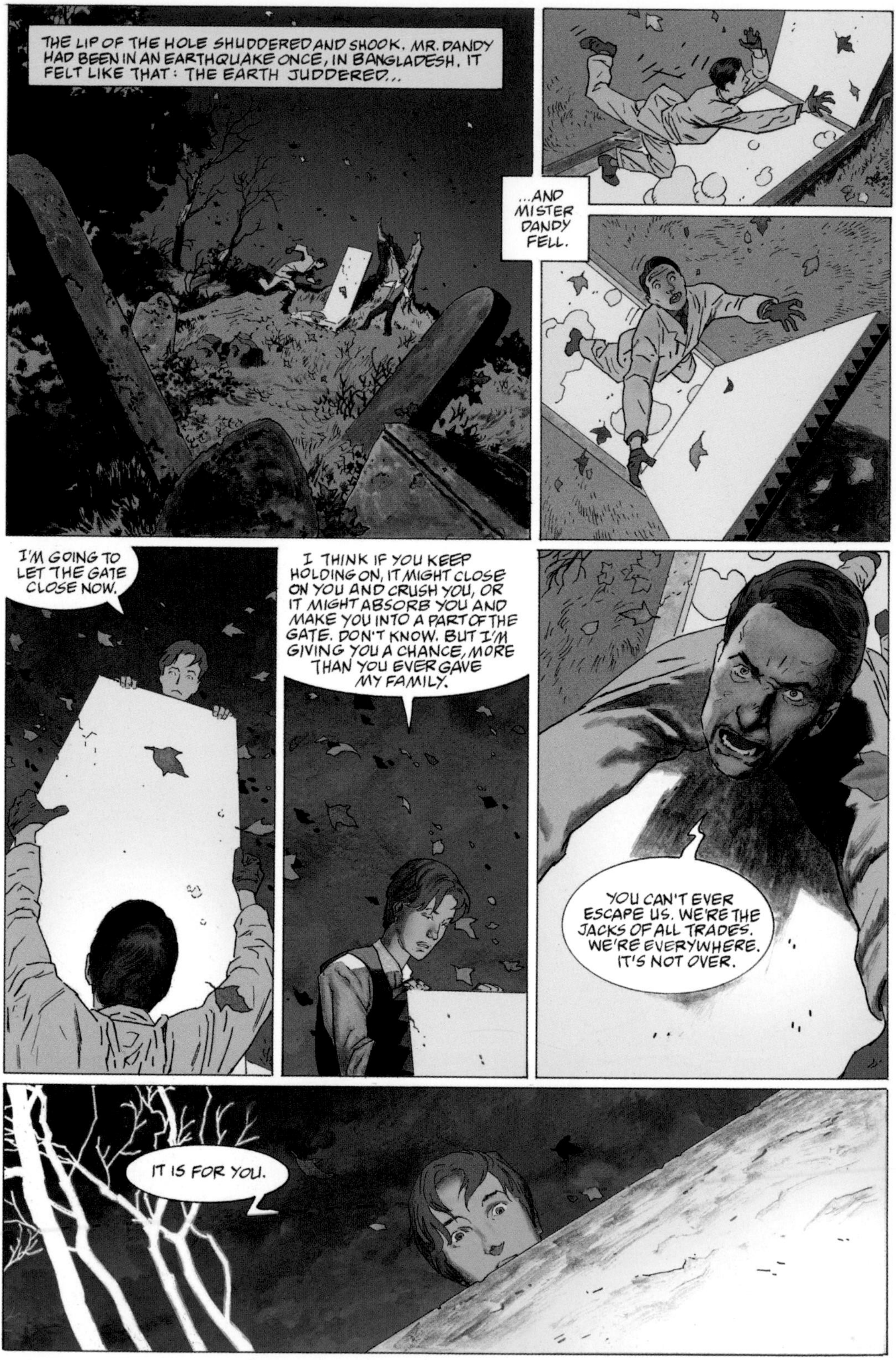
THE LIP OF THE HOLE SHUDDERED AND SHOOK. MR. DANDY HAD BEEN IN AN EARTHQUAKE ONCE, IN BANGLADESH. IT FELT LIKE THAT: THE EARTH JUDDERED...
...AND MISTER DANDY FELL.
I'M GOING TO LET THE GATE CLOSE NOW.
I THINK IF YOU KEEP HOLDING ON, IT MIGHT CLOSE ON YOU AND CRUSH YOU, OR IT MIGHT ABSORB YOU AND MAKE YOU INTO A PART OF THE GATE. DON'T KNOW. BUT I'M GIVING YOU A CHANCE, MORE THAN YOU EVER GAVE MY FAMILY.
YOU CAN'T EVER ESCAPE US. WE'RE THE JACKS OF ALL TRADES. WE'RE EVERYWHERE. IT'S NOT OVER.
IT IS FOR YOU.

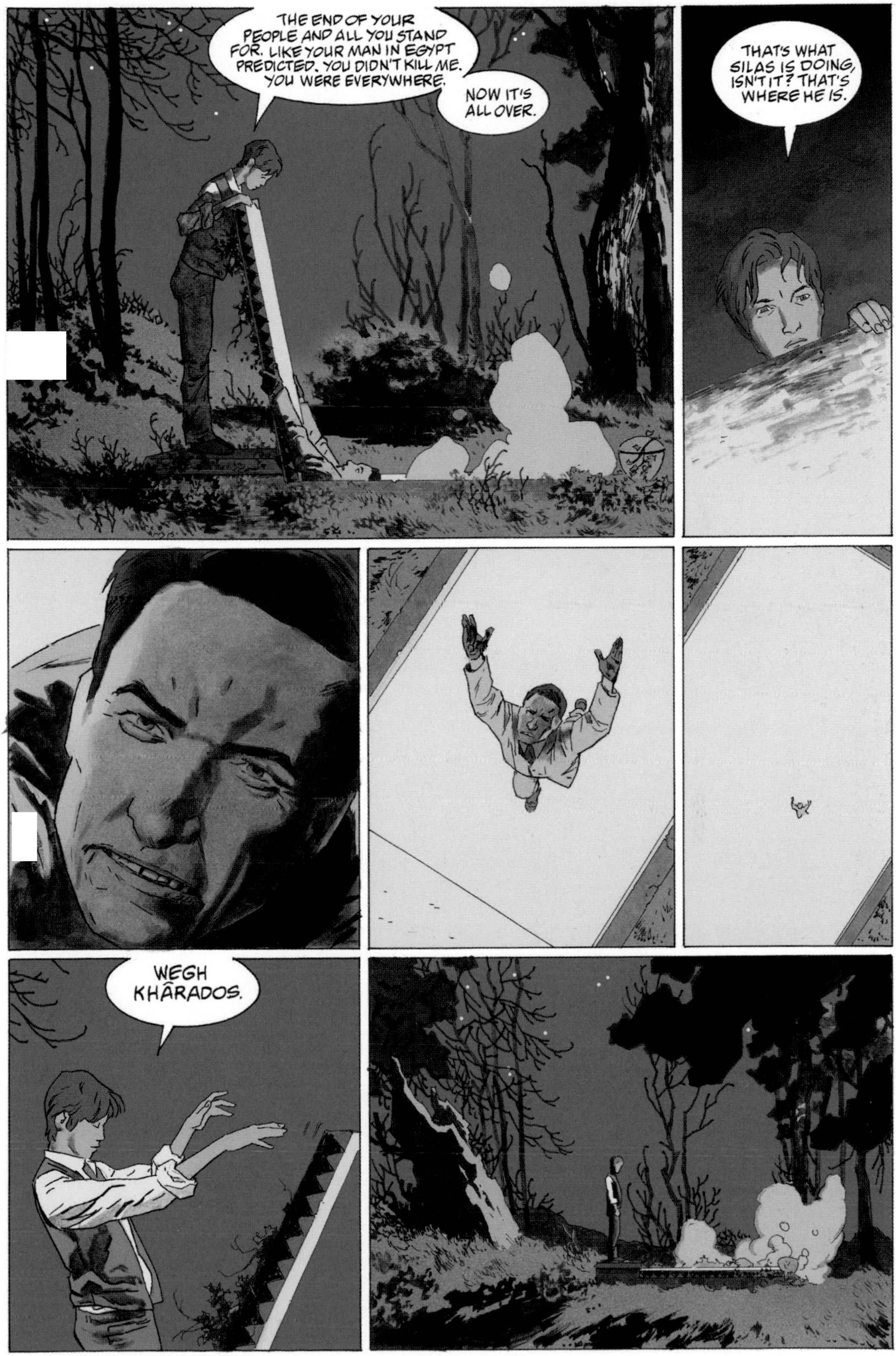
THE END OF YOUR PEOPLE AND ALL YOU STAND FOR. LIKE YOUR MAN IN EGYPT PREDICTED. YOU DIDN'T KILL ME. YOU WERE EVERYWHERE.
NOW IT'S ALL OVER.
THAT'S WHAT SILAS IS DOING, ISN'T IT? THAT'S WHERE HE IS.
WEGH KHĀRADOS.

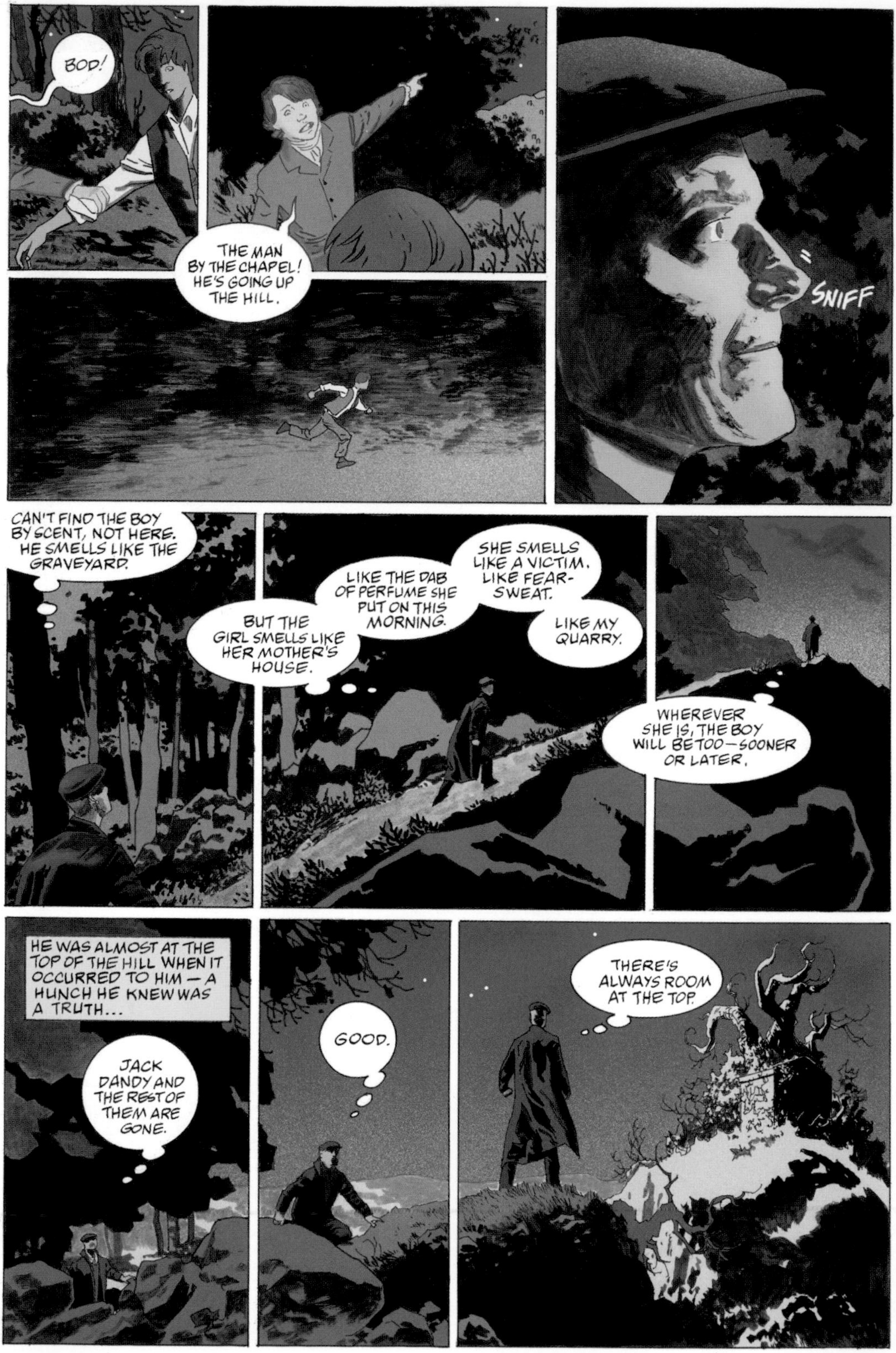
BOD!
THE MAN BY THE CHAPEL! HE'S GOING UP THE HILL.
SNIFF
CAN'T FIND THE BOY BY SCENT, NOT HERE. HE SMELLS LIKE THE GRAVEYARD.
BUT THE GIRL SMELLS LIKE HER MOTHER'S HOUSE.
LIKE THE DAB OF PERFUME SHE PUT ON THIS MORNING.
SHE SMELLS LIKE A VICTIM. LIKE FEAR-SWEAT.
LIKE MY QUARRY.
WHEREVER SHE IS, THE BOY WILL BE TOO—SOONER OR LATER.
HE WAS ALMOST AT THE TOP OF THE HILL WHEN IT OCCURRED TO HIM — A HUNCH HE KNEW WAS A TRUTH...
JACK DANDY AND THE REST OF THEM ARE GONE.
GOOD.
THERE'S ALWAYS ROOM AT THE TOP.

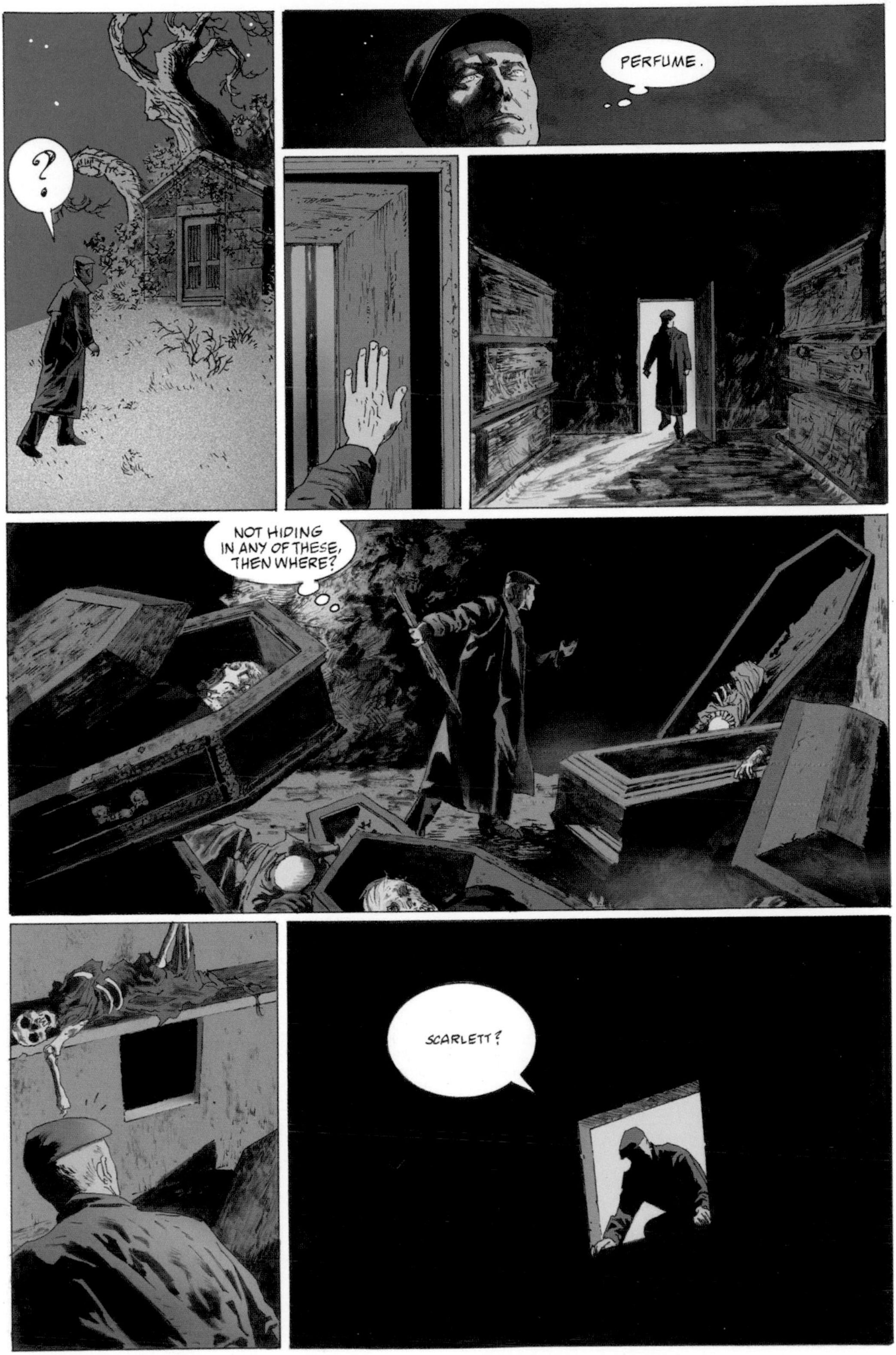
?
PERFUME.
NOT HIDING IN ANY OF THESE, THEN WHERE?
SCARLETT?

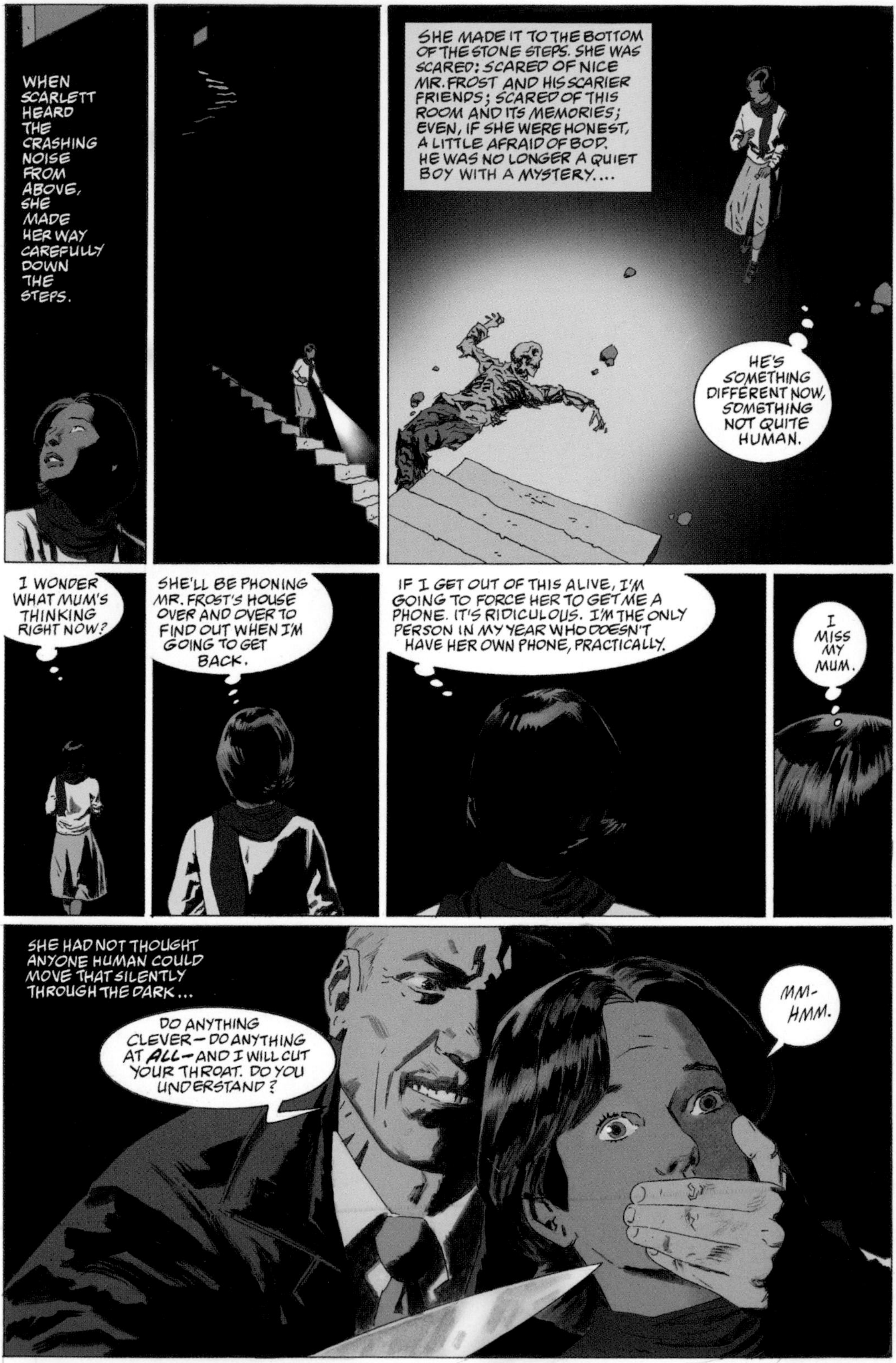
WHEN SCARLETT HEARD THE CRASHING NOISE FROM ABOVE, SHE MADE HER WAY CAREFULLY DOWN THE STEPS.
SHE MADE IT TO THE BOTTOM OF THE STONE STEPS. SHE WAS SCARED: SCARED OF NICE MR. FROST AND HIS SCARIER FRIENDS; SCARED OF THIS ROOM AND ITS MEMORIES; EVEN, IF SHE WERE HONEST, A LITTLE AFRAID OF BOD. HE WAS NO LONGER A QUIET BOY WITH A MYSTERY....
HE'S SOMETHING DIFFERENT NOW, SOMETHING NOT QUITE HUMAN.
I WONDER WHAT MUM'S THINKING RIGHT NOW?
SHE'LL BE PHONING MR. FROST'S HOUSE OVER AND OVER TO FIND OUT WHEN I'M GOING TO GET BACK.
IF I GET OUT OF THIS ALIVE, I'M GOING TO FORCE HER TO GET ME A PHONE. IT'S RIDICULOUS. I'M THE ONLY PERSON IN MY YEAR WHO DOESN'T HAVE HER OWN PHONE, PRACTICALLY.
I MISS MY MUM.
SHE HAD NOT THOUGHT ANYONE HUMAN COULD MOVE THAT SILENTLY THROUGH THE DARK...
DO ANYTHING CLEVER—DO ANYTHING AT ALL—AND I WILL CUT YOUR THROAT. DO YOU UNDERSTAND?
MM-HMM.

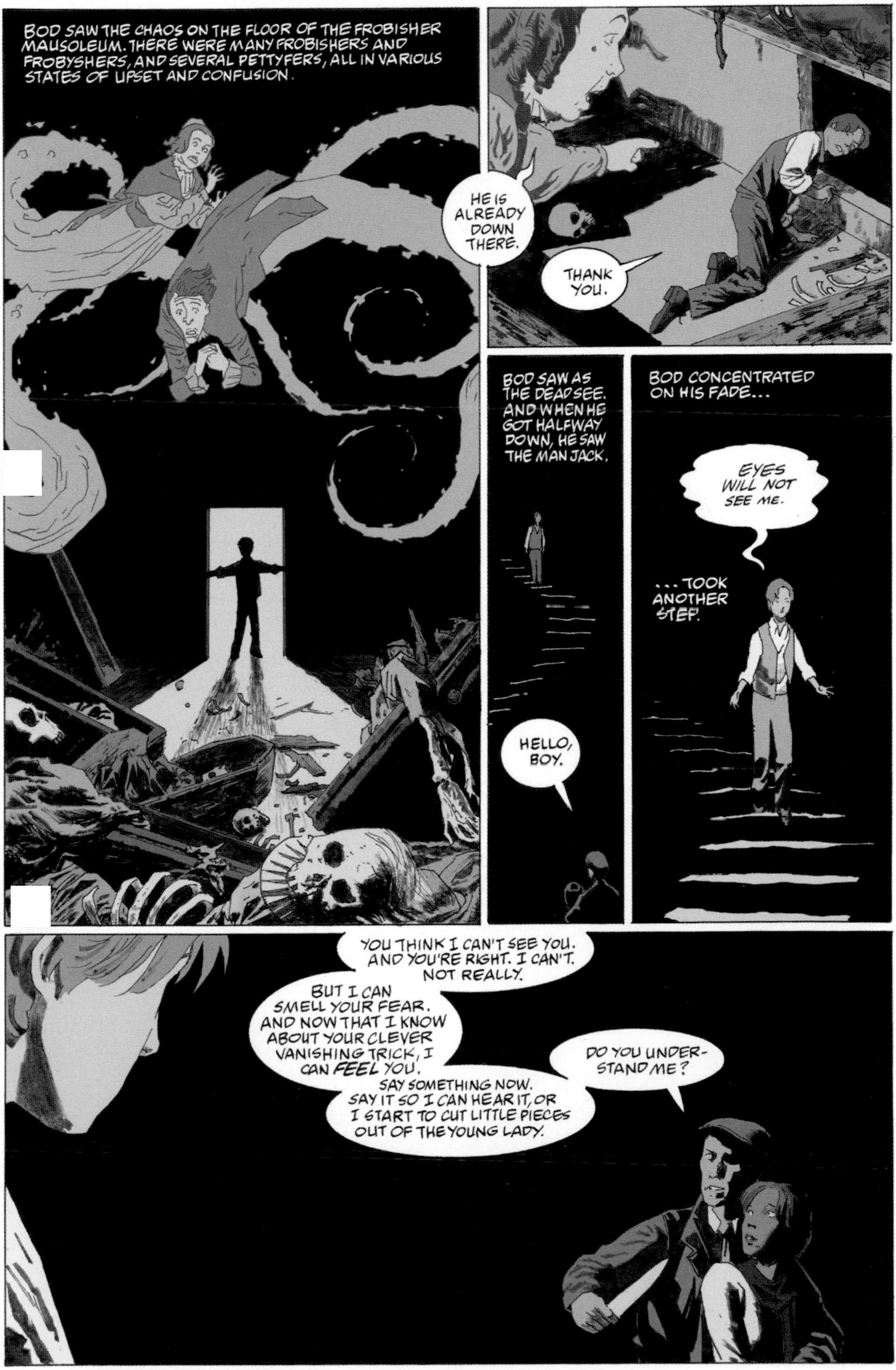
BOD SAW THE CHAOS ON THE FLOOR OF THE FROBISHER MAUSOLEUM. THERE WERE MANY FROBISHERS AND FROBYSHERS, AND SEVERAL PETTYFERS, ALL IN VARIOUS STATES OF UPSET AND CONFUSION.
HE IS ALREADY DOWN THERE.
THANK YOU.
BOD SAW AS THE DEAD SEE. AND WHEN HE GOT HALFWAY DOWN, HE SAW THE MAN JACK.
HELLO, BOY.
BOD CONCENTRATED ON HIS FADE...
EYES WILL NOT SEE ME.
...TOOK ANOTHER STEP.
YOU THINK I CAN'T SEE YOU. AND YOU'RE RIGHT. I CAN'T. NOT REALLY.
BUT I CAN SMELL YOUR FEAR. AND NOW THAT I KNOW ABOUT YOUR CLEVER VANISHING TRICK, I CAN FEEL YOU.
SAY SOMETHING NOW. SAY IT SO I CAN HEAR IT, OR I START TO CUT LITTLE PIECES OUT OF THE YOUNG LADY.
DO YOU UNDERSTAND ME?

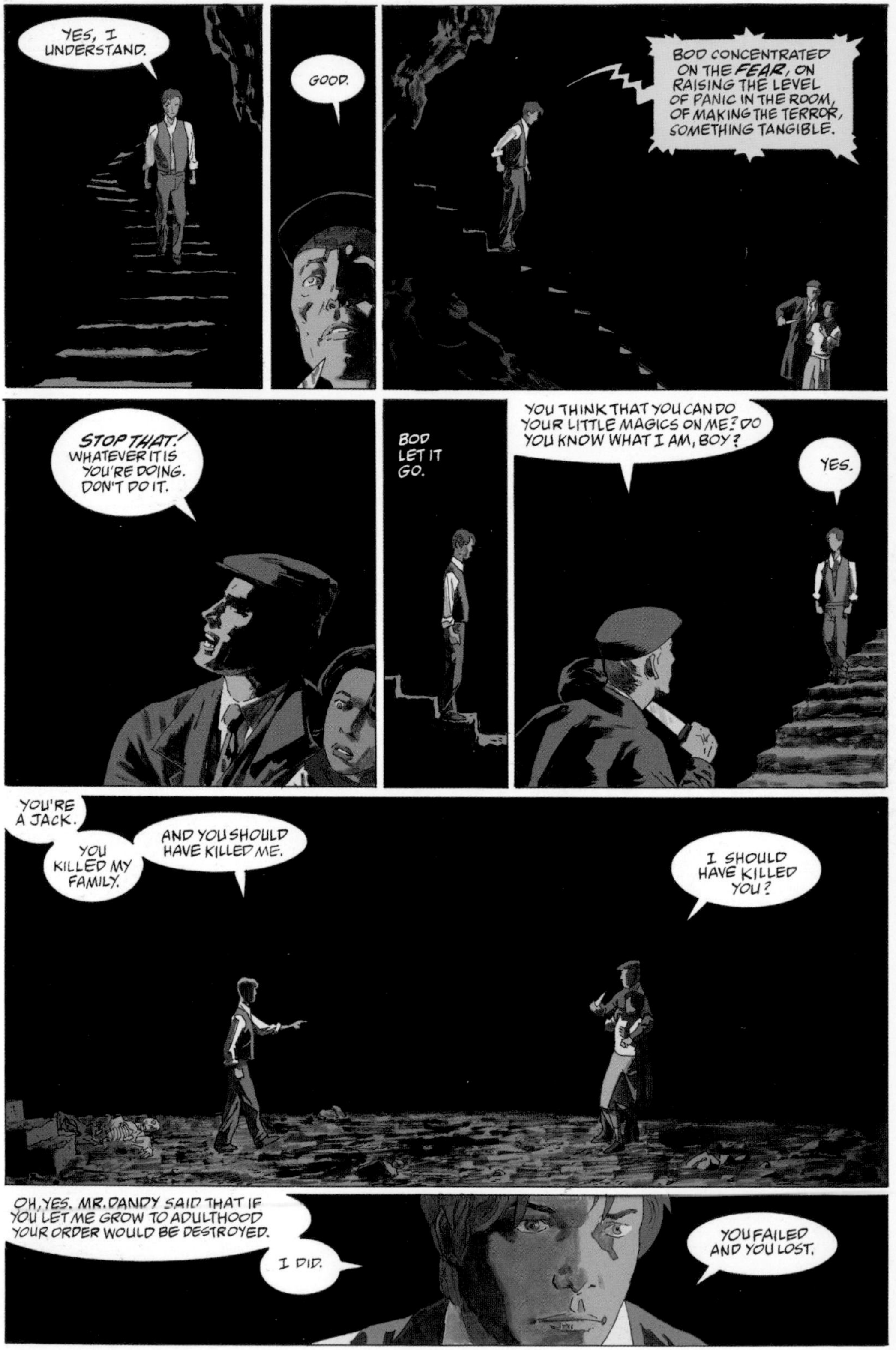
YES, I UNDERSTAND.
GOOD.
BOD CONCENTRATED ON THE FEAR, ON RAISING THE LEVEL OF PANIC IN THE ROOM, OF MAKING THE TERROR, SOMETHING TANGIBLE.
STOP THAT! WHATEVER IT IS YOU'RE DOING. DON'T DO IT.
BOD LET IT GO.
YOU THINK THAT YOU CAN DO YOUR LITTLE MAGICS ON ME? DO YOU KNOW WHAT I AM, BOY?
YES.
YOU'RE A JACK.
YOU KILLED MY FAMILY.
AND YOU SHOULD HAVE KILLED ME.
I SHOULD HAVE KILLED YOU?
OH, YES. MR. DANDY SAID THAT IF YOU LET ME GROW TO ADULTHOOD YOUR ORDER WOULD BE DESTROYED.
I DID.
YOU FAILED AND YOU LOST.

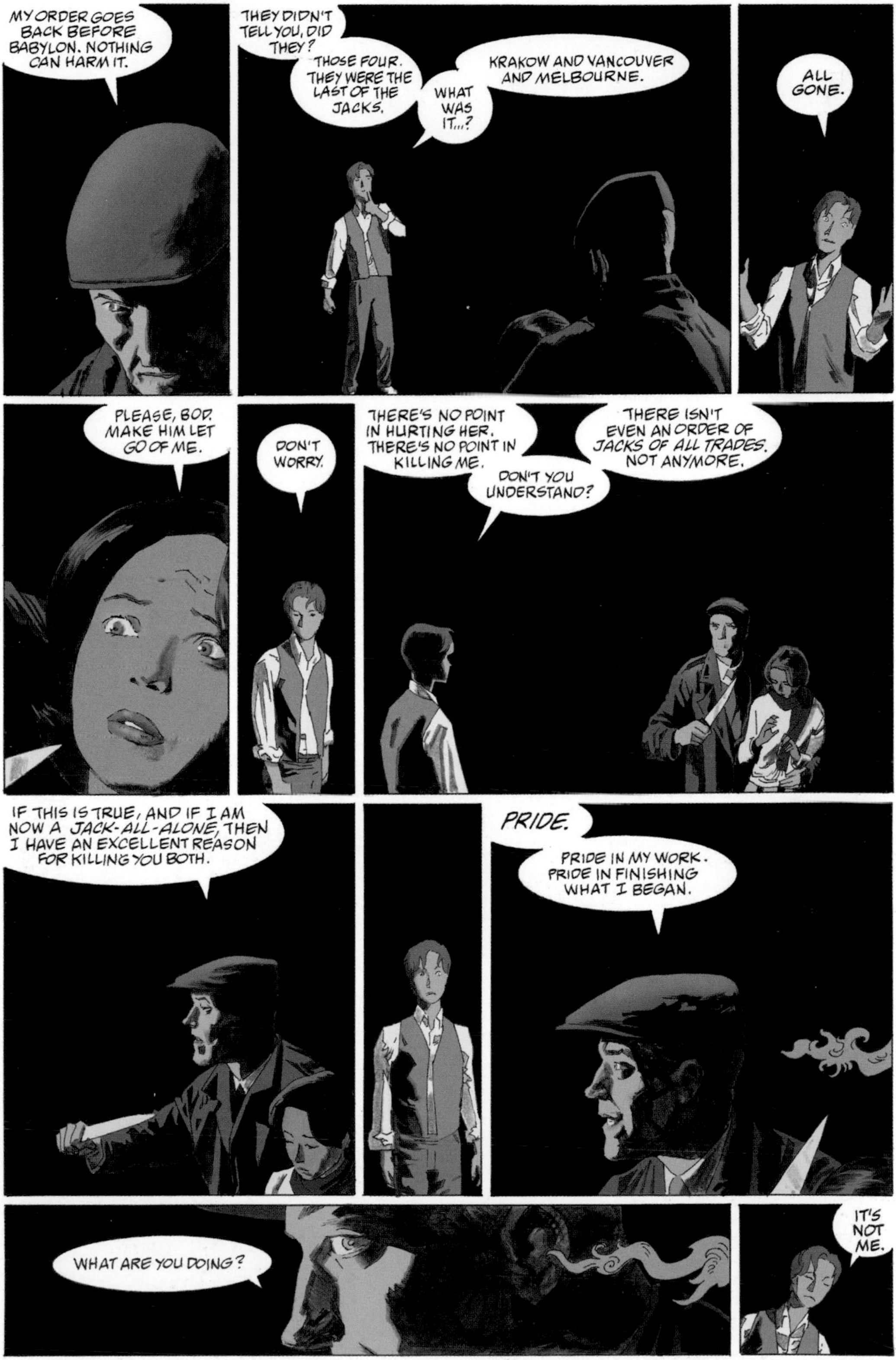
MY ORDER GOES BACK BEFORE BABYLON. NOTHING CAN HARM IT.
THEY DIDN'T TELL YOU, DID THEY?
THOSE FOUR. THEY WERE THE LAST OF THE JACKS.
WHAT WAS IT...?
KRAKOW AND VANCOUVER AND MELBOURNE.
ALL GONE.
PLEASE, BOD. MAKE HIM LET GO OF ME.
DON'T WORRY.
THERE'S NO POINT IN HURTING HER. THERE'S NO POINT IN KILLING ME.
DON'T YOU UNDERSTAND?
THERE ISN'T EVEN AN ORDER OF JACKS OF ALL TRADES. NOT ANYMORE.
IF THIS IS TRUE, AND IF I AM NOW A JACK-ALL-ALONE, THEN I HAVE AN EXCELLENT REASON FOR KILLING YOU BOTH.
PRIDE.
PRIDE IN MY WORK. PRIDE IN FINISHING WHAT I BEGAN.
WHAT ARE YOU DOING?
IT'S NOT ME.

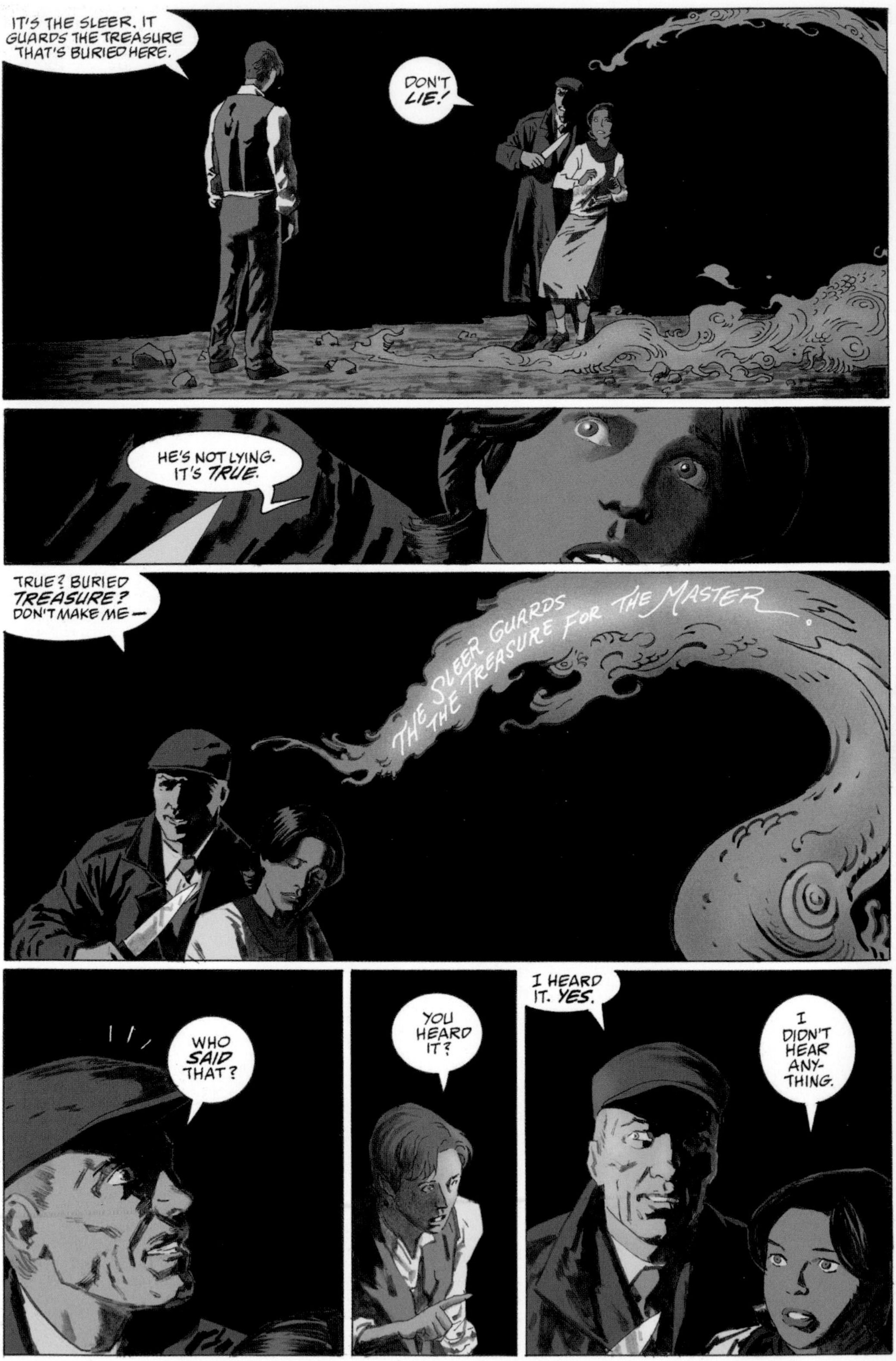
IT'S THE SLEER. IT GUARDS THE TREASURE THAT'S BURIED HERE.
DON'T LIE!
HE'S NOT LYING. IT'S TRUE.
TRUE? BURIED TREASURE? DON'T MAKE ME—
THE SLEER GUARDS THE TREASURE FOR THE MASTER.
WHO SAID THAT?
YOU HEARD IT?
I HEARD IT. YES.
I DIDN'T HEAR ANY-THING.

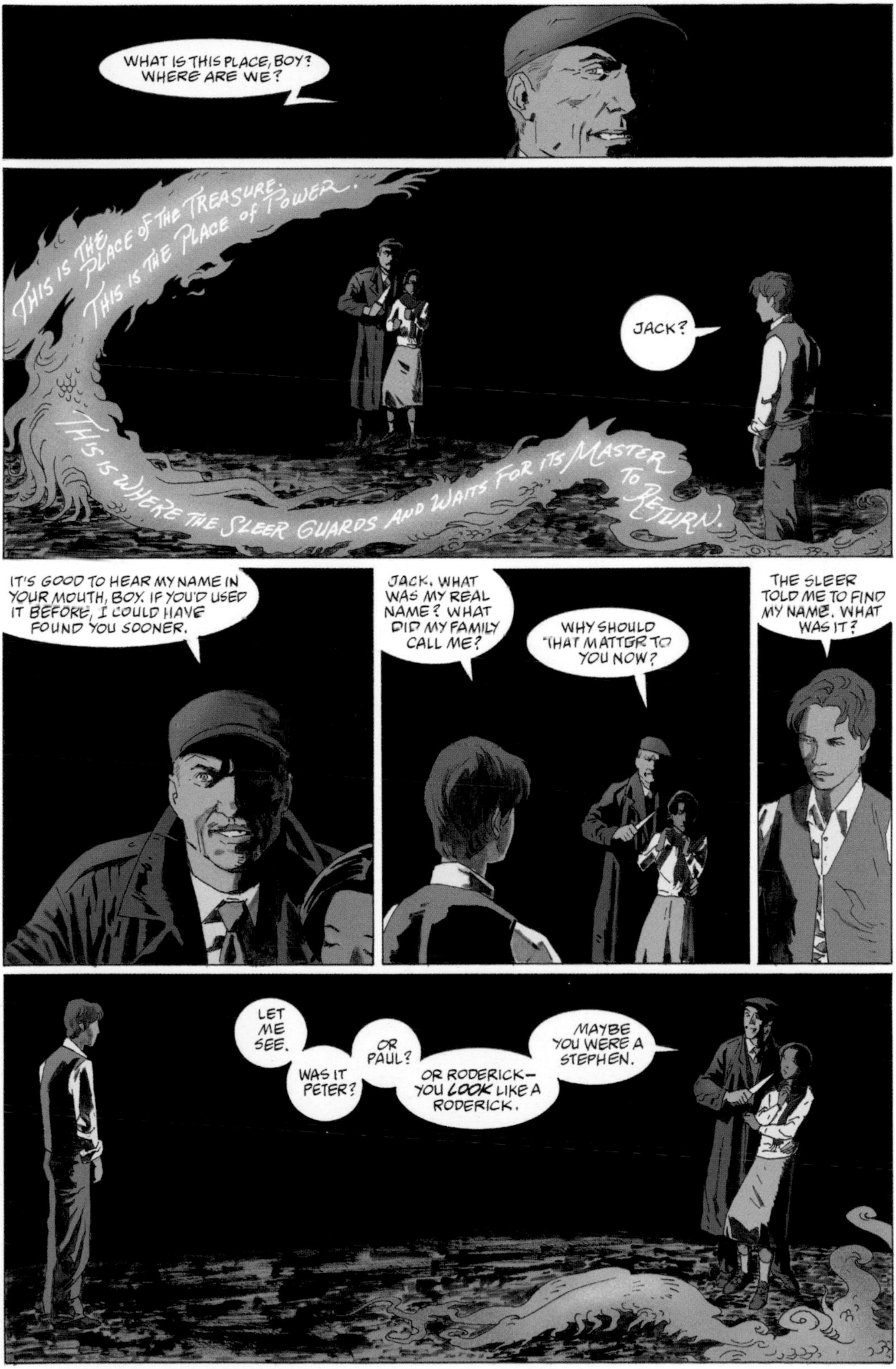
WHAT IS THIS PLACE, BOY? WHERE ARE WE?
This is the Place of the Treasure. This is the Place of Power.
This is where the Sleer guards and waits for its Master to Return.
JACK?
IT'S GOOD TO HEAR MY NAME IN YOUR MOUTH, BOY. IF YOU'D USED IT BEFORE, I COULD HAVE FOUND YOU SOONER.
JACK. WHAT WAS MY REAL NAME? WHAT DID MY FAMILY CALL ME?
WHY SHOULD THAT MATTER TO YOU NOW?
THE SLEER TOLD ME TO FIND MY NAME. WHAT WAS IT?
LET ME SEE.
WAS IT PETER?
OR PAUL?
OR RODERICK– YOU LOOK LIKE A RODERICK.
MAYBE YOU WERE A STEPHEN.

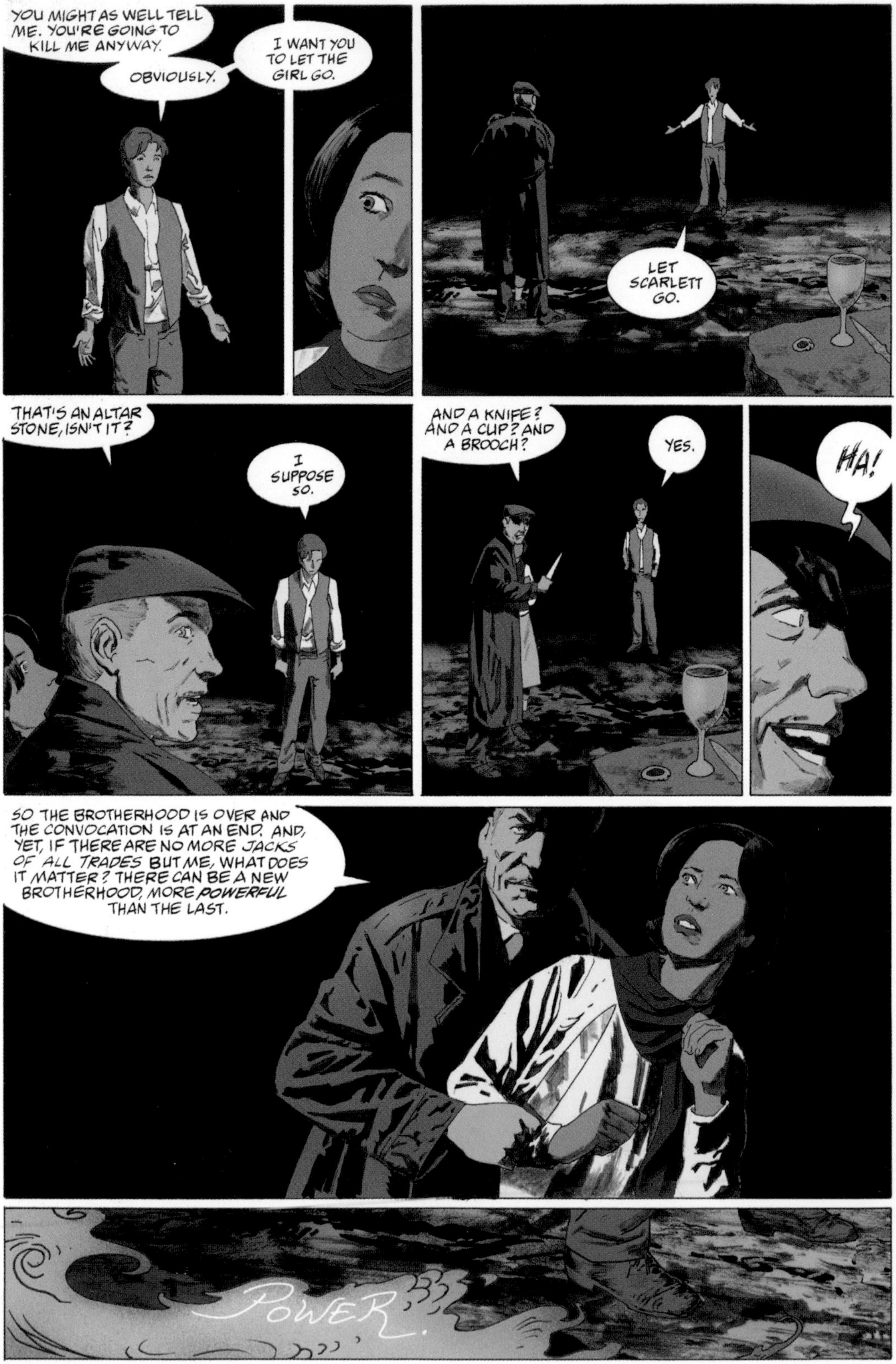
YOU MIGHT AS WELL TELL ME. YOU'RE GOING TO KILL ME ANYWAY.
OBVIOUSLY.
I WANT YOU TO LET THE GIRL GO.
LET SCARLETT GO.
THAT'S AN ALTAR STONE, ISN'T IT?
I SUPPOSE SO.
AND A KNIFE? AND A CUP? AND A BROOCH?
YES.
HA!
SO THE BROTHERHOOD IS OVER AND THE CONVOCATION IS AT AN END. AND, YET, IF THERE ARE NO MORE JACKS OF ALL TRADES BUT ME, WHAT DOES IT MATTER? THERE CAN BE A NEW BROTHERHOOD, MORE POWERFUL THAN THE LAST.
POWER.

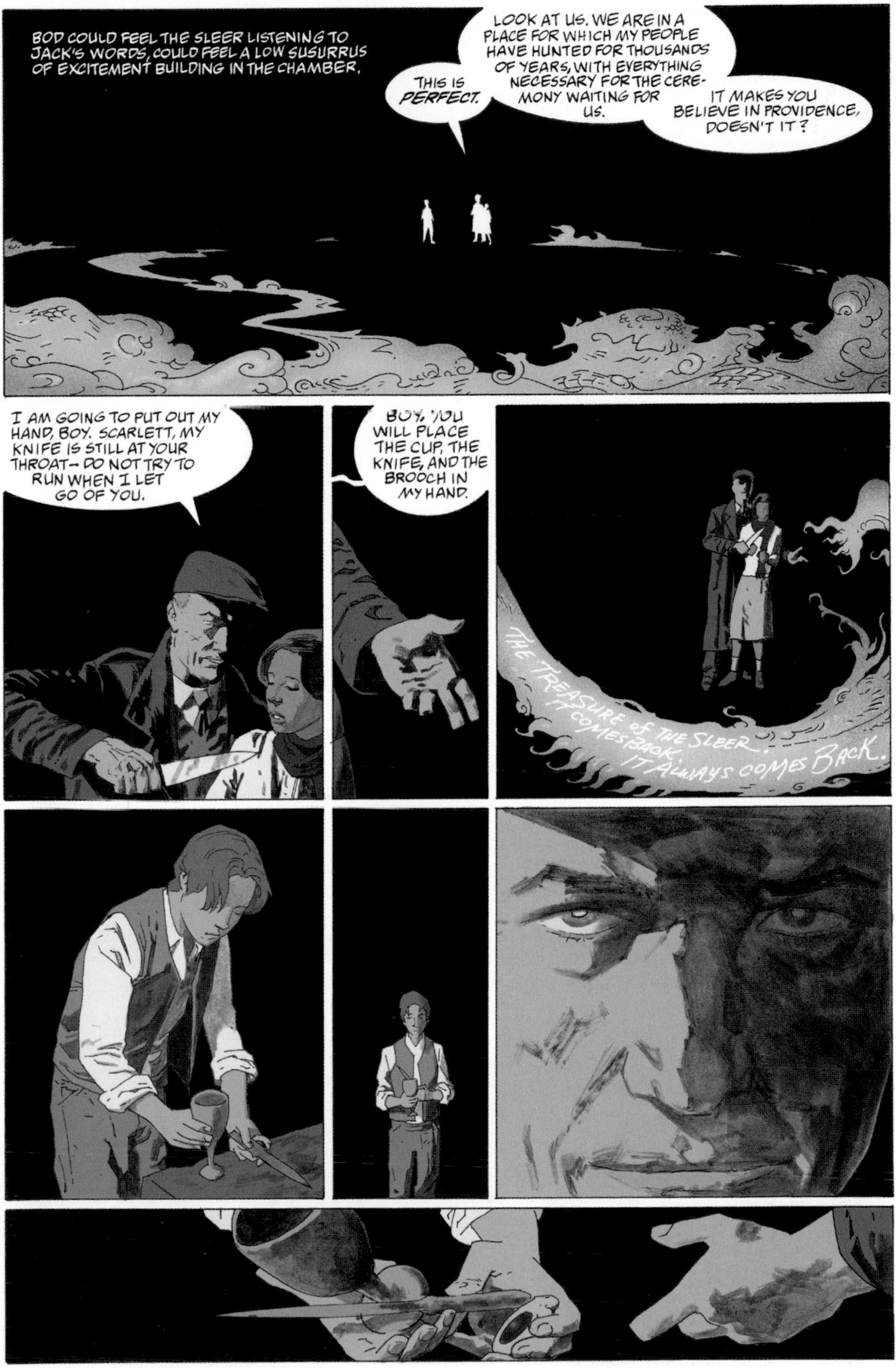

BOD COULD FEEL THE SLEER LISTENING TO JACK'S WORDS, COULD FEEL A LOW SUSURRUS OF EXCITEMENT BUILDING IN THE CHAMBER.
THIS IS PERFECT.
LOOK AT US. WE ARE IN A PLACE FOR WHICH MY PEOPLE HAVE HUNTED FOR THOUSANDS OF YEARS, WITH EVERYTHING NECESSARY FOR THE CERE-MONY WAITING FOR US.
IT MAKES YOU BELIEVE IN PROVIDENCE, DOESN'T IT?
I AM GOING TO PUT OUT MY HAND, BOY. SCARLETT, MY KNIFE IS STILL AT YOUR THROAT-- DO NOT TRY TO RUN WHEN I LET GO OF YOU.
BOY, YOU WILL PLACE THE CUP, THE KNIFE, AND THE BROOCH IN MY HAND.
THE TREASURE OF THE SLEER. IT COMES BACK. IT ALWAYS COMES BACK.

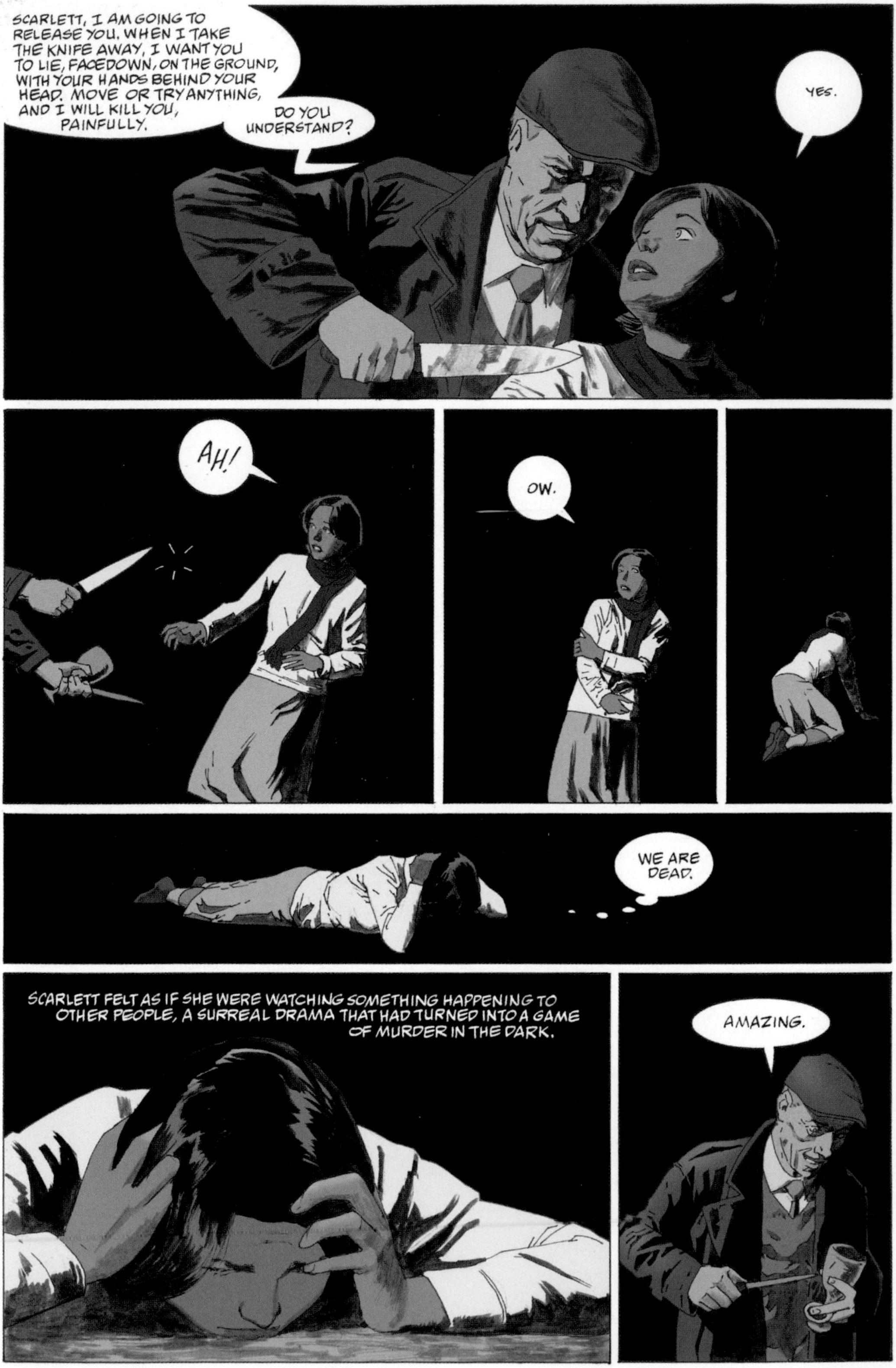
SCARLETT, I AM GOING TO RELEASE YOU. WHEN I TAKE THE KNIFE AWAY, I WANT YOU TO LIE, FACEDOWN, ON THE GROUND, WITH YOUR HANDS BEHIND YOUR HEAD. MOVE OR TRY ANYTHING, AND I WILL KILL YOU, PAINFULLY.
DO YOU UNDERSTAND?
YES.
AH!
OW.
WE ARE DEAD.
SCARLETT FELT AS IF SHE WERE WATCHING SOMETHING HAPPENING TO OTHER PEOPLE, A SURREAL DRAMA THAT HAD TURNED INTO A GAME OF MURDER IN THE DARK.
AMAZING.

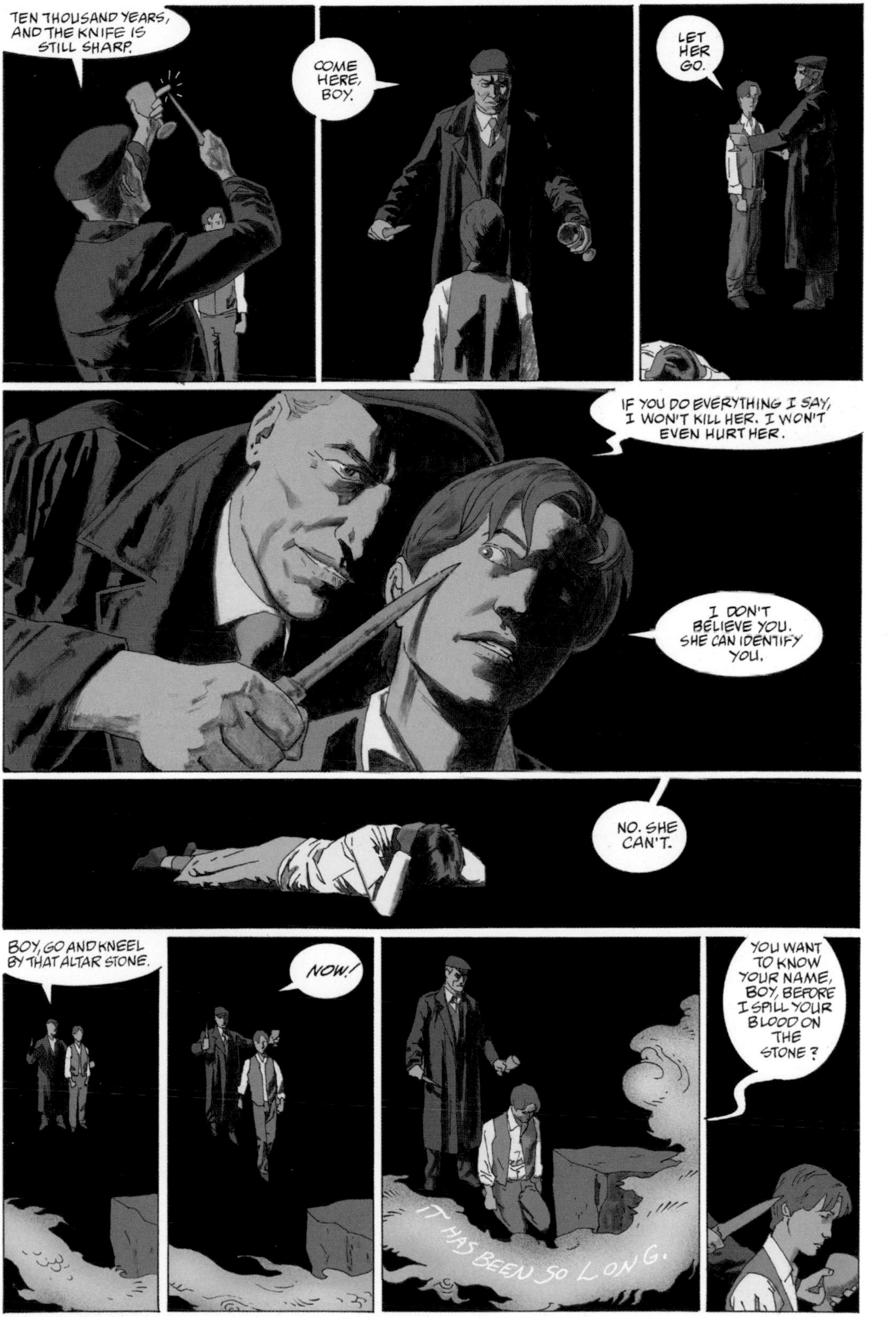

TEN THOUSAND YEARS, AND THE KNIFE IS STILL SHARP.
COME HERE, BOY.
LET HER GO.
IF YOU DO EVERYTHING I SAY, I WON'T KILL HER. I WON'T EVEN HURT HER.
I DON'T BELIEVE YOU. SHE CAN IDENTIFY YOU.
NO. SHE CAN'T.
BOY, GO AND KNEEL BY THAT ALTAR STONE.
NOW!
IT HAS BEEN SO LONG.
YOU WANT TO KNOW YOUR NAME, BOY, BEFORE I SPILL YOUR BLOOD ON THE STONE?

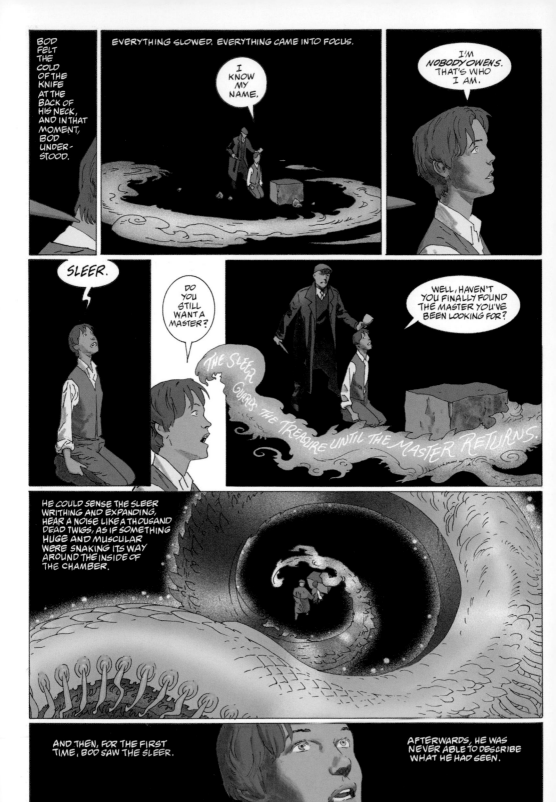

BOD FELT THE COLD OF THE KNIFE AT THE BACK OF HIS NECK, AND IN THAT MOMENT, BOD UNDERSTOOD.

EVERYTHING SLOWED. EVERYTHING CAME INTO FOCUS.

I KNOW MY NAME.

I'M NOBODY OWENS. THAT'S WHO I AM.

SLEER.

DO YOU STILL WANT A MASTER?

WELL, HAVEN'T YOU FINALLY FOUND THE MASTER YOU'VE BEEN LOOKING FOR?

THE SLEER GUARDS THE TREASURE UNTIL THE MASTER RETURNS.

HE COULD SENSE THE SLEER WRITHING AND EXPANDING, HEAR A NOISE LIKE A THOUSAND DEAD TWIGS, AS IF SOMETHING HUGE AND MUSCULAR WERE SNAKING ITS WAY AROUND THE INSIDE OF THE CHAMBER.

AND THEN, FOR THE FIRST TIME, BOD SAW THE SLEER.

AFTERWARDS, HE WAS NEVER ABLE TO DESCRIBE WHAT HE HAD SEEN.

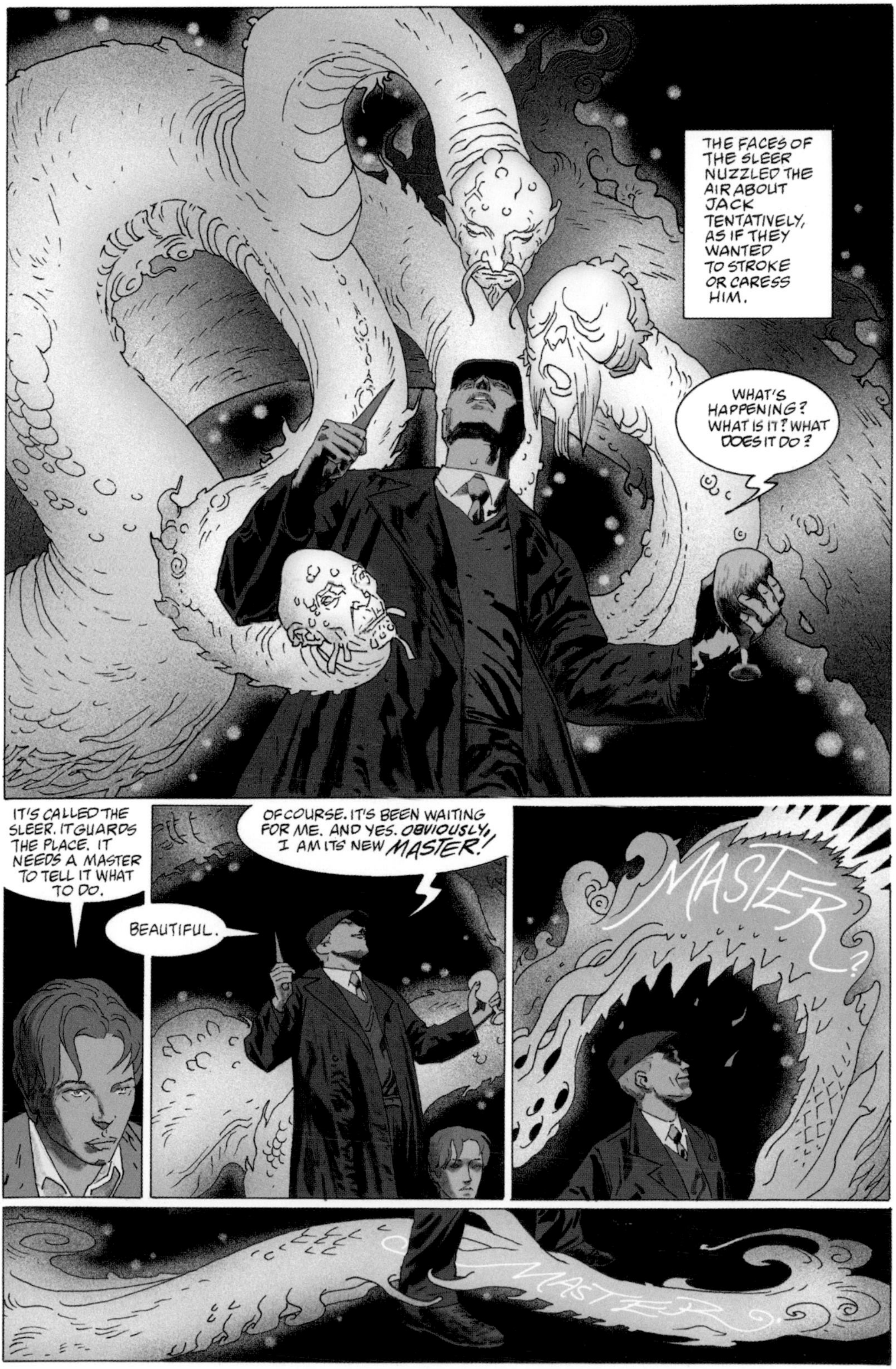
THE FACES OF THE SLEER NUZZLED THE AIR ABOUT JACK TENTATIVELY, AS IF THEY WANTED TO STROKE OR CARESS HIM.
WHAT'S HAPPENING? WHAT IS IT? WHAT DOES IT DO?
IT'S CALLED THE SLEER. IT GUARDS THE PLACE. IT NEEDS A MASTER TO TELL IT WHAT TO DO.
OF COURSE. IT'S BEEN WAITING FOR ME. AND YES. OBVIOUSLY, I AM ITS NEW MASTER!
BEAUTIFUL.
MASTER?
MASTER.

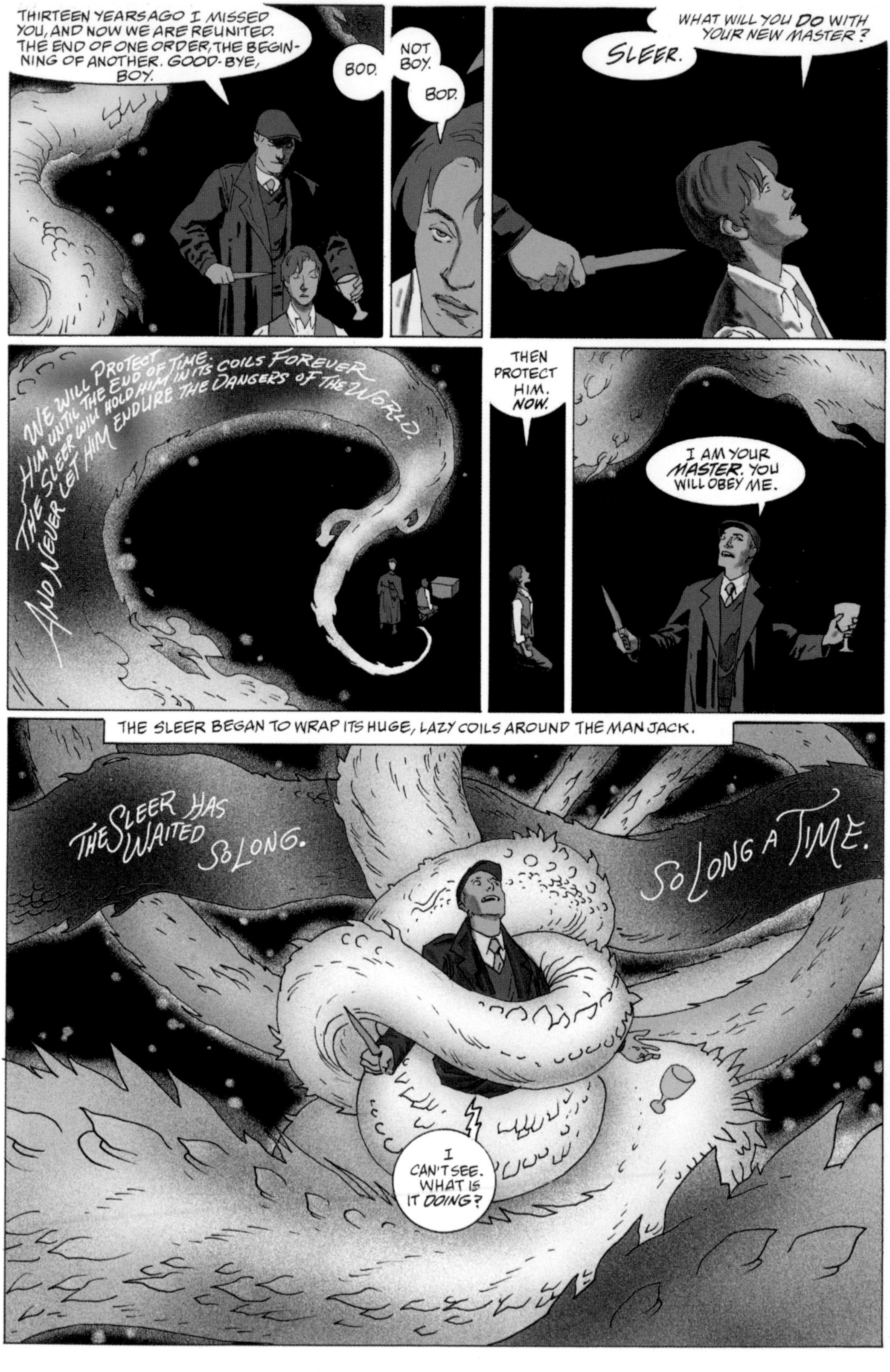
THIRTEEN YEARS AGO I MISSED YOU, AND NOW WE ARE REUNITED. THE END OF ONE ORDER, THE BEGINNING OF ANOTHER. GOOD-BYE, BOY.
BOD.
NOT BOY.
BOD.
SLEER.
WHAT WILL YOU DO WITH YOUR NEW MASTER?
WE WILL PROTECT HIM UNTIL THE END OF TIME.
THE SLEER WILL HOLD HIM IN ITS COILS FOREVER
AND NEVER LET HIM ENDURE THE DANGERS OF THE WORLD.
THEN PROTECT HIM. NOW.
I AM YOUR MASTER. YOU WILL OBEY ME.
THE SLEER BEGAN TO WRAP ITS HUGE, LAZY COILS AROUND THE MAN JACK.
THE SLEER HAS WAITED SO LONG.
SO LONG A TIME.
I CAN'T SEE. WHAT IS IT DOING?

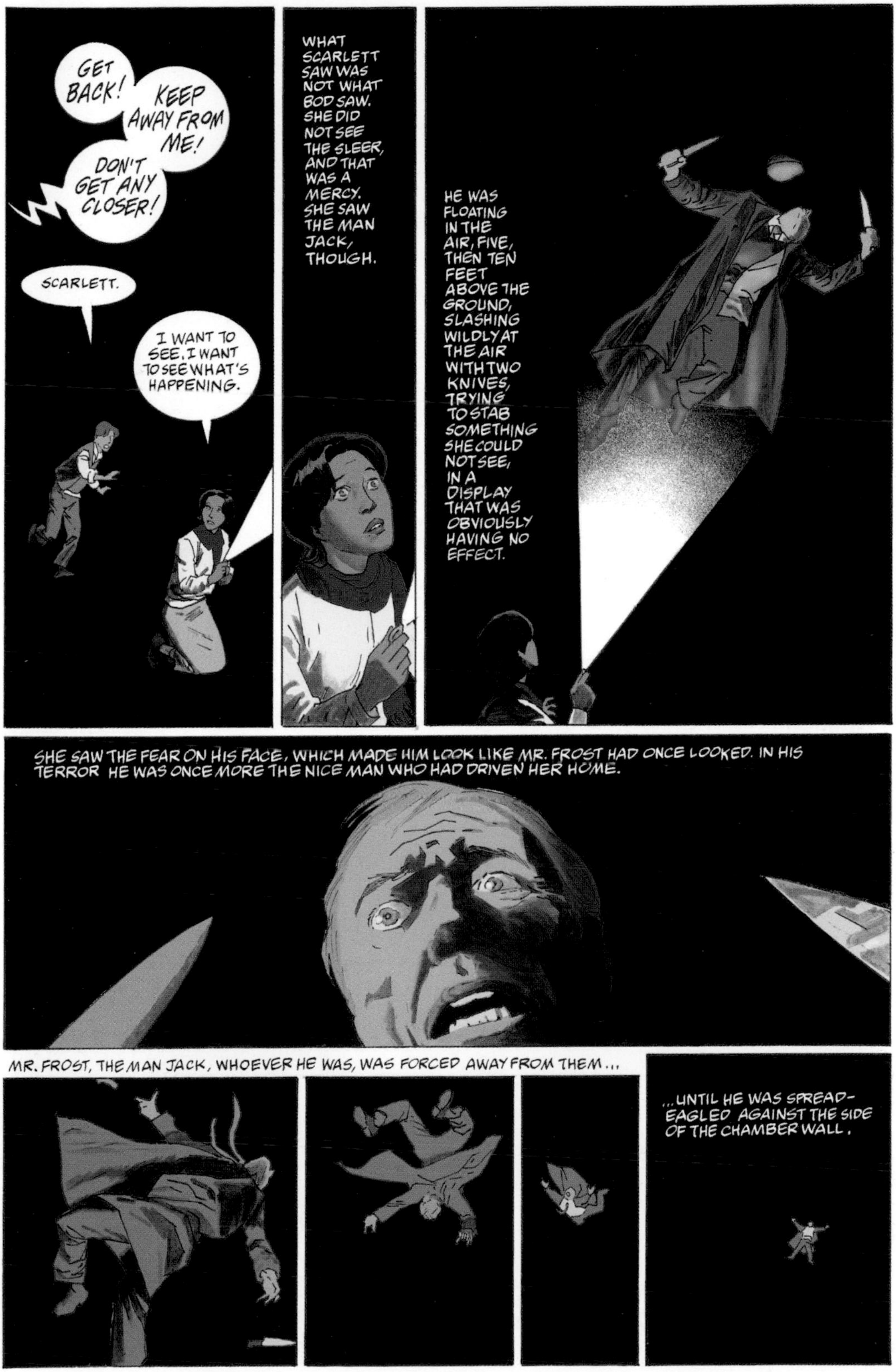
GET BACK!
KEEP AWAY FROM ME!
DON'T GET ANY CLOSER!
SCARLETT.
I WANT TO SEE. I WANT TO SEE WHAT'S HAPPENING.
WHAT SCARLETT SAW WAS NOT WHAT BOD SAW. SHE DID NOT SEE THE SLEER, AND THAT WAS A MERCY. SHE SAW THE MAN JACK, THOUGH.
HE WAS FLOATING IN THE AIR, FIVE, THEN TEN FEET ABOVE THE GROUND, SLASHING WILDLY AT THE AIR WITH TWO KNIVES, TRYING TO STAB SOMETHING SHE COULD NOT SEE, IN A DISPLAY THAT WAS OBVIOUSLY HAVING NO EFFECT.
SHE SAW THE FEAR ON HIS FACE, WHICH MADE HIM LOOK LIKE MR. FROST HAD ONCE LOOKED. IN HIS TERROR HE WAS ONCE MORE THE NICE MAN WHO HAD DRIVEN HER HOME.
MR. FROST, THE MAN JACK, WHOEVER HE WAS, WAS FORCED AWAY FROM THEM...
...UNTIL HE WAS SPREAD-EAGLED AGAINST THE SIDE OF THE CHAMBER WALL.

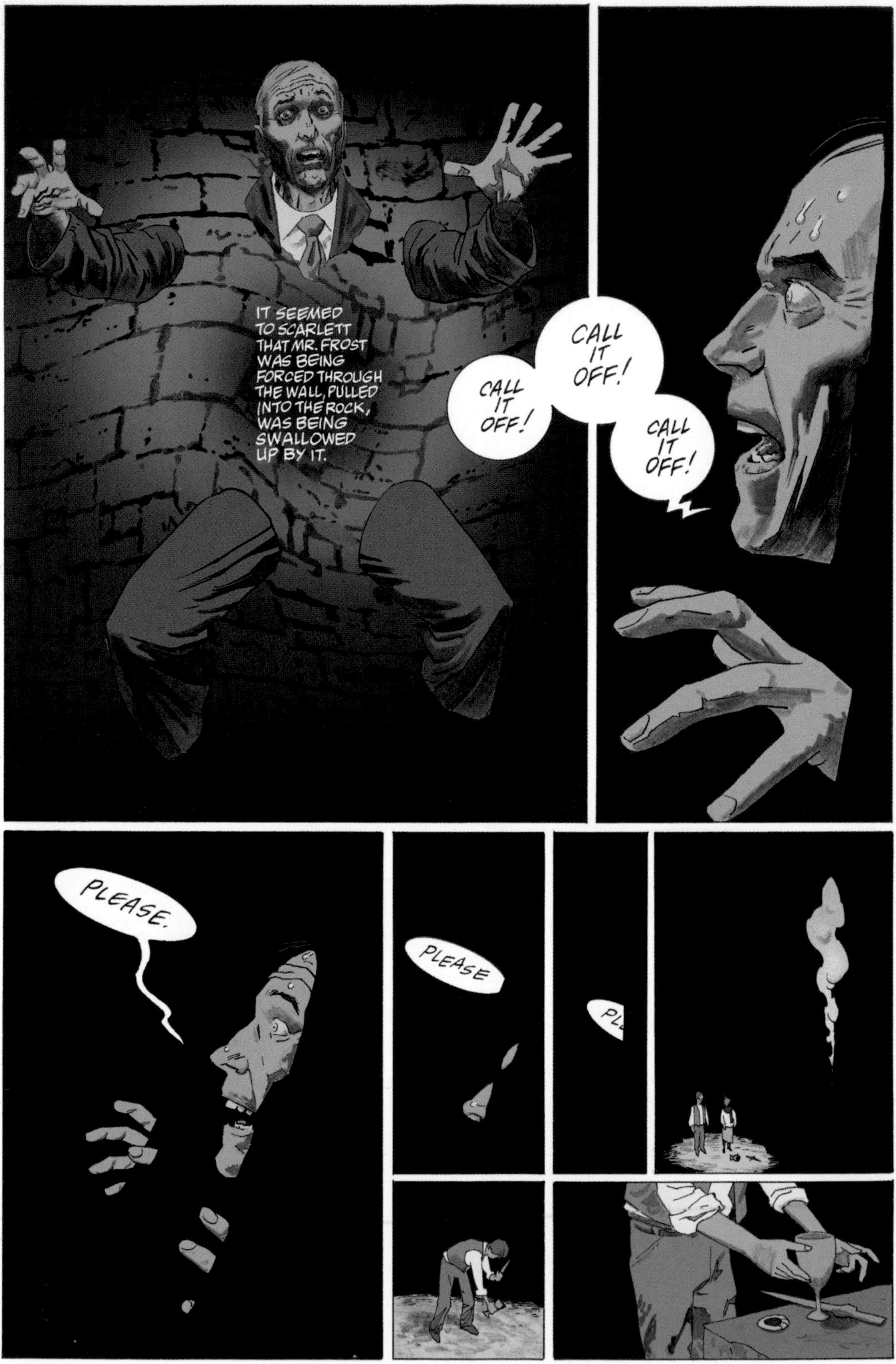
IT SEEMED TO SCARLETT THAT MR. FROST WAS BEING FORCED THROUGH THE WALL, PULLED INTO THE ROCK, WAS BEING SWALLOWED UP BY IT.
CALL IT OFF!
CALL IT OFF!
CALL IT OFF!
PLEASE.
PLEASE
PL

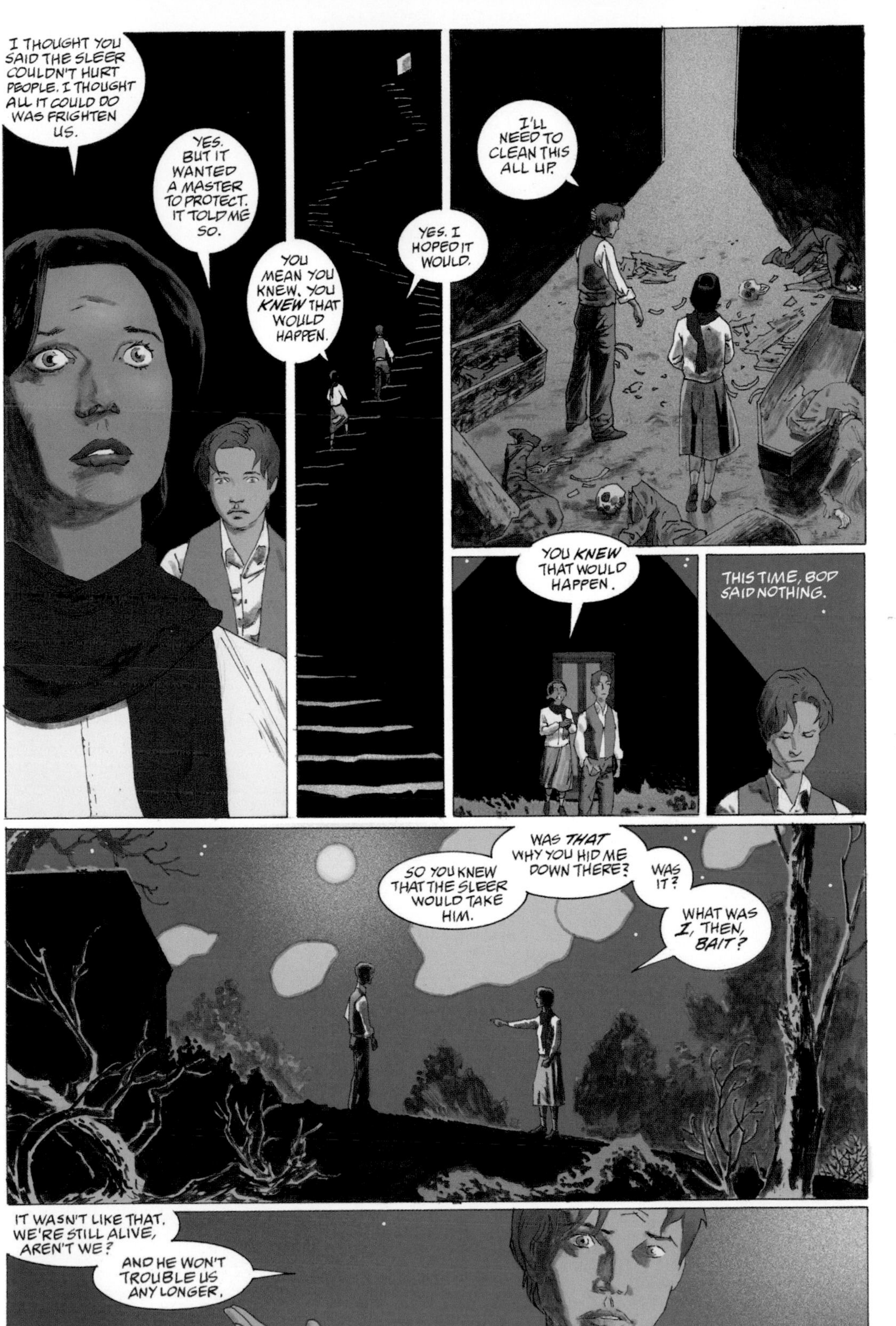
I THOUGHT YOU SAID THE SLEER COULDN'T HURT PEOPLE. I THOUGHT ALL IT COULD DO WAS FRIGHTEN US.
YES. BUT IT WANTED A MASTER TO PROTECT. IT TOLD ME SO.
YOU MEAN YOU KNEW. YOU KNEW THAT WOULD HAPPEN.
YES. I HOPED IT WOULD.
I'LL NEED TO CLEAN THIS ALL UP.
YOU KNEW THAT WOULD HAPPEN.
THIS TIME, BOD SAID NOTHING.
SO YOU KNEW THAT THE SLEER WOULD TAKE HIM.
WAS THAT WHY YOU HID ME DOWN THERE?
WAS IT?
WHAT WAS I, THEN, BAIT?
IT WASN'T LIKE THAT. WE'RE STILL ALIVE, AREN'T WE?
AND HE WON'T TROUBLE US ANY LONGER.

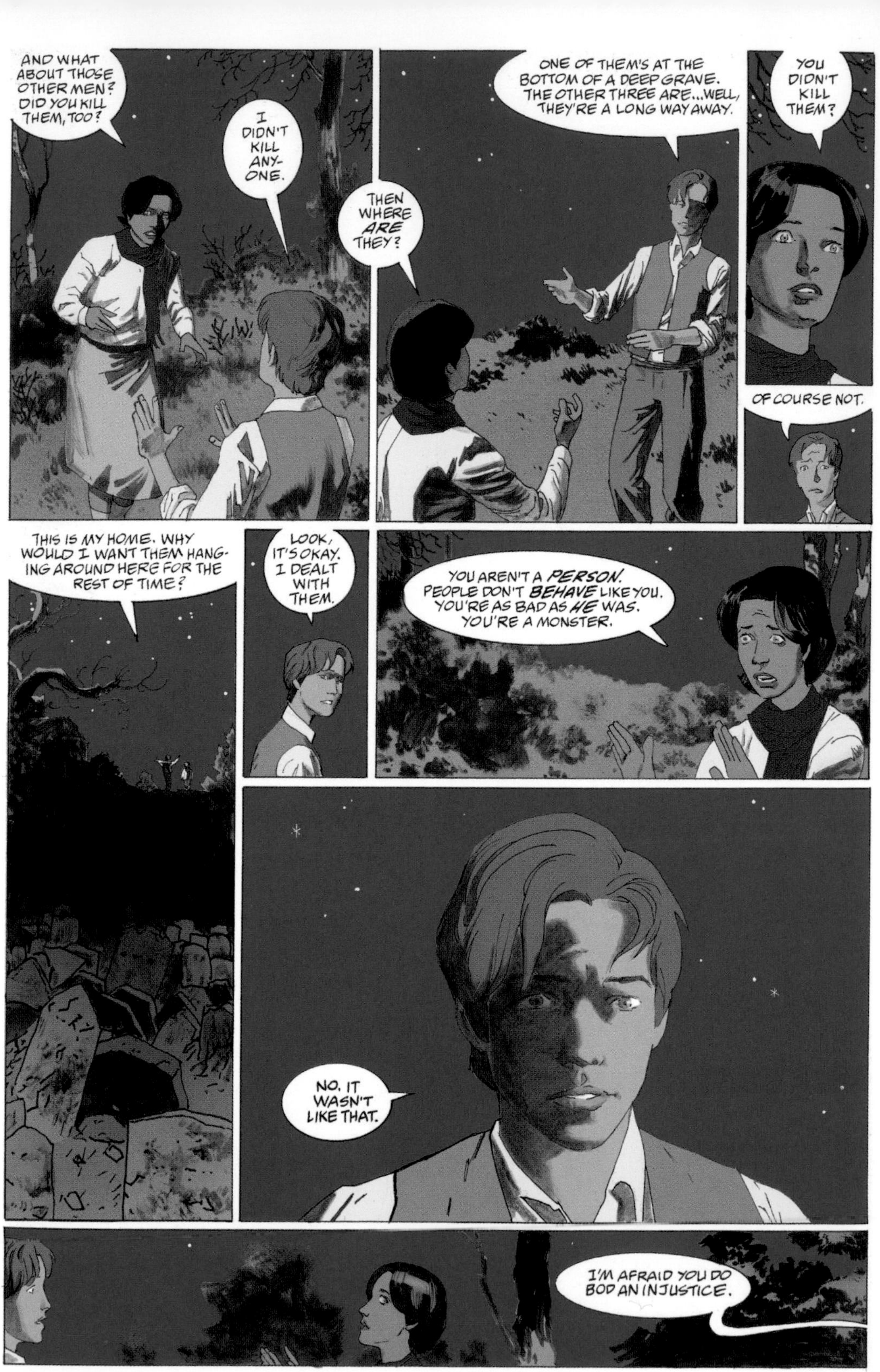
AND WHAT ABOUT THOSE OTHER MEN? DID YOU KILL THEM, TOO?
I DIDN'T KILL ANY-ONE.
THEN WHERE ARE THEY?
ONE OF THEM'S AT THE BOTTOM OF A DEEP GRAVE. THE OTHER THREE ARE...WELL, THEY'RE A LONG WAY AWAY.
YOU DIDN'T KILL THEM?
OF COURSE NOT.
THIS IS MY HOME. WHY WOULD I WANT THEM HANG-ING AROUND HERE FOR THE REST OF TIME?
LOOK, IT'S OKAY. I DEALT WITH THEM.
YOU AREN'T A PERSON. PEOPLE DON'T BEHAVE LIKE YOU. YOU'RE AS BAD AS HE WAS. YOU'RE A MONSTER.
NO, IT WASN'T LIKE THAT.
I'M AFRAID YOU DO BOD AN INJUSTICE.

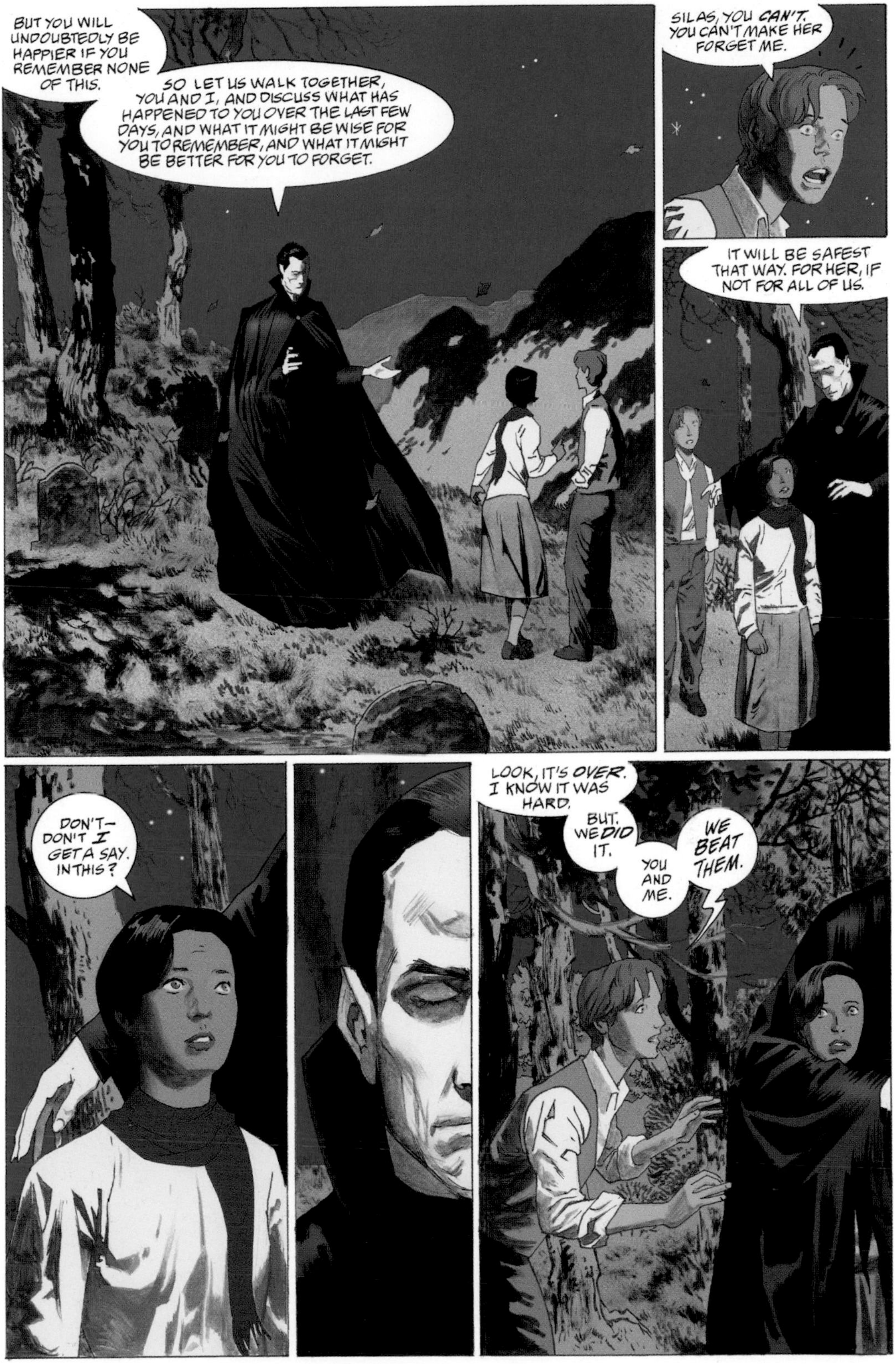
BUT YOU WILL UNDOUBTEDLY BE HAPPIER IF YOU REMEMBER NONE OF THIS.
SO LET US WALK TOGETHER, YOU AND I, AND DISCUSS WHAT HAS HAPPENED TO YOU OVER THE LAST FEW DAYS, AND WHAT IT MIGHT BE WISE FOR YOU TO REMEMBER, AND WHAT IT MIGHT BE BETTER FOR YOU TO FORGET.
SILAS, YOU CAN'T. YOU CAN'T MAKE HER FORGET ME.
IT WILL BE SAFEST THAT WAY. FOR HER, IF NOT FOR ALL OF US.
DON'T— DON'T I GET A SAY IN THIS?
LOOK, IT'S OVER. I KNOW IT WAS HARD.
BUT. WE DID IT.
YOU AND ME.
WE BEAT THEM.

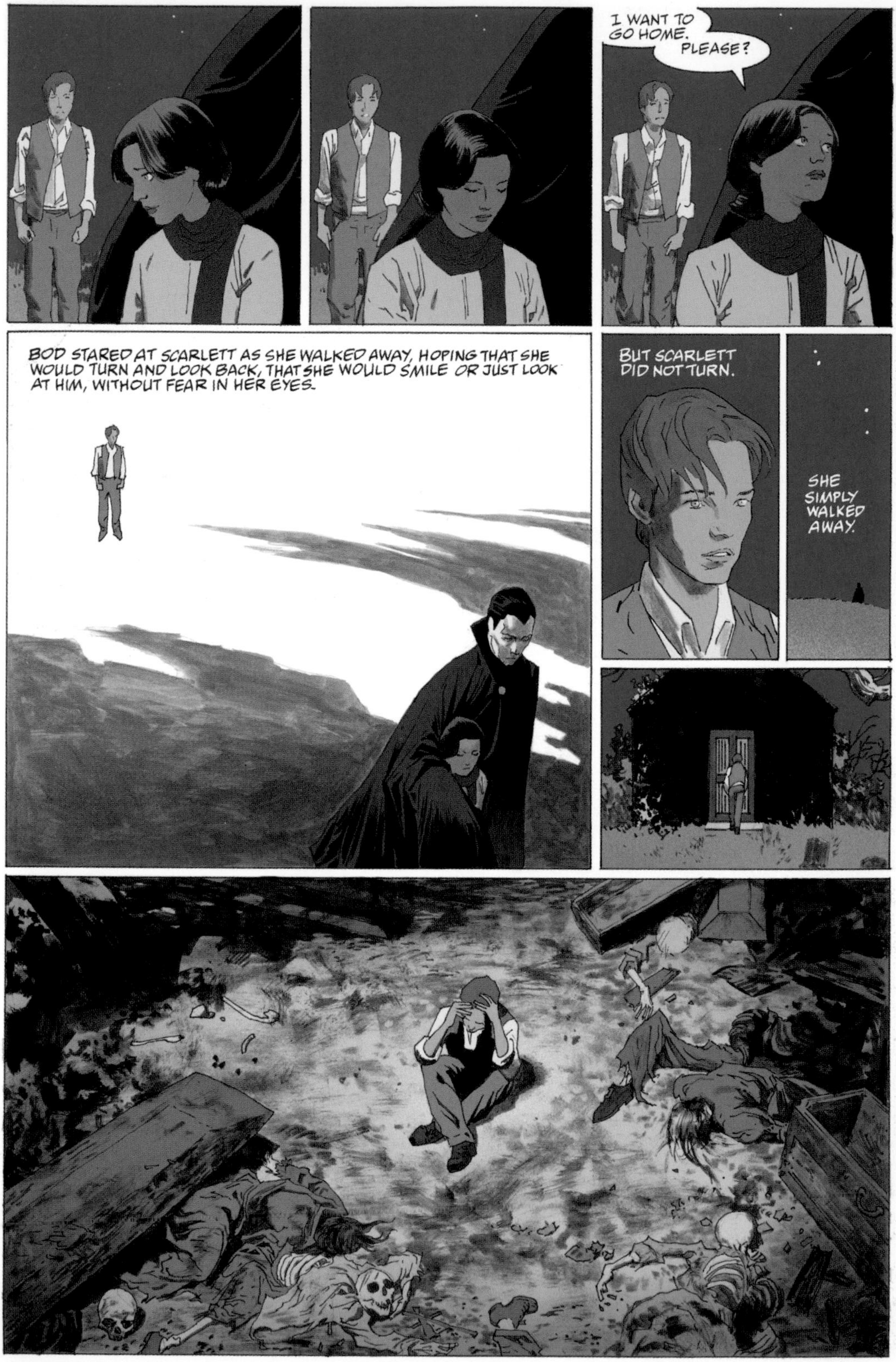
I WANT TO GO HOME. PLEASE?
BOD STARED AT SCARLETT AS SHE WALKED AWAY, HOPING THAT SHE WOULD TURN AND LOOK BACK, THAT SHE WOULD SMILE OR JUST LOOK AT HIM, WITHOUT FEAR IN HER EYES.
BUT SCARLETT DID NOT TURN.
SHE SIMPLY WALKED AWAY.

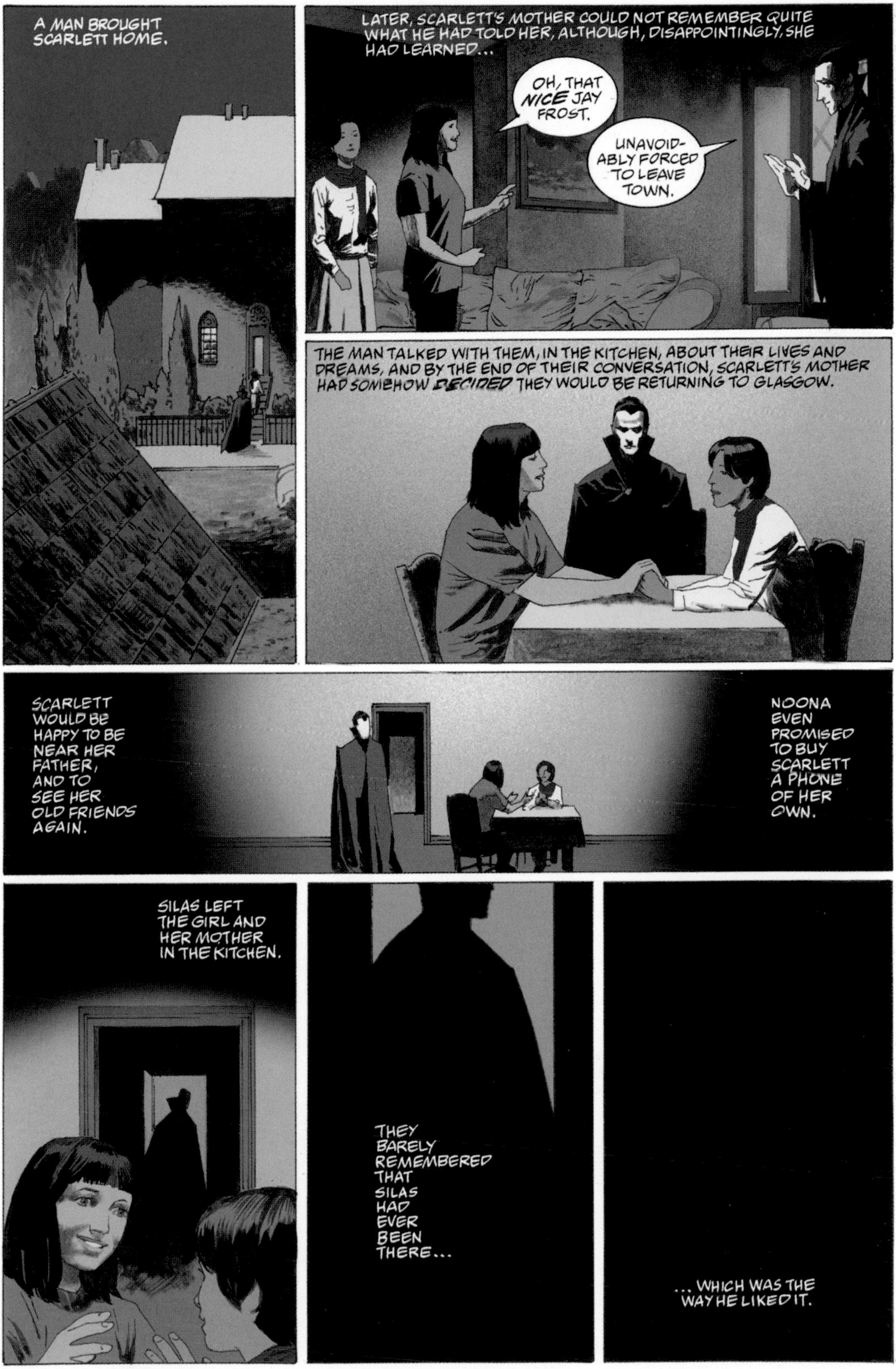
A MAN BROUGHT SCARLETT HOME.
LATER, SCARLETT'S MOTHER COULD NOT REMEMBER QUITE WHAT HE HAD TOLD HER, ALTHOUGH, DISAPPOINTINGLY, SHE HAD LEARNED...
OH, THAT NICE JAY FROST.
UNAVOIDABLY FORCED TO LEAVE TOWN.
THE MAN TALKED WITH THEM, IN THE KITCHEN, ABOUT THEIR LIVES AND DREAMS, AND BY THE END OF THEIR CONVERSATION, SCARLETT'S MOTHER HAD SOMEHOW DECIDED THEY WOULD BE RETURNING TO GLASGOW.
SCARLETT WOULD BE HAPPY TO BE NEAR HER FATHER, AND TO SEE HER OLD FRIENDS AGAIN.
NOONA EVEN PROMISED TO BUY SCARLETT A PHONE OF HER OWN.
SILAS LEFT THE GIRL AND HER MOTHER IN THE KITCHEN.
THEY BARELY REMEMBERED THAT SILAS HAD EVER BEEN THERE...
...WHICH WAS THE WAY HE LIKED IT.

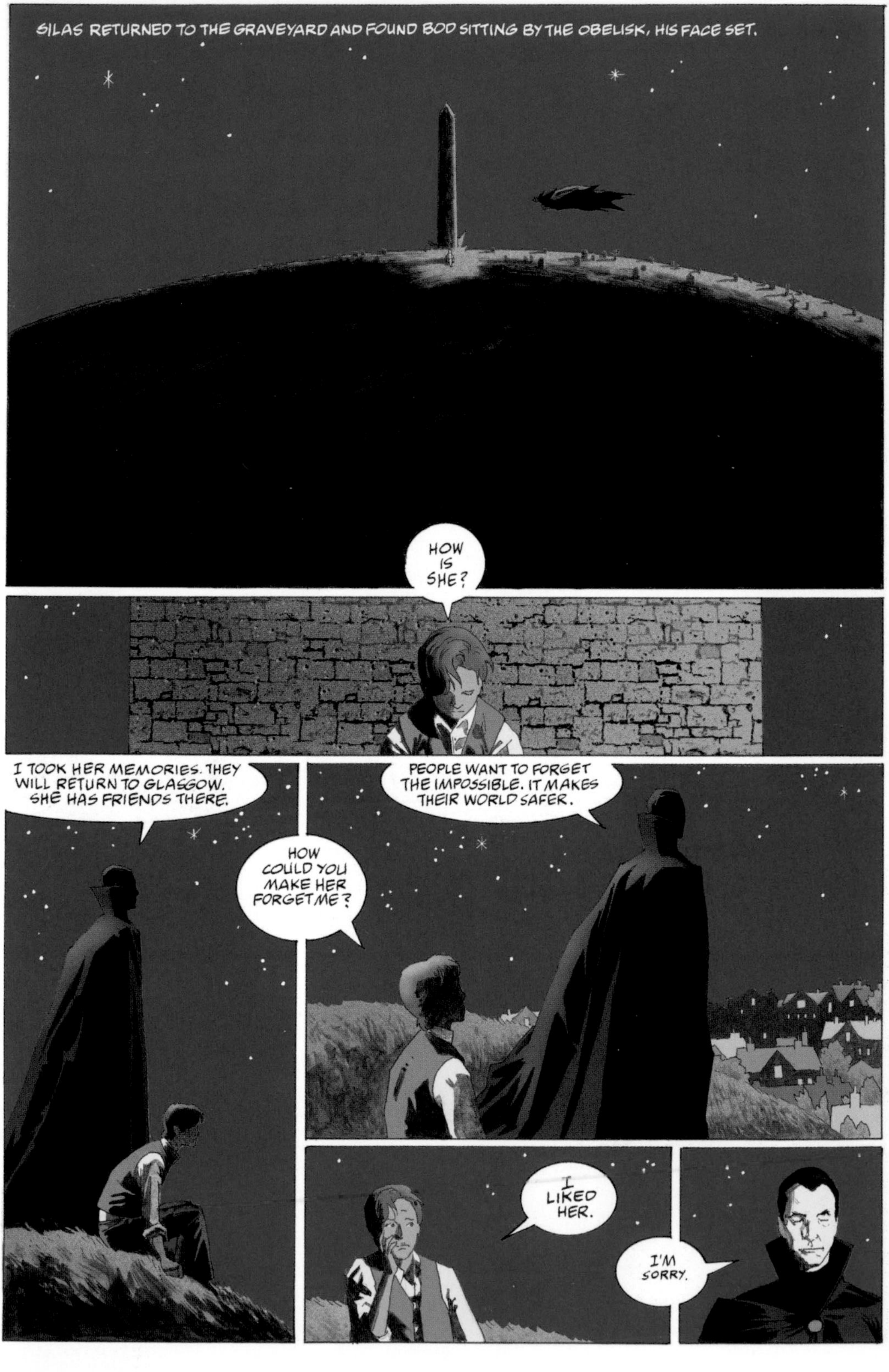
SILAS RETURNED TO THE GRAVEYARD AND FOUND BOD SITTING BY THE OBELISK, HIS FACE SET.
HOW IS SHE?
I TOOK HER MEMORIES. THEY WILL RETURN TO GLASGOW. SHE HAS FRIENDS THERE.
HOW COULD YOU MAKE HER FORGET ME?
PEOPLE WANT TO FORGET THE IMPOSSIBLE. IT MAKES THEIR WORLD SAFER.
I LIKED HER.
I'M SORRY.

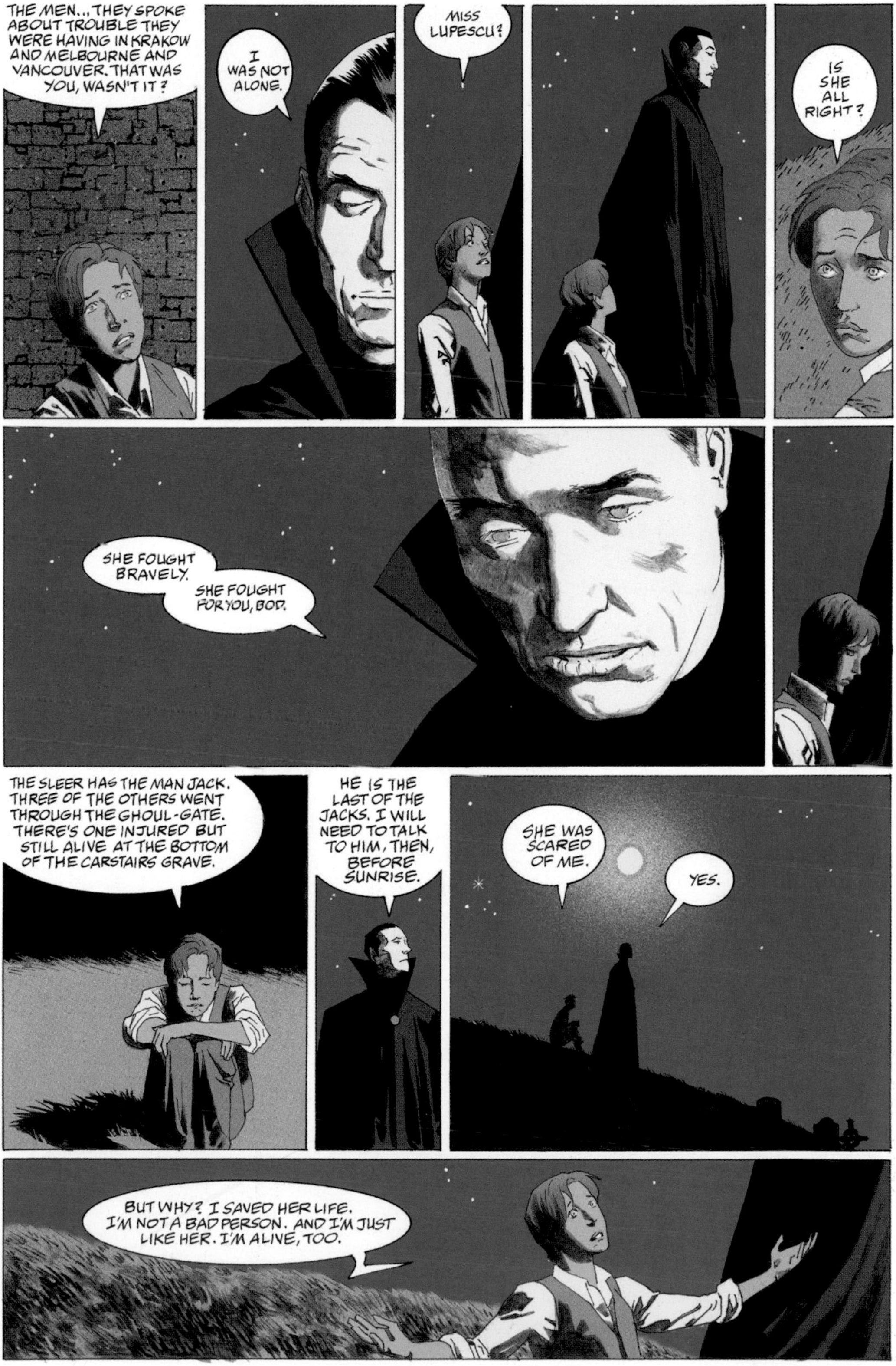
THE MEN... THEY SPOKE ABOUT TROUBLE THEY WERE HAVING IN KRAKOW AND MELBOURNE AND VANCOUVER. THAT WAS YOU, WASN'T IT?
I WAS NOT ALONE.
MISS LUPESCU?
IS SHE ALL RIGHT?
SHE FOUGHT BRAVELY.
SHE FOUGHT FOR YOU, BOD.
THE SLEER HAS THE MAN JACK. THREE OF THE OTHERS WENT THROUGH THE GHOUL-GATE. THERE'S ONE INJURED BUT STILL ALIVE AT THE BOTTOM OF THE CARSTAIRS GRAVE.
HE IS THE LAST OF THE JACKS. I WILL NEED TO TALK TO HIM, THEN, BEFORE SUNRISE.
SHE WAS SCARED OF ME.
YES.
BUT WHY? I SAVED HER LIFE. I'M NOT A BAD PERSON. AND I'M JUST LIKE HER. I'M ALIVE, TOO.

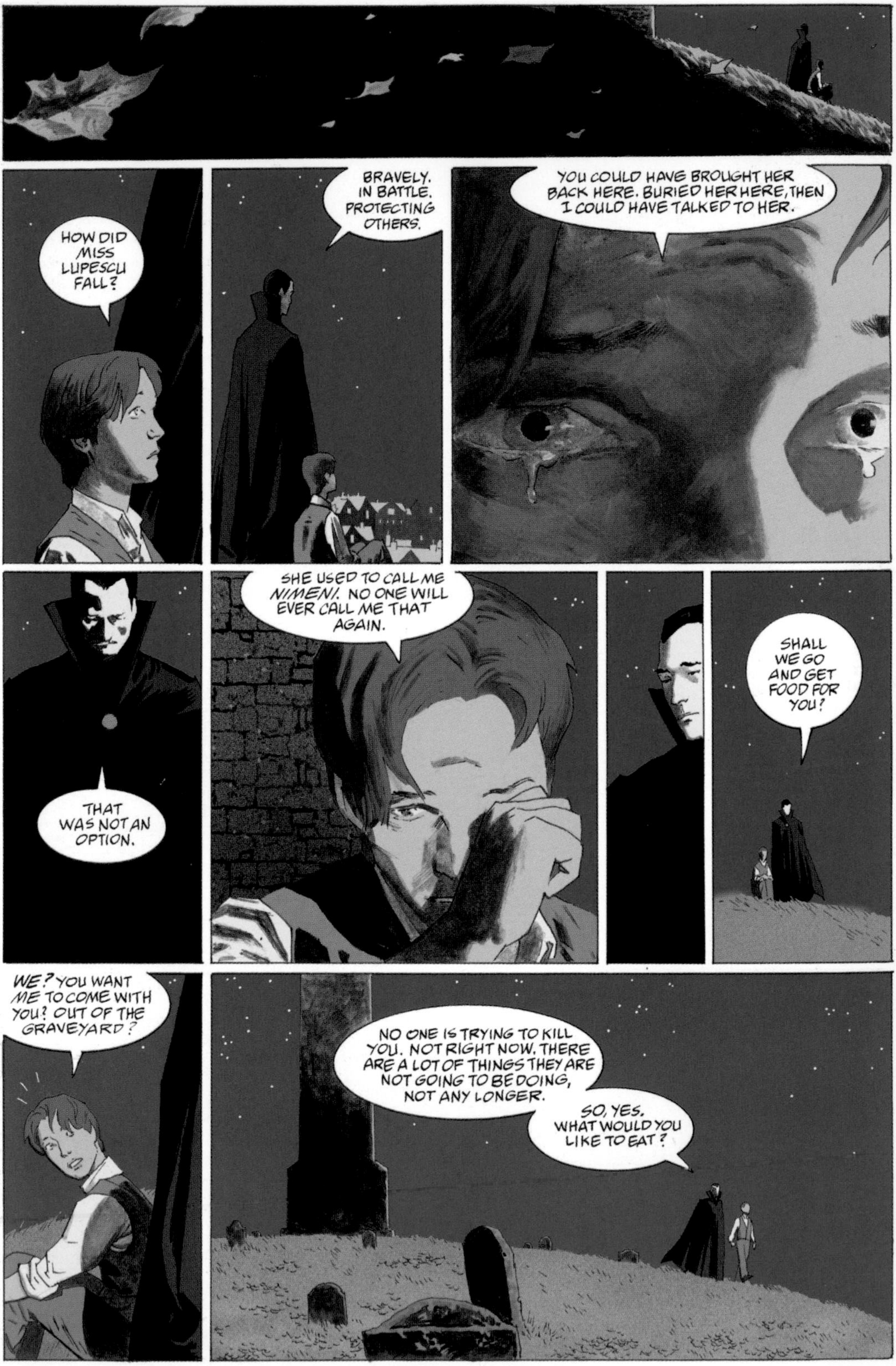
HOW DID MISS LUPESCU FALL?
BRAVELY. IN BATTLE. PROTECTING OTHERS.
YOU COULD HAVE BROUGHT HER BACK HERE. BURIED HER HERE, THEN I COULD HAVE TALKED TO HER.
THAT WAS NOT AN OPTION.
SHE USED TO CALL ME NIMENI. NO ONE WILL EVER CALL ME THAT AGAIN.
SHALL WE GO AND GET FOOD FOR YOU?
WE? YOU WANT ME TO COME WITH YOU? OUT OF THE GRAVEYARD?
NO ONE IS TRYING TO KILL YOU. NOT RIGHT NOW. THERE ARE A LOT OF THINGS THEY ARE NOT GOING TO BE DOING, NOT ANY LONGER.
SO, YES. WHAT WOULD YOU LIKE TO EAT?

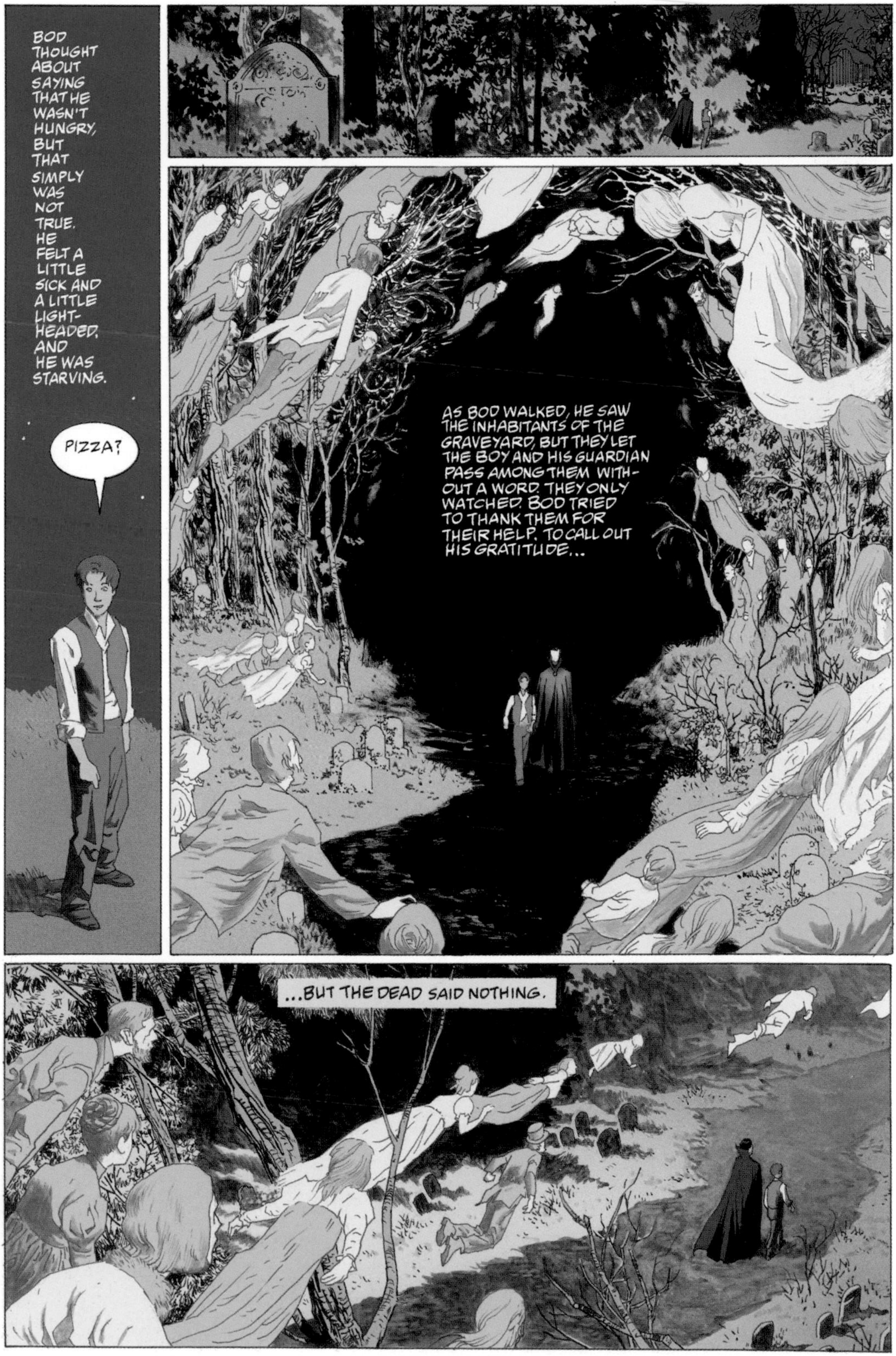
BOD THOUGHT ABOUT SAYING THAT HE WASN'T HUNGRY, BUT THAT SIMPLY WAS NOT TRUE. HE FELT A LITTLE SICK AND A LITTLE LIGHT-HEADED, AND HE WAS STARVING.
PIZZA?
AS BOD WALKED, HE SAW THE INHABITANTS OF THE GRAVEYARD, BUT THEY LET THE BOY AND HIS GUARDIAN PASS AMONG THEM WITHOUT A WORD. THEY ONLY WATCHED. BOD TRIED TO THANK THEM FOR THEIR HELP. TO CALL OUT HIS GRATITUDE...
...BUT THE DEAD SAID NOTHING.

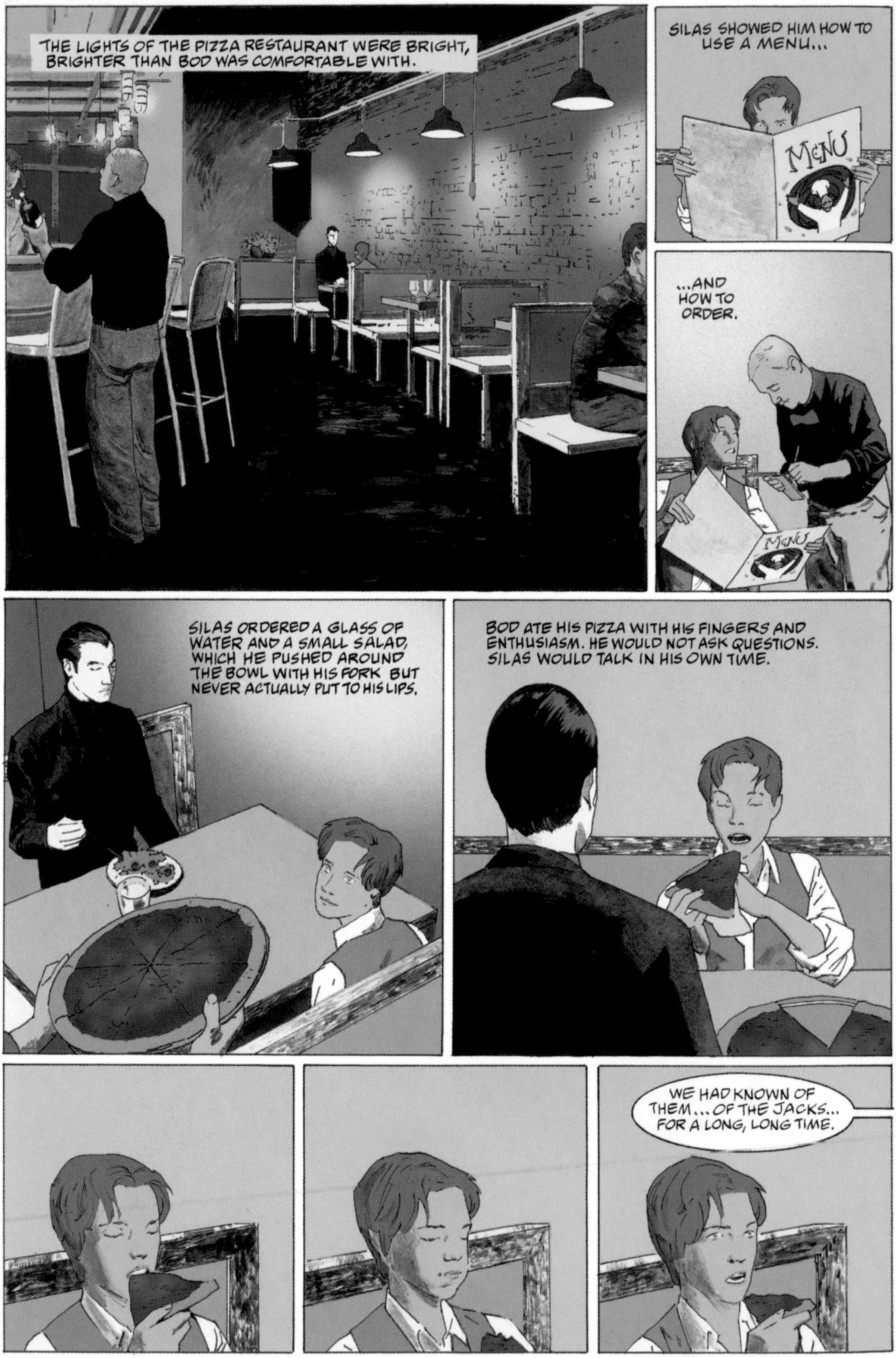
THE LIGHTS OF THE PIZZA RESTAURANT WERE BRIGHT, BRIGHTER THAN BOD WAS COMFORTABLE WITH.
SILAS SHOWED HIM HOW TO USE A MENU...
MENU
...AND HOW TO ORDER.
MENU
SILAS ORDERED A GLASS OF WATER AND A SMALL SALAD, WHICH HE PUSHED AROUND THE BOWL WITH HIS FORK BUT NEVER ACTUALLY PUT TO HIS LIPS.
BOD ATE HIS PIZZA WITH HIS FINGERS AND ENTHUSIASM. HE WOULD NOT ASK QUESTIONS. SILAS WOULD TALK IN HIS OWN TIME.
WE HAD KNOWN OF THEM... OF THE JACKS... FOR A LONG, LONG TIME.

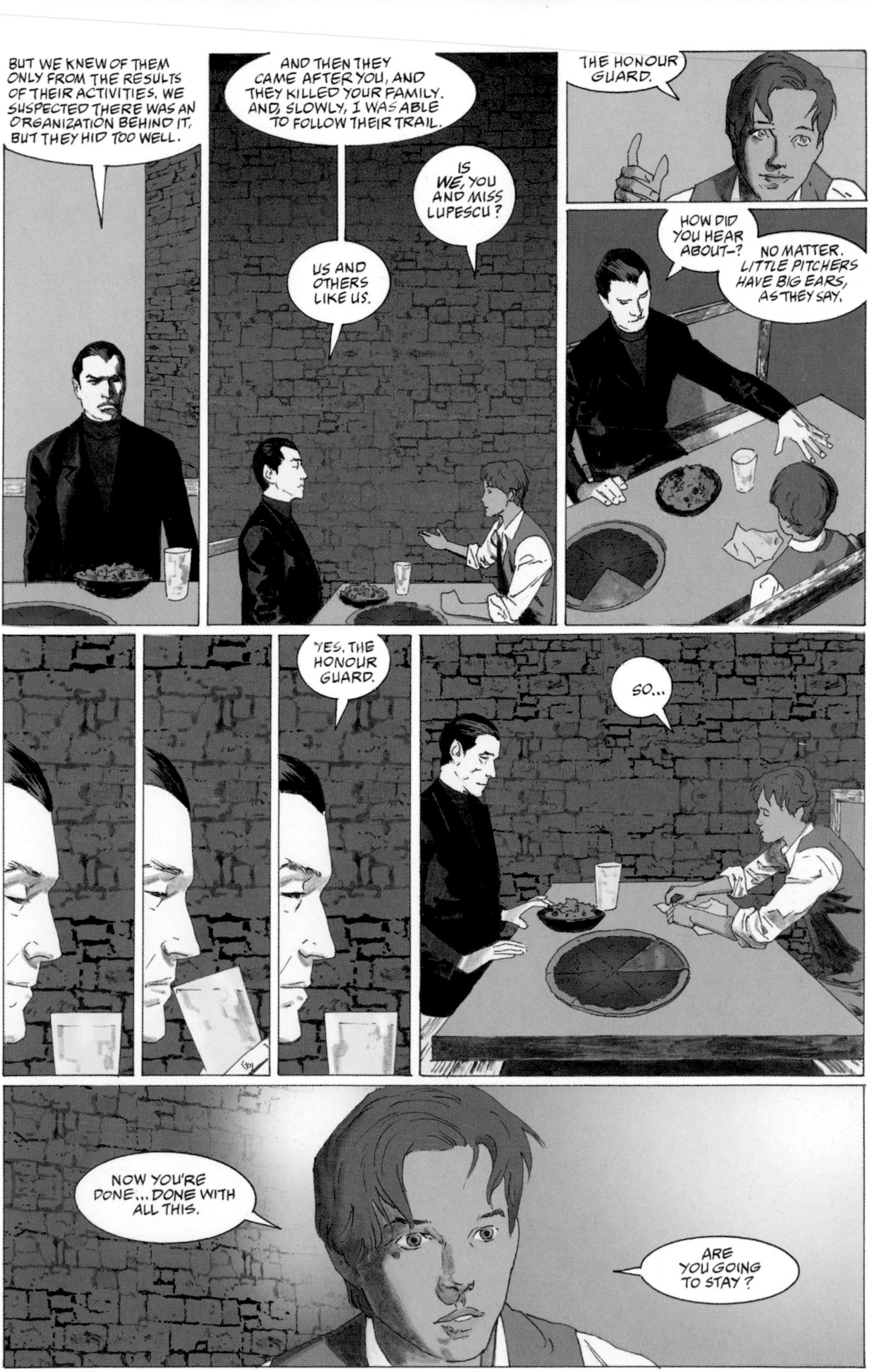
BUT WE KNEW OF THEM ONLY FROM THE RESULTS OF THEIR ACTIVITIES. WE SUSPECTED THERE WAS AN ORGANIZATION BEHIND IT, BUT THEY HID TOO WELL.
AND THEN THEY CAME AFTER YOU, AND THEY KILLED YOUR FAMILY. AND, SLOWLY, I WAS ABLE TO FOLLOW THEIR TRAIL.
IS WE, YOU AND MISS LUPESCU?
US AND OTHERS LIKE US.
THE HONOUR GUARD.
HOW DID YOU HEAR ABOUT–?
NO MATTER. LITTLE PITCHERS HAVE BIG EARS, AS THEY SAY.
YES. THE HONOUR GUARD.
SO...
NOW YOU'RE DONE... DONE WITH ALL THIS.
ARE YOU GOING TO STAY?

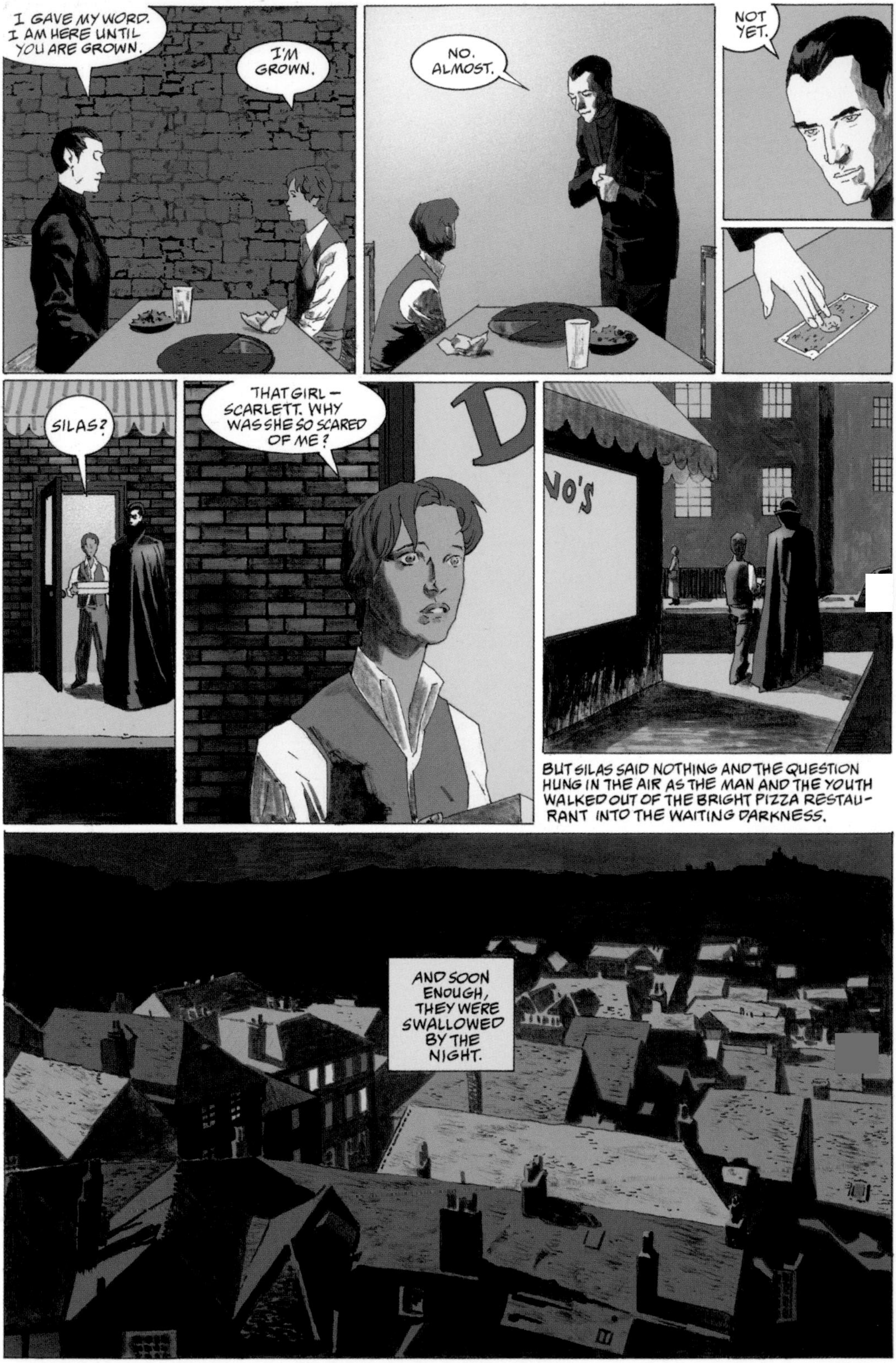
I GAVE MY WORD. I AM HERE UNTIL YOU ARE GROWN.
I'M GROWN.
NO. ALMOST.
NOT YET.
SILAS?
THAT GIRL — SCARLETT. WHY WAS SHE SO SCARED OF ME?
NO'S
BUT SILAS SAID NOTHING AND THE QUESTION HUNG IN THE AIR AS THE MAN AND THE YOUTH WALKED OUT OF THE BRIGHT PIZZA RESTAU-RANT INTO THE WAITING DARKNESS.
AND SOON ENOUGH, THEY WERE SWALLOWED BY THE NIGHT.

8
Leavings and Partings

Illustrated by P. Craig Russell, Kevin Nowlan, and Galen Showman

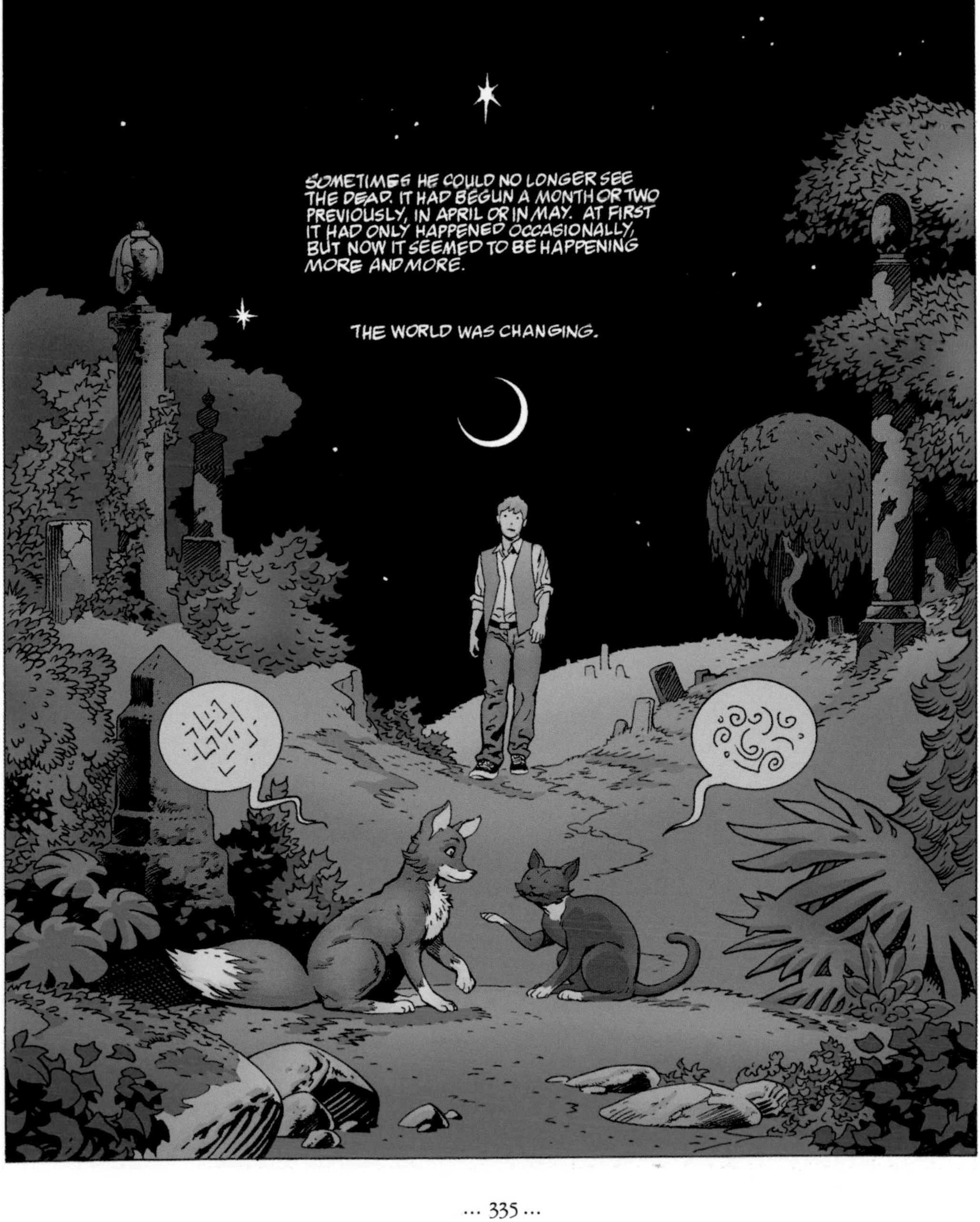
SOMETIMES HE COULD NO LONGER SEE THE DEAD. IT HAD BEGUN A MONTH OR TWO PREVIOUSLY, IN APRIL OR IN MAY. AT FIRST IT HAD ONLY HAPPENED OCCASIONALLY, BUT NOW IT SEEMED TO BE HAPPENING MORE AND MORE.
THE WORLD WAS CHANGING.

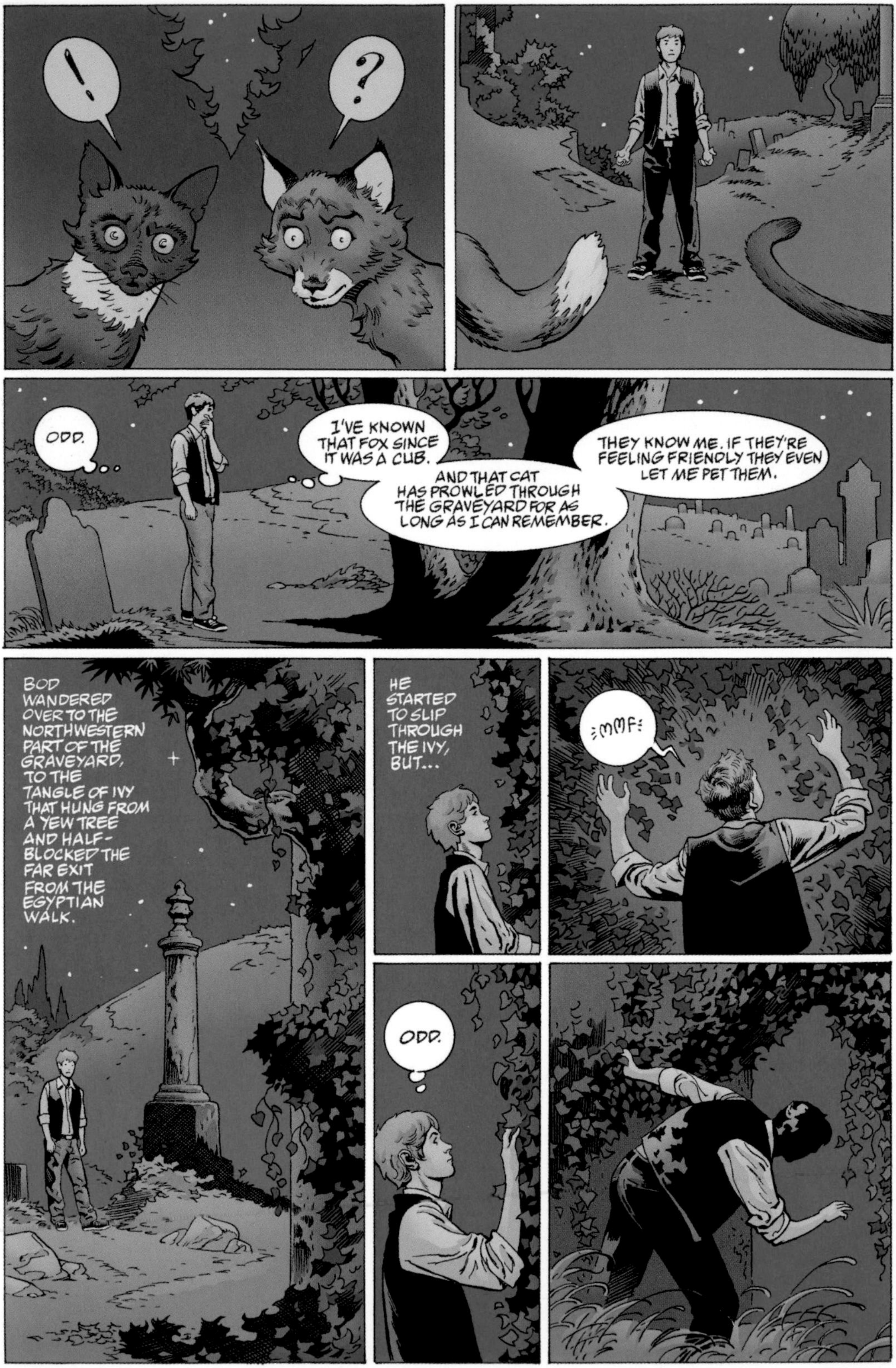
!
?
ODD.
I'VE KNOWN THAT FOX SINCE IT WAS A CUB.
AND THAT CAT HAS PROWLED THROUGH THE GRAVEYARD FOR AS LONG AS I CAN REMEMBER.
THEY KNOW ME. IF THEY'RE FEELING FRIENDLY THEY EVEN LET ME PET THEM.
BOD WANDERED OVER TO THE NORTHWESTERN PART OF THE GRAVEYARD, TO THE TANGLE OF IVY THAT HUNG FROM A YEW TREE AND HALF-BLOCKED THE FAR EXIT FROM THE EGYPTIAN WALK.
HE STARTED TO SLIP THROUGH THE IVY, BUT...
MMF
ODD.

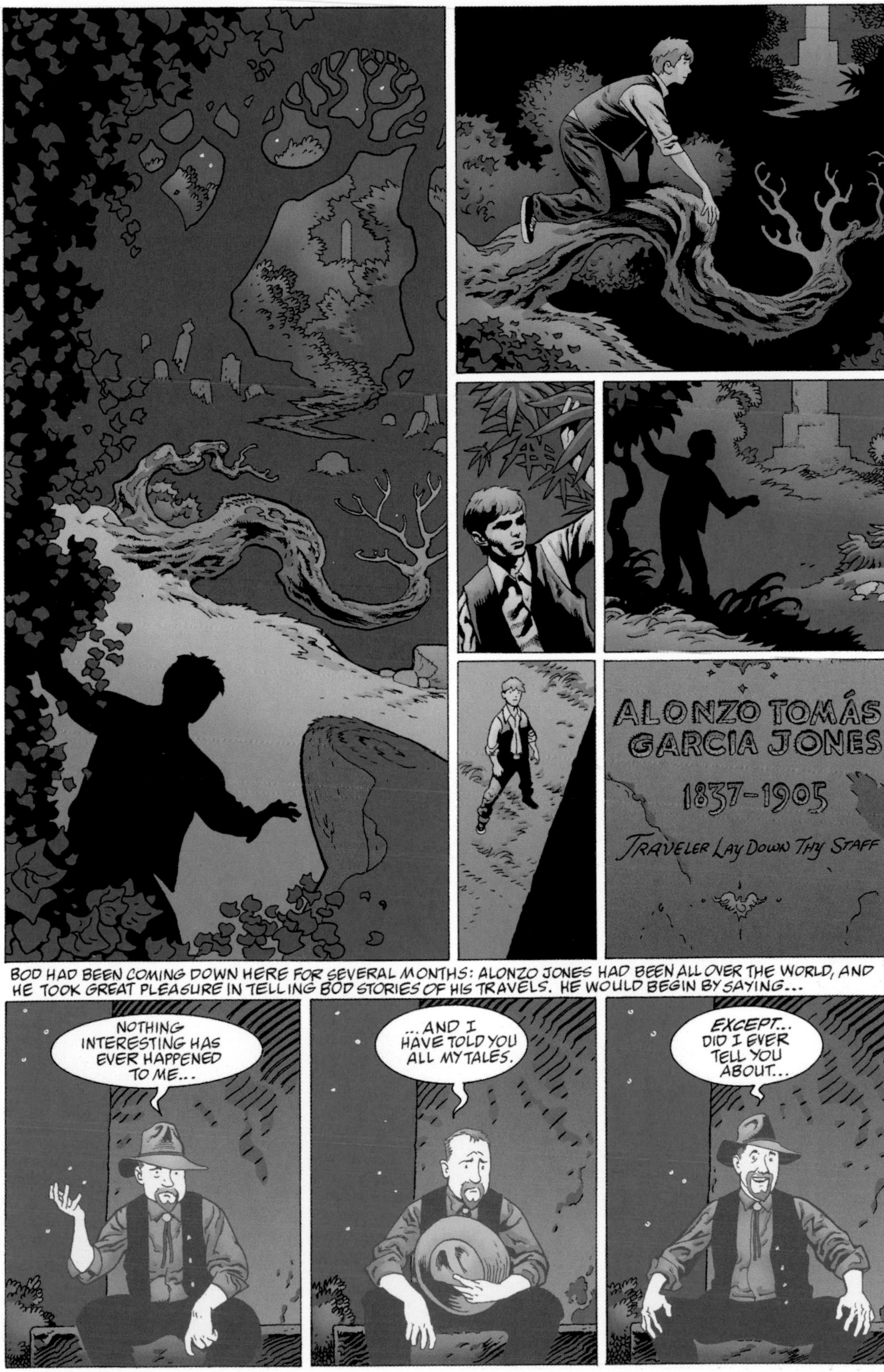
ALONZO TOMÁS GARCIA JONES
1837-1905
TRAVELER LAY DOWN THY STAFF
BOD HAD BEEN COMING DOWN HERE FOR SEVERAL MONTHS: ALONZO JONES HAD BEEN ALL OVER THE WORLD, AND HE TOOK GREAT PLEASURE IN TELLING BOD STORIES OF HIS TRAVELS. HE WOULD BEGIN BY SAYING...
NOTHING INTERESTING HAS EVER HAPPENED TO ME...
...AND I HAVE TOLD YOU ALL MY TALES.
EXCEPT... DID I EVER TELL YOU ABOUT...

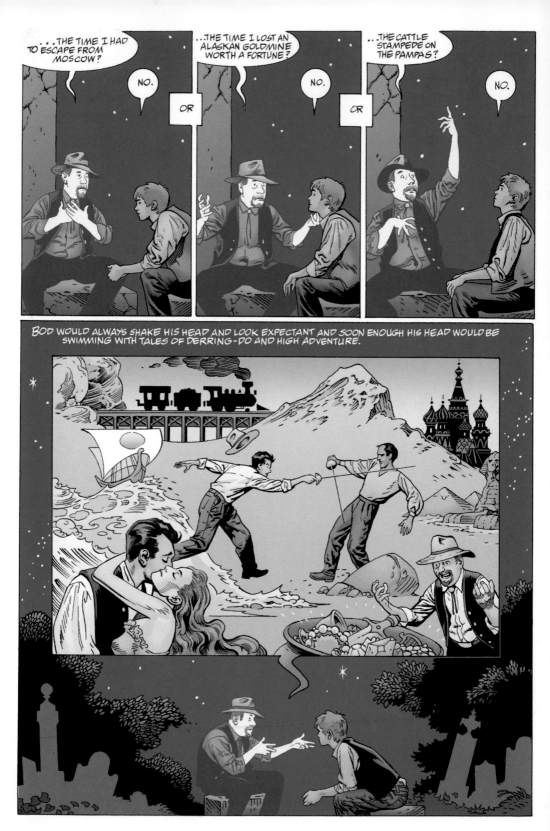

... THE TIME I HAD TO ESCAPE FROM MOSCOW?

NO.

OR

.. THE TIME I LOST AN ALASKAN GOLDMINE WORTH A FORTUNE?

NO.

OR

.. THE CATTLE STAMPEDE ON THE PAMPAS?

NO.

BOD WOULD ALWAYS SHAKE HIS HEAD AND LOOK EXPECTANT AND SOON ENOUGH HIS HEAD WOULD BE SWIMMING WITH TALES OF DERRING-DO AND HIGH ADVENTURE.

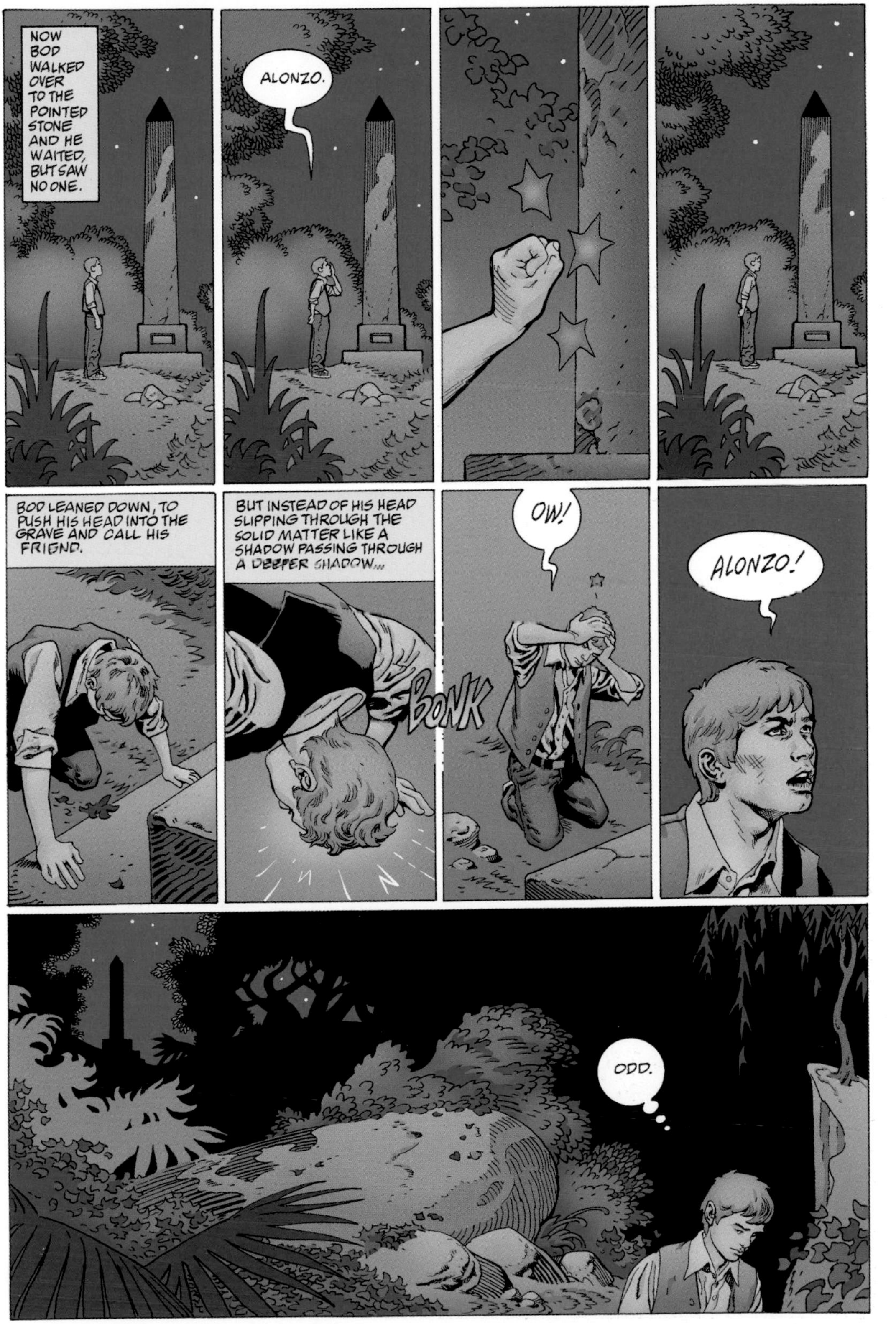
NOW BOD WALKED OVER TO THE POINTED STONE AND HE WAITED, BUT SAW NO ONE.
ALONZO.
BOD LEANED DOWN, TO PUSH HIS HEAD INTO THE GRAVE AND CALL HIS FRIEND.
BUT INSTEAD OF HIS HEAD SLIPPING THROUGH THE SOLID MATTER LIKE A SHADOW PASSING THROUGH A DEEPER SHADOW...
BONK
OW!
ALONZO!
ODD.

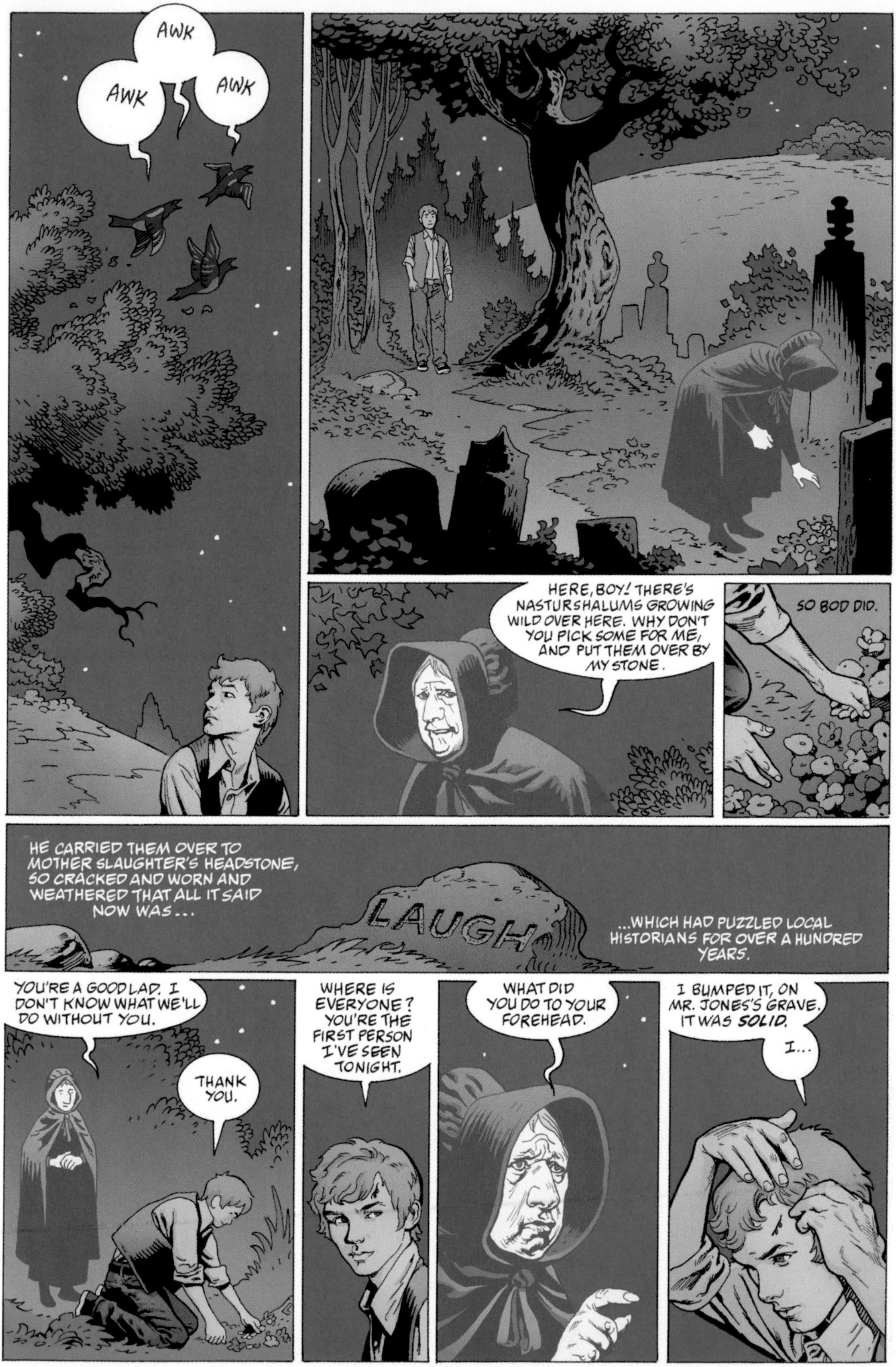
AWK
AWK
AWK
HERE, BOY! THERE'S NASTURSHALUMS GROWING WILD OVER HERE. WHY DON'T YOU PICK SOME FOR ME, AND PUT THEM OVER BY MY STONE.
SO BOD DID.
HE CARRIED THEM OVER TO MOTHER SLAUGHTER'S HEADSTONE, SO CRACKED AND WORN AND WEATHERED THAT ALL IT SAID NOW WAS...
LAUGH
...WHICH HAD PUZZLED LOCAL HISTORIANS FOR OVER A HUNDRED YEARS.
YOU'RE A GOOD LAD. I DON'T KNOW WHAT WE'LL DO WITHOUT YOU.
THANK YOU.
WHERE IS EVERYONE? YOU'RE THE FIRST PERSON I'VE SEEN TONIGHT.
WHAT DID YOU DO TO YOUR FOREHEAD.
I BUMPED IT, ON MR. JONES'S GRAVE. IT WAS SOLID.
I...

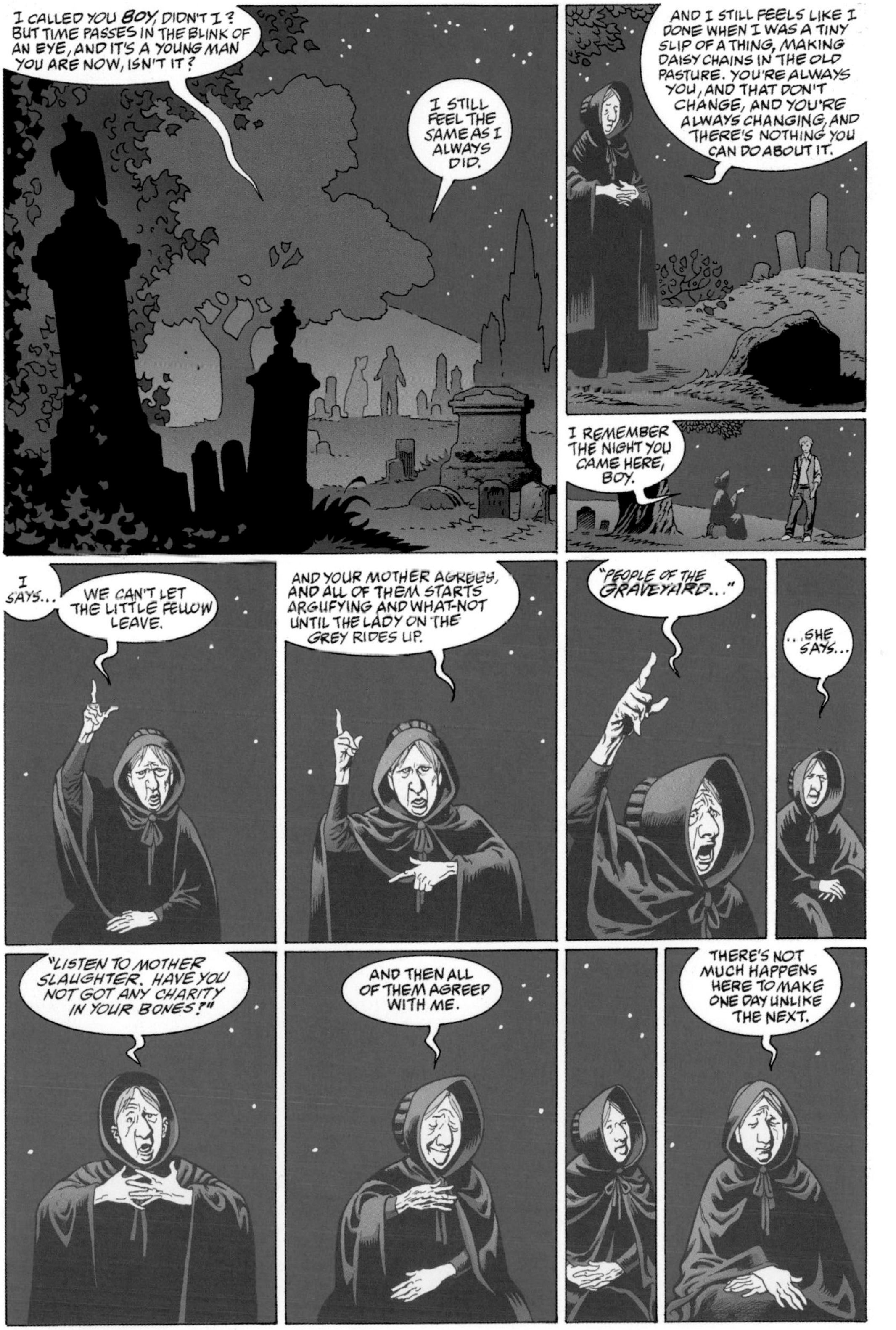
I CALLED YOU BOY, DIDN'T I? BUT TIME PASSES IN THE BLINK OF AN EYE, AND IT'S A YOUNG MAN YOU ARE NOW, ISN'T IT?
I STILL FEEL THE SAME AS I ALWAYS DID.
AND I STILL FEELS LIKE I DONE WHEN I WAS A TINY SLIP OF A THING, MAKING DAISY CHAINS IN THE OLD PASTURE. YOU'RE ALWAYS YOU, AND THAT DON'T CHANGE, AND YOU'RE ALWAYS CHANGING, AND THERE'S NOTHING YOU CAN DO ABOUT IT.
I REMEMBER THE NIGHT YOU CAME HERE, BOY.
I SAYS...
WE CAN'T LET THE LITTLE FELLOW LEAVE.
AND YOUR MOTHER AGREES, AND ALL OF THEM STARTS ARGUFYING AND WHAT-NOT UNTIL THE LADY ON THE GREY RIDES UP.
"PEOPLE OF THE GRAVEYARD..."
...SHE SAYS...
"LISTEN TO MOTHER SLAUGHTER. HAVE YOU NOT GOT ANY CHARITY IN YOUR BONES?"
AND THEN ALL OF THEM AGREED WITH ME.
THERE'S NOT MUCH HAPPENS HERE TO MAKE ONE DAY UNLIKE THE NEXT.

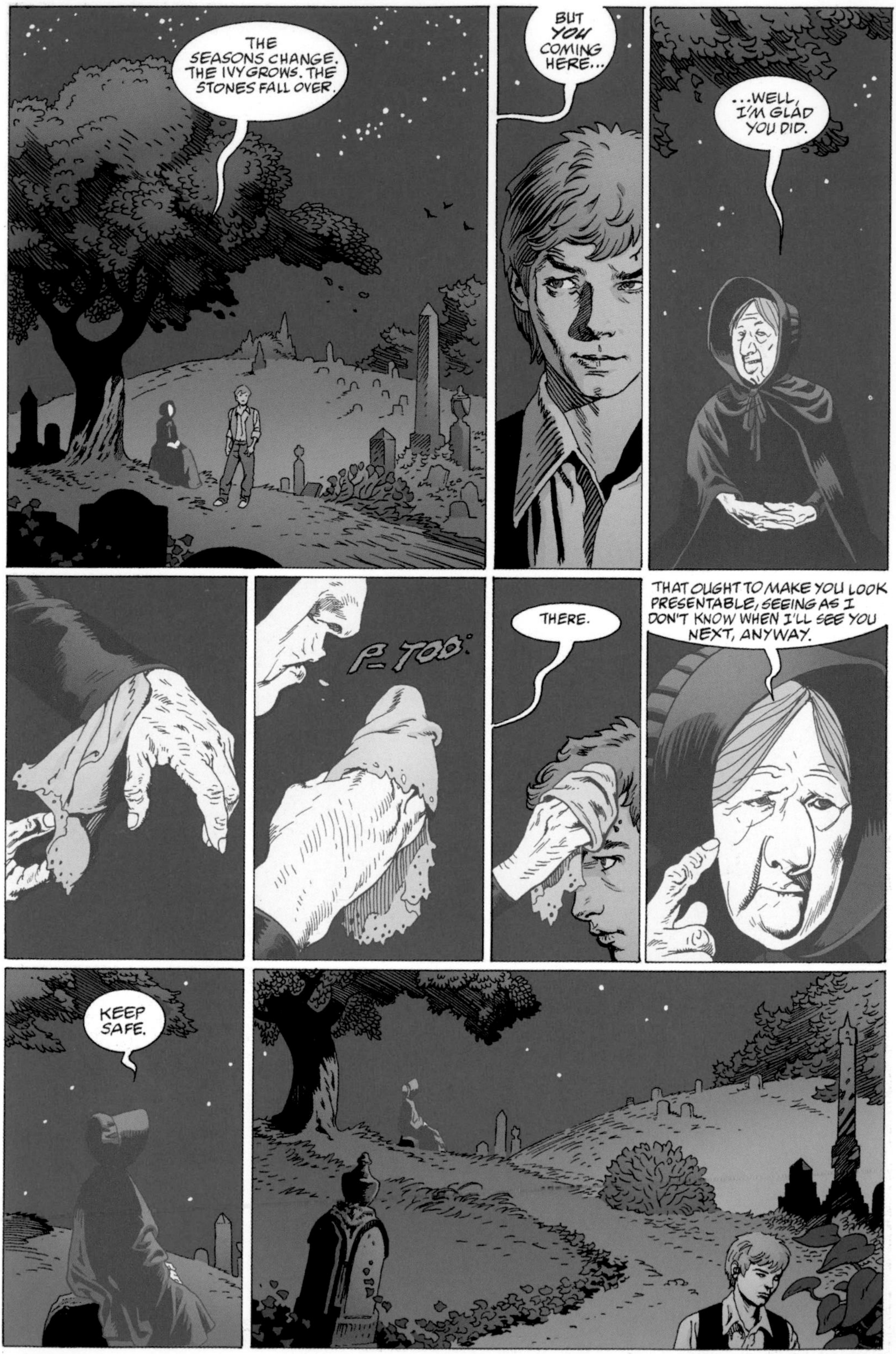
THE SEASONS CHANGE. THE IVY GROWS. THE STONES FALL OVER.
BUT YOU COMING HERE...
...WELL, I'M GLAD YOU DID.
P-TOO!
THERE.
THAT OUGHT TO MAKE YOU LOOK PRESENTABLE, SEEING AS I DON'T KNOW WHEN I'LL SEE YOU NEXT, ANYWAY.
KEEP SAFE.

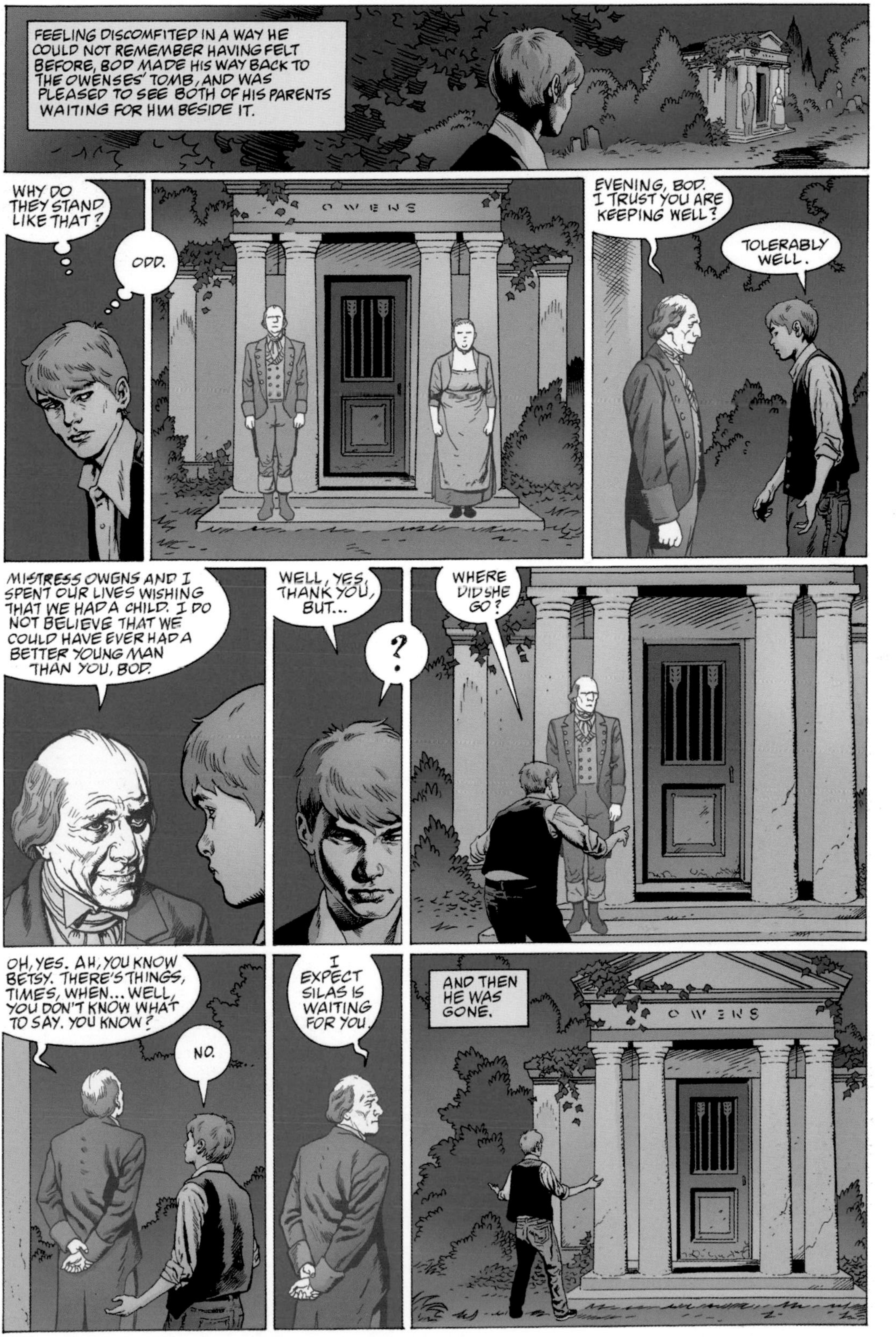
FEELING DISCOMFITED IN A WAY HE COULD NOT REMEMBER HAVING FELT BEFORE, BOD MADE HIS WAY BACK TO THE OWENSES' TOMB, AND WAS PLEASED TO SEE BOTH OF HIS PARENTS WAITING FOR HIM BESIDE IT.
WHY DO THEY STAND LIKE THAT?
ODD.
OWENS
EVENING, BOD. I TRUST YOU ARE KEEPING WELL?
TOLERABLY WELL.
MISTRESS OWENS AND I SPENT OUR LIVES WISHING THAT WE HAD A CHILD. I DO NOT BELIEVE THAT WE COULD HAVE EVER HAD A BETTER YOUNG MAN THAN YOU, BOD.
WELL, YES, THANK YOU, BUT...
?
WHERE DID SHE GO?
OH, YES. AH, YOU KNOW BETSY. THERE'S THINGS, TIMES, WHEN... WELL, YOU DON'T KNOW WHAT TO SAY. YOU KNOW?
NO.
I EXPECT SILAS IS WAITING FOR YOU.
AND THEN HE WAS GONE.
OWENS

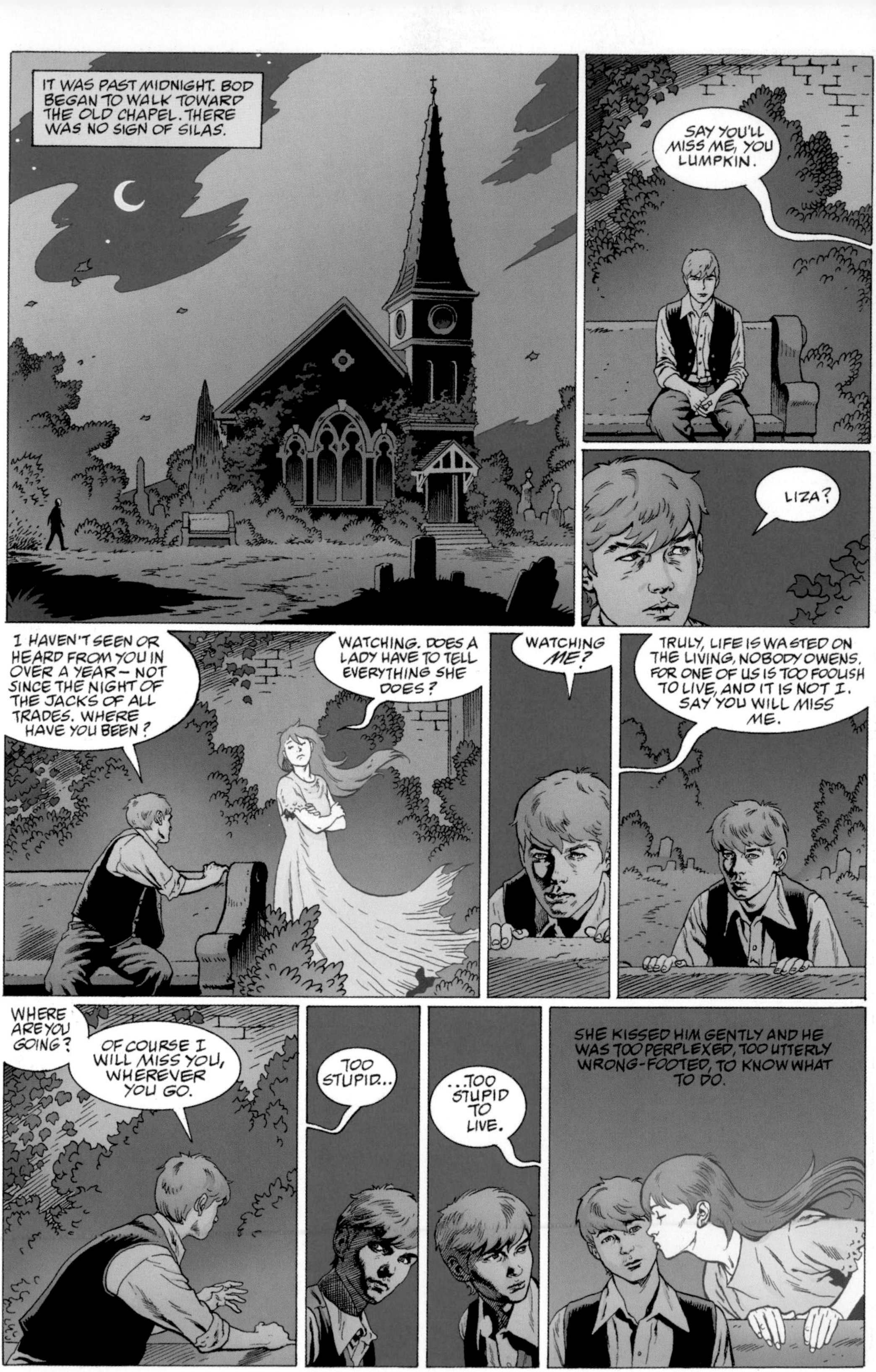
IT WAS PAST MIDNIGHT. BOD BEGAN TO WALK TOWARD THE OLD CHAPEL. THERE WAS NO SIGN OF SILAS.
SAY YOU'LL MISS ME, YOU LUMPKIN.
LIZA?
I HAVEN'T SEEN OR HEARD FROM YOU IN OVER A YEAR— NOT SINCE THE NIGHT OF THE JACKS OF ALL TRADES. WHERE HAVE YOU BEEN?
WATCHING. DOES A LADY HAVE TO TELL EVERYTHING SHE DOES?
WATCHING *ME*?
TRULY, LIFE IS WASTED ON THE LIVING, NOBODY OWENS. FOR ONE OF US IS TOO FOOLISH TO LIVE, AND IT IS NOT I. SAY YOU WILL MISS ME.
WHERE ARE YOU GOING?
OF COURSE I WILL MISS YOU, WHEREVER YOU GO.
TOO STUPID...
...TOO STUPID TO LIVE.
SHE KISSED HIM GENTLY AND HE WAS TOO PERPLEXED, TOO UTTERLY WRONG-FOOTED, TO KNOW WHAT TO DO.

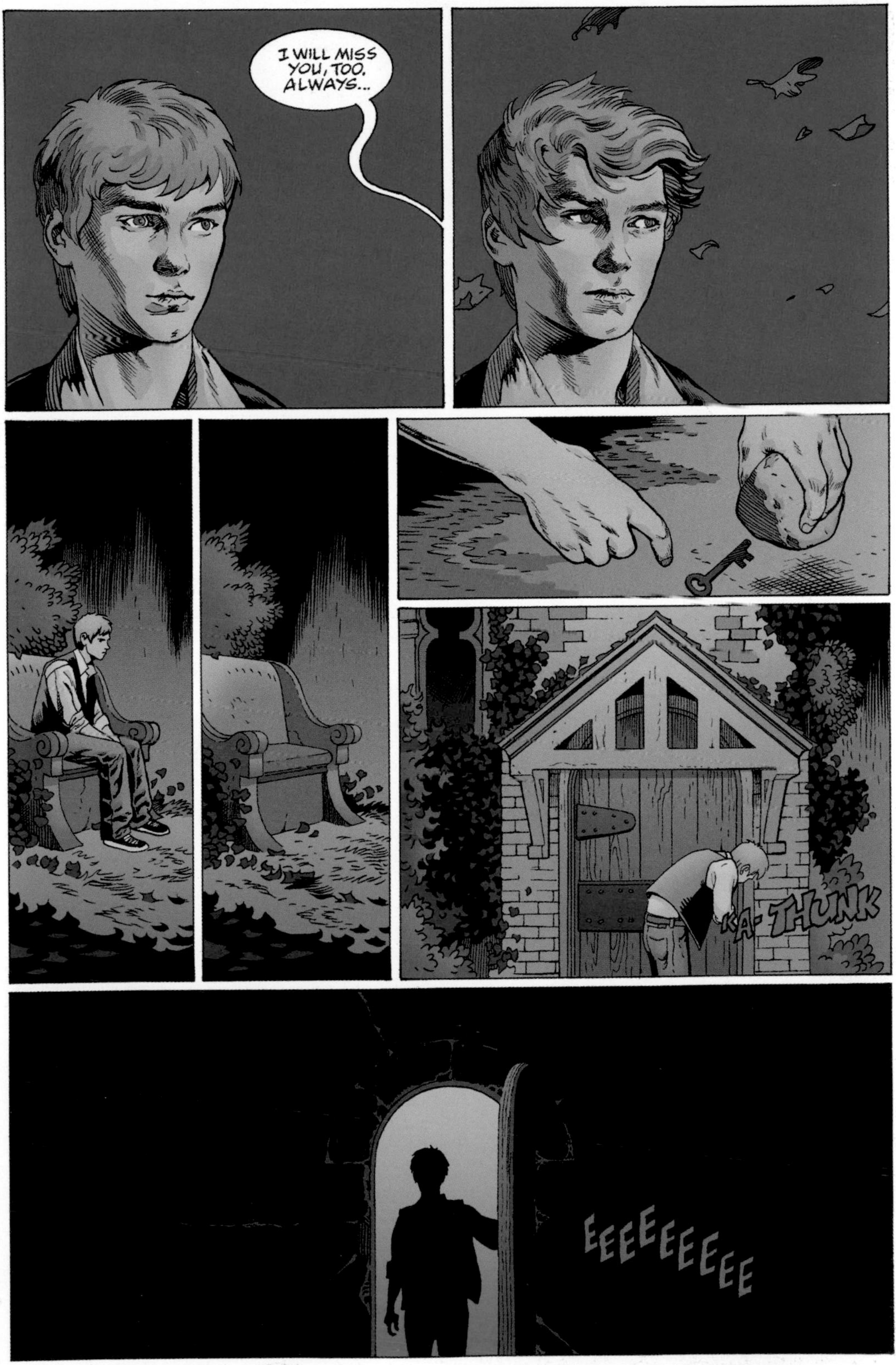
I WILL MISS YOU, TOO. ALWAYS...
KA-THUNK
EEEEEEEEEE

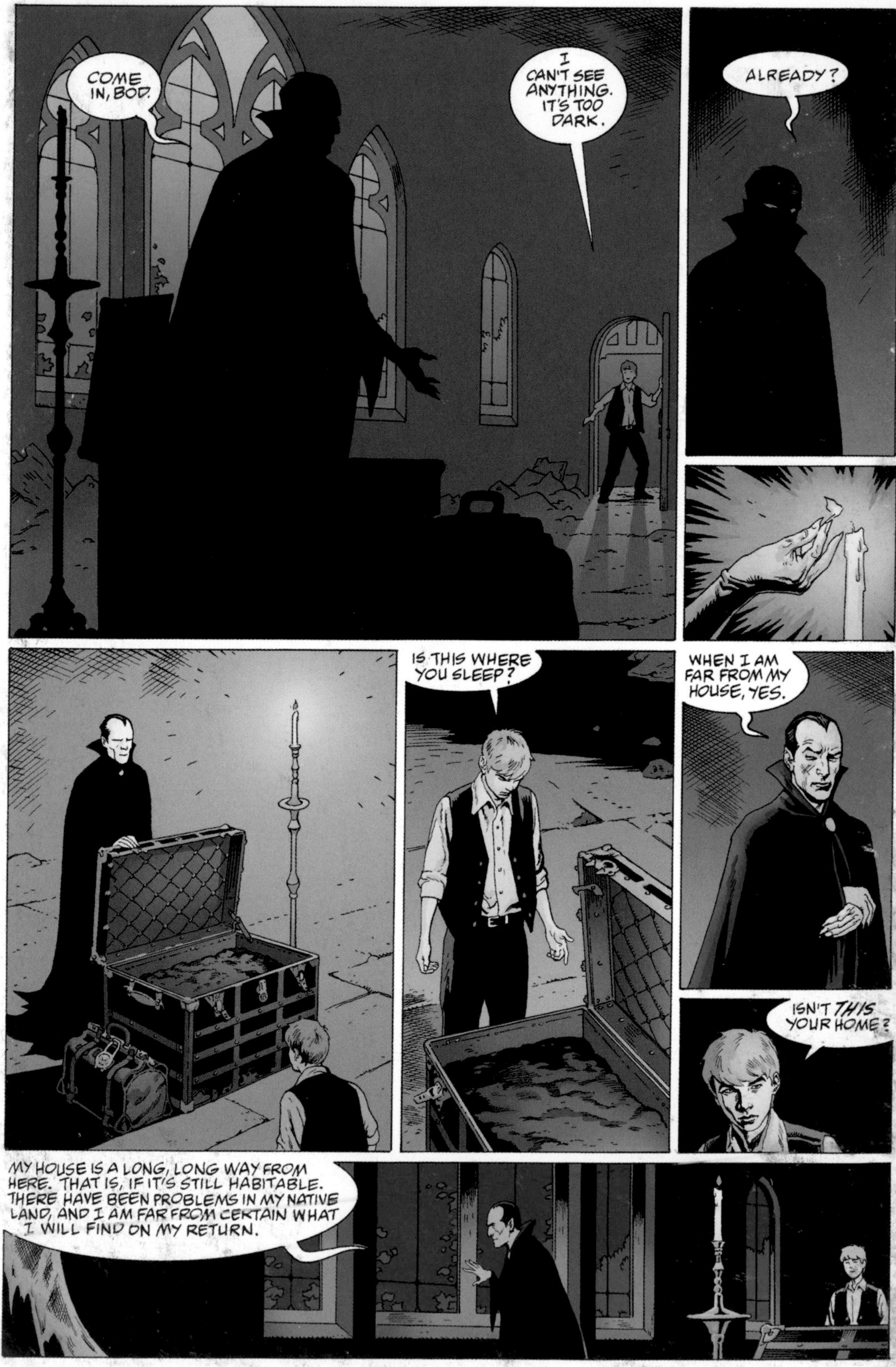
COME IN, BOD.
I CAN'T SEE ANYTHING. IT'S TOO DARK.
ALREADY?
IS THIS WHERE YOU SLEEP?
WHEN I AM FAR FROM MY HOUSE, YES.
ISN'T THIS YOUR HOME?
MY HOUSE IS A LONG, LONG WAY FROM HERE. THAT IS, IF IT'S STILL HABITABLE. THERE HAVE BEEN PROBLEMS IN MY NATIVE LAND, AND I AM FAR FROM CERTAIN WHAT I WILL FIND ON MY RETURN.

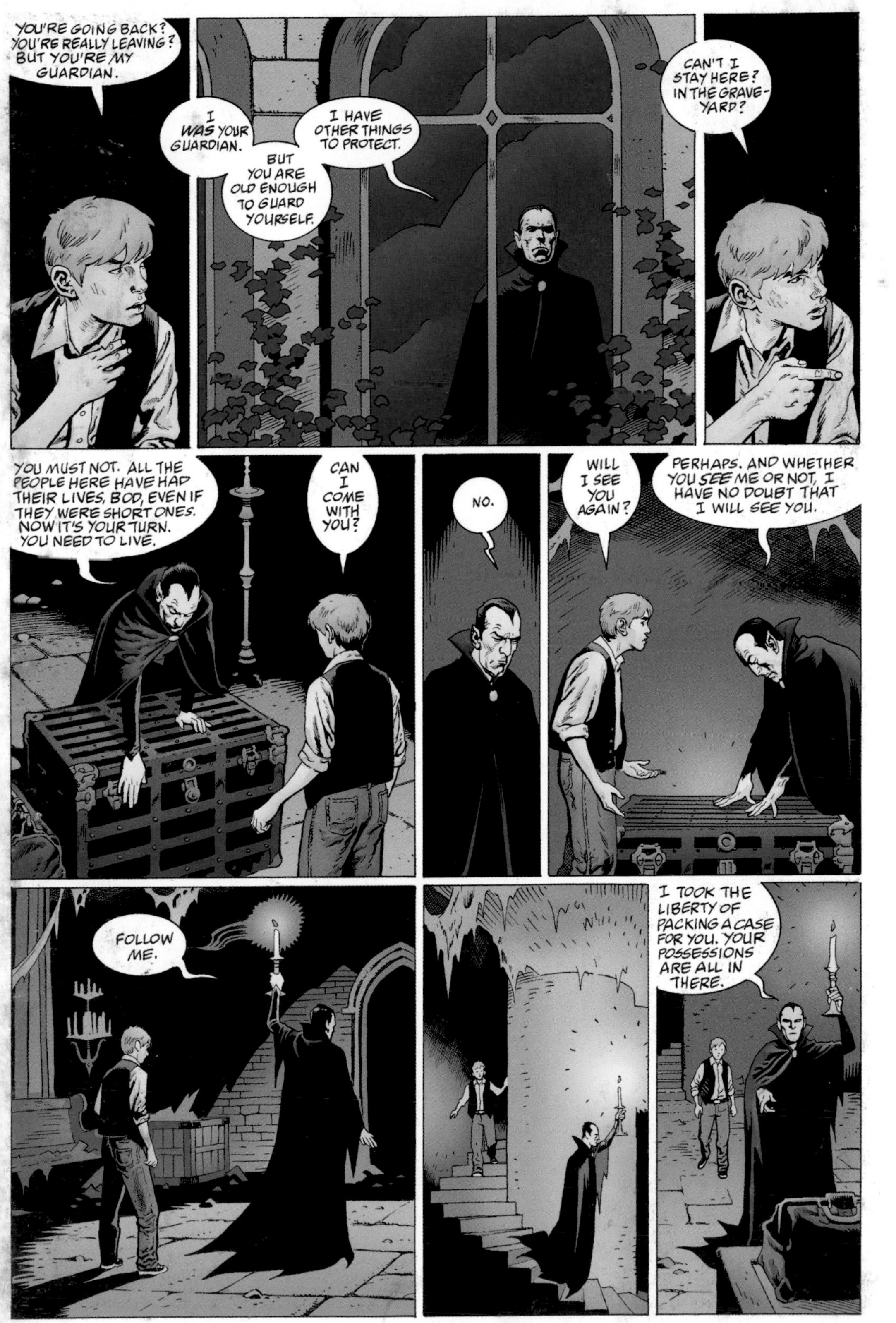
YOU'RE GOING BACK? YOU'RE REALLY LEAVING? BUT YOU'RE MY GUARDIAN.
I WAS YOUR GUARDIAN.
BUT YOU ARE OLD ENOUGH TO GUARD YOURSELF.
I HAVE OTHER THINGS TO PROTECT.
CAN'T I STAY HERE? IN THE GRAVE-YARD?
YOU MUST NOT. ALL THE PEOPLE HERE HAVE HAD THEIR LIVES, BOD, EVEN IF THEY WERE SHORT ONES. NOW IT'S YOUR TURN. YOU NEED TO LIVE.
CAN I COME WITH YOU?
NO.
WILL I SEE YOU AGAIN?
PERHAPS. AND WHETHER YOU SEE ME OR NOT, I HAVE NO DOUBT THAT I WILL SEE YOU.
FOLLOW ME.
I TOOK THE LIBERTY OF PACKING A CASE FOR YOU. YOUR POSSESSIONS ARE ALL IN THERE.

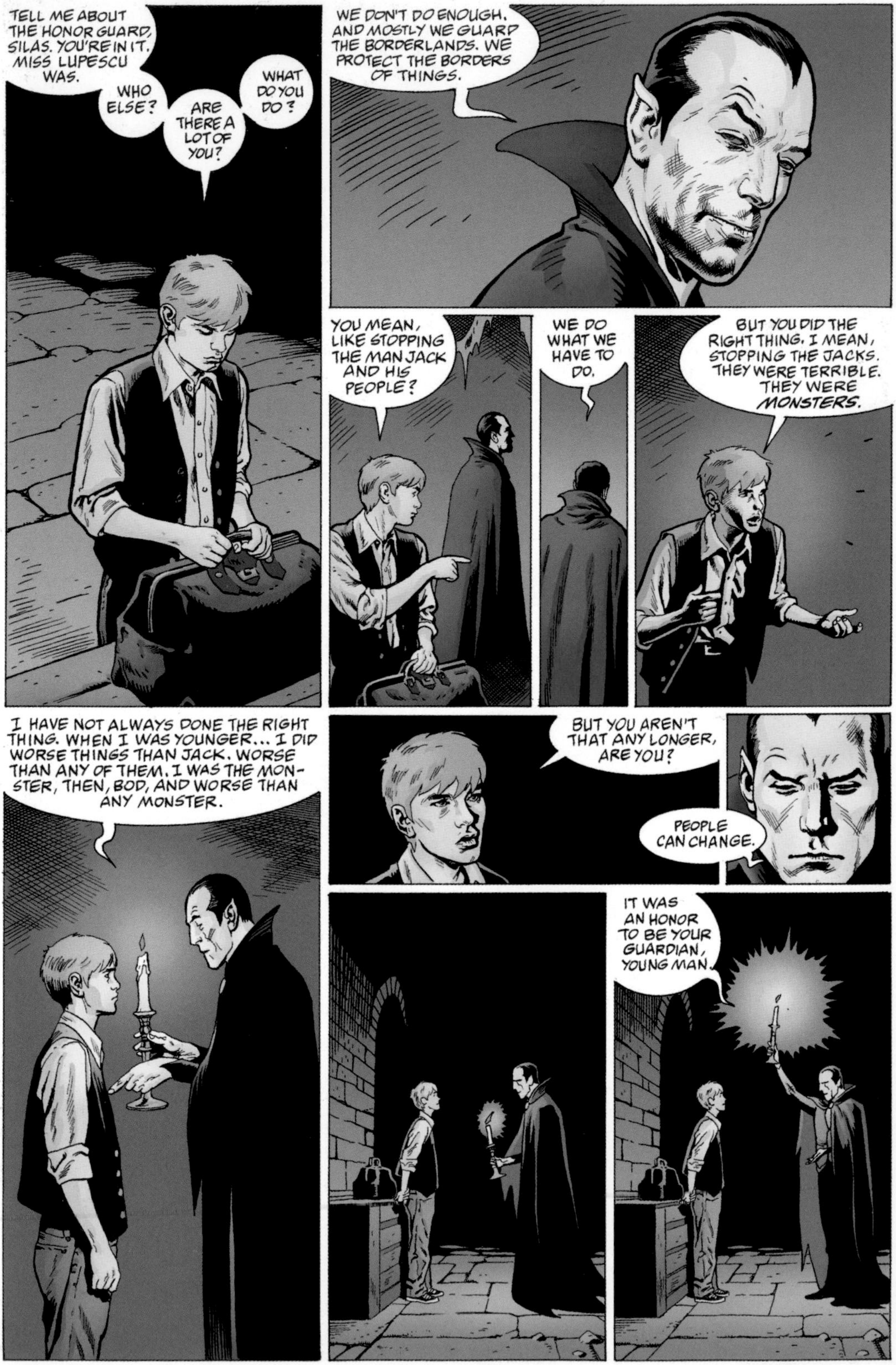
TELL ME ABOUT THE HONOR GUARD, SILAS. YOU'RE IN IT. MISS LUPESCU WAS.
WHO ELSE?
ARE THERE A LOT OF YOU?
WHAT DO YOU DO?
WE DON'T DO ENOUGH. AND MOSTLY WE GUARD THE BORDERLANDS. WE PROTECT THE BORDERS OF THINGS.
YOU MEAN, LIKE STOPPING THE MAN JACK AND HIS PEOPLE?
WE DO WHAT WE HAVE TO DO.
BUT YOU DID THE RIGHT THING. I MEAN, STOPPING THE JACKS. THEY WERE TERRIBLE. THEY WERE MONSTERS.
I HAVE NOT ALWAYS DONE THE RIGHT THING. WHEN I WAS YOUNGER... I DID WORSE THINGS THAN JACK. WORSE THAN ANY OF THEM. I WAS THE MONSTER, THEN, BOD, AND WORSE THAN ANY MONSTER.
BUT YOU AREN'T THAT ANY LONGER, ARE YOU?
PEOPLE CAN CHANGE.
IT WAS AN HONOR TO BE YOUR GUARDIAN, YOUNG MAN.

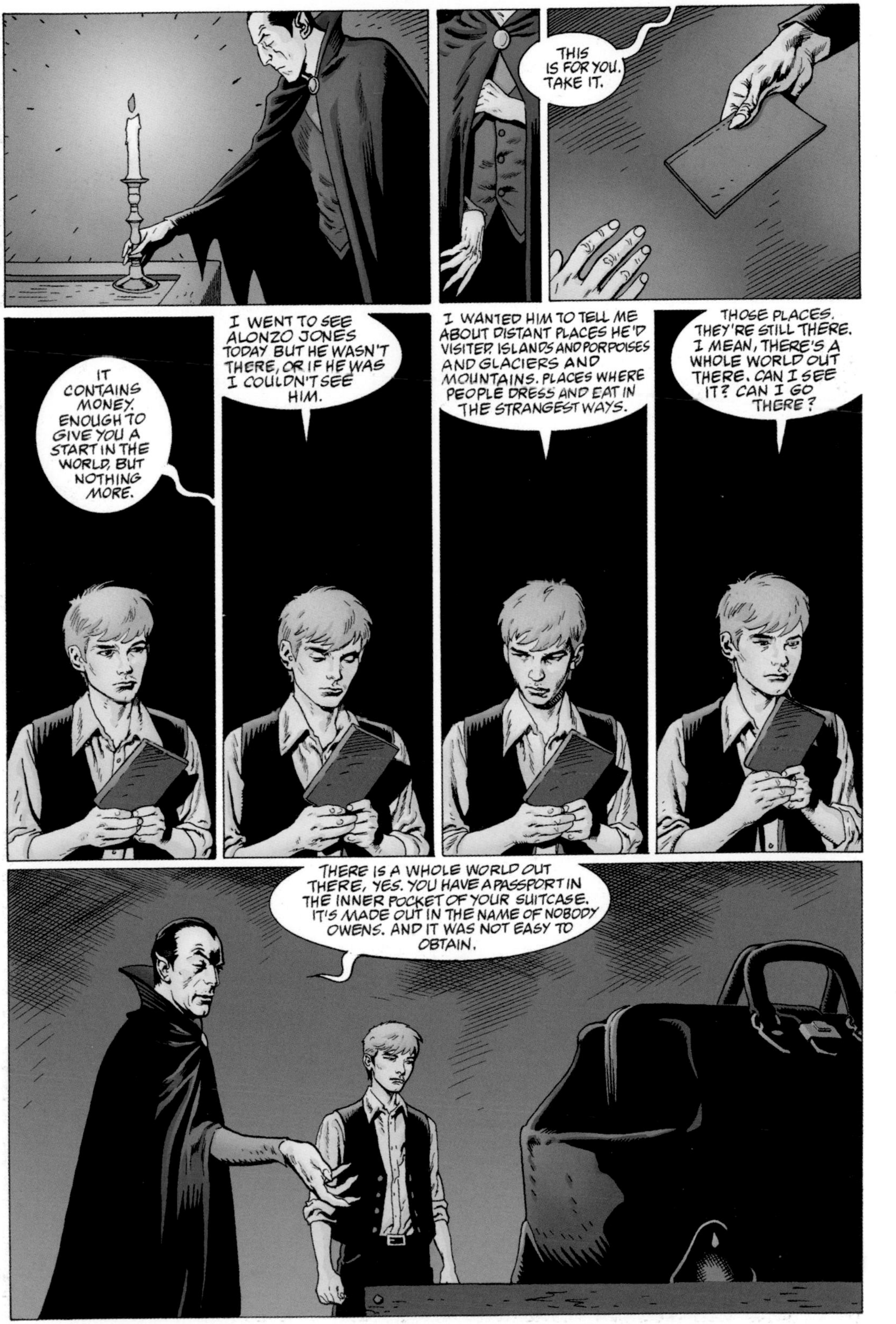
THIS IS FOR YOU. TAKE IT.
IT CONTAINS MONEY. ENOUGH TO GIVE YOU A START IN THE WORLD, BUT NOTHING MORE.
I WENT TO SEE ALONZO JONES TODAY BUT HE WASN'T THERE, OR IF HE WAS I COULDN'T SEE HIM.
I WANTED HIM TO TELL ME ABOUT DISTANT PLACES HE'D VISITED. ISLANDS AND PORPOISES AND GLACIERS AND MOUNTAINS. PLACES WHERE PEOPLE DRESS AND EAT IN THE STRANGEST WAYS.
THOSE PLACES. THEY'RE STILL THERE. I MEAN, THERE'S A WHOLE WORLD OUT THERE. CAN I SEE IT? CAN I GO THERE?
THERE IS A WHOLE WORLD OUT THERE, YES. YOU HAVE A PASSPORT IN THE INNER POCKET OF YOUR SUITCASE. IT'S MADE OUT IN THE NAME OF NOBODY OWENS. AND IT WAS NOT EASY TO OBTAIN.

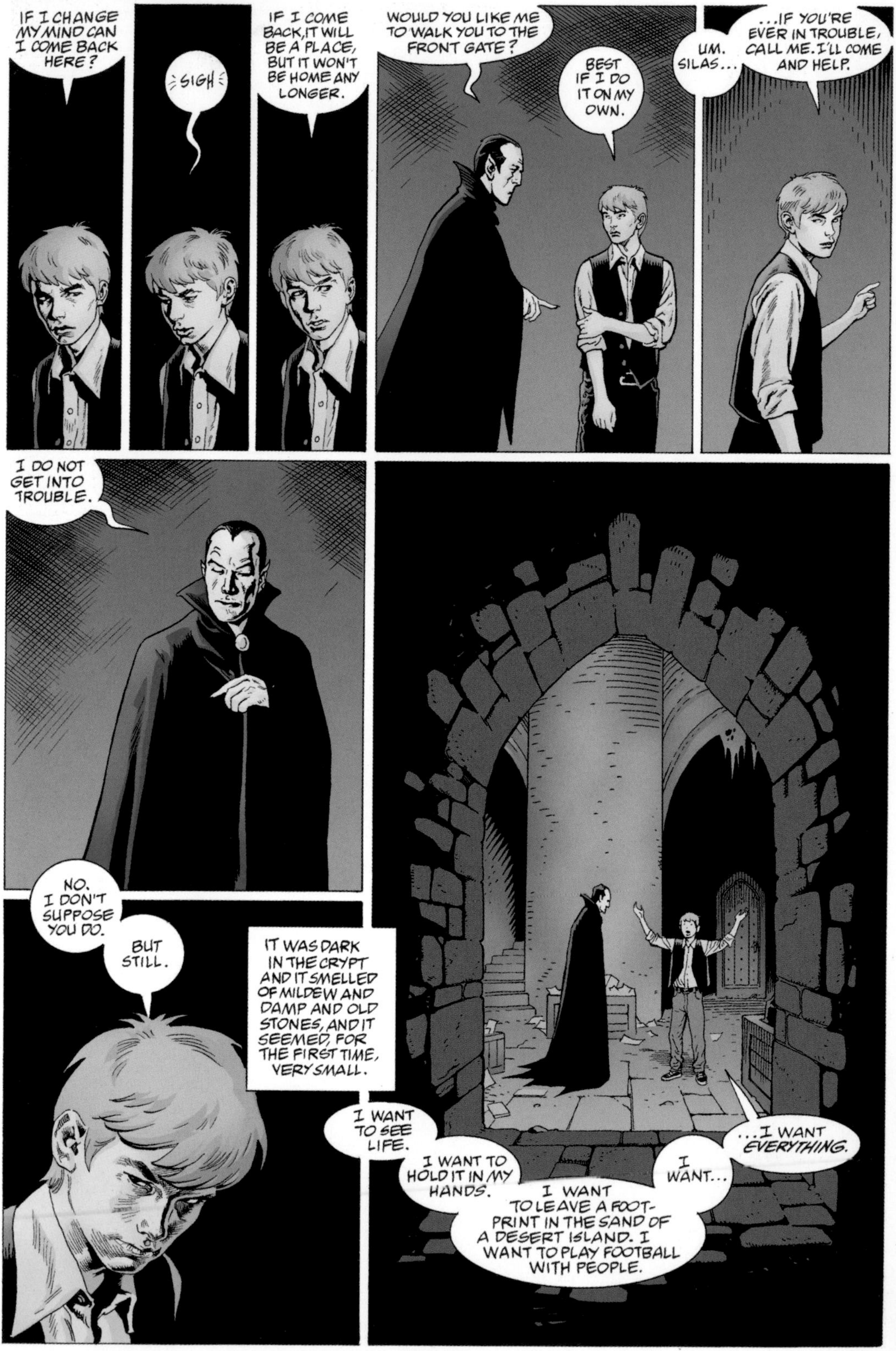
IF I CHANGE MY MIND CAN I COME BACK HERE?
SIGH
IF I COME BACK, IT WILL BE A PLACE, BUT IT WON'T BE HOME ANY LONGER.
WOULD YOU LIKE ME TO WALK YOU TO THE FRONT GATE?
BEST IF I DO IT ON MY OWN.
UM. SILAS...
...IF YOU'RE EVER IN TROUBLE, CALL ME. I'LL COME AND HELP.
I DO NOT GET INTO TROUBLE.
NO. I DON'T SUPPOSE YOU DO.
BUT STILL.
IT WAS DARK IN THE CRYPT AND IT SMELLED OF MILDEW AND DAMP AND OLD STONES, AND IT SEEMED, FOR THE FIRST TIME, VERY SMALL.
I WANT TO SEE LIFE.
I WANT TO HOLD IT IN MY HANDS.
I WANT TO LEAVE A FOOTPRINT IN THE SAND OF A DESERT ISLAND. I WANT TO PLAY FOOTBALL WITH PEOPLE.
I WANT...
...I WANT EVERYTHING.

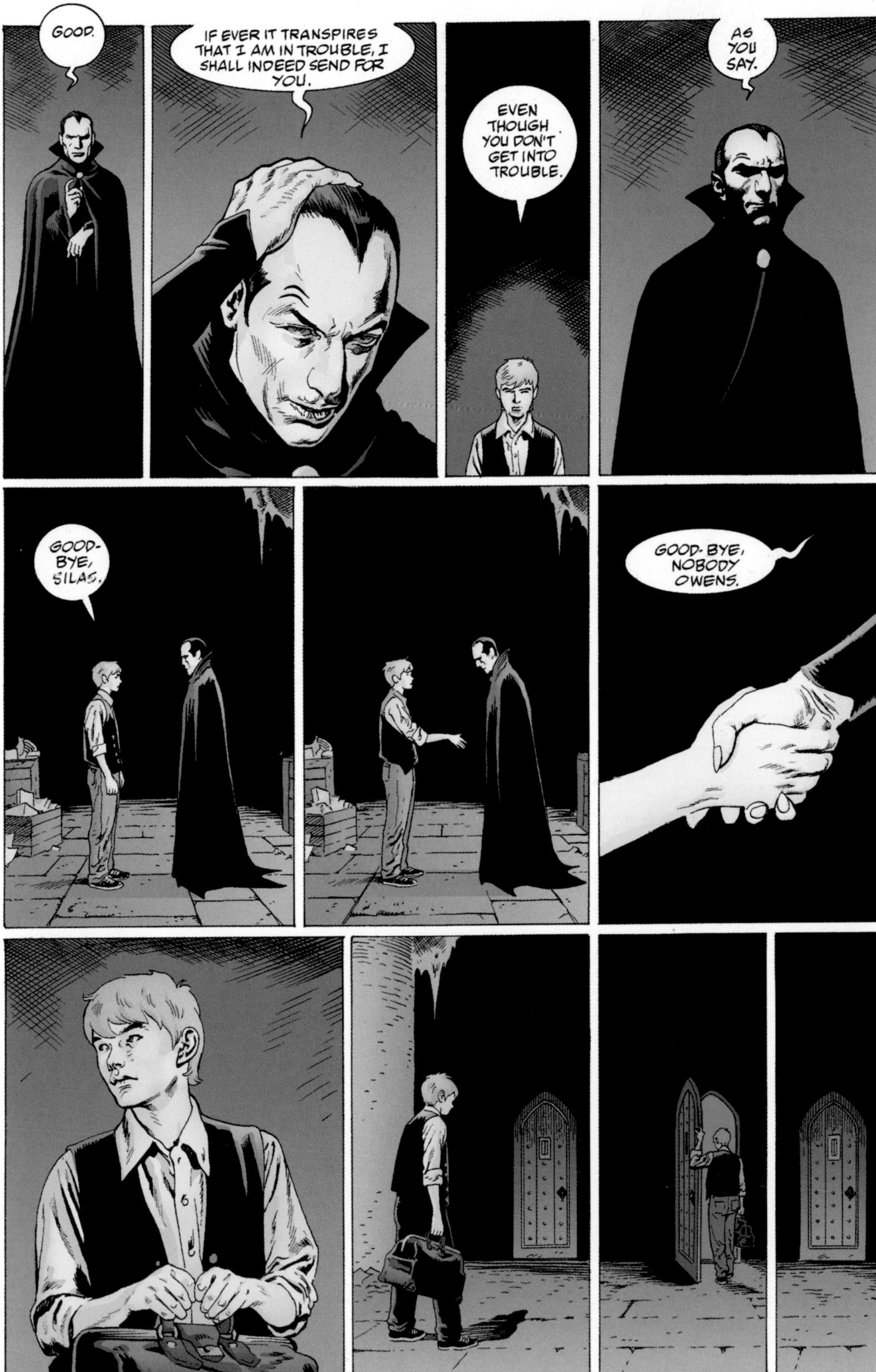
GOOD.
IF EVER IT TRANSPIRES THAT I AM IN TROUBLE, I SHALL INDEED SEND FOR YOU.
EVEN THOUGH YOU DON'T GET INTO TROUBLE.
AS YOU SAY.
GOOD-BYE, SILAS.
GOOD-BYE, NOBODY OWENS.

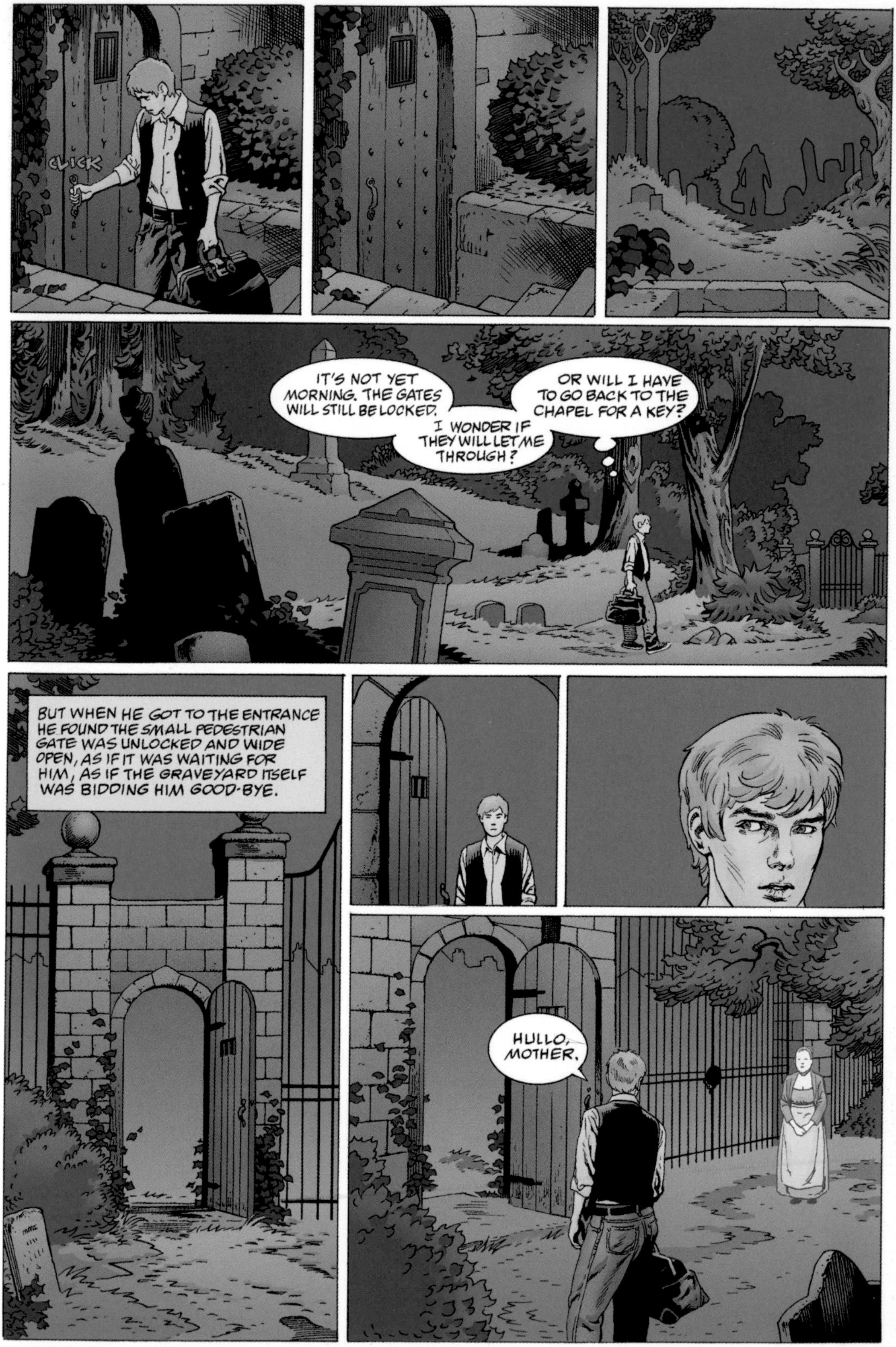
CLICK
IT'S NOT YET MORNING. THE GATES WILL STILL BE LOCKED.
I WONDER IF THEY WILL LET ME THROUGH?
OR WILL I HAVE TO GO BACK TO THE CHAPEL FOR A KEY?
BUT WHEN HE GOT TO THE ENTRANCE HE FOUND THE SMALL PEDESTRIAN GATE WAS UNLOCKED AND WIDE OPEN, AS IF IT WAS WAITING FOR HIM, AS IF THE GRAVEYARD ITSELF WAS BIDDING HIM GOOD-BYE.
HULLO, MOTHER.

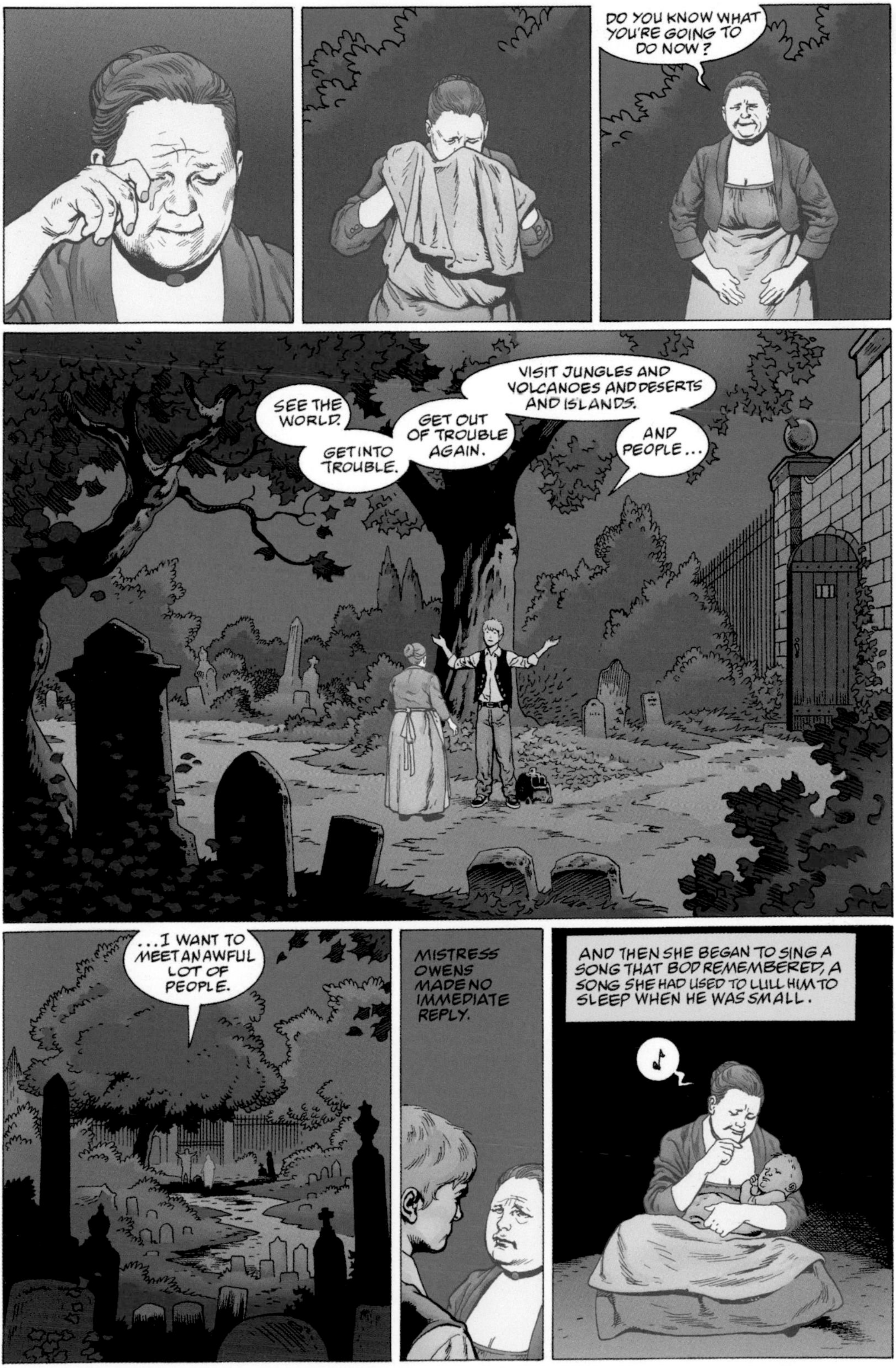
DO YOU KNOW WHAT YOU'RE GOING TO DO NOW?
SEE THE WORLD.
GET INTO TROUBLE.
GET OUT OF TROUBLE AGAIN.
VISIT JUNGLES AND VOLCANOES AND DESERTS AND ISLANDS.
AND PEOPLE...
...I WANT TO MEET AN AWFUL LOT OF PEOPLE.
MISTRESS OWENS MADE NO IMMEDIATE REPLY.
AND THEN SHE BEGAN TO SING A SONG THAT BOD REMEMBERED, A SONG SHE HAD USED TO LULL HIM TO SLEEP WHEN HE WAS SMALL.

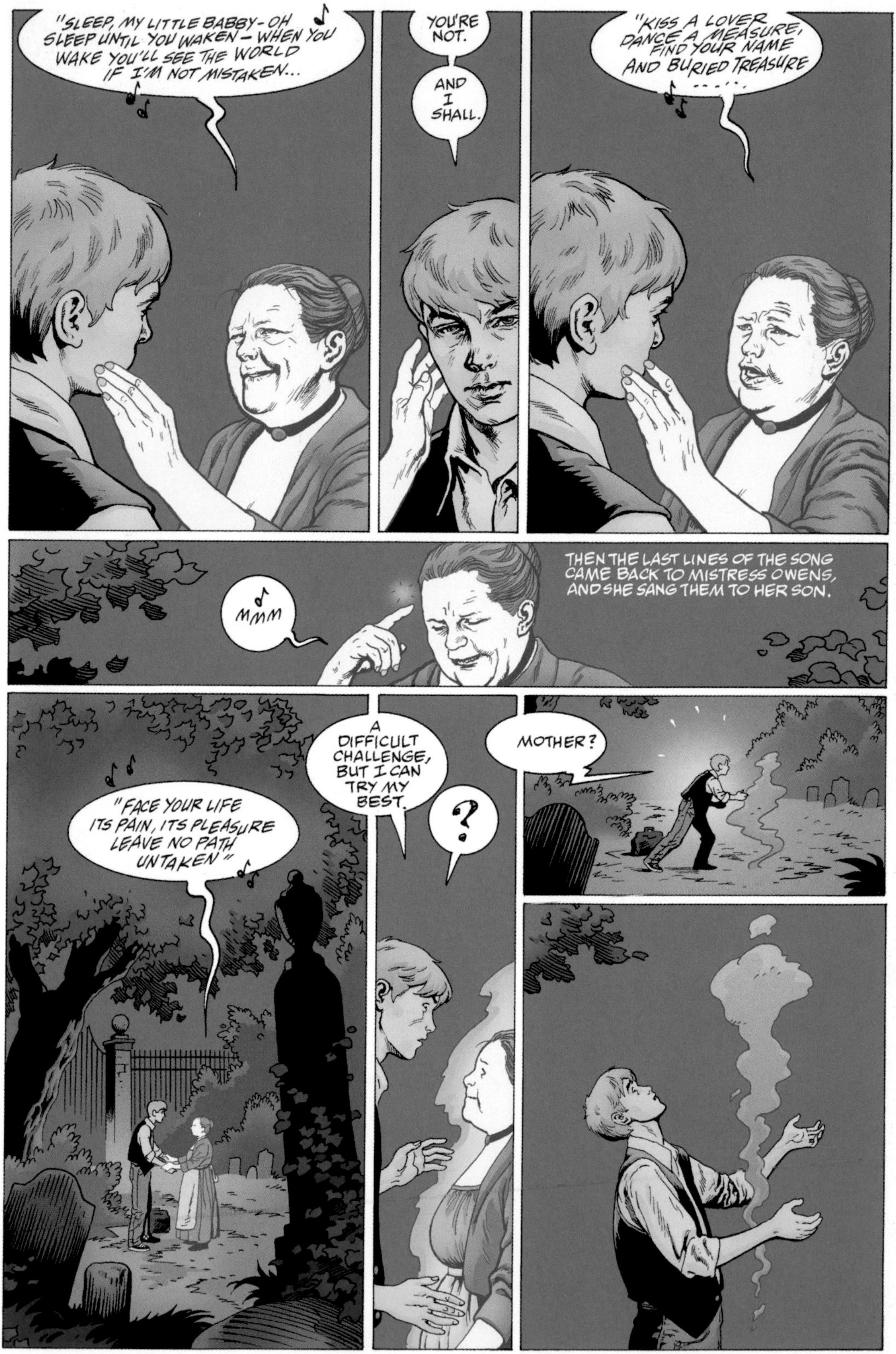
"SLEEP, MY LITTLE BABBY- OH SLEEP UNTIL YOU WAKEN - WHEN YOU WAKE YOU'LL SEE THE WORLD IF I'M NOT MISTAKEN...
YOU'RE NOT.
AND I SHALL.
"KISS A LOVER DANCE A MEASURE, FIND YOUR NAME AND BURIED TREASURE ....
MMM
THEN THE LAST LINES OF THE SONG CAME BACK TO MISTRESS OWENS, AND SHE SANG THEM TO HER SON.
"FACE YOUR LIFE ITS PAIN, ITS PLEASURE LEAVE NO PATH UNTAKEN"
A DIFFICULT CHALLENGE, BUT I CAN TRY MY BEST.
?
MOTHER?

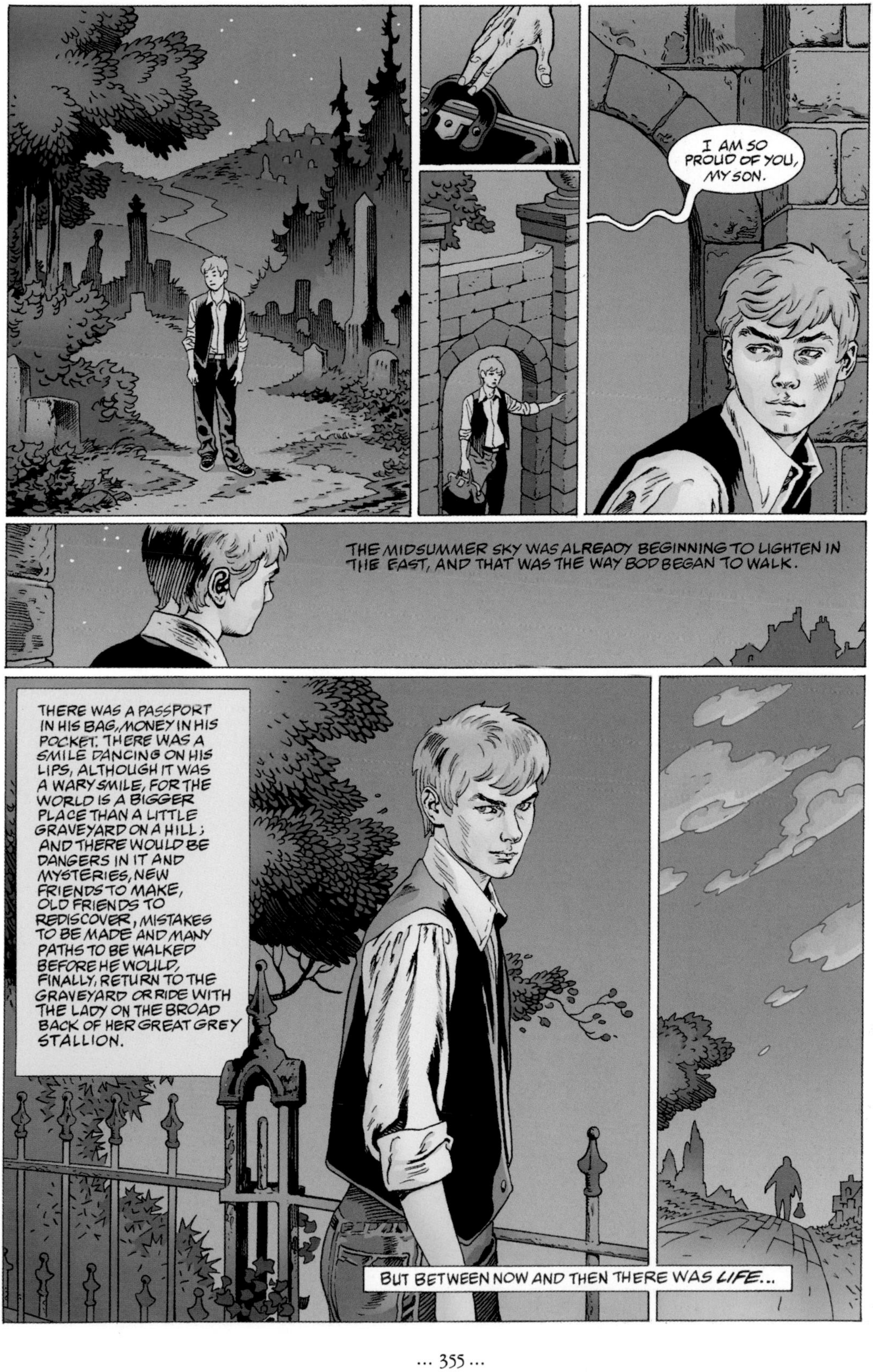
I AM SO PROUD OF YOU, MY SON.
THE MIDSUMMER SKY WAS ALREADY BEGINNING TO LIGHTEN IN THE EAST, AND THAT WAS THE WAY BOD BEGAN TO WALK.
THERE WAS A PASSPORT IN HIS BAG, MONEY IN HIS POCKET. THERE WAS A SMILE DANCING ON HIS LIPS, ALTHOUGH IT WAS A WARY SMILE, FOR THE WORLD IS A BIGGER PLACE THAN A LITTLE GRAVEYARD ON A HILL; AND THERE WOULD BE DANGERS IN IT AND MYSTERIES, NEW FRIENDS TO MAKE, OLD FRIENDS TO REDISCOVER, MISTAKES TO BE MADE AND MANY PATHS TO BE WALKED BEFORE HE WOULD, FINALLY, RETURN TO THE GRAVEYARD OR RIDE WITH THE LADY ON THE BROAD BACK OF HER GREAT GREY STALLION.
BUT BETWEEN NOW AND THEN THERE WAS *LIFE*...

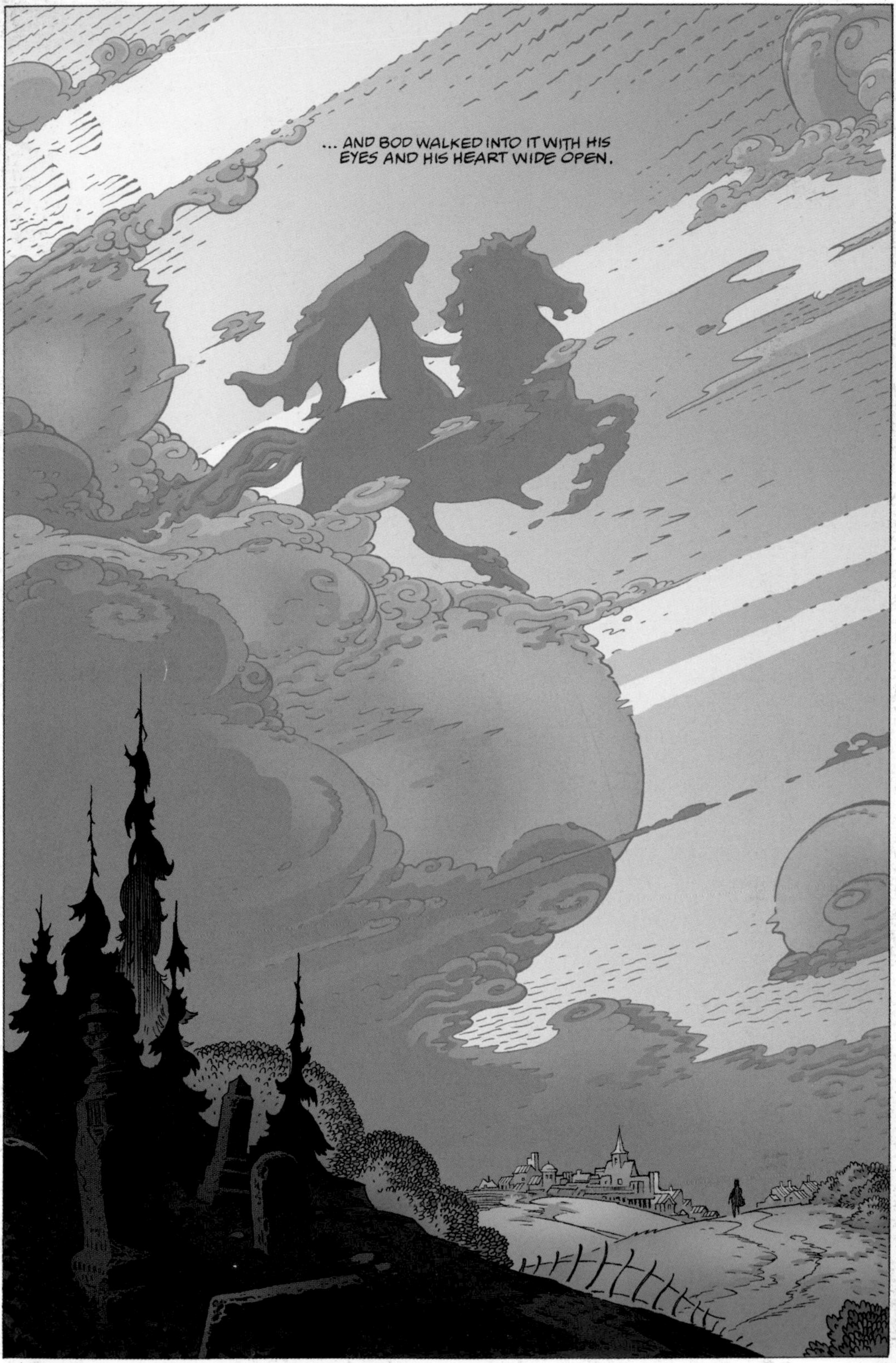
... AND BOD WALKED INTO IT WITH HIS EYES AND HIS HEART WIDE OPEN.

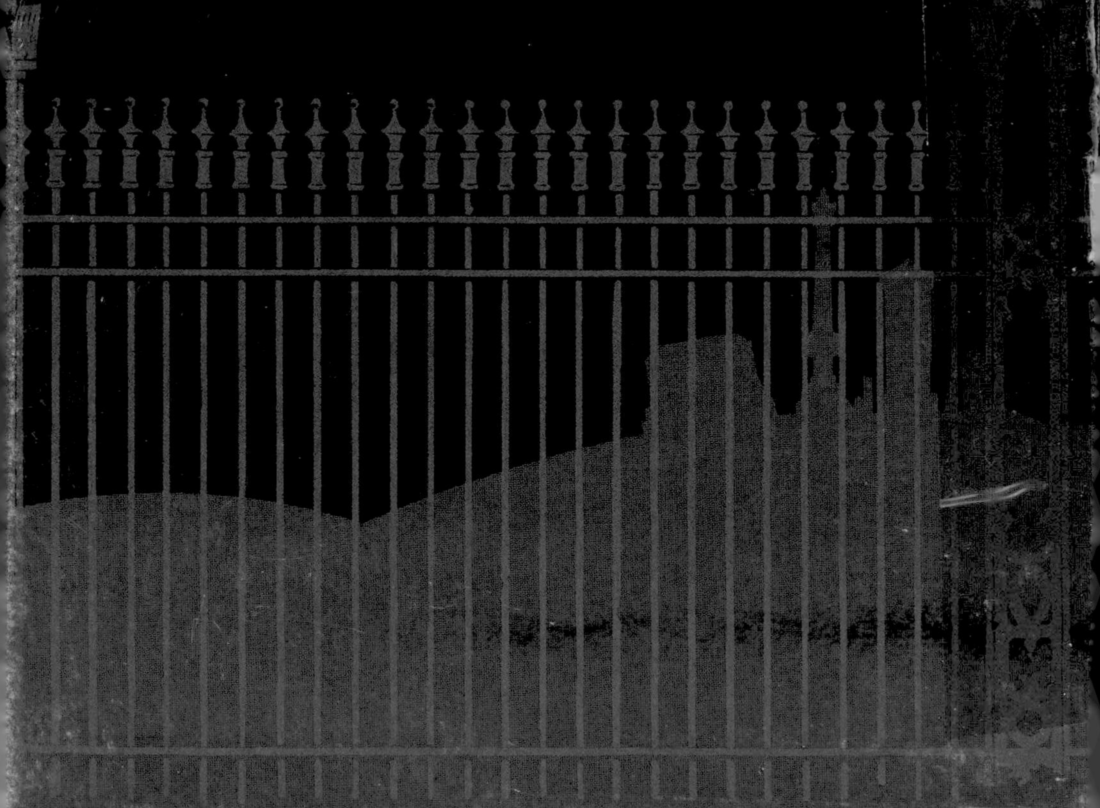

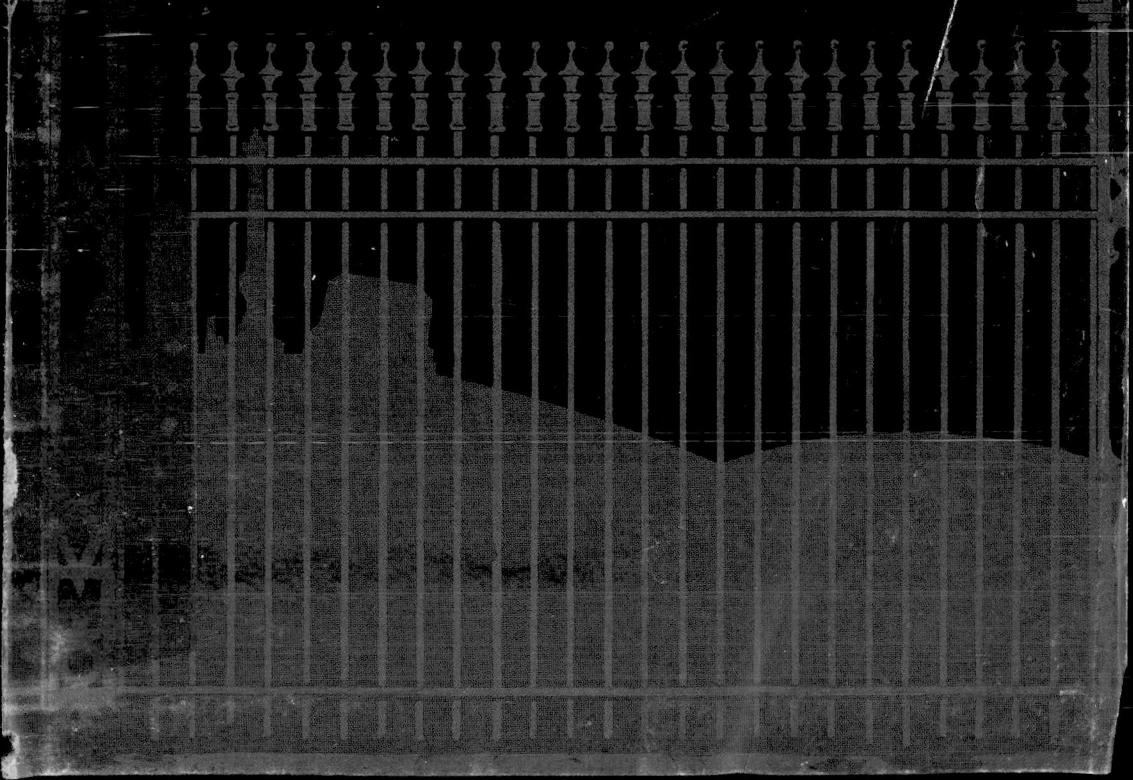